Sickness and Health

SICKNESS AND HEALTH

Colin Douglas

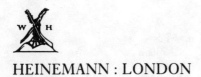

HEINEMANN : LONDON

William Heinemann Ltd
Michelin House, 81 Fulham Road, London SW3 6RB
LONDON   MELBOURNE   AUCKLAND

First published
Copyright © Colin Douglas 1991

A CIP catalogue record for this book
is held by the British Library
ISBN 0 434 20424 2

Phototypeset by Deltatype Ltd, Ellesmere Port
Printed in Great Britain by Mackays of Chatham PLC,
Chatham, Kent

PROLOGUE

June 1979

Max looked round again. 'Terrible waste.'

'Sixty two, was he? Sixty three?'

'Not that. The crowd. Just his sort of do. Everyone he'd want to have a word with about this and that. The girl from the Medical Students' Council who might come in handy for next year's ball committee. The poor chap whose department had to go ... "No hard feelings, I hope, Willie. Early retirement's the thing now, we're all green with envy ... And how *is* Muriel?" And all those really old buggers – dements of distinction who probably wouldn't know him from Adam or the undertaker, but he's so good with them. Was. "This way, Sir Alastair. You *are* looking well. Fishing's the secret, as you've always said ... No. This way, I think." '

Max Cathcart lowered his voice. An old man in a long black coat and white silk scarf went slowly past them. He was gaunt and stooped and his arms scarcely moved as he walked. The thumb and index finger of his nearer hand rubbed restlessly together and his steps were short and shuffling. He had Parkinson's disease, probably not on treatment. Dr Andrew Scott noted it neutrally: with the right pills the old man, who seemed to be around eighty, would probably walk a bit better but not really live any longer.

'Christ,' said Max. 'It's Gorgeous George.'

The old man turned his head, tortoise-like, beamed a deliberate cadaveric grin at Max and shuffled on.

'At least his hearing's all right.'

Andrew Scott watched the stooped, retreating figure. Years ago, Dr G S M Gordon had been a showman-clinician, a consultant at the Institute who had taught students simply in order to demonstrate his towering superiority over them. He had retired quite unlamented twelve or thirteen years previously and was heading for a small group of similarly old men in similar coats who were

3

nodding and shaking hands at a spot that would ensure them early entrance as soon as the doors of the crematorium opened.

'It must really cheer them up – all those old buggers you thought were dead, I mean – turning out for a lad in his sixties and having a cackle about the vicissitudes of life, then off to the New Club for a good lunch. Where were you planning to have lunch, Scott?'

'Hadn't thought about it.'

'Who's the guy in the Homburg? Or is it a fedora?'

'Surgeon. Did thyroids until the drink caught up with him.'

'Chipper. Chipper somebody. "Just chip away, boy, don't worry about the blood . . .' Chapman. And his drinking mate who got to be President of the College. And old Ratho. Looks as if he's just wet himself. Yes, the lords of creation, as it was then. God, it takes you back. But the great thing about Edinburgh medicine is that there's always a new lot of old buggers waiting to take over.'

Scott looked round the growing crowd. 'I suppose so.'

'I didn't mean Lennie.'

'No.'

'Great chap. How did you hear? You didn't come back specially, did you?'

'No.'

'But it's a great way of catching up with things. And then lunch with me. How about the Cafe Royal? That's probably where Lennie would have wanted people to go. Robbie rang me on Thursday night . . . Nice of him, but he seemed to be taking it all very personally.'

'That's how I heard too. Robbie. Phoned on Thursday. We had a couple of words as if I'd been away for the weekend then he told me. Solemn stuff. Suddenly, at home.'

'Same here. Said he thought I'd probably want to know and kept calling him Professor Lennox. And then the funeral arrangements. All very rambling and Robbie-ish. Even told me parking here was never a problem, mad bugger. Must be here somewhere. Everyone is.'

Everyone was. Two or three hundred had gathered around the entrance to the crematorium and there were still a few minutes to go. 'Lots of women,' said Max. 'Only really good blokes get a lot of women at their funerals. There's Aunty Jean . . . Poor old thing. She'll probably stay out here for years and years, like Greyfriars

4

Bobby.' Mrs Wigton, a comfortable Edinburgh widow in her fifties, had been Professor Lennox's secretary, and in that capacity the confidante and soother of hundreds of variously troubled medical students and the keeper of almost as many secrets as her late boss. She was standing with two girls in their early twenties, presumably medical students of the kind that had come in useful for ball committees. All three were upset.

One of the girls looked a bit like Sandy: sufficiently so for Scott to wait until she turned a little away from Mrs Wigton and into profile. She was not Sandy, who in any case, Scott reminded himself rather belatedly, would arrive for her father's funeral in the first of the large black saloons of the cortege. For Scott, a lot of girls still looked like Sandy.

'An odd story, according to Robbie. Very odd in its way . . . You're not listening, Scott, you're leering at those birds with Aunty Jean. Gospel according to Robbie. Lennie gets up in the middle of the night, goes to his study – something he never does, at least not in the middle of the night – sits for hours, decides to go back to bed, takes a wrong turning and falls downstairs. Instant total death. Biggish stair, apparently. Well, you've seen it, we all have. Margaret's wakened by the noise, worries, goes and looks and there he is. Worse than poorly, in fact a lot worse. But not over the bannister or anything gruesome. Just straight down the stairs.'

'Yes. Robbie sort of explained it. Amazing how he always knows that kind of thing.'

'I thought he was going to read me the post mortem report, but it's one for the procurator fiscal so nobody knows, not even Robbie. But the proc. must be quite happy or they wouldn't be burning him.'

'Suddenly, at home' sounded nicer, and Professor Lennox had been a very nice man. A line of black cars drew up, doors opened and slowly and untidily the mourners began to move. Ahead of the crowd that had been waiting, in the little huddle of the remaining Lennox family, Sandy, pale and calm, walked up the last few steps into the crematorium with her mother beside her, clutching her arm and sobbing.

The slow move forward had taken Scott and Max closer to the group with most experience of such occasions, the very old, very properly dressed men of medicine whose number now included Dr Gordon. 'He's next.' Max nodded towards one of them. He had lowered his voice again, but perhaps not enough. 'Lorimer.' Dr Lorimer, once a physician-potentate, now long retired, had seen medicine from the thirties, when it was all style and hardly any science, through the briefly miraculous era of penicillin and on into its current bewildered fragmentation into myriad subspecialities and the unwilling care of the elderly. He was still recognisably a gentleman physician, but his shirt collar looked three sizes too large. Scott, who had just returned after a year away from Edinburgh, looked to Max for an explanation.

'Lymphoma,' Max mouthed. 'Found a lump. Had the rays, the pills, the lot and doesn't want any more. So he's next.' Scott remembered a tale from long ago and the village where he had spent his childhood. Funerals there had been affairs everyone knew about, with all the blinds lowered in the windows on the main street and a procession, led by a horse-drawn black-and-gilt hearse, down the steep hill to the riverside graveyard. A grim winter had accounted in turn for four or five of a band of worthies who had grown old together since their return from the First World War. At the graveside yet again, one of the surviving handful had begun to cough and splutter and had had to lean against the hearse. Another was reported to have shaken his head and muttered gloomily: 'Tam next. Hardly worth the bother o' getting him back up the hill . . .' As they entered the crematorium Dr Lorimer began to cough. Shakily, Gorgeous George Gordon steadied him.

Inside, ushers were at work and Scott and Max found themselves firmly down the centre aisle and into the second front row of a small block of seats in the transept, facing the pulpit and looking across the front rows of the main seating, where the dead man's family was already settled. On the left was the broad maroon baize surface, surrounded by six sentinel brass stanchions and awaiting the mortal remains of Professor G R Lennox DSC MB ChB FRCS FRCPE FRCSE; on the right the solemn, seated rows: hundreds of people surprised and sorrowful at being in that place on that day for that reason, among them the Principal and Vice-Principal of the University, a dozen or more clinical and pre-clinical professors and scores of other medical people, from the young self-conscious girls with Aunty Jean through every successive stage of medical life to the ancient semi-professional mourners in long coats, now grouped solidly near the front just across the aisle from Margaret Lennox,

6

Sandy, her brother and two women in late middle age sufficiently like Lennie to be presumed to be his sisters.

An organist improvised uncertainly. People were still coming in and the ushers fussed here and there, trying to close gaps in the middle of rows to make space for the older members of the growing group of mourners standing at the back. From that group a youngish man, blond and bearded, suddenly strode alone down the centre aisle, turned left and made it clear to those in the row just in front of Scott and Max that he expected to be accommodated there.

'What a shit,' Max murmured. The beard was new. The rest, especially the cool progress down the aisle and the presumption of a welcome in the front row, was pure Gus. ' "Let me through," ' Max whispered hoarsely, ' "I'm the dead bloke's ex-son-in-law". God, what a shit.'

Gus Ratho, one of the people Scott considered it quite pleasant not to have seen for twelve months, was a clinical immunologist, a young consultant a couple of years senior to him and Max, who had married Sandy in the early seventies. Their separation and divorce had been a complex, unpleasant and unusual matter for the Edinburgh medical bourgeoisie. Sandy, who must surely have noticed his entrance, was looking straight to her front.

Scott, who had not seen her at all for about eighteen months, saw her now in profile and at leisure. Even allowing for the circumstances, she looked a little older and thinner than he had expected. Her hair was the shortest he had ever seen it, shorter even than when she had been a very schoolgirlish new medical student, earnest in the reading room with a big shopping bag with lecture notes and sheet music sticking out. As they waited Scott thought about all the ways she had had her hair and tried to decide which he had preferred, hesitating for a few agreeable moments between medium length and spread out on a pillow and longer and whipping around her naked shoulders when she was on top and letting herself go. The latter, he thought, then looked over towards her again and found that Gus Ratho's head was in the way.

Gus had glanced at Sandy too. It had all been very difficult. He had seen the death announcement on the second page of *The Scotsman* two days before and felt mildly upset that this should have been the first he had known of the whole business. Of course there had never been any doubt that he should attend the funeral. His father was here and most of the Edinburgh doctors he regarded as being in any sense comparable to himself were also present. The Lennoxes and the Rathos had been close for many years, far longer than he had known Sandy, and he had remained very fond of Margaret despite everything. And though Sandy's feelings were naturally to be taken into consideration they were only part of larger and much more significant social context.

Choosing a tie had also posed problems. Had he still been family, so to speak, black would have been the obvious choice. Nowadays friends tended simply to wear dark ties, although of course the more senior men like his father and Dr Lorimer stuck to the older tradition, and very well it suited them too. That morning, after some thought, Gus had plumped for the tie of the Royal College of Physicians of Edinburgh, with its dark blue ground and discreet little centaur motif in green. Lennie had worn it a lot, and a good number of the other younger consultants had chosen it for today's occasion too, probably for similar reasons. True, it had been a present from Sandy, but that could hardly be helped, any more than sitting in a place where he virtually had to stare at her could. The last two years had been very difficult, very difficult indeed, but looking across at his ex-wife, her brother, the aunts, Margaret and so on Gus had to admit to a little pang at not being there among the chief mourners at what was likely to be the largest Edinburgh medical funeral for some years.

The organist improvised with increasing desperation. Sandy wanted to look round to see if they were coming but didn't. Her mother took her hand gently and squeezed it, whether comforting her or seeking comfort she did not know. Gus should have stayed away. A nicer person would have, but then a nicer person would still have been her husband and been here with her. When he had appeared, striding bumptiously across to a front seat, Sandy had thought immediately of squash, a game she had never played. Once, after one of their lesser rows, she had had to go in to work with a black eye and had told someone who asked about it that she had got it playing squash. For weeks afterwards the girl had kept pestering her to fix up a match or game or whatever and Sandy, who always thought of herself as a basically truthful person, had felt quite guilty. She glanced across at him again. His new beard was horrible, but in its way quite suited him. And behind him Andrew, after a mysterious absence of more than a year, had reappeared with a nice tan.

The first indication that proceedings were under way was a change in the music. From his nervous vamping the organist switched to a confident elaboration of the Dead March from Saul, then the little procession came into view: the clergyman, followed by the coffin topped by a single wreath and borne by four pale men in worn black suits. The five moved smoothly down the aisle, passing the front row and reaching their destination at precisely the moment Handel and the organist would have wished. As two of them covered the coffin with a maroon drape, unfolded from behind and loosely supported by the six brass stanchions, Sandy and her mother looked steadfastly ahead.

The cleric, a New College professor and former University chaplain, announced a psalm: the hundred and twenty first. There was a fluttering of unfamiliar pages and the congregation rose. Among the ancients Lorimer and Georgeous George shared a hymnbook in a way that made it look as if they were propping each other up. As they began to sing a sudden shaft of sunlight through stained glass lit on Dr Lorimer, turning his face an unearthly green. 'I told you,' Max muttered. 'He's next.'

> 'I to the hills will lift mine eyes,
> From whence doth come mine aid.
> My safety cometh from the Lord
> Who heaven and earth hath made . . .'

Early in the third line the singing faded badly. A tricky high note emerged with some nasty near-misses and sorted out the regular churchgoers from the crematorium casuals. In the transept Gus Ratho, definitely one of the former, winced but strove to ensure that his own contribution would not be found wanting. After all, choral singing was one of the outside interests listed at the end of his curriculum vitae, a useful little touch which had encouraged friendly questioning at job interviews throughout his junior hospital doctor career and had the additional merit of being true.

To Scott's mild embarrassment, Max, with whom he was sharing a hymnbook, was making no attempt to sing but acting instead like someone who had never seen the Scottish metrical psalms before: hogging the book and browsing among the long extravagances of

9

the 119th psalm, shaking his head in puzzlement, perhaps over the twenty two sub-headings. Not that it mattered to Scott, who found himself recalling without effort the words for all four stanzas of the 121st as the music unfolded.

'The Lord shall keep thy soul; he shall
Preserve thee from all ill.
Henceforth thy going out and in
God keep for ever will.'

They sat down. Dr Lorimer's face reverted to its previous unhealthy colour. 'Amazing' Max whispered, still immersed in the one hundred and nineteenth psalm. 'It could take hours and hours, but it might come in handy when they've got the bodies mixed up, or somebody's forgotten to sign the cremation papers.' Gus Ratho looked round from the seat in front: the head boy quelling disorder with a glance. Max made a face.

'Blessed are they that mourn: for they shall be comforted.' The clergyman's voice, familiar from University services long ago, rose over the quiet hum of the organ pump. 'The souls of the righteous are in the hand of God, and there shall no torment touch them. They are in peace.' He paused, looked upwards to the stained glass window above the coffin, and raised his voice. 'And I saw a new heaven and a new earth: for the first heaven and the first earth were passed away; and there was no more sea . . .'

Sandy sniffed. Her father had quite liked the sea, joined the navy rather than the Army in 1940 because, as he had put it ever afterwards, he liked his comforts and thought it was far better to be drowned once in a while than have to sleep in a puddle every night.

'And God shall wipe away all tears from their eyes; and there shall be no more death, neither sorrow, nor crying, neither shall there be any more pain: for the former things are passed away . . .'

Did it hurt to break your neck? Robbie's version of events, as relayed to Scott, was that Lennie had fallen downstairs and been found a few minutes later by his wife, conscious and still breathing but otherwise completely limp. A spinal cord transection at that level was not necessarily fatal but, in the eyes of many people who knew about it, not worth surviving either. Had Lennie and his wife, also a doctor, made their own assessment and decided as much? Whatever they had thought or said in the few minutes in which something might still have been done, Lennie had died, suddenly at home, at the foot of the stairs at about five in the morning. Scott tried to remember the last time he had seen him.

The clergyman turned to his congregation. 'Friends, we are gathered here this morning, each with our own memories of Gavin Lennox. Summoned together suddenly, in sorrow at his sudden passing, in our hearts we remember a man to whom so many of us had at one time or another so much cause to be grateful. As students, colleagues, patients, friends and family we mourn him and remember him: for his kindness, his ready wit, his great knowledge and his enthusiasm for his calling of medicine, his contributions to its scientific advancement, his teaching both in the lecture hall and at the bedside, and for the humanity, application and ingenuity he brought to the last of his many professional tasks, that of administration.

'There have been many beloved physicians, perhaps fewer beloved administrators, but it is a measure both of Gavin's greatness and of his humanity that over what was to be the last decade of his working life he served in that capacity with such conspicuous success, perhaps by exercising the selfsame qualities of leadership and example which had so distinguished his wartime career as a surgeon lieutenant, Royal Naval Volunteer Reserve . . .'

Max was silent and thoughtful, the hymnbook now closed in his hand. An ugly row with an especially bone-headed obstetrician in the fifth year of the medical course had led to a meeting at short notice with Professor G R Lennox, at that time Clinical Dean and penultimate arbiter of the destinies of those who had made it beyond third year. Max, who had been on one of Lennie's little committees and had been to his house more than once for drinks before the Faculty Ball, had expected a token interview, a joke and perhaps even a cup of tea brought in by Aunty Jean. He had emerged instead with a new understanding of what was meant when a Naval court martial sentenced someone to be severely reprimanded.

'. . . and culminating in the award of well-merited Distinguished Service Cross, one of comparatively few awarded to medical officers of the RNVR. The war over, and after a brief but happy spell in general practice in Moniaive, Gavin was summoned back to Edinburgh by his old chief to serve as clinical tutor in the then emerging speciality of endocrinology, a discipline in which he was to earn such distinction. But it was the establishment of the National Health Service in 1948 that was to capture the imagination of Gavin Lennox and so many of his generation. His personal ideal of medicine as a service to people, to all the people, was about to become reality on a national scale, and he threw himself into its development with a zeal that few could match. Singled out as a consultant at an early age to set up a department. . .'

Gorgeous George, Scott noted, was grinning again and his eyes were glistening: had he too perhaps been once an idealist, an enthusiast for the new order of medicine? It would have been hard to guess from his behaviour on the wards in their first term of clinical teaching, but perhaps idealism had been commoner in 1948 when Lennie and his colleagues, back from the war, had, as the clergyman recalled, turned an Edinburgh poorhouse into a flourishing teaching hospital in less than five years.

Sandy, who had once astonished her kindergarten teacher by announcing that her father had been a doctor at the Institute before he was sent to the poorhouse, remembered what fun he had been when they were little, even when he said things like that which caused as much confusion as amusement, and began to cry.

'. . . but above all we remember with gratitude his energy, his vision and his unfailing consideration for everyone who came into contact with him. To Margaret and the family, whose loss is immense, our sympathy and our prayers reach out as they face their bereavement . . . Let us pray.'

Gus Ratho believed in prayer. He bowed his head and closed his eyes and pressed his hands almost flat together in full sight of the congregation. In its small way, it was an opportunity for witness. Most of them, he noted in a quite unintended peep, were content simply to bow their heads, only the more devout quarter or so closing their eyes. The only praying hands he could see were his own and Professor Munro's.

'Father of mercies, and God of all comfort; look in Thy tender love and pity, we beseech Thee, on Thy sorrowing servants. Enable them to find in Thee their refuge and strength, a very present help in trouble, and to know . . .' Munro's voice, a fine baritone instrument used with skill and, it seemed, sincerity, took them a lot nearer the moment of committal, that relinquishing of mortal remains that Sandy had so irrationally feared. Again she felt her mother's hand on hers.

'Forasmuch as it hath pleased Almighty God to take unto Himself the soul of our brother here departed, we therefore commit his body to be dissolved . . .' At the touch of a button and with a hushed whisper of well-used municipal electrical equipment, the coffin was lowered and the maroon drape sagged amid its six brass standards. Sandy's mother squeezed her hand. 'Ashes to ashes, dust to dust, in sure and certain hope of the resurrection to eternal life, through our Lord Jesus Christ . . .'

In the moment of quiet that followed, the connoisseurs on the left at the front were turning to one another and nodding. The thing had been well done. The clergyman had either known Lennie quite well or gone to a lot of trouble to bone up on him. Lennie had been young and keen and done a lot for Edinburgh and for medicine and that had come across, and Margaret must be as happy as could be expected in the circumstances: not like some of them, who left you wondering if you'd turned up at the wrong funeral.

The clergyman, perhaps aware of his success, turned once more to a high stained glass window and allowed his voice a little more resonance. 'And I heard a voice from heaven saying unto me, Blessed are the dead which die in the Lord, that they may rest from their labours, and their works do follow them . . .'

Gus Ratho had been disappointed. Apart from things straight out of the book the spiritual content of what had been said was negligible. The officiating clergyman, the Reverend Professor Munro, had been first and foremost a golfing crony of his ex-father-in-law and a minister only for the purposes of weddings such as his own, and it had shown, although most of those present would hardly have noticed the difference.

'And now let us conclude by giving thanks for the life of Gavin Ronald Lennox in the singing of his favourite hymn, John Bunyan's fine call to faith, *Who would true valour see?*' As the tune, one of the first she had ever known apart from nursery rhymes, started up, Sandy, although she had chosen it herself, wanted to howl. He had sung it in the bath, and when he was sailing, and he had made up silly poems to it, and only when she had tried to do that herself had she discovered how difficult it was. She bit her lip as they stood up, and as they sang tears began to flow.

'Who would true haggis eat?
Go to MacSween's.
A lovely tea-time treat
    With spuds and beans.
No sausage can compete,
Corned beef nor potted meat.
Black pudding cannot beat
    MacSween's haggis.'

A spirit had flown free. She was laughing and crying but that was all right because it would look like just crying. The rest of the congregation, all unaware of the private significance of the hymn to the family, was enjoying it too; the cheery defiance of the god-besotted tinker's verses and the steady, tramping tune were right for them, and right for Lennie too.

'Who would true valour see?
Let him come hither.
One here will constant be,
    Come wind, come weather
There's no discouragement
Will make him once relent
His first avowed intent
    To be a pilgrim.'

George Gordon and Dr Lorimer stood together through the hymn like veterans at a regimental reunion, prouder and straighter than before, singing it and meaning it and enjoying it like an old marching song. Watching them, Scott saw that, and George Gordon's tears and Lorimer's huge wasted frame and realised: there was a regiment, a regiment with rules and drills and customs, with heroes and rogues and fallen comrades and overseas battalions and centuries of tradition and a very high opinion of itself, perhaps even with reason. And he and Max, like Lennie, Lorimer, Gorgeous George and forty or fifty or a hundred other people here were part of it. It wasn't a bad regiment to belong to and when somebody like Lennie died it rallied round with a good turnout. All it needed was a name, and if it were to have one it would have to be something like God's Own Edinburgh Doctors.

'Hobgoblin nor foul fiend
Can daunt his spirit;
He knows he at the end
    Shall life inherit.
Then fancies fly away;
He'll fear not what men say;
He'll labour night and day
    To be a pilgrim.'

The last note died away, the congregation stood with bowed heads and the clergyman raised his right hand in benediction. 'The grace of our Lord Jesus Christ, the love of God, and the communion of the Holy Spirit be with you all. Amen.'

In the front row Sandy felt better. Professor Munro, now waiting to escort them to the door, had been the right person to ask and had been terrific, with mum and with the practical details and with what he had said and how he had said it and she would tell him so. They moved back down the aisle in slow time, between rows and rows of people standing waiting, Sandy holding her mother's arm, her brother following. As they did so it came back to her with a jolt that Professor Munro had once asked her, in church and in front of an awful lot of people, 'Do you, Alexandra, take this man to be your lawful wedded husband, to have and to hold?' But that had been a long time ago, and not even Gus would think of blaming the minister.

The organist had required a little persuasion about the music he was playing now. It was another favourite of her father's, one he had sung to its own words with no funny poems, and it was solemn and familiar even if it was a little unusual in the context. When Professor Munro had come round to plan things they had discussed hymns and music. Everything had been decided except the last music and mum had suddenly said 'I know. He wanted it at our wedding and I put my foot down, and we had a silly row about it and he said "Oh, all right, but I'm definitely having it at my funeral." So he can. "For those in peril on the sea ..." ' Everyone had laughed, then Professor Munro had said 'Oh, there's probably quite a lot to be said for it at weddings . . . That bit in the middle? ". . . and bid the angry tumult cease, and give, for wild confusion, peace . . ." ' and they had laughed at that as well.

Behind the family the aisle filled slowly as people began to move out, talking quietly, standing back and making way for one another and nodding to friends and acquaintances. Gus smiled politely at Scott and rather pointedly ignored Max. A little man with a limp hobbled behind a clutch of notables from the Institute, mainly consultant surgeons and physicians. Scott knew him but couldn't immediately place him. Definitely not an Institute notable, but something to do with the medical school. The man caught Scott's eye and gave a quick skewed nod that helped a lot: he was a servitor, the one who for years had emerged from the porter's lodge every hour of the working day to unlock a long cupboard on the east wall of the quad and signal the passing of time, the beginning or end of a lecture-hour, by a few tugs on a bell-pull protected from mischievous students by means of the locked cupboard. 'Ars longa, vita brevis' said the motto on the maroon clock high on the wall beside the bell. Lennie had walked under it a dozen times a day going to and from his office, and the little bell-ringer had come to his funeral.

Margaret Lennox, her daughter and her son stood in that order to the left of the door as the crowd emerged, shaking hands with people, talking briefly with friends and hearing gruff words from men and women unknown to them but somehow touched by Lennie's death. Ahead of Scott, at the front of the slow, informal queue, Gus was doing his repulsive sincere thing with Margaret, holding her elbow and looking closely into her face for far too long. Scott wondered if he was going to try anything like that with Sandy, and how she might handle it if he did. She was spared as Fiona, another girl from their year now also separated or divorced or something, stepped behind Gus and embraced her with a consoling hug. It was a hint not even Gus could ignore. He nodded at Sandy's brother and walked away.

Max was behaving now. As he reached Margaret he shook hands with her and murmured something about Lennie being a great chap. Margaret smiled and said 'Thanks for coming along, Max,' in a way that reminded Scott of drinks at their house just before the graduation ball. 'And Andrew.' A brief nod informed Scott that there were still a lot of people behind him. He turned towards Sandy and their eyes met. She looked just tired and a little red-eyed. She shook his hand then seemed to stop in mid-handshake as though she were about to say something.

Scott, who knew her very well indeed, was trying to work out what she was going to say when he noticed her left hand. There was a new wedding ring, thinner and brighter than its predecessor. That was a surprise. She let his hand go, gave him a tiny smile and turned to the next person in the queue, a greyish lady in her seventies with the air of a retired senior nurse.

Outside, people were standing around much as they had done before the service, but more cheerfully. 'See what I mean,' said Max. 'Just his kind of do. Not the same without him bobbing up for a little word here, there and everywhere.' It was true. Professor Lennox, a quick, slight man of middle height, with a twinkling smile and soft, rather hoarse voice, had always been around: at meetings, on committees, arranging this and that and generally oiling the wheels of the variously ancient and unwilling components of that complex piece of human and institutional machinery known as the Faculty of Medicine.

'Boys, isn't it awful . . .' Aunty Jean, in a stiff black suit and purple blouse, had appeared from the crowd and stood in front of Max as though expecting to be embraced. Max obliged. 'Oh, Max, it's all absolutely dreadful! Of course Margaret rang me first thing the next morning, what else could she do? And I don't think I've ever been so shocked in all my life. At least with Mr Wigton . . .' Aunty Jean always referred to her late husband as if they had just recently been introduced '. . . At least with Mr Wigton I got plenty of warning, with his condition. But poor Professor Lennox . . . We'd left the office talking about what we had to do next day as usual, and as usual he dropped me off at Holy Corner, it being a Tuesday, and the next thing is Margaret's phone call. Such a dreadful shock. The whole office is still . . . stunned is the only word for it, boys. Not because things weren't in order. They were, they always were. One of his basic principles, from the Navy, we always said, although he hates the word shipshape. But so many people, so many committees just *depend* on us. It's simply awful, boys. And here we are at the funeral and I still can't believe it. People so depend on us.' There was a pause and Mrs Wigton pursed her lips. 'Max, dear, you've got your car here, haven't you? This place is so dreadfully far out.' Max winked at Scott over Mrs Wigton's head, mouthing the words 'Cafe Royal' and signalling one o'clock with an upraised index finger, then offered Aunty Jean his arm and was gone.

Gus Ratho had joined his father and some of his friends. Dr Lorimer, who was probably getting on for ninety now, looked at him in a puzzled kind of way. 'Gus Ratho, Dr Lorimer . . . Perhaps it's the beard . . .'

'Yes, yes, Gus. Knew you straight away. But shouldn't you be over there with your wife?'

Gus nodded and smiled politely. Dr Lorimer was getting very old now. Not that he hadn't achieved a great deal in his time, particularly on the committee side, and most of the consultant establishment owed him a lot, quite literally, but there would be no point whatsoever in going into any detail. 'You're looking well, Dr Lorimer . . . Father says you always . . .'

'It's his putting that lets him down. Still quite a drive for his age, but he won't take my advice on putting . . .'

'Awfully sad about Lennie . . .'

'Who?'

'Professor Lennox, Dr Lorimer.'

'We always called him Gavin. D'you call him Lennie, Gus?'

'Well, yes, Dr Lorimer.'

'Hm . . . And how's Sandy taking it? Must have been a terrible blow for her . . . Particularly the way he went . . . And he was always so close to Sandy. So how's she taking it?'

'Bearing up, as we all must in the . . .' Gus responded to an imagined urgent summons from somewhere beyond the old man's shoulder and said 'I'm sorry, Dr Lorimer, you must excuse me . . .'

Scott scanned the crowd, recognising a lot more people as he did so. The odd thing about having been away for a while was that some people had changed a lot, some hardly at all. The professor of anatomy looked the same, indeed the same as he had done sixteen years before, when he had first appeared in front of his class of innocents, wielding a huge, expensive book he had written himself and recommending it with a phrase much quoted since: 'It is my privilege to dispense good advice, just as it is yours to ignore it'. Lennie was said to have been instrumental in reducing his share of the curriculum from nine hundred to five hundred hours but grudges were not borne. A girl who had been much lusted after in third and fourth year had over the past year acquired, for whatever reasons, an obvious indifference to how she looked. Max might know something about that. And the strange man from pathology with a line in bow ties was looking madder than ever.

'No trouble parking, then?'

Scott turned round. 'Oh. Hello, Robbie.' Robbie Roberts – pale, with lank reddish hair and one shoulder a bit higher than the other – was someone who had never changed. While a lot of people in the year had been socially clumsy and physically awkward when they had started the course together more than fifteen years ago, only Robbie had stayed that way. As usual when he talked, he was smiling a lot and looking around for other people to talk to as well.

'I rang as many people as I could find who might be interested . . . Mainly from our year but even then there are a terrific lot. But lots came. Nice for Margaret. And Sandy. Poor Sandy. The awful business with Gus and now this. And of course the kid. Which is doing really badly, by the way. I know the girl in the neuro-developmental paediatric clinic, the one who saw her at their first attendance. You might know her too. Liz. Big girl from the year below us. Very grim, according to Liz. Not something they see very often and I can't remember exactly what it's called, but grim. You know. Nappies till you're twenty, and apparently shouts all the time. Poor Sandy.'

'Poor Sandy.'

'Margaret's bearing up. Does the grannying bit to give them a bit of a break now and again. But after Lennie, I don't know . . .'

Robbie was an exact contemporary of Max and Scott, a local boy who at the age of seventeen had crossed the street from George Heriot's school to Edinburgh University's Medical Faculty and shown early promise by winning prizes no one had ever heard of in anatomy, physiology and biochemistry. As a houseman he had acquired a reputation for following the line of least resistance with predatory staff nurses and then talking too much about it afterwards over lager and lime in the pub. His intended career in surgery had faltered and he was now an anaesthetist whose work took him all round the hospital and kept him nicely up to date with gossip. In due course, and as part of catching up with events, Scott would have a pint with him.

'Oh,' said Robbie. 'Must have a quick word with Fiona . . .' He was off. Scott glanced over at Sandy and her mother, whose duties at the door were almost complete. Sandy was holding an old lady's hand and laughing. When she and Scott had been together she had laughed a lot.

The party over, the crowd outside was thinning rapidly. Gus set off for his car feeling angry and confused. Dr Lorimer, his father and someone else were getting into Dr Lorimer's silly maroon Bentley coupe, probably heading for the Scottish Arts Club for a heavy lunch and an afternoon sleep. The Lennoxes, with Professor Munro in tow but, curiously, minus Sandy, were standing looking jolly pleased with themselves. It had certainly been quite correct, indeed mandatory, for him to attend and to be seen to attend, and Margaret had obviously appreciated a word from him. But Sandy still had a lot to learn. Perhaps coming to terms with her father's death would be a useful and ultimately meaningful spiritual experience. He glanced at his watch. If he missed lunch, which was no bad thing, there might just about be time to go back to the Southern via the medical library and dig out a few more references for his chapter of Dr Bennett's book.

Scott walked slowly under the trees, thinking again about Lennie's last hours in his study at home, in the middle of the night. He found his white Renault and joined a slow queue easing past a line of parked cars in a kind of leafy one-way system. Suddenly, with the sort of para-normal awareness that had often happened with Sandy, he spotted her, tiny in his rear-view mirror, on foot and alone, hurrying along a gravel path looking anxiously ahead. She passed within a few yards of him, stopped at a shabby grey Escort estate and got in. As the queue eased forward again Scott's car passed hers on the left. She was sitting in the front near side seat, reaching round towards the back. In the driver's seat was a man with short dark hair and a pale tweed jacket. In the back was a baby seat into which was strapped a large and active child, blonde and red-faced, now around two years old. She was bobbing and writhing so vigorously that the grey Escort was actually shaking on its springs, and from her there came an almost continuous high-pitched shriek, whether of agony or delight or mere mindless survival it was hard to tell.

To his surprise, Scott arrived at the Cafe Royal first. He sat for a while with a gin and tonic, browsing on the peanuts and gherkins and crisps and thinking about the whole business of coming back. A handful of regulars, hard-drinking, vaguely literary lawyers who had been sitting in more or less the same seats a year ago, pressed swiftly on with large whiskies. By twenty past one Max had not appeared. Scott was in no doubt about the time or the place. The most likely thing was that Max had gone by mistake to the Abbotsford, their other habitual city centre pub. Also to be considered was an intervening chance encounter with someone with whom lunch might be more interesting, at least in the sense that it might lead to an afternoon in bed; for a queasy moment Scott even considered the possibility that an inconsolable Aunty Jean, not much over fifty and in fair shape for her age, might prove to be consolable after all. One could never quite be sure with Max.

Scott slowed up on the crisps and things, made his second drink last a long time and wondered yet again about coming back. A year had passed and the same people were sitting in the same pubs and drinking the same things, admittedly at somewhat inflated 1979 prices. The sameness of it all was somehow both a reproach – something irrational about being absent from one's place of duty – and a threat. How long did it take to get like the little group of lawyers and how long did you stay that way if you did? By any standards they were pitiable, but because this was Edinburgh and they were lawyers who sometimes wrote things for the papers they probably thought they were the heirs of the Enlightenment. To stop thinking about that Scott turned his mind to his various reasons for having gone away but found that depressing too. After one day back at home he had seen Sandy for about twenty minutes and remembered more or less everything about her.

'Sorry about that . . . Aunty Jean's fault.' Max had been talking almost all the way from the door, so loud that all the lawyers were looking across at them. 'She went on and on and just wouldn't get out of the car. Seemed to think she should at least have been asked to join the family for lunch. And basically she's mad as hell at Lennie for dying. No job, no power, no lift to Holy Corner on Tuesdays. No getting to know who's in trouble and who's on the fiddle and who's a tiresome drunk they're trying to sack. And she's probably made a very big mistake about what's going to happen next. Treated Mike Irving like shit for years and now he's going to be the next Lennie. And he's got a nice sensible secretary already who's good and even good-looking . . . "Of course I'm not for one moment implying that there's anything going on between them . . . Jews are normally very careful about that sort of thing, especially with blondes. But it's been noticed around the office they're very, very close ... And there are so many things in our files that are really Edinburgh matters ... Delicate things ... You know the kind of thing, Max ..." But she wouldn't tell me. Just sat there. Yes, thanks. I'll have what you're having if you're having another before lunch. You've told them, have you? And delicate means dirt. I really tried to get her to open up a bit but she came over all grief-stricken so eventually I just leaned across her and opened the door. "You will keep in touch, won't you, Max," she said, so that might mean some dirt later. Yes ... Sorry I'm late.'

They were given a corner table well away from the drunks in the bar. A waitress in an old-fashioned black dress told them the oysters were nice today and Max decided that Lennie would have wanted them to have oysters and a half-bottle of champagne to start with. Thereafter free will prevailed, Max ordering something complicated with kidneys, Scott – rather thoughtlessly – a grilled sole, of which Max made grim and obvious sport.

'So let's see what's happened that you might be interested in. Oh, yes. Stuart MacGregor and Fiona have split up. You might be interested in that. I mean you always sort of fancied Fiona, didn't you?' Max drenched an oyster in tabasco and slurped it down, then coughed, winced and took a gulp of champagne. 'We're definitely going to have to do something about you ... "Unmarried senior registrar, flat and car, nice bloke, cuddly but lonely, seeks woman who does a turn, for caring relationship possibly leading to breakfast on Sunday." ' He laughed, started coughing again and poured himself more champagne. 'Sorry. We should have ordered a bottle ... And another thing. Quite interesting, really. Gus Ratho got the big brush-off.'

Scott was always careful to sound rather distant when anything to do with Sandy came up. 'Didn't that one break up a while ago?'

'Not Sandy. Fiona. Dirty beast. Got nowhere and serve him right.'

'Really?' Scott recalled the little tableau at the door: Ratho and Margaret, Fiona and Sandy.

'Yes. According to Robbie ...' The details lasted comfortably until the turbigo and grilled sole arrived. In due course Scott got an opportunity to enquire about Robbie himself.

'Bad scene. Well, baddish. Jobs coming up and he's being told not to bother. I mean, that's got to be bad news. If your own teaching hospital as good as tells you to bugger off, and you don't want to go and you haven't done anything to deserve it, and it's not just one job we're talking about, but two or three now, you begin to wonder what's wrong. Why does your face not fit? Or, what it really means, why has it suddenly started not fitting? That could get through to a chap eventually. And it's getting through to Robbie. He doesn't go on and on about it, but you can tell, and it's got to the point where you don't ask him how things are any more, because you know the answer already. Not at all like the boy wonder who cleaned up in second year. Remember all that? Humphrey? "Knock knock." "Who's there?" "Humphrey." "Humphrey who?" "Humphrey Heriot's, and I've just won all the prizes." '

The champagne problem was solved by the ordering of another bottle. Max and Scott sat until almost three then went for a walk, in the course of which Max, pausing sometimes to point things out as though Scott were a tourist, continued with his briefing on recent developments in Edinburgh medicine. By the end of the afternoon Scott still wasn't sure whether he was glad to be back or not.

I

WE ARE
MAKING
A NEW
WORLD

December 1949

The man lying on the examination couch looked at his feet as if he had never seen them before. 'Yes. You could be right, Dr Lennox. Maybe a wee bit blue, especially that one.' He pointed accusingly to the left. 'It's the worst. In bed as well. I could be up half the night with it, even with the sleeping tablet, but if it's not that one it's that one. Could that be right, doctor? It moving from one foot to the other? And the cold weather doesn't help. And like you said, walking up a hill. But it's not the gangrene, is it?' Gavin Lennox shook his head and the man smiled. 'Couldn't be doing with the gangrene. Came through the war, not that one there, the Great War, I mean, without a mark and I'm not going to start now. So that's all right.' He lay back on the battered leather examination couch and smiled.

They were half way through a morning clinic in the Royal Charitable Institute's Medical Out-Patients Department. The cubicle was shabby and cold but the patient, naked from the waist down, did not seem to mind. Dr Gavin Lennox, in his early thirties, trim in his white coat and as usual comfortably in control of things in a way the students admired but did not fully understand, smiled back at Mr Lawson. 'Now if I might just . . .' He laid a hand on the man's left foot. Mr Lawson looked surprised.

'Something wrong?'

'Not at all, doc. You've got nice warm hands.'

'And you've noticed this foot's colder, Mr Lawson . . .'

'Oh, yes, doc. Well, *she* has. Like a block of ice, she says.'

'And your toenails, Mr Lawson . . . Notice anything about them?'

'Definitely, doctor . . . Yes, definitely.' The students waited with interest. The man chuckled. 'Canny reach them like I used to . . .'

'Quite,' said Dr Lennox in an officer-like voice that usually quelled patients like this. 'I see . . .' He bent over the man's feet with the students. 'Nails yellowish, pale, thickened and flaky. Skin thin, dry, scaling. And look.' He rested a finger for a moment on the purplish red at the base of the left toenail. 'See how slowly the colour returns? And the pulses . . . Mr MacLeod?' The older student, dapper in his demob suit, raised his hands and shook his cuffs back, a Harley Street touch perhaps wasted on Mr Lawson. 'May I, sir?' He ran his fingers down the tendons on the front of the man's ankles in the approved fashion, right then left, the more normal first, then felt on the inside of each ankle just above the heel. 'Dorsalis pedis and posterior tibial pulses absent on the left, posterior tibial diminished on the right, right dorsalis pedis normal, Dr Lennox.'

'Thank you, MacLeod. Anything else?'

'Oh. Of course.' He lifted each knee from the couch, feeling behind it for the pulse. 'Diminished on the left.'

'Anything else?'

'Oh sorry. Excuse me, Mr Lawson.' The student turned back the man's shirt and felt for pulses in the groins, pausing in thought or embarrassment. 'Never mind, son,' said Mr Lawson. 'We've all got to learn our trade.'

'You're being very patient with us,' said Dr Lennox, more officer-like than before. 'Normal, both sides,' said the student, retreating gratefully. 'Good,' said Dr Lennox. 'Though it's conventional, at least until you've passed a few more exams, to start at the top and work down. Now another test . . . Mr Lawson, can we just raise your legs a bit. . . ? Look. Left goes pale a good deal quicker . . . As we'd expect. And something else. Mr Lawson, I'd like you just to sit round with your legs hanging down . . . Thank you. So it does look as if the circulation's not so good on the left, as I'm sure you're already aware. So perhaps the best thing now would be to get you into the ward for a little while. How do you feel about that?'

The man sat on the edge of the high, narrow couch in his shirt tail looking thoughtful. 'Is this arterial insufficiency, doctor? Is that what you're trying to explain?'

'Well, yes.'

The man nodded slowly. 'You mean like the King?'

'Exactly,' said Dr Lennox.

'Me and His Majesty . . .' said the man. 'I saw it all in the paper.' He smiled again. 'So when's the operation?'

Dr Lennox paused. Jackson, the younger student, was laughing quite unprofessionally, but there would be time enough over coffee to grill him about the origin and course of the arteries supplying blood to the lower limb. 'Let's not get too far ahead of ourselves, Mr Lawson. His Majesty had a number of tests before anything in the way of an operation was done, and if you agree, as he did, I think we could get on with them most quickly if you would come into the ward.'

'Now, doc?'

'Oh, I think there would be plenty of time to go home for your toothbrush.'

The man's left leg, still hanging down, was now an unpleasant shade of purple, but he sat contentedly, still taking the measure of his new-found affinities with Royalty. 'And all this is on the National Health?'

'Quite definitely.'

'Him and me?'

'Well, yes.'

'Really?'

'Strictly speaking, Mr Lawson, as you're probably aware, one shouldn't really discuss the affairs of one patient with another, but as His Majesty's recent health has been so widely reported I don't think I'd be breaking any confidence in saying that yes, he was operated on by National Health Service staff, from this hospital actually, and the whole thing went very well. I believe the Board of Governors has recently received a letter from the Palace expressing His Majesty's great satisfaction.'

'Oh, I would do that too,' said the man. 'If everything went well.'

'So shall we say ward twenty five? Around two o'clock?'

The man showed no signs of moving. There were a number of other new patients to be seen. 'I thought it was done in London.'

'You're quite right, Mr Lawson. People went down specially from the Institute. But since you already live in Edinburgh . . .'

'Sure, doc . . .' The man sat forward on the edge of the couch with his elbow, hand and chin in the pose of Rodin's 'Thinker', then looked up brightly. 'Learmonth. That's the name. Mr James Learmonth, the Edinburgh surgeon. He was in all the papers. So I'll be getting him too?'

'Very likely, Mr Lawson. Now aren't you getting a bit cold sitting there?'

' "By appointment to his Majesty the King", eh. . . ? But I suppose he pays his stamp like everybody else.'

'I wouldn't know.'

'You know I wasn't in favour of National Health . . .'

'Give it a chance, Mr Lawson. We'll certainly do our best. And there'll be plenty of time to have a chat about things when you come into the ward.'

'And the king gave him a knighthood, didn't he?' Mr Lawson reached for his trousers then paused again. 'I'll maybe send him a bottle of whisky.'

'That's entirely up to you, Mr Lawson . . . Look forward to seeing you again this afternoon.' As Mr Lawson shuffled out in his bare feet, with his socks and shoes in one hand and holding his trousers up with the other, Lennie had an idea. 'Jackson? You'll be around ward twenty five this afternoon, won't you? How about clerking in Mr Lawson for us? I'm sure you'll learn a lot. And of course you can present him on Dr Lorimer's round on Monday.' Jackson paled most gratifyingly. 'Now . . . Who's next? There were dozens out there half an hour ago.'

The next patient was a weedy youth who had been turned down for National Service in the lowest medical category and advised to see his own doctor about his chest trouble. And since he didn't have a doctor he had come up to the Institute's Medical Outpatient Department. He was a disappointed man. 'It wisnae National Service I was interested in. Eighteen months is nothing. I was going tae join up. My faither and my uncles were all Cameronians and I knew I had a wee bit of chest trouble but so had my uncle and he was mentioned in dispatches. And this army doctor pulled me out of the line and said son, you're one of the lucky ones . . . But I wasnae. I wanted in. I telt him, while he was sounding my chest, and he just telt me to shut up.'

Lennie calmed him down, asked him a few questions then invited Jackson to examine him. The student percussing the man's skinny chest, tapping away quite competently and finding a big dull area on the left which had presumably persuaded the army doctor that he was surplus to the requirements of national defence. The man's fingers were abnormal too, bulging at the tips and under the nailbed, something the student noticed for himself. 'Right, Jackson, he's got finger clubbing and a stony dull patch on the left. And of course the occasional fever on the history. So what's he got?'

'Koch's infection?' Jackson used the term for TB that the patients were supposed not to know.

'Nonsense. MacLeod?'

'Empyema?'

'Almost certainly. With a Koch's empyema mentioned as a hundred to one outsider to spare your colleague's feelings. And what are we going to do?'

'Drain it?'

'*We're* not. It's chronic. Physicians don't touch them. Not runny enough, so nothing comes out of our little tubes. Needs to see a thoracic surgeon.' Lennie returned to the patient. 'We'll get you X-rayed today and up to see a surgeon to drain some mucky stuff out of your chest probably next week. In a couple of months you'll feel better than you've felt for years . . .'

'Could I go back?'

'Hm?'

'For the Cameronians, sir. If I get this fixed . . .'

'Well, yes. Might well be worth a try. Now let's get you a chit for your X-ray.' A moment later the youth wandered out with his shirt over his arm, his military hopes revived. Lennie and MacLeod, who had both spent time with the colours, smiled. Jackson, who had not, and for whom the recruiting sergeant waited if he failed his exams just once more, tried unconvincingly to smile too.

Dr Lennox got up and looked out of the room. In the waiting hall Sister Dewar surveyed her eight wooden benches and two dozen or so patients. 'Sister. . . ? Sorry we're a little slow this morning.' Sister Dewar nodded, first in the manner of absolution towards Lennie then commandingly at a woman seated alone and apart under the 'No Spitting' notice.

'Miss Cuthbertson,' said Sister Dewar.

'Thank you, sister,' said Dr Lennox.

The woman was tall and thin and perhaps in her early fifties, carefully but not expensively dressed and wearing a dark velvet hat with a towering bow at the front. Lennie showed her in. 'Dr Lennox . . .' The woman smiled discontent. 'I was expecting Dr Lorimer. Dr Simmie went to some trouble to . . .'

'I'm seeing you on behalf of Dr Lorimer, Miss Cuthbertson.' Lennie smiled and took her arm. 'I'm afraid Dr Lorimer is unavoidably out of Edinburgh today. But please sit down . . . May I take your coat?' The patient looked from one medical student to the other and back again, her disappointment deepening. 'Miss Cuthbertson . . . We occasionally have medical students sitting in with us, but if you'll excuse them . . .' MacLeod and Jackson got up and as they left heard Lennie muttering something about it being well past their coffee time.

Miss Cuthbertson sat forward on her chair as though she had not yet decided to settle for what was on offer. Lennie sat back and smiled again. 'Dr Lorimer asked me to look out for you particularly and convey his apologies. Dr Simmie is an old friend of his, but alas . . .' He paused to convey weighty reasons best left undiscussed.

'Yes?'

'London. But of course if you insisted, perhaps early next month he might . . .'

'What did you say your name was?'

'Lennox, Miss Cuthbertson.'

'Dr Lennox, Dr Simmie gave me to understand that a woman in my position, as he put it, would be treated as though the National Health Service simply didn't exist. As he put it.'

'Oh.'

'The courtesies remain for our own, Miss Cuthbertson, were his exact words. Dr Lennox, I should explain I am a medical secretary. I have worked closely with your profession for nigh on thirty years.' She clicked open her handbag and scrabbled inside it. 'Dr Lorimer is the man for you, he said, and I shall write this morning. Dr Lennox, I have been sitting out there for an hour and a half while people with rights but no manners have coughed and jostled, laughed and joked and strolled around half-naked as though this were a public swimming bath.' She unfolded her handkerchief just in time for the first of her tears. Lennie got up, moved one of the student's chairs and sat down beside her with a hand lightly on her shoulder. In cases like this you gave in early and lied like hell just to get on with things. 'My dear Miss Cuthbertson, my profound apologies . . . Dr Lorimer showed me Dr Simmie's letter before he left and I had intended to ask Sister Dewar to let me know as soon as you arrived. My mistake completely. I'm so sorry . . . Now, if you'll excuse me for one moment . . .' He slipped out and returned from the front desk with a letter which began 'This miserable and often troublesome woman . . .' and was addressed simply to 'The Doctor,

MOPD, The Royal Charitable Institute'. He settled in his usual seat and folded the letter into the pocket of his white coat. Miss Cuthbertson smiled.

There was one more preliminary matter. They talked briefly of her career and established Dr Lennox's credentials through their mutual acquaintance with a number of distinguished local practitioners. Thereafter the story emerged quite quickly. She had been losing weight. Her appetite had been poor. That had been the first thing she had noticed, perhaps as much as a year ago. She just didn't feel like eating now, far less cooking. And more recently if she ate even a little, really by forcing herself, she felt full. But no pain as such, just a full feeling, and perhaps a bit of an ache recently, more to the left than in the middle, and it was that and all the weight she'd lost that had finally convinced her it wasn't all just nerves and made her go to Dr Simmie, who was really more like a friend than a doctor. Dr Lennox nodded.

Under the twinset, blouse and perfume she was quite grubby. She sat shivering on the examination couch and the chaperone nurse who had been called in hurried to get a blanket over her as quickly as possible. Her tongue was furred and her teeth irregular and badly decayed. At the root of her neck, just above the collarbone on the left, was a little clutch of firm irregular lymph nodes, none more than a quarter of an inch across, but of fatal significance all the same. For the sake of form he asked her to lie flat and placed a hand on her upper abdomen. Beneath the left ribs was a firm craggy lump. She winced as he pressed it.

'It's mother I'm worried about,' she announced. 'She has no one else.' She put her clothes on again and the nurse left. She sat opposite Lennie and asked him if he thought she had cancer of the stomach. Again he nodded. 'I've typed letters about it for thirty years. And I've seen from the letters what happens, so I suppose I ignored it at first but I can't any more. And it's my mother I'm worried about.'

It was all very sad, but not anything that could be sorted out in MOPD. Lennie sat for rather more than the decent minimum with her. Mother and daughter, mother now senile and incontinent, lived in a three-roomed flat at the top of a tenement stair somewhere off Gorgie Road. The daughter's job brought in a little money and a little respectability. When she died the old lady would be helpless and on her own. 'I've seen letters about people like that,' said Miss Cuthbertson, 'but I never thought there would be one about my own mother. ' "infirm and destitute . . . It is a statutory obligation of the Medical Officer of Health . . ." And then the poorhouse. And whatever you call it, it's still the poorhouse. And she'll know what's going on because she's not all that senile.' There were more tears.

The woman had only months or even weeks before her. She needed to be allowed to get on with what was left of her life and to try to get something organised for her mother, then perhaps come into the Institute when she couldn't go on any more. She would be looked after kindly and the name Lorimer would be used freely. Lennie tried to explain how the old poorhouses had been reorganised, some becoming hospitals within the Health Service, and how care in them had improved and was expected to improve still further. He would write to Dr Simmie and try to telephone him as well, and if Miss Cuthbertson would kindly make an appointment at the front desk to see him again in two weeks at Ward Twenty Five Out Patients they could keep in touch. She pulled her odd, threatening hat on, patted her eyes once more with her sodden handkerchief and left the room quite composed.

The students returned and the rest of the morning passed harmlessly enough. A drayman with quinsy was referred a hundred yards up the hill to the Surgical Out Patients Department. An insurance clerk with ulcer dyspepsia said to be resistant to treatment turned out on closer inquiry not to be taking anything like enough of his tincture of belladonna. Jackson distinguished himself further by getting very muddled about the function of the various nerves in the forearm, the patient being an anxious young man who had wakened up with a paralysis causing his right wrist to droop. Lennie interrogated both quite amiably, quickly demonstrating the neurological ignorance of the former and the cause of the mysterious paralysis of the latter. The patient had fallen asleep after an evening of passion, his partner sleeping most of the night on his right arm. He was reassured about what had happened, how his trouble would sort itself out over the next few hours or days, and how it was nothing to do with what he was most worried about, something he called galloping paralysis of the insane. When he had gone Lennie explained to the students that the syndrome was known, from more regular circumstances in which it had also been found to occur, as bridegroom's palsy.

They were sitting discussing that and a few of the other nerve compression syndromes when Sister Dewar came in. 'Dr Lennox, I wonder if you could possibly . . .' From the waiting hall came the sound of voices raised in anger. Lennie got up and the students followed him. 'Scotland's miracle hero, unfortunately,' Sister Dewar murmured as they went out. The waiting room was empty except for a woman who was shrieking and a man, seated in a wheelchair, who was shouting. Both, it seemed, were drunk. 'Ah, yes . . . A Mr Gilchrist, I think. We'll see what we can do. Again.'

The woman addressed Lennie. 'He says he's worse. The worse for drink, if you ask me. Look at the state of him. "Take me up tae the Institute," says he. "It's a medical opinion I need, no' you yellin' at me." '

'Right enough,' said the man. 'She's took the words oot o' my mooth. Half-crippled and pains everywhere, and I have tae put up wi' her.' With his left hand he pulled a bedraggled newspaper cutting from his shirt pocket. 'I'm Scotland's miracle hero, and look at the treatment I'm gettin'. It widnae be allowed under the Geneva convention, the things she does tae me.' He thrust the clipping towards Lennie, who took it politely and opened it up with some care. 'Ah, yes. Thank you, Mr Gilchrist . . . If I might just read this. Ah, yes . . .' The newsprint, now barely holding together, was eight years old and told how 'dashing Pte Rab Gilchrist of Thornybauk, Edinburgh had a miracle escape in the fierce fighting round Dunkirk last month, escaping death by less then half an inch as a Boche bayonet entered his neck. Scotland's miracle hero is now making good progress in an Edinburgh hospital . . .'

'He's a drunken waster and I'm fed up with him,' said his wife.

'I wonder if we might have a chat, Mrs Gilchrist, in just a moment. Now, Mr Gilchrist, what can we do for you?'

'I have this Brown-Sequard syndrome, from a partial cervical cord injury off a bloody German . . . Paralysed all down the one side, cannae feel a thing right all down the other . . . Lucky to be alive, they said.' He paused to shake his left fist at his wife. 'They didnae know about her . . . And I need rest and physiotherapy.'

Mr Gilchrist was a familiar figure in MOPD and on the wards. He came up from time to time, usually drunk and following a domestic crisis. His injury and his neurological deficits, which he had described quite well, were adjudged sufficiently interesting to merit admission once or twice a year for teaching purposes, and he knew it. Sister Dewar was nodding. Lennie took Mrs Gilchrist aside for a confidential account of how things had been going at home. Her breath was ripe with fresh and stale whisky. A rest would do her good, and another batch of students would master the intricacies of the Brown-Sequard syndrome of partial cord transection. That was arranged and Lennie and the students crossed the Institute's courtyard heading for the wards.

On the way Jackson asked about the King's illness. 'Last March,' said Lennie 'A great local sensation. Sad for the King, of course, but awfully good for the Institute. He's got peripheral vascular disease, quite bad on the right, according to all the best gossips, and the chaps in London had the unprecedented common-sense and modesty to ask the national expert even though he doesn't work in London. So James – now *Sir* James – was summoned to the presence, with a couple of chaps from Harley Street, of course, in case his accent needed translation, that kind of thing. He'd taken his toolkit and had a good look, did all the things we're going to do to Mr Lawson, and decided His Majesty would be none the worse for a sympathectomy. Then it got a bit complicated. All the best West End hospitals wanted to stage the show, Edinburgh was out of the question and the King hates hospitals anyway. I think he decided himself. Get it done at home. So they chose a great big room half way up the north face of Buckingham Palace, had it scrubbed out, draped all the chandeliers and Rembrandts and got a table, some lights and things, really made it quite a decent theatre. And at this end hampers and hampers of stuff were got ready, and I think a few humble folk up here might even have done their bit – for the good of their circulation, of course – by way of dress rehearsals, because being an expert on something isn't necessarily the same as doing a lot of it. They even laid on a special train for them: James, the gasman and an especially fearless theatre sister, plus all the hampers with two of everything and a few understudies in case anyone got flu. Quite a party, by all accounts. So there they were in Buck House, with the King snoring comfortably under the ether, James chiselling into the depths in search of the right bits to snip, with a senior registrar at each elbow to make sure everything went right, and of course the Archbishop of Canterbury, best cassock, cope and mitre shrouded under theatre kit, standing just outside the door in case it didn't. But it all went terribly well. And as Mr Lawson pointed out, if His Majesty's paid his stamps it'll all have been on the National Health.'

For their own separate reasons MacLeod and Jackson had extended their medical clerkships beyond the end of the autumn term and into the Christmas vacation, and both were enjoying it rather more than they had anticipated. Compared with normal term-time teaching it was, as Lennie had remarked after a ward round with Dr Ratho earlier in the week, more like medicine and less like mass entertainment. In the normal course of events twenty students trailed from bed to bed in the footsteps of a distinguished consultant physician who from time to time and more or less randomly fished out one of their number for public sacrifice. In MOPD they sat in tiered rows, perhaps as many as sixty at a time if the junior clerks were there as well, while the consultant, centre stage front, demonstrated his diagnostic wizardry on a tongue-tied, half-naked patient whose willing participation seemed somehow to have been taken completely for granted.

With Lennie now it was quite different. He took time and showed them things, and because there were only two of them they got much closer to the patients, who in turn opened up and became far more interesting. MacLeod, who had been a patient himself quite recently and still sometimes saw things from the patient's point of view, especially appreciated that. Jackson, on a Dean's warning and two weeks ago uncertain whether he wanted to continue in medicine, had thought about things again and decided to persevere, not simply to avoid trouble with his father. Lennie had made being a doctor look interesting again, so he would stick at it and perhaps be summoned to Buckingham Palace himself one day, although he had yet to decide in which particular specialist capacity.

As they approached the ward Dr Ratho emerged from it, escorted by Michael MacNair, the house officer. Dr Ranald Ratho, although the junior consultant on the firm and still in his forties, was strong on protocol, insisting on the little rituals such as the one now in progress. In his hat and overcoat, he was leaving the Institute probably on his way to his private patients in Moray Place. The houseman half a pace behind him, an ex-Royal Signals captain of unusually left-wing views, was carrying his briefcase for him and would do so as far as the car, and was performing that duty with a show of the elaborate tolerance to be found in the minders of aristocratic lunatics. Ratho, tall, aquiline and well-tailored, strode along unaware of MacNair's little parody. When he saw Lennie and the students he stopped, raising a gloved hand. Lennie quickened his pace. 'Sir?'

'Ah, Lennox . . . I was wondering what had kept you. Just taking the family off to Kinnell for a few days. Then Christmas in Edinburgh, of course. And I believe you know that Dr Lorimer's been detained in London for a couple of days more at least.' Ratho leaned over towards Lennie and their respective retinues drew back. 'Difficult case, I believe. One where Dr Lorimer's opinion seems greatly valued by our London colleagues. Does the name Spens mean anything to you. . . ? Mmm, thought it might. All very tricky, but it seems that our senior colleague might be of great assistance in ensuring . . . a satisfactory outcome.' Ratho grinned and almost winked. 'Tricky case, Spens, but Dr Lorimer's involvement can only do us good.'

Mention of the Spens business seemed to upset MacNair, who glowered at the back of Ratho's collar then glanced across to see how Lennie was reacting. For the moment Lennie ignored him: the matter would no doubt be raised again soon, in circumstances in which MacNair could safely vent his feelings.

'Oh, and Gavin . . .' Ratho came closer, the brim of his Homburg almost touching Lennie's forehead, and signalled in the direction of the students behind. 'Thanks awfully for looking after the lame ducks and black sheep . . . on top of everything else. Dr Lorimer appreciates it enormously. Mentioned it on the telephone from London this morning. And he's looking forward to seeing you at Christmas . . . You'll bring the family in, of course.' He paused and smiled his Moray Place smile. 'Gavin, thanks awfully . . . Goodbye.' He swept off with MacNair, a foot shorter, hurrying in his wake.

Lennie and the students walked on. 'Another big Institute case in London, Dr Lennox?' Jackson asked, knowing he probably shouldn't have. 'Something of that sort, I imagine, Jackson . . . Way above my head.' Lennie smiled. He had private views on the Spens business but would not from choice discuss them with either his seniors or his students. 'And probably yours too. Now, how about a quick cup of coffee, and when Dr McNair joins us we can get to grips with the inpatients? Agreed. . . ?' There was no enthusiasm and Lennie knew that: an early lunch would have suited them better but a ward round would do them more good. In the doctors' room a couple of scones remained from Dr Ratho's morning coffee and Lennie passed them round with some ceremony, insisting that out of term-time students were young colleagues who needed to be looked after, and no, he didn't feel in the least inclined to have one himself. By the time MacNair rejoined them they were happy again. MacNair was not, whether because of the Spens business or at the prospect of an unexpected ward round before lunch it was not clear.

Lennie pressed a coffee on him. 'You're probably right, Michael, but perhaps a bit ahead of the times. I quite agree that all that stuff about seeing sir to his car's getting a bit old-fashioned nowadays, but our seniors seem to quite enjoy it and it's fairly harmless. And like most things in medicine, it's not as bad as it used to be . . .' He launched into another of his yarns: something about a competition they had once had as houseman to see who could slam the door of a consultant's Rolls-Royce hardest, which culminated in sir getting angry and getting his gears mixed up and reversing at speed into a wall. '. . . and the mark's still there, and we're, um, rather proud of it to this day.' Lennie chuckled and the students laughed out loud. The yarn even seemed to cheer MacNair a little. 'Come on, Michael,' said Lennie. 'Finish your coffee and let's take a stroll round. And shouldn't we organise a late lunch in the Residency. . . ? Our young colleagues to join us, of course, if they'll allow me the honour. I'll ring the butler now, while you're finishing your coffee.' He got up and MacNair smiled, at the Rolls-Royce yarn and at Lennie, doing a Rommel again: dropped in it at short notice, but bouncing back with a mixture of charm, arm-twisting and the imaginative use of facilities not strictly under his control. He was good and he knew it and he would move up from clinical tutor to assistant physician soon and he deserved it. And the Residency butler wouldn't mind about the late lunches, because he liked Lennie too.

'Right, Jackson. End of the bed stuff. Mrs Arbuthnot's just come in, I believe, and neither of us has seen her before. So I'd like you to tell me what's wrong with her.' Jackson stood with the others in the ward's only single room looking sheepish. Mrs Arbuthnot was sixtyish with yellow hair and a yellowish tinge to the whites of her eyes. She smiled and fluttered her eyelashes. Lennie made his own quick appraisal: almost certainly an alcoholic and probably some kind of hysteric as well, but that was beyond the scope of the kind of medical square-bashing Jackson was enduring as a last alternative to being thrown out of medical school. There was something more obvious. Her skin was thinned and pale, her body angular and wasted and her hands shapeless and floppy like the paws of a dead mole. 'Yes, Jackson? Sorry, Mrs Arbuthnot, I should have introduced myself and these young men, who would be greatly helped if you would allow them to take a quick look at your hands and arms. Would you mind? No? Carry on, Jackson . . .'

Mrs Arbuthnot held out her right hand as though Jackson were about to fall upon his knees and kiss it. At least one of Lennie's diagnoses was confirmed. 'Such a pleasure to be able to do something in return,' she fluted. 'After all that Dr Ratho's done for me. Dr Jackson, is it? I don't think Dr Ratho told me about you.' Jackson smiled and blushed and took the proffered hand, soft and almost boneless to feel. 'Um. Arthritis,' he mumbled. 'Martyr to it, Dr Jackson . . . Or is it Mr Jackson, for the time being at least? I should perhaps mention that Dr Ratho *didn't* say anything about medical students . . . when we talked in his rooms in Moray Place about my coming in for spinal pumping treatment . . . But I assume all *that* will be done by someone fully qualified . . . A Dr Lennox was mentioned . . .' Mrs Arbuthnot fluttered her eyelashes again.

Lennie nodded. 'Indeed, Mrs Arbuthnot . . . Dr Ratho did mention that you were coming in . . . I'm Dr Lennox, and I've been looking forward to meeting you . . . Now, if you'll excuse us, we must press on, and I'll pop back later in the afternoon to discuss your treatment in detail with you . . . With a little more privacy, I'm glad to say . . . But for the moment, please do excuse us . . .' Mrs Arbuthnot waved her little floppy hand and they moved on. Lennie and MacNair exchanged glances. Dr Ratho should have mentioned a case like this, however much his haste to be off shooting pheasants in Perthshire before dark. He had established the doubtful habit of seeing people privately in his rooms in Moray Place, arranging with the ward sister to have them brought in to the ward as NHS patients with some airy plan of investigation and management, yet omitting to say anything to the doctors who would actually be carrying it out. It was a disagreeable routine to which people had adapted, but this patient posed one or two special problems: there were now firm suspicions she was a hysteric and a drunk, and treatment by spinal pumping for rheumatoid arthritis was probably best left to the diminishing number of doctors who still believed in it.

When they were out of earshot Dr McNair was apologetic but uninformative. The lady had arrived accompanied by a chauffeur carrying her personal effects at eleven that morning. No, there was no letter from Dr Ratho or the referring general practitioner. And yes, sister had known she was coming but had assumed Dr McNair did too, and when the staff nurse was helping her to unpack there had been a bottle of gin among the nighties. The staff nurse pursed her lips and nodded. She was from the North and knew a lot about drink. Lennie would go back later and try, on behalf of his stylish but cavalier superior, to make some sense of it all. The next patient, in the first bed on the left in the main ward, was for the moment in rather deeper trouble.

She lay on a cardiac bed that folded in two places to form a kind of broad, shallow chair, allowing her to remain semi-recumbent: propped up to make breathing as comfortable as possible but with legs hanging low to allow the accumulation of fluid for tapping. Mrs Murray was in the last stages of rheumatic heart disease and she knew it. She had suffered rheumatic fever in childhood and become breathless in the course of her first pregnancy. A heart murmur had been discovered. Wasted and gasping now, she was dying in early middle age because the pumping action of her heart could no longer overcome the inefficiency of its valves, first damaged by an illness when she was ten. Lennie asked for screens to be brought and they examined her, listening to the various squeaks and rumbles from the wrecked valves and the moist crackles from her sodden lungs. Her legs were pale and hugely swollen but fluid was draining satisfactorily from the multiple incisions McNair had made that morning. Lennie replaced the covers and took her pulse again, mainly so as to touch her. 'You're being very brave and patient with us, Mrs Murray . . . And you should begin to feel a little easier soon.' She shook her head. 'And we can make jolly sure you get a good sleep tonight . . . That'll help a bit.' He took her medicine chart from the hook above the head of the bed and put her evening dose of morphine up from one quarter to half a grain. As they moved on a few gentle questions from Lennie revealed that Jackson was under the impression that rheumatic heart disease, as endured by Mrs Murray, and rheumatoid arthritis, as demonstrated in Mrs Arbuthnot, were closely related conditions. 'I know the nomenclature's a bit misleading, Jackson, but as your reading takes you beyond the list of chapter headings I think you'll find there are some very interesting differences. So bone up on both of them tonight and we'll talk about them again tomorrow. Who's next, Michael?' MacNair paused. 'Sorry, Dr Lennox ... The last lady, with rheumatoid arthritis, Mrs Arbuthnot ... Dr Ratho did say something about her, just as he was leaving. The spinal pumping thing. That's what she's here for. It didn't mean much to me, but when she mentioned it . . .' Lennie nodded. 'We'll sort all that out shortly, Michael. Ah, yes. Miss McCracken ... How are you today?'

The patient, a pale blonde girl in her late twenties, opened her eyes, looked round and beamed adoringly up at Lennie. 'Marvellous, no other word for it, Dr Lennox. I feel marvellous and Dr MacNair says my blood count's coming up again, that's twice running, nearly forty percent now and my tongue's stopped hurting and my appetite's come back and I feel stronger and if this goes on I'll get home again and I think I'm even putting on weight and . . . and . . .' Lennie moved a little nearer and she seized his hand. ' . . . and I know now I'm not going to die . . .' She lay back and sobbed, tears streaming past her ears and on to her hair and the pillow. Lennie patted her hand and she sniffed moistly and collected herself a little. 'I'm sorry, but it's the first day in more than two years that I've felt like this ... And you've just no idea ...' Lennie nodded. 'Well, all you have to do now is rest and get better, and so far as we know that's the end of it. And I think we're almost as pleased about all this as you are . . .' She smiled through her tears, sniffed again and begun to laugh. 'And the most marvellous thing is never having to look at another raw liver sandwich in my whole life ...' 'Quite,' said Lennie. 'That's certainly something to look forward to.' She broke down again and hid her face in the staff nurse's starched apron. Lennie muttered something about lots of rest meantime, and they moved on.

'Interesting,' said Lennie. 'The stuff actually seems to work.'

The students looked at one another and then at Lennie. 'So let's press on . . .'

They pressed on, and made it round both wards and across to the Residency quite neatly for the late lunches booked at two o'clock. As they waited for Morris to bring their fishcakes Jackson asked about the anaemic girl. Although Jackson was the kind of student who might reasonably be suspected of asking questions to avoid being asked them himself, the case was an interesting one. The girl had been sent up from Roxburgh about three years previously by a very sharp general practitioner who had made the diagnosis on clinical grounds alone, even though the girl was unusually young for her illness. She was blonde and blue-eyed, had a sister who had become anaemic during pregnancy, and had presented just feeling tired but admitting on questioning to having a sore tongue. Dr Lorimer had seen her and brought her in for investigations. Her haemoglobin had been thirty percent and a marrow biopsy had confirmed a diagnosis just as bad as leukaemia: pernicious anaemia, with a maximum life expectancy of around two years. Then liver therapy had come along, and the poor girl had had to eat a pound or so of raw liver every day just to avoid getting worse. She had been very, very brave, soldiering on at home with her gruesome diet, coming in from time to time for observation and tests. Her blood count had rarely gone below thirty, but liver therapy was an ordeal that some patients could not bear. The previous year Lennie had seen a man die rather than struggle day after day with the cold, bloody, slimy chunks. Exhausted and ghostly pale, he had simply given up and faded on into death.

The fishcakes came with cauliflower and a thin cheese sauce. Lennie carried on with his story. 'Then a couple of bright chaps thought it might be nice to find out what it was in the raw liver that was helping, and set to work. One of them ground his way through four tons of the stuff, proteolysing it, extracting it, extracting the extract and so on, eventually getting about a gramme of some pink stuff . . . Amazing when you think about it, makes needles in haystacks look quite rewarding. But luckily a little of it goes a long way. This girl's had less than a milligramme altogether, and look at her . . . No one's quite sure exactly what it is yet but they've sort of thought of a number and called it vitamin B12. And thank god she stuck to her guns with the liver, because she's probably one of the first half dozen cases in Scotland to get the stuff . . . Now then, Jackson, what are the other common causes of a macrocytic anaemia in young women?'

The Residency in early afternoon was quiet, a club for young gentlemen at a time when most of them were at work. Lennie, MacNair, MacLeod and Jackson sat at leisure over a pudding described as Charlotte Russe, and conversation turned eventually to the absence in London of Dr Lorimer. MacNair was surprisingly well-informed. Spens, he assured them, was not a case but a scandal. The work of the Spens committee had been discussed and deplored at the Socialist Medical Society he attended on the few occasions when his houseman's duties permitted it, and in his view the whole business should have been stamped on firmly by Nye Bevan as soon as Corkscrew Charlie and his gang had raised it. And if Lorimer was getting involved it meant Scotland was going to be blighted too with an idea that might just about pass muster in London, where standards of medical ethics were notoriously low, but which didn't make any sense at all north of the border.

Jackson had another question and MacNair answered it. 'The Spens awards, laddie, will let Charlie Moran do for the National Health Service what Al Capone did for the business life of Chicago . . . The whole mafia apparatus of secrecy, money, influence and threat, help your friends and punish your enemies, not with concrete socks but with straightforward bribery and blackmail, and they've even got the taxpayers to pay for it . . . They've actually done it . . . Bevan really has given him the money, so now he must be looking for a Scottish hit man, and why not J D K Lorimer? Vice-President of the Edinburgh College, old enough to matter, young enough to be around for a useful space of years. Reliable conservative and keen mason. Well done, Charlie. But he's probably hedged his bets with someone in Glasgow too . . .'

'So they're some sort of prize. . . ?'

'That's what they'll try to tell people if they can't keep them completely secret . . . Make it sound like a Nobel prize for medicine, recognising outstanding achievement. But they're nothing of the sort. They're handouts, big pay-rises, even added on to your pension. *Their* pensions. For merit, they say, or to compensate for giving up private practice, which they won't anyway. Or to instil a sense of competition for glittering prizes . . . But if they're giving us three reasons, all different, then they don't really believe any of them themselves, and deciding who gets them will be the biggest joke of all . . . So nobody wants anything to do with them . . .'

'D'you think so, Michael?' said Lennie. 'Is that what they're saying at the Bolsheviks Club?'

'Oh, they'll get people like Lorimer in. Suits him to have a reputation for controlling how much the other consultants get paid, and you can see why. But really nobody else . . . There have been dozens of letters in the British Medical Journal, every single one against.'

Lennie gave up on his Charlotte Russe. The Spens awards might have been what Aneurin Bevan had meant when he had said he would fix the leaders of the profession by stopping their mouths with gold. In effect they were now in charge of a great deal of public money, to be disbursed to themselves and selected colleagues in the form of secret pay and pension increases, some of them very lavish indeed. But it was hard to see the thing ever working except as an officially recognised system of corruption counter to all the principles of fairness and equality that the NHS stood for. Lennie loathed it but didn't want to talk about it. 'Now I can't think what the students must be thinking of us. Moaning about money when thanks to the blessed Nye we hardly ever have to mention it nowadays . . . A great improvement, in my opinion, the salaried service, but it's amazing how many of the patients haven't quite cottoned on . . . Old ladies keep offering me boiled sweets and asking if they might knit me a pair of socks or bring me in some baking . . . Come on, chaps, I'll see La Arbuthnot myself. Michael's got plenty else to do. And Jackson, it's your pleasant duty this afternoon to persuade Mr Lawson that what was good enough for His Majesty in March is good enough for him in December . . . Thank you, Morris. We'll get out of your way now. No . . . No coffee, thank you very much.'

The students mumbled their thanks to the butler and the four made their way along the main corridor of the Residency again. 'The pictures are rather fun,' said Lennie, stopping suddenly to peruse a group photograph, one of the dozens hanging frame to frame in double rows on both sides of the corridor. 'That's our lot. A thin wartime crop. And Dr Lorimer in his Oxford bags is just along here.' They browsed along the rows of pictures, incidentally spotting youthful versions of one or two other members of the Institute's senior staff, going right back to sepia groups of only eight or ten, the elegant young residents of the nineties with centre partings and tight, high-buttoned suits, until the recorded past stopped abruptly at the top of the back stairs. As they trooped down into the courtyard again Jackson thought about Lennie as a houseman and about the confident young dandies in sepia who must mostly be retired or dead now, and decided afresh to go on with medicine after all.

Mrs Arbuthnot was happy to see Lennie again. She lay in the single room in a pink bed-jacket perhaps specially purchased or crocheted for the occasion. Her unpacking had been completed. On her locker were a couple of perfume sprays, a silver cigarette case and lighter, a bottle of Rose's lime juice three quarters full, a bowl of fruit and a formidable stack of lending-library novels. She was bright-eyed and quite cheerful now and once more extended a droopy hand. 'Dr Lennox, Dr Ratho spoke so highly of you . . . "A young man who will go far, Mrs Arbuthnot . . . We hope for great things from him . . ." So how kind of you to come at only . . . two thirty, is it? But the nurses have been terribly sweet and under-standing and have made me as comfortable as anyone in my condition could possibly be in the circumstances . . . Was it an emergency, Dr Lennox? One of these life and death affairs you people have to deal with every day? I suppose one shouldn't really ask . . . But I hope you managed to fit in some lunch. You know I think the war had that effect on people . . . They started to skimp on proper lunches . . . They'll pay for it in ulcers, we always said.' She giggled and Lennie made a mental note to examine her eyes closely, something not perhaps strictly necessary but at least offering a leisured opportunity to smell her breath; and the night nurses might also be invited to check up on the bottle of Rose's lime juice while Mrs Arbuthnot was asleep.

'And how did all this trouble of yours begin. . . ?' Mrs Arbuthnot smiled and lay back and looked at the ceiling. Lennie waited and a long silence followed. 'Sometimes,' said Mrs Arbuthnot, 'some-times I think I should simply sit down with pen and paper and write the whole thing down once and for all . . . People do that. They find it helps them to understand, and it might help their fellow-sufferers too, and of course . . .' She turned towards Lennie with a little saccharin smile. ' . . . so many busy doctors would find it saved their precious time . . .' She paused and Lennie nodded. 'Archie Ainslie knows my case inside out, of course, and I'm sure he would have told Dr Ratho . . . And Dr Ratho was sweet and completely understanding and took all the time in the world and made lots and lots of notes . . .' Her eyes filled with tears and turned ceilingwards again. 'You see my difficulty, Dr Lennox . . .'

'I know it's distressing for you, Mrs Arbuthnot, but please try . . .'

'And Dr Ratho's sure that spinal pumping treatment's the answer . . . He said it's what everybody has in America. "It's for the few, Mrs Arbuthnot," he said. "Selected cases only, we insist, but there have been some remarkable successes with it and yours might be just the type of case to gain most . . ." ' She turned to Lennie again and fluttered her eyelashes. 'I'm ready, Dr Lennox . . .'

Lennie sat back in his chair. 'Quite, Mrs Arbuthnot . . . But as I'm sure Dr Ratho explained to you, it's not something we rush into and since I shall be doing it – if it turns out there are indeed no special risks or problems – I would appreciate the opportunity to get to know about your various troubles at first hand.' Mrs Arbuthnot reached for her cigarette case, flipped it open, threw a cigarette between her lips with remarkable dexterity then picked up her lighter and fumbled with it for a few poignant moments. 'Would you mind, Dr Lennox? There's a dear . . .' Lennie obliged, she inhaled deeply then puffed long twin plumes from her nostrils. 'I have a theory about rheumatoid arthritis, Dr Lennox . . .'

As Lennie watched and listened it occurred to him that perhaps the treatment proposed was what was needed. Spinal pumping, which involved a spinal tap and the repeated withdrawal and replacement of cerebro-spinal fluid, worked if it worked at all as a kind of drastic placebo, and placebos in general were said to have their most dramatic effects in hysterics who believed in the treatment being offered. Perhaps that was what Dr Ratho had had in mind, though it would have been helpful if he had said so. Mrs Arbuthnot's theory, something both complicated and imprecise concerning nervous tension and astrological influences, added nothing to what Lennie knew already about rheumatoid arthritis, but her exposition of it proved helpful. A background account of fifteen years of symptoms, her innumerable medical encounters and her travels round the more expensive mudbaths of pre-war Europe corroborated in detail the diagnosis first made when she had offered her hand to Jackson for examination. The woman was a pitiable hysteric, a professional invalid building out from real disease and disability to an unnecessary but all-encompassing way of life. With a husband rich enough to indulge her and her family gone she had taken up arthritis as a career and, presumably, drink as a solace. If Dr Ratho had known all that it would have been helpful of him to pass it on and if he hadn't it was just as well someone had come to grips with it now. Eventually Lennie reached for his ophthalmoscope and was rewarded with a generous whiff of freshly consumed gin.

When he had finished examining her he made up his mind. The simplest way forward was to do what both Mrs Arbuthnot and Dr Ratho wanted, give her two or three bouts of spinal pumping if one didn't put her off it altogether and then send her home in time for Christmas to boast of its miraculous success. 'Well, Mrs Arbuthnot, I think we should go ahead and start treatment tomorrow . . .' She interrupted him with a delighted little shriek and a bit of floppy hand-clapping. '. . . assuming nothing alarming crops up on one or two routine tests. Monday afternoon suit you? We'll just take you over to a room across the passageway with a group of nurses to help us and I'll slip a needle into your spine and draw off some fluid, pop it back in again and repeat the process every few minutes for about an hour . . .' Lennie watched her carefully as he spoke but if anything she appeared keener. 'Then the same again on Wednesday, and probably Friday. Three treatments should be more than adequate, and I'm rather assuming that you'd prefer to be home for Christmas . . .' Mrs Arbothnot nodded in radiant dumbshow, hugged herself and reached for another cigarette. Perhaps for a week or so she would be happy.

Over tea Lennie discovered that Sister had formed views already. 'Patients like that don't know when they're well off, Dr Lennox. She has everything she needs at home and she arrives here with a chauffeur and three suitcases as though we were a hydropathic spa and proceeds to treat my girls like parlourmaids. Very silly of her, because Dunnett, my senior staff nurse, found gin among her nightclothes, you'll know that, she'll have told you. But the rules for the Mrs Arbuthnots of this world are exactly the same as they are for

Judy O'Grady, Dr Lennox. In my view and in the view of the Institute's Board of Governors and I have already told her so.' Sister put her cup down with some force. There were rules and she believed in them. A notice at the ward entrance, a formidably printed document under glass, summarised them and outlined her powers and often reminded Lennie as he passed of the Articles of War posted in HM ships. There was no specific mention of mutiny, but singing, whistling, gambling of any form and the consumption of intoxicating liquors other than on medical advice could all result in summary ejection after one warning. There was even a clause which specified that able bodied patients would undertake such domestic duties as the Ward Sister shall from time to time direct, again supported by the sanction of instant dismissal. Lennie thought about that and decided that, although Ranald Ratho almost certainly wouldn't approve, scrubbing out the kitchen would probably do Mrs Arbuthnot just as much good as spinal pumping. Perhaps on some other occasion.

The following day Jackson was still shaky on rheumatic heart disease but well up to standard on rheumatoid arthritis. Puffed up with newly acquired knowledge he was sceptical about the treatment planned for Mrs Arbuthnot. Lennie found himself defending it without enthusiasm. 'We're more or less agreed that no one knows what causes rheumatoid so, in theory at least, anything might help. There's a school of thought that says it's a kind of nervous dystrophy and spinal pumping's based on that. A few chaps have reported quite good results, usually in conjunction with something else, but the last thing I read on it wasn't very keen. BMJ a few months ago. Six cases. The only patient it helped was . . .' Lennie lowered his voice and glanced around. '. . . a nursing sister. The point they seemed to be making was that it worked on people who wanted it to work . . . But there's still a fair bit of that in medicine generally, not just in the chronic diseases. You want to watch, Jackson? See if she takes up her three suitcases and walks? No one would be more delighted than I if she did.'

On Monday afternoon they took Mrs Arbuthnot across to the procedure room and she lay on her side with her knees as close to her chin as comfort and her disease allowed and Lennie painted her lumbar spine with antiseptic, draped her and scrubbed up. Jackson watched and listened, marvelling at his ability to get a difficult patient first to behave herself, more or less, then to submit to all this. Lennie worked away with some local anaesthetic then with a long needle and worried that she might actually be enjoying it. Her spine was difficult but he got in first shot and clear cerebrospinal fluid – gin clear, the neurologists called it, quite appositely for a case such as this – welled slowly back as soon as he withdrew the needle's obturator. Jackson's admiration increased. The procedure dictated that twenty cubic centimetres of the fluid be drawn off into a syringe then replaced by pushing it straight down the needle again: twenty cc's twenty times in an hour was the standard routine and a lot of people found it uncomfortable. Mrs Arbuthnot lay quietly, gripping Nurse Dunnett's hand and murmuring sometimes about not wanting to be a bother to anyone.

At last Lennie withdrew the needle and strapped a pad to the little puncture wound, turned Mrs Arbuthnot onto her back again and asked her how she felt. She pursed her lips and paused and eventually said 'Better? Yes, probably . . . Except for a slight headache.' Lennie, who had expected to be told either that she had suddenly felt fitter than she had done for years, or that she would never go through all that again even if it meant she had to live in agony till she was a hundred, simply assured her that was common and nothing to be alarmed about, but that she should rest flat for the next twenty four hours or so. She thanked him and was taken back across the passageway to her single room.

Early the following morning, not long after two o'clock, MacNair was summoned from sleep in his Residency bedroom by a knock on the door. 'Sorry to disturb you, sir . . . The ward would like you to go across, sir . . . A Mrs Arbuthnot's not so well.' The porter, one of the older ones, seemed genuinely apologetic. 'Thanks . . . I'm on my way . . .' MacNair got up, dressed quickly and hurried downstairs, across the frosty courtyard and on to the ward. In the sideroom with Mrs Arbuthnot were two student nurses, one holding her quite firmly round the shoulders, the other stroking her hair and telling her there was really nothing to worry about. The nurse in white cuffs left the blue-collar in charge still holding Mrs Arbuthnot round the shoulders and went outside with MacNair. 'She was fine when we came on, Dr MacNair . . . Just a bit of a headache after her spinal thing and asleep by eleven o'clock, then about an hour ago she rang her bell and shouted when we didn't get there right away, but she's done that before . . . Then when nurse went in she said she had a headache and felt terrible. Her temperature was a bit up. Ninety nine point five. Then she started being very noisy and shouting about her sore head, and asked us to put out the night-light because it was hurting her eyes, so we sought medical help.'

When they went back in Mrs Arbuthnot was calling the first year student nurse a thieving tart and striking out at her. 'I shall pay my bill first thing tomorrow, write to the manager and tell my lawyer, young woman . . . Hotel or whorehouse, I hardly care, I shall certainly never be back . . . Where's Hector? Hector?' MacNair moved quietly towards her. 'Mrs Arbuthnot . . .'

'Where's Hector. . . ? Hector? Whoring around again, you can be sure . . . It's the only reason we come to these ghastly places . . . Hector!'

'Mrs Arbuthnot, you're in the Institute for treatment for your arthritis, and your husband's at home.'

The patient sat up straight and glared at MacNair. 'Young man, don't presume to advise me on my husband's whereabouts. He's at Jenny's, up in Albert Terrace . . . Couldn't wait to get me in here . . . I can tell. Thinks he's getting Christmas off too but he's not . . . I'll be out and I'll see a solicitor and he'll soon find out whose money it is . . . And so will his little Jenny. Now leave me alone, it's the middle of the night and I'm quite upset. Sorry to have got you all out of bed but I'm really quite all right, considering everything, and I'd dearly love to get some sleep.'

'But Mrs Arbuthnot, if you've got a headache . . .'

'. . . then it's just as that pleasant young man this afternoon said it would be . . . Kindly put the light out and go back to bed, Dr MacNair. You know it's the middle of the night but these girls still have lots of work to do.' She winked at the nurse in charge. 'Don't you, girls? Lots of lovely work. . . ? Now kindly run along, all of you, and let an old woman get some sleep.'

'Maybe she's just had a bad dream,' said the first year nurse when they were outside again. First year nurses did not address doctors directly when third year nurses were present, even if they had something sensible to say. 'It's her temperature we're most concerned about, Dr MacNair,' said the third year nurse, to regularise matters. MacNair nodded. 'And she's really no idea where she is half the time. She was a bit like this last night, but nowhere near so bad . . . Dr MacNair, we were wondering if she could have meningitis. You know, after the spinal thing . . .'

MacNair shook his head. 'Shouldn't have . . . Lennie's very good . . . But I suppose there's a faint possibility . . . Could you please check her temperature, nurse, but first I'll go over her again . . .' As MacNair led the way back in the nurse in charge nodded to her junior colleague. Mrs Arbuthnot lay awake and alert and was lucid and cooperative while the houseman asked her about her symptoms and examined her. There was nothing in all that to support a diagnosis of meningitis and a few minutes later the senior nurse reported that Mrs Arbuthnot's temperature was normal. MacNair left the ward unsure as to whether or not the whole thing had been some kind of little tussle and if so who had won. When he had thanked the nurse she had replied 'Thank you, doctor' in a way that reminded him of how a certain Signals sergeant had used 'sir' as a term of contempt.

At four MacNair was summoned to the ward again. Mrs Arbuthnot's temperature had gone up to one hundred point four, she was drowsy and her headache was worse. On close questioning she was prepared to admit that the light hurt her eyes and her neck was now a bit stiff. This time MacNair did not hesitate but asked the nurse in charge to get things together for an urgent diagnostic spinal tap. She smiled and said 'We're all ready, doctor.' Though drowsy and stiff Mrs Arbuthnot cooperated well and MacNair, kneeling uncomfortably and sweating with anxiety about what he was attempting and what he might find, got in first time too. He drew out the obturator and waited. At the butt of the needle a drop formed slowly then fell, crystal clear, into the waiting glass tube. Clear cerebrospinal fluid did not harbour pus, and without pus Mrs Arbuthnot could not have meningitis. He took the sample to his little laboratory, spun it down, stained it and looked down his microscope with some confidence. There were a few normal lymphocytes, and all was well. He went back to the nursing station to pass on his findings. Mrs Arbuthnot did not have meningitis. She had a sore head and a temperature and was a bit confused but she did not have meningitis, and he now felt sufficiently confident about what was going on to write her up for a couple of aspirin tablets. And if that didn't sort her out Lennie would be back on the ward in a few hours and he could turn his superior mind and greater experience to the problem. At six thirty MacNair walked back across the courtyard and upstairs to bed.

By eight thirty he was on the ward again, in the doctors' room trying to find enough sharpened and sterile needles to begin his blood round, when Sister came in. She stood in front of him, a good six inches taller because of her heels and her hat, and so close he could smell her soap. 'Dr MacNair . . . I wonder if you are aware that Mrs Arbuthnot is not only quite unwell but seeing wee grey creatures running up and down the walls . . . She's hearing things that aren't there and shaking and sweating and has had an intermittent low elevation of temperature overnight. And since I wouldn't be at all surprised if she went on to have a fit I have taken the precaution of drawing up some paraldehyde . . . I wonder if you could come and see her, Dr MacNair?'

Diagnosis was not, of course, a nursing responsibility and Sister had been quite careful to observe that convention. MacNair returned in her wake to Mrs Arbuthnot's sideroom feeling very foolish indeed. The patient, with a nurse seated at each side of her bed, was leaning forward and staring straight ahead. She did not at first look round, but when MacNair closed the door behind him she jumped as if she had been shot at then stared in terror at the wall again, clutching her bed-jacket and muttering to herself. He leaned towards her. 'Mrs Arbuthnot . . .' Wild-eyed and dishevelled, she turned to face him and suddenly focussed. 'Get away . . . You're all in it . . . You and them together. They're jumping cold and grey and I don't like it one bit. Call them off and get out . . . Hector? Where are you? Hector! Come back . . . Hector!'

A white enamel kidney dish containing a large syringe lay on the bed table. Sister stood silently waiting. MacNair picked up the syringe and she nodded at the staff nurse on the patient's left. 'Mrs Arbuthnot,' said the staff nurse, 'we're just going to give you a wee injection. In your bottom . . .' Sister nodded again and the staff nurse moved swiftly, pulling Mrs Arbuthnot's shoulders round and down so that suddenly she found herself lying on her side. The second nurse pulled back the bedclothes then the first reached down and got her right arm behind the patient's knees, doubling her up with her left buttock jutting up but still half-covered by a short nightie. The second nurse twitched it clear and Sister smiled at the houseman. 'We find that with patients like this quickest is kindest. Dr MacNair. . . ?'

An evil-smelling drip of paraldehyde oozed from the syringe on to his hand. The stuff was foul and sticky and had to be given in uncomfortably large injections to produce sedation and giving it slowly didn't make it any less painful. MacNair swabbed a little patch of skin with meths then stabbed his needle in. From somewhere under the staff nurse Mrs Arbuthnot gasped briefly then howled in pain. 'Just a wee prick,' said the staff nurse. 'It'll be all over very soon.' Slowly the syringe emptied. Mrs Arbuthnot whimpered then gasped again as MacNair pulled it out. The staff nurse let her out of the armlock and stroked her hair. 'You'll get a nice wee sleep shortly, dear, and probably wake up feeling fine . . .'

'Don't you dare dear me, miss. When Dr Ratho hears of this there's going to be the most unholy row . . . It's a common assault and I have an excellent lawyer, as you will shortly find . . .'

Sister stood with her hands folded in front of the bib of her apron. 'Staff nurse, I think Mrs Arbuthnot is temporarily not herself, so we'll get her across to Incidental Delirium until she feels a little better. I've already spoken to Sister and she's only too happy to take her. And Dr Ratho will no doubt find time to visit his patient over there when he eventually returns from his weekend . . . Thank you, Dr MacNair, I'm sure we can manage now until the porters come. But a ward like this is no place for a patient in the throes of delirium tremens.' Sister smiled at her nurses. 'As I'm sure Dr MacNair will agree . . .'

When Lennie came in MacNair explained what had happened. Lennie was philosophical. 'One can understand Sister's point of view and strictly speaking she's quite right. And if you agreed you agreed. There isn't much we could have done to head off the trouble before it happened, other than not bringing her in in the first place, I suppose. The Ratho side of things isn't a pressing problem for the moment, so we'd hope to calm her down and slide her out to the comforts of home in good time for Christmas. And people don't normally go to their lawyers when it involves admitting to a bottle a day . . . So not to worry, Michael. We'll take good care of her and you'll be surprised how quickly everyone will want to forget about the whole unfortunate business . . . We'll nip across and see her after we've cast an eye over the deserving poor. So who's in trouble this morning?'

In the single room just vacated by Mrs Arbuthnot Mrs Murray was dying. When the doctors came in her husband sprang from his chair and stood smartly frowning to his front. Her children simply looked more miserable and bewildered and were shepherded out along with their father by the staff nurse. Lennie stooped over and said softly 'Mrs Murray . . . Dr Lennox here . . .' She lay half-conscious, pale and almost still, her breathing shallow and alternately fast and very slow. 'Mrs Murray . . . Are you in pain?' She shook her head a fraction of an inch each way. He laid his hand on hers and said 'We're around, Dr MacNair and I, if there's anything you need . . . Now I think your family are here, so we mustn't interrupt . . .' Mrs Murray nodded again and closed her eyes. Lennie squeezed her hand. The junior nurse sniffed and blinked then set to with unnecessary zeal, fluffing up the pillows and fiercely straightening out the counterpane where the little boy had been sitting on it.

The children went back in and Lennie had a word with Mr Murray, who was still trying to stop himself standing to attention. 'She's as comfortable as we can make her, Mr Murray . . . A brave woman who's been through a great deal over the last few years.' 'She's very grateful, doctor, for everything that's been done,' said Mr Murray. 'Her brother and sister have been informed of her condition and are on their way in. Thank you very much, doctor.' Lennie nodded and the man squared up, turned and walked smartly back to the bedside. The now civilian Mr Murray was facing up to the death of his wife in the week before Christmas and was doing it the way he knew best, just soldiering on. Lennie, MacNair and the staff nurse moved away.

Without students or consultants the ward round was quick and effective and there was still time to talk to patients. The formerly anaemic girl from the Borders had put on some make-up but messed it all up by weeping again. An old lady with a stroke who had come in overnight was eager to show MacNair how much her hand had improved but to her obvious puzzlement still couldn't speak. MacNair watched how Lennie handled that and was once again impressed. The patient seemed to recognise words quite well, so Lennie first asked her if she knew what she wanted to say but couldn't find the words, at which she nodded vigorously, then talked to her normally thereafter, with lots of questions phrased so that she could reply either by nodding or shaking her head. As they made to leave she clutched Lennie's hand and kissed it and MacNair realised how much better he could have handled things when he had admitted her, even though it had been in the middle of the night.

By coffee time the students had still not arrived. In the privacy of the doctors' room MacNair raised the subject of Lennie's rumoured promotion. Lennie was diffident. 'It's actually only an associate assistant physicianship . . . Sounds dreadful, doesn't it? Like one of those ridiculous quarter-rung promotions people got in things like the Imperial Viennese Tramways Inspectorate. Herr Unter-ober-unter-obersomething, waiting years to drop an unter. But that's the way they do things here, and the rumours are a bit of a nuisance. Knives come out . . . Nothing personal, of course, but if dishing you is the only thing they can think of to annoy some old enemy who's backing you, then dished you'll be. The innocent occasionally suffer, I suppose, but deserving chaps too, I'm sure, so one shouldn't complain. But no, I'm certainly not banking on it . . . Not absolutely sure I want to go on in hospital medicine . . . And I actually enjoy my tutoring.' MacNair listened to that and found it plausible but probably not true: Lennie was ambitious and clever, and with the beginnings of a family he needed the money and security of a promotion. But being Lennie his style was to play the whole thing down and act the part of the amateur jockey: stub out his cigarette, jump on a horse and win the Grand National as though by accident.

The students arrived and were sent on to the ward to prepare a couple of endocrinological cases each. Mrs Arbuthnot was no longer the kind of case they should be seeing as part of their extra tuition. Lennie and MacNair walked up the long winding corridor that joined the medical and surgical houses of the hospital to the block just behind the Surgical Out Patient Department that accommodated the Incidental Delirium ward. They knocked and waited and eventually a grey-smocked porter with a large bunch of keys on a chain let them in. 'Sister's busy,' he grunted. 'You don't mind waiting.' It was a more of a statement than a request. The wire-meshed door was locked behind them and they stood in the corridor. 'She'll not be a minute. Just a discharge to custody . . .' The porter shambled off. Visits to ID always conjured up for

56

MacNair the seedier rituals of military discipline: dealing with MP's who regarded the rest of the army as the enemy; explaining to bemused drunks what they'd done after they'd left the NAAFI; leaving cells behind and realising again that the smell of freedom was just fresh air. The association was strengthened by the appearance of the ID Sister, a large and permanently angry woman now followed by three uniformed men walking in untidy line abreast, the outer two well turned out and wearing peaked caps, the man between slouching along hatless and reluctant, his arms tugged forward by handcuffs. MacNair remembered suddenly that Mrs Arbuthnot had arrived on the ward with a chauffeur, 'as though we were a hydropathic spa'.

They waited as papers were signed and changed hands and the door was unlocked and locked again, then Sister turned to Lennie. 'Dr Lennox . . . Yes. The DT's from twenty five, I think.' Lennie nodded. 'Give me a common rapist any day,' she sniffed, turning back into the ward. 'At least they come with extra staff . . . Her ladyship's in the side ward, and fortunately she's got it to herself today. Ate her porridge, moved her bowels and no complaints. Paraldehyde again at ten for agitation and threatened fits. And the paraldehyde's hardly touched her, which clearly means she's got a very substantial habit . . . Here we are . . . Mrs Arbuthnot, dear, some doctors for you . . . And please don't do that. Having the sheet over your face means something quite special in hospital . . . That's better. Please don't do it again. No complaints, dear? Good. Dr Lennox, can I just leave you to it? We're exceptionally short-staffed today.'

From the adjacent main ward came a hubbub of distress and derangement: more than one male voice sobbing, and a curious repetitive upward triplet of something like laughter. Mrs Arbuthnot opened first one eye then the other. 'It's been like that all morning, Dr Lennox. Never a moment of quiet the whole time. And the grey thing's still running around, actually threatening people. And I've been attacked, you know. Girls from the hotel. Hector's girls, I think . . . I wouldn't put it past him. You only have to ask yourself who stands to gain most from my death. So I'm most awfully glad you've come, Dr Lennox. I suppose Dr Ratho sent you.'

'Yes, Mrs Arbuthnot . . . And I'm sorry you've been so upset. You mentioned grey things . . .'

'It was far worse in the hotel, Dr Lennox. Lots of them and all over the curtains and wallpaper. But here it's just one. A big one, almost human . . . And another attack. They try to stifle you, and stab you, and then they let you go and say they're nurses.' Mrs Arbuthnot propped herself up on her elbows and looked suddenly sleepy. 'But I know, Dr Lennox . . . I know . . .' She looked round and yawned then smiled with considerable charm. 'You must excuse me, Dr Lennox. It's long past my bedtime . . .' Lennie sat down on the bed and said quietly 'Best to get some sleep if you feel like it, Mrs Arbuthnot . . . We'll pop in again later and see how you are . . . And I'm sure there's nothing all that terrible going on . . . Nothing we can't sort out quite quickly between us when you're feeling better . . . so perhaps the best thing to do now is just relax . . . That's it . . . Good . . .' She lay back and closed her eyes, murmured 'Goodnight, dear' and fell asleep.

The porter unlocked the door for them and they were out in the fresh air of the lower surgical corridor again. 'Best thing for her,' said Lennie. 'A bit of a snooze. We'll bring her back across as soon as she's slept that lot off and is compos mentis again . . . Tomorrow, with any luck. But Christmas at home is a less certain matter. Pity, because I don't think she's the sort of case Dr Ratho wants lying around over the weekend reminding people of the . . . less fortunate side-effects of placebo therapy, so to speak. But we certainly can't leave her there . . .' MacNair, if his opinion had been asked, would have agreed. Mrs Arbuthnot had been admitted from Moray Place because Ranald Ratho had been stumped. Now things had got out of hand and she was far more ill than she had intended to be, a drunkard unmasked and raving in a locked ward used mainly by criminals and lunatics. And his own contribution had not been particularly helpful. 'It's funny,' he said as they were passing the door of the Residency, 'she talks about her husband all the time but there's been no sign of him since she came in.' Oh, I don't know,' said Lennie. 'Might explain a lot.'

Three days later, on the day before Christmas Eve, Mrs Arbuthnot was transferred back to the now vacant single room on ward twenty five. There was no more talk of whorehouses, hotels and lawyers. She lay pale and ill, eating and drinking little and pathetically grateful for everything that was being done for her. Too weak to smoke, she needed help even to sip what Sister described as 'permitted fluids' from an invalid cup. Her buttocks had suffered much from paraldehyde and had broken down to form a large, foul-smelling pressure sore. She was uncomplaining when the nurses packed it with eusol soaks in an effort to clean it up, but its size and the speed of its appearance prompted Sister to speculate aloud that Mrs Arbuthnot was about to turn her face to the wall. At visiting hour her husband, a short dapper man wearing a tie identified by Lennie as that of the Royal Company of Archers, sat briefly with her and then explained at length how he had been unexpectedly detained abroad in pursuit of an export order but was pleased to see that his wife was making good progress. His regards were to be passed on to Ranald Ratho. Later on in the afternoon the nurses found Mrs Arbuthnot sobbing.

'I rather think Sister approves of Christmas being on a Sunday,' said Dr Hutchison Hunt through a mouthful of mince pie. A consultant in his fifties, senior to Ratho and junior to Lorimer, Henry Hutchison Hunt dropped in to the wards from time to time on his way between clubs. Though nominally in charge during the absence of his two colleagues, he was, from the point of view of the junior staff, neither findable nor worth finding. 'You can see her point . . .' He took a gulp of sherry. '. . . and if she had her way she'd make it a permanent arrangement. "Far less trouble for all concerned, Dr Hunt, especially if we're going to go like the English and turn it into full scale day off. But at least having it on a Sunday minimises the disturbance to the routines of the ward."' Dr Hutchison Hunt sniffed, flared his nostrils and stuck his nose and chin forward all at once, just as Sister did when she was making a particularly forceful point, then smiled. 'It'll be interesting to see what happens next year . . . And how are you, young NacNair? Bearing up under the strain of your time in the house?' MacNair nodded. Hutchison Hunt still had his eye on the door. 'Best job in medicine, apart from being a consultant, of course. They're *your* patients. You know every one of them and when you go round in the morning you can tell from the look in their eye what sort of night they're had. And when you go round again after the cocoa of an evening they'll confide their every last secret to you.'

Michael MacNair, who had only a couple of months still to do on the ward, smiled and said nothing. 'How's the Mess?' Said Hutchison Hunt. 'D'you still have dining-in nights. Mess silver out, speeches and odes, a guest or two from the consultant staff? Great times . . . You know for some reason they made me Keeper of the Virgins.' Misty eyed again, he shook his head. 'Great sport, Malcolm, great sport. And afterwards I won the trolley race, pushed by the Faither of the Mess – terribly nice chap, died in Changi, poor fellow – probably as drunk as ever he was in his life . . . I mean in the trolley race, not . . . not in . . .'

'Ah . . . MacNair . . .' The door, which Hutchison Hunt had been eyeing anxiously throughout, was opened with great force and J D K Lorimer strode in. 'A merry Christmas to you, Michael . . .' MacNair leapt to his feet just in time for Lorimer's emphatic clubman's handshake. 'Oh . . . And you, Henry . . . How nice to see you . . .' Hutchison Hunt started to get up, a fuddled, pink Mr Toad in a green suit. 'A merry Christmas, Joe . . .' he muttered. Lorimer had already turned once more to the houseman. 'Michael . . .' Lorimer boomed. Hutchison Hunt settled sheepishly into his chair and reached for another mince pie. 'Michael, I gather you and Lennie have done a terrific job over the last couple of weeks . . . Much appreciated, and I want you to know it . . . As Ranald Ratho probably told you, I've been stuck in London on one of these committees without which, it seems, our National Health Service would grind to a halt . . . And I would have resented it all a great deal more if I hadn't been confident that all was well on the home front . . . So thank you, Michael.' A broad, well-manicured hand grasped MacNair's left shoulder and shook it amiably. 'And a happy Christmas to you . . . Is Dr Lennox about yet? I suppose we're all a little early, strictly speaking.'

J D K Lorimer was a large and squarely handsome man who was quoted as having said that to get on in medicine you needed brains, good looks and money. ('I was born with the first, developed the second shortly after puberty and ten years later quite fortuitously married the third.') Now in his early fifties, he had got on in medicine to the point of hardly ever having to do it at all. As senior consultant on the unit he took his teaching and ceremonial functions seriously but delegated clinical chores with firmness. Committees and examination duties often took him south and abroad, and when in Edinburgh he spent much of his time at the Royal College of Physicians down on Queen Street. 'And how was London, Joe. . . ?' Hutchison Hunt asked when he had finished his

60

mince pie. 'Oh, the usual, Henry . . . The same old gang, saying more or less the same old things, I suppose, but it's progress if they feel that these days they have to say them in the presence of a Scot, a Northerner and a man from the Ministry. And London looks as if it'll still be full of holes twenty years from now . . . We really were jolly lucky up here . . . So, yes, I'm glad to be back, and just as well too. Mustn't miss Sister's little soiree . . . Miriam's on her way . . . Got nobbled on a League of Friends matter just as we were leaving the Board of Governors' coffee do . . .'

Christmas tradition on the ward was that the medical staff assembled in the doctors' room and on the stroke of noon progressed to Sister's parlour where a little party, lasting exactly one hour, ensued. Old hands knew the form. Transients such as the houseman were fully briefed, and MacNair had in the pocket of his white coat a little bottle of a rather austere perfume wrapped in an offcut of Christmas paper. He would receive in return a cheap fountain pen and a bottle of ink, to be handed over with a time-honoured remark about good handwritting being simply good manners. He would be, he had worked out, probably around the fortieth recipient of both gift and advice. Tradition dictated also that this was a family occasion: though Sister was single or, as she put it, married to her ward, anything less than a full family turnout by her guests would be regarded as an insult to her hospitality. MacNair, single at thirty, was anticipating the gathering without enthusiasm. Hutchison Hunt, very much a bachelor and perhaps fifty now, had made some kind of point in his own way by being drunk already.

'Peep peep! Merry Christmas! Peep peep!' The door of the doctors' room crashed open and a small fair-haired boy sitting in a shiny green pedal-car propelled himself swiftly into the room and around the large desk in the middle. 'Peep peep . . . Out of the way . . .' Houseman and senior consultant moved obediently aside and the car, a fair facsimile of the latest open-topped Austin tourer, swept around the desk once more then headed straight for the armchair occupied by Hutchison Hunt, jolting to halt against its padded leather. 'Merry Christmas, uncle Henry . . .' Hutchison Hunt looked down over the arm of the chair at his assailant. 'And a merry Christmas to you, young man . . . Santa seems to have been extremely kind to you.' The little boy put his head to one side.

'Granny Kinnell had it sent from Jenners. But it was under the Christmas tree, if that's what you mean. What did you get?'

'Socks and ties, mostly . . . This is one.' Hutchison Hunt fingered a green silk tie patterned with stirrups and riding crops. 'That's quite nice,' said the little boy. 'And I expect you have a car already.' 'I do indeed, but nothing like as splendid as yours, Angus . . . Now I wonder if you know everyone . . .' The boy reversed his car a little way and manoeuvred it in the vicinity of Hutchison Hunt's armchair. 'I'm just going to park first . . .' He did so and got out. Hutchison Hunt stood up. 'Now I believe you already know Dr Lorimer . . .'

'Merry Christmas, Dr Lorimer.'

'And a merry Christmas to you, Angus.'

'But I don't think you've met Dr MacNair . . . Michael MacNair, one of our colleagues here on the unit. Angus – Angus Ratho, of course – visits us every Christmas . . . has done for years . . . Michael . . . Angus . . .' The door opened again and Lennie, accompanied by his wife and a little girl, came in. Hutchison Hunt, by now thoroughly enjoying himself, carried on with the introductions. Margaret Lennox had met Dr Lorimer but not Angus or the houseman. The little girl did not seem to know anyone, but stood politely while Hutchison Hunt introduced the men present in order of seniority, starting with Lorimer and finishing with Angus Ratho. 'Alexandra, this is Angus . . . Angus Ratho . . . Alexandra Lennox . . . But I believe many of Miss Lennox's friends actually call her Sandy.'

'Hello, Sandy.'

'Hello, Angus.'

'How old are you?'

'I'm three.'

'I'm five and I've just taken delivery of a brand new car . . . Would you like to come and look at it?' The two went off towards the armchair by the window and Hutchison Hunt smiled and laughed then cornered Lennie. 'Lennie, you've done a terrific job over the last couple of weeks and we're all terribly grateful.' He lowered his voice. 'And I don't think it'll come as any surprise to you to hear that you're being very strongly backed for the assistantship, not least by me. It could turn out to be a very happy Christmas indeed, for the pair of you.' He winked at Margaret. 'Mince pie, anyone? Ah,

Ranald . . . Just in time for a quick one before Sister's little do. A mince pie, that is . . .'

Ranald Ratho shook his head and glanced round the room. 'Merry Christmas, Ranald,' said Hutchison Hunt. Ratho nodded. 'And to you, Henry.' Ratho was alone and not at all relaxed. 'Mopsy all right, Ranald?'

'Unfortunately no, Henry . . . Decided to dig in at Kinnell until the New Year, and I can't say I blame her . . . Really been quite frail . . .'

'Gastritis again?' Hutchison Hunt, who suspected Mopsy Ratho of drinking almost as he did himself, regularly used enquiries like that as a kind of forward defence.

'We're actually going to get some cardiography organised, and probably ask Rae Gilchrist to see her.'

'Oh dear . . . But nothing serious, I hope . . .'

Lennie, with one eye on Sandy and Angus and the green car by the window, watched and listened discreetly. Mrs Ratho's delicate health was known to him, and did not make the inevitable conversation with her husband on the subject of what had happened to Mrs Arbuthnot any easier. If he had thought about that particular patient at all since his return from Kinnell it would most probably have been in terms of her being happy at home, her invalidism having been temporarily indulged and dramatised, with an agreeable fee somewhere on the way from her bank account to his. And of course a consoling aspect of the care of chronic illness in private practice was that such fees were recurrent for the foreseeable future. Ratho shook himself free from Hutchison Hunt and proceeded to a stagey exchange of greetings with Lorimer just as Miriam Lorimer arrived to complete the party. The senior consultant called the room to order simply by looking round, and they moved on, only about five minutes late, to Sister's parlour.

Sister too was unseasonably tense and and preoccupied, Mrs Arbuthnot's death having upset her a lot more than she would have anticipated. Her sympathies, negligible to begin with, had grown substantially when Mrs Arbuthnot had returned from Incidental Delirium with that appalling pressure sore, and further still when the husband had appeared and made it perfectly obvious why the poor woman had been driven to drink far more than was good for her. And the details of her last hours and messy demise, just after supper on Christmas Eve, would have been harrowing enough in their own right even if everything else about her stay in the Institute had been perfectly straightforward. Dr Lennox was not to be held responsible and had done his best when things had got difficult, and young MacNair was neither worse nor better than the average medical houseman. He needed telling but when he was told he did fine. No, the man to blame was the man who had telephoned in from Moray Place ten days or so before. 'Delightful lady, sister, just a little bit arthritic and in need of our special attention. I'm sure you'll find her quite charming. We'll just pep her up and get her home in time for Christmas . . . Thank you so much, sister . . .' And not the slightest mention that she was really a private patient whose proper place was up in Cameron Wing paying seven guineas a week and drinking as much as she felt like. *And* they were five minutes late. Christmas or no Christmas, it was time someone had a word with Dr Ratho.

By twelve thirty it was clear to Lennie that Sister's little party was not going to improve. MacNair's socialist convictions had surfaced vividly after a couple of glasses of sweet brown sherry, so Lennie stood by him, partly out of curiosity and partly because letting him talk like that to anyone else in the room could only lead to serious trouble. Margaret and Miriam were deep in the kind of conversation to be expected at this time of year between the lady of the manor and the wife of the better sort of peasant. Angus and Sandy had found a friend in Henry Hunt, who was sitting between them doing simple ante-room conjuring tricks, and Sister, after a quiet but animated chat with Ranald Ratho, seemed somehow to have gone off the boil. As MacNair ground on about why mutualisation of the industrial assurance companies was not only a very poor substitute for outright nationalisation but would actually inflict substantial damage on Labour's electoral prospects, the nature of another conversation in the room gradually dawned on Lennie. Lorimer and Ratho had clearly not spoken at length for a few weeks and were now quietly running through an agenda of some importance. The Spens awards had gone through and would happen in Scotland too and Lorimer would have a great deal to do with who got them. A bright young man from London was interested in moving to Edinburgh and had some claim to Scottish connections, his father being a Scots Guards brigadier or perhaps brigade-major. And although it was not exactly stated that the placing of this young man was a quid pro quo in relation to the Spens machinations, Lorimer did seem to be saying he enjoyed the backing of a number of influential London physicians. It occurred immediately to Lennie that if the young man in question was all that good the leaders of the profession in London would probably want to hang on to him, but there were in Edinburgh medicine young men like that too: labelled, usually unbeknown to themselves, for export only. The bad news concerned the job for which it appeared the young man was the ideal candidate: that of associate assistant physician at the Institute.

In MacNair's view Herbert Morrison and his gang were proposing mutualisation because they knew it would take the companies off the nationalisation agenda, discredit Bevan and thus ensure that a dozen more nationalisation projects would go under. In Ratho's, Lennie had shown himself to be simply not cut out for medicine the way it was done in the Institute, and a job in poorhouse doctoring would not only suit him better but make way for a potential consultant whose commitment to the continuation of private medicine could be taken for granted. And fortunately the Board had decided to upgrade another poorhouse and call it the Southern General: Dr Lennox would get something better suited to his inclinations, if not immediately then quite soon enough. Lennie listened carefully and took all that in, nodding politely as MacNair demolished Herbert Morrison's case on the nationalisation question.

Morrison was lucky, and would survive. Lennie would not: what he had just overheard marked the end of his career at the Institute. Lorimer and Ratho went on to discuss other more pressing matters concerning possible candidates for the Vice Presidency of the Committee of Physicians of the Royal Charitable Institute. Lennie stood silent. He had done his best, with no illusions about how much good it would do him. He had looked after the patients, taught the students and covered up for the various absences and shortcomings of his senior colleagues, but that had not been enough; in the larger medical world powerful forces were at work. Now that he knew, the important thing was to make sure no one thought it mattered to him. Without in any way drawing attention to himself, he finished his warm brown sherry, agreed with MacNair's final point and moved to rescue his daughter, tactfully if at all possible, from Hutchison Hunt's left knee.

June 1950

Years later it occurred to Robbie that if you didn't know Edinburgh very well 1 Thistle Place was a very good address. It had everything – the unmistakable national emblem, strong hints of the Georgian graces of the New Town and of course the much sought after number one – everything that went to make the kind of address the Secretary of State himself might choose if he wasn't already stuck with a flat half way along the south side of Charlotte Square. Long after his mother finally moved he sometimes thought about that address, perhaps on thick notepaper of the kind people had printed for private practice: Dr Robert Keir Roberts, BSc MB ChB FFARCS, across the top, with 'Rooms, 10 Moray Place' and on the right 'Residence, 1 Thistle Place, Edinburgh'.

The earliest thing he could remember about the address was how difficult it was to pronounce. He had known it when he was two, but even when he had started at primary school it still sometimes came out with a lot of unwanted f's that made the teacher smile and left him wishing there was time to explain that it was a nice place to live, just hard to say properly. Number one was at the end of the street nearest the canal, so near that when it was quiet you could hear men talking on the barges. The other end of the sixty yard street led nowhere, but over the wall and the big houses in that direction was the road you had to cross to get to school. Behind was a lane that led up the side of the brewery, also hard to pronounce, and there were really nine families living at 1, Thistle Place.

The backs of the odd-numbered side of the street faced southwest, which meant that the kitchens were sunny from the middle of the day until evening. The top flats, eighty seven steps in four flights from the close, were sunniest of all. Their neighbours were a man who worked in a bank and his mother who never went out, and a lady with no husband or children but who was quite nice.

Robbie's parents, if ever they had thought about it, would probably have agreed that, with lots of sun, quiet neighbours and an inside toilet, their flat at 1 Thistle Place was as good an address as they could reasonably have hoped for.

If they had been asked, they would both said that they hoped for better for their children. Children were going to have it better, and right enough, as Robbie's father would have put it: even working class children. He was a railwayman, lucky to have got a start in the thirties, working his way slowly up to fireman and then driver, with the usual interruption but back on the job in 1945. He believed in making the trains run on time, but by democratic means, and believed in the railways belonging to the people, and in children not going cold and hungry, and in the right to education and in the right to health. His squad had spent two long years in the Western Desert planning the post-war British economy and social order. That the Attlee government had broadly agreed with them had come as a bit of a surprise.

There were two children with quite a large space in between, and quite right too, considering he'd been in the desert: Margo from before and wee Robbie afterwards. Margo was eleven and bright, tall for her age, nearly as tall as her mother, and in the last class at the primary school where Robbie had just started. The problem had begun because she was bright and in the last class of the primary school. Her father had been asked to go up to the school to talk to the headmistress about Margo, and knew before he went that there was no question of her being in any kind of trouble. He had seen her report cards: class work and conduct always in the top grades, comments straining to avoid sounding the same as last time but using the words 'excellent' and 'outstanding' quite a lot anyway.

What the headmistress wanted to discuss was scholarships. She explained that free education at a Corporation high school such as Boroughmuir was good, probably as good as anywhere in the country, but that there were other schools, schools in Edinburgh, attended by people from all walks of life, that offered pupils like Margo opportunities that the ordinary corporation schools could not match. And for Margo, if she did as well as was expected in the entrance examination, that education would be free, with the possibility of extra help with money for books and uniforms. Perhaps Mr Roberts would like to think about it, talk to Mrs

Roberts and to Margo and then decide. And he might be interested to know that he was the only parent she was speaking to on the subject this year.

He thought about it all the way to the depot. Free education was free education. What was free education with extra opportunities and help with uniforms and books in a school where the other parents were paying? Would that be supporting something he didn't believe in, or would opposing it just be putting his own beliefs before his child's best interests? He discussed it with his wife after the kids were in bed and still didn't know what was right. His wife thought Margo should try but, as she said, going in for an open examination wasn't the same as doing well in it. They agreed in the end to discuss it with Margo and then let her decide for herself.

Robbie overheard a little of this and on the way to school Margo explained a bit more, about blazers and music and school libraries as big as the one on George the Fourth Bridge. It sounded as if she wanted to go, and someone else would have to take him to school. She read the extra books for the exam, usually lying on the hearthrug in front of the kitchen fire, and told him about them on the way to school and back.

When her father saw the way she was working at preparing for the exam and heard her talking about it he found something else to worry about. How would she take it if she didn't get in? Was it fair to raise her hopes if wee girls all over Edinburgh, some of them actually in the school already, were preparing, most likely with better help, to compete for what was probably only a handful of these scholarships, and if she didn't get one would she spend the whole time at Boroughmuir thinking it was somehow second best, and she a failure? A few weeks before the exam it looked as if the strain was beginning to tell. Margo wasn't exactly ill, but not her usual self either.

Robbie had noticed too. Going up to school she wasn't talking as much, and once they had been half way across the big road and a lorry had suddenly appeared and he had had to snatch her hand, running ahead and tugging her to the far pavement. Afterwards she had cried and asked him not to tell mum, because she was supposed to be looking after him. Then she said her head hurt. That night her mum gave her half an aspirin and put a cool damp dishtowel across her forehead, and her dad said she should have a night away from her books.

In the morning the headache had gone away. It was just eyestrain, her parents decided, but she had read nearly all the books on the teacher's list and she had a good memory. A bit more spelling and arithmetic and a few more practice essays for the headmistress would make the best use of the time still left, and spare her eyes. The headache came and went, but was never as bad when it had just started. Privately John Roberts concluded that Boroughmuir High School would have been fine all along: really free education, and she would know people there from the wee school. Margo was still not herself and not eating properly, but he decided that worry and eyestrain would explain everything and the holidays would see the end of it. He wrote to Mrs Mulholland in Pittenweem confirming their holiday booking for the trades fortnight.

The week before the examination he took Margo up to have a look at the school, walking there and back so that they would have plenty of time to talk about things and, if it seemed the right thing to do, decide to withdraw from the examination. There was no one about so they went in and walked round a playground that was more like a park and Margo said she liked it, but on the way home she complained of a sore neck.

Her neck was sorer the next day, sore and a bit stiff. Mrs Roberts took Robbie and Margo to school, handed a note in for Margo's teacher and took her straight up to the doctor's surgery at the top of Viewforth. In the waiting room, where they had to sit for an hour and a half, Mrs Roberts worried that Margo might catch something that would stop her sitting the exam. There was a whole family with impetigo and an old man with a cough who should have been seen first and got out of the place because of the risk to the children. People eyed each other, memorising who had come in before them and who after and looking round to check every time the door of the doctor's room, which was really just the back shop, opened to let someone out. There weren't enough chairs and Margo sat on her mother's knee, clinging to her in a way she hadn't done since she had had the measles.

When they got in Dr MacPhail was nice to them but in a hurry because they all knew how many people there still were outside. He asked how Margo had been getting on at school and she told him about the exam, how she'd been working for it, about the eyestrain the week before, and how her neck hurt now. 'Let me see,' he said, looking into her eyes. 'Ah, yes. A wee bit red . . .' They had talked about how much she had been reading, and he advised cutting down a bit and using a better light. Mrs Roberts had then told him how Margo lay on the hearthrug most of the time she was reading and he shook his head. 'Very bad posture, especially for wee girls. Eyestrain . . . and neck strain.' He made a note on Margo's card and popped it back into its stiff brown National Health envelope. 'You'll have some aspirin? Try that. Half a tablet only, three times a day. And a bit less reading.' He patted her head as he got up to show them out. Going back down Viewforth she wanted to walk slowly.

They went home rather than back to school. If she began to feel better she could study just as well there, and if she didn't she could go to bed with a chopped boiled egg in a cup with some margarine if she felt like it. Her father, in his uniform ready to go out, was unimpressed. She wasn't just not right, she was ill. They put her to bed and went back through to the kitchen and he heard in detail what the doctor had said and done. They agreed she should stay off school and in bed and they would know whether the aspirin was helping by the time he came back from his work.

Margo ate only half the boiled egg, lay restlessly for an hour or two then fell asleep. When it was time to go and collect Robbie her mother asked Miss MacHardy from next door to come in and sit with Margo for a wee while. She did her hair and came through with her knitting and when she saw Margo lying asleep, pale and sweating, she asked if she was constipated or if her troubles were starting. Mrs Roberts hurried out and met Robert at the school gate and rushed him home as quickly as she could. When they got back Margo had wakened up and looked a wee bit better and Miss MacHardy was looking pleased with herself.

Robbie sat on her bed till teatime, playing snap with her and then I spy, which was never very good in their bedroom because they had played it there so often. After tea and another half aspirin she said her headache was a good bit better but her neck still hurt and she just wanted to go to sleep. He went through to the kitchen and lay in front of the fire with his reading book until his mother told him to sit at the table because it was better for him. When she was putting him to bed Margo woke up and complained about the light, so he lay in the dark, listening to his mother just telling a story instead of reading one.

70

It was past midnight when John Roberts got back from the depot. Margo was sitting on her mother's knee in the big chair in the kitchen with a wet dishtowel covering her forehead and most of her face. She was shaking and whimpering and when he asked her she said her neck was hurting more than ever. He lifted the dishtowel from her forehead and she screwed up her eyes. Except where the cloth had been, her skin was hot to touch. He asked her to open her eyes again and she started to cry. The aspirin wasn't working and eyestrain and neck strain didn't make sense with a fever. The girl was ill, maybe seriously ill, and they could either wait till morning or try and get help that night. Her mother was for waiting. Margo had been as ill once before, all night, with the start of the measles, and as right as rain the next morning apart from the spots. They pulled her nightie up looking to see if there were spots, maybe from chickenpox this time.

Should they go to the doctor's house, along Polwarth practically at Myreside? Not at the risk of waking Dr MacPhail in the middle of the night to be told a bit more about eyestrain and neck strain, they decided. Her father would take her up to the Royal Hospital for Sick Children. They wrapped her in a blanket and he carried her downstairs, her mother accompanying them as far down as the first landing then going back in case wee Robert woke up. He could try the short way and walk all of it, which would probably take longer, or stick to main roads in the hope of a taxi, from Tollcross at least, where there was an all-night rank.

He carried her nearly half a mile along Gilmore Place, with never a taxi in sight. A bit before one o'clock and just short of Tollcross a strange thing happened. He was passing the RAMC headquarters, Margo getting heavier in his arms, as some kind of party was breaking up. A drunk lieutenant colonel in mess dress, swaying across the pavement to his car, almost knocked Margo from his arms, apologised, then looked closely at her, and at John Roberts in his British Railways uniform and nodded. 'Sick chicks or Institute? Fine . . . Come on . . . Get in . . . Take you there myself . . .' He drove fast through the deserted summer night, turning round in his seat to ask odd things about Margo's illness: her speech, and had she trouble hearing, how long the light had hurt her eyes, had she developed a squint since this started, and did anyone in the family have chest trouble? At the side door of the Royal Hospital for Sick

Children he let them out, bowing and taking off his hat and muttering about probably better not to come in himself, best of luck and the like. John Roberts, who had never had much time for the RAMC or for lieutenant colonels, said thanks very much and had to work quite hard to stop himself crying on the way in.

A porter went for a nurse who took one look at Margo and sent the porter for a doctor. While they were waiting she took her temperature, then a boy of twenty or so, blond and untidy from his bed, came hurrying down and tried talking to Margo but now she wasn't making any sense. He asked John most of the questions the RAMC colonel had asked and a few more, then went back to Margo. He put his hand gently under her neck and tried to lift her head forward. Her neck was stiff and she moaned when he tried it again. Then he tried to look in her eyes with a tiny light, the nurse holding her head still as she moved drowsily. He gave up and turned to John again. 'And you're sure this has been coming on for about three weeks now?' The short answer, all nonsense about exams and eyestrain set aside, was yes. 'We'll take her in here, just till tomorrow, and do tests on her spine, for meningitis, I'm afraid . . . And she'll almost certainly be taken up to the City in the morning. We'll get her into the ward now.' John went back to where Margo lay on the trolley and held her hand. As they waited he could hear the doctor on the phone. 'Yes. An isolation room . . . Yes, even if you have to move somebody . . . A girl. Eleven . . . A TB meningitis.'

When he came back he knew he had been overheard. 'Yes . . . Sorry. Almost certainly . . . the kind of meningitis you get with tuberculosis. But the people at the City will go into everything about . . . finding out how she got it.' John Roberts held his daughter's hand tighter but there was no response. The two men looked down at her. She lay just as if she were asleep, breathing normally. How she got it was hardly the most important question, at least for now. 'I should explain,' said the houseman, 'I'm just on for emergencies, and not an expert on this, but it's not as bad as it used to be. I mean . . . she's got a better chance than some. She's not gone deaf or blind and she's talking, so it might be all right. And they've got the new American drug at the City and they're using it for meningitis and a lot of them are doing well . . . I'm sorry, Mr Roberts.'

It was the middle of the night and the boy was out of his depth.

There would be somebody else in the morning, after the tests, and he would try to see them before his work, and then the girl would go to the City where they were experts, if only at watching people die of TB. He had known it was TB meningitis from about half way along Melville Drive, when the RAMC man had asked him if there was anybody in the family with chest trouble. There wasn't, but it was obvious what he was talking about and you could catch TB in trams, at school, anywhere, and now Margo was going to die of it. 'It's called Streptomycin,' said the doctor, looking suddenly pleased with himself. John Roberts didn't know what he was talking about. The doctor smiled. 'The American drug they're using at the City. And it's really good.' They followed the trolley up through gloomy corridors to the ward where a nurse in a huge starched cap was waiting for her. Ten minutes later he was walking home again with the blanket over his arm and Margo's nightie folded in his pocket.

Next day she was moved to the City Hospital, miles out to the south. When her mother went up on the bus to see her a ward sister told her that Margo was as well as could be expected and sat her down and explained about visiting and keeping in touch. Visiting was twice a week but coming in as often as that just upset the children and the number system had greatly improved keeping in touch and saved a lot of unnecessary travel for families. Every patient had a number, and every day the hospital phoned the offices of the Evening Dispatch with changes in condition. If your child's number wasn't in the paper that meant their condition was unchanged and there was no need to worry. Condition improving was obviously good news, condition deteriorating meant just that, but might not be too serious. Very seriously ill, unfortunately, meant that the patient's condition was very serious. Very serious indeed. And for the sake of simplicity dying, unfortunately, was included with very seriously ill, but attempts were always made to get in touch with parents directly too. The ward sister checked a column in a large ledger and wrote Margo's name and number there and on a slip which she handed to Mrs Roberts. 'Most people find it a very convenient system. Evening Dispatch, Mrs Roberts. Usually at the bottom of the page, near the back. And everybody can keep in touch with their child's progress daily. For tuppence.' The sister smiled and laughed. 'Now would you like to come in and say goodbye to Margo?'

In the ward were two long rows of beds and the place was quieter than you could ever have imagined anywhere could be with twenty or thirty children. A few lay awake and watchful, many more were asleep or worse. Mrs Roberts followed the sister's firm squeaking footsteps across the polished floor to a bed half way down on the left where Margo lay, pale and ill, with the sheet right up to her chin, her cheeks sunken and her wee mouth pathetically dry. She touched her hair, which was nice and tidy, and her eyes half opened. 'Margo's as well as can be expected, Mrs Roberts. Not, you know, very seriously ill . . .'

Buying the evening newspaper became a matter of life or death. Quite often Mrs Roberts found herself waiting at the newsagents for the van with the first edition. There was no news of Margo, but a nasty moment when someone with the number just before hers appeared on the very seriously ill list. A week after she had gone in John Roberts arranged to have time off work and went up to the City hospital to see for himself. In the childrens' ward he sat with Margo for the full half hour, holding her hand and listening to her talk about the scholarship exam and the books she had read. She was better than he had expected: unaware she had missed the exam but saying sensible things about the books. Her speech was clear, and she wasn't deaf and she seemed to be able to see properly and she said the pain had gone away. When the bell rang her eyes filled with tears and she reached out to him. Her arm had got a lot thinner in quite a short time.

'Mr Roberts?' A short, red-haired man in a white coat was waiting for him at the door of the ward. 'Mr Roberts, if we might just have a word . . .' The man held out his hand. 'Jameson. Jimmy Jameson. Really would like a quick word with you. About Margo, obviously. How about outside? Bench there in the sun.' John Roberts was steered briskly out on to the grass in the direction of a long rustic seat under a tree. The little man sprawled in one corner of it, squinted cheerfully up at the sun then turned to him. 'Sorry. Should have explained. Been looking after Margo since she got here . . . Thought I'd grab you for a chat, if that's all right. Tricky business, TB meningitis . . . I understand you already know that's what she's got. But we've managed to get hold of some stuff that seems to help it. You may have noticed she's a bit brighter. We're looking at that, and one or two other things, and the stuff really seems to be making a difference.'

John Roberts just nodded, because if he had spoken it might all have got a bit emotional. Dr Jameson, his left foot twisted up to rest on his right knee, rattled on. 'Streptomycin. American, originally. Actually kills off the bugs, which is great progress. One or two problems with it. It's got to be injected, which is a bit sore. And for Margo, with her meningitis, it's got to be injected into the spinal fluid, which can be jolly sore. But she's game and it's doing her good and we're . . . fairly hopeful about the whole business. Which is something new in TB meningitis.'

'Thanks, Dr Jameson. Thanks very much . . .' John Roberts sat in the sun under a tree crying like a baby and sniffing and saying sorry. The doctor was unembarrassed. 'We're doing what we can. It's still . . . a bit tricky. Nothing's certain, as ever with tubercle, but so far it's all quite encouraging. How are people taking it at home? There's a little chap too, isn't there?'

They sat in the sun and John Roberts told him far more than he had expected to about Margo and her school career, the exam and the beginning of her illness, how their own doctor had treated it and even about the strangely helpful RAMC officer. Then the doctor had asked again about the family, especially Robert, and about the house, and any relatives who might have been ill lately, and about anyone else who came round to the house regularly. John realised what was happening and didn't mind. How Margo had got it was important, and in a kindly, purposeful way this doctor, who sounded a bit like General Montgomery on the wireless, was doing his best to find out. Eventually he sat up a bit straighter. 'Well, Mr Roberts, the sensible thing would obviously be to get you all X-rayed . . . Yourself and your wife, and little Robert, so I'll get one of our girls round to see you and fix things up. Not only to track down where it's coming from but to make sure anyone else who's got it starts on the treatment early . . . because we can do a lot more now. As you've seen. So thank you, and I'm awfully glad we've had a chance to talk.'

Mr Roberts was encouraged but that evening wrote to Mrs Mulholland in Pittenweem cancelling their holiday. Margo would still be alive at the trades fortnight, getting slowly better in hospital with the new treatment, and they would be in Edinburgh to visit her and see her gradually getting back to her normal self. And they might still manage a late holiday if things went on as well as they were doing. When he told Robert a bit about that he asked if he could go and see Margo next time, and cried when he was told that really he couldn't, because that was one of the rules of the City hospital. To cheer him up John told him about Dr Jameson who was making Margo better, what he sounded like, how he had asked all about 'the little chep', and how he was going to send a lady to see them all and take pictures to make sure they were all right.

The lady came the next week and they all went to a clinic in the shadow of the castle and stood in front of a big machine with their arms up having their pictures taken. They heard the following week that everything was all right. Then Margo's number appeared in the evening paper under the heading 'Very Seriously Ill'. John went up to see her. She was dying. Dr Jameson sat with him on the same seat under the tree and said how sorry he was, because things had been going so well. The problem was that streptomycin worked only as long as the bugs were killed by it, and if they developed something called resistance the disease advanced again, as it had done, sadly, in Margo's case.

On the day of her funeral Robbie was put in his best clothes but did not go to the cemetery. Instead he spent the afternoon with Miss MacHardy. The lady had come to her house too and she had been to the clinic beside the castle to have her picture taken. They talked about hospitals and doctors and getting your picture taken. Robert decided that afternoon, though he did not tell anyone then or later, to get all the scholarships in the world and be a doctor and find a cure for things like eyestrain and neckstrain. The following week Miss MacHardy went off for a long holiday in the country for the good of her health, and for several months after that Dr Jameson's lady kept in touch and everyone had their picture taken again.

November 1950

Lennie parked his car unnecessarily far from the main entrance to the Southern General and walked slowly back to it. He was early and he didn't like being early, and he was even beginning to wonder if he should be going at all. It had all been a little odd. Dr Burton-Smith, medical superintendant for the Southern, had rung him up at the Institute half way through his second last week there and in the course of a suspiciously jovial phone call had invited him to lunch. 'Nothing formal, old boy . . . Just drop in for a bite and a natter . . . Important for you to know you're wanted here. Good show . . . Main entrance, and we're half way up the grand staircase. Twelve thirty? Jolly good show . . .'

Lennie had accepted, and only later had done a little checking up on Dr Burton-Smith. He had, it seemed, a reputation for being a bit of a phony, as should have been obvious as soon as he had said his name: the Navy had been infested with hyphenated Smiths and Lennie's experience of them had been almost entirely unsatisfactory. And besides, whoever heard of a poorhouse with a grand staircase? Lennie walked along a dank alleyway between the main building and a strange two-storey corrugated-iron detached block, freshly labelled Wards 23/23a but with faded military signboards in Polish still flanking its doors. Somewhere inside an old woman with a strong Scottish accent was shouting again and again for somebody called Netty.

By contrast, the entrance hall was rather grand, as indeed was the staircase. Opposite the main door it rose broad and shallow from the polished black and white marble floor in a way that made Lennie think immediately of the finale of a pre-war production of Cinderella, then split to left and right at a half-landing and led on up to first and second floor galleries. Its bannisters were elaborately carved oak and a series of workmanlike Victorian portraits of men in black coats – presumably municipal worthies such as the Guardians of the Poor – looked down from the walls. As Lennie climbed from the half-landing a door opened above and to the left, and the gallery echoed to the trit-trot of a short, heavy lady hurrying solicitously towards him in high heeled shoes.

'Dr Lennox? Oh, good. Dr Burton-Smith's expecting you . . . He'll be ready for you in just a moment . . . Would you like to come into my office and sit down . . . He really won't be a moment.' He followed her along the gallery, past a notice saying 'Offices of the Medical Superintendant: All enquiries to Mrs Roddie, second door on left.' The short fat lady opened the second door on the left, showed Lennie in and said 'We're awfully glad you've been appointed here, Dr Lennox. I'm Mrs Roddie, secretary to the Medical Superintendant, and I'll be happy to help you in any way I can when you join us . . . Dr Burton-Smith will be just a moment . . . Please take a seat.'

Lennie thanked her and sat down. There were one or two odd things about the office. It was extremely tidy, with no signs of work in progress. On the wall above the desk there was a pinboard covered with little notices all of which were all in shorthand. To the right of the typewriter lay a bunch of keys more in keeping with high office in the Bastille than with a minor secretarial post in a modern hospital. Mrs Roddie sat down on a swivelling chair, picked up the keys, folded her hands in her lap, swung round to face Lennie and threw him a large smile. When the smile had lasted so long as to be almost embarrassing she suddenly said 'You must be awfully pleased to have been appointed to the Southern, Dr Lennox. And against such competition.' Another smile followed.

The facts concerning Lennie's departure from the Institute were probably quite well known around the Southern but there was no cause to be ungracious. 'Happy to be coming here,' he murmured. Mrs Roddie reacted as though he had delivered an epigram that would have silenced Oscar Wilde: she threw her head back and shook with genteel but well-nigh uncontrollable laughter. 'I know Dr Burton-Smith is really looking forward to meeting you,' she said when her delight had eventually subsided via a painful diminuendo of girlish tinkles. 'I'll tell him you're here.' Lennie, marking her down as around fifty, mad and possibly dangerous, got up and prepared to meet the man who appeared to think he was his new boss.

The moustache was large and the handshake firm, with a knuckle-grinding masonic twist to it, which Lennie, though not a mason, returned as a matter of course. 'Dr Lennox? Johnny Burton-Smith's the name.' He chuckled and let Lennie's hand go. 'Bit of a mouthful, so most people just call me Tiger. Take a pew, old boy. Good to see you. Small one before lunch? Just name your poison . . . Got sherries, dry and not-so-dry . . . Or a spot of mother's ruin? You know I think I could even do a pink gin for an old Navy man . . . You only have to say the word . . .' Lennie, who would rather not have had anything but abandoned that option as not worth the trouble in the circumstances, decided on a dry sherry and while his host was pouring it looked around. The room was large and comfortable, panelled in the same dark oak as the stair. Its windows faced south towards the Pentlands and the desk, currently buried deep in drifts of untidy foolscap, was actually a long table. Dr Burton-Smith, now the medical superintendent of the newly constituted Southern General Hospital, occupied the boardroom of the former poorhouse.

Lennie's enquiries had prepared him for a certain amount of military nonsense, but not on anything like the scale he now encountered. The panelled walls of Burton-Smith's office were hung with rows of framed photographs of airfields, of single aircraft and whole squadrons in flight, of smoking wreckage littering runways, of aircraft being maintained or ammunitioned, of ground-crew posed woodenly looking skywards, of enemy cities variously pockmarked or obliterated, and of course photographs of Burton-Smith himself, seated thoughtfully or commandingly at a series of desks, chatting with senior officers and parading past neatly made beds in service hospital wards. As well as the photographs, there were displayed around the room gleaming 20mm brass shellcases, chunks of propeller blade mounted and labelled, the inevitable ashtray-machined-from-piston-head and perhaps half a dozen squadron shields: all the usual schoolboy souvenirs, in fact, but here comprising the collection of a chubby schoolboy of about forty-five who ought to be growing out of it.

When Dr Burton-Smith came back with a dry sherry Lennie happened to be looking at a picture of a light bomber. 'Mossie Mark 23,' said his host helpfully. 'Amazing bloody crate. Photo recce and Pathfinder. Climb like a homesick angel and still give you 350 mph

at 30,000 feet. Nothing could touch it till the Me 262 popped up
... And the chaps who flew them were bloody amazing too.' He
paused in noble-browed nostalgia, a tear for fallen comrades not far
away. 'Great days, Dr Lennox, great days . . . Chin chin.' He raised
his glass and saw off most of a large gin and orange. 'There was a
comradeship about then that we don't seem to have managed to
carry over into the palmy days of peace . . . But welcome to the
Southern, which is why we've invited you up for lunch. We've never
actually had a senior registrar here before but we're all in favour of
progress so we're certainly going to look after you. You're
supernumerary, as I understand it, and since you'll be a consultant
in a year or two it's important you get all the experience you feel you
need, in any field you want, and these days that certainly includes a
dash of administration.' He twinkled comradeship. 'And I can
certainly help you there . . . You know, we've actually given some
thought to how a senior registrar ought to be looked after, a matter
to which our clinical colleagues in the West Wing may not yet have
turned their attention . . .' He came forward on his chair and turned
suddenly serious. 'You may have difficulties ahead, I should warn
you, Dr Lennox, but I want you to know, and I really mean this . . .
You can always rely on Tiger. With me at least, I think you'll find
that everything's on the level.'

Lennie sipped his sherry and smiled and nodded, which seemed
to suffice, though a bit of masonic gesturing around the neck with
the sherry glass would probably have pleased his host more.
Burton-Smith beamed and finished his gin and orange. He was
wearing, Lennie noted without surprise, an RAF tie. As Lennie's
informant had remarked, 'Funny old business, war. He went off to
it as plain J B Smith, the poorhouse doctor, and came back from it
four years later as the intrepid Squadron-Leader Johnnie "Just call
me Tiger" Burton-Smith. And the funniest thing about the whole
business is that he spent most of it as MO to one of their jails,
somewhere in darkest Norfolk, I think. So watch him.'

'Another little sharpener? It's a Cape fino . . . Practically
impossible to get hold of now unless you know somebody . . .'
Lennie managed to nod appreciation but at the same time, by
putting his glass down firmly, to avoid incurring another sherry.
Burton-Smith drained off the end of his gin and orange and
smacked his lips. 'Spot of lunch? I'll just let the indispensable Mrs

Roddie know where we're going . . .' Instead of roaring at the secretary's door as Lennie had expected, he got up, opened it quietly and said 'We're off to lunch, Davina . . . If you'd kindly tell them downstairs, thanks awfully . . . No interruptions on any account . . . Then a tour of the station.' He smiled and nodded affectionately and closed the door. 'This way, Lennie . . .' He ushered his guest towards a door at the other end of his office. 'A truly remarkable woman, you know. Backbone of the hospital service, people like Davina, and little thanks they get for it. And I think you'll find that having her on your side is a great advantage in the . . . coming struggle.'

The National Health Service was just over two years old and, generally speaking, it seemed to be doing quite well. Slowly but surely the old patchwork of hospitals – charity and private, municipal and wartime Emergency Medical Service – was being reorganised in a fair attempt at Bevan's ideal of a comprehensive health service for all, free at the point of need. Doctors of Lennie's generation, who had little love for what had gone before, found themselves fitting in easily: there were a few sensible rules, no day-to-day worries about money and compared to medicine in the Forces – all too well known to most of them – it was bliss. Others found it harder, especially the stuffier sort of pre-war consultant and the hordes of office doctors who, under the old regime, had each been allowed to run their own stuffy little shows. As he followed his host in to lunch, Lennie made a firm diagnosis: Burton-Smith was one of those.

The door opened on to another oak-panelled room, a comfortable little lounge with a table already set for lunch for two. 'Sit ye down, sit ye down, sit ye down . . . Um. No. That's actually *my* seat. Lovely . . . Welcome to my humble board, Dr Lennox. We *have* managed to salvage a little from the remorseless advance of socialist egalitarianism.' On a gilt-edged officer-class institutional plate at each place lay two sardines on a little piece of toast. Burton-Smith shook out a napkin as though cracking a whip. 'Tuck in. And besides, if you and I were to appear in the paupers' dining-hall . . . Sorry, staff canteen.' He winked roguishly. '. . . all manner of idle speculation might ensue.' He leant closer. Was the room suspected of harbouring a hidden microphone or two? 'I don't mind telling you, Lennie, that I regard it as a matter of some importance that facilities for discreet conversation with colleagues continue to be maintained.' He poured each of them a glass of white wine from a small carafe and picked up his fish knife. 'Let me explain . . .'

When the sardines were eaten Burton-Smith lifted a little silver bell near his right hand and rang it vigorously. A moment later a servant in white apron and mob cap appeared with a chafing dish, set it down, removed the fish plates and reappeared with two large dinner plates so hot as to be practically glowing. 'Thank you, Mrs Lowther.' The servant, a fat, red-faced woman, performed a little sarcastic curtsey and retreated. 'Now what have we today. . . ? Lennie, if you would be so good . . . There's a bottle of plonk. There, on the sideboard . . .' The plonk turned out to be a claret with an impressively dirty label and the chafing dish had concealed a roast pheasant and a profusion of braised vegetables. Smacking his lips again, Burton-Smith carved and served as one who did so regularly, while Lennie poured the claret, giving himself only a decent minimum but filling his host's glass to the brim.

What Burton-Smith was explaining was more or less what Lennie had expected him to explain. The National Health Service, regardless of whether or not it was going to survive the next general election, was, his host had announced, no more the sum of its parts, and its most important components by far were undoubtedly the old municipal hospitals. 'Poorhouses they may have labelled us, but we came into it because we had been promised a fair deal and we were fool enough to believe we would get one . . . But what happened . . .' He had lowered his voice again and leaned so close across the little table that Lennie could smell his sardines, his soap and his sweat. 'What happened was that our political lords and masters were persuaded by the silver-tongued sirens of Harley Street to sell us down the river . . .' His jaw clenched and his voice narrowed to an envenomed whisper '. . . to the teaching hospitals . . . Lock, stock and barrel . . . A hundred years of service down the drain in an afternoon's committee work . . . We came into it to escape from them, to set ourselves up to tackle them on something like an equal footing, instead of having to act as rubbish-dumps for their many and glorious failures . . . But from the minute we join it was perfectly clear what they were up to . . . They're treating us like occupied enemy territory . . . "Go in there and sort 'em out, bring 'em up to scratch if you can, get rid of 'em if you can't, and if any of 'em make trouble make a bloody good example of 'em . . .' Burton-Smith put down his knife and fork. 'And that's what they're trying to do to me,' he said quietly and with great emotion, his mouth still full.

Lennie listened politely. The best lunch that had come his way for some time was turning out to be one it was not easy to enjoy. After a long silence he said 'Is it really as bad as that?' Burton-Smith seemed to take that not as politely phrased disagreement but as a request for further details.

'Worse, probably. At least in the past it was all quite honest and above boards. "You take our disasters, look after them till they die and don't ask too many questions." Nothing very exciting in the way of medicine, but at least they had to be polite to us. No, Lennie, it's the sheer bloody arrogance of the way they're going about things now . . . That bloody man sitting in the Institute ringing up his friends on the old boy network . . . "Got another poorhouse to sort out, Henry . . . Be a good chap and come up to Edinburgh and give us a hand . . . No question of *us* doing it . . . None at all, not even given the chance . . . And some little pipsqueak from St Guy's who happens to have been the Grand Panjandrum's houseman in 1936 gets told a cock and bull story about how the Edinburgh poorhouses are all being turned into teaching hospitals overnight, come and join us, it's only a question of winkling out a few last pockets of resistance and they're ours . . .' Burton-Smith frowned, pursed his lips, spat out a piece of birdshot and resumed his peroration. 'Well, here's one pocket of resistance that's going to hold out for a bloody long time yet . . . And as the Southern General's first senior registrar, Dr Lennox, *you're* going to help us . . . Cheers.' He winked, passed his third glass of claret a couple of times across in front of his throat and drained it in one.

The pudding was a disappointment, a pallid dough sown with a sultana or two and drowned in watery custard. Burton-Smith smacked his lips a lot and had two helpings before ringing his little silver bell for coffee, over which they discussed the newly established medical unit of the Southern General Hospital. The medical superintendant had little to say in its favour and had evidently already fallen out with almost everyone involved. Its chief was a particular disappointment to him. 'Lauder wouldn't have lasted ten minutes in the scruffiest RAF station in creation . . . Look at him. Holes in both his socks half the time. Straw on his shoes, literally. Keeps hens, you know, a smallholder, really, not a physician at all, and dresses the part. A tweed jacket from a jumble sale and six months between haircuts. I used to get the occasional doctor like that here, before the war, usually meant a drink problem, naturally, but I'd give them one week to improve. One week, and I meant it, then out. And in the RAF it'd be a matter of charges being brought, for sound military reasons of course. I mean, you can tell everything you need to know about a man from the state of his buttons. But this chap, a bloody consultant sent from on high to show us how it's done, dammit, and the bloody gardeners look smarter than he does . . .'

Lennie listened patiently. Everyone knew that Rob Lauder dressed like that and no-one minded. For Lennie, his presence at the Southern was one of the major consolations of exile, and his legendary scruffiness simply one of the components of the scene, as it had been from his student days before the war. Burton-Smith stirred several spoonfuls of brown sugar into his coffee. 'And his chums from St Guy's are just as much trouble, even if they do own a couple of good suits . . . But I think we've dished them this time . . .' Lennie waited for details but his host just smiled and nodded. 'Taught them a lesson, all of them. They forget that when the chips are down I'm in charge here and the Board looks to me, for action as well as for advice, where the Southern General is concerned. So it doesn't pay the West Wing to try and pull one over on Tiger . . . As they will very soon learn. Now, how about a stroll around the station? As we used to say at Manston . . .'

The medical superintendant led the way downstairs and out into the sunshine. 'Let's head East first. Circular tour. Start with the boiler-house, end with the morgue . . . You clinical chaps forget about the basics, but in administration you can't afford to, even for a minute . . .' Though chubby and well-lunched, Burton-Smith walked quickly, talking about the building and its history, mentioning an architect Lennie felt he ought to have heard of and sometimes getting a bit technical about the drainage difficulties of the site. In the boilerhouse he spoke sharply to a stoker whose use of coke he felt to be excessive in relation to the mild weather, then explained to Lennie the details of a plan to improve the heating system over the course of the next ten years or so if money became available. They left the boiler room via an underground passageway full of warm pipes and hissing steam that reminded Lennie vividly of his various duty trips into the bowels of HM destroyers. They surfaced eventually via a stairwell opening on to a gloomy corridor.

'The surgical department,' said Burton-Smith, sounding for all the world like a lift attendant. 'General and orthopaedic surgery, gynaecology and our planned ophthalmology unit.' He turned to Lennie with his conspiratorial grin again. 'The latter development something of a coup. One in the eye – if you'll forgive the expression – for our lords and masters in the Institute, whose little unit is cramped and falling down and may have to close, I understand from a structural engineer brother, at very short notice indeed. So we are thinking ahead, and could accommodate forty ophthalmological beds with a site for a new operating theatre right next door as soon as the stable block, a structural embarrassment of our own, sadly, can be knocked down.'

Lennie murmured gentle appreciation. The medical super-intendent stopped and grasped him by the shoulder. 'Dowding won the Battle of Britain by thinking ahead . . . I'm proud to think that my job here is rather like his. Not out there in the heat of combat, but up in my office, weighing up the issues, considering what must be done and how we must tackle it. Thinking, thinking, planning ahead . . . As you will see for yourself shortly, Lennie.'

The linoleum was cracked and the floorboards beneath it rank with the stale urine of decades. Burton-Smith strode on. 'And you'll notice how we've completely got rid of the poorhouse colours, the dark brown and cream our predecessors purchased by the barrel . . . My own idea, this.' He waved a hand in the air. The corridor walls were done in pale grey, with a blue-grey ceiling and steel-grey doors. Lennie felt suddenly that he knew as much as he ever wanted to about the interior decoration of RAF prisons. They climbed two flights of stairs, passing on the landing an old lady with bandaged legs and a hat pulled down over her eyes who looked as if she were lost, but Burton-Smith did not seem inclined to stop and help her. 'Our proposed neuro-surgery department . . .' He nodded in the direction of a ward door secured with a large padlock and chain. 'Another disaster area down the way . . . So again, like Dowding, I have planned ahead. A few minor repairs, a matter of roofing that would take only months, and all this could be available to them. I have already mentioned the matter to a brother – in both senses, since the man concerned is a trade unionist as well, though I emphasise a thoroughly decent fellow – who sits on the Board, and simply await word that my offer is about to be taken up. And Sir Norman Dott himself is, I have reason to believe . . .' Burton-Smith grinned again and winked and adjusted his tie.

It was all getting rather tedious. Suddenly the bare corridor terminated at a pair of swing doors and they were back in the main entrance hall, crossing it via the second floor gallery. If this were indeed the half way point of the tour (and the main building of the Southern General seemed to be symmetrical about its administration block) the lunch looked to Lennie like turning out to be a very hard-earned one indeed. They crossed the gallery and after the brief splendours of its oaken bannisters and black and white marble far below went through another set of swing doors into yet another featureless and malodorous corridor. 'Enemy territory,' said Burton-Smith quietly, 'though of course there are one or two helpful friends within it.' They descended one staircase and climbed another shortly afterwards and it became clear to Lennie that the route might have been chosen with a view to avoiding something or someone. Eventually they were back on ground level, heading outwards along a corridor that led at last into a dismal courtyard. 'That was the West Wing . . . Our medical department,' said Burton-Smith. 'I expect they'll show you round in a bit more detail when you commence your clinical duties . . . In due course. But now . . .' He brightened up. 'The morgue.'

They crossed the courtyard and opened a large grey door. 'Might be easier if you just followed me,' said Burton-Smith, setting out along a gloomy corridor with walls of bare brick. 'Walton!'

'Sir?' A small, tidy man with carefully brushed greying hair and an anxious expression scuttled out of a room hardly bigger than a telephone booth. Burton-Smith smiled. 'Lennie, this is Walton, one of our longest serving and most reliable employees . . . Dr Lennox is our newest . . . Starts the week after next as our first senior registrar . . . How long is it now, Walton, that you've been with us?'

The mortuary attendant, who seemed to be in his early sixties, smiled ingratiatingly. 'I started here on, I think, the fifth of May, nineteen thirteen.' He smiled again and rubbed his hands. 'And how are we today, sir?'

'Busy as ever, thank you, Walton . . . And you?'

'A number of poor souls, sir, but nothing at all out of the ordinary for the time of year . . .' Once more the man smiled first at Burton-Smith and then at Lennie and rubbed his hands. 'Twelve, sir.'

'And cremations?'

'Seven, sir . . . At least. There is one case where the relatives have in their distress yet to agree among themselves . . . Though of course I may hear from the undertaker at any minute . . .'

'Indeed, Walton. May we go in?'

'Of course, sir . . . Of course.'

The mortuary attendant led the way into a large room one wall of which was occupied by a vast old-fashioned refrigerator with four tall zinc doors. The attendant opened first one then another, revealing labelled, sheeted corpses neatly on shelves, their heads pointing towards the doors. Some were fully covered, some had yellowish waxen faces peeping out from the folds of the sheets. At each door Burton-Smith leaned forward and closely inspected any uncovered face, nodding each time. When the last door was closed they proceeded to a desk where an old-fashioned office pen, an inkwell and little sheaf of forms awaited the attention of the medical superintendant.

'A formality, Lennie, but a very important one and perhaps the most solemn part of my daily routine here. Some medical superintendents delegate the signing of cremation papers . . . This one, never. It's a matter of enormous medico-legal consequence if ever anything goes wrong, as I'm sure you're aware. Nothing has, so far, at the Southern General, but I like to think that if it did I'd be the very first to pick it up.' The mortuary attendant smiled and nodded. As Burton-Smith signed his way through the little stack of papers it occurred to Lennie that, since each signature attracted the standard fee of one guinea, such conscientiousness was not without its rewards. And besides, what did the doctors who had been looking after the patients think? In most hospitals the cremation papers were signed by them, and the fees, it had to be admitted, sometimes came in handy.

In a few moments they were out in winter sunshine again, walking by a trim lawn and neatly-tended flower beds towards the two cypress trees and the traffic island that marked the front of the administration block. Lennie, having found little on the tour that merited favourable comment, said something nice about the gardens. 'Yes,' said Burton-Smith, 'one of several departments that function admirably because they come under my direct control. Give them to a committee and within six months you'd have some awful muddle of cabbages and weeds and of course acres of uncut grass . . . I don't mind admitting that I went off to the war thinking I knew a lot about administration but came back knowing a hell of a lot more . . . Things work when someone's in charge, and there's no reason why the whole hospital shouldn't run as smoothly as the best bits of it run now . . . It's an uphill struggle, Lennie, but a worthwhile one, as you'll find out when you join us.'

As they climbed the steps to the main entrance a senior porter in a peaked cap stood smartly to attention. 'Afternoon, sir . . . Sir . . .' The second sir was directed at Lennie, who nodded an acknowledgement. Burton-Smith barked 'Afternoon, Connacher . . .' and suddenly speeded up into an odd little charade of senior-officer-rushing-into-HQ-to-change-course-of-war, in which Lennie was presumably playing a small supporting role as some kind of ADC. To maintain this impression they rushed all the way upstairs and slowed only as they went along the gallery to Mrs Roddie's office. Here Burton-Smith's manner again changed suddenly. 'Davina?' he said softly, going into his secretary's office as though reporting to her and assuring her he had not spent an unnecessarily long time over lunch. 'There have been one or two messages,' she said firmly. 'The Regional Drainage Engineer rang . . .' She lowered her voice in a way that indicated the matter was one at a level of secrecy far beyond the security clearance of mere ADC's. Burton-Smith leant close to listen and nodded anxiously. Lennie, still outside the door, could have sworn he heard him say 'Really, Davina? So what shall we do?' but was not quite near enough to be absolutely certain. The door was gently closed from within.

Lennie stood for a moment wondering if circumstances were now such that he could decently leave but was concerned that no opportunity had arisen for thanks and farewells. A few minutes later Dr Burton-Smith and his secretary came out again. Both were smiling. 'Now, Dr Lennox,' said Burton-Smith, 'I'm sure that before you go you would like to take a quick look at your office . . . Not really ready yet but we're going to make jolly sure it is by the time you join us a week on Monday . . . Davina?' Mrs Roddie fiddled with her gaoler's keys and the three moved a few yards along the gallery to a door one beyond that of the medical super-intendent's little lounge. 'Just getting sorted out for you,' said Mrs Roddie, as though to explain the tea-chest full of dusty oddments standing by the door. 'I think you'll be very comfortable up here with us.' In the time it took her to deal with two separate and substantial locks, both of which looked as though they had just been installed, Lennie noted to his puzzlement a number of bibles and other devotional works among the junk in the tea-chest. He was shown into a spacious, well-lit room that had been stripped bare, even of linoleum and curtains. A painter's dust sheet covered a heap of furniture in the middle of the floor. 'We'll have it completely redecorated and furnished for you next week ...' Mrs Roddie flashed her saccharin smile again. 'We're so looking forward to you joining us here, Dr Lennox.'

Another masonic handshake at the top of the stair and it was all over. Lennie walked back to his car with the feeling that so far he had had only rather a one-sided view of life at the Southern and that a number of very odd things required an explanation or a context or both. The business of the room was particularly disturbing: his attachment was quite definitely to Rob Lauder's medical unit, not to the hospital and certainly not to its administration, and if he needed an office at all – and to his knowledge no senior registrar in Edinburgh had one, whether he needed it or not – it would be one down near the clinical coal-face in the West Wing. And whose possessions had been dumped unceremoniously in a tea-chest to make way for his? On his way back down through Morningside to the Institute and the afternoon diabetic clinic Lennie wondered about all that and decided to have a chat quite soon with Lauder himself.

By chance an opportunity arose on the evening of the Saturday before Lennie was due to start at the Southern. At a gala performance of a local amateur Gilbert and Sullivan production in the King's Theatre he and Lauder happened to meet in the Circle Bar at the interval. Lennie's wife, who had not met the celebrated Dr Lauder, had liked him but afterwards confessed to being disappointed by his appearance (He had been wearing a perfectly respectable dinner-suit and ordinary patent leather shoes with no hint of agriculture about them). While the wives chatted Lennie had quickly gone over with his boss-to-be some of the odder points about his recent visit to the Southern. The matter of the office in the administrative block particularly intrigued Lauder. 'Strangest thing,' he said. 'We'd got a little place for you right next to our teaching room, and suddenly the locks are changed, but nobody gives us any keys and then one day the poor bloody padre turns up, glum as they come, with a tea-chest full of kit, saying it's his new office, not that he'd asked for one, but the medical superintendant's secretary thought he would appreciate being a bit nearer the patients . . .' Lauder ran his fingers through his mop of straggly hair and burst out laughing. 'So that's what they're up to . . .'

'I thought it was a bit odd.'

'The kind of thing that happens all the time, sadly enough, but we'll sort it out somehow . . . So what did you think of Tigger?'

'Gave me a nice lunch and a walk round the place. Eager to impress, I thought . . . Seems to have quite an efficient secretary.'

'Davina? There are times when she seems to have quite an efficient medical superintendent . . . Poor old Bullshit-Smith, still hasn't quite got the point about what's really happening at the Southern, but *we're* having lots of fun. He'd take you on his tour of the station . . . What did you think of the place?'

'It was odd,' said Lennie. 'Went round the whole hospital, didn't see a single patient.'

Lauder laughed again. 'Patients? We've got hundreds . . . as you'll see on Monday.'

'Except in the mortuary . . . That seemed quite busy . . . And a lot of paperwork there too . . . Forms and things, for the medical superintendent . . .'

Lauder raised his eyebrows. 'So you actually saw him at it . . .'

'Yes . . . Lots . . . All very odd.'

'Tricky area, Lennie. Of course it's bloody outrageous but there's very little anyone can do . . . Hundreds of fees a year, too, but very tricky when you . . .'

'Quite,' said Lennie, thinking suddenly of the pheasant and claret lunch and a gleaming Alvis parked by the main door of Southern General. 'But if it's all fair and above board . . . And if he declares it in his income tax . . .'

All over the Circle Bar heads turned as Lauder let out a whoop, slapped Lennie on the back and then gripped his arm. 'That's it! I bet he bloody doesn't . . . Thanks, Lennie. We've got him. . . !' He roared with laughter and slapped Lennie's back again. A bell rang somewhere, summoning them once more to the dress circle and the remainder of their evening with a restrained Edinburgh version of 'The Pirates of Penzance'.

June 1955

Although the wall was too high for the position to be really comfortable, Andrew Scott leaned against it with his right arm along the top, enjoying the warmth of its rough, unmortared stone and flaking yellow-and-grey lichen. He was ten, and quite small for his age, but his arm, manfully tanned and grimy almost to the elbow with dark grease from scores of fleeces, looked like a real worker's now. On the other side of the wall the old man waded around among the swirling sheep, examining ears and fleeces and fleece markings, reaching down sometimes to grab a dark, bony leg and look under a hoof for footrot, but always alert to events on the other side of the wall, listening for the shout that brought him every few minutes to the bolt-hole with its greasy wooden portcullis. In a string of linked pens beyond him hundreds more sheep, mainly blackface and crossbred ewes, stood tight-packed, panting in the heat, still unshorn.

Scott leaned proudly on the wall, waiting by the other side of a bolt-hole. The old man was called Davy and had a great respect for education. Over the morning break they had talked about education in general, and about learning Latin, a grand thing in his opinion. Scott, who had not quite started on that yet, or on French – also a grand thing – had nonetheless agreed. Then the old man had told him the Latin word for a sheep was *ovis*, and according to his information they sometimes got ovine infections, so knowing a bit of Latin was probably useful for things like that. Across the wide shearing-pen, in the blue haze to the west beyond the main valley, a string of peaks shimmered. The sun was lower now. The old man had asked him during the morning break if he had ever thought about becoming a vet. They did a lot for farmers and he had never known one that didn't have a grand car too: Lagondas, some of them, he'd heard tell.

It was the second time that day that Scott had been advised about his future. If ye can talk and think and count quick, Mr Merkland had told him in the course of the long, lurching trailer-ride up from the road, ye'll be a grand wee auctioneer. And auctioneers, it seemed, had a good life: travelling, organising things, and doing well at it. He had then started singing numbers in quickfire, rhythmic chant, his voice rising as the sum in pounds went from large to immense, then paused and announced, just as auctioneers were supposed to, 'going . . . going . . . gone . . . for twa hunder and eichty poun' . . . tae the polisman wi' the wee moustache that jist blew his nose . . . Oh. . . ? No' a bid, sir? No? Ye could change your mind yet, sergeant . . . She's a sow ye'll be proud o' . . .' Scott had found that very funny, but had also been flattered that Mr Merkland should have told him what was really quite a subtle, grown-up story.

Mr Merkland, a knotted white handkerchief protecting his head, was at the first place on the right, sitting calmly with a big old blackface ewe sprawled in front of him, its head under his left arm. He was clipping as steadily as ever, rolling the fleece back as he went to reveal the short, evenly ribbed, startlingly white wool beneath. His sheep always seemed less trouble, his effort less conspicuous and though he never hurried he kept pace easily with men perhaps even forty years younger. He was almost finished, Scott noted, but Torwatletie was ahead of him so he would not be the first to need a rough sheep. Scott would take one to Torwatletie; Alec, the other boy, to Mr Merkland. Davy, his pipe gripped wetly between toothless gums, looked over the wall again, taking in the same information at a glance.

To Scott Mr Merkland had proved a surprising friend. At first – perhaps still – more his father's friend, he had taken to dropping in at the manse when he was in the village, having a cup of tea and sitting talking for ten or fifteen minutes. Often his daughter played after school with Scott's older sister, and some of his visits were to collect her, but he always seemed quite happy to discuss things – cars, school, anything – with Scott. One day he had come to pick up Fiona, his daughter, and had asked, quite incidentally it seemed, though he must have at least raised the possibility with his parents first, if Scott could come up and help at Netherton, stay the night – it was a Friday – and help a bit more on the Saturday.

Friday evening had been quite interesting, feeding hens and

store cattle almost until it was dark. The best bit had been Saturday morning, getting a cow and calf ready for the show. The cow, a shaggy black beast, massive and round, had stood patiently being shampooed until its coat was smothered in foam, with Fiona and Scott on one side and Mr Merkland on the other working the lather into its coat, moving slowly down from spine to belly. Then Scott had been asked to rinse it with a hosepipe while Fiona and Mr Merkland did the calf, and then, the biggest surprise of all, he had been invited to take them for a walk to dry. Astonishingly, the cow had gone quietly with him: a huge swaying, dripping creature docile on a loose halter, padding quietly after a boy of ten who had never before been given responsibilities remotely approaching those of that moment. Behind her, the calf trotted, neat and clean and happy to follow its mother anywhere. As instructed, he took them to the road-end, a quarter of a mile or so away, turned and brought them back. By the time they were in the byre again the three were like old friends. The coats of cow and calf were combed to fluffy, gleaming wonder, their hooves polished with oil and they were ready for the journey to the show field and the judges that afternoon. They had not won, though to Scott's admittedly inexpert eye they had looked every bit as good as the pair that did.

Beyond the open gate at the far end of the shearing pen there was a huddle of hungry and bewildered lambs. Each time a ewe was released from a shearing stool it stood for a moment, shook itself then bolted for the opening and the lambs, nosing among them until one, or sometimes two, leapt from the mob and locked on to her udder. By mid afternoon the group of lambs was smaller but more desperate, and the ewes, engorged with milk, more eager than ever to be out amongst them. Torwatletie, a gruff, grudging man known only by the name of his farm, had a stool at the far end of the row of shearers. He finished his sheep, tossed its fleece to one side, thumped it in the flank and it bounded off towards the lambs.

'Roughie!'

Davie nodded and raised the slatted door blocking the bolt-hole. A big blackface ewe was nudged forward by the others then ran at the gap. Scott was ready, crouching outside to grip it before it built up speed. It saw him, dodged off to the right in front of Mr Merkland and gained a yard or two that might prove embarrassing. If it ran wild round the pen the sheep on stools already got restless, and if it escaped at the far end unshorn that was little short of a disgrace. Alec, the other catcher – older, bigger and faster than Scott – might cut in and save the day but that too would mean dishonour and Scott, not a farmer's son, was already an outsider of suspect value. He leapt at the ewe in time to grip it, his right hand connecting firmly with a horn, but not in time to stop it. It kicked and lurched onwards and he went down but his grip held. For a moment it stood still then lunged, dragging him on his knees across the cropped grass. Without letting go he got to his feet again and gripped its other horn. If you did that and hauled their front legs off the ground you could steer them anywhere you wanted.

The ewe, wild-eyed and panting, its dark muzzle streaked with spittle, reared up of its own accord and twisted round. They fell and rolled together more than once and after an uncertain, bruising tussle in which Scott's only aim was to hang on he found himself standing again, somehow on the ewe's other side but more in control. It twitched and butted up, flicking its rough, curved horns around to wound or escape, succeeding in neither. Scott, preoccupied now with keeping hold of it and getting it across to Torwatletie, was nonetheless conscious that he was being watched. A number of the shearers smiled and nodded or shook their heads. Mr Merkland winked. The little rodeo ended when the ewe, still angry and kicking and butting, was handed over and hauled up on to the stool. Torwatletie gripped it and snipped at the air with his shears before taking a long, expert cut under the fleece along its belly. 'Aye, laddie . . . She'll maybe like a wee rest noo.' Walking back to the bolt-hole he noticed his right knee was grazed and bleeding. Mr Merkland caught his eye and nodded, perhaps approvingly. Scott resumed his place, leaning against the wall.

Mr Merkland finished the ewe in front of him and it ran off towards the lambs. Instead of asking for another he signalled to Davy with the gesture of a glass raised to his lips. Davy clambered over the wall into the shearing pen then led Scott and Alec across to one of the two tractors and trailers that had brought men and equipment up to the abandoned farm for the day. Beside the trailer were two crates, one of beer, one of lemonade. Each was covered with a wet sack that had been dipped in the stream every hour or two throughout the day. Davy set to work with his two assistants, pouring beer and lemonade to make shandy in twenty or so pint glasses, still greasy despite an afternoon rinse in a spring at the previous day's venue. As each shearer finished his sheep he sat back with his drink. Some stretched their legs, or lay out on the stools with their caps over their eyes. The break would last for twenty minutes. When they restarted at four they would work for perhaps two hours more, until the sheep in the outer pens were all sheared, then they would lurch down the five miles of rough track and narrow metalled road to Netherton.

To Scott the afternoon break was probably the second best part of the day, coming a good bit behind the lavish farmhouse lunches, a matter of display and rivalry between the wives of the various tenant farmers and proprietors taking part in the week-long round of shearing. A fizzy, beer-tinted drink of lemonade, especially on an afternoon as hot as this one, was something you looked forward to, and by four o'clock you were tired, you had done a lot and what was left to do was a manageable stretch, even with a few aches and pains and a grazed knee. Davy poured, and Alec and Scott went back and forward across the pen with full and empty glasses, more welcome than when they were bringing sheep, then lay in the sun with the others until Mr Merkland raised his hand and snipped his sprung steel shears in the air above his head to signal the last start of the day and a little rush of work for the boys as all the shearers began again more or less at once.

The sun sank further, the pens emptied and the day ended with a batch of a dozen or so rams: big, wide beasts with thick, curling horns, stronger but less nimble than the ewes. On Davy's instructions Alec and Scott worked together, one on each side, taking them slowly and carefully to the remaining shearers while others rested or began to load the trailers and pack the last of the wool, throwing fleeces up into the mouth of an eight foot long bag swinging under a thing that looked like a gallows in a Western. One man, an unfortunate with the hottest, stickiest task of all, worked away inside the bag as he had done all day, catching the rolled fleeces and passing them down to trample them tight, rising out of the bag as it was filled and pausing occasionally to try to dig sheep-ticks – a special risk of the job – from his skin.

The last of the rams ran free and the more particular shearers worked with oil and whetstone to sharpen their shears for next day. The huge bags of wool were loaded on to one of the trailers and secured with rope and gradually everything was cleared away, leaving only trampled grass in empty sheep-pens beside an abandoned upland farmhouse. Men stood around, smoking and talking. A shepherd with a pair of collies returned from some expedition that had ensured that the right flocks would graze on the right hills for the next few months and the little convoy, tractors and trailers and a couple of army surplus jeeps, set out down the track not long after six.

Scott sat on a woolbag at the front of the first trailer, between Davy and Mr Merkland, who had swopped his handkerchief for his usual tweed cap. He was in cheerful form, answering Scott's questions about ticks and the wool market and why Margree, the untenanted farm up the hill behind them, had been abandoned. 'I was brought up in a place like that mysel', Andrew,' said Mr Merkland. 'Nine mile tae walk tae the school. And my mither put chicken grease tae dress my hair because there was neither money nor shop for anything else . . .' Scott felt sudden pity for the man beside him, even though everyone said he was the richest for miles around. 'And see what it did for me . . .' Poker-faced, Mr Merkland pulled his cap off and bent forward to display his bald white scalp, then he and Davy burst out laughing. Scott, puzzled at first, joined in. Mr Merkland explained more about Margree. 'The lads nowadays, the tenants, they're asking for better and getting it. A single man needs company and a wife would never look at it. They want a' thing electric these days, and piped water, and Margree's no' worth it. So we manage fine from Netherton . . . Davy here enjoys a twenty mile walk wi' his dog . . . In the mornin', ye ken, before his work . . .' The old man on Scott's right nodded and chuckled and sucked noisily on his pipe.

The tractor and trailer swung down a green track by a stream. Scott sat content, tired and comfortable enough on the woolbag, leaning on another one just behind and hanging loosely on to one of the securing ropes, watching the blurred, worn tyres of the little grey Ferguson tractor below. Mr Merkland asked him what his mother thought of him earning a living, a question Scott took to refer to their previous conversation about being an auctioneer, then solemnly told him how much it would cost her to keep a lad of his size, and how he should hand over his wages to her the next evening as soon as he got home. Scott, who had assumed that his week with the shearing squad was a treat, like getting to shampoo the cow, found himself once more surprised by Mr Merkland, and turned his mind to a number of other things he might do with his first pay packet, depending on its size. Mr Merkland sat back and began to sing. 'My brither was a baker loon, he rose at four in the mornin' ...' A goosander, scared from the stream by the little convoy, clattered aloft and flew off up the far side of the valley.

'Davy!'

The old man on Scott's left had slumped, his head down near his knees, teetering as though he might fall forward and under the trailer. Mr Merkland moved swiftly, leaning across Scott to grab Davy's shoulder and steady him. 'Stop!' he shouted. 'Stop, Tam ...' The driver did not hear. Mr Merkland and Scott yelled more loudly and the driver looked round, saw what was happening and drew up. The old man had been sick and was spluttering and coughing. Scott scrambled back out of the way as Mr Merkland slapped him on the back and pulled him round to lie on his side on the woolbag. 'Davy ... Davy, lad ...' The old man lay still and hardly breathing. His face was pale and his eyes were half-shut. Scott watched as Mr Merkland loosened his collar stud and gently slapped his stubbly cheek. 'Davy, lad ... Dinnae ...' The old man shook his head slowly from side to side, then lifted an arm to clutch his chest. 'Are ye sair, Davie?' The old man nodded and closed his eyes. 'Andrew, son ... There's a wee first aid box in the black kist in the other trailer ...' Scott clambered down, wondering if Mr Merkland had thought of that as a tactful means of getting him out of the way while he and the driver – who was now standing on the towbar looking quite ill himself – and old Davy, the man most concerned, got on with the grown-up business of death.

The jeeps were far ahead now and still going. The second tractor had drawn up and the men from its trailer joined those of the first in an anxious circle looking up to where Mr Merkland and Tam, the driver, were trying to make Davy comfortable on the woolbag. Scott hurried through them to the back of the second trailer and found the black tin trunk, opened it and rummaged, among knives and boxes and bottles of terebene and marking fluid, for the first aid box: a square khaki tin with a red cross on a round white background. It was too small, too disappointing, to do any good. Feeling efficient rather than simply inquisitive, Scott opened it and checked its contents. There was a round cardboard pillbox with 'Aspro' scrawled across the top, some adhesive tape whiskered with dried tobacco, a dun-coloured roll of bandage and a tiny bottle of brandy. It would not help, but he hurried back round to the towbar and clambered up to hand the box to Mr Merkland.

Davy had been straightened out and was lying on his back on the first woolbag, his head to one side and cradled in the driver's arm. There was a line of sweat in the stubble on his top lip and his eyes looked calmly beyond the two men bent over him and out into the blue above the hills. Scott held the box open for Mr Merkland, who took the brandy bottle, flipped open its little brass top and held it to the dying man's lips. Some spilled down his chin but enough went in for Davy to feel it. His mouth closed and his lips made tiny, moist, contented movements. 'Fine, Davy . . . Fine . . .' Mr Merkland's hand, large and dark, stroked the old man's brow. Suddenly Davy's eyes closed. Mr Merkland nodded, patted the pale stubbly cheek and wiped away a trickle of brandy from the dead man's chin.

About a dozen men stood silent, their question answered. First one, then another took off his cap. Mr Merkland folded the old man's arms across his chest and stepped to the ground. Scott followed him, blinking and sniffing because workmen did not cry. He found himself standing closer to Mr Merkland than he would have done if he'd thought about it, and was glad when Mr Merkland put an arm around his shoulders, a tweedy sleeve smelling as much of sheep as sheep did. The tractor engines idled on, gurgling against the upland stillness of the green track. No one spoke. Mr Merkland slowly took off his cap and bowed his head and the others followed. After a moment he looked up again as though he were about to speak. The men waited and watched. Instead of speaking he began to sing, in the same light pleasant voice that Scott had heard a few minutes before, the others joining in, at first uncertainly, then steadily and even tunefully:

> 'The Lord's my shepherd, I'll not want . . .
> He makes me down to lie.
> In pastures green, he leadeth me,
> The quiet waters by.'

By the second verse they were flagging, but they all knew the third, that began 'Yea though I walk in death's dark vale', and took it firmly to the end. They fell silent and Mr Merkland nodded benediction and dismissal then turned to the driver. 'A haup, Tam. Cover Davy, and we'll get on.' A tarpaulin sheet was found in the back of the trailer and three men wrapped the body, securing it with a couple of loose turns of rope in the hollow between two woolbags. The convoy began to move again, the first trailer now a high, jolting hearse, the second a conveyance for a huddle of subdued, surprised mourners.

Uneven grass gave way to a single track metalled road but they speeded up only a little. In the huddle on the second trailer Mr Merkland talked about Davy, who had been eighty two, and a shepherd all his days apart from four years in the army in France and Mesopotamia. The uncle of Mrs Merkland, he had come to live with them at Netherton when his wife had died ten years before and had worked around the place because he had enjoyed it, doing a bit less as he had got older, '. . . but he aye looked forward to the clipping.' Scott thought about that, and wondered if the day in the sun had been too much for the old man, then asked Mr Merkland what he thought. 'Andrew, son, you couldn't have kept him away . . . And if ye'd tried he would have told you he'd never missed yin, bar the war, for seventy year, and he'd never had a day's illness in his life, bar shrapnel.' Scott thought a bit more about it and then about the long bundle among the woolbags on the trailer ahead, and decided Mr Merkland was right.

When they got back to Netherton Mrs Merkland, who was waiting in the courtyard and had had no warning of her uncle's death, cried a bit. The men stood around not quite knowing what to do then went up to Mrs Merkland one at a time and said gruff, kind things about Davy. It occurred suddenly and absurdly to Scott that each of them still, in a kind of a way, depending how you looked at it, contained a shandy poured that afternoon by the dead man. And all day they had sheared sheep released by him for the boys to catch, and some of them had joked during the breaks about his pipe, a curly old black thing with a little shiny, perforated lid and a uniquely pungent tobacco. He had been at sheep clippings for seventy years. And an hour previously it had taken him only a few minutes to die.

But there were formalities too, it seemed. Mr Merkland phoned for the doctor to come up to confirm the death officially, and within ten minutes Dr Girdwood had driven from the village in his green

MG, examined the body as it lay, still atop the woolbags, and given permission for it to be moved. In an odd sort of way it had been very considerate of Davy to have died on the trailer: anywhere else would have caused great trouble if you weren't supposed to move a body until the doctor arrived. Scott resolved to check up on that, but meanwhile he watched as Mr Merkland and two others carried Davy's corpse into the house, standing beside Fiona, who was crying a bit too, but not putting his arm round her.

With the corpse inside the house they made a start on unloading the wool and getting things ready for the next day. Usually when that was finished Mr Merkland phoned the manse so that Scott's father could drive up and collect him. Obviously it was different today. Mr Merkland was busy because of Davy and it might be simpler just to walk the three miles even though he was quite tired. Scott was still thinking about that when Dr Girdwood came out of the house and asked him if he was heading back to the village. Scott started to explain about the usual arrangement but the doctor shook his head. 'Jump in. You'll be home in five minutes.' He was a famously fast driver. Scott jumped in.

The car, an open-topped MG TD in British racing green, familiar in the village and much envied, roared into life and Scott settled back into the leather seat. A head-spinning turn took them out of the courtyard and in what seemed like only seconds they were at the road-end a quarter of a mile away. As they drummed along the main road Scott began to wonder again about the old man's death, on the trailer, far from anywhere, and if anything could have been done to help him. It was difficult to think of a way of putting it so eventually he just asked if the doctor thought the old man had been frightened.

'Hard to say,' said the doctor over the noise of the road and the wind. 'D'you see it?'

'Quite a lot . . . He just was sick, then fell and Mr Merkland caught him . . . And he sent me for the first aid box and when I came back he was quite peaceful. His chest was sore though.'

'Heart attack, almost certainly . . . Might have known he was going . . . Some people do . . . But it was all over in a couple of minutes. And among friends. Lots of us would settle for that, Andrew . . . There are some Spangles in the glove compartment if you'd like one.'

Scott found the Spangles among a jumble of cigarette packets and maps, had one himself then offered the doctor one, put them back and thought about settling for different kinds of death, something he'd thought about before, but never with quite the crisp enthusiasm that the doctor had just shown. He probably knew a lot about it. There was a longish pause in conversation. The MG TD had featured as the cutaway engineering drawing in the middle of the *Eagle* only a few weeks before: a British racing green just like the doctor's, with all the important inside bits visible and numbered, and a key to the numbers underneath the picture. Being in one was more interesting when you knew where everything was.

'I believe you're to be congratulated,' said the doctor as they neared the village. 'A small matter of an examination. Congratulations.'

'Thanks,' said Scott, making it sound casual. The qualifying exam results had just come out and at the end of the holidays he would go to the county academy and do French and Latin as well as everything else, unless another exam in Edinburgh the following week determined otherwise. They were going down the main street now and Scott found himself hoping someone from his class would see him in the doctor's car even though he knew that was a bit silly. As they turned left at the cross someone did: Robert Findlay, who would probably be quite jealous and might even punch him around a bit because of it, and he had definitely seen them.

They stopped at the end of the manse drive. 'It's good for the school,' said the doctor. Scott didn't know what he was talking about. 'What is?'

'You. In the exam. Coming first in the county.'

'Did I?'

'Gosh. Maybe you're not meant to know. But . . . people talk. So perhaps you shouldn't. Talk about it, I mean. But congratulations anyway.'

'Thank you, Dr Girdwood. And thanks for the lift.'

Feeling suddenly stiff and weary, Scott walked up the drive to the manse. What the doctor had said was interesting, and opened up possibilities beyond being an auctioneer, but when all was said and done – as the headmaster, almost certainly the source of his information, might say – Kirkcudbrightshire was only a wee county.

June 1955

Lennie paused in the cool of the archway, combed his hair, checked the deep gloss on his best Royal Navy shoes and stepped out into the sunshine of the quad just as a servitor he had not seen before emerged from the porter's lodge to ring the bell. The man was limping, and walking behind him Lennie found himself thinking rather automatically about the diagnosis: not the shortened, flaccid leg of childhood polio, nor the dead swing of an artificial limb, nor the rigidity of a fused knee joint or the painful waddle of an arthritic hip. As the man turned and reached up with the key to the odd little coffin-like box on the wall that stopped students mischievously signalling an early end to their lectures Lennie saw his boot: short, high and inwardly curved. He had talipes equinovarus, one of the commonest variants of club-foot. Lennie checked his watch just as the bell stopped ringing and the man caught his eye and smiled. They were both right.

Across the quad half a dozen medical students were sitting in the sun on a broad stone balustrade, in a row like sparrows on a wire. One waved and Lennie recognised her as a girl who had just spent three weeks on an attachment at the medical unit at the Southern and had done well there, even under the close scrutiny of Lauder and himself in a mock finals exam: a nice girl with green eyes who had picked up a heart murmur everyone else had missed. Now real finals loomed and most of the sixth year students were in libraries, or sensibly sunning themselves between times like the ones opposite; and Lennie too was facing a little test, an interview for a consultant job at the Institute, and all on a day too hot for study or for wearing an interview suit or for sitting in a room answering questions on which the next thirty years of your career depended, but in the circumstances you went along quite uncomplainingly. A deep, arched doorway offered shade and a cool stone stair led up to the floor where the appointment committee had been convened.

The job was not ideal but Lennie was not in a position to be too particular: after more than five years at the Southern as a senior registrar and a couple of disappointments with more conventional jobs, he had been advised to apply for anything remotely suitable, and at least this one would allow him to stay in Edinburgh. The problem was that no one seemed to know exactly what the job entailed – or, if one thought positively, the main advantage of it was that whoever was appointed could make of it more or less whatever he pleased. It seemed that the advertisement that had appeared in the BMJ was an interim compromise in the course of a long squabble between the University and the Institute, with the real contest being deferred until someone was actually appointed to the post.

It would have been easier for the Institute's physicians if Henry Hutchinson Hunt had been anything other than a hopeless boozer. His consultant sessions could have been better defended if he had been seen on the wards more regularly and less drunk. By the time he died – sober, curiously enough, and of a heart attack while trying to rescue a small boy from a canal – he had almost ceased to pretend to be working at all, simply dropping in on the wards at deliberately inconvenient times, enquiring blandly if everything was all right then pushing off again to one of his clubs with an airy assurance that he would be glad to come in at a moment's notice if there were any problems. To Lennie's knowledge, no member of the junior staff had ever felt the need even to try to locate him. The wards had continued to run fairly smoothly but after his death – reported in the local press as a heroic sacrifice on the part of a dedicated healer – a number of people had insisted on asking why a man who had worked around two hours a week required to be replaced by one who might want to work forty or fifty, and the University had spotted an opportunity, by means of the joint appointment now about to be made, to increase its influence in the Institute.

On the first floor a note scrawled on a piece of foolscap pinned to a door signified the candidates' waiting room. Lennie paused in the corridor. From within came a low moaning noise, a nasal ululation that rose and fell irregularly but not unattractively, carrying hints of the exotic and perhaps oriental, of snake-charming or the call of the faithful to prayer. Lennie listened to the sound for a moment, guessed what it was and from whom, and then went in. To the left of the door was a row of four chairs. A dark, portly man in a voluminous black suit was lying on his back across them with his head towards the door. His right hand, fingers tensely spread, was pressed to his right cheekbone, his eyes were closed and his lips held firmly together. The weird sound, a kind of hummed dirge, filled the little room. Lennie stood unnoticed. The dirge gave way to a brisk progression of cheerful, strutting cadences complete with quite competently executed grace-notes then suddenly there was silence. The man folded his arms across his chest, smiled with his eyes still shut and let out a long, happy sigh. 'Like it, Lennie?'

'The last bit's quite jolly . . . But as you know, Sam, I'm not an expert.'

'Indeed no.'

There was a pause. The man opened his eyes, took a large pair of horn-rimmed glasses from his breast pocket and put them on but did nothing to indicate that he might be about to get up and thus give Lennie somewhere to sit. 'A new one?' Lennie enquired politely.

' "Bridie's Farewell to the Cardiology Department of the Royal Charitable Institute, Edinburgh",' said the man. He smiled again. 'First performance.'

'Privilege to hear it, Sam. But you should have brought your pipes, marched round the quad a bit and cheered us all up.'

Dr Bridie shook his head at what was clearly a preposterous suggestion then sprang to his feet and smiled. 'Please take a seat, Dr Lennox. As you know, committees like this reserve the right to keep you waiting, muck you about, probe your weaknesses, undermine your strengths, raise your hopes, dash them, transform your career in the twinkling of an eye or blight your life for ever. And take all afternoon about it. So please have a seat, Dr Lennox, and one of our hostesses will join you at your table shortly.' Lennie laughed and sat down.

Sam Bridie had been a senior registrar for at least a year longer than Lennie and now claimed to have worn out a new suit purchased and used only for consultant interviews. He was a disappointed man: his career had faltered for a variety of reasons, some of which he reported with strange, inverted pride, some of which he would have been reluctant to recognise at all. He had done a lot of cardiology but no one of influence seemed to regard him as a cardiologist, so he had made belated attempts to broaden his training. This was the second occasion he and Lennie had competed at interview and it was possible there would be others. His waiting-room banter, Lennie thought as he settled down, might eventually become tiresome.

Sam was still smiling to himself, perhaps in contemplation of his latest pibroch, perhaps rehearsing some neat phrase to explain to the committee his odd and extended senior registrar career. Or had he already decided to emigrate? Quite a number of people like him, having failed to achieve a consultant post in a decent teaching hospital, had concluded therefore that Britain was finished and settled eventually in some unheard of town in Australia or Canada. He was sitting one seat away from Lennie, in his interview suit (an angular, loose-fitting, double-breasted job that made Lennie think of the late Ernest Bevin), portly in profile, his black hair sleeked down with Brylcreem, and he had started making funny noises again: not mouth-pibroch but a breathy whistling sound with no recognisable rhythm or tune. To stop him Lennie asked a vague question about the fourth candidate, the one from Glasgow whom he knew had pulled out the day before.

'Withdrawn,' said Sam abruptly, as though some personal slight had been involved. 'It's between you, me and the Lord's anointed. With all the traditional disadvantages of the alphabet heaped upon my innocent head . . . As usual.'

'Come on, Sam.' Lennie remembered a similar conversation at one of their previous interviews.

'No. It's deadly serious. Our senior colleagues have all the concentration and recall of gnats on heat, so that anyone with the sense to be called Yuill-McGrigor is fresh in their minds when the discussion begins and therefore thoroughly deserves the job. You probably haven't noticed, Lennie, comfortably in the middle of the alphabet as you are. So the Lord's anointed, for that reason among others, will take the palm today.'

Yuill-McGrigor was the promising young man recruited from London for the job Lennie had mistakenly expected to be his some years before. He had, according to Lennie's information, gone down only moderately well in the Institute, where his manner with patients was criticised not so much for being condescending, which it was, but for being, in local terms, frankly incomprehensible. His scientific promise was yet to be fulfilled and he was said to spend a good deal of time in pursuit of grouse, salmon and deer, though whether the latter would work for or against him at interview depended very much upon who was sitting round the table. The withdrawal of the man from Glasgow simplified things a lot, Lennie decided: if Ratho and Lorimer wanted to maintain the tone of their unit with a gentleman-physician and succeeded in carrying the committee, Yuill-McGrigor would get the job; if, however, one or two key people speaking for the University interest could convince a majority that a bit of teaching and research experience would be more useful in the post than an endless supply of Jermyn Street shirts, then there was a chance that Lennie and Margaret might that evening be opening the bottle of champagne her father had sent them, as he put it, just in case. Sam, sadly for him and not only because of his suit and his funny noises, was just no longer a serious applicant.

The candidates had been summoned to attend at half hour intervals, starting with Dr Bridie at two o'clock. At twenty past two Tony Yuill-McGrigor – tall and thin and elegantly droopy, like the subalterns ranged over ante-room furniture in old *Punch* cartoons – wandered in. He pulled a chair out of the row and sat facing the other two. Sam glowered at him then grunted 'They're late.'

'I shouldn't take it personally, Sam. They'll be delighted to see you in there once they've got themselves sorted out . . . And I gather our Glaswegian colleague decided against a trip to Edinburgh today . . . So they've really got half an hour in hand . . .'

Sam frowned and nodded and started his silly whistling noises again. Yuill-McGrigor turned to Lennie. 'What do you think, Lennie? Bit of a discussion because it's one of these new joint appointments? A mixed committee, so people have to get know each other? University chaps, Institute chaps, and I believe the Health Board is represented too . . . Though not by anyone one has come across. A lay member, and an administrative medical officer of some sort . . . D'you know him, Lennie? A Dr Smith?' Sam rolled his eyes and whistled and twiddled his thumbs. 'D'you know him, Sam?' Sam raised his eyebrows and pursed his lips in manner designed to indicate that though discretion was preferable there was much he could divulge if pressed. 'Was there something. . . ?' said Yuill-McGrigor.

'Oh, nothing serious,' said Sam. 'Certainly nothing criminal . . . that could be substantiated. Some minor difficulties in a previous post. Not anything that couldn't be sorted out with a word here and handshake there. But his accomplice got three years.'

'Really, Sam?'

'Two, with remission. A model convict, I understand. Most helpful in the prison hospital. But I'm not an expert on the case.' Sam smiled and glanced meaningfully at Lennie. 'But altogether a most interesting one. You mean you haven't heard, Tony? A little piece of private enterprise at the Southern General that came to light when for some reason the tax inspectors decided to take a closer look at the personal finances of the medical superintendent. And all sorts of interesting things began to crawl out from under stones. Mortuary attendant goes to jail, does not pass go, does not collect any more jewellery from the deceased or kickbacks from the Worshipful Company of Undertakers. Three years, he got. And our friend in there, every bit as guilty but a little more circumspect, got twenty.'

'Twenty years?' gasped Yuill-McGrigor, in the manner of a very astonished young subaltern in an old *Punch* cartoon.

'Yes,' said Sam solemnly. 'Sentenced to twenty years as an administrative medical officer at the Health Board. No remission but full pension rights at the end of it, of course. Not a bad chap, actually . . . And the whole business did him no real harm . . . Maybe even some good. He sobered up a lot, I believe, and even stopped using a ridiculous double-barrelled name he'd thought up for himself . . .'

'Really, Sam?' Yuill-McGrigor subsided further into thought and the three candidates sat, in silence except for Sam's odd noises, until a minor official of the Faculty of Medicine appeared at the door shortly before three o'clock. 'Dr Bridie?' Sam sprang up again, shook out his Ernie Bevin suit, straightened his tie and marched out. Lennie and Yuill-McGrigor, each aware that the other was his sole serious rival, relaxed considerably and for an hour or so enjoyed a wide-ranging discussion of the Health Board's recently published proposals to replace the Institute, a crowded and dilapidated mid-Victorian charity hospital, with something more suited to modern scientific medicine and the care of patients in the middle of the twentieth century.

They were eventually interrupted by the little official. 'Dr Lennox?' he intoned from the door like a stage butler. 'Good luck, Lennie,' said his main rival as he rose to go. 'Thanks, Tony . . .' On the way along the corridor Lennie checked his turnout: tie, cuffs, strategic buttons and a last glance at his lucky Royal Navy shoes. Another door opened and he found himself in a long, sunny room overlooking the quad. Seven middle-aged and elderly men were sitting in a semicircle at the far end of a large oval table. Shaky MacKenzie, Vice-Dean of the medical faculty, was in the chair, just as Lennie had expected, and rattled quickly through the introductions. On either side of him were Lorimer and Ratho, then Professors Cairnie and Maguire, then an unknown, a Mr Williamson, lay member of the Board and, from his demeanour and his lumpy suit, a trade unionist; and opposite him Smith, or Bullshit-Smith, as Lennie would always think of him, thinner and less flamboyant than before, and touching the knot of his tie just to make sure that Lennie had not forgotten their fraternal bond. 'Please sit down,' said old Shaky.

Lennie sat down and glanced round them again. Williamson would prove resistant to Yuill-MacGrigor's charm. Lorimer and Ratho needed careful, courteous handling if their true preference was to be overruled by the others. Of the two professors Cairnie, the more difficult and important, was the more likely to stay awake. Smith smiled as Lennie discreetly returned his signal. There was hope. Shaky cleared his throat. 'Now I think you are familiar with the usual procedure, Dr Lennox, and I shall proceed directly by inviting Professor Maguire to open the formal interview. Professor Maguire?'

For half an hour Lennie fielded questions carefully devised by the two opposing camps to cause him maximum discomfort. Too strong a reassurance to the University people on the subject of teaching and research would give Lorimer and Ratho sufficient ammunition to finish him off; any lack of commitment to the Health Service component might leave room for Yuill-MacGrigor to be appointed as a thoroughly agreeable colleague, a potential academic who might grow into that side of the job: a notion that would suit Ratho and Lorimer quite well and leave them free to spend a lot more time on committees and golf. The trick was to pitch it down the middle and hope that in doing so he could still carry the support of the trade unionist. There was some comfort from Williamson's reaction to events: he showed every appearance of devastating the genteel hauteur of Ratho and Lorimer: if he regarded the interview as the extension of the class war by other means, Yuill-MacGrigor was in trouble.

Mr Williamson was the last to question Lennie. He wanted to know how the candidate, as he called him, felt about the Board's proposals to replace the Institute with a more modern hospital. That was tricky. Was he in love with the present building, a rambling exercise in rococo Scots baronial, Lennie wondered, or was he set on tearing it down as a relic of the patronising charity of the Victorian bourgeoisie? Lennie started cautiously, pointing out that there was a lot of goodwill towards the Institute in its present form at its present site, and noted that his interrogator had begun to look a little impatient, which was helpful. He could then proceed to point out that, although the building had reflected the best and newest of ideas in hospital design in the 1860's when it was built, medicine had changed a great deal since then. Perhaps the Health Service owed it to itself and its patients to build something now that represented as big an advance as the present Institute had done in its time. Williamson seemed pleased, but such radicalism was not going down well on the right flank of the firing squad, where Lorimer and Ratho were muttering together.

'But of course the problem from our – the Board's – point of view,' said Williamson, 'is that the doctors can never agree among themselves about what's to be done, and when, and above all where . . . What could you do about that, Dr Lennox?'

Lennie smiled and said something about independence of mind being an outstanding characteristic of medical men, especially in the older teaching hospitals. Smith was grinning broadly and even Lorimer allowed himself a little smile. 'So what would we do, Dr Lennox?'

'Whatever you do it won't be easy, but if it's made clear that things can't go on for ever as they are at the moment, with people just muddling along with a bit more overcrowding each year and odd little extensions tacked on here and there, then discussion might have to become a bit more definite. So perhaps the Board should set a date for opening a new hospital. The centenary year. . . ? 1970, is it? That would give us five years to decide and ten years to build something, on the same site or somewhere else . . .' Ratho was muttering to Lorimer as though Lennie had just proposed the immediate demolition of the Royal and Ancient College of Physicians on Queen Street. Lennie smiled again and added 'Or would that be rushing things a bit?'

Williamson seemed both pleased and amused. 'And just one last question, doctor . . .' The little man narrowed his eyes. 'What would you do about the problem of private practice?' The last phrase came out with a wonderful collection of rolling r's and a tone which seemed to equate the matter with an outbreak of bubonic plague. Lorimer and Ratho were listening with renewed interest. That, Lennie decided, was most likely what the pre-interview fight had been about. A very tricky one. 'Strictly in relation to this post,' he began, 'it seems unlikely that any problems would arise. As seems clear, anyone who was appointed would have his work cut out . . .'

'Yes, yes, doctor . . . But the broader question . . . How is it that some of our senior medical staff can get away with having the best of both worlds. . . ? A salary from the Board and the chance to use, and sometimes abuse, the facilities of the National Health Service for the benefit of their private business outside . . . What would you do about that, doctor. . . ?'

'I certainly can't speak from any personal experience in the matter,' said Lennie, thinking of the misfortunes of his senior colleague's patient, Mrs Arbuthnot, 'though I understand most of the points about private practice and the NHS are covered in the national agreement reached when the Health Service was set up . . . An agreement whose terms should be strictly observed, of course, and if necessary enforced by . . . by . . .'

'Quite', said Shaky from the chair, as Lorimer and Ratho relaxed again and Smith seemed to be enjoying their discomfiture. 'I think the candidate has made his position on private practice quite clear.' Mr Williamson coughed and nodded and settled back in his chair. Lennie realised belatedly that the question had had nothing to do with him, and that Williamson's aim had been simply to embarrass Ratho and Lorimer. And why not? His interrogator, squat, barrel-chested and wheezy, was almost certainly a miner as well as a trade unionist: a man with a visceral belief in the principles of the Health Service and a deep suspicion of the smoother professionals within it. He was indignant, and rightly so, about the corrupting division of loyalties that private practice engendered and if, in his capacity as a Board Member, he wanted to rebuild the Institute in a field next to the Gilmerton Miners Welfare Hall, he was only doing his job as a local politician. But now he was looking at Lennie as though he had just designated him the people's candidate for the post in question.

Lennie relaxed. Old Shaky asked him if he had any questions for the committee, a formality to which the traditional response was no. Shaky then thanked him for coming along and expressed a hope that the committee would be in a position to communicate its decision at around five o'clock. Lennie thanked the chairman, glanced round the group at the other end of the table, smiled, got up and left. Only when he was out in the corridor again did he realise how hot it had been in the interview room. Instead of going back to the waiting room, with its risk of an hour or so of Sam's funny noises, he went downstairs and out into the quad again, crossing it and leaving through an archway that opened on to the tree-lined walk separating Edinburgh University Medical School from its great teaching hospital, the Royal Charitable Institute, formerly the Royal Charitable Institute for the Care of the Indigent Sick: the place Lennie had always, since he had first entered it as a student in the thirties, imagined himself working happily for years as a consultant. In less than an hour he would know.

The afternoon was still and warm and Lennie, uncomfortable and perhaps conspicuous in his best suit, had not really thought about how he would pass the time until the committee made up its mind. The obvious thing would have been to go back to the waiting room but Sam and the heat and, he had to admit, a certain amount of tension, ruled that out. He wondered for a moment about spending some time in one of the medical bookshops in Teviot Place or in the museum on Chambers Street, but decided eventually to go for a short walk instead. In the interview room Yuill-McGrigor would now be coming under fire from Comrade Williamson and perhaps Professor Cairnie, who had let slip some quite serious reservations about him in the course of Lennie's visit to his department. And then there was the discussion. Would Smith hold firm in his Southern and other loyalties? Or was he by some remote chance aware of origins of the complex train of events that had precipitated his downfall at the Southern and his move to the

Board? And what of Ratho and Lorimer? Would they, in the genteel squabbling that passed for objective professional evaluation on these occasions, make the most of the convention that those who had to work with the man appointed got rather more than their fair share of influence in discussion? In a corner like that, and in the secrecy of an appointment committee, they could smear Lennie civilly but effectively enough: 'not *quite* the kind of chap we had in mind for the job, talented though he undoubtedly is . . .' 'Clever, I grant you, but just a *shade* difficult . . .' And a single unfortunate case, like that of poor old Mrs Arbuthnot, could easily be considered offence enough. But there was nothing Lennie could do about any of that now. He bought an *Evening Dispatch* with no serious intention of reading it and went and sat in the sun in Greyfriars churchyard, looking out over ornate, lichened grave-stones shimmering in the heat haze to the looming grey bulk of the Castle and a reef of thunderclouds beyond, until quarter to five, when he got up and strolled back to the medical school and the waiting room at the top of the stairs.

As Lennie opened the door both Bridie and Yuill-McGrigor twitched anxiously round in their seats then relaxed again when they saw who it was. 'Sorry, chaps. Thought I'd just pop back to hear how things turned out . . . Obviously no news yet.' Sam was rumpled and sweating and clearly suffering both from the heat and the suspense. Tony was bearing up better but was by no means as dapper as he had been two hours earlier. Lennie looked at his watch. Shaky had said around five o'clock and it was now ten to. But then Sam had been listed for interview at two and had not actually gone in until almost three. Lennie settled down again, in the chair that Yuill-McGrigor had moved in order to make a more conversa-tional grouping. And at least Sam wasn't making any funny noises now.

Just as the bell in the quad was ringing for five o'clock the door opened and Smith appeared. 'Dr Lennox. . . ?' he said. 'The committee would be most grateful if you could come along again . . .' Lennie got up. He had a consultant job, and at the Institute too. 'Jolly good show, Lennie,' said Yuill-McGrigor. 'Yes,' said Sam, 'Jolly good show . . . Jolly good show, old chap.' Out in the corridor Smith seized his hand. 'Brilliant interview, Lennie. Let me be the first to congratulate you.' The masonic handshake was the warmest

Lennie had ever encountered. Lennie squeezed a pudgy knuckle with his thumb and smiled.

When Sandy came out of school at quarter past three her mum and her little brother were waiting for her as usual. They walked down the main road and then along under the chestnut trees and past the cemetery gate and down into Plewlands Gardens and home but when they got there she noticed one or two more odd things. The table-cloth in the dining room had been changed, from the usual maroon tassely one to a lacey one that only came out for grown up dinner parties, and her toys had been tidied up more than usual. And usually when it was as sunny as this she went out to play in the back garden but today when she had taken off her blazer and hung it up her mum seemed to want her to stay inside. Then her brother said there was a secret and he wouldn't tell her, so she bullied him a bit when her mum was in the kitchen and he told her they had made marzipan while she was at school but she wasn't getting any, and he had because he had helped. There was another secret, so she bullied him a bit more and he told her that big grandpa had sent them some fizzy wine that children didn't get.

A grown up dinner party would make most sense, Sandy decided while they were having milk and biscuits before Children's Hour, and why hadn't her mum just told her as she usually did? They would go to bed early and lie awake and listen and have nice leftovers the next day. But there might be a bit more to it than that, because her mum and dad had been talking a lot in French for nearly a week, which they didn't usually do just for dinner parties, and because her dad had been really fussy about his shoes (his very best shoes) before going out to work that morning. After their milk and biscuits but still before Children's Hour James started to talk a lot of nonsense about going into a big house with mum and an old lady. It sounded as if he was making it all up so she told him that and then he said he wouldn't tell her any more even if she wanted him to, because really it was a secret. When she sat on him with a cushion he said it was a big house and they had walked upstairs and there was another stair with lots of little rooms after that, and there was a dog and the old lady had smelt smoky. Sandy decided he wasn't making it up after all, but it was all very odd.

Their mum had been busy in the kitchen, probably putting something for the dinner party in the Rayburn, but came through when it was time for Children's Hour and they listened to Aunty Kathleen and some singing by school choirs, then there was a Tammy Troot story, a good one with lots of funny voices. Then the most unusual thing of all happened: their dad came home early, before the weather and the bells for the news on the wireless, and their mum ran out into the hall to see him first, again very odd, and they were laughing and even shouting a bit. James and Sandy went out to look and dad had lifted mum up in the air and they were both still laughing. She was saying 'I knew you would' again and again and he said 'Its just as well I did . . .' and laughed a lot. James rushed in and tried to cuddle all their legs at once, then they had a wild, laughing, family cuddle, even though Sandy still had really no idea what it was all about, and wanted to know.

Her father picked her up and hugged her. 'They're letting me out of the poorhouse,' he explained, still laughing. 'I'm going back to work in the Institute.' 'Oh,' said Sandy. 'Is that all?' He laughed even more and threw her up in the air, something he hadn't done for a long time, and caught her and hugged her again. They went into the kitchen, which was very tidy and the kitchen table had a tablecloth on too, and there were some tall glasses and a dish of marzipan home-made sweeties and they all had one, then their dad started to open the fizzy wine, which was complicated because it had paper and wire on the top, a bit like a ginger beer bottle, then it opened with a huge bang and he and mum laughed again, and mum poured lemonade for the children, then made them hold their glasses up and say 'To dad's new job.' That was probably what all the French had been about, and perhaps he would like to work at the Institute again.

They had more marzipan sweeties then they all got into the car and went down the hill and along the road to church but not as far, with mum and dad in the front talking about a house and James sitting in the back beside Sandy looking pleased with himself because all his secrets had been true. The car turned off the main road and stopped. They got out and opened a door in a grey stone wall and walked up a path that was more like a tunnel because of huge plants on both sides and their mum rang the bell on a maroon door. They waited for ages then a wee old lady with a cigarette came to the door and looked at them all then smiled and asked them in. Sandy wasn't sure but her mother held her hand. The hall was nice, with a shiny floor and a big staircase that went up and up, and a window in the ceiling right up at the top and a great big stained glass window, big enough for church, opposite the stair and covering it with patchy, coloured light. The old lady coughed as she went from room to room with everyone following her. The kitchen had a Rayburn, bigger than theirs, with a sleeping brown dog that woke up and wagged its tail when they came in.

They went upstairs, right to the top, and there was a nice white corridor and four little rooms in a row. Sandy heard the old lady saying something about it being ideal for children up here, and her own had always been very happy, so she went back along the corridor and found the biggest of the little rooms, the one she would have if they really were coming here. Then they went down one floor and strolled around some more. The old lady seemed to be quite proud of the house, even though bits of it weren't very clean, but the rooms were nice and Sandy could see her mum and dad talking happily together as if they liked it and they really were going to move from Plewlands Gardens. James was trotting happily around too, opening cupboard doors and generally being too big for his boots because he'd been there before. While they were all standing on the middle floor landing talking he went up to the old lady and took her hand and asked if he could see the dog again. The two of them started off downstairs, with Sandy following. Everyone seemed very happy. Sandy looked back and saw her mum and dad standing at the top of the main stairway. They were holding hands and kissing.

II

VICTORIES
OF SCIENCE

October 1963

Down one side of the hall was a long table with plates of sandwiches and cakes. At the far end, by the platform, stood a group of a dozen or so middle aged men in suits and a couple of young men in academic gowns. They were chatting easily, as though used to this sort of thing but in no great hurry to get started. The new medical students, to be welcomed at what was described in the programme as a tea party given by the Dean of the Faculty of Medicine, were still thin on the ground, clustered aimlessly near the door and scarcely doubling the numbers of their hosts opposite. Most of them, Scott noted with concern, were wearing blazers of stiff new navy serge with the University crest bright on the breast pocket. Perhaps it was all going to be a bit more like school than he had assumed. Certainly the tea-party venue, the debating hall of the University Union – with its leaded windows, polished floor and gilt-lettered rows of names and dates of past office-bearers – had the weary all-purpose air of a school assembly hall. Perhaps the Dean had summoned them simply to tell them to observe the timetable with strict punctuality, walk smartly between classes and refrain from depositing confectionery wrappings in stairways and corridors.

A couple of girls came in, wearing the kind of frocks people wore to end of term dances at school; at least it was co-educational. Scott stood by himself, wondering how long the whole thing would last and if it would ever overcome the strange sadness of its first impact. Suddenly a crowd of perhaps twenty confident young men in sports jackets and dark suits made an entrance. They were talking loudly and laughing, as though they knew their way around already and had dropped in just to show everyone how to go about enjoying a tea party with the Dean. It occurred to Scott as they passed that they might even be drunk. The University Union boasted, someone had said at dinner the previous evening, the longest bar in Western Europe. Trying it out over lunchtime might have been the fast, fashionable thing to do on the last Friday before the proper start of first year medicine.

Most of the noisy new arrivals wore sports jackets, so perhaps the people with blazers were simply the kind who arrived on the dot for Dean's tea parties and there really weren't very many of them after all. A tall girl in a pale pink suit came in by herself and, since no one else was looking at her, smiled at Scott. She was wearing bright red lipstick and her hair, gingery-orange and at odds with everything else, was permed into a huge elaborate globe. Scott smiled back, which proved to be a mistake. She said 'Do you know everybody already?' 'No . . . Not really,' said Scott. 'Met a couple of people last night . . . At dinner in hall.' That sounded more self-assured than he had intended. The girl made a face and said 'You Scots all seem to know each other. It's not fair. Look.'

The big group had remained together and was in loud conversation with itself. 'I think they're all from Edinburgh,' Scott said. The girl frowned. 'But it's such a small country . . .' Scott did his best in unpromising conversation. People continued to arrive but the group of twenty was still making more noise than all the rest put together. A short, red-faced youth left them and walked uncomfortably back across the hall towards the door and a voice started to sing 'We know where you're going . . .' repeating the phrase again and again to the tune of 'Ring-a-ring of roses'. The singing and laughter followed the defector until he had disappeared. 'And you all have such a good time,' said the red-haired girl peevishly.

'Stick around, baby . . . You could have one too.' A short slender man with a Beatles haircut and a dark, vaguely Beatles suit had joined them. 'The Scots have been having a great time for ages. Since . . . before the Romans. That's why the Romans left, in fact. Couldn't stand the pace.' Scott wondered how long his halting efforts with the girl had been overheard. She laughed and turned to the newcomer, who smiled and said 'Where are you from, baby? Huh? No . . . Talk a bit more and let me guess.' The interrogator's accent, Scott decided, was basic Glaswegian with a bit of American learnt from films. The girl smiled and enunciated 'In Hertford, Hereford and Hampshire, hurricanes hardly ever happen . . .'

'I guessed as much.'

'I'm actually from Virginia Water.'

'Quite a lot can be done for that nowadays, you know. Especially now you've come to Scotland.'

Scott laughed, but the girl sucked her cheeks in and flounced fragrantly off towards a trio of girls in school-party frocks. The Glasgow Beatle was unconcerned. 'She's gonna have to learn to take a joke if she's really gonna stay in medicine.' He stuck out a hand towards Scott. 'Max Cathcart.'

'Andrew Scott.'

'That's a hulluva suit, Andy. I'm kinda interested in suits and that's what we call a Bulgarian diplomat number. Tropical weight. Where the hell d'ya get it?'

Much later, towards the end of a long evening, Scott realised he should have said he got it second-hand from a Bulgarian diplomat in Caracas. At the time he had simply told the truth: that he had had it made to measure by the best tailor in Bolgatanga, but he hadn't been very good.

Max was not interested in Bolgatanga or why Scott had been there. 'You sure he had a measuring tape?' He pulled a little at the lapels of Scott's jacket, undid its top button and smoothed it down by tugging the hem at both sides very much as the man in Bolgatanga had done. 'There . . . That's a bit better. I mean, this is the Dean's tea party we're at, not some third-rate embassy knees-up in Congo-Brazza. Great. So where are *you* from, as they say at these things? Jeeze, it's not as if I was rude to her . . .'

'I'm sure she'll get over it . . .'

'If you come from somewhere that sounds silly you should either not tell people or put up with it when they take the piss. I know. I'm from Auchenshuggle.'

'You're kidding.'

'As good as. Take the Auchenshuggle car and we're a hundred yards from the second last stop. Hit Auchenshuggle, stranger, and you've rode that streetcar too far . . . And I know where I've seen you before. Dinner last night. We're both in Irving Hall. Great.'

Auchenshuggle was somewhere in the east of Glasgow. Scott was pleased with his little bit of accent-spotting but continued to worry about his suit. No one in the hall was wearing anything quite like it, other than a member of the little group at the far end of the hall; a slim, middle-aged man getting a bit thin on top and also wearing the famous three-coloured stripy Edinburgh medical tie that Scott had learned only that morning to call blood, liver and pus. His suit was pale and light-weight like Scott's, but expensive-looking and probably neat enough to protect him from having Max fiddling with his lapels and shoulders and top button; although with Max, Scott found himself thinking already, one never knew.

No one had started on the tea and sandwiches. Again, that was a bit like school, or a church social. With grim little tea-ladies in black dresses and white aprons stationed at intervals behind the table with their arms folded, no student, not even one of the Edinburgh drunk set, had yet reached towards the plates on the long table. A full quarter of an hour of the Dean's tea party had passed and nothing much had happened. Max, Scott decided suddenly as they waited, was Jewish and his dad had a tailoring business, probably not too successful, somewhere in Glasgow.

At the far end of the hall the platform party had quietly mounted the rostrum and stood side by side looking out over their audience. Those nearest noticed first and a hush spread backwards through the hall, the big drunk clique settling down last. An old man in the centre of the line tapped thunderously at a microphone. 'Sorry about that,' he said, too close and loud. 'I know that for the past two days you have endured a great many welcomes. This is perhaps the last but I hope the most personal. Welcome to the Faculty of Medicine of the University of Edinburgh.' There was some half-hearted stamping of feet, tolerated with evident puzzlement by the speaker. 'May I as Dean and on behalf of all the teaching staff welcome you. You are here because on the evidence available to us we think you have it in you to make doctors, even good doctors. Few faculties anywhere attract better-qualified first year students. And that's just as well, because medical knowledge advances as never before. Some of you, I have no doubt, will in your turn lead medicine on to further great advances . . .' Scott glanced at Max, who was listening intently with his chin up and his eyes half-closed . . . 'But that, of course, is once you've mastered the basics, starting on Monday. So may I say good luck, and wish you well, and may I also assure that you will not be exposed in such numbers to such loosely structured thought until the hour of your graduation.' The last bit had been half thrown away, with a quick informality that cast irony on all that had gone before. Max was still looking as though he had been touched by some higher vision of himself. The dean coughed once more into his microphone. 'Now there are a number of other people up here who wish to talk while you remain so easily impressionable. I hope they will be brief. Mr Ratho?'

A fair-haired young man in a black gown tasselled with gold approached the microphone. 'Mr Ratho is the First Junior President of one of our revered local institutions, indeed the oldest medical student society in the world, the Ancient Society of Physic . . . And also, I believe, a medical student in the second year of the course.' The young man bestowed on the Dean a smile with something servile about it. 'Thank you, Professor Logie . . . My name is Angus Ratho, and I'm representing the Society this afternoon because our Senior President is at present abroad on a scholarship elective. As the Dean has already kindly pointed out, the Society has a long and distinguished history. But I am here today to tell you that it is only as good as its present membership and that as medical students in Edinburgh you should be aware of the opportunities, privileges and indeed responsibilities the Society offers you . . .' The man's microphone manner was polished, indeed a great improvement on the Dean's, but what he had to say was, it seemed to Scott, a rather strange plug for what sounded like a distinctly odd set-up. The Society had been formed in a tavern centuries ago but now had extensive premises of its own and an important library. Dress was formal for the main meeting of each term. Women were not admitted. The annual membership fee was counted in guineas, and many former presidents of the Society had gone on to distinguish themselves in medicine both at home and abroad. Max was still rapt. When the oily young man sat down he whispered to Scott. 'I'm going to join. The suit's no problem. I might even be president.'

The First Junior President of the Ancient Society for Physic was followed at the microphone by someone who clearly loathed him, a senior medical student called Malone who spoke on behalf of the Students' Representative Council in a demotic Scots accent strikingly contrasted to Ratho's. He urged the first year students to make full use of their democratic rights in free and open elections – open, naturally, to women as well – to choose year representatives to negotiate, through the Medical Student's Council, with the Faculty and the University. He sounded sensible and sincere and Scott marked him a lot higher than his predecessor. The girl in pink, he noted, was unimpressed, but the Dean had been listening intently and nodding as Malone had spoken.

A few administrative matters, largely to do with bicycle sheds, were dealt with then tea was announced. The Dean descended and headed straight for the noisy group of men. Others from the staff delegation fanned out among the students, joining in the loose queues that formed opposite each tea lady. Max went off to patch things up with the girl in pink, or possibly to start afresh with her female companions. Scott, having just returned from a year with VSO in West Africa, decided to talk to one of the overseas students. A small Indian with glasses and a dark suit with too many buttons, all of them done up, stood looking bewildered at the back of one of the queues. There was a line of sweat on his top lip and he flinched as Scott said hello.

'Good afternoon.' He spoke softly and glanced round as though in fear of being overheard. 'How are you today?'

'Fine, thank you.' There was a silence that bothered Scott more than it did the little Indian. 'Good speeches, I think,' he said eventually. Scott said something approving about the Dean and Malone. The Indian smiled. 'Democracy is wonderful thing. We have it now in my country. Somewhat.'

To Scott that probably made him Indian rather than Pakistani but he was proved wrong. The man giggled. 'My country is not India, though near it.' Scott guessed Ceylon and was wrong again. 'I am from Male. Capital and principal island of the Maldive Archipelago. You are English?'

'Sort of. Scottish, really.'

'It's near.' The man went silent again. Scott stuck out his hand and was rewarded with a textbook handshake from a small moist hand. 'Scott. Andrew Scott.'

'Easy to remember. Scott the Scottish. Look. Now we are having tea.'

'There you are, boys,' said a tea lady with yellow hair and an ancient powdery face. The man from Male took some sandwiches, balanced them in his saucer and went off towards an open space. Scott followed. 'I am Ali. Mahmet Ali. A common name in Male,' he announced when he had eaten one sandwich. 'Our government has given a scholarship in medicine. One only.'

'To Edinburgh?'

'Of course. The British high commissioner, His Excellency MacLaughlan, was quite certain. It is not good?'

'I hope we won't let you down,' said a middle-aged voice close behind them. There was a juggling of tea cups and more shaking of hands. 'Jameson. Jimmy Jameson. On the staff here. Clinical dean, actually, but my proper job is being a cough doctor. Now where are you chaps from?'

'Different places,' said Ali. 'Our friend is Scottish. I am from Male.'

'Oh, yes . . . In the Maldives. By the Laccadives. First on the left as you're coming home round India.'

'You have been?' Ali's eyes were wide.

'Sort of dropped in on a troopship once. Lovely spot . . . Now, there's a chap over here I've just been talking to you really ought to meet. From Ceylon, just around the corner from you. Please excuse us.' Dr, or possibly Professor, Jameson smiled at Scott in a way that seemed to indicate approval for his gallant but inexpert attempts to make an overseas student welcome and swept off with Ali. To Andrew's surprise, there was not much difference between them in height.

'I don't know what's wrong with the women here today.' Max had reappeared and was talking with his mouth full. 'About twenty of them and they're all we've got. They're just going to have to improve as we go along. First the big pink one, then one with specs and spots and a flowery frock, I mean I thought I was really doing her a favour. From Airdrie too. Turns out she's going to be a missionary in Nyasaland and wanted to know if I knew of a good evangelical church here in Edinburgh. I said I'd look around for her. Will it always be like this, I ask myself. I shoulda stayed in Glasgow. Home cooking and the brush-off from girls you know. Hey, this tailor of yours is doing all right.'

Another of the staff contingent, the man in the lightweight suit and Medical Faculty tie, was doing the rounds and just taking his leave of a nearby group of blazers who seemed to be standing to attention as he did so. He approached Scott and Max. 'Hello . . . How are you?' His handshake was warm and dry. 'Gavin Lennox. Endocrinology. So we won't actually be seeing very much of each other for a few years yet. But I try to get to these bunfights when I can. Meet the new people and try and keep in touch as they go along.' Scott and Max introduced themselves to him and Max eyed his suit. 'Only just got here,' said Lennox. Max looked puzzled. 'This time on Wednesday I was in Kaduna . . . in Northern Nigeria. We've got a link with the medical school there and we do what we can to help. Got here straight from the airport. All set for Monday?' Scott and Max both hoped so. 'You might find it a bit more like school than medicine for a year or two. But don't be put off. The teachers are mainly doctors, and human too.' He glanced quickly around. 'Even the anatomists. So where have you come from?' Max mentioned Glasgow and Hutchesons' Grammar. Scott said that he'd been away from school for a year, teaching in West Africa. 'Really?' said Dr Lennox. 'Nigeria?'

'Next door but three. Ghana. Up north.'

'Good thing to get away from it all for a while. Get your knees brown, as they say. Enjoy it?'

Scott thought of the tin-roofed classrooms full of earnest mission-boys, and the taste of mangoes and sweetcorn from the school garden. 'It was all right for a year.'

'We should probably encourage more of that . . . Pushing off for a while before you begin. My lot got their travelling courtesy of the crown and its enemies, and I think everybody who came back enjoyed it . . . So what about you, Max? Have you travelled?'

'Well, just Israel. Couple of months in the summer.'

'One of those kibbutz things?'

'That's right.'

'So how was communal living?'

Max thought of a large Swedish girl called Irma who had groaned enthusiastically during and usually snored a lot afterwards. 'Interesting, but not for everybody. They say that themselves. But it works for them and they're very proud of it.'

'You know, you're not just a bright lot, you're an adventurous lot too. Amazing the places people have been. The Dean's really rather proud of you already. "All those chaps who could equally well be atomic scientists or senior wranglers . . ." But medicine's going to need you.' Max and Scott waited politely for an explanation. 'It's all getting so complicated. When I started – there I go again, more than half way to the pension – there were about six pills that worked and ten that didn't and hardly any specialties. Most of medicine was just jollying things along, and we were all terribly ordinary. But it's all got much more interesting and complicated . . . A new specialty a month, I should think, for another couple of decades at least. Cybernetics rearing its elegant head. Computers and whiz-bang new lab tests . . . So to handle all that we're going to need all the senior wrangler material we can lay our hands on.' Dr Lennox paused. 'Max, Andrew. Welcome to the club. It's a good one. See you again in a year or two.'

He was gone. Scott began to feel better about his suit and his West African connection. Dr Lennox had gone to work on a particularly unpromising group of girls only a few yards away. 'Look at them,' Max groaned: 'Hairy legs, sensible flatties and dresses like the loose covers on my grandma's three piece suite. And can you please direct me to a really strict Christian place of worship? More tea, vicar?' They went for a top-up and the tea was dark and barely lukewarm. The sandwiches and all the better cakes had gone. People had started to leave. The man from Male was in earnest conversation with a slightly larger version of himself, possibly the man from Ceylon. The tall girl in pink had found a small but attentive audience of blazers and looked vacuously radiant. Scott, who had spent much of the previous year alone and in silence, reading, fishing or just walking in the dusty plain around the school, recalled something from Thomas a Kempis to the effect that parties were bad for you and decided to go for a walk by himself before dinner in hall in a couple of hours' time.

He made his way downstairs and out past a decrepit uniformed doorman. To the right was an odd, tight little pattern of tenement-lined streets with small, old-fashioned shops and pubs and, on a corner site, a three storey drapery shop with a window display where everything cost a penny or halfpenny less than the next pound up: coats, five pounds, nineteen shillings and eleven pence; shirts, nineteen and elevenpence halfpenny and the like. Scott wandered happily round the block a couple of times, eventually going into a little bookshop with a white-painted rhinoceros head hanging outside. Inside there was a clutter of shelves and series of rooms on different levels and thousands and thousands of books, every one a paperback. He browsed contentedly, reading quite a lot of a book of love poems a bit more explicit than anything he had come across before, but funny and clever too. He bought it, and a Huxley novel, and made his way back beyond the Union to the Medical School and its quad, where lectures would start on Monday. They had been shown quickly round that morning but Scott was happy to look again and check where things were and just be there on his own in a pleasant place that would soon become familiar. The anatomy department was easy: a huge doorway with 'Anatomy' carved in its lintel and, for further reassurance, the immense skeletal rump of an elephant clearly visible in a first floor window immediately above. Biochemistry, unknown to mid-Victorian architects, was somewhere to the right, perhaps masquerading as 'Practice of Physic', and physiology was off to the left from the tunnel leading out on to Middle Meadow Walk. A clock, surveying all beneath from high on a sunny wall, warned with its inscription 'Ars longa, vita brevis'.

As Scott emerged from the tunnel into the sunlight of a broad, tree-lined walk he faced a third Victorian institutional building, a huge turreted complex of three-decker pavilions on a walled site sloping south towards the park. It was, he knew, the Royal Charitable Institute, formerly the Royal Charitable Institute for the Care of the Indigent Sick, and its appearance was at once formidable and captivating. For a brand new medical student it was still very much in the future but that only made it more intriguing: the first two years of the course were really just a novitiate leading up to the term you entered it. The rest of the five year course, it seemed, revolved around it. Craggy and black with soot, it loomed through the trees ahead, a grim crow-stepped northern fortress frowning across at the medical school's Florentine palace only a hundred yards away. In its windows cannon-mouths would have been unremarkable. If the hospital Scott's mother had eventually emerged from had been like something left over from a POW camp, and the one in Bolgatanga some kind of gentle tropical barracks, this was a grubby, grim citadel, a symbol of might and deterrence on another scale altogether: medicine's own Edinburgh Castle.

As Scott stood looking at it a man in a greasy overcoat staggered and dropped limply just in front of him and lay staring up into the trees above. Scott knelt by his head, although the first aid course for medical students did not begin until the following week. Meanwhile there were faint memories of things learned in the school scout troop three years before. The man was fifty or so, unshaven and not clean. Scott thought of the old man at the sheep clipping and looked for obvious signs of life or death, then the man began to breathe in little gasps. Someone else, a blonde girl smelling far nicer than the man on the pavement, knelt close beside Scott. 'Maybe I can help,' she said. 'I'm a nurse.' She flicked lightly at the man's face with her fingers and he grimaced then coughed. 'I'm no' an epi-holic,' he announced, his eyes suddenly focussing on her. 'I'm an alco . . . an alco-leptic.' The girl laughed. 'What do you take for it?'

'Whisky, hen. Just whisky. Huv ye got some on you?'

The girl laughed again and shook her head. The man turned his bloodshot gaze on Scott. 'You, son? Naw. . . ? Well maybe gie's fourpence for a cup of tea.' He sat up of his own accord and sniffed loudly. ' "Delayed shell-shock. Ye'll have tae take good care o' yersel' ", the MO said. Fourpence, son.' He made it sound like a fixed charge for a service already rendered. Scott and the girl helped him to his feet and Scott reached in his pocket and gave the man a shilling, less than a tenth of what he had just spent on books he did not really need. The blonde girl smiled and shook her head again, as he himself would have done if she had been a brand-new tourist handing out shillings to all the skinny, clawing beggars in Bolgatanga market. 'I'm sure he'll be all right' she said, picking up her bag. 'Are these your books?' As Scott retrieved them and thanked her two policemen descended on the drunk and began to haul him towards a police box at the top of the hill. The girl shrugged, then turned and hurried towards a gate in the fortress wall ahead.

'You should have stayed, Andy,' said Max. 'It got quite interesting towards the end. Had a chat with that guy from the Society. He says the thing is to join right away. Lots of guys don't until third or fourth year and miss out on a lot of important stuff. What he means is he got to be something really quickly. And I had a word with a biochemist. Really dull. I guess a lot of them are, otherwise they'd be doing more interesting things like . . . like immunology.' They were standing behind old-fashioned wooden chairs at the long tables of the dining room in Irving Hall. Everyone else had fallen silent and Max's views on biochemists were now widely known. He looked round to find out why no one else was talking and the Warden at the high table intoned 'Benedictus benedicat'. With a great clatter of chairs about sixty hungry young men sat down to eat.

Over haggis, beans and chips, Max told Scott about his proposed career as an immunologist. 'Apparently you do an extra year, same as you can for biochemistry and boring stuff like that, but unlike them it helps you later ... In the clinical stuff, I mean, because immunology is where it's all happening. That endocrinology bloke, the one with the suit like yours, as good as said so. New specialty, the old buggers don't understand it, but it really, really matters, because all the diseases you can't explain yet are going to turn out to have some kind of immunological basis ...'

Scott could not recall Dr Lennox having said anything quite so detailed, though he had talked in general about the rise of lots of new specialties. 'Diagnosis too. It's developing all the time. You used to do it by questions and rummaging around for lumps, then there was X-rays and sending pints of blood and wee-wee to the lab. In future all that's going to be immunology too.'

'Really?'

'Yeah. And there'll be immunological treatments. I mean, there are some already, anti-serums and things. But quite soon you'll get your immunology sorted out and that'll be it. "Thanks, doc, I feel great now ..." Yeah, immunological cures. That's the way medicine's heading nowadays.'

Scott listened respectfully. Although he could follow what Max was saying, he himself had had no idea of the potential of the new speciality. Should he have taken a tea-chest of advanced biology books off to Ghana for reading when he wasn't explaining to Thomas Aquinas Akanlu and Co how to dissect a cockroach for their O-levels? Or should he have persuaded his parents to get him an airmail subscription to *Scientific American*? And would everyone else in next Monday's classes, even the hairy-legged girls from Airdrie, be so formidably well-informed? Over the ginger pudding, Max talked about immunological protection for ailing tissues and the selective destruction of cancer cells by enhanced immunity, and how quite soon every hospital would have its department of immunology and there would be professors of it with big departments, and the important thing was to get into it early. 'It's not just a fashion, like narrow trousers and a single vent. More fundamental than that. A big trend, like the two piece suit. You gotta join or go bust, but join early and you make a million.'

The plates were cleared away by a fat lady who told Max not to swing his chair on its back legs like that. While they waited for coffee Scott decided to try to find out how Max had come to know so much about immunology, asking him how long he'd been interested in the subject. 'Since school, really. The only bit of biology that did anything for me . . .'

'But all that clinical stuff . . . We didn't really . . .'

'Oh, that . . . Yes.'

'And how it's going to develop. . . ?'

'Yes. All that. Well, you heard that endocrinologist . . .'

'But he didn't . . .'

Max lowered his voice. 'That Ratho guy . . . From the Society I'm going to join . . . He really knows his way around, and immunology's where it's at . . . I mean, I've been thinking about it for myself as well. Since this afternoon . . .'

The coffee arrived and Scott declined it. 'Wrong, Andy,' said Max. 'We're going drinking. So you gotta have coffee first. Counteracts it. Better have two cups, because I met this Edinburgh guy and he's going to show us the nightspots . . .'

Scott had made a resolution, based on his orderly, almost monastic experience in Africa, to lead a quiet life in Edinburgh: working, reading and probably walking a lot, at least until he had settled in and passed a few exams. He hesitated. 'Just a quiet pint in a few pubs,' said Max. 'Lovely evening for it. An excuse for a bit of a walk round town. Nothing outrageous. I mean, it's the Sabbath, isn't it. . . ? Mine anyway.' With a feeling that Thomas a Kempis wouldn't have approved, Scott agreed.

Robbie left the Dean's tea party and made his way home to Thistle Place alone. If he had been starting the afternoon again he would have done it all a bit differently, but the trouble with going from George Heriot's school to Edinburgh University was that so many other people did as well, and the people you had been to school with were not necessarily the people you wanted to spend the whole of your time in medical school with too. And despite the Dean's sandwiches he was really hungry now, That had probably been the first mistake, spending his lunch money on a pint and a half of beer – a pint more than he had ever drunk before – but in the circumstances it would have been very hard to do anything else without looking completely silly. And going up from the biggest bar in the Northern Hemisphere to the debating hall with the Heriot's crowd in order to meet other people had been another serious error. Still, his mum would ask if he had met the Dean and he could say he had. What he would not tell her was what a disappointment it had been: Professor Logie had been loud and silly and looked and sounded as if he too had had a drink instead of his lunch, perhaps for years and years. It was like meeting your headmaster in a pub and finding he was just a drunken old bore. Eventually he had got away from them all, talked for a couple of minutes with a sensible man who'd just flown in from somewhere in Africa where he was a visiting professor and then met the odd chap from Glasgow, the only first year medical student he had talked to whom he had not known already from school. Sadly, that had been another mistake. Robbie, who had never lied to his mother about anything important, was going to have to find some way of telling her he was going out to spend Friday evening in a pub, or perhaps even a series of pubs, something his father had never done in all his life.

'We're actually not very religious,' said Max. 'I did all the bar mitzvah stuff, but everybody does. Well worth it and it keeps everybody happy. Just a party where you do a turn and all your aunties say my how you've grown and it seems like only yesterday he was in nappies, oy vey, and everybody gets to see if you've got new furniture.'

'Cathcart isn't a very . . . Jewish name . . .' said Scott over the noise of the pub.

'It is now,' said Max. 'My grandfather, my father's father, Grandpa Yehudavitch, settled in the South Side, just off Cathcart Road. A nice name for a road or anybody, he thought, everybody can pronounce it. It's kind of caught on in the family. All my second cousins are called Argyle and Buchanan and things like that.' Scott wondered about that, and decided Max was exaggerating. 'Confuses the enemy. I mean, wee Rachel and Hymie Sauchiehall . . .' Max laughed. 'Who would ever guess?'

At the other end of the bar was an African, a tall, high-cheekboned man of a shade the boys called proper black, and probably a Hausa though his face was unmarked. Scott found himself wanting to talk about his year in Ghana, so he asked Max what the kibbutz had been like. Max thought again about Irma's big brown body and its neatly marked little white target zones, took a long gulp of beer and said 'Great. More Jewish than anywhere, even

Whitecraigs, but less religious . . . Nobody talked about it though . . . Being Jewish, I mean. Well, nearly nobody. Until this crazy wee German kid rolled up. Sixteen, blonde china-doll job, nice wee body and shouldn't have been there at all. A guilt complex. Her dad worked in the West German Board of . . . Oh. Here he is . . . Robbie!'

Max did the introductions. 'Robbie, this is Andy, who's just back from doing his white man's burden stuff in Nigeria. Andy, there is nothing about Edinburgh's night life that Robbie here cannot show us . . .' Scott and Robbie shook hands. Robbie – gawky and pale, with untidy reddish hair – was looking round as though he had never been in a pub before. 'Great,' said Max. 'Pint, Robbie? Andy's buying . . .' The pub was loud and getting louder. At the far end, a tall man with a moustache and glasses stood with his eyes closed, swaying gently back and forward and singing. 'I thought we'd start here,' said Max. 'It's a really famous pub. Poets come here, loads of them.'

According to Max, the next pub, Greyfriars Bobby's, was almost as famous and its name commemorated a dog that had belonged to Robert Burns. There were no poets. It was full of drunk Norwegians and the music was so loud as to be painful. They had a pint anyway, but as they left Robbie took Scott aside and said it had nothing to do with Burns, and the dog had belonged to a man, just someone ordinary, who had been buried in the churchyard and it had stayed where its master had been buried until it had died too. Scott had read something along these lines once, perhaps in a primary school reading book, which after two pints of cold, fizzy beer came back with remarkable clarity. He agreed with Robbie, and while Max crossed the road in front of the pub to show them the statue of the dog, a mournful bronze creature with something of the Pekinese about it, he and Robbie decided that two pubs were probably enough and they could take a walk around the middle of town and Robbie would make sure they all got back to the vicinity of the first pub, only a few hundred yards from the Medical School, the Institute and Irving Hall, by about ten o'clock.

Max led them past the statue and on to a street that turned mysteriously into a bridge, intersected below first by a narrow lane forty or fifty feet underneath then by a vast rectilinear chasm that opened out westwards into a kind of square. They passed a kilt shop and a religious bookshop specialising in the more rabid forms of anti-Catholic pamphlet. Scott lingered in front of it, looking at neat stacks of 'The Anti-Christ of Rome' and 'The Heresy of Mariolatry' and thinking of the tin-roofed cathedral and the calm, fragrant ritual of benediction and the shock when he had realised that the reason the man in the other corner at the back was finding it difficult to pick up the rosary he had dropped was that he was a leper with no fingers.

'Come on, Andy . . . Here it is. Look . . .' Max and Robbie were standing in front of a nondescript office building looking up. Max was pointing to the top of the facade, where in the dusk a couple of sculptured stone birds crouched. As Scott caught up he patted a brass plate on a dark, glossy door. 'This is it . . . The Ancient Society of Physic. The thing I'm going to be president of. You know. Dinner jackets and no women. And that's probably the tavern where they used to meet in seventeen-something. We should probably . . .'

Across the road was a very ordinary-looking pub occupying the ground floor of a drab Victorian office block. Scott and Robbie shook their heads. 'OK', said Max. 'Maybe some other night . . . How about a walk around? There's supposed to be a castle near here.' Robbie knew a quickish way round to the castle, which involved cutting along a kind of pavement that became a curved gallery hanging higher and higher over a steep little street, with shops and churches, that snaked down to the open square, which Robbie explained was the Grassmarket, where they used to hang people, and his school was just on the other side. They walked on, crossed a road, climbed a long flight of stone steps and found themselves, as Robbie had promised, on the Castle Esplanade, looking out towards distant moonlit hills. In the foreground was a huge dark jumble of variously spiked and turreted buildings. 'That's it,' said Robbie. 'See. My school. The medical school. The institute. Everything, really.'

'One more pub,' said Max. 'I need a piss.' To oblige him they stopped briefly in one called the Ensign Ewart and found themselves once more on the street with streets running underneath it. They passed the Society's rooms again and Max touched the brass plate for luck, then Robbie started to talk about it being time he was thinking about getting home, and how he would have invited them for coffee but it was a bit out of their way since they both lived in Irving. There was a dangerous moment when Max said he really did feel like another coffee and that would be a great idea, but Scott thanked Robbie for his kind offer and said they really ought to be getting back to Irving, where the doors were locked at eleven o'clock, a regulation of which Max seemed unaware. Then they both thanked Robbie for their tour and said they'd see him on Monday, and he loped off in the direction of Thistle Place, down the road that separated the Institute from his old school.

Scott and Max stood at the street-corner opposite the police box. The easternmost bastion of the Institute, a crow-stepped, turreted hulk of three looming storeys, towered over everything. Scott thought again of the drunk who had collapsed and the little nurse who had done all the sensible things and then tripped off unconcerned into the dark fortress. 'Let's go in,' said Max. Scott said nothing. 'It's a teaching hospital,' said Max. 'For medical students. We're medical students.'

'We are on Monday,' said Scott. 'Anatomy, physiology and biochemistry.'

'But basically we're medical students. And medicine's an all day, all night thing. Come on. There's plenty of time.'

A huge illuminated clock-face high in a tower at the heart of the citadel read twenty to eleven. 'Not much.'

'Quick look round and straight home to Irving. Come on, Scott. Irving men hang together . . . The main gate's along here.'

They walked along the front of the hospital to paired wrought iron gates separated by an unlit and probably empty lodge. 'Easy,' said Max. 'And if anybody wants to know, we could be visiting our grandmother who is dangerously ill. But basically it's a matter of just keeping walking whatever happens. Right?'

Inside the gates and across a wide courtyard with a couple of vaguely classical statues of men in heroic poses, a broad flight of steps led up to an arched doorway in the base of the clock tower. They were approaching the steps when a man in a dark uniform and peaked cap emerged from the doorway and came down towards them. 'Keep walking,' Max muttered. 'Remember your poor grandmother.' As they passed the man turned momentarily then went on his way. 'Told you,' said Max. 'Straight ahead when we get inside.'

'Why?'

'So we don't have to stand there discussing it.'

Suddenly they were through the door and walking across a high, well-lit hallway floored with chequered black and white tiles. To left and right the black and white floor extended down long corridors. Straight ahead of them, on a wood-panelled wall, hung an enormous oil painting of Queen Victoria, seated, with an assortment of dogs playing round her feet. 'Evening, ma'am,' said Max. 'Left, and then down those stairs.'

They passed a series of stern marble busts in niches then walked down a stairway lined with gilt-lettered subscription lists and found themselves in a short, much less grand corridor that turned aimlessly left and then right and ended in swing doors that led outside again on to a raised walk with a lawn and some trees on the right and a sloping glass roof, reflecting the moon, on the left. Scott glanced back. Behind them the clock-tower loomed. 'Max . . .'

'Don't worry about a thing. Interesting, isn't it? And being able to find your way around this place at night and really quickly might save a life some day. I mean really save a life.'

The walkway curved round to the right and joined another in a T-junction one floor above ground level. To left and right were more of the big three-decker pavilions. 'Go right,' said Max, 'then straight ahead. OK?' The next pair of swing doors led into another well-lit hallway. As Max and Scott went in a couple of nurses, uniformed and cloaked and carrying baskets with knitting things and magazines, were trying to come out. There was a brief, silly, traffic-jam with Max being stylish and gallant and the nurses giggling. Inside the hallway they stopped. A corridor led off into a dimly lit ward, in the middle of which a nurse sat at a desk, watchful under an Anglepoise lamp. 'That's a ward,' said Max.

Scott looked back at the clock-tower. Max had turned his attention to a board by the ward door, white-painted and about two feet square, to which four name-plates were fixed by small brass screws. 'There you are. The ward's medical consulting staff. The . . . the consultings. Could be us some day. Dr M J Cathcart. Dr . . . Dr A Scott. You got another initial, Andy? You gotta have initials in this business. One's no good. Look. Mostly they've got three . . . Dr H J S MacLean. Dr J I P Herriot . . .'

'I'm A D F,' said Scott.

'Great. You'll make it. But I bet none of those guys is an immunologist. And that's where it's all happening in medicine these days.'

The night nurse at the desk got up and came a little way towards the entrance of the ward. Max and Scott withdrew on to another moonlit walkway and stood discussing their careers until a church clock somewhere started to strike eleven. Fortunately the Irving man who had told Scott about the door being locked had also told him what you did if you were caught out. They strolled back through the hospital confidently, as though their grandmother had rallied unexpectedly, and made their way down a stable lane behind Irving Hall, over the back wall, through the garden and up to the window of one of the ground floor bedrooms, conveniently accessible from a herbaceous border. The occupants of such rooms were expected to get up when wakened by tapping on their windows and admit latecomers without complaint. As Max had said, Irving men hung together.

March 1966

Although he knew you weren't meant to, Gus found the girl attractive: only physically, of course, because the truth was that mentally she wasn't up to much and probably never had been. But her hair was long and dark and she had big brown eyes and nice regular teeth, and she lay back on the pillows smiling at him with one hand stretched out towards him and the other up just at the neckline of a rather low cut nightie. 'Honestly,' she said, 'I'm doing my best,' then laughed in a way that made her breasts wobble a lot. She wasn't wearing a bra, which of course made it worse. Gus shifted in his seat. 'I'm really sorry, Dr Ratho . . .' she said. 'But I think being in hospital for so long would make anyone a bit stupid, don't you?'

Strictly speaking Gus should have explained that he wasn't really Dr Ratho: not yet, anyway, although he was more than half way through the medical course and, if everything went according to plan he would get a PhD as well quite soon. He smiled at her to show that he wasn't in the least upset or impatient, and she started to finger the little bow at her neckline as if she might be trying to undo it. Like a lot of them, she had rather clumsy hand movements.

'So let's just whiz through a few of the simpler questions, shall we? The absolutely basic things. Age, Miss Lyle . . . What age are you?'

She smiled again, a really lovely smile that made Gus swallow hard and check that his ballpoint pen wasn't leaking. 'Nineteen,' she said. 'Well, nearly twenty now.'

'We'll call it nineteen,' said Gus. 'And your job? What was your job?'

The girl looked puzzled, 'Dance. I'm a dancer. Obviously a student still, but just put dancer.'

'You're a dancer,' said Gus, scribbling it on his form. A lot of them were like that, always speaking about how they would get back to work and telling you all the things they were going to do when they were better.

'And what I'm really interested in is ballet. And I know what everybody says: you'll just end up in the chorus, not everybody can be Moira Shearer and all that, but I don't mind . . . I never wanted to. I love ensemble work . . .' She tilted her head slightly to one side and spead her arms outward, palms up and a little wobbly, and for an eerie moment Gus could imagine her drifting on tiptoe across a stage in a perfect line of dancers. She laughed. 'You'll have to come and watch me, Dr Ratho.'

'Yes, indeed . . .'

'Especially if you're the one who's going to cure me.'

'Quite. And now there are a lot of questions about where you've lived. Abroad, that kind of thing.'

'I *love* travel,' she squeaked.

'Really?' It was all getting a bit silly because she seemed to be regarding the whole thing as an excuse for the kind of social conversation that helped to while away a boring afternoon in hospital, but unless he was reasonably civil he would never get to the bits that mattered and the whole thing would be a waste of time. 'But have you ever lived abroad for any length of time?'

'Ages,' she said, lying back on the pillow again. 'Some dreadful places. But dreamy ones too, like Cyprus and Malta. And the worst was Aden. D'you want to know how long, and when and all that?'

'Strictly speaking, yes.' Gus braced himself and she launched into a long list of places, with gushy accounts of the weather and the swimming and the social life and everything except which regimental studs had had her on the beach. After the first three he tilted his papers a bit and just pretended to write.

'. . . then daddy got Lowland HQ, which he'd always wanted, being a Royal Jock, and we moved here and I left school and started in dance. In London. But that's not abroad.'

'Now I have to ask you about things you eat . . .'

'That's easy. They like us thin and strong, like horses for the flat, so lots of thin things, tiny steaks, salmon, all that, and hardly anything to drink . . .'

'I see. And for some reason we're particularly interested in potatoes . . .'

'Well, I'm not,' she said, laughing again, her nipples bigger than before. Gus swallowed hard, annoyed at her for being clever as well as sexy, and tried to concentrate on the difficult bit of the questionnaire. 'Miss Lyle . . . We were talking a moment ago about how all this began . . . The very first thing that went wrong . . .'

'Boring,' she said, putting on a little girl face.

'But what I'm trying to get at is the details, Miss Lyle. For our research, actually, and if it's going to help anyone it has to be based on the facts . . . The facts of the case and the things we find in your blood . . .'

She sniffed. 'Now you're making me sound like a dog with worms . . .'

'I'm so sorry, Miss Lyle . . . I really don't mean to upset you, and when I said . . . things in your blood . . . just now it was only a rather simple way of putting something that's actually very complex . . . I certainly didn't mean to upset you . . .'

She had closed her eyes and folded her arms. Gus began to get frankly angry, not just annoyed with her flirtatiousness and her evasiveness but angry that she simply wasn't even trying. The most infuriating thing of all was that Roger Killick had told him she would be easy, not ga-ga or weepy or giggly or drooling so much that you couldn't understand a word. 'You'll enjoy her, Gus,' he had said. 'Good looker, quite interesting case. Rapid onset, paraplegic now, but a bright lass who'll give you lots of good information.'

'Miss Lyle?' She opened her eyes. 'Miss Lyle, perhaps I should have explained a bit more at the beginning. The idea of all this is to improve things for patients by improving our knowledge of how all this starts. And of course we rely absolutely on the information we get from patients, entirely confidentially and given voluntarily of course, and the idea of my research project is to see if the things that happen in really well-documented cases tie up with the things that are happening in the blood and the . . . the cerebrospinal fluid. In fact if you want to know the details we're looking at how diet, previous illnesses, foreign residence and the progress of the disease correlate with certain changes in the blood, mainly to do with immunological responses. It's really the only hope of finding any kind of cure.' Now she was looking at him a bit more respectfully. 'So perhaps . . .' She smiled again: only a polite, social smile, but at least she was going to carry on helping him with his Honours Immunology project. 'Just going right back to the beginning . . .'

'A funny feeling. A sort of . . . dead feeling in my skin.'

Gus ticked the appropriate box. 'Where?'

'Malta.'

'Miss Lyle . . .'

'Oh sorry. I thought you wanted to know all about where I was . . . The travel bit. Sorry. In my leg.' Gus found the box and ticked it. 'My left leg, actually . . . The silliest business, really . . .'

'And when was that?'

'In the morning. The morning after.'

'Sorry. Miss Lyle, was it years ago, or months?'

'Malta. So it would be . . . Sixty two? Yes. Sixty two. I'd been, um, snogging half the night in a car. Risky in Malta, but there was really nowhere else. I'm not embarrassing you, Dr Ratho, am I?'

'Not at all.'

'Next morning half my leg was numb. If that's what it does to you, I thought, I'll just stick to horses.' She laughed again. 'And gradually it went away, in about a couple of weeks. And a great relief too, if I may say so. And the next thing was I broke a plate.'

'That's what I was going to ask you. The next incident.'

'I'm telling you . . . At a party. A scruffy, Sunday-evening tapas do at home. The kind of thing colonel's ladies put on to stop the young officers just drinking themselves silly in the mess. A hot buffet thing, and I was giving out some plates and a chap, a nice chap, dropped one, and actually swore. Then another chap sort of juggled one. It was really quite funny . . .' She laughed but less happily than before. 'Then another winced and I thought, that's odd, maybe it's me. And I put down the rest of the plates, and . . . smelt burning. Me. My fingers. And I couldn't feel them.'

'Quite.' Gus ticked another box, and another. 'And when was that?'

'Six months later? Less? Malta again. I could work it out for you . . .'

'We'll call it sixty two again.'

'No. January sixty three.'

'That's near enough . . .'

'I thought you said . . . Sorry . . .'

Gus squirmed again. Now she wanted to be more scientific than the scientist. The sensory stuff, with dead patches and loss of heat sensation, didn't matter much because you couldn't really measure it. The paralysis was what was interesting, and in a severe, fairly rapid case like this you could expect a clear history of weakness and then look objectively at the relationship between power loss and the cell culture results, which was exactly what his project was going to prove. He skipped a few rows of boxes and sat back. 'Miss Lyle, just to get things straight, when was the last time you could actually walk at all?'

She took a deep breath as though she was going to sneeze, but instead howled: a long, piercing wail that had everyone in the ward looking and the ward sister racing across the few yards from the nursing station so forcefully that the floor shook. 'Mr Ratho!' she towered over him, her frilly cap quivering and her face white with rage. '*Mister* Ratho! I have no objection to students conducting courteous and tactful interviews with patients on the ward . . .' She paused, and Gus was about to say something emollient. 'But when a young whipper-snapper like you with neither tact nor common-sense charges in and spreads havoc as you have done here I have no alternative but to insist you leave immediately . . . Get out! Now, Fiona, dear . . .' She sat down on the bed and the wretched girl threw her arms round her. 'There there . . . Nurse! The screens, dear. Thank you, nurse . . .' Gus grabbed his papers and left the ward, deliberately slowing down as soon as he was in the corridor, then walking with studied calm back to the laboratory. He was angry, especially because there were so few patients he was going to get complete data on, but it was hardly his fault that the ward sister hated everything to do with Dr Killick and the Clinical Neuro-Immunology Unit, and still less his fault that multiple sclerosis patients got easily upset and quite often cried for nothing.

Sandy Lennox washed her hair and dried it and then began to wonder what girls wore to meetings of a society that had never allowed girls at its meetings before. She opened both her wardrobes and sat on her bed in her bra and pants thinking it would have been clever to have had a chat with some of the others from her year who were going, to decide on a party line. Somebody was sure that most of the men didn't wear dinner jackets any more, and that helped a bit: at least you didn't have to wear something long and silly that meant a taxi, but it didn't help an awful lot. And thinking what other girls would probably wear was interesting in a bitchy sort of way: who would dress up to make them wish they'd had women in the

Society for years; who would be aggressively frumpy to show they didn't care, and who would manage the same effect without actually thinking about it. In the end she decided on the kind of thing you'd wear at home if the Queen was coming to tea – quietly expensive, maroon, good but not noticeable – then had a silly moment when she was sure everybody would have discussed it and decided except her, and she'd be quite wrong.

She did her face and decided it really didn't matter what she wore, because thinking about it just made an issue of it, and it was only a club, though one with funny rules and, if they had decided to admit women because there were a lot of them about nowadays and they needed the subscription money, you could turn up in denims and the pullover you shampooed the dog in and they would just have to lump it unless your cheque bounced. So there. But there was also something about an informal party in the Society's new rooms after the lecture bit, so she did a good job on her hair and a subtle job on her lips and went downstairs feeling quite glamorous and on the way out told her mum she wasn't sure when she'd be home, and not to wait up.

Gus was quite proud of what he'd done for the Society already in his year as President. Though he would have been the first to admit that he had not been greatly in favour of letting the girls in, it was clear that medicine as a whole was going that way and there was no point in fighting it. The Society had to move with the times and almost everyone on Comitia had been in favour of change, although that might have been because of a slimy bit of lobbying on the part of little Cathcart and his crowd. The main thing was that, when the final decision had been taken, lots of people had congratulated him on the way he had chaired the discussion that had changed the Society more than any other in two hundred years. The season's programme was another source of some pride. As Convenor Actorum the previous year, Gus had planned it in some detail, with regard both to its educational value and its usefulness in cultivating contacts. Now he was reaping his reward: very few undergraduates could say they had chaired lectures by a Nobel prize winner in medicine, by the leading medical journalist in the UK and by – tonight's lecturer – old Bielby, a recently knighted local academic surgeon.

It was all very civilised, as indeed it was meant to be. You wrote well in advance, on impressive notepaper and enclosing a glossy brochure on the history of the Society, emphasising how honoured it would be etc, and making sure that anyone coming from a distance knew they would be well looked after in a good hotel. On the day you met them and made sure they enjoyed the traditional dinner preceding the lecture. Once more that had gone well. The North British was not just convenient; in terms of wines, menu and service it did the kind of old-fashioned things that eminent men liked, and the expense was a minor consideration given that the Society was footing the bill. Sir Edgar Bielby, whom Gus had known slightly already thanks to his father, had turned out to be quite a pleasant old boy, basically an unimproved Yorkshireman and obviously still beaming from his New Year's Honours knighthood, but, despite his scientific reputation, still very much an outsider in Edinburgh medical politics, where all the more important things were decided mainly away from committees and almost exclusively by people who'd known each other for decades before he'd arrived.

They had come up in a taxi from the North British to the Royal College of Surgeons, where the main lecture was being held, and the great man had just gone off to check his slides and, as he coyly put it, think of something to say. Gus stood in the foyer with his case, looking a little bit lost. Eventually the college bedellus got the point, coming over and saying 'Can I help you at all, sir?' Gus looked surprised and said 'Actually, I'm chairing the lecture tonight . . . Senior President of the Ancient Society of Physic, you know. And I was wondering if there was somewhere I might, um, get togged up.'

The man smiled and said he was sure the college President wouldn't mind if a fellow-President just popped into his robing room for a moment, which was exactly what Gus had wanted him to say, then led him to an agreeable little room with a couple of armchairs, a coatstand, a long mirror and the inevitable portraits of men in mutton-chop whiskers and college gowns. On a writing table were three decanters, which proved respectively to be port, sherry and malt whisky. Gus took off his overcoat, lounged in one of the armchairs looking at himself in the mirror opposite for a moment, then opened his case, hung up his overcoat and put on his presidential gown: black velvet with two rows of gold tassels, an altogether grander affair than that of the First Junior President.

Then he extracted the Society's weighty, silver-gilt medallion of office from its pocket in the case, slung it round his neck, adjusted it and checked the general effect in the long mirror. He combed his hair, buffed up his shoes a bit using a College of Surgeons brush set by the coatstand and pulled a card from his top pocket to check his notes for the evening's introductions. His first little jeu d'esprit, he knew, would get the best reaction. '*Ladies* and gentlemen . . .' If change was inevitable, he told himself in the mirror, clutching the lapels of his gown in statesmanlike fashion, he, Angus Pottinger Galbraith Ratho, might as well take credit for it in front of as large an audience as possible.

When Gus emerged the great man was huffing and puffing and pawing the ground a bit, with the College bedellus standing by and doing his best to soothe him down. Gus murmured 'I'm most awfully sorry, Sir Edgar . . . For a ghastly couple of minutes I thought I'd lost this . . .' He fingered the medallion . . . 'So sorry . . .'

'My dear boy, I'm just being a typical nervous speaker . . . Aren't I, Forrest?'

The bedellus, whose name, Gus thought, was almost certainly Chisholm, smiled and nodded and glanced conspicuously at his watch. 'Is it time. . . ?' said Gus.

'When you're ready, sir,' said Chisholm. Speaker and chairman followed the bedellus along a lavishly carpeted corridor towards the doors of the College's main hall. The bedellus threw them open and bawled 'Prray be up-standing for the Prre-sident of the Ancient So-ciety of Physic of Edin-burrrgh . . .' The waiting audience shuffled to its feet. The hall was almost full, which meant around two hundred, and a lot of the girls had turned out, which of course was nice. Gus, taking care to look nervous and diffident, led the speaker on to the rostrum and stood modestly fingering his medallion of office while the great man seated himself, with much huffing and puffing, in the chair beside the lectern. '*Ladies* and gentlemen . . .' There was a gratifying ripple of applause.

Sandy, sitting quite near the front with some others from second year, sat listening and was impressed. She had known Gus Ratho for ages, because of their families, and had always thought of him as a bit wet, but he seemed to have improved recently and he had done his little speech and the introduction thing quite nicely: nicely enough for her to tell him so, in a friend-of-the-family sort of way, at the party afterwards if she got the chance and if she decided to go. The lights went down and the surgeon started off his talk by explaining a bit about the history of immunology, quite interesting things about people sewing bits of animals on to other animals ages ago and how the bits did all right to start with then began to fall off after a few days. He had a distracting habit of looking round to see what slide was on the screen and talking up to the pictures of white mice behind him rather than down to the medical students in front, but he was obviously knowledgeable and enthusiastic and when he got on to talking about people who were dying of kidney failure he began to sound like Sandy's idea of a proper, caring doctor. The pictures of the operations at twenty times life size were a bit much for some people, with huge fingers in puddles of blood twelve feet across and vast kidneys being plumbed into gaping holes in the patients, but the end result, a slide of a happy, well-looking lady at home, was fine by everyone. 'And here's another . . .' said Sir Edgar as a slide of two men playing golf came up. 'Now d'you see that terribly ill-looking chap on the left? That's my senior registrar.' A lot of people laughed. 'The patient's the other one,' he went on, 'Three up at the fourteenth. And it's Luffness, for those of you who find golf more interesting than current fashions in the management of renal failure.'

Gus sat in the throne-like College chair looking round and up at the slides: not a good place to see things from, but quite good for being seen. The ward sister's crazed assault on his research project that afternoon was, he decided, only a minor irritant, the kind of thing bitter old spinsters did now and again to show they had power. And her shouting like that in the ward was really quite unprofessional, regardless of who she was shouting at. It was actually quite sad. Even poor Fiona hugging her was probably the first time for years that anyone had touched her other than as a matter of strict social necessity. And what she appeared to have forgotten was that students became houseman, and then registrars and senior registrars and consultants, so that some day she might very much regret what she had, in the heat of the moment, said to someone doing important research in her ward.

The great man wasn't doing too badly. The gathering Gus looked out on from his throne – probably the biggest the Society had ever attracted, and certainly the first mixed one – sat attentively, rows of upturned faces lit by the slides on the screen. And the dinner had gone quite well, with Roger Killick, the consultant immunologist at the Institute, who was there as President's guest, obviously enjoying it too. Roger had been one of the great man's first house surgeons in Edinburgh, and had prompted his standard anecdotes with quiet skill and traded conference horror stories quite amusingly. It was really all quite straightforward, Gus reflected as the slides came and went: when the time came in a couple of years to apply for housejobs he could append to his application to Sir Edgar's unit a fairly informal note mentioning the fact that they had met over dinner on the occasion of his address to the Ancient Society of Physic. And in conversation over dinner he had made perfectly clear his commitment and expertise in the vital new field of immunology.

A slide went up, a hugely magnified account of the microscopic battlefield of the rejection process: standard stuff with massed, warring cells from a failing kidney graft, stained red and blue, technically quite a good picture. Gus thought of the slides he himself had shown the Society a few weeks before in the course of his Presidental lecture, *Multiple Sclerosis: Cellular Locks and Immunological Keys*. His own pictures hadn't actually come out very well, because of some technical problems with the wavelength of the immuno-fluorescence, but, as Roger Killick had pointed out, an undergraduate audience needed to grasp only the broad principles, and some of Roger's own slides of something similar in rats got the general message across with a far higher technical quality. And, as Roger had assured him, no one had come rushing up after his talk saying 'Hey, Jimmy, those looked mair like rat lymphocytes tae me.'

The great man's immunology was a bit rough and ready, Gus concluded when his attention returned to Sir Edgar's lecture. Although it was possible he was toning it down a bit for undergraduates he was skipping lots of important details and he seemed to have decided that his anti-lymphocytic serum was a major advance, a view not widely reflected in the literature Gus had been reading as background material for his own project. Still, the most important thing was that he was an immunologist of sorts, and an influential local one with a good housejob at his disposal, and that Roger Killick, who had been very keen to spend some time with him, seemed to be enjoying the evening too. Gus scanned the audience – easily and comfortably done from the Presidential throne – and found him again, sitting in the second row between Hymie Cathcart and another little creep from that year, Roberts, the one who spent most of his time in Casualty.

The great man was getting well into the whither-now-everything section of his lecture, speculating on what means might be available to manipulate and suppress immunological responses in the 1970's and 80's: the kind of crystal ball-gazing exercise that elderly scientists indulged in as a substitute for continuing effort, but at least it meant he was probably within striking distance of the end of his lecture. Gus reached for another little card in his top pocket and brushed up on his vote of thanks by the light of the last slide as the speaker launched into a coy little tribute to the Society's recent constitutional advance. '. . . and may I, as a somewhat conservative but nonetheless admiring immunologist, congratulate the Ancient Society on its own recent experiment in, um, attempting to incorporate, how shall we put it, some slightly alien living material. As I learned over a most agreeable dinner before this lecture, this was not achieved without a certain amount of what we might term, um, inflammatory response, but looking around this audience with, um, a fairly experienced eye, I can assure you that there appear to be as yet no significant features of, um, rejection . . . Mr President, members of the Society, um, *Ladies* and gentleman, thank you for your kind attention . . .' He sat down and Gus led the audience in warm and prolonged applause.

'We didn't always live here,' said the thin, dark little man who had just handed Sandy a glass of wine. 'We're sort of descended gentry. We couldn't really afford our ancestral home any more. It happens a lot . . . And then some developers wanted to knock it down, so they paid us to push off and look at us now. Just rented. Isn't it squalid?'

He was piling it on a bit, Sandy decided. All the other student societies she'd been to met in dusty former church halls with uncomfortable seats and doubtful toilets. This lot had a huge flat, two flats really, ground floor and basement, and it was clean and nicely decorated and full of people having quite a good time. He had an odd accent, half Glasgow, half something else.

'But at least we've managed to hang on to one or two bits of our furniture . . . And if you sit on that sofa yours will be the first female

. . . body . . . to have sat upon it for at least two hundred and thirty years.'

'Really, Max?' Sandy sipped her wine, a student white served quite warm, and remained standing.

'D'you know lots of people here?'

Sandy decided it would be very pompous of her to say she'd known the President since she'd been about four. 'Not really.'

'Andy . . .' He was reaching for the nearest of a group of three boys. 'Andy, come and meet one of our new lady members. Sandy Lennox, Andy Scott . . . Andy's new too. Same year as me but only joined last term.'

'Hello.'

'Hello, Sandy.'

'Andy's all right,' said the half-Glaswegian. 'He's in favour of women.' Sandy must have looked puzzled, because he went on to explain 'In the Society, I mean. Lots of people weren't . . . You should have heard the arguments. Everything from the toilets and what would they wear, down to silly stuff like distracting serious chaps working in the library. You know, with their chatter and gossip, or making eyes at us. Then when we'd discussed all that they said OK, associate members. But what the hell does that mean, we said, they can join but can't go for a pee? So we held out for full membership and got it for you.'

The chap seemed to want to be congratulated on his amazingly advanced social thinking. Sandy said nothing, which didn't seem to make any difference. 'The ladies' loo is the little one at the back downstairs,' he said as though she had just asked. Sandy turned to the one who had just joined them. 'What did you think of the lecture, Andy?'

'Oh . . . Interesting. You know, in a where-will-it-all-lead kind of way.'

'Pancreas,' said Max, the half-Glaswegian. 'Total, utter cure for diabetes.'

'But what about all the other things diabetics get. . . ?' said Andy. 'All the circulatory stuff, gangrene and things.'

'Simple,' said Max. 'Either get 'em early, before it all happens, or bring 'em in late and give them a complete eighty-thousand mile service. Parts and labour, all on the NHS. Pancreas, we got. You got bad legs? Legs too, we got. How many you want? How wide?'

Andy looked as if he wanted to make a serious point while Max just wanted to be smart. Sandy listened a bit more. She was already quite accustomed to being used as an audience while medical men, from professors like her dad down to students like these, had conversations like that, and was beginning to suspect that the real reason they had decided to admit women to membership of their silly society was just so that they could have lots of new people to bore. She started to look round for a reasonable means of escape. Gus was in a corner surrounded by a crowd of girls already, so that wasn't much help. It might even have to be the little loo at the back downstairs, because they had started talking about heart transplants. Suddenly Max grabbed one of the big bottles of student white and rushed off to top people up. 'Hello again,' she said to Andy. 'I'm one of the new lady members.' He laughed, and they talked for quite a long time: about the foibles of the anatomy teachers; about West Africa, where he'd taught for a year between school and starting in medicine and she'd lived during the school holidays while her dad had been a visiting professor at Kaduna; and about Vietnam, on which they agreed. Eventually, when the queue for Gus had gone down a bit, she excused herself and went over and told him he'd done a good job. He seemed pleased to see her.

Scott topped up his glass and went downstairs to the basement, where it was darker and people were more drunk. Someone, probably Max, had organised some music and among the book-shelves of the Society's library there was a little clear space, about three yards by four, where half a dozen couples were dancing. As Scott's eyes adjusted he noticed a few more people, in odd corners among the floor-to-ceiling bookshelves, not dancing. Among them was Robbie, leaning against a shelf of 1890's Lancets looking sorry for himself and talking to a sensible girl from the year below, Theresa, who seemed to be trying to cheer him up. Both their glasses were empty, and Scott's arrival with a full one prompted Robbie to offer to go up and get Theresa some more wine. She handed him her glass, he found his own and ascended the little cast-iron spiral staircase uncertainly into the light. 'Is he all right?' Scott asked.

'Not terribly,' said Theresa. 'Worried about his mum, and his career, and whether he should do an Honours year or not, and if he does whether it should be anatomy or bacteriology, because bacteriology gives out more firsts but anatomy's more useful. And girls. Which he needn't be, because Margaret Auld's nuts about him. She's upstairs and he'd only have to go within six feet of her.'

'Does he know that?'

'I was getting round to it. How are you?'

'Reeling from the shock of women in m'club.'

'You're kidding.'

'They'll be letting them into the laundrettes next . . .'

'Andrew.'

A few months previously Scott, who knew Theresa vaguely from having coffee sometimes in the Catholic Students' Chaplaincy, had met her by chance in a Marchmont laundrette, where they had had an agreeable hour sitting watching their respective washes and talking. Afterwards she had invited him up to her flat for coffee. Scott had decided a drink might be more sociable, so with their plastic bags of washing they had dropped in at an off-licence on the way. On Theresa's bed, a narrow, ascetic mattress on the floor, overlooked by a spiky crucifix and a bookshelf of devotional works, they had drunk a bottle of Spanish Sauterne then fallen to sleepy, friendly cuddling with the radio on. The evening had passed pleasantly enough. Theresa, it seemed, had principles, but in practice they turned out to mean only that she could not in conscience reciprocate the kind of patient, expert dalliance she so enthusiastically encouraged from him. Nevertheless she was warm and clean and eager and enjoyed herself a lot. Scott, philosophical about the kind of deprivation her upbringing was imposing upon him, could see the funny side too, and contrived to bring her to a crucifix-rattling climax just as the announcer closed down the station and a recording of a fine old-fashioned military band launched into the national anthem. She had come to, so to speak, to its dying strains and had giggled and writhed and pummelled his naked chest out of indignant embarrassment at the irreverence of it all, but they had remained friends. 'How are you, Theresa?'

'Fine thank you, Andrew. Quite intrigued by all this. I mean, it's really quite ordinary, if you take away the robes and big medals and so on. You've no idea what people said about you . . . Stories about silly initiation rites, human bones as gavels, all kinds of funny jiggery-pokery behind the damask curtains . . . I think most people are here out of curiosity and probably won't bother to come again.

You're so ordinary. Gus Ratho without his robes on is just another bright young Edinburgh boy on the make, only more so. Thinking ahead to his housejob with Sir Edgar, I shouldn't wonder.'

In some ways Theresa was quite sophisticated, Scott decided. They talked a bit more about Gus Ratho, who in her opinion should have gone to a medical school well away from his father's sphere of influence, if indeed one could be found, and also about which of the medical units in the Institute offered best all-round experience for the first term of clinical teaching. Eventually she took his glass and downed a biggish sip and handed it back, remarking 'I don't know what's happened to Robbie.' Scott finished his wine and, as Theresa had presumably intended, put his arm round her and steered her the few feet to the cleared space where people were dancing. Quite soon Robbie came down the spiral staircase again, without wine and closely following Margaret Auld. After them came Gus with the nice blonde girl who had lived in West Africa. Gradually the little dance floor became quite crowded. Theresa snuggled comfortably against Scott, her cheek close and warm on his chest, her fingers inside his shirt. The music became slower and quieter and Scott recalled the speaker's surmise about the Society's nervous adjustment to the realities of medicine of the Sixties: signs of rejection were indeed minimal.

Gus was enjoying himself too. The evening had gone well and Sandy, whom he vaguely remembered from when they were children and from seeing her around the medical quad, was bright and amusing to talk to. Although she was a good nine inches shorter than he, she was, as his mother would say, decorative: a classification which came somewhere between comely and stunning in her scheme of things but definitely signified approval. She dressed well and danced as well as the circumstances required. There were one or two other quite important things about her, Gus had to admit to himself as they circled slowly in the hot darkness of the Society's basement library. Her father, recently appointed to a new chair of endocrinology at the Institute, was very much a coming man on the scene and although Gus's father did not entirely approve of him was said to be a leading contender to succeed Jimmy Jameson as clinical dean. Gus held Sandy closer, and was surprised at the warmth of her response.

Max, who had recently started to work seriously on trying to give up nurses, had not had a good evening. Sitting beside Roger Killick at the lecture had been all right, but Edinburgh's second most famous immunologist had rushed straight off at the end to congratulate its most famous one, so there hadn't really been much of a chance to talk to him. The party, which he had told Gus he'd take care of, was all right so far, but not any better than that. There had been one or two worries about the sound system and the guy from first year who had been paid to change the records had turned out to have some weird enthusiasms: people could take only so much of *Eleanor Rigby*. The booze had been the big problem. From last year's accounts he knew the kind of money that went on cosy little dinners for the chosen few. He had seen bills for twelve, even fifteen pounds and had tried to push the booze budget up a bit but the Custos Aeris – acting, he was sure, on Gus's instructions – wasn't having any of it. So they had had cheap white plonk and even then it had run out. Still, it would all be sorted out in the very near future: as Senior President of the Society of Physic, Maxwell Jacob Cathcart would show them what could be done. And meantime, since he was definitely trying to give up nurses, there was this wee Polish number, possibly Jewish and if so the first woman he had ever looked at that his mother might have approved of: Irena, pronounced Ee-ray-na. In the darkness, to the strains of *Eleanor Rigby* third time round, he moved his hands from the small of her back to the large of her bum. 'How about you and me getting away from all these crowds and people,' he murmured, and felt her head nodding against his cheek in reply. He squeezed her and patted her. 'Just give me ten minutes to wrap this lot up. Then your chariot awaits.'

'Is this it?' she said when she saw it. Max had a lime green Mini-van of which he was very proud, and for this evening he had washed it and cleaned the inside and even taken the mattress out of the back.

'Right,' said Max. 'It's a very convenient town car, and we're not going very far.'

Ee-ray-na sniffed and gathered a long, full skirt around her for the descent into the passenger seat. 'Where do you live, Mac?' She asked as they hit the main road and Max opened it up a bit.

'Max. Marchmont, same as everybody.'

'That's actually quite handy for dropping me off.'

'Where do you live?'

'Ventnor Terrace.'

It was nowhere near being on the road to Marchmont but there was still a chance. 'In a flat?'

'No, Max. With my parents, of course . . . Because my father is old-fashioned . . . A typical cavalry officer . . .'

'I actually make very good coffee.' They had reached the traffic lights where they would have to turn right for Marchmont. She laid a hand on his arm. 'Some other night, Max, dear. I have a migraine . . .'

'Caffeine's just what you need. Pharmacology, last term.'

'Not tonight, Max, dear.'

Even though the lights were still at red Max made up his mind and cancelled his right turn signal and when the lights turned green gunned off and swept through Newington, corners and all, at about fifty, getting to Ventnor Terrace in one minute flat. 'What number you want?' he asked, doing his New York taxi-driver number.

She told him and they pulled up with a stirring shriek of rubber. He leaned over towards her to do the polite minimum in the circumstances. 'Now Maxie,' she said, putting an index finger on the tip of his nose. 'Naughty boy.' She took his hand and opened it and peered down at it. 'So much heart line, you want to rush me. Naughty Max.' She ruffled his hair, pecked his cheek, then murmured huskily 'But we can see each other again soon.' When Max said nothing she got out of the car and stood waving prettily under a streetlamp as he roared off in the general direction of Marchmont, unsure quite where he was going until he had worked out who was on a night shift that night and who wasn't. And if her dad was a gallant case of failed suicide on a horse she probably wasn't even Jewish anyway.

Gus and Sandy had slipped quietly away from the party and walked along Chambers Street and down Candlemaker Row towards the Grassmarket, where Gus had his flat. It was all a bit odd. Sandy was assuming he had asked her and he was assuming she would go, and it was all happening as if she did this sort of thing all the time. At the foot of Candlemaker Row they turned left and round the corner into a curious scene, far busier than anything else she had seen in Edinburgh at that time of night except during the Festival. It was like one of those crowded untidy Scottish pictures of a market day in the country, except it was dark and the crowd, grouped round a police box and a public toilet but spreading out over the road as well, consisted of drunks and tramps and down and outs and a couple of policemen, some awful-looking women, probably tarts too drunk or too old to be any good at it, and a separate younger, cleaner, louder lot coming out of an archway and standing around and getting into cars: a late audience from the Traverse, she realised. Gus held her hand tighter and they headed into the crowd against its stream. 'I'm up here,' he said. 'It's not usually quite as Bohemian as this.'

They went through the archway and into a courtyard with the theatre entrance at the far end then climbed four flights of stairs. On the way up Sandy decided that she was a bit surprised Gus lived here, but that she approved of it too. She would have guessed New Town, one of the smaller streets to the North, and she would have been quite wrong. He opened his front door and switched on the lights. It was all white and modern and had stripped pine varnished floors and central heating. They passed a little windowless room with a desk and lots of books and came to a lounge that looked out over the Grassmarket and up to the dark, curving walls of the Castle. Gus took her coat and Sandy stood in the dark looking down on the street-lit crowd below.

Gus came back and switched on a table lamp. 'Amazing view,' Sandy said. 'Is that why you got it?'

'Partly. And the sillier reason is that it was near the Society. But then the Society had to move. But it's still awfully near everything . . . And dad had wanted to put a little bit of granny's money into property. Worked out quite well, really . . . Coffee, Sandy?'

'Um, yes thanks. Not too strong for me.'

'Gosh. Please sit down.'

He went off again and Sandy decided that he probably needed someone like her more than he thought. On the way down he had said all sorts of odd things about how the evening had gone and what different people there had thought of things, and about what his parents thought, and the importance of doing things properly and not just lettings things happen. Things going wrong, like the wine running out a bit early, annoyed him and he blamed someone else for that but as the chap in overall charge he still felt responsible. All a bit boring actually, thought Sandy, but sad too, as if he was still finding out who he was and where he was going. And if he knew that was what she thought he'd be furious, because she was still just a little girl in second year. While she waited for coffee she really didn't want she wondered about what sort of girls he normally went out with: probably wildly pretty ones who had nothing to do with medicine and were a bit dim, she decided, and they would think he was simply marvellous, which he wasn't really, but wouldn't be able to give him the kind of help he needed now and for the forseeable future.

When he came back they sat on his nice low modern sofa, practically at opposite ends, and had coffee and polite conversation. Part of his trouble, Sandy decided, was that he was too handsome for his own good. His hair was fairer than hers, and he had a nice profile with maybe just a bit too much chin, but his teeth were marvellous. As they talked she tried to imagine him without his clothes on and he came out as lean and fit in a boyish sort of way, and pale with bits of nice golden hair here and there.

'So while it's really as good as finished, it would be nice to have just a few more patients, maybe another ten or twenty, because some of the trends are interesting but don't actually mean a lot unless I get the numbers too. And we're looking for people who are doing really badly, so the measurables are there and the lymphocyte things are right up. As Roger says, no point in looking when the horse has bolted. And some of the patients are actually quite difficult. You know, silly and weepy. And time's getting on.'

Sandy was tempted to say yes, it jolly well was, and it was past her bedtime and did he have a bedroom somewhere and did he want to come too? Instead she listened patiently to some of the problems he had had trying to interview people with multiple sclerosis and get the samples he needed from them. 'You'd be astonished, Sandy . . . They forget important things, and give you a jumble of things they wish were true and lose control and then can't tell you a thing.' As he listened it occurred to Sandy that he was talking so much because he was nervous and didn't quite know what to do next, and might even be quite new to it all, which was possible and probably something else he'd be furious with her for understanding too well. She let him talk quite a lot more then got up to look at the view again and asked him casually from the window if he happened to have any gin and tonic, because she'd like a drink. They both went to the kitchen, which was as nice as the rest of the flat, and they made two drinks and went back to the sofa and sat a bit nearer each other. It was progress of a sort.

At nearly midnight and after another gin and tonic Sandy stood up in a kind of make-or-break way and said she mustn't be too late home. Gus stood up and put his arms round her and they kissed and then went and looked out of the window for a while, kissing and cuddling as well. When he had done quite a lot of that and got excited enough for her to feel him through their clothes he began to look at her in a too-shy-to-ask sort of way, so she put her hands under his jacket and pulled his shirt up so she could feel his naked back and he came gratifyingly alive and held her close and kissed her a lot. As they went to his bedroom, which was neat and modern and white like the rest of the flat, she wondered if he was assuming that she was as new to all this as she suspected he was, and decided to proceed tactfully, as if she might be.

They lay on his bed still dressed, which was a mistake and slowed things up a lot, then rolled around a bit with him doing a bit more, and a bit less badly, but not doing her dress much good. She took it off in two seconds flat then, because it was the kind of thing you would wear if the Queen was coming to tea, folded it neatly on a chair. Soon they were naked in bed and about time too. He was slow and shy and it was all difficult enough without starting to bother him about contraception. And anyway, she thought in a silly way, human reproduction wasn't until next term. They would take a chance this once, on the grounds that accidents happened mainly to people who took them all the time. She lay under him making little encouraging noises but trying not to sound too experienced. It was all a bit difficult.

Gus closed his eyes. It was all rather complicated. Sandy was charming, in her bright, cheerful, sensible way, but she just wasn't his kind of girl. No doubt his mother would approve, and no doubt his father would stop muttering about Gavin Lennox in quite the same terms when he took her home to meet them, but that didn't actually help very much in a situation like this. And now she was stroking his neck and making these odd, rather expert little movements while he was struggling just to maintain a presence. And if he told her he'd actually done very little of this before, certainly none of it with the kind of girl he'd be remotely likely to want to take home, she'd think he was hopelessly wet and probably a bit silly too, so he kept his eyes closed and thought about the tall, stunningly beautiful girl he had interviewed that afternoon, the dancer with hopeless multiple sclerosis and the long, lovely body that was simply a lot nicer than Sandy's, which was all right but a bit squat and stocky. That made a useful difference, or at least it did until Sandy responded by doing a number of even more expert things that really made him begin to wonder all over again. It was all very difficult.

Walking across the Meadows on the way back to Marchmont Scott and Theresa held hands and took their time and talked mainly about the party. 'Our lot did all right, I suppose,' said Theresa as they passed under the arch of whale jawbones at the edge of the park. Scott said that made it sound like a hockey match and she laughed. 'Mainly with people from your year. Irena and Max . . . Trish and the chap with acne.'

'Barnetson.'

'Robbie and Maggie. I'm sure it's something to do with knowing your own lot too well, from when they were spotty youths straight from school, and seeing them being silly in anatomy. That and the Allure of the Older Man. You know. We sort of hope you'll be a bit more grown up.'

'We're doing our best.' Scott remembered what Max had said a long time before about the women in their year, and about being stuck with them. There probably was something less risky about girls if you could tell them which were the best medical units to apply for and reassure them that despite all the rumours most people passed physiology first time. 'And if we're no good there's always the year above.'

'Sandy and Gus,' said Theresa.

'What's she like?'

'Interested?'

'Just curious.'

'Bright. Ambitious. Works hard.'

'And wants to be a professor like her dad?'

Theresa thought about that and then said 'Probably not. But definitely a professor's wife. And she'd be rather good at that.'

As they neared the street where Theresa lived she held his hand tighter and seemed to speed up a bit. On the pavement outside her door they stopped and Scott put his arms round her. 'Aren't you coming up for coffee?' she asked, her voice muffled in his lapel.

Scott looked at his watch. 'Isn't it a bit late?'

'Just a quick one.'

'Oh, all right . . . And if we're really quick we'll still catch the national anthem.' She laughed and punched him and nuzzled his neck, then they went up the stairs two at a time.

April 1966

Scott and Robbie had been advised that George Gordon's firm was a good one for the third term of fourth year, once you knew the basics and were looking for a bit more in the bigger specialties. On the wards of Drs Gordon, Smail and Pattullo the junior staff were keen, you saw a bit of gastro-enterology, some kidneys and a fair bit of general medicine too, and if you were lucky old Gorgeous George himself didn't appear too often. He made a point of taking the first junior clinic himself, going round the group asking what your father did and what school you had attended. Except in the unlikely event of everyone having been to Glenalmond, Fettes, Strathallan or the Edinburgh Academy, he said his piece about the social decline of medicine, then, if there were any girls in the group, went on to say something about medical women and town dogs being doomed alike to a lifetime of fundamental unhappiness. The aim of the exercise was to make boys from the lower orders squirm and girls of any description cry. It was as predictable as it was rehearsed, its endurance a bizarre entrance fee to an otherwise satisfactory clinic. Overseas students never applied.

Robbie, having survived the confession of a railway inspector father and Heriot's School, was thriving on it. He had befriended the houseman and had started coming in early to help him with his blood round. He went back in the evenings on admitting nights and clerked patients just to give a hand, even though that was expected only of senior students, and every time he came across a new diagnosis he looked it up in one of the huge textbooks he had bought with his prize money from second year. Most of the rest of the clinic vaguely resented all this enthusiasm, but Scott, who was interested but not fanatical, quite enjoyed it. He learned a lot just from having coffee with Robbie.

He was talking now about the pick of the catch from the previous night: a young woman from a mental subnormality hospital who had come in with a urinary tract infection but had also turned out to have one of the rarer causes of a low IQ. Robbie, having clerked her in at eleven the previous evening, had gone home and read up on her diagnosis and some related conditions and was actually now getting a bit boring about it all.

'So she's unusual because her fits are quite easily controlled. And her skin things aren't too bad. Some of them get them up to an inch across, usually where she's got them, around the nose and on her cheeks. And she's one of the brighter ones, because she can actually talk . . .'

'But it's not very common, is it?'

'Less than one per cent of subnormality . . . And her urinary tract infection's a lot better, just overnight, so not a true pyelo-nephritis.'

'Lucky old her.'

'She's twenty.'

'So back to the nuns, today or tomorrow . . .'

Robbie laughed. 'Yes, that's what you'd think, but everybody's very excited about her. Mean to say, Bourneville's disease. Pretty rare, but the wee lumps round the fingernails are diagnostic, so I was kind of on to it right away. And apparently they're keeping her to use in membership exams, and the registrar's going round saying you see about one in a lifetime and he's obviously read up all about it. Good teaching hospital case, really. Like the chap with keratoderma blenorrhagica.'

They were sitting on an enclosed lawn, a little enclave of green in the crowded jumble of buildings comprising the Institute. The registrar, a thin man with big glasses and endless reserves of wet-lipped enthusiasm, had spent most of the first session of the morning on the woman with Bourneville's disease, stressing the rarity of the condition and also, curiously, its importance. Scott had listened to a long explanation of its imperfectly understood genetic basis, its various clinical manifestations and its unhelpably gloomy prognosis and had wondered why they had to know so much about something they might never see again. As they had stood for more than half an hour round the patient, it occurred to him that they were being taught about the common things only when the registrars ran out of uncommon things to teach on. 'How's Maggie?' he asked, at least partly to avoid learning any more about keratoderma blenorrhagica.

'Oh, all right. A bit shaky on neuro-anatomy.'

'Oh?'

'It's quite worrying. We were talking about thalamic pain . . . You know, the kind of thing you sometimes get after a stroke. Hadn't a clue about the thalamus. Not a single clue. And it's not difficult. Deep brain stuff. Final common path of sensation and all that. Anterior, medial and lateral nuclei . . . All very logical, but hadn't a clue.'

'Really?'

'Oh, she'll probably pass,' said Robbie, sounding like a professor of anatomy on the verge of disillusioned retirement.

'And apart from that?'

'What?'

'How's Maggie?'

'Oh. Yes. Pretty well. We usually work in the Society library till about ten, unless the unit's admitting. It's quite comfortable and there's practically everything you need.'

'Isn't it a bit difficult with you living at home?'

'Oh, we manage. She's in a flat in Polwarth. Five minutes from us. I'm usually home by eleven . . . Come on, Andy. Time, gentlemen, please. Medicine calls. Senior registrar case presentations.' They got up, and the rest of the clinic, the less keen, who had been sitting a little way off, began to get up too. They straggled back inside, along the corridor and upstairs to the teaching room on the female ward of Gordon's unit and sat chatting, waiting for the senior registrar, MacInnes, a harassed man who quite often clutched involuntarily for his cigarette packet as much as a quarter of an hour before the end of a teaching session, to come and hear a couple of cases from them.

At ten past eleven the door opened and a voice said 'Come'. No one entered. The door had simply opened and was now held open by an invisible hand, and the voice, that of George Gordon himself, invisibly commanded the students to rise up and follow him. A few students, among them those who had been designated to prepare cases for presentation, grimaced as they moved outside to where he was waiting in the corridor, a tall, bald man in a good dark suit with a flower in its buttonhole. 'Gentlemen . . . And of course ladies. Forgive me, ladies. Gentlemen, my first task today is to convey the apologies of our colleague Dr MacInnes, whose dearest wish it was to teach you this morning but who has been called from our midst by . . .' He paused and smiled, the magician who alone knows what is to be pulled from the hat. '. . . a happy event, or should I say an impending happy event. He is at present with his dear wife, *enceinte* but approaching delivery, we understand, by the minute and only a few hundred yards away within this hospital. A perfect husband but, alas, an absent teacher. So!' He put his right arm across his middle and bowed from the waist. 'May I humbly beg your indulgence this Thursday morning. I am not he whom you expected, but one called from afar at the shortest of notice . . . For we know not the hour nor the day . . . And I understand that one or two of you have some . . . *cases* to present?'

Helen, a small, quiet girl with glasses, was clutching a sheaf of ruled notepaper and shifting uneasily from one foot to the other. MacInnes' teaching style was relaxed and untidy, a matter of helpful digression, woolly encouragement and reproach rarely going beyond puzzlement that something had been missed or misinterpreted. You did your best and he helped you improve on it. With George Gordon it was different. To Scott, an occasional Traverse attender, Gordon was theatre, but bad theatre: a curious blend of the ringmaster and the magician, in a performance devised to control and mystify, with students and patients interchangeable at his whim, victims and audience too.

'Shall we begin?' Helen clutched her notes more tightly. Morris, a mild, plump youth from Falkirk, pulled some paper from his pocket. 'The case, my young colleagues, the case and its presentation . . . The very grammar of medicine, the articulation of that sometimes overwhelming mass of impressions, suspicions, deductions, hunches, hypotheses and rarely, oh so rarely at your stage in medicine, *conclusions* about what it is that has brought that patient along to you, a medical practitioner . . .' He folded his arms, leaned back and smiled again, then snapped round like a gunfighter. 'You, miss! I see you have a case . . .'

'Mr-MacClintock-is-a-seventy-six-year-old-retired-green-grocer-widowed-and-living-alone-who-noticed-blood-and-mucus . . .'

'My dear girl . . . My dear, dear girl. Relax. Just relax. You have a delightful voice and you have clearly done a great deal of meticulous preparation, but you are not doing yourself justice. You are simply not doing yourself justice . . . And you are not doing yourself justice *because*. . . ? Because you are nervous. You must learn to relax. And we must help you. So why, I ask myself, why do we not go now and have the pleasure of meeting this gentleman, this veteran of a lifetime's purveying of vitamins and roughage to the people? I am sure nothing could serve you better because nothing can substitute for the reassuring presence of the man who stands at the heart of this drama . . . the patient!' He smiled his magician's smile. 'Lead on, dear girl . . . *We* shall follow.'

They reached a bed more than half way down on the left of the ward, in which an old man lay reading a newspaper. He folded it as they approached, pulled himself up on his pillows and smiled. No one smiled back. Helen straightened out her notes and started again. 'Mr-McClintock-is-a-seventy-six . . .'

'No, no, my dear . . . You must stand *here*. The *place d'honneur* on the patient's right, looking out to us, whom you are addressing, and speaking up confidently and clearly, just as though you were a houseman . . . I'm sorry, house*woman* . . . And I your chief . . . The time is morning, the day, that following an admitting night. We are in some haste as there have been many admissions. Your chief looks to you now for a concise but comprehensive account of the problems afflicting a patient who has just come into his care and for whom he is already responsible . . . So let us begin again . . .'

'Mr-MacClintock-is-a-seventy-six-year-old-retired-and-widowed-greengrocer-living-alone-who-noticed-blood-and-mucus-in-his-stool . . .'

'Ah! We must pause. Do I hear correctly? In? Or are my ears deceiving me? *In?* Are we to assume that this decent tradesman, this fastidious seller of foodstuffs, as a matter of daily routine and in contradiction to all normal conditioning, goes poking around *in* his stools? Dissecting them? Filleting them? Looking to see what's inside them? Because that's what you're trying to tell us, girl . . .' His voice dropped. '*That* is what you *said*.' He turned ostentatiously from Helen to the far end of the half-circle of students. 'Gentlemen, clinical description, if it is to be worth anything at all, must be precise . . . I think our colleague, had she reflected, would have said *on*. I *am* right, my dear, am I not?'

He turned once more to where Helen had been standing. She was already half way down the ward and still retreating. His smile of concern changed instantly to slack-jawed mime-surprise. No one laughed. He grinned, a death's head over a magician's suit. 'Well, gentlemen,' he said, 'perhaps one of *you* has prepared a case.'

Morris raised a hand. Gordon nodded curtly to Mr MacClintock and they all moved back down the ward to the bedside of a heavy, greying man with a hare lip. Uninterrupted by Gordon, Morris gave a workmanlike account of how Mr Lockhart, an author of some kind, had been coming down the steps of his club after lunch three days previously and had experienced crushing central chest pain and acute shortness of breath. He had collapsed and been brought in to the Institute as an emergency via the Casualty Department. His pain had gone and his breathlessness had almost gone. He had never had any previous such illness and his only previous treatment related to his cleft palate and hare lip. Gordon listened, upright and alert, his arms folded and his shoulders back as Morris' account of the case drew to a close. '. . . so in summary, a fifty-three year old previously healthy man with an acute myocardial infarction complicated by atrial fibrillation and acute left ventricular failure, responding well to therapy with morphine, digoxin, diuretics and anticoagulants.'

'Thank you, young man. A fairly adequate account of a common and distressing problem with, in this instance at least, a happy outcome . . .' The patient raised an eyebrow. 'But where is he now. . . ?'

'Sir?'

'Where is the patient now?'

Morris looked puzzled. 'Well, sir, he's . . . in hospital.'

'A shrewd piece of clinical observation, if I may say so . . . Anyone?'

'He's in bed,' said Betty, the remaining girl.

'Thank you, miss. You have retrieved the reputation of your sex. And drawn suitable attention to the major omission in our young colleague's account of the modern therapy of the condition. Bed rest. Thank you, m'dear. Despite all the might of our proliferating therapeutic armamentarium still a major weapon in our fight against this scourge of modern man. Not six weeks of strict bed rest as our recent predecessors insisted, with the poor chap lying in terror for his life lest the ward sister spot his furtive efforts to pour himself a glass of water, or even three as some of my more conservative contemporaries still maintain.' He drew himself up. 'Ten days.' He grinned down at the patient. 'With the freedom to pour yourself as many glasses of water as you like. And how are you feeling today, my dear chap. . . ?'

'Well, thank you,' said the man, his speech defect a hollow whistle with each word.

'A mere seven days to go. And how did you enjoy your breakfast?'

'Delicious,' said Mr Lockhart, in what was probably an excess of gratitude for porridge, a roll and tea in a thick cup.

Gordon frowned and moved to the head of the bed and took down the drug chart. 'Hm . . . Yes. Thought so.' He turned to the students. 'If a patient can still eat his breakfast three days after we have commenced digoxin . . .' He paused with his hand upraised. '. . . we are quite simply not giving him enough.' Mr Lockhart was looking up as if he might be about to speak again but was not encouraged to do so. 'And if you are not giving him enough you might as well not be giving him any . . . And yet here we have fast fibrillation, a threat to life itself that can be controlled only by adequate doses of digoxin . . .' The man raised himself up a little, once again as though to speak, then lay back. 'Nausea . . .' Gordon used the word with relish. 'Nausea is a side-effect of digoxin so useful as to be almost classifiable as an effect . . . At least we can tell when our patient has had enough.' He grinned and looked slowly round his student audience, the normal prelude to the singling out of a victim. 'And perhaps, young colleagues, we should remind ourselves of some of its other side-effects, hm? Some views, please . . .' No one volunteered. 'A view from the manse, perhaps?' Eyes turned on Scott. 'Um, visual things, sir. Seeing yellow and green . . .'

'But, Mr Scott . . . Surely, being a son of the manse, you have the greek.'

'Xanthopsia.'

'Quite. Now, perhaps a view from . . . the engine-shed?'

Robbie grinned. 'Vomiting, diarrhoea, weight loss and mental disturbance. Occasionally abdominal pain. And of course the effects on the heart – fast and slow arrhythmias and premature beats – all of which are made worse if the patient is potassium-deficient . . .'

Gordon beamed back at him. 'Admirable, Mr Roberts.' He

twinkled roguishly. ' "Oi'll geeve it foive." ' It was a passable version of a catch-phrase from a pop music personality who had been off the air for some time. No one laughed. 'So let us hope that Mr Lockhart enjoys his breakfast a little less tomorrow.' With a cheery wave to the patient he led his clinic on up the ward.

'Jimmy's amazing,' said Max. 'Charges around like there's no tomorrow. A bit eccentric, of course. The very first day we were out there he rushed up with an armful of chest X-rays – "Morning. Jameson's the name. Here you are . . ." – and starts handing them out, one X-ray each. All very odd. Then he says "Follow me" and rushes off down a corridor, out a little door and on to a big patch of grass. "Lovely day," he says. "Tutorial outside. Grass a bit damp. So we'll sit on these old chest X-rays." So we sit around on them, out in the sun like some mad picnic, all very nice, the girls flashing their thighs and the man rattling cheerfully through the hundred and one jolly things you can get free with your lung cancer . . . And then his ward rounds. Madly social. Like, it's not just the pneumonia that gets him fired up, it's the social stuff. He really wants to know who's looking after the old lady's cat while she's in with pneumonia. And who's looking after the lady next door's children while she's looking after the cat. So they tend to go on a bit. Apparently one time they were grinding round the ward, worrying about the bronchitis, the plumbing, the cat and the new gas cooker, with regular dips into recent advances in applied molecular biology for the benefit of the overseas post-graduates – gathered round him like flies, from countries you've never heard of – and time's going on, not that he'd notice, and it's one o'clock and people are beginning to think about lunch. Then it's half past one and people are getting bloody hungry. Then its quarter to two and he says "Gosh, that time already . . . How about breaking for a spot of lunch?", and Sam somebody, a registrar or something, mutters from the back row "Lunch? I didn't know they fed the bugger, I thought they just wound 'im up . . ." But he's OK. And serious about immunology. Says it's going to be really big in asthma. Breakthroughs on the way. So I kind of wondered about that, because you can't be interested in the immunology of everything at once, and there's a lot of asthma about.'

' "Boy immunologist brings hope to millions." '

'Piss off, Scott. It's getting serious. Been to see the man and all that. He was quite encouraging. Says he's hoping to expand his honours group to six, if he can maintain the quality. It should be all right.'

They were drinking in the pub nearest the Institute and Irving House. It was busy and a small shaggy man, the top of his fiddle lost under his beard, was playing jigs and reels and things in the little alcove on the way to the toilet. Scott was waiting with an empty glass for Max to realise it was his round.

'What about you?'

'Yes, please,' said Scott, pushing his glass across.

'I meant an honours year. You still trying for one?'

'I think so. Maybe physiology.'

'They're all mad,' said Max. 'A professor who's the only guy in the world who uses words like dysdiadochokinesia in casual asides, and lot of mad inventors in smocks in the basement. Try bacteriology. Not a lot of people want to do it so they hand out a lot of firsts. Or you might even get into immunology. I mean if he's going to take six of us . . . And he's a very bright guy, obviously going places.'

'What's he like?'

'Killick? Well, bright. Senior lecturer at thirty four, reader at thirty eight. His own unit. Well, virtually. Still a sort of branch of Pathology and Neurology, but his own thing, and the only show in town. That's bright . . . So I went to him and said all the stuff about meeting him at the Society, and hearing about the course from Gus, and how I'd been interested in immunology for years . . . I was actually there for half an hour. Well, quarter of an hour waiting to see him, then the same again with him. In the Clinical Neuro-Immunology Unit. Amazing place, up above Endocrinology, in a lot of huts on a flat roof. Saw Gus too, actually. Slogging away there in the lab . . . Beginning to panic about final honours, I guess, because he was a bit grumpy. Oh. Another pint?'

'Thanks. Export.'

'Sure.'

Max reached the bar just in time. Behind him, advancing from the door, came half a dozen young men in tartan waistcoats with a couple of fierce-looking women in tow. They hailed the barman, waved cheerfully to the fiddler and couple of other people in the pub and generally gave the appearance of taking the place over.

'Bloody poets,' Max muttered as he returned with their drinks.

Sandy sat on her bed and counted again even though she really didn't need to. She had never been late in her life and nine worrying days could no longer simply be put down to worry: nine days since she should have started and nineteen since her visit to Gus's flat in the Grassmarket, so eight months and so many days until it was born, if that was what was going to happen, and almost six years till it could go to school, and about seventeen before it could begin going to bed with whichever sex it wasn't and start the whole thing off all over again. And if it had any sense it would be a boy.

The day after her visit Gus had phoned and been quite sweet, talking as though the room was full of people or the phone was being tapped but asking her if she would like to come with him to a private view and then a film the following Friday. She had gone, and met one or two people she had vaguely known from school, then they had held hands through *A Man for All Seasons* and he had driven her home and come in for a coffee and sat with mum and her in the kitchen, as though he were one of the family, doing quite well and not talking about himself too much. As she had seen him off the premises he had asked her out again, although it had been more like giving her a list of all the things in his diary for the rest of term that he needed a partner for. They had gone down the tunnel of bushes to the side gate and he had kissed her quite keenly in the dark before roaring off in his boy racer. As she watched she had rather wished she was going with him, for more and better sex with reasonable precautions, but it was nice that he had talked to mum. But all that was before she had been worried, and the last time she had seen him she had been only slightly worried. Tonight, she decided, might be interesting.

Over breakfast, while a man on the radio went on and on about a panda in a zoo which couldn't have pups or whatever, poor thing, she took stock. She was a medical student, 20, as they said in the papers. Her boyfriend, if that was what he really was, was a medical student, 22. Her father, 49, described as a medical practitioner and professor of endocrinology, had sensibly married her mother, 47, also a medical practitioner, yonks before they had her, as people had tended to in those days, sensible old them. It was when she got round to Gus's parents that it all got a bit difficult. Her own mum would be sensible, because of her work and how she basically was; his was sloshed all the time. Her dad might mutter a bit; his would go off the deep end, or whatever Vice-Presidents of Royal College of Physicians did to express their extreme displeasure. It was very hard to imagine them all gathering happily round for a quick little wedding and taking cheerfully to a bit of premature grandparent-hood, if that was what was going to happen. And maybe, still maybe, all this worry was about nothing, which would be unbelievably marvellous, because normal, uncomplicated life could just suddenly begin again. Sandy looked across the table at her mum and dad, who were swapping pages of the *Scotsman* so they could both read it at once, and nearly burst into tears.

Gus took a sterilized pipette and dipped it into a solution of the bean stuff that was supposed to transform lymphocytes into big, lively antibody-producing cells, drew up a tiny amount and transferred it to the tissue-culture that might or might not contain viable lymphocytes from the blood of someone with early and aggressive multiple sclerosis. Cell culture work, he had decided some weeks before, was not the stuff of which good undergraduate research projects were made. You needed to be fanatically patient and fastidiously clean, because if you weren't things just didn't grow, and inoculation of all the bean stuff in the world wouldn't make any difference.

In theory it had all been very simple. If multiple sclerosis was a disorder of immunity there would be evidence of the disorder in the immune system. You would be able to detect signs that the body was itself producing things that damaged the sheaths of nerve cells and so crippled and killed people like Fiona, or the boy he had started with, Mark, whose disease had been so active that he had died already. The method Roger had chosen had been adapted from one the haematologists used quite routinely now. The trouble was that even if you discounted all the difficulties of cell culture, there wasn't much you could do about the shortage of lymphocytes in the nervous system. You got only a few in cerebrospinal fluid, so they had decided he should try to use lymphocytes from the patient's blood as well. If Gus were to be honest with himself, they were actually using them instead, because so few of the lymphocytes from cerebrospinal fluid had been any good. But with the title of the project fixed in advance and the introduction, already written, referring to cerebrospinal fluid lymphocytes, there wasn't much scope for manoeuvre. One made the best of it.

Gus discarded the pipette for re-sterilisation and swirled the cell-culture dish with a neat flick that mixed the culture medium without spilling it, then marked its label with the date and time of the phytohaemagglutinin inoculation and put it back in the incubator to grow, if indeed there was anything in it that was still alive. He removed the next dish, put it on the bench in front of him and began to wonder if he wouldn't be making better use of his time by just pushing off to the library. The project, after all, counted for only about a third of the marks used in grading for honours, and if what he really wanted was a first there were more marks lying around in the library, so to speak, than in the laboratory. The alternative, an option with much to be said for it, was to cut a few corners on the project, so that he wouldn't be wasting time on what was after all a less important part of the overall assessment, and make up for it with a really honest effort to do as well as possible in the written papers and the oral exam. He simply marked the label of the second dish and put it back in the incubator. That, Gus decided, was not only cutting a corner but facing the facts. Whatever else the bean stuff did for lymphocytes, it didn't raise them from the dead. As he was closing the incubator Cathcart wandered into the laboratory, quite typically without knocking.

Cathcart, who seemed to be sniffing around looking for Roger, sat down uninvited at the lab bench and started to quiz Gus about his project, saying a number of uncomfortable things about the difficulties of doing anything that relied on a supply of lymphocytes from cerebrospinal fluid. He had been in the audience when Gus had addressed the Society, so he knew the basic ideas and experiments, but from the sound of things might even have looked up a few of the references for himself. His basic point, that the things that happened in multiple sclerosis tended to happen in places where there weren't any lymphocytes you could get at, was all too true. He sat there looking a shrunken version of the most Jewish Beatle, chewing gum and waving his hands, talking with a Glasgow accent and telling him, Angus Ratho, now rather more than three quarters way through an honours course in immunology, where he had gone wrong.

'Lymphocytes are great if you can get 'em, Gus. It's just there aren't that many of them about . . . What about all those other cells you get in the brain and the spinal cord? I mean I know you can't actually go digging for them . . . Well, maybe you could, if they happen to be having brain surgery for something else. But what about those cells you get in there, not actual neurones . . . Yeah. Got it. Oligodendrocytes. That's probably where the real action is in multiple sclerosis. Have you thought of them, Gus? I mean it's probably a bit late for your project . . . But I was actually thinking of doing some neuro-immunology myself next year, you know, when I'm in the honours immunology course. D'you reckon your basic technique, the thing you're doing with the lymphocytes, when you can get hold of them, would work with oligodendrocytes?'

'That's a jolly interesting idea, Max . . .' Gus tried to make it sound impatient but not impolite. 'Actually, Max, I'm in the middle of doing some phytohaemagglutin inoculations, and the timing's fairly critical.'

'Great. I can give you a hand. I mean, if I'm going to be doing it myself with oligodendrocytes next year it'd actually be very helpful . . .'

'Sorry, Max. Kind of you to offer, but cell culture's such a terribly unforgiving business. These are living things one is dealing with, and every minute counts . . . but awfully nice of you to drop in. I'm sure Mrs Gillsland will know where Roger is if he's not in his office. She's just along the corridor. Second door on the right.'

Although Max had taken the hint he was still hanging around the department, which meant that instead of pushing off to the library Gus had to stay in the lab kicking his heels, with a few cell-culture bits and pieces lying around in case the little shit came back or even just put his nose to the glass in the door. Eventually he inoculated a few more dishes more or less to pass the time, and on a lab notepad jotted down some of the things that he would concentrate on reading in detail once he did get a chance to get over to the library, where it would have been useful to be able to spend the whole evening. Unfortunately, he had already committed himself to picking Sandy Lennox up at seven thirty for the Distressed Practitioners' Benevolent Fund spring reception in the College of Physicians.

Sandy lay in her bath and thought about her first proper boyfriend, a very organised young man from Daniel Stewart's who was now a supply officer in the Navy and still wrote to her sometimes from all sorts of exotic places, and with whom this sort of thing would just never have happened. They had met at a friend's house when they were both still at school and she had invited him to their last end of term dance and for most of a dreamy summer they had gone around with a crowd doing nice things that everybody's parents mostly approved of, like swimming and films and parties at each others' houses. After six weeks together they had discussed it sensibly and decided to go ahead, being sensible, and he had organised everything and it had all been very easy and lovely and sometimes when she thought about it she still missed him. He was somewhere on the other side of the world now, calmly organising things in a ship that would never suddenly find itself running out of potatoes or short of sailors or behind with its correspondence, and with him she had never been worried once.

Being sensible about being worried was something she was gradually learning. There was no point in panicking or confiding in anyone or even looking worried enough to invite the kind of questions that inevitably resulted in a revealing cover-up. The only sensible thing to do was wait a bit longer, until it either definitely was or definitely wasn't, and then tell Gus, not trying to tie him down or make him feel guilty, but because he had a right to know before anyone else and it might even bring out the best in him. In the short term, meaning tonight, the sensible thing to do was to aim for business as usual: doing a reasonable job eating and drinking for the benefit of the Distressed Practitioners, and looking after Gus, whose research project was getting a bit difficult in the home straight and who had his big-deal honours immunology finals coming up, not just boring old things like her bacteriology, which you could have learned at school if they lent out the bugs.

So there was no point in lying in the bath wondering how long you would go on looking like that. Sandy got up and dried herself, glancing at the mirror but trying not to, and then got dressed – semi-posh, early summery – and went downstairs. Mum and dad were in the first floor sitting room, having a sherry and talking before dinner, which was one of the nice things they did that Sandy had always thought of as worth copying herself later on. Her dad smiled as if he was surprised and pleased to see her, and her mum looked approving and asked her if she would like a wee sherry. She took one and they sat around like people in a play awaiting the arrival of the still unwitting perpetrator of the dark deed behind the awful secret that the audience knew about already from Act One.

* * *

'Sandy, dear . . . How marvellous! Of course I remember you. And Gus has talked *so* much about you. And how good of you to turn out for my poor DP's . . .' Sandy shook a gloved hand and smiled and nodded. Mopsy Ratho grinned, showing some lipstick on her teeth. 'People think we can just forget about them because of the NHS and all that, but they have lots of special things to face that only the Fund really understands . . . Marvellous, dear, have a wonderful time.' She paused in a fuddled way as though she had run out of things to say that didn't need thinking about, then suddenly brightened up. Speaking straight to Sandy she said 'And why don't you and Gus join us later? Just a few committee people and some friends, for a bite at the Cafe Royal. . . ? Ranald would be *so* pleased.' From the corner of her eye Sandy could see that Gus wasn't keen but couldn't object, so she wondered about making her swotting an excuse for them both not going, then thought it would sound feeble because everybody, including them, was going to be quite drunk quite soon. Before she could say anything Gus was smiling bravely and saying it would be lovely, which was sweet of him, and if it didn't go on too long they might still manage a quiet hour in his flat on the way home. She smiled and thanked Mrs Ratho properly and they stood there like a happy young couple until she started looking around over their shoulders. 'Marvellous, darlings,' she breathed, 'but must circulate . . . See you later . . .' She teetered off into the crowd, tall and skinny and drunk. Gus smiled bravely again, and Sandy took his hand and squeezed it. Maybe she would forget all about them and they could just push off and go straight to bed.

'Gosh, yes . . .' said Gus. 'Wonderful news, isn't it?'

'And they should get a jolly good hospital for fifteen million pounds . . .' said Professor Jameson.

'Not quite as much as that, dear . . .' said his wife. 'Fourteen million, three hundred and eighty five thousand was the figure quoted in the *Scotsman*, I think you'll find.'

Professor Jameson screwed his face up briefly, as though trying to visualise the newspaper in detail. 'I'm sure you're right, dear . . . And if they'd only stick another fifteen bob on the end of it they could get a nice brass knocker for the front door.'

Sandy thought that was funny and laughed out loud, which cheered Professor Jameson up after his wife being so tough on him.

'But the main thing is,' said Gus, 'they're getting on with it. Not perhaps as big as everyone had hoped . . .'

'Eight hundred and sixty beds compared with nine hundred and eighty at present,' said Mrs Jameson, 'but a viable unit that could be extended if necessary . . .'

'Might be a bit messy having the builders in for ten years though,' said Professor Jameson. 'That's what really worrying the chaps who work there. One can certainly sympathise . . .' He put a hand on Sandy's sleeve. 'Just had two weeks of them for a new bathroom at home. The kind of thing that might persuade a chap to settle for the hospital he's got.'

'And a quite senior official at the Board's in charge of the whole project,' said Esmee Jameson. 'Someone called Smith. Such a reassuring name.'

'Quite. But I think it's awfully important for the Institute to stay where it is,' said Gus. 'Even if it does mean a bit of an upheaval while they're building the new one. People would be prepared to put up with that for the convenience of a central site . . . More for the patients than for anyone else of course, and then there's the continuity of a great tradition . . .'

'Come on, Gus, you're sounding like the chairman of the Board of Governors already. Nothing sacred about hospitals, either where they are or what they're called. Accidents of history, most of them, hardly any of them what we need today. Take the Institute, the legacy of a fashionable Victorian charity . . . Or those dozens of Emergency Medical Service places that got thrown up in convenient fields away from the bombing during the war. And now you want to put all that money into a cramped, sloping site so difficult it'll take ten years to finish?'

'Oh, well . . .'

Sandy felt a bit sorry for Gus again. Professor Jameson was treating him, she realised, as an equal: throwing arguments at him that were real and difficult and not just cocktail-party chatter. He smiled and turned on her. 'So how would you spend your fifteen million, Sandy?'

'Oh, gosh.' Sandy had heard some of the alternatives discussed at home and tried to remember them. 'Well, I know some people think you could shift the Meadows, so to speak. Build it all on the flat bit next to where it is now, move in when it was finished, and then put grass where it was before.'

'Hm,' said Professor Jameson. 'Good thought, Sandy. Two problems. One, millions of people get very strange whenever anyone wants to mess around with the Meadows. Two, you'd have to build about fifteen storeys if you wanted ten showing above ground when you'd finished . . . Awfully soggy, the Meadows.'

'I'd be terribly concerned about losing all the valuable links with the University in any major move away,' said Gus, sounding grand again. 'I know in my own field we're awfully keen to stay in touch with the pure scientists . . .'

'No problem, Gus. Do what we do. Couple of tame scientists on site. That and using the phone a lot . . . But it's jolly cosy, I expect, working in a hospital where every time you open a broom cupboard some struggling new department falls out.'

Sandy laughed again but Mrs Jameson was beginning to look as if she might be about to take her husband away, which was a pity because he was good fun and not in the least bit drunk. He was allowed one last contribution. 'My own view is that the whole matter be put in the hands of the Medical Students Council . . . If past form is anything to go on they're the only chaps who'll actually still be around when it all eventually gets built. But for some reason most of my professorial colleagues disagree.'

'Now, darling, we really must have a word with the Szymanskis. So do excuse us. Lovely to see you both . . .' Professor Jameson gave them a friendly nod with his face screwed up and followed his wife off in the direction indicated. Sandy began to feel the tiniest bit funny but immediately stopped herself thinking anything silly. It was too soon and anyway evening lightheadedness was nothing to do with morning sickness, much more to do with a sherry and a glass of Distressed Practitioners' fizzy wine on an empty stomach. Gus laid his hand on her shoulder and said closely in her ear 'Are you all right, Sandy?', which definitely did make her feel funny. She said she was, and wasn't Professor Jameson good fun, and was there something to eat somewhere.

They found someone with a tray of little sausage rolls. Gus had a couple and Sandy had four without thinking much about it, which made her worry about herself all over again. Then they talked to Tommy Johnston, a surgeon she knew because he went fishing with her dad and quite often sat drinking whisky in the kitchen at home afterwards. Gus didn't know him, so she introduced them and he grilled Gus about why he was doing a year off in immunology when he could be getting on with the serious business of medicine. Gus handled him quite well, allowing for his rough surgical ways, which were an affectation anyway, and quickly moving the subject round to fishing, something he knew much more about than Sandy had suspected. Then the surgeon's wife, a consultant dermatologist, joined them and they talked about their two children, who were surprisingly young, just finishing primary school. 'Only way to do it in a doctor-doctor marriage, Sandy,' said Tommy 'That's if you both want careers rather than jobs.' He clamped a hand affectionately on his wife's nearer buttock. 'Postpone the pleasures of parenthood until you're very near too old to go crawling round the floor.' Gus laughed nervously. Sandy took a deep sip of fizzy wine some of which went up into her nose and brought on a fit of coughing. Tommy slapped her back while his wife, who knew mum quite well, might just have been raising an eyebrow.

To Sandy's relief the quick bite in the Cafe Royal did not materialise. Mopsy had begun to feel unwell again and Ranald Ratho had had to take her straight home from the reception. Gus did not seem very concerned, but muttered something about the added strain of organising things when you didn't do it very often. Sandy felt sorry for him and decided to try to have an honest chat about it all one of these days, which would be sensible and helpful and not particularly disturbing for him since everyone knew anyway. For now she held his hand while they walked to the car. As they were driving across George Street she said she was hungry so Gus turned suddenly off into Rose Street and they went to a Greek place there that he knew. They sat at a little table and played footsie while they were waiting to be served, and because of the wine and possibly being pregnant Sandy began to feel very possessive about Gus, and imagining that they were married already and having a nice honeymoon somewhere on a Greek island and had left all their troubles in Edinburgh. It was silly but it passed the time, and even when she stopped thinking about it she was still happy because she could quite easily have been in the Cafe Royal for a long loud meal with a lot of drunk people, instead of which she was here with Gus to herself, having a nice quiet dinner on the way to bed.

Gus, who had been to Greece already, was helpful with the menu, and they had egg and lemon soup then kebabs and rice and just coffee, dark and bitter, and eventually left the restaurant and went back to the car. This time he took her hand, and asked if she would like to pop up to his flat, as he put it, and when they got there it was all a lot easier than it had been before, for reasons that Sandy afterwards found both strange and obvious. They didn't actually bother with coffee since they'd just had some, but sat on the sofa looking out at the Castle and talking about his mother, who had been drinking a lot for as long as he could remember, but probably a bit more lately and definitely far more now than was good for anyone. He described how she topped herself up all the time, with sherry until lunchtime and gin thereafter. She was hardly ever drunk – tonight had been a bad night – but never really sober either. She managed things at home because everyone pretended not to notice and there was a good cook-housekeeper, and she survived on her committees because she chose her friends and timed her drinking carefully. Sandy first wondered how it felt to live like that then understood more clearly why Gus had set up on his own in a flat when his parents had a perfectly good big house in Murrayfield. As he talked about home, and what it was like when Mopsy, as he called her, was just being her normal self, ie drinking about a bottle of sherry and a bottle of gin a day, Sandy felt utterly sorry for him and infinitely more sympathetic about a lot of things. He came from the kind of home that people envied, and expected you to be happy in and proud of, and he had been miserable and insecure there and had got out as soon as possible, but couldn't really get away and was still ashamed of it. His mother, who was foolish and ill together – it hardly mattered which came first – was a disaster for herself and her family. Sandy could forgive him a lot of things because of that: his diffidence, his vanity and his shallow ambition. He had never had anyone he could trust, and he would be a better person now that he had. And if God had any sense she wouldn't be pregnant after all.

'Sorry, Sandy,' he said after a long silence. 'My little local difficulties must be very boring for you.' She shook her head and put her arms round his neck and looked into his eyes and then kissed him because it was a lot easier than saying patronising things like 'I understand, my darling, and always will, say nothing more about it.' They stood up and he put his arms round her because he still wasn't very good at saying he wanted her to go to bed with him. This time they undressed first and he was an awful lot better at the preliminaries: quick and loving and obviously dying for it. When she was aching for him he stopped suddenly and reached over for something from the drawer of his bedside table. 'Best to take some precautions, Sandy. Be an absolute disaster if, um, anything happened.'

'This is the dirty turret,' said Robbie. 'We don't come in here much except to watch . . . Registrar jobs like big abscesses, really dirty ulcers, that kind of stuff. And the nurses use it too, mainly for chemical warfare.'

Scott had understood all of that except the last bit. Robbie laughed. 'Against the dreaded clockwork dandruff. It's worth seeing. Once anyway, if you can go straight home and have a bath afterwards. They strip them off, douse them with the powder, leave them for a while to let it work then go in, still in their plastic pinnies of course, and drag them off for a bath round the back. And see, it's all tiled so you can more or less hose it out afterwards.' Scott nodded. 'The nurses do all the really rough stuff. You can see why. And over here . . .' They moved a few yards across the semi-basement that housed the Institute's Casualty Department. '. . . the clean turret. Evening, Terry . . . Terry, this is Andrew, in to learn the rudiments, so he'll probably be coming along to you shortly. Andrew, Terry.'

A short, sleek, reddish-haired man in a white coat with its top pocket stuffed with assorted pens, spatulas and scissors looked up from his task and smiled. 'See you shortly, Andrew.' He stooped forward again and frowned in concentration, halfway along an eight inch laceration in a tattooed forearm and pulling its edges together with another black, blood-slippery stitch. The patient, a young man with long greasy hair and variety of fresh-looking facial bruises, was looking the other way and whistling through his teeth. 'That's the kind of thing you should start on,' said Robbie as they turned to go. 'Long, straight laceration, not on the face or anything and with a good blood supply. Forearm's not bad. It's the shin you've got to watch. Transverse pre-tibial lacerations are a nightmare, especially if the flap's facing the wrong way . . . But stuff like that's dead easy.' Robbie laughed again. 'Provided he's not too fussy about getting the edges of his tattoo neatly joined up.'

'And the chap doing it . . . What's he? A registrar?'

'God no. Not sure what he is. I mean he just comes in. A

volunteer, I suppose . . . Might be a hairdresser or something. Not sure, but a bloody marvellous stitcher. Taught hundreds of people. Have you done a lot of oranges?'

'Sorry?'

'Oh. Never mind, you can only learn so much from them. I mean they don't bleed or jump about or vomit over you, do they? But some people stitch up fresh orange peel before they start here. But there's no substitute for the real thing, and Terry's your man . . . So, continuing the grand tour . . . Hello, Jeannie. That's Jeannie. Staff nurse. Loves the dirty turret stuff, so worth keeping on the right side of.'

After several invitations Scott had agreed to join Robbie in his usual Friday evening routine, which was to spend the hours between seven and midnight in the Casualty Department. According to Robbie you learned a lot, met a lot of registrars, got to see some really ill patients, learned applied anatomy and even got to sew it up again, and it was usually a lot more interesting than going to the pictures. That afternoon Scott and Robbie had gone to meet the surgeon in charge for a kind of official introduction and vetting. Mr Gillon, a gruff, bald man in a tiny, cluttered office in a warren of corridors at the back of the department, had looked Scott over, asked him what school he had gone to and what exams he had failed in the medical course so far. Scott's answers must have been satisfactory, because he had then been told he could come in on one night a week, preferably with Robbie, for a probationary period of one term after which he should come and see Mr Gillon again. Less than three hours later he was there in his white coat, if not actually ready for action at least ready to watch while others did their stuff.

'And this is the Intensive Care Area.' They stood looking into an empty room with a big light hanging from the ceiling and some shelves crowded with impressive bottles and shiny tools. 'Actually it's not very intensive, as you can see. But it's all right for now and the Department's going to be the first bit of the Institute to be replaced when they rebuild it. Jock Gillon's chuffed to bits with himself. Ah. Yes. And this is the exciting stuff. All the major casualties that are on their way are put up on that board. Just names and something to say roughly what they are. Like RTA for road traffic accident. So the alert student . . .' Robbie grinned again. '. . . always keeps an eye on that board.'

For the moment it was blank. They moved on. 'We don't go in there very much.' Robbie indicated another, larger room furnished mainly with trolleys and curtains. 'It's lying-down patients, all the medical emergencies, and some surgical ... Hello, Jinty ... Another staff nurse ... And usually the GP's phoned the case in already. In which case their names would be on that board. No. The other one. See? Easy when you get a hold of it once. Uh-oh.' Robbie cocked an ear. High on the wall above, a small plain loudspeaker had clicked into life and begun to hiss and crackle. 'Sounds like some action.' Within the ethereal, egg-frying noises a voice croaked. 'What's that?' Scott asked. 'Sshh. Listen,' said Robbie.

The voice said something indistinct. A staff nurse arrived in a flurry of white and peered up at the loudspeaker just as it fell silent 'Aitchman or Aitken,' said Robbie. 'Bleeding ulcer. Half an hour.'

'Thanks, Robbie,' said the staff nurse, writing 'Aikman – GI bleed – c. 8.00 pm' on the board. She disappeared into the Intensive Care Area.

'See?' said Robbie. 'The system works. The ambulance men radio them in and Jinty will have everything set up. And this is Minor Trauma. You know, the kind of stuff that walks in. Sprained fingers and cut ankles, as they say in the trade. So it's really where you should try to pick up your experience.' They moved on into a big room with three of its walls taken up by little screened cubicles like confessionals for the afflicted. Robbie nosed around, glancing at notes scribbled on the clipboards that seemed to accompany each patient. 'Let's just see if there's something you might want to have a crack at, a simple slash somewhere only their closest friends will see. No. Not that. And certainly not that. Sorry, Andy. And the rest is all "Please X-ray . . ." Sorry. But on the other hand it's not even eight o'clock yet, so don't worry, you'll get your chance, I promise you. Oh. Hello, Bert. You in here tonight?'

'Just covering while the senior house officer's off eating.'

'I see. Bert, this is Andy Scott . . . My year. In for a bit of Casualty experience. He's seen Jock and all that. Keen to do a bit of stitching if you see anything suitable.'

The registrar nodded and Robbie led Scott on through the department. It was all rather odd. Robbie, a third year student, was acting as if he were a permanent and fairly senior member of staff. Even odder, everyone else seemed to accept him more or less at his own valuation. Scott thought about it and realised that his friend could quite well have been around the place longer than many of the medical staff, because his Friday sojourns had begun eighteen months before and most of the Casualty Department's medical staff served for six months or at most a year. And Robbie was still so engagingly and eccentrically keen about it all, as if he had what the priests in Bolgatanga referred to as 'a vocation within a vocation': the kind of wild but harmless enthusiasm – such as touring the bush with a mobile cinema showing Shakespeare films to bewildered aboriginals – that usually meant the chap was overdue for a bit of home leave.

But there was probably more to it than that. Robbie had mentioned once that he thought having seen things and done things in Casualty would probably help a bit with his intended career of surgery. Over coffee in the lounge at the back Scott raised the subject again. Robbie elaborated with curious modesty. 'Surgeons are funny folk. As soon as they see what medals you've got – especially in things like physiology and pharmacology – they start convincing themselves you're no good because you spend all your time in the library. So, more than most people, I need all the practical experience I can get . . . And it gives you stacks of things to look up as well. Medical as well as surgical. Saw a case of erythromelalgia a couple of weeks ago . . . You'd never see that on the wards in a hundred years.' Scott looked interested, because the quickest way of learning rarities was to let Robbie explain them. 'A circulatory thing. Red bumps on your fingers and toes that go away by the time you've got an appointment at Medical Out-Patients. Not important, but quite interesting really. Harmless. You tell them that and they're quite happy. What about you, Andy?'

'Hm?'

'Your career. Still heading for psychiatry?'

'Psychiatry?'

'Oh. I'm sure you said you were going to do psychiatry. On that mad pub-crawl with Max, just when we started.'

Scott had vague, embarrassing recollections of wanting to be a psychiatrist; worse, of having told people. 'Must have been the fifth pub. Don't remember a thing about it.'

'The third. You wanted to understand things.'

'Did I? I'm not sure now that they do.'

'Psychiatrists? Probably not. And Max was going to be an immunologist.'

'Still is. Plotting to get into honours with that chap Killick.'

'Good luck to him. A shit by all accounts. It's funny. I wanted to find the cure for TB.' Robbie stretched and yawned. 'But Jimmy Jameson and his crowd beat me to it, so I'm going to be a famous surgeon instead.'

The lounge was a bleak, windowless room at the back of the department. It smelt of stale coffee and cigarettes. There was a kettle, some mugs, a selection of battered and unmatching armchairs and a couple of dog-eared newspapers. Not much in itself, Scott thought as he sipped his coffee, but being there in a white coat and vaguely waiting for something to happen was progress: a long march from the dissecting room with its tattered, acrid corpses and mad demonstrators; an equally useful distance from tutorials in the basement with strange physiologists whose rooms looked like the cells of a forgotten civilisation of mechanically-minded hermits; an improvement even on the rituals of ward teaching, which was medicine made easy by the registrars or, as in the crazed posturing of George Gordon, wildly impossible, a pastime fit for demigods alone. Here, as Robbie said, you not only saw things, you did things too, even if it was only a couple of stitches somewhere that wouldn't show.

They finished their coffee and strolled round the department again. Though it was still well before nine things had definitely livened up. Two policemen stood holding a drunk, his trousers dripping sadly, at the front desk. Behind them a skinny youth was dabbing a gashed lip with a handkerchief that might be a risk in itself and behind him was a little old lady holding her wrist. One of the policemen seemed to recognise Robbie, who greeted him warmly. Scott listened as they had a short, disjointed conversation about an assault case in connection with which charges were now pending ('We kent wha did it, ken . . . Jist a question o' gettin' a wee statement oot o' the bidie-in, ken what that's like . . .'). As they proceeded up the corridor Terry emerged from his clean turret.

'Robbie, I've got just the case for your friend . . . Andrew, is it? Just on the point of popping round to see if you were still round the back. It is Andrew, isn't it?'

Scott nodded. 'On you go,' said Robbie. 'I'll leave you to it.'

'This way, Andrew.' Scott followed Terry down a vapour trail of Old Spice back to the clean turret, where a florid-complexioned middle-aged lady lay on a trolley smiling happily up in the direction of the ceiling. 'Hazel, dear. Here's the young man I mentioned . . . Hazel's what you might call one of our regulars. You don't mind me telling him, do you, Hazel? And just show us again, dear. Let's have a peek.'

Hazel hiccoughed and stuck out her right arm. Terry flicked a gory gauze dressing from her forearm, revealing a three-inch laceration still oozing from its edges. 'See, Andrew. Beer glass trouble again . . . I keep telling her, it's the company she keeps. Could have been worse, though. Last time she came in she'd sat on one, hadn't you, dear?' Hazel hiccoughed again. 'You gonnae do it or are ye no'?'

'Any minute now, Hazel . . . We'll just get our gloves on, won't we?' Terry opened a packet containing a pair of rubber gloves and indicated that Scott should do the same, then he put them on, deftly avoiding any contact with their outside surface, and watched as Scott fumbled to do the same. 'You'll get the idea,' he breathed. 'I'll just take you through it gently, seeing it's your first time.'

'Is he a student?'

'In a manner of speaking, Hazel. And we all have to learn our jobs. Even yours . . . So for a little thing like this, Andrew, I'd suggest a three-nothing black silk. Probably about eight or nine stitches. The usual mistake is to put in too many to start with. That and too tight. Have you tried it with an orange, Andrew? No? Straight into the real thing? Why not? Most people do these days . . . There we are, an integral suture. Nice little curved needle, and your three-nothing black silk's permanently threaded already. See. And a quick click . . .' He snapped a pair of forceps on to the needle ' . . . and you're off. Oh. Very well. I'll do a couple just to give you the idea. All right, Hazel? Just a little one. There!'

He flicked the point of the needle through the skin edge and into the laceration, then up through the skin on the opposite edge, did something fast and precise with suture, forceps and a pair of tweezers and was pulling a knot tight before Scott could really see how it was done. 'Now there's a little pair of scissors, Andrew, if you'd care to snip that . . . Lovely. Well, a bit on the short side, actually, but nobody's perfect. One more from me and then it's your turn. Watching again? There we are . . . Over to you. Andrew.'

Scott took the forceps holding the needle and prodded the skin edge much as Terry had done. It scarcely dimpled. 'Oh no, Andrew, our Hazel's a tough girl. You'll need a bit more of your strength than that.' He had come unnecessarily close, his Old Spice oppressive even in competition with Hazel's stale booze and staler clothes. 'Like this.' His gloved hand enclosed Scott's and drove the needle through skin for him. 'But it's actually a bit easier going the other way . . . No. Not so far out. Ideal. Now, push! Good. Well, near enough. Just pull on through, Andrew. And now for the difficult bit, but remember, everything comes to he who practices. And it's not just your old Boy Scout left over right and under. Look.'

Terry stood behind the bar-stool thing that Scott was sitting on, looking closely over his right shoulder. 'There we are. In and out. That's the first bit. Bit of a jerk, not too tight. All right, Hazel? Now your loop . . . Pop through with your forceps, nip the end, and a little tweak. Gentle but firm, I always say. It's living skin we're dealing with. Lovely. Your first stitch. Shall I trim it, sir?'

With a smile and flourish Terry snipped away the redundant black silk thread. 'Now you're absolutely on your own, Andrew. Or shall we just do one more together?' Because of the Old Spice and the heavy breathing and the fact that being helped by Terry meant being practically embraced by him, Scott thought he might try the next one on his own. Halfway through it Hazel absentmindedly used her right hand to scratch herself, which slowed things up a bit, but the stitch when he finished it, pulling the knot tight, looked much the same as the other two. Terry's praise was muted but Scott slogged on, his clumsiness diminishing with each new effort, until the gap in Hazel's forearm had been closed by eight stitches, six of them his own. A bit more fussing by Terry with a swab, a soapy wash and a spray with some stuff like nail-varnish signified the end of the procedure.

To Scott's surprise Hazel thanked him as she clambered down from the trolley. 'Thanks very much, son. And all the best. Maybe see you again.' He smiled and nodded then took off his gloves and flicked them into a waiting bin as though he'd been doing it for years. 'A pleasure, Miss um . . . Hazel . . .'

'Cheerybye, dear.' She waved at Terry and shuffled off down the corridor with a little card of instructions about tetanus which she seemed likely to ignore. 'Dirty old cow,' said Terry. 'But all right for a bit of practice . . . For the likes of you.'

There was no one else who needed the kind of stitching that Scott could now offer, so he went back through the department to the lounge, where Robbie was sitting with a couple of the staff nurses, one of whom was in the middle of rather a complicated account of a patient who had been in the department that afternoon. ' . . . so the third time she came back with this arm with nothing much wrong with it Ronnie was going to kick her out but she was quite a nice wee woman and obviously worried, so I sat her down and asked her what she thought was wrong with her arm . . . It's a bit sore there, she said, and there's that lump and I'm sure it's getting bigger. So I said no, everybody's got a lump there . . . It's normal. Look. There's mine. And let's see your other wrist. I'll show you. And she had this funny leather glove on the other hand. Hadn't taken it off all morning. Well, she said, that's the problem, dear, I've only got one arm. And the other one was this wooden thing with a leather covering . . .' She giggled and Robbie was rolling about in his chair guffawing. 'She'd lost it, see? From some kind of cancer of bone. You could see why she was worried. So I got Ronnie back and he was great, really nice to her . . . And when she went away he said "Sorry, staff. But this is a busy department and we really can't be expected to spend a lot of precious time counting everybody's arms."'

'What a hoot,' said Robbie, writhing with delight. 'Sit down, Andy. You know Jeannie? Liz?' Scott sat down and Liz, who had listened to her friend's story with obvious concern and not laughed much at the end, offered him a crisp.

'How'd you get on with Terry?'

'Hm. Odd bod.'

Robbie laughed again. 'Odd as the proverbial nine bob note . . . The thing is not to upset him, or he flounces and everybody has to do their own stitching. Was that Hazel in there?'

'Yes . . . Hazel somebody . . .'

'You should have heard him the time she sat on a glass. "Beats me how she earns a living . . . Even before all this . . . " What had she done this time?'

'Oh, just an arm.'

Jeannie sniggered and Robbie said 'Yes, you got off lightly, young Scott . . . Is there anything interesting coming in, Jeannie? Time we got Andy into something a bit more exciting than Hazel's arm, eh?'

'Couple of things for the admitting surgeons, but it's still only . . .' She turned the little pendant watch on the bib of her apron up so that she could see its face. '. . . nine o'clock? Gosh. Come on, Liz. Back to the suffering millions.' The two nurses tidied up after their snack, washing their coffee cups and even the teaspoons they had used. 'See you, boys . . . We'll let you know if there's anything . . .'

'Thanks . . .' Robbie lolled back in his armchair. 'Jeannie's great and Liz is all right,' he pronounced, almost before the door had closed behind them. 'They run this place, the staff-nurses. There are a couple of sisters too, who don't seem to do very much, and an amazing woman who'll look in later. Deirdre, the deadly night-sister. You have been warned. But she doesn't come on till ten.'

'Hello, young man . . . Never expected to see you in here in your spare time . . .'

Scott turned round. 'Oh. Hello, Jamie.' Jamie Wilson, now a final year student, had once occupied one of the rooms on the ground floor at the back of Irving Hall, and had a wide circle of friends who at one time or another had clambered through his window. 'Just looking around . . . With Robbie.'

To Scott's surprise, Robbie, who seemed to know everybody, didn't know Jamie, so he introduced them, explaining how he knew Jamie. 'Ah,' said Robbie, 'the old Irving mafia. Can't get away from it.'

Jamie sat down. 'What brings you here?' Scott asked.

'Oh, just a bit of amateur toxicology. A wee project I'm trying to finish, on catecholamines in sedative self-poisoning . . . Started it in my elective but didn't get enough patients. Another half a dozen more should do it.'

'If people only knew, they'd try harder . . .' said Robbie. 'Help medical research. Take an overdose.'

'God knows, plenty of people just do it anyway. But it's the times they choose. Evenings and weekends, when men of sense would rather be doing something else.'

'Is there one coming in?' Robbie asked. It occurred to Scott that Jamie, perhaps inadvertently, had slighted Robbie's vocation within a vocation. Typically, Robbie hadn't noticed.

'GP phoned the medical registrar on call half an hour ago. And he rang me because I've been badgering him all day about this.'

'So what's the poison?' Robbie was being enthusiastic again.

'Methaqualone.'

'Oh. The dreaded Mandies. That's Mandrax, Andy. Filthy stuff that gives you the nastiest sleep of your life.' He laughed again. 'Or maybe the last. Twenty percent mortality in some series. They need to be washed out – that's dirty turret stuff – and watched pretty closely because they can go from coma to fits and back twice in ten minutes.'

'Very good, doctor,' said Jamie, smiling quietly at Robbie's performance. 'But let's get our priorities right . . . The first thing is a blood sample. For these catecholamines of mine . . . So how's life with you, young Scott?'

'No use complaining.'

'Which unit are you with?'

'Gordon, Smail and Patullo.'

Jamie laughed then said 'No, not a lot of use complaining. But some of the juniors are quite sane.'

'What about you, Jamie?'

'Revision term. Quite enjoyable. You meet all the people you haven't seen since the rotations began. And swotting's all right. You come across all sorts of things you've vaguely wondered about for years. And there's a morning lecture course, with the whole of medicine flashing before your eyes in about six weeks. So they all make a bit of an effort, and even tell you what's important and what's not.'

'Sounds marvellous. What about housejobs?'

'Oh, not too bad. Sir Edgar's unit for surgery . . .'

'Gosh. Well done, Jamie. And medicine?'

Jame coughed modestly. 'Sir Ronald's.'

'You're kidding,' said Robbie. 'You've got to be kidding. That's amazing. How d'you manage that?'

'Oh,' said Jamie, going a little pink. 'Don't really understand it myself. Strangest thing, really. But I suppose it might have been something to do with the old Irving mafia.' He chuckled and Robbie looked from Scott to Jamie and back twice over, a reaction which seemed to afford Jamie more quiet amusement. Scott, already familiar with Jamie's style, was amused too. If Jamie had got two of the best housejobs going, a double that very, very few newly qualified doctors pulled off, he had done it because he was efficient and organised and hardworking and bright and had done well in exams all through the course, and had managed all that without being in the least unpleasant about it. He would do well, and nobody would mind.

'How about a coffee, Jamie?' said Robbie suddenly, very much as though Jamie's forthcoming housejobs changed everything.

'Oh, thanks, Robbie. They said twenty minutes, but she's coming from quite far out.' Robbie made coffee, asked about milk and sugar, got it right, stirred it and handed it over as though Jamie were a chief already. Eventually, at about quarter to ten, Liz, the staff nurse, appeared at the lounge door. 'Dr Wilson? There's an overdose they said you wanted to see . . .' Jamie got up. Strictly speaking he wouldn't be a doctor for another eight weeks or so, but the staff nurse was right: he was the kind of sensible, bright chap that could have been one for years already. Scott and Robbie got up and followed him.

The woman on the trolley in the dirty turret was pale and deeply unconscious. She wore a pink nightie and lay on her side under a departmental blanket. A student nurse stood by her, stooping over her and listening at her elbow with a stethoscope as air hissed out of the blood-pressure cuff round her upper arm. 'It's a bit tricky, staff. Seems to be going up and down, but mainly low. Eighty over something.' The staff nurse checked it and marked a chart. 'We'll call it eighty five. But definitely down on what it was . . . And still right out of it . . . Clare. . . ? Mrs Gillsland . . . Wake up, dear . . .'

'Who's seen her, staff?' Robbie had moved towards the patient's head and was pinching her earlobe firmly. 'Hm. Pretty flat.' Her hair, long and the colour of gingerbread, had fallen across her face, so Robbie swept it to one side then flipped a pen-torch from his pocket and shone it into her left eye. The pupil was wide but contracted down with the light. 'Hm. Who's seen her, staff?'

'Well, nobody. Everybody's sort of busy. We've told the med. reg. but he's dealing with a coronary and . . .'

'Right. Let's get a drip up.' The staff nurse ran saline from a bottle on a drip-stand through a giving-set, shook the bubbles out and waited. Robbie reached for one of the little syringe things used for getting into veins. There were three lying side by side on the staff-nurse's tray, one green, one pink, one beige. He hesitated.

'Perhaps I can give a hand,' said Jamie, lifting the green one, snapping it open, testing the syringe and sliding the cannula into a vein on the forearm below the blood pressure cuff. 'D'you have a twenty mil syringe, staff?' He was handed one, connected it to the cannula without spilling a drop of blood, filled it and set it aside. Then he secured the saline drip into the cannula and stabilised it with strips of adhesive tape. 'I'd just keep it open, staff. Perhaps the most important thing is just to have a quick look at her and then try to wash her out.' Jamie checked her scalp, muttering something about people who looked like overdoses sometimes turning out to be head injuries, checked her pupils again with Robbie's torch, tested some tendon jerks and then, with the staff nurse's help, rolled her over so he could listen to her chest. He folded his stethoscope. 'Do we know how many she took, or when? Is there a GP's letter?'

It was on the clipboard, under the blood-pressure chart, and the GP who had written it thought she had taken between twenty and thirty Mandrax sleeping tablets some time between five thirty and six thirty. There was a PS. 'I should have mentioned in our telephone call that Dr Roger Killick, Royal Charitable Institute, may be interested in this case.'

Robbie, who had been reading over Jamie's shoulder, looked at Jamie. 'Is that who's supervising your research?'

'Certainly not,' said Jamie.

'Of course. He's an immunologist. But what's he doing. . . ?'

'Nothing immunological . . . She actually works here, this girl. With Killick . . . But from the story she would be well worth a washout.'

'I've done lots of those,' said Robbie. 'Dozens.' The staff nurse was nodding, which was reassuring.

'More than I have,' said Jamie. 'Maybe if you let the med. reg. know the details he'll ask you to go ahead . . . And say I've had a quick look at her too. But he might prefer to come along and do it himself. Certainly mention the Killick angle.'

'What's all this about?' said Robbie. 'What exactly am I supposed to tell him?'

'Tricky,' said Jamie, looking round in a way that suggested he was swearing all present to silence on the matter. 'Of course consultants at the Institute don't have mistresses, but if they did this girl would be Roger Killick's.' The student nurse's eyes widened. 'Works here, for him. They're married . . . You know, but not to each other . . . Oh, it might be simpler if I rang the med. reg. myself. And you'll be wanting some blood for routine investigations and a methaqualone level, won't you, doctor?' Jamie took four blood tubes from the staff nurse's tray, filled them from his syringe, labelled them with the patient's name and handed three back to the staff nurse. 'I'll ring him straight away. You're all set up for a washout?' The staff nurse nodded and Jamie left. Robbie was eyeing the thick red rubber tube, the funnel, the half-gallon jugs of water and broad stainless steel basin evidently used for washing out the stomach contents of patients who had taken an overdose.

Had it not been for that equipment, and the staff nurses, and the fact that she was lying on a steel trolley with barred sides in a constricted, completely white-tiled room with something of the gas-chamber about it, the woman under the blanket could simply have been enjoying an early night. She lay on her side, pale and relaxed, almost pretty, breathing steadily with an occasional light, musical snore. As Scott stood waiting for whatever it was that was going to happen next he noticed one or two other things about the trolley. The surface under the mattress on which the patient lay was a curved sheet of metal, ringed by a steel tube frame hinged at the forward edge, the one under her head. At the other end, emerging from under the sheet metal and curving down into the frame of the trolley, was a kind of ratchet arrangement evidently designed to tilt the patient into a head-down position. And at the level of the patient's chest and knees were two sets of broad leather straps. Both the nurses had started to put on big plastic aprons and white rubber boots.

'Robbie?' A woman from the reception desk popped her head round the door. Unabashed by the evolving execution-shed ritual, she smiled and said 'That was the med. reg. on the phone. He's on his way . . . Soon as he can . . . And could you please just start washing her out . . .'

'Thanks, Betty . . . OK, girls, we're off. You probably think it's a hell of a size of a tube, Andy, but it's got to let the pills and Chinese carry-outs and stuff like that come back up . . . Right, girls?'

The nurses first lifted the departmental blanket then rolled it tightly round the patient, pinioning her arms by her sides. When that was done they laid her on her side again, tucked her hair up under a plastic shower-cap, buckled the leather straps around her, raised the foot of the trolley and placed a steel basin on the white-tiled floor underneath her head. Robbie, by now also in white wellies and plastic apron, stuck a hand in one of the jugs. 'You want it warm, you know, body temperature, because most of these people are in enough trouble without getting hypothermia. So let's have a go . . . What goes down must come up, as they say. Unless you've left it too late.'

He picked up the red tube, which was at least an inch in diameter and about three feet long, and gently opened the patient's mouth. She stirred, first like someone waking from peaceful sleep, then angrily, rolling and writhing against the restraining blanket and straps. Her eyes opened briefly and she gagged and spluttered. Robbie took his hand away from her mouth and nodded to the staff nurse. 'All right, dear,' said the staff nurse. 'Just a wee tube in your throat . . . Help get the tablets up . . . All right?' The nurse held the patient's head tightly, a hand on either side, and Robbie tried again. Again she gagged and shuddered. 'OK, staff, I suppose we'll just have to . . .' The student nurse took over from her colleague, restraining the patient's head while the staff nurse inserted in the patient's mouth a curious device, a bit like ratcheted forceps, but with rubber-padded curved attachments that fitted around the patient's upper and lower front teeth and forced her jaws apart. She moaned and writhed and kicked helplessly as the gadget clicked home and held, leaving her gaping and disfigured, defenceless against the tube.

'There we go,' said Robbie, slipping it down effortlessly. 'Funnel and first jug, please.' A wide plastic funnel was fixed into the exposed end of the tube and half a gallon of salty water, poured steadily, swirled down out of sight. For a few moments nothing happened, then the girl's shoulders shook and her legs kicked helplessly against their strap. The end of the tube, now hanging free over the basin, spurted pints of cloudy fluid. 'Great,' said Robbie. 'Any pills?' The fluid drained freely then dwindled to a slow drip. The staff nurse picked up the basin, swilled it around a bit, squinting into it like someone panning for gold in a western, then looked up. 'Food debris, a few possible pills.'

'Great. Funnel and second jug please.' The patient's eyes

opened, in terror and disbelief, then closed again. The student nurse handed Robbie another heavy stainless steel jug brimming with warm saline. He turned to Scott as he poured. 'Basically you just slosh away till you get clear fluid back . . . But her problem might be blood levels . . . You know, from what she's absorbed before we could get at her. But this is what she needs right now, even if it doesn't actually look very nice.'

As the fourth jugful was coming up, almost clear, the door opened again. 'Hello, Robbie.'

'Oh, hello, Matthew.'

'Thanks, but I think I'd better take over . . .'

'Nearly there. Not a bad return, and clearing now.'

'Yes . . . But just let me finish her, will you? Jamie Wilson's just rung me. Bloody GP. He left out a major fact when he phoned me about this. Jamie filled me in . . . Oh. It's her.'

'Apparently a secretary in the Neuro-Immunology Unit . . .'

'Yes, yes. I mean I've seen her around the place, but I didn't know . . . Look, let's just give another jug so she had a registrar washout, OK?'

The staff nurse was nodding. Robbie stood back as Matthew, the admitting medical registrar, donned boots and apron and, with rather less style than Robbie, poured another four pints of warm saline down the tube and watched it come rushing up again and into the basin on the floor.

'There we are . . . Crystal clear. And you've taken blood? Good. Filthy bloody stuff, Mandrax . . . Any fits?'

'No,' said the staff nurse.

'Not yet,' said Robbie.

'Bloody hell,' said the registrar. 'I was due to hand over at ten, and now this. And bloody Killick. Does he want telling or does he not want to know? And if he does am I supposed to ring him at home and leave a message with his wife, or what? He might know already, I suppose. Has he been in, staff?' The staff nurse shrugged her shoulders.

'And where the hell am I supposed to put her?'

'Why not the admitting medical unit?' said Robbie, grinning happily at his own common sense. 'Which unit's on?'

'Colquhoun, Phemister and Killick.'

'I see,' said Robbie. 'Oh God.'

'Right,' said the registrar.

'And who's actually on call?'

'Bloody Killick.'

'Yes, Matthew,' said Robbie, grinning again. 'I see your problem. Oh well. Anyway . . . We've washed her out for you. And Jamie Wilson had a quick look at her. She seems fine.'

'So he said. But I better go over her again.' They took the tube out and released the clamp holding the patient's jaws apart. The registrar leaned over and gently slapped her on one cheek. She opened her eyes and stared up at him and coughed. 'Bloody Killick.'

'Oh, hello, Mrs Gillsland,' said the registrar. 'You know you're in hospital? Good.' She sniffed and coughed again. The student nurse released the leather strap and staff nurse removed the absurd flowery pink plastic shower-cap and smoothed her hair. 'You did fine, Mrs Gillsland, dear . . . You're going to be all right now.' She shook her head in firm disagreement, then sniffed and her shoulders began to heave again. The staff nurse comforted her as she sobbed and as her sobs turned to long, baying howls. The registrar stood biting his lip then made a decision. Silently, but in the clearest possible terms, he indicated that the students should leave.

'Rather him than me,' said Robbie as they walked back past reception. 'I wonder what else has drifted in . . .'

Gus was rather proud of his laboratory notebook. It was just an ordinary square hard-covered five shilling lined notebook of the kind he had used at school for years, but it symbolised two and a half terms' work and would also now with any luck form a very useful part of his honours degree assessment. On the front cover was his name and the title of his project. Inside, the first half summarised the clinical details of all the patients he had seen, reducing their variously sad and complicated tales to neat columns of tabulated data headed by anonymous numbers, and in the second half were records of his laboratory work: detailed day-by-day descriptions and counts of his cell cultures and their progress, pictures of successfully transformed cells and photomicrographs of his immunofluorescence work. He was particularly proud of the latter – big, glossy black and white pictures with shining confident haloes against a dark background like galaxies in outer space, showing how the labelled antibody gathered around the target cells. He was almost as proud of his laboratory notes. Lots of people were careless about things like that, just charging on with their experiments and writing things up a week at a time, which could easily be represented as failing to keep a proper record of what you were doing. Every day's work in Gus's book was separately documented, with the date at the top just like a primary school writing-lesson. And since no two days were quite the same the style of his handwriting varied just a bit, as though the notes had been written in different postures, at the bench and or at the desk, or sometimes when he was very tired and sometimes when he wasn't. For similar reasons he was using different pens, mainly cheap ballpoints, perhaps the same one for two or three days then changing from black to blue, or from fresh to faint and nearly running out. It was all going quite well. He picked another pen from his little collection, checked his diary to avoid obvious mistakes such as working on Easter Monday, and launched into his record of the last few weeks' work, referring back to the previous term's figures to make sure that the gradual improvement in the yield of transformed lymphocytes was creditable rather than frankly improbable. And once again Roger Killick, who in some ways had as much to gain as Gus from a successful honours immunology project, had been very helpful with the photographic material.

He did another week's figures then, since finishing one's project meant tidying up on the equipment side as well, rinsed out a batch of tissue culture plates, swilling the cells that may never have been any good anyway down the lab sink and putting the plates to one side for the technician to deal with in due course. Then, since it was all part of the job and a lot easier than working on his lab notebook, he tore up some of the rough pencil notes he had made at the time of the very earliest experiments, away back in November just after he had learned the basic techniques. Though only a few pages, they had been quite useful over the course of the morning; now they were just so much junk. He threw the fragments into the waste paper bin. It was quite astonishing how much accumulated in a laboratory over the course of only two and half terms, so instead of going straight back to his notebook Gus attacked a couple of shelves and the worktop by the window, quickly filling his waste paper basket and starting an overflow in a cardboard container that had once held the big bottles of cell culture medium. When that was full he returned to the main task of the day, this time using a fading blue pen that with luck might, in the interests of even greater authenticity, run out in the course of a single set of results.

Gus completed his experimental work with some satisfaction. He relished tidiness and finishing things. His project, he felt, would not now let him down and there were still four weeks in which to bone up on general immunology for the written exams. Such work he found easy. You simply read as much as you could in the shortest possible time before the exam, taking notes and revising your notes more frequently as the exam approached: an obvious, effective technique which had served him well ever since first year, getting him exam results that few could rival. If it worked again, and there was no reason to believe it wouldn't, and if his project was to be assessed by an external examiner who, Roger had assured him, would be unlikely to demand details and even more unlikely to understand them, then he would get a first class honours degree, at worst an upper second. A first would be preferable, Gus thought, sitting for perhaps the last time in a now tidy laboratory, but even an upper second would allow him to pursue neuro-immunology to PhD level and thus assure him a flying start in academic medicine.

As the end of the academic year approached life for Gus was definitely becoming a good deal tidier in a number of ways. The Society's programme was almost complete. He would chair a specimen night, traditionally rather a drunken affair when people presented odd and silly cases, sometimes in verse or accompanied by funny slides, and then an AGM at which the only business of note was to stop Max Cathcart being elected to succeed him as President. Neither should present any particular problems, and Gus would leave having presided over the best lecture programme in years, and having revolutionised the Society by opening it to women. There was probably little point in ever going near it again.

There was one other problem, though in the natural course of events it would have been expected to solve itself over the course of the long vacation. The trouble was that Sandy Lennox had made absolutely no mention of leaving Edinburgh over the summer. While everyone else was talking endlessly about clerkships in Michigan or Montana, or hitch-hiking to Kabul, or going off on international work-camps to help people who should probably be helping themselves, Sandy had nothing planned. He had been half-expecting her to go back to Kaduna for a couple of months, and had perhaps been mistaken in telling her quite early on that he was already committed to staying in Edinburgh over the summer to work with Roger on some preliminary ideas for a major project that might well eventually form the basis of his PhD. He wished now that he had kept quiet about his own plans, because it was perfectly possible that that was why she had decided, in her doggy way, just to stay around. It wasn't that she was in any way unpleasant. If anything she was *too* good, too relentlessly cheerful and wholesome and patient, as if she knew she was good for him and would go on being good for him for ever whether he wanted it or not. However, because it would be upsetting and complicated, and because of a number of commitments of the kind where a partner was expected, there was nothing much he could do about it until the end of term. A few weeks more – a couple of dinners, a party or two, a few more of her quite enjoyable visits to his flat and a possibly tricky Sunday lunch – would see the thing to a natural break of sorts, but it would all have been a good deal simpler if she had been going away.

For Sandy, knowing beyond all possible doubt had come as a relief of a sort. It stopped her thinking silly, escapist things about how wonderful it would be if she weren't, and forced her to make plans about how to handle things from now on. She did not, she had to admit, have much to go on. There had been a girl in fifth year at Easdaile, a missionary's daughter, a boarder who had led an adventurous life for a term or two, who had begun to put on a bit of weight and started wearing her blouse outside her skirt and then disappeared suddenly, rumour had it to have her baby and then give it away to a couple who wanted one but couldn't and then come back to school. She had never returned. Abortion Sandy had known about quite early, probably when she was only about seven, because her parents made a point of explaining quite directly any words in the newspapers that she didn't understand, and a doctor some-where in Newington had lost his job for doing one. Her view of abortion was a bit more sophisticated now. Occasionally girls mum looked after at her clinic went for them, if they'd been raped (another newspaper word) or if there was a serious risk to their physical or mental health. But she felt fine, and now that she definitely knew, her mental health if anything was a little better.

Did it help if your boyfriend might go off his rocker because of it, fail his exams and ruin his career? Or if his mum would probably drink herself to death in about an afternoon? Sandy sat on her bed again with both her wardrobes open, running an eye over the things that didn't really need a waistline even though that stage was still quite a long way off. But at least she had decided when, where and how to tell Gus. After lunch they would go for a drive, and she would insist on going to North Berwick, and they would walk along the beach and she would tell him somewhere miles from anywhere, so that it was just them and they would have time together, out of doors and beside the sea, to agree which it was to be.

In a magical ideal world, of course, they would just go ahead, and be happy and grateful and somehow get on with things, both of them in medicine and defying Tommy Johnston's forthright and unsolicited advice, coping somehow with the fact that they had started a new person. The trouble with that was everybody else, and little things like having to take a year out of the course and get married in circumstances neither of them would regard as ideal and that their families, especially his, would regard as ill-advised or downright disgraceful. The missionary's daughter approach, of having a person and then giving them away, if that was what had really happened, wasn't something she'd thought about in detail because it just wasn't right. For Sandy it was going to be all or nothing, nothing being finding some way of getting an abortion; and, she had decided ages ago, whatever happened she was going to stand by Gus.

Sandy suddenly stopped thinking about it – something else she had taught herself to do over the last couple of weeks – and went downstairs to help her mum get ready for the kind of Sunday lunch that would normally have been quite straightforward and enjoyable. They were having Gus and the Jamesons and a new senior registrar with wife: Gus because he was her boyfriend and also what her father called, in inverted commas, a prominent student; the Jamesons because it was now official that dad would be taking over from Professor Jameson as Clinical Dean, a job he would be good at and quite enjoy now he wasn't zooming to and fro between Edinburgh and Kaduna all the time; and the new senior registrar on his unit because mum and dad were very conscientious about that sort of thing. Sandy set the table and did the clever folding bit with the napkins, then when everything was ready sat in the kitchen with mum and dad, passing the Sunday newspapers around.

The Jamesons arrived first, because, as Professor Jameson said, even after nearly twenty years in Edinburgh they still hadn't got into the habit of being late. They all went up to the lounge and had a sherry and talked, happy because Jimmy was handing on an agreeable job to his chosen successor and because they were all friends anyway. Esmee Jameson sat on the sofa with Sandy and asked sensible questions about how the modified curriculum was working out, and conveyed her view that eight hundred hours of anatomy was still about four hundred too many, and better things could be done instead. She was in favour of psychology for medical students, possibly with a bit of philosophy and maybe even some sociology, if that could be made to include field trips to slums, jails and peripheral housing estates. Sandy thought a bit of that might be fun and more use than some of the things they had had to do, and agreed with Mrs Jameson not simply from politeness or a distaste for pickled corpses.

When the doorbell rang again Sandy went down hoping for Gus. Instead it was Dr Dyker, the senior registrar, with a very pregnant wife. Sandy did her stuff despite a ghastly sinking feeling, and showed them upstairs, following the vast, waddling Mrs Dyker, who could only have been in her late twenties but had quite bad varicose veins and was breathless by the time they reached the landing. She put her on the sofa next to Mrs Jameson, who would no doubt have firm but useful views on pregnancy, put Dr Dyker next to mum then went round topping people up. When she had done that, and pulled out the piano stool so she could sit near Professor Jameson, she got a sudden, silly premonition that Gus wasn't just late, he wasn't going to turn up at all.

'Well, Sandy . . . D'you think Smith has met his match?'

'Sorry, Professor Jameson . . .'

'Ian Smith. D'you think Wilson's going to sort him out at last?'

'Difficult, isn't it? But I suppose he's in a better position now . . .'

'Gosh, yes, Sandy . . . Couldn't agree more. But it would be an awful lot easier if you could just send a gunboat up the Zambesi, hm?'

Sandy smiled and thought about her supply officer. The doorbell rang again. She went down and it was Gus, with a big bunch of flowers for mum, and looking super despite all his swotting. They had a quick, happy kiss behind the door then went upstairs, where they stayed for only a minute before coming down again for lunch. Mum was being her usual organised self, and put Mrs Senior Registrar and Esmee on either side of dad, Gus between herself and Esmee, Senior Registrar on her right and Sandy between him and Jimmy, which was fine because Jimmy was fun and Gus was perfectly capable of doing a good job with Mrs Jimmy, even at her toughest.

Over the soup the new people got the weight, as dad would put it, and had to tell everybody about moving from Aberdeen, which Mrs Jimmy talked of as if it were in Lapland, and about finding a house in Edinburgh and of course about the coming happy event: when, where and which did they want. Everyone was kind and welcoming, and to Sandy's surprise Gus joined in rather nicely, even with the happy event bit, which was quite clever of him considering he was single and, even if he didn't even know it yet, not so very far behind. When they had got through all that and the soup Sandy and mum collected the plates and brought through the trolley and everyone was obviously quite relieved it was going to be good old fashioned Sunday lunch: roast potatoes, Yorkshire pudding, cabbage, roast beef (MacSween's finest, regular customers only) and lots of good gravy, with dad splashing a bit of claret around.

When everybody had everything Sandy, like a good Easdaile girl, turned to the man on the other side and chatted him up a bit. Dr Dyker was nice but awkward, with unruly hair and a red, outdoor face which, with his suit and his accent – rural Aberdonian – made for an overall impression of a ploughboy got up for church. That proved to be misleading: he played the cello and had been to India and had done lots of things for the Campaign for Nuclear Disarmament in Aberdeen. As he talked Sandy kept one ear on what was going on on the other side of the table. Mrs Jameson was putting Gus through it on third world population growth, a topic evidently sparked by his mentioning that he intended to try next year for a Kaduna scholarship, so it served him right. Now he was learning a lot about African urbanisation, mortality rates and practical contraception for rural areas in underdeveloped countries.

After the pudding they went upstairs again for coffee and for a while people were full and a bit quiet, then Professor Jameson asked

Dr Dyker what it was like coming to work in the Institute after Aberdeen Royal Infirmary. He went pink and said he was glad to hear that they were going to replace it soon. Professor Jameson enjoyed that a lot. 'Jolly tactful way of putting it, Gregor, if I may say so. Of course up there you've got those sensible thirties buildings. Granite, plenty of space and all in jolly good order . . . Been there once or twice to examine, that sort of thing. So yes, a bit of a come-down for you. But we *are* doing our best . . . If you'd asked me a couple of months ago I'd have said that doing our best didn't amount to much more than discussing the new Institute every ten years or so . . . But this time it's different. Budget earmarked, chaps working on the plans, bit of a rumpus for a year or two, then the Queen cutting a ribbon somewhere and we'll have a hospital to be proud of at least until the end of the century.'

'Sounds wonderful, Jimmy . . .' said Mrs Jimmy in a school-marmish way. 'But how do we know what we're going to need then?'

'Ask the chaps. Gus? What sort of hospital do you want to be working in in the year 2000?'

'Gosh. Tricky. You know I've been thinking about that. Probably a . . . flexible one. You know, one that has an outside shell, and floors, and services and all that, but the kind of internal structure you can alter . . .'

'Jolly good. Care to elaborate?'

'Well, who knows what's going to be needed? Certainly nobody would have predicted the need for immunology services even as recently as ten years ago, so we're in a prefab on the roof, trying not be noisy upstairs neighbours to Professor Lennox's department. And half a dozen other units are in the same boat, on people's roofs and in their basements and so on. So you build knowing how much you need, roughly, but with only the vaguest idea what, because it won't be very difficult to adapt . . . A flexible hospital, in other words.'

'Jolly good,' said Professor Jameson. Sandy had listened carefully to all that and had been quite impressed. Dr Dyker was shaking his head a bit. 'You don't agree, Gregor . . .'

'It's all these funny wee units that worry me,' said Dr Dyker. 'That was beginning to happen in Aberdeen too, everybody settin' up their ain wee place wi' a nice notice board outside, and their own secretary and a grand set of notepaper and forms, and the chap runnin' it callin' himself the director, when he could have been spending the same money better as part of a larger department.'

'Well, Gus? What would you say to that?'

'Obviously one can't speak of the situation in Aberdeen . . . But down here we seem to be finding that, um, independent initiatives, especially if they're a bit innovative and specialist, don't seem to be encouraged by the larger departments. Or, as in the case of the Neuro-Immunology Unit, are really breaking new ground that no single department could reasonably take responsibility for. And I understand that funding is sometimes easier if there's one clearly identified unit involved. Dr Killick's proposals for work on pre-senile dementia, I know . . .' Sandy was afraid that now he was going to get a bit boring, but noticed that her father was actually paying close attention to what Gus was saying. '. . would look a bit odd coming from a non-clinical department, which is where most immunology has been based, as I understand it, in most medical schools.'

'Yes, tricky one, I suppose . . .' said Jimmy. 'But are you chaps really going to sort out dementia? That's jolly good news.'

It was Gus's turn to go a bit pink. 'Well, Roger's view is that there are some quite strong pointers to an immunological basis . . . Some of the microscopic features are practically diagnostic, and with techniques evolving all the time it's certainly worth trying to raise some money to look at the ideas in detail.'

'Hmm. So when old buffers like Lennie and me get a bit forgetful we'll just trundle along to your place – assuming of course we can remember where it is – roll up our sleeves and get a shot of anti-amnesia serum and everything comes flooding back. Sounds absolutely marvellous . . .'

'Darling . . .' Mrs Jimmy was looking a bit stern again. Gus laughed and said 'Probably won't turn out to be quite as simple as that, Professor Jameson. Unfortunately . . . But we certainly have to pursue all the clues the new techniques throw up.' Gus had said enough and seemed to have recognised that for himself. Mum started making noises about more coffee and Sandy got up to deal with it. General conversation dwindled, then dad and Jimmy went into a little huddle of their own, probably a quiet mutter about something to do with clinical deaning, as Jimmy called it. Gus looked across to Sandy and gave her a big smile

At about three the Jamesons showed signs of polite restlessness, and by half past Sandy and Gus were sitting in the MG Midget with the top off, heading for North Berwick. Despite mum's protestations, Gus had actually been quite helpful with the first bit of tidying up, then they had been packed off to get some fresh air, something mum attached a lot of importance to in the run-up to exams. They zoomed through Musselburgh and out along the twisty coast road, a happy couple in a red sports car doing the kind of thing that Sandy had always thought of as being done only by people in cinema adverts, except that in adverts nobody was pregnant. At North Berwick they parked at the harbour, spent a silly ten minutes clambering about on a red sandstone sea-wall that wasn't really broad enough to walk along safely, then they set out for the beach walk on which Gus was going to hear about something that had been bothering Sandy over the last few weeks.

Unfortunately he had some worries too, and that took about half a mile. Roger's secretary had gone off sick and then resigned suddenly and was threatening in some unspecified way to make life difficult for the Neuro-Immunology Unit. It was all rather complicated, to do with a big grant application, the dementia one he had mentioned over lunch and which would help a lot with his PhD. The woman had been absolutely essential and the application was only half-complete. A lot of the data was at quite a critical stage and Roger had been getting fed up with her even before she had gone off sick, but she had done a lot more than most secretaries. A lot of important stuff was more in her head than anywhere else, which meant that even if they could find somebody it would all be very difficult for at least a few months and the deadline for the grant application was quite near. From the sound of things it seemed to Sandy that a sick woman wasn't getting a lot of sympathy, though she didn't feel it would help to say so there and then: they were getting quite near the place where she had decided to tell Gus, a pointed black rock quite far down the beach that had been a pirate castle when they were kids.

A family was coming along the beach towards them, a mum and a dad with a baby sleeping in a stroller and a boy of about seven in front of them, dancing from side to side with his eyes shut, waving his arms and clicking his fingers as if he was being a pop star in his head. Gus stopped talking as they passed. The mum smiled at them. They reached the rock. Sandy stopped and faced Gus, holding both his hands. 'Gus, I'm pregnant.'

'Hullo? Lennie?'
    'Yes.'
'Jimmy here. Sorry to bother you at home.'
'It's all right.'
'Not too early?'
'No, no.'
'Good. Reference the small problem we discussed over coffee yesterday.'
    'Killick?'
'Yes. I'm at the office. Thought I'd just have a snuffle round before I push off to Guatemala. And there's the most astonishing letter here. Confidential and all that. From his secretary, and probably a good deal more, if you see what I mean . . .'
    'Yes . . .'
'A Mrs Gillsland. His former secretary now, I suppose . . . Extraordinary stuff. Hard to know exactly how to take it, but if even a quarter of it's true . . .'
    'What sort of stuff?'
'Gosh. Where does one start? Six pages of it, but to take the main points . . . The only decent results come from a graduate scientist who never gets a mention . . . Those lovely pictures he produces are largely bogus . . . Most of his lab data's sucked out of the end of his thumb, so his dementia grant application is science fiction in search of major funding . . . He's too cosy by half with the people he buys his equipment from and his accounting methods would make your hair stand on end. And of course she's writing separately to the Inland Revenue. That enough?'
    'It's a lot, but . . .'
'Yes, yes. "Hell hath no fury" and the like.'
    'Quite.'
'"Lilies that fester" and all that . . . I know.'
'And he's not about to go off to a chair anywhere, is he?'
'Not so far as I know.'
'Tricky.'
'Jolly tricky.'
'Not sure, Jimmy.'
'The answer's probably a quiet little committee. A very quiet little

committee. Chaired by you, I'd imagine, on behalf of the Dean.'

'Should we . . . talk about it again?'

'Of course. Soon as I get back. Just thought you might like to think about it. I'm, um, taking the letter off with me.'

'Good.'

'Be nice to have something interesting to read on the plane. Regards to Margaret, and thanks awfully for lunch . . . And of course Esmee sends her love . .'

'Thanks, Jimmy. Enjoy Guatemala . . .'

Lennie put the phone down and Margaret turned over. 'What time is it?'

'Oh, half past six.'

'D'you think all that's true?'

'Probably.'

'Gosh.'

'I know . . . Gus.'

'Shouldn't do him much harm. He's only a boy. But Killick . . .'

'He must know it's coming.'

'Poor chap.'

'If only he'd looked after his women . . .'

'Too early for tea?'

'No, but I'll get it.'

'No, I will. I'm . . . looking after you.'

To no one's surprise, Gus got a first in Immunology. Sandy too did well academically, and when term had ended was admitted briefly to the care of a gynaecologist in Glasgow, a friend of her mum's. Dr Ross was grey-haired and cuddly and had had four children of her own. She certified that Sandy's mental health was at grave risk if the pregnancy continued and terminated it accordingly. A few weeks later Sandy went off on a hastily arranged two month clerkship in Kaduna.

Scott, at the end of his probationary term in Casualty, reported in Mr Gillon's cluttered office for his review appointment. They talked generally then Scott was told that he was regarded as a steady and useful chap who would be welcome to give a hand in the department next term if he felt so inclined. He thanked Mr Gillon but explained that he would rather not continue meantime, as he would be concentrating on his honours physiology year. He was asked if he had any thoughts or worries about the department, and mentioned Terry and the way he treated patients and others. Mr Gillon wanted details and was given them. He sighed and picked up a large brass paper knife. 'The man's an anomaly and probably a liability. He was here when I inherited this place and a lot of people find him useful . . . But thank you, Andrew, for reminding me about him.' Shortly afterwards Terry was thanked for his years of devoted and unpaid service to the Institute, and disappeared.

October 1968

'But more importantly to you, to us, as medical students, the Medical Students' Council has direct access to the Medical Faculty, to represent your views on educational and other matters. Your year representatives – once you've elected them, of course – will join the Council and become involved in all that, as your representatives. So if you think you'd like to stand we look forward to getting your nomination papers later in the term. And of course everyone should try to vote. Um, thank you.'

Professor Jameson bobbed to his feet. 'Thank you, thank you so much, Andrew . . . I'd very much like to endorse all that, from the other side of the table, so to speak. We value the views of our student colleagues on the liaison committe very highly. And when it seems that half of Europe's students are sitting in, chucking paving stones or burning things down to get their points across, we're jolly glad here in the Faculty of Medicine at Edinburgh to find ourselves somewhat ahead of the field. So are there any questions for the chairman of your Council?'

One of the very few boys wearing a suit raised his hand. 'You, sir,' said Professor Jameson. 'The gentleman in navy blue near the front . . .'

'Is this in any way political, please?'

'Andrew? Are you political? I mean your council, of course.'

Scott hesitated then decided to assume that the questioner meant party political. 'Nobody on the council represents any particular political standpoint, if that's what you mean . . . The issues involved – like whether or not students should have to live in during the whole of the Obstetrics and Gynaecology attachment – probably wouldn't interest any of the major political parties very much.' There was a useful ripple of amusement. 'So, generally speaking, no.'

'Quite,' said Professor Jameson, smiling broadly. 'They're all political with a small *p* . . . Like us. That answer your question? Splendid. Anyone else? No. Well, let's go on now to one of our more venerable institutions. I'm going to ask the Senior President of the somewhat quaintly named Ancient Society of Physic to say a few words . . .'

Scott sat down, stuffed his notes into his jacket pocket and checked his watch. He had kept strictly to his three minutes including questions, had not dried up or got confused and could therefore now relax. Another year's worth of medical students had had a short introduction to their democratic rights and responsibilities. It was not a duty that Scott had anticipated for himself. He had got into student politics fairly late, somewhat by accident and as a result of trying to find out where to complain about something. A series of muddles about junior surgical attachments had culminated in a week of idle chaos for half a dozen students and Scott had been delegated, in the course of one of their endless coffee breaks, to complain to one of their year representatives. He discovered from an apologetic chairman of the council that no such representatives existed, and to his surprise had been co-opted before he could get off the phone.

Since then it had all been quite interesting and not particularly difficult or demanding. From his earliest youth he had been aware of committees and roughly what happened on them, from hearing long discussions at home about the minutes of the kirk session, the machinations of the Womens' Guild and the doings of their various sub-committees. At school he had been secretary of the literary and philosophical society in his final year and later, in Irving Hall, because he had quite often been seen to be reading novels, he had found himself with sudden and total responsibility for the library committee. The Medical Students' Council had held no great surprises. After a few meetings the secretary, in fear of failing all his third year exams, proved to be actively seeking replacement. When he had served a year as secretary Scott was the only person around who knew enough about what was going on to succeed the retiring chairman. It was now a matter of some concern to him that quite recently, when he had been on the council for almost exactly two years, a further vehement complaint had been received about the chaotic and idle junior surgical clerkship which had prompted his entry into student politics in the first place. He had never got round to doing anything about it. He pulled out his diary and scribbled something in it to remind himself in time for the next faculty liaison meeting.

'. . . and with due respect to the Dean, we've never felt we had to apologise for our name. Physic is just the word for what physicians do, in other words medicine as opposed to surgery. And we're ancient – this is our two hundred and twenty-second annual session – and we're a society. So why not the Ancient Society of Physic?' Max turned to Professor Jameson, who clutched his brow in comic repentence. 'But the name of the Society doesn't matter an awful lot. It's what it stands for . . . The fellowship, the commitment to medical learning and, um, things like that. And the Society's rooms and library, to which every member has a key, are a comfortable, central place to study and relax, to be with friends and to . . .' Max hesitated ' . . . and I should have mentioned that for the past few years membership of the Society has been open to women . . . A change everyone agrees has been for the better.'

The audience stirred restlessly and Scott realised that the idea of a student society that did not admit women probably didn't make much sense to them. Max shouldn't go on about it, even if he had been a great pioneer in his time. Though he would hate to be told so, he was beginning to sound middle-aged. The eighteen and nineteen year olds standing around in the Union debating hall eyeing the sandwiches and each other and listening to the speakers only very intermittently were quite different from the batch five years earlier that had included Max and himself. For a start almost half of them were women. And as a group, with a few exceptions like the chap in the navy blue suit, they looked as if they had just returned from a mass pilgrimage to places like Berkeley and the more fashionable ashrams of India. The girls had long hair, tiny skirts and loose tops with strange badges, the men flared denims with patches signifying peace and flowers. It was all very different. Would Max be provoked to circulate through the tea ceremony dispensing advice about suits with a bit of a taper, lapels just so and trousers, OK, flared if you must but let's not get carried away, huh? Or would the Dean at some point feel compelled to remind them that patients might not be quite ready for the style they embraced, comfortable, colourful and charming though it might be?

Scott wondered about that and decided that in an odd sort of way Jimmy Jameson, the new Dean, seemed to be enjoying them. He was new and so were they and whatever they looked like now they were no doubt all great passers of exams, and by the time they got near the patients fashion would have moved on anyway. As Max waxed commercial about the Society's membership fees Scott sat on the other side of the Dean and wondered what the new lot was making of the people on the platform, if indeed they were thinking about them at all. They looked as if they weren't. Max ended lamely with a plug about the Society's reduced subscription rate for MacKay's Lending Library and sat down. Again the Dean bobbed up. 'Questions, hm? Anyone?'

There were none. The dean of bicycle sheds did his turn more or less exactly as Scott remembered it then Professor Jameson said something about everybody being jolly patient after a hard week of being welcomed everywhere and given the party line on everything, but this party was essentially a tea party and would people please just help themselves. Max and Scott, with Professor Jameson and the others from the platform, descended to circulate. 'Thanks, chaps,' said the Dean, with one hand on Scott's elbow and the other on Max's. 'Ideal contributions. Short and snappy. Awfully good of you both to come along and do your stuff. You will stay for a spot of tea, won't you? Meet the new chaps . . . And girls . . .' Max nodded vigorously. 'Jolly good show . . .'

Soon Scott found himself talking to a tall girl from Roedean who was so bland and confident about everything that quite quickly he turned out to be the one who was being put at ease. She asked him how he liked Edinburgh, how long he had been involved in student politics and what he intended to specialise in when he qualified. She was cool and pretty and quite hypnotically attentive and Scott was beginning to get boring about not knowing what he wanted to do at the end of it all when Max suddenly appeared and asked her where she'd got her beads. She smiled down at him and murmured something about Nepal. Max said he'd never been there but vowed it was a place he had always meant to visit. Scott slipped away and for some minutes he wandered, among groups of colourful, confident young people talking mainly about travel and Vietnam, eventually with a vague intention of talking to the man in the demob suit who had asked him the question about politics. He was not to be found. Scott settled instead for a trio of rather staid young men from Ulster, where a small riot had just occurred. They assured him that things would settle down very quickly in the province if the people there were just allowed to get on with it on their own, away from all the interference of the British press and the BBC.

'Good,' said Dr Huntly. 'Good of you to drop in. And may I say how much we appreciate your fitting a bit of the rough and tumble of surgical life into what is clearly a very busy schedule. But from the Dean's tea party to Mrs MacGrotty's piles 'tis but a short step. We're glad you made it.'

'Have I missed anything?'

'Nothing serious. We've explained to people. They understand. It's no trouble. But now you're back we can get on with things again.'

Scott realised that it would have been in his interests to have been less specific about the reasons for his absence from the unit on the afternoon of an admitting day. Huntly, Sir Edgar Bielby's senior house officer, was enjoying himself. He sat back in his chair. 'There was one in my year. I suppose every year has one, like you have a year schizophrenic and a year idiot. Our year politician was an Irish Fifer, communist and good-cause man. Mulvaney? Malarkey? Malone? Yes, Malone. Astonishing chap. Fitted in a bit of medicine between committees. But I'm afraid that for comrade Malone it's going to be . . .' Huntly shook his head sadly. '. . . public health. Nothing else for it, if you've spent your entire undergraduate career explaining the social causes of disease to a lot of bored and uncomprehending consultant physicians and surgeons. But I suppose he might enjoy it. And he used to do what you do. Forever skipping off to tea with Deans, sub-committees on the last stages of capitalism and the like. And there are quite a number of units in town where that sort of thing doesn't go down at all well.'

'So has anything come in?'

'Gus is seeing a comely but acute abdomen, probably a straightforward appendix. Your student colleague is holding his nose and admitting a black foot. I'm management, at least for the time being. So we're coping, but good of you to ask, young Scott, and we'll probably need you later.'

They were sitting in the doctors' room of the male ward of Sir Edgar's unit. Its window looked out through autumnal branches to the Medical School opposite. Below, a pedestrian rush-hour had begun, filling the broad avenue between the trees as students and office workers set out across the park to the nearer southern suburbs. Huntly stretched back further in his chair and put his feet up on the desk. 'Do they still tell them to work hard and play hard?'

'I suppose so. The Dean didn't, but somebody must.'

'One of our lot tried it. Odd chap who'd been in the RAF. Went like a train all through first term of first year. Did everything from distance running to debating and actually kept up with the work as well. Next term he did nothing. Moped around looking lost. Third term he disappeared. Didn't even sit the exams. Manic depressive, I suppose, looking back on it, but nobody knew the words then. Just dropped out and disappeared.'

Scott hung up his jacket and put on his white coat. Huntly sat looking out of the window. There was a short textbook of general surgery on the desk, a dog-eared paperback edition of a book described by one of their lecturers as a duffer's guide to surgery. Scott picked it up, sat down in one of the armchairs and started to read up on what duffers needed to know about black feet.

'Not sure, really. A twinge, just, to begin with. Then more of an ache, very definitely coming and going a bit. But hard to put a precise time to when it all began.'

'Even roughly . . . Was it months ago, or just weeks?'

'I'd say months. Before the Festival. A couple of months?'

Scott nodded and wrote that down. 'Anything make it worse?'

'Such as?'

'Fatty things, maybe.'

'Which I normally try to avoid anyway.'

'Because they disagree with you?'

'Because they make me fat.'

'But if you did eat fatty things . . .'

'The pain would come on. And a bit of sickness.'

'Feeling sick or being sick?'

'Maybe both. Usually just feeling sick.'

'And always the same place. . . ? The pain, I mean.'

The woman nodded and patted herself with her left hand somewhere up under her right ribs. That was helpful.

'And this time what happened? To the pain, I mean.'

'It didn't go away. It stayed and got worse, so I called the doctor.'

'You'd never seen him before about this?'

'Her. No. What could my GP do about my gall-bladder?'

Scott wrote that down too, verbatim. It was a diagnosis he was working towards even if he hadn't quite got there yet: definitely in his top three, probably at the top. He nodded.

'So that's what I've got, is it?'

'Could well be,' said Scott.

The woman smiled. 'My son's a medical student, in third year. He says the worst bit's when the patients think you're a doctor.' Scott laughed and the woman laughed too then winced. 'Sorry,' she said. 'I didn't mean it like that. And you're probably further on.'

'A bit,' said Scott. 'What about other things, like your weight?'

'I told you. I have to watch it.'

'Yes, but is it going up, or just staying the same.'

'Oh, just put staying the same.'

'And – going back to when you got sick – was there ever any blood in it?'

'No. And I'm sure I'd have noticed that.'

'And what about your urine. . . ? Has that ever been darker than usual?'

'Should it be? I mean if I've got a gall-bladder. . .'

'Sometimes it gets dark if the bile isn't getting through normally. Did you happen to notice?'

'Just put normal for that too.'

'Now some more questions . . . Things I should actually have started with. Your work, please?'

'Teacher.' At least she smiled when she said it. They talked briefly about that then plodded through the long list of routine questions about chest and heart symptoms, headaches, blurred vision, dizziness and numerous other items that people in surgical wards didn't seem to get as often as people in medical wards. That was as it should be. The woman was fit and middle aged and had nothing wrong with her except an inflamed gall-bladder. She had come in with right upper quadrant abdominal pain, nausea and a fever. She would be better soon. They would treat her with antibiotics until the inflammation settled then send her home to come back and have her gall-bladder out at leisure, or they would decide to go in that night and get the whole thing over. The decision, and so far as Scott knew there was not much in it either way, would be presented as the only possible thing to do in the circumstances. That was another odd thing about surgeons: they had strong views that they didn't seem to wish to discuss at length. The used 'always' and 'never' a good deal and wanted to get on with things rather than temporise or agonise the way the physicians did. And they seemed to enjoy operating for its own sake, which might be the determining factor more often than they would care to admit.

Scott finished his questions and checked back and filled a few of the more important gaps, like previous illness and family illnesses like diabetes, then drew the screens and started to examine Mrs Peters. She was plump and vaguely blonde, the 'fair, fat, fertile and forty' sort of woman said to be particularly prone to the complaint, though Scott was sure he had read something somewhere suggesting that this too was just another bit of unverifiable surgical folklore. She was still hot to touch and her pulse was fast. He did a few of the things that were more for medical than surgical admissions, like checking her pupils and her hearing in each ear, felt her neck and armpits for lumps, checked her breasts too, sat her up and sounded her chest then, when she lay down again, nearly flat with only one pillow, examined her abdomen.

It was white and a bit flabby, with stretch marks from the chap in third year and his two younger sisters, and there were no obvious lumps. He laid a hand flat on the place furthest away from the trouble and palpated his way round from left lower to right upper quadrant. Just under the ribs on the right she was very tender, but there was no mass, no firmness from a distended gall-bladder. That was all right, in fact probably a good thing, since if the gall bladder were to be easily palpable it was more likely to be something serious: a sign described by a Frenchman whose name Scott could not immediately recall. The most likely diagnosis was still cholecystitis, an inflamed gall-bladder. For the sake of completeness he checked again in the place where duodenal ulcers usually hurt most, just above the navel, and then checked on a few more things she obviously didn't have, like strangulated hernias, and finished the abdominal bit of the examination by listening with his stethoscope for bowels sounds, which were present and normal.

The rest of the examination was easy, routine stuff with hands, tendon hammer and blood pressure cuff, until the last little ritual, the rectal examination, which demanded a bit more ceremony. Scott excused himself, found the ward's rectal tray and got a staff nurse to help and chaperone. He pulled on a plastic glove and started to explain to the patient what he was going to do. She said she knew all about it and turned promptly on her side, still talking in her teacherish way: 'Absolutely no problem as far as I'm concerned, so just get on with it . . . I can assure you that after three babies you learn how to leave your dignity at the hospital door.' Scott got on with it, with a residual sense of enormity about what he was doing to a member of the teaching profession and the mother of an unknown junior colleague, not that thinking things like that helped. There was nothing amiss. The colour of the stool was indeed normal. Scott thanked Mrs Peters and took the specimen obtained off to the ward's cramped and malodorous laboratory, where a chemical test involving eerie purple fluorescence failed to flicker in the dark, thus ruling out significant internal bleeding.

'Thanks awfully, Andrew . . . I've just had a quick look at Mrs Peters myself, so if we could flick through what you've written I might add a scribble . . .' Scott was sitting at the desk in the doctors' room finishing off his admission notes. Gus pulled a chair up and lifted the first page. 'May I . . ? Good . . . Yes. Ten weeks, I think, rather than two months . . . And quite important to say that the pain didn't radiate anywhere else. You really should know about shoulder-tip radiation, shouldn't you? Not uncommon with cholecystitis. And it would do no harm to have a few more details on family history . . . Probably not crucial in this case, but at your stage its a question of getting into the habit of doing things properly . . . And you, um, haven't tested her urine yet, have you? An acute inflammatory episode like this might well be the first clinical appearance of diabetes, and if she's for an anaesthetic tonight . . . You're aware of the importance of all that . . . So we'd be awfully interested in whether or not there was sugar in her urine, wouldn't we?'

We would, thought Scott, and as soon as the lady favoured us with a pee we could do something about it. Most housemen were a little more overtly grateful for the efforts of senior medical students on the wards, and so far this admitting day Gus had reserved the easiest case, the girl with an appendix, for himself. Harry, the other student, had spent an hour or more with the strange old man whose leg was going to have to come off and who seemed to be going into DT's as well. Scott had fielded Mrs Peters. Gus had spent an agreeable twenty minutes or so with a nice girl who could probably have been sorted out in ten, and now he was getting his kicks from being superior on the finer points of work he had largely avoided himself. 'But thanks awfully, Andrew. When you're a houseman yourself you'll really appreciate having the occasional student around on a busy waiting night . . . Now if I might just have the notes. . . ?'

Scott sat back while Gus used a flashy gold-trimmed fountain pen to add a magisterial paragraph that simply summarised his own account of the case. 'Thanks awfully, Andrew . . . Now I don't think there's anything more on its way in meantime, so let's check with Sam and find Harry and perhaps go and eat. Ever eaten in the residency?' Scott shook his head. 'It's . . . quaint, but terribly handy, and eating together gives us a chance to discuss things. I'll just ring down and make sure it's all right.' Scott listened while Gus used his considerable charm on a member of the Institute's domestic staff who seemed to need a little persuasion. He put the phone down and smiled at Scott. 'Everything's fine, Andrew. But she'd prefer us sooner rather than later. I think Sam's over on the male ward . . . And of course Harry . . .'

Scott took the hint and went off to find the senior house officer. Sam Huntly was sitting at the bedside of the man who needed an amputation and was trying to persuade him it would be a good thing to get on with it. The patient, an unshaven and ill-kempt little man probably in his seventies, fingered the permission slip and looked from it to Sam and back again. 'And what's this about "any other necessary procedure" . . . ? Does that mean you can do what you like to me once I'm out for the count?'

Sam shook his head. 'It's a formality, just to cover various emergencies. Not important. The main thing is to do something about your leg.'

'Well, anything you can do that might help it . . .'

'Mr Hurst, as I've tried to explain, the best we can offer is an operation to limit the damage . . . As I said, removing the leg, saving as much as possible, probably taking it just above the knee . . . It must be pretty uncomfortable the way it is now.'

Whatever it felt like, it smelt dreadful: a sickly, choking, sweetish odour filled the sideroom and had been noticeable even from the door of the ward. Sam, to his credit, did not seem to let it bother him, but sat close to the man's bedside with a pen ready for him as soon as he decided to sign. 'It's a fairly routine matter, Mr Hurst, but it would be best to get on with it . . . The longer it's left the more problems might arise . . .'

'Like what?'

'Well, there's infection . . .' Sam stood up and lifted the covers from the bed-cage that protected the man's left leg. A new and dreadful wave of the stench flooded the room. 'You see? The red edge there? That could be quite serious.' Scott looked over Sam's shoulder. The leg below the knee shaded in colour from red to purple to black. The foot was a wasted, slimy claw with a brownish stain spreading on the sheet below it. 'I see what you mean,' said the patient. 'You're talking gangrene, aren't you?'

'That sort of thing,' said Sam. 'So best to get it early. We'd be glad to help.'

'And what if the operation goes wrong?'

Sam replaced the covers and remained standing. 'It's actually one of the simpler operations, Mr Hurst. Safe, quite quick and you'll feel an awful lot better after it.'

There was a long pause then the patient looked up. 'I knew it was about fifty-fifty for that leg, doctor. You will be doing the operation yourself?'

'Myself and another chap,' said Sam. 'You'll feel an awful lot better afterwards.'

'Will I?'

'When it's done most people say they would have had it earlier if they'd known. They just feel so much better, you know, without a bad leg . . .'

'And it could go right through my system. . . ? If I didn't . . .'

Sam nodded. The man spread out his hands and looked at them then sighed. 'OK, doc . . . Let's go.' He moved as though to get out of bed and appeared puzzled that Sam did not help him.

'All I need just now is your signature, Mr Hurst. It'll take an hour or two to get things ready but we'll certainly get on with it as quickly as we can. So if you can just sign the form. There, and I'll witness it.'

The old man took the pen and, in a round clear hand, wrote Jas. Walton. 'I thought your name was Hurst, Mr Hurst?' The patient tapped the side of his nose and said 'I've got one or two names, doctor.'

'Well, can it be Hurst meantime, since that's what we've been using so far? Be a lot simpler for everybody.'

'Fine by me,' said the man, scoring out his first signature and writing J. Hurst in narrow sharply sloping copperplate below it. 'But most people just call me Jimmy.'

'Thanks, Jimmy. We'll get on with it in an hour or so. And meantime I'll organise an injection that'll help the pain and maybe settle your nerves.'

'I'm not worried, doctor.' The man laughed and then coughed. 'Seen it all. Used to be a mortuary attendant.'

As the four walked down to the residency Sam answered some of Scott's questions about the case. 'It happens because they keep hoping it'll get better, so they leave it so late they know they'll lose it, which is another reason for not coming up. I've seen one or two others, but none as bad as that ... And it helps if your brain's wasted with drink.'

'Really?'

'He's probably drunk more often than he's sober, and the sedative, anxiolytic and mild analgesic properties of alcohol are too well described for me to bore a man of your experience with them yet again. Poor old bugger lives in a lodging house, his mates bring in the booze, everybody stays pissed and it's only when the smell gets too bad they actually bring him up. Or maybe his money ran out.'

'And the two names?'

'Or more. Again, he wouldn't be the first. One jump ahead of the law or the income tax most of his life, probably. Bigamy, things like that. You could check with Casualty. They've got a decent list of aliases for most of their regulars. But the problem isn't who he is, it's getting his leg off. You should come into theatre, Andrew. You, me and the registrar should manage what we've got. Leave Gus and Harry in the front shop for a couple of hours. All right?'

'Whatever you like, Sam,' said Gus. 'Happy either way.' Harry, the other student, seemed cheered at the prospect. Perhaps he'd already had enough of Walton alias Hurst and his doomed, malodorous leg. They proceeded downstairs past walls crowded with the orderly gilt-lettered records of 18th-century charitable donations, arrived at the heart of the Institute and turned off one of its main corridors through a doorway Scott had seen many times but never entered. A modest brass plate at eye level read 'Residency'. On the wall of the dingy corridor inside was a long vertical board with the name of each resident and beside it a little sliding panel which signified whether he was in or out: an anachronism now that everyone carried bleeps, Scott thought, but Gus flicked the one marked 'Dr A G P Ratho' stylishly across as he passed. 'This way, please . . . Unless . . .'

Scott took him up on the invitation, and was shown down a corridor lined with dusty group photographs of residents from the thirties and forties to an old-fashioned gents' loo with vast porcelain stalls and neglected brass fittings. On the way back along to the dining room he paused at one or two of the photographs with the vague idea of looking for people who might still be around the place. A short, angry woman with a hairy upper lip and a pink uniform overall emerged from the dining room, glared at him and snapped 'Are you a late extra supper wi' the surgeons?' Scott nodded. 'It's on the table . . .' she said as she disappeared into a pantry. '. . . gettin' colder.'

Gus, Sam and Henry sat together around the end of a long table in a wood-panelled room decorated with several dozen more of the group photographs. Supper was a thick brown stew served with solid hemispheres of mashed potato and a helping of soggy cabbage. Scott ate it anyway. It tasted a little better than it looked, but not good enough to redeem the overall disappointment of the occasion. Being a resident in the Institute was the goal of every reasonably ambitious Edinburgh medical student and most of them failed to achieve it. The Residency, a building older than the Institute itself but incorporated within it when it had moved to the site some time last century was an essential first staging post in any worthwhile career in medicine. All that had made the door with the brass plate one of special interest and importance. Having gone through it once, as a visitor and temporarily useful junior, Scott now found its mysteries an anti-climax, the place beyond it old-fashioned and shabby and smelling of bad plumbing and stale food. Even the heavy EPNS salt-cellar was clogged with damp.

Harry, the other senior student attached to Sir Edgar's unit, was talking about an exam he was about to sit. Half-listening, Scott began to wonder if he had missed something important on a faculty notice-board, but when he paid more attention soon realised it was nothing to do with the medical course. Harry, who was from Bathgate and did not seem to have distinguished himself much in the course so far, had applied for membership of a society for people with exceptionally high intelligence. Sam was probing him a bit. 'So it'll be like the thing we saw at the end of primary school? Sums and difficult words, with a few of those which-picture-comes-next questions for people who are intelligent but not very good at words and sums? That kind of thing?'

'Well, the preliminary test, the one you have to pass before you sit the real thing, was quite interesting . . . No problem really, so I'm going straight on to the main test . . . The first thing was a mixture of things . . . Series of numbers, logic puzzles . . . Tests of abstract thinking . . . Things like that . . .'

'And there'll be prizes if you're really good, presumably . . .'

'I don't know . . . The main purpose is to see if you're intelligent enough to join . . .'

'And what do they do, all these intelligent people, once they're in the club? Do they have meetings to solve the world's problems and save the rest of us the trouble, or what?'

'Well, they certainly have meetings.'

'And if you fail can you re-sit? Or do they give out badges. "I flunked Mensa". Seriously, young Harry . . . What if you fail?'

Harry looked thoughtful then said, 'I'll join the masons.' Sam nodded sympathetically. Harry scooped up some stew and cabbage. 'They're quite big in Bathgate.'

Talk turned to the evening's work and Sam explained about how operating lists were planned. 'Surgery's meant to be clean but a lot of it isn't, especially on waiting nights. So what we'll plan for is an orderly retreat from cleanliness. Three cases. Dirty, dirtier and downright bloody filthy. That's the appendix, the gall-bladder and the leg in that order, in case you're wondering. I've told them we'll start with the appendix at eight. Seen one, Andrew?'

'Not yet.'

Sam seemed disappointed by that. 'See one, do one, teach one,' he intoned. 'The three sacred steps to higher surgical wisdom and true holiness.' He looked at Scott again and brightened up. 'But maybe you've seen an amputation?'

Scott chewed his last mouthful of stew carefully, swallowed it and said no. The fat lady in pink bustled in and took their plates away, returning with the pudding, a solid mixture of sponge and jelly topped with artificial cream. Even Gus raised an eyebrow. 'It's Charlotte Russe, Dr Ratho,' said the woman sharply. 'I thought ye liked it.'

Shortly before eight Sam led the way into the operating suite. He and Scott stripped and showered and put on the slack white pyjamas on offer then scrubbed up, Scott for the first time. 'I'm not sure all this kills germs,' said Sam, 'but it keeps theatre sister happy. Look. Finger by finger. And each finger has four sides . . . Knuckles and nails seem to be dens of exceptional bacteriological depravity. No. More like that. Yes. No hurry. This is when your average surgeon works out what he's actually going to do once he gets in there. Then hold your hands up so the nasty germs drip off your elbows on to the floor. Good lad.' Sam, with his hands held up and apart, marched solemnly towards a staff nurse who was holding a green gown outspread. 'Introibo ad altarem Dei . . . Thanks, love. Watching, Andrew? And they actually like tying you up. Now . . . No-touch technique. Staff thinks I mean her, but it's actually how to get your gloves on without touching the outside. Astonish your friends on wintry mornings.'

Slowly and awkwardly, and helped quite a lot by Sam's banter Scott was transformed. Masked, hatted, scrubbed, gowned and gloved, he followed the SHO into the bright empty space of the operating area to await the first patient. She arrived, half-naked and already stertorously asleep, under the care of an anaesthetist and a theatre orderly. Sam swabbed her abdomen with foamy, brownish liquid in big house-painting strokes, covered her with green drapes until only a six-inch square of skin was showing, then cut down into skin with a single firm sweep of the scalpel. Scott, standing at his elbow, swallowed heavily and took a couple of deep breaths, reminding himself there was worse to come. Curiously, that moment was the worst. After the skin was parted the disturbing connection with normality was severed and what he saw was new and interesting: the glistening viscera that slithered like big, sluggish worms, the blood vessels pulsing red and the appendix itself, a vestigial organ here thickened and tense like a septic finger. Sam worked and Scott held things with a retractor as he directed. His skill was engrossing, more so even than the internal landscape in which he practised it. He parted healthy tissue, pausing now and

221

then to curb bleeding with a sizzling diathermy electrode, mobilising the appendix until it stood out, clamped above and below where it would be severed, the long purse-string stitch round its base ready to be drawn tight to close the large intestine as soon as it separated.

'There, lad. Nick that without nicking my finger and its yours.' Scott was handed another scalpel, slid it between the clamps and watched as appendix fell away with the uppermost clamp. Sam nodded. 'It's thanks to you she'll pull through, doctor, but I'd be happy just to tidy things up for you . . .' He tucked the stump in, tightened the long suture until all that was left was a grey dimple in the large intestine, swabbed the wound dry and closed it with easy, confident stitches: catgut for the peritoneum, black silk for the deep fascia and a clever, single spiralling stitch that went the length of the skin wound and hardly showed at all when he was finished. The girl was wheeled away and they took their gloves and gowns off and went for coffee in a little windowless sitting-room beside the shower. The case that followed, Sam explained, was registrar stuff and Duncan, his immediate superior, would be coming in shortly. Students, however, were welcome on such occasions as second assistants and came in quite useful for holding things open so the grown-ups could see properly.

The next operation was both more serious and a lot less fun. Duncan, a tall, morose man, scrubbed in grim silence and worked away in Mrs Peters' abdomen with a kind of joyless determination, communicating in words of one or two syllables ('Swab', 'Retract', 'Suction') like a surgeon in a film. Sam, no longer in charge, was subdued and silent. For Scott it was a long hour and a quarter. True, working up there under the liver with blood vessels and bile ducts crowded together above a swollen, inflamed gall-bladder was complicated and dangerous, but it seemed to Scott that the tension and silence didn't help. If Sam and Duncan and the theatre sister who handed them the things they asked for had all hated each other the atmosphere would have been no different. It relaxed only a little when the gall-bladder was eventually freed: a dull, slimy little pouch of pus and gravel cut loose and dumped in a stainless steel bowl, to be prodded and inspected like a newly landed fish. When they finished the registrar went straight home, muttering something about checking up by phone later and not even pausing for a coffee in the little lounge before he left. Perhaps he and Sam really didn't get on.

Sam's good cheer returned immediately. He despatched a theatre orderly down to the dining room for sandwiches and while they were waiting talked, with a little prompting from Scott, about the registrar. 'Getting to the bitter stage, maybe. Failed another senior registrar interview last week, probably his fourth or fifth. A less determined chap, or one with a wee bit more insight, might be starting to turn his mind to other things than surgery . . . Radiology, I suppose, or chiropody, or sisal-planting in the Lesser Antilles . . . It's entirely up to him, of course. He can cut, as you saw, but he's such a miserable bugger even when he's got nothing to be miserable about. And I think even Sir Edgar may have noticed . . . Little things like not laughing at his jokes, but they mount up, especially when there are a dozen other chaps around who can cut just as well and spread a lot less in the way of gloom . . . Something to do with his potty-training, no doubt, but not the kind of thing you can ask about and in any case far too late for anything to be done. So don't be a miserable bugger, young Scott, like your dumb friend who's probably going to end up as a West Lothian GP and Grand Imperial Wizard of the Bathgate masons.'

As they sat and chatted it seemed to Scott that surgery as a career had its attractions: the preference for action; the visible results of septic organs detached and despatched to pathology for a vindicating final dagnosis; the backstage cameraderie in which the larger, career-shaping truths of medicine were shared in warning and advice by people it might actually be quite fun to work with. The theatre orderly appeared with sandwiches – ham and pickle, chicken and tomato – and Sam thanked him in appalling French, which to Scott's surprise the man acknowledged in appalling English ('No troo-belle, m' sieur, don't mention eet . . .') as though the exchange were part of some long-running comic-waiter joke of the kind that developed in little groups that worked closely together. It was only when they were half way through the amputation that Scott realised the orderly actually was a Frenchman whose English, though not as bad as he sometimes pretended, was frequently eccentric.

The procedure was a rough one and the Frenchman had the worst of it. The patient lay gassed and oblivious, his stinking leg wrapped from the knee in green towels and held by the orderly while Sam worked to sever it at mid-thigh level, cutting back into its depths so that the raw end of bone left when he sawed through the femur would be cushioned by generous flaps of skin and muscle. 'You see the idea, young Scott . . . Not one of our most up-to-the-minute tricks. The chap who did several hundred of them in an afternoon at Waterloo would probably recognise it but might think we were a bit slow, n'est-ce pas, Jacques?'

'What eez zees, heh, Waterloo . . . ?'

Eventually blood vessels were tied off, nerves neatly snipped, the bone sawed through, the leg detached and the flaps pronounced viable. The failure of blood supply that had preceded the man's gangrene did not, it seemed, extend to the thigh, where blood vessels thumped with life, muscles bled when cut and the skin edges oozed to Sam's complete satisfaction. He dabbed the wound dry and closed it with big loose stitches and thanked the anaesthetist and theatre sister. Scott, who had had little to do except look and occasionally hold things out of the way with a retractor, was impressed. A man who would have died a miserable death had been tidied up and now, admittedly minus a leg, would live. It was half past ten on a Friday night. Appendix, gall-bladder and the foul, decaying limb, each already neatly labelled for the pathologist on Monday morning, no longer posed any threat to life or health. The last patient was wheeled away and the theatre staff moved in to scrub and clean. The list was over.

Back in the female ward the lights were dimmed and the evening shift of nurses had handed over to a night shift of only three, a third year student nurse and two even more junior colleagues, who moved quietly about checking readings and worrying over intra-venous infusions while the two rows of recumbent patients watched or dozed or slept. Sam and Scott and the third year nurse went quickly round, spending most time with the appendix girl and Mrs Peters, who lay on her side snoring heavily. In the limited official vocabulary of nursing, both were comfortable, and there was nothing about the pulse, temperature or blood pressure of either to suggest that anything was amiss.

In the doctors' room of the male ward Gus sat alone. Sam asked what had happened to Harry and grunted disapprovingly when Gus reported that he had gone home. Scott, who had been thinking of excusing himself at the first opportunity that offered itself, changed his mind. To leave a surgical admitting night before midnight was perhaps to invite a reputation for being fit only for general practice in West Lothian. They went into the ward. In the first bed on the left lay a man perhaps in his sixties. Gus smiled and said 'The only new patient, Sam . . . A Mr Tulloch. Came in at quarter to ten. His GP had rung me earlier. Straightforward acute retention of urine. Previously quite well.'

'How much when you catheterised him?'

'I'd actually only just finished clerking him, Sam . . .'

'Hmph.'

'Everything's organised just to slip a tube in . . . He's not in much discomfort . . . I knew you'd be along any minute and thought Andrew might like to . . .'

Sam turned to Scott. 'Ever done one?' Scott nodded. 'The sooner the better . . . I'll tell nursey you're an expert and you'll let me know straight away if you get into trouble. Nurse?'

Scott had been taught how to intubate the male bladder by an omniscient and omnicompetent Indian house officer in the medical unit of a hospital near Glasgow where he had spent two weeks avoiding the rigours of manse life over Christmas the previous year. He had learned a lot, and there were a number of procedures, like venepunctures, bone marrow biopsies and catheterisations, in which he was competent because he had practised them at Hairmyres and because he could still hear in his head Dr Chakrabati's patient and detailed instructions unfolding as he performed them. Scott talked briefly to Mr Tulloch and explained what he was going to do. A nurse appeared with the appropriate set of paper towels, tubes, bottles and dishes on a trolley, he washed his hands and put on a pair of rubber gloves and a softly Indian tape-recording in his head began 'First thoroughly wash the penis, remembering of course to retract the prepuce if present . . .'

The student nurse helping him seemed to have done one or two of them before too, and everything went reasonably smoothly. Nobody dropped anything, and when she held a swab with a dab of lubricant on it he extruded the tip of the catheter from its sheath, coated it then slid it a good distance into the man's urethra without any difficulty, indeed without encountering any significant resistance at all. That was odd. If the man couldn't pee the working assumption was that his prostate was large and his urethra tight. A moment later the clear polythene sheath the catheter came in began to fill with urine. The nurse held a cardboard container ready and Scott let the open end of the catheter, its cover and such urine as had already appeared fall into it. The flow continued for a few more seconds then stopped. That was very suspicious. If Mr Tulloch was serious about having urinary retention he would have to produce two or three pints at least.

'Look,' said the nurse, pointing to the paper towel covering most of the man's abdomen. 'Hm,' said Scott, 'I think I'd better get Dr Huntly to come and take a look . . .' The stiff white paper square through which the intubated penis coyly peeped was bobbing up and down, not much, perhaps only a few millimetres, but quite definitely moving. The lower abdominal swelling which everyone had assumed was a bladder was pulsating, something the bladder did not normally do. Scott hesitated then laid a gloved hand firmly on the paper-covered lump. The pulsation was regular, firm and unequivocal to the touch. 'It's a bit sorer when you press it,' said Mr Tulloch.

'Sorry . . . I'm just going to get Dr Huntly to have a look at you, Mr Tulloch.'

The man smiled. 'So you said, son.'

'Sorry. I'll get him right away.'

The nurse began to tidy up, as nurses seemed to without being told, and Scott crossed the darkened ward to where Sam was just finishing at the bed opposite. 'Yes, lad? You just went right ahead and did a prostatectomy? Good. All the less to tackle tomorrow . . .' Gus laughed and so did the third year nurse. 'I got in all right but there wasn't much urine,' said Scott. 'A hundred cc's at most. And you might want to have a look at his belly . . .' They all went back to Mr Tulloch's bed. Sam uncovered him and inspected his pale abdomen with its curious throbbing fullness and then laid on a hand, nodding to himself. Gus looked distinctly shifty.

'So it's not my water?' said Mr Tulloch. Sam nodded again and pushed the sheet further down, feeling in the man's groins. 'Are your legs a bit sore, Mr Tulloch?'

'Kind of numb, maybe.'

'Yes . . . Well, I think we'd better get on with things tonight . . . I'm going to ask one of the senior surgeons to come in. An expert, really, in the kind of thing you need. A bit of what we call vascular surgery, surgery on the blood vessels. The kind of thing it's better to get on with more or less straight away, if that's all right with you.'

'So what's wrong?'

Sam explained, as gently as anyone could, that the big artery in the back of the abdomen, important because it carried the blood supply to both legs, had begun to stretch a bit and needed to be repaired urgently before the blood supply to the legs got any worse. As he spoke Scott thought of the leg they had just removed and wondered what it would be like for the man to rot from the waist down, though morphine would probably spare him from the worst. Mr Tulloch, who presumably didn't know any of that, looked thoughtful. 'Just go right ahead, doctor,' he said quietly. 'We'll get you something for the pain straight away,' said Sam, 'and something to calm your nerves.' Gus smiled and nodded and picked up the man's drug chart from the end of the bed.

Back in the doctors' room again, Sam read the GP's letter, flicked through Mr Tulloch's case notes, made some emphatic alterations to Gus's account of the abdominal findings, added a couple of paragraphs of his own at the end then picked up the phone and asked the operator to get him a number which he seemed to know off by heart. 'Sam Huntly here, Sir Edgar. Sorry to bother you at home, sir . . . Got a vascular emergency, a chap of sixty eight, good previous health, with a leaking abdominal aneurysm. Six hour history of pain. Pulsatile and expansile lower abdominal swelling, femoral pulses present but diminished, no immediate risk to distal tissue and he's agreed to surgery. Sir. Very good, sir. Yes, I'll get him in . . . Midnight, sir. I'll see everything's ready.' Scott looked at his watch. It was quarter past eleven. Sam turned to Gus. 'No stopping him, even at his age. I'll tell the theatre bods. And perhaps you could let Duncan know he's first assistant for a big pair-of-trousers job with His Eminence, starting promptly at midnight. You might as well mind the shop out here until things settle then push off to your bed . . . Andrew?'

'Yes?'

'You probably won't have seen a leaking aortic aneurysm snatched from the jaws of death.'

'No.'

'Now's your chance. Well, midnight is. OK?'

From curiosity and an aversion to the idea of general practice in West Lothian, Scott agreed and was immediately sent to take blood from Mr Tulloch for emergency investigations and cross-matching. Sam sat down at the desk in the doctors' room to ensure by a series of phone calls that everything that was meant to happen by midnight would happen by midnight, so that Sir Edgar could simply walk into the operating theatre and get on with it. When Scott came back with his blood tubes Sam was still on the phone, evidently to an anaesthetist. '. . . previously fit chap, no known diseases, medications or vices of significance, eight centimetre aneurysm, maybe, but getting bigger even as we speak. So if you don't mind coming in, Joe, because it probably is a senior registrar kind of job, not one for the duty SHO who's on for appendices with a bottle of ether and a red spotted hankerchief . . . Thanks, Joe . . . Sir Edgar will be pleased. See you soon . . . No, he sounded quite pleased . . . And he'll make it sound as if it happens every second night . . . Right . . . Thank God it doesn't . . . Cheers.'

'Ah, good lad . . .' Sam picked a handful of assorted blood forms from a stand on the desk and took the tubes from Scott. 'We'll start with BTS. Give 'em details . . . They're like the milkman. Want to know why you want eighteen pints instead of your usual two. And can you ring for a porter? It's three one three. Thanks, Andrew.' As Sam scribbled Scott remembered a few more things about aortic aneurysms and what happened to people with them. Most of it was bad. Without an operation they all died; with one, some of them made it, but probably not many. No one seemed to have explained that to Mr Tulloch. Did he have a wife and family who ought to know? Was he the kind of chap who might like a word with a priest before things went any further? That was another side of surgery that Scott found less vivifying: a tendency to minimise difficulties, to act as if everything was a matter of routine and as if most of the routines worked well and safely most of the time. Did patients prefer that kind of brisk optimism? Did it spare them knowledge that would only alarm them? And was there any way of finding out how much they wanted to know without first disclosing what kind of trouble they were in? The more Scott thought about it the more obvious it became why surgeons went about it the way they did. He could not imagine himself sitting on the bed of a suffering, trusting man and going through the grim facts of it all, perhaps being asked some painfully searching questions. 'What are his chances, Sam?'

'Grim if we do, appalling if we don't. So we do. And the boss is actually quite good at it. It just takes a bit of time.'

For fear of sounding less than keen, Scott did not ask how long. In the event Sir Edgar came in at midnight. Everything was ready for him: the patient asleep on the table, Sam, Duncan and Scott standing waiting with the theatre sister and her assistant. He made a long abdominal incision, from ribs to below the pounding mass but side-stepping the umbilicus in a neat little curved diversion, and gently moved everything out of the way to reveal a bruised, gory, pulsating bulge in the lower aorta, starting just below the arteries to the kidneys and extending a bit into the main artery to the right leg. It all took time, so much that Scott began to think that most of the operation was really just a preparation for the operation itself, the actual vascular repair. Living tissue had to be mobilised and yet preserved, treated with care and kept moist and warm by packs that had to be constantly changed. Little blood vessels had to be tied off or cauterised with the diathermy probe. Sir Edgar, grunting and sometimes humming long, strange airs that might once have been opera, worked happily and even sometimes chatted as he worked, less than Sam had done but a lot more than Duncan. Odd and various topics, such as hi-fi equipment, Rhodesia and Japanese cars, arrived from nowhere and were dropped just as suddenly. Scott, who had been introduced briefly just before they began, was puzzled to be asked abruptly what medical students thought of the workings of the Abortion Act, and relieved to realise only moments afterwards that Sir Edgar was more interested in the latest spurt of blood than he was in the answer.

By half past one everything was ready for the main part of the procedure, the vascular repair. Sir Edgar, puffing and wheezing a bit and still giving forth odd snatches of opera, worked deep in the abdomen to isolate the weakened, swollen blood vessel, clamping it off with large, padded forceps and then freeing it from the spine behind, working his way down to the point where it bifurcated to form the two main arteries to the legs. Sam's phrase about 'a big pair-of-trousers job' made sudden sense. The shape of the piece to be removed was an upside-down Y, its stem considerably wider than the legs, and therefore approximately trouser-shaped. The graft to be inserted, a similarly Y-shaped object constructed of woven man-made fibre, lay ready on the theatre sister's trolley. By two the business of sewing it in had begun: a long, meticulous struggle to join the stump of the old man's aorta to the stem of the prosthesis, and make the join blood-tight, and then to do the same at the severed end of each of the iliac arteries. Sir Edgar, large and heavy, stooped and turned to join good new material to doubtful old stuff, with tiny stitches done in a puddle of blood at the bottom of a deep dark hole. He did not hurry. Happy little grunts told his assistants when the work was going well, long silences and occasional testily indrawn breaths denoted difficulties. By four he was ready to ease the clamp that held the healthy aorta just below the twin arteries going off to the kidneys. The little dacron trousers filled and he eased the clamp further. The graft bulged and began to throb. He chuckled happily, then stopped as the puddle of blood welled deeper. Something, probably the uppermost suture line, was leaking. He leaned down and twisted round trying to see where the blood was coming from as Duncan used the suction probe to empty the steadily reaccumulating puddle. Eventually he sniffed, shook his head and reapplied the clamp. 'Sorry, chaps. Thought we were home and dry. We're not. Thank you, sister.' He was handed forceps and a curved, threaded needle. 'We'll just double up a bit round the back here . . . Thank you, Duncan.' He was sixty and he was doing difficult, even desperate, emergency surgery. It was long after midnight and things were going wrong and now he was going back in to try and retrieve them. How tired was he? How disappointed? And if things went badly, how long could he go on?

Three quarters of an hour later he eased the clamp again. Once more the graft expanded and once more it leaked, this time at one of the lower suture lines. Again he clamped the aorta and reinforced a line of stitches. Scott watched with the rest as the slender thread pulled fabric and blood vessel together and the old man flicked more and more of his neat little stitches into being. And every stitch demanded skill and judgement. Mr Tulloch had developed an aneurysm because his arteries were weakened by a process of fatty degeneration far more widespread then the aneurysm itself. If the surgeon were to pull too hard the stitch would simply cut through, but if it were left loose enough to avoid that risk completely then the suture line would never withstand the pulsing pressure of blood. Sir

230

Edgar, puffing a little, straightened up again and watched as Duncan sucked away all the blood around the operative site, then leaned in again and gradually released the clamp. The graft filled and pulsated and this time did not leak. Sir Edgar glanced round his team of helpers, looked back into the wound, saw that it was still dry and nodded, then stood back and straightened up and flexed his arms and moved from one foot to the other as though he had been suffering from cramp for quite a long time. They waited for several minutes to be absolutely sure everything was holding. When he stooped again to begin the long slow business of closing up he was humming the toreador song from *Carmen*.

By half past five they were closing the wound, but the anaesthetist was not quite happy. Mr Tulloch's blood pressure had failed to come up as expected, and the most worrying possible explanation for that was bleeding at the graft site. Sam was detailed to check the patient's pulses at knee and ankle and reported that all was well. Even if the graft were leaking a bit it was still doing its job. The anaesthetist checked his readings again and reported no improvement but no deterioration either. Sir Edgar decided to wait and see, so for a further half hour they stood by in readiness to go in again if they had to. For Scott it was a low point: had they finished or were they about to start again and be in there for hours more. The sky beyond the towers of Heriot's school began to lighten. Just after six the anaesthetist reported a sustained and healthy rise in the patient's blood pressure. Sir Edgar ordered that the man be taken back to the ward and watched closely. The operation was over.

In the doctors' room a strange euphoria took over. Sir Edgar, Duncan, Sam and Scott sat with tea and toast. They had endured and prevailed and the patient had lived. A sixty year old surgeon had worked all night and in doing so had saved a life of a sixty-eight year old patient and passed on some of his skill to others. Scott, a witness and occasional holder of things out of the way, felt somehow part of it too. In the armchair Sir Edgar, unshaven, sports-jacketed and tieless, was jovial and relaxed: perhaps being a distinguished surgeon was lonely, and something like this a treat for him. He talked and joked and even got up to pour everyone's second cup of tea. As it grew light outside it somehow mattered less that no one had been to bed. In an odd sort of way they were having a party now, and no one wanted to go home.

At seven Sir Edgar got up and suddenly sounded like a consultant again. 'Duncan, I wonder if we might go round now, and call it my ward round for the day . . . Scarcely worth coming in again for ten o'clock. Shall we check on Mr Tulloch and cast a quick eye over the rest of them and leave it at that?' The party was over. They all got up, trooped into the male ward and started at the aneurysm patient, whose readings were now entirely reassuring and who snored placidly under the influence of morphine, watched by a nurse responsible for him alone. Sir Edgar inspected his urine output as collected in the catheter bag, felt for his pulses, scrutinised his drug chart and all the other documentation in unnecessary detail and thanked the nurse with some ceremony. He was enjoying himself.

The next patient was the man whose leg had been removed the previous evening. He was awake and watchful and grinned as the doctors approached. 'Yes, Duncan?' said Sir Edgar.

'I think Dr Huntly . . .'

'Sam?'

'Mr Hurst came in last night, sir. Ischaemic left leg. Rather a late presentation, but above-knee amputation quite straightforward, sir.'

'Good, Sam. A bit of orthopaedic experience often comes in handy, hm?' Sam nodded. Sir Edgar turned to the patient. 'And how are you this morning, Mr, um, Hurst?'

The man grinned more fiercely than ever and tried to prop himself up on one elbow. Sir Edgar sat down on his bed and tried to indicate that the man should rest. 'I want to shake your hand,' said the patient, still struggling to sit forward. 'I want to shake the hand of the man that saved my life . . .'

'Sam . . . Dr Huntly here's the chap you want. But glad to hear you're pleased.'

The man was not to be put off. He struggled forward, seized Sir Edgar's hand and fell back on to the pillows again. His grin had become frankly insane. 'I used to work in hospitals . . . Call me a founder member of the National Health Service . . .'

'Really?'

'Southern General Hospital, Edinburgh. Before, during and after the war.'

'Splendid . . .' Sir Edgar made a gentle attempt to escape the man's grip. It seemed to tighten.

'Call me a fallen angel, but I worked with doctors once.'

'Quite,' said Sir Edgar, at last breaking from the man's grasp.

'You'll maybe know him . . . A Dr Smith?'

'Now that's a fairly common name, in medicine as elsewhere.'

'The bastard should have gone to jail . . . Same as me.'

Sir Edgar got up, nodding contentedly. 'And your leg's all right, Mr . . . Mr um . . .'

As they moved on Sam muttered about a drinking problem and possible DT's. Sir Edgar laughed. 'Quite. Anyone else, Duncan, or is that it for the men?'

In the female ward both the girl who had had appendicitis and the woman who had had her gallbladder removed were sore but grateful. Sir Edgar was jolly and gallant, apologising for the informality of the occasion and the earliness of the hour. The staff nurse who accompanied them clearly did not approve, but she had not been a party to the long struggle of the night. She shepherded Sir Edgar off the ward as though he were some kind of benign but not entirely trustworthy eccentric. At the top of the stairs he thanked Duncan and Sam and even Scott, whom he addressed as 'Mr . . . um . . .', before tripping off downstairs humming another of his tuneless fragments of opera. Duncan, miserable as ever, followed him down. Sam and Scott went back to the doctors' room on the male ward. Scott asked about Gus and the original diagnosis. 'Some houseboys don't look beyond the GP's letter,' said Sam. 'Especially if they're smug, idle and under the impression that housejobs are just a chore on the road to inevitable glory. But little things like that are beginning to take the shine off young Dr Ratho.'

'You wouldn't tell Sir Edgar . . .'

'God, no,' said Sam. 'I'd never do a thing like that. No . . . I told Duncan. He'll pass it on.'

As Scott took off his white coat and reached for his jacket he suddenly felt tired. It was Saturday morning and not yet eight o'clock. He could go back to the flat and sleep till lunchtime and then resume something like normal life. It had all been very interesting. To his surprise Sam thanked him for staying on and going into theatre for the aneurysm. 'And of course it'll do you no harm if you're thinking of applying for a housejob here,' he added. '. . . especially if old Tulloch actually makes it.'

'Mr Chairman?'

'Hello?'

'Andrew?'

'Oh. Hello.'

'Sandy here. Gosh, I haven't just woken you up or anything?'

'Yes, but it's all right.'

'Are you sure? I could ring back.'

'What time is it?'

'Nearly half past twelve. Are you all right?'

'Fine.'

'Really sorry to disturb you. Was it a wild night out?'

'No. Honest work. Admitting night. Amazing, really. All-night stuff with Sir Edgar, saving a life. Well, watching him.'

'I'm impressed . . . Andrew, I've just been down to the SRC. One or two things in our box, so I thought I should ring you . . .'

'Fine.' Sandy Lennox had been secretary of the Medical Students' Council for as long as Scott had been chairman, and was very organised about it. Her phone calls were short and clear, and her minutes of meetings crisp and sensible, with lists of things for people to do before next time and phrases like 'there was a general discussion' when people had been talking nonsense. She got on with things quickly and quietly and Scott found her very easy to work with. 'So what's new?'

'A long boring letter from the Scriba of the Society, mainly about the Ball so I just dealt with it, but it's done, in case Max asks you. And a sort of shifty reply about compulsory residence in gynaecology attachements. Says emergencies are common and important. Not what the survey showed, and it's on the agenda already. And an odd thing inviting you to the opening of the very first bit of the new Institute. Notice is a bit short, which is the main reason I rang you on a Saturday and spoiled your beauty sleep.'

'When?'

'Tuesday, four o'clock. Looks as if someone suddenly thought, oh, yes, what about some students? Can you go?'

'Um. Think so.'

'OK. I'll RSVP it for you. Four o'clock, the neuropathology suite, boring speeches and tea will be served.'

'Is that what it says?'

'Sort of. And it's that little new bit at the back of the mortuary.'

'I know, and I can just picture it. Wee sausage rolls laid out on the slabs . . .'

Sandy laughed. 'Was it really all night?'

'For some of us. Gus was minding the shop but it went all quiet out there so he got to go to bed. And Sir Edgar was actually pretty good. Took his time, but sorted out a very messy abdominal aortic aneurysm. We finished about six and hung around a bit to see if it would leak, but it didn't, so everyone got home in time for breakfast.'

'I'm really impressed, Mr Chairman.'

'How's the Southern?'

'All right. Dr Lauder's lovely. Worries about the wee old ladies and keeps up to date as well. And so lovably scruffy. I keep having to stop myself offering to darn his socks.'

Scott laughed. 'But they're teaching you some medicine too?'

'Gosh yes. Lots. And Dr Lauder turns up the most amazing stuff. An old lady came in who looked like a stroke but wasn't quite right. He had a peek and prod at her and said, hmm, what about TB? TB meningitis? And it was. So she's doing quite well now on triple therapy. And her occupation, that's the oddest bit of all. She was a cockle-gatherer.'

'A what?'

'You know. Cockles and mussels alive, alive-o. Sent in from somewhere away down the coast and she gathers shellfish for a living. So we're all having a wonderful time, and plotting about how to get his housejob.'

Scott sat cold and naked and listened happily to Sandy rattling on about the Southern. She was being less businesslike than usual, which was fine since no one was in a hurry. Lots of people, especially girls, liked Rob Lauder's medical unit. It was friendly and scruffy and efficient, like its senior physician, and it still offered genuine general medical experience when most medical units were specialising, teaching more and more about less and less for students who didn't want to be specialists, or at least not yet. Sandy's chances of a housejob there were probably quite good. She was bright and competent and even vaguely good-looking – a combination known to appeal to Dr Lauder at housejob interviews – and having the Clinical Dean as your dad probably helped a bit too, in its quiet Edinburgh way.

'. . . and his outpatient clinics are amazing. People come in and sit down and tell him all their troubles first, and they chat about all

that for a while before they get round to the medical bits. And he's
not afraid of dying people . . . You know what I mean?'

'Think so.'

'Spends time with them, listens and chats as if he was their last
ever new friend. It's just so different from the Institute that it's like
discovering medicine all over again. I really want to be a doctor . . .'

'. . . when I grow up.' There was a short silence. 'Sorry.'

'You're right. I shouldn't chatter on to a busy chairman . . . But I
am enjoying it.'

'Good. And thanks for dealing with all that stuff. What did Max's
lot want?'

'Something boring to do with bars and money. It was all in the
files of last year's Ball committee. I suppose they've just lost theirs.
So I put them right tactfully and it should be all right, and you can
tell Max if you see him.'

'Thanks.'

'How's surgery?'

'I keep thinking I might want to be one. Not sure. The SHO
seems to have quite a nice life, but the registrar's miserable. And I
haven't seen the senior registrar yet. How's Gus enjoying it?'

'So-so. Doesn't say much. Likes Sir Edgar and doesn't like the
SHO . . . And Tuesday's all right?'

'Tuesday?'

'The opening thing. Sausage rolls on the post mortem tables. It's
chairman and secretary too, so I'll try and get down from the
Southern in time. See you there, Andrew, if you remember.'

'Oh. Yes.'

'And we can have a look at some stuff for the faculty liaison
committee. I'll bring the file.'

'Oh. All right. Thanks, Sandy.'

'Bye.'

'Bye.'

On Monday morning the ward round started with Mr Tulloch.
He was drowsy still, but probably sufficiently alert to realise that a
lot of doctors now viewed his case as interesting and important. He
smiled sleepily as Sir Edgar introduced himself, leaned over him,
called him 'my dear chap' and asked how he was feeling. Then a
nurse pulled back the covers and the shroud-like gown to expose a
pale, swollen abdomen with a strip of wound dressing extending

from the ribs to the shaven remnants of pubic hair. Sir Edgar borrowed his senior registrar's stethoscope and listened, grunting and sniffing in a way that might have drowned all but the loudest sounds from within the patient, then grinned and nodded, took the stethoscope from his ears and handed it back to its owner. Next Sir Edgar turned his attention to his urine bag slung from the frame of the bed. He lifted it, weighed it in his hand, held it up to check the amount it contained against the black volume markings on its edge then put it down. Again he appeared content. For aortic aneurysm patients, a pint or so of cloudy, bloodstained urine could mean the difference between life and death. Scott, who had inserted the catheter in the first place, even before the proper diagnosis had been made, experienced his own moment of craftsmanlike satisfaction. Then the nurse drew the covers from the Mr Tulloch's legs and Sir Edgar, with more wheezing and grunting and odd semi-musical noises, pawed his knees and feet in search of pulses, nodding and smiling to himself with each successive confirmation of the restoration of blood flow. He straightened up and the nurse covered the patient once more.

'Well done, my dear chap.' said Sir Edgar 'Awfully well done. If you can just bear with us for a few more days of, um, rest and observation, I should have thought that, um, all being well, um, we might be thinking about getting you home to Mrs, um . . .' Sam whispered helpfully and Sir Edgar nodded. 'Mrs Tulloch. Perhaps towards the end of the week after next.' He stepped closer to the patient again and took his hand. 'And what about the pain? We're treating that adequately, are we?' Mr Tulloch looked thoughtful, perhaps even frowned. Sir Edgar swung round and fixed on his senior registrar, who had returned that morning from holiday and had presumably never seen the patient before. 'Kenneth?'

The senior registrar, a tall, sallow man whose freshly laundered white coat, in order to be long enough, was wide enough to go round him twice, smiled and said 'I'm sure it's all been taken care of Sir Edgar. Duncan?'

The registrar looked surprised and turned to the ward sister who pointedly avoided his gaze. Sam lifted a clipboard with a drug chart from the end of the bed. 'Mr Tulloch had thirty milligrams of Omnopon approximately six-hourly over Saturday and . . . most of Sunday.'

'Let me see, Sam.' Sir Edgar seized the clipboard with his left hand and slapped it firmly with his right. 'Where are the students, Kenneth? Ah, yes.' Without thinking about it, Scott found himself standing more or less to attention. 'Mr um, Mr . . .' Again Sam whispered helpfully. 'Mr Scott . . . Ah, yes. Of course. Mr Scott. Whatever surgical skills you may go on to develop, you can be sure that unless post-operative pain control is adequate your patients will only rarely be grateful to you. Mr Tully here, snatched only two days ago from the jaws of, um, a potentially tricky illness, can hardly be expected to feel kindly towards us if we have neglected to think of his resultant pain. My dear chap . . .' Sir Edgar had turned to the patient again. 'Are you in pain just now?' Mr Tulloch looked around the semi-circle of faces at the end of his bed then gave a tiny nod. 'We'll get you something for it right away.' Sir Edgar handed the clipboard to sister, who handed it, along with the keys of the drug cupboard, to the staff nurse, who in turn excused herself from the ward round.

'And now, my dear chap, how did you sleep last night?' Mr Tulloch had not slept well. Gus was sent off to retrieve the drug chart from the staff nurse. 'Rest,' said Sir Edgar, 'rest and sleep and the relief of pain . . . I don't know if any of you have any experience of the receiving end of the business of surgery. I should say straight away that I have, and while sparing you the details I can assure you that for the sake of my patients I dearly wish it had happened some decades earlier.' The patient's hand was clasped again. 'Mr Tully, may I say simply that I know how you must feel . . . So perhaps one of our students . . .' Sir Edgar peered round the semi-circle. 'You, sir . . .' Harry, who had been standing idly by, in the manner of one who had already decided against a future in surgery, was taken aback. 'Sir?'

'Yes, you . . . Mr um . . .' This time Sam did not help. Sir Edgar's irritation increased. 'You, sir . . .'

'Yes, sir?'

'You, sir . . . The hypnotic of choice in the post-operative patient. Yes? Quickly. Drug of choice?'

'Soneryl, sir?'

'What?' The word came out as a kind of long, strangled, whooping grunt. A couple of mighty roars and the movie proper would begin. Harry bit his lip. The senior registrar smiled happily

238

and the ward sister, probably the most experienced witness of such drama, was looking as though she expected it might all take some time. 'A barbiturate?' Sir Edgar pronounced the word syllable by syllable, with precision and infinite contempt, his head rolling around on his shoulders as he did so. 'A barbiturate, boy?' Harry nodded. The drug he had named for the job was not unreasonable: perhaps getting a little old-fashioned now, but still widely used and probably the staple hypnotic in at least half the wards in the Institute.

If Scott had been asked the question he would have answered similarly, on the assumption that Sir Edgar's views on drug therapy were probably rather conservative. It would have been a serious mistake. 'Poison!' His neck writhed and his shoulders heaved. 'A poison both acute and chronic, strewn around this hospital, I grant you, by night nurses pushing drug trolleys positively groaning with that and similar poisons . . . But a poison all the same.' He lowered his voice and closed in on his victim. 'They all are. Every single barbiturate could be dropped from our pharmacopoiea without detriment to anyone except the occasional unfortunate with epilepsy. Ah, Gus . . .' The houseman had returned and handed Mr Tulloch's drug chart to his chief, whose rage subsided as quickly as it had arisen. He smiled. 'Thank you, Gus . . . Now, what shall we prescribe to make sure . . . My God! Good God, man, what's this?' A large forefinger prodded the top line of the drug chart. Sir Edgar drew a mighty breath. *'Soneryl?'* The MGM lion could not have done better.

Half an hour later, on the way down to the outpatient clinic, Sam talked a little more about Gus. 'No idea what he's going to end up in, but it's not going to be surgery. Turned up in August as if he was doing us all a great favour and didn't really mind our accents and our rough ways. Got up the chief's nose by chatting about immunological matters he seemed not actually to know very much about. And whatever the old bugger's faults he's not one for bull-shitters. So missing the aneurysm and using the great surgeon's least favourite pill on his most favourite patient really isn't going to affect his career very much at all . . . D'you know him?'

'Vaguely. His girlfriend's in our year. And he was big in the Society of Physic.'

Sam grunted. 'He would be. But the great thing about surgery as a specialty is that shits like him get found out pretty quickly and go off and specialise in something else.' As they arrived in the outpatients department Scott reflected that a speciality without people like Gus might be quite agreeable, but was that enough to make up for having people like Duncan, and the senior registrar and, on a bad day, Sir Edgar?

The neuropathology place was signposted on a series of makeshift cardboard notices beginning at the front door of the drab and malodorous two-storey building that housed the Institute's mortuary and post mortem room. Scott walked quickly through its dim corridors. The rich, half-sweet smell of death was everywhere, conjuring up mad pathologists and pale opened corpses, their faces pulled down so that their skulls could be opened, and the variously bored and nauseated students who, in the course of clocking up attendances at the compulsory twelve post mortems, stood around trying not to yawn, faint or vomit. Suddenly the shabby, brown-painted corridor ended in a pair of double doors, on the other side of which a broad, bright fluorescent-lit foyer opened. By the doors a glossy maroon notice board announced, under the crests of the university and the Institute, 'Departments of Neurology and Pathology: Webster Neuropathology Research and Teaching Suite'.

Scott had arrived just in time to join a short queue of people in suits moving into something labelled 'Lecture and Demonstration Theatre'. The place was bright and fresh, smelling of new wood and paint and carpeting, and there were seats for about forty people, most of them filled already. At the front was a screen and a neat modern lectern, behind which a dapper, rather plump, grey-haired man with a little moustache was pushing buttons in an attempt to control a slide projector shining through a window above the back row of seats. Beside him another, older man, the Chairman of the Board of Governors, an anatomy professor famed for the length of his sentences, stood smiling as though such technical trouble were a routine and agreeable preliminary on these occasions. Eventually a picture appeared, a huge outdoor tableau of Victorian pomp with carriages and plumed dignitaries, then disappeared again leaving the screen blank. The man with the moustache nodded. The older man tapped the lectern.

'Good afternoon, ladies and gentlemen. As chairman of the Board of Governors of the Royal Charitable Institute of Edinburgh, may I welcome you to an event of historic significance in the life of this great hospital: the opening of the first phase of a massive building programme which, when it is complete, will make the Institute – already one of the most distinguished centres of medical teaching and research in the world – also one of the most modern and well-equipped. Our little gathering today celebrates both an achievement – the opening of these compact, up-to-the-minute facilities for teaching and research in the vitally important field of neuropathology, made possible by a most generous donation from Mr Webster, happily present today . . .' The speaker paused and nodded and smiled at a decrepit figure crouched over a walking stick in the front row. '. . . both an achievement and great beginning – that of the complete reconstruction on its existing site of a one thousand bed teaching hospital. But first things first . . . Mr Webster, ladies and gentlemen, it is my privilege today to accept on behalf of the Board of Governors of the Royal Charitable Institute of Edinburgh the Webster Neuropathology Teaching and Research Suite. Mr Webster himself has stipulated a minimum of ceremony. He is by nature a retiring man, indeed a man of few words, but may I say pre-eminent in philanthropy and abundantly generous in this particular instance. He it was who, in conjunction with Dr Killick – who but for his well-merited promotion to the first chair of immunology at the new medical school in, um, Penang would have been with us today – saw our need for new facilities in this vital and fast-moving field of clinical science, and made the whole thing possible in a remarkably short space of months. Mr Webster's generosity speaks for itself. We have today first rate new research and teaching premises in a spot where only eighteen months ago stood an obsolete incinerator and its attendant fuel dump. Mr Webster, we thank you from the bottom of our hearts . . . And if the example set by this project in terms of speed of construction and standard of finish can be emulated for the duration of the whole of our immense rebuilding programme we shall consider ourselves very fortunate indeed . . .' The speaker paused. 'But here to tell us all about that is the man charged by the Board with the formidable responsibility of heading the planning team . . . A physician and administrator of vast experience and expertise in these complex matters . . . Dr Smith, from the offices of the Regional Board. Johnny, over to you.' The chairman smiled and moved to a seat in the front row, leaving the floor to the dapper, grey-haired man, who coughed modestly, thanked him and said 'First slide, please, if we may . . .'

The horse drawn carriages reappeared and Scott realised that they stood in what was now the consultant car park in front of the main door of the Institute. The broad flight of steps was flanked by men in dark suits and white gloves, and a few civic dignitaries and military officers escorted a small, stooped figure, undistinguished and clad also in black, who was about half way up to the door. 'Her Late Majesty Queen Victoria,' Dr Smith announced, 'officially opening the new Royal Charitable Institute of Edinburgh in 1868. It was quite a party, commemorated by a plaque just on the right as you enter that selfsame door today. The building that we know and love was a wonder in its time, a great improvement on the cramped and insanitary infirmary sickrooms that preceded it.' Dr Smith paused and struck a noble pose, not unlike that of the statue on the right at the foot of the steps. 'It is our privilege today to witness the beginning of another leap forward.' He looked up at the screen and pressed a button beside the little lectern at the front. There was a dull click. The carriages still waited and the plumed officers remained, stooped over the little monarch half way up the steps. He pressed the button again. Still nothing happened. The audience seemed on the whole sympathetic. One with more students in it, Scott reflected, would have reacted differently. Dr Smith abandoned his pose and went angrily at the button as though trying to get his money back from a jammed phone-box. Meanwhile the chairman of the Board of Governors had moved quietly from his seat and through the little auditorium to the projection booth up at the back. For a few moments the screen went dark, and with it the whole room, then a splendid vision in white and green and blue, an artist's impression of an immense and futuristic building surrounded by lawns and trees and basking under an idyllic sky, burst into view. 'The new Royal Charitable Institute of Edinburgh,' said Dr Smith, a little hesitantly.

It was the size of a city block, occupied the whole site of the present Institute and consisted of a pattern of six hexagonal flat-roofed towers, each six storeys high, linked by a spread of lower but equally futuristic building interrupted here and there by neat little islets of green, each flecked with trees. The edifice was dominated by the towers, which were white and horizontally striped with grey and black to signify their generous belts of window, and which, but for their immensity, could have been examples of a design considered but rejected by the manufacturers of Liquorice Allsorts. In the entire picture there were no people, although given the scale of the thing the artist could have got away with a few ant-like specks; nor were there cars or other vehicles, apart from a single ambulance at an entrance half way down one side, occupying roughly the spot where the horses had been standing in the previous picture.

To Scott the simple geometry and bright, flat colours owed more to the art of the comic strip than to any foreseeable reality in hospital design. Hospitals were complex, untidy and crowded. The Institute itself was like a sporadically developed but now hopelessly over-crowded mediaeval walled town. Dr Smith's picture, officially the shape of things to come, displayed something that was not simply unlikely; it was incredible. If a little green man with a bulging forehead had been shown alighting on the top of one of the towers in a flying sauceboat he would not have looked at all out of place. Scott glanced round the audience to see how other people were taking it. The chairman sat back, quizzically polite, like someone compelled by the presence of proud parents to endure a dreadful child. A couple of physicians muttered together. Sandy, sitting at the other end of the same row, caught Scott's eye and looked as if she were about to start giggling. It might be fun to talk to her later.

'Ladies and gentlemen . . . I give you our new hospital, the Royal Charitable Institute of Edinburgh. And I think . . .' Dr Smith raised a pointer and singled out a little cube in the middle of one of the green spaces, dwarfed by the adjoining towers. '. . . as they so helpfully put it on those splendid maps for tourists in the bus shelters on Princes Street . . . *You* are *here*. In the Webster, as I am sure we shall soon be calling it, a small but important part of the spendid finished product we see here . . . A building which, I think you will agree, Mr Chairman, will immediately put us on the level of any teaching hospital in the world . . .'

He smiled confidently round his little audience. 'And if our projection facilities are indeed still behaving, I think . . . Yes.' He pressed the button again and another view, by the artist who had done the previous one and a good deal before that for Dan Dare in the *Eagle*, appeared. The two central towers loomed high over an important looking entrance. The lone ambulance featured again, a little larger this time. 'Here we have another impression . . . The approach to what will be the finest Casualty Department in Great Britain, possibly in Europe . . .'

A few more of the audience seemed to have abandoned any attempt to connect what was being shown with what might happen. An old surgeon, an agreeable, somewhat rustic man now approaching retirement who still lectured his undergraduate classes on the merits of cauterisation as a treatment of piles, was chuckling to himself. Dr Smith listed some of the delights of possibly the finest Casualty Department in Europe – six examination and treatment rooms, an overnight stay ward, three emergency theatres and direct access to an intensive care unit – and Scott recalled the practical simplicities of the clean and dirty turrets, the friendly coffee room at the back and the generally cheerful scruffiness of the existing arrangements. They were, he decided, under no immediate threat. Another slide, a blueprint plan of the whole building labelled to show the location of all the main departments and specialties, appeared. 'And I hope that as each of you looks for your own place in this general scheme of things you will not be disappointed at what you find . . . Of the six main ward blocks . . .' The pointer swung grandly. '. . . two are surgical. Here . . . And two medical. Here . . .'

Dr Smith paused. The door of the lecture theatre had opened slowly and someone had slipped in, but instead of going quietly to the back as people were meant to, the newcomer stood against the door as though intent on preventing anyone from leaving until he allowed it. In the glow from the screen he shifted uncomfortably, a little man in a rough brown coat or perhaps dressing gown, unkempt and angry. And there was something very odd about the way he was standing. Scott looked again. The man definitely wore a dressing gown rather than a coat, and pyjamas rather than trousers. He was standing awkwardly because he had a crutch tucked under each shoulder, and he was standing on one foot because he had only one leg.

Dr Smith ignored the interruption and resumed his account of the new Institute. 'And in the top three floors of this one . . . Obstetrics . . . With gynaecology, so to speak, down below . . . And lastly . . . Here . . . A block with facilities for ophthalmology, dermatology, oto-rhino-laryngology, maxillofacial surgery and venereology . . . A corner of the Institute we are already beginning to think of as the, ahem, Tower of Babel . . .' There was a small chuckle from somewhere near the back, then a snarl from the dishevelled man standing at the door. 'Brother Smith?' The speaker ignored him. The slides moved on and a ground plan with a timetable for the gradual replacement of the whole hospital appeared, each section labelled with its projected date of completion, somewhere between 1970 and 1976. Dr Smith explained that one or two problems might be encountered in the course of construction. Those still listening were now either bored or frankly disbelieving. The man at the door shook with anger. 'Brother Smith!' he roared. 'Traitor to the craft! Son of Jubelum!' Dr Smith conceded that mud and, in dryer weather, dust might all cause minor difficulties, as would noise. 'Mocker of the Great Architect who is not mocked . . .' shouted the man at the door. The effect on the audience was minimal. If anything, more people were now paying attention to what Dr Smith was saying. 'Where were brotherly love, relief and truth,' roared the intruder, 'when I went down?' He shook his fist at the speaker and the screen, then made as though to strike out with a crutch. In doing so he crashed painfully to the floor, cursing as he fell, then lay against the door, shaking with rage but no longer trying to interrupt. Only then did Scott recognise him: he was the amputee from last week's admitting night, the old man from the lodging house. Dr Smith had changed slides again. Scott got up and moved to help the man, who might conceivably be having a belated bout of delirium tremens, and got there at the same time as an older man from near the front. As they knelt together over the slumped, splayed figure, who had now added indecent exposure to his list of offences, Scott recognised his fellow first-aider as Professor Lennox.

'His bowels should be burnt to ashes and scattered before the winds of heaven,' said the man.

'Quite,' said Lennie. 'But let's try to get you a bit more comfortable . . . And perhaps some fresh air?'

'Mr Walton?' said Scott, who had suddenly remembered the man's name. 'Are you in any pain?'

'My leg's a bit sore. Nothing terrible.'

'But you probably shouldn't be overdoing it meantime,' said Lennie. 'You know Mr Walton, Andrew?'

'Well, he's a patient from ward six,' said Scott.

'Splendid. Perhaps we could help him out into the fresh air, and then, Andrew, if you could perhaps just ring the ward. I'm sure they must be terribly worried about you, Mr Walton.'

While Dr Smith assured people that access and things like electricity and water supplies to functioning wards and departments could be almost one hundred percent guaranteed for the most of the construction era, as he called it, Lennie and Scott managed to get their patient upright and out of the little lecture theatre. They sat him down on a bright modern sofa in the foyer outside and Scott went off to find a telephone, leaving Lennie chatting to him about his operation. On the ward he had not been missed. The staff nurse who was in charge promised to send someone down with a wheelchair as soon as possible. Scott, who vaguely knew the girl and had expected her to be grateful, was surprised when she made it sound as if he were to blame for the whole troublesome business.

When Scott got back to the Webster suite Lennie and the patient were sitting side by side, chatting like old friends. Lennie explained. 'It turns out that Mr Walton and I worked together at the Southern once, rather a long time ago . . . ' Mr Walton chuckled happily then broke down in a fit of hideous coughing. Lennie steadied him with one hand and with the other made a glass-lifting gesture accompanied by a questioning movement of one eyebrow. Scott nodded. The man's coughing fit subsided. Lennie smiled at him and said 'And as part of his rehabilitation Mr Walton was just taking a little stroll around the hospital . . .'

'Nice wee place you've got here,' said the patient. 'I've always been very interested in mortuaries . . .' The three chatted about the Webster suite and the rebuilding project generally until a porter and a student nurse arrived from ward six and took Mr Walton away. He was wheeled out in style, sitting smartly with his crutches sloped over his right shoulder and waving a cheerful goodbye to his new friends. 'Pity he couldn't have stayed for a cup of tea,' said Lennie as he went. 'You know, representing the patients, as it were. Quite an interesting chap in his way. A complicated hard-luck story of course, but a lot more interesting to talk to than most of that lot in there.'

A tea-lady arrived pushing a creaking trolley with an urn, milk-jugs and cups. Lennie glanced at his watch. 'Hardly worth going back in, I should have thought. How's student politics, Andrew. . . ?

246

You must be awfully busy these days, rushing from demonstration to demonstration and trying to fit in a bit of medicine as well.' Scott laughed. It wasn't like that and Lennie knew it wasn't like that. Sandy probably got teased in the same way when she went home, but medical students had not had much to do with the various sit-ins and minor disturbances that had, over the previous term, assured Edinburgh that it was still part of the university life of Europe as a whole. A lecturer in Chinese who was rumoured to be a recruiting agent for the secret services had had his filing cabinet turned out and his status confirmed, and for a heady couple of nights people had slept in sleeping bags on the carpeted floor of the office of the university secretary, the latter incident ending when that official had led a dawn strike comprising a dozen of the fitter servitors who simply bundled four or five bleary and half-naked students out on to the stair and changed the lock on the door. Thereafter world revolution, at least in Edinburgh, had been cancelled owing to lack of interest.

'It's all right,' said Scott.

'Would youse two like a cup of tea?' the domestic enquired. 'While it's fresh.'

Lennie thanked her but thought it might be best to wait for the rest, who would be out shortly. The women clattered away quite contentedly with her cups and saucers then asked Lennie if he thought she ought to start pouring for everybody to avoid a queue. He looked at his watch again and nodded, then turned to Scott. 'Andrew, I know you're right about gynaecology compulsory residence. Piece of nonsense and should have been stopped years ago. Clever of you to have done a survey and got the figures you so kindly sent us, but with a – shall we say rather tense? – senior lecturer holding the fort between professors, the moment may not be quite ripe . . . Acting heads of department can be so terribly sensitive, so if you could just give it a term or so, keeping it on the agenda by all means, but not putting too much pressure on what is after all only a interim regime . . . And it would be rather nice to give the new professor – whoever he is, and there are a number of outside candidates – the opportunity to get off to a good start by doing something sensible and popular with the students. If you see what I mean . . .'

Scott saw exactly what he meant, but could hardly go straight back to the Medical Students' Council with the glad tidings that the problem was solved, though not immediately, because the paranoid dimwit who was causing all the trouble would probably not now be getting the chair. Instead, to buy a bit of time without seeming to give in, Scott decided he would suggest that his letter could be best dealt with by another survey, this one looking at the sort of emergencies people were being made to stay around for, not just how often they happened. 'I was wondering,' said Lennie. 'Have you thought of doing another of these useful little surveys? When people are arguing from entrenched positions there's nothing like new information to get them thinking again . . . and of course to keep the issue on the boil. For example, what *kind* of emergencies is it that are coming in?' Scott said he thought something like that could be arranged over the next term or so. The door of the lecture theatre opened and people came out and began to cluster in a broad line in front of the woman with the teapot. 'Now if you'll excuse me, Andrew . . . Must just have a quick word with Alan Thorburn over there . . . But a little more information next term might be just what was needed. Thanks awfully . . .'

Scott made a note on a card and put it in his top pocket, another useful thing he had learnt from watching Lennie in committees. Justice in the matter would prevail, slowly, and now it was his job to help slow things down. But the news about the acting head of department was entirely gratifying: a bone-headed, vindictive and vacuously ambitious obstetrician, with whom Scott had just happened not to get on at all well in their sole clinical encounter, was heading for the biggest disappointment of his life. Student politics had its compensations after all. He joined the queue for tea just behind Sandy, who looked round and seemed pleased to see him. Had she had the treatment too, Scott wondered as they stood waiting, or were Lennie's methods more defined than that? In a corner Alan Thorburn, acting head of the department of obstetrics and gynaecology, was listening very carefully to what Professor Gavin Lennox, professor of endocrinology and clinical dean of the Edinburgh University medical school, had to say on the subject of whatever it was he had wanted to have a quick word about.

'Well, that was all very interesting,' said Sandy, as though signifying an official start to conversation.

'Was there anything important in the last bit?'

She glanced round and said quietly 'No. It all went quite dull . . . after the cabaret. Who was he?'

'Mad chap from our ward who's just had his leg off. Used to work at the Southern. Your dad knew him.'

'Really?' Sandy smiled. 'I must ask. And what was all that stuff about mocking the architect?'

'Don't know. Maybe he just didn't like it. You know, the new Institute. Lots of people won't.'

'I suppose so. But he didn't seem to think much of Dr Smith either.'

'He was perfectly all right once we got him out. Pretty tough chap, though. Got down here on his own from the ward, only three days post-op. So what did you think of it? I mean the new Institute.'

'I agree with your patient.'

Scott laughed. On the smart new sofa thing under a large framed print of the Institute's eighteenth century premises, now the Department of Physiology's animal house, Mr Webster, the man who had given however many thousand pounds to build a little brick box with a couple of labs and a lecture theatre that somehow symbolised another rebirth of the Institute, was sitting looking vacantly ahead, a middle-aged female companion at his side. The chairman of the Board of Governors approached them with a cup of tea in each hand. The lady took both, and the chairman sat down on the other side of Mr Webster, who continued to lean on his walking stick and stare blankly to his front. Scott recalled the chairman's rather uninformative introductory remarks. He had heard that Roger Killick was leaving but had not heard any of the details. Penang, if it was where Scott thought it was, was not exactly the kind of place people went to from choice. It might be worth asking Gus, both about that and about the mysterious elderly donor, for whom the description 'a man of few words' seemed curiously flattering. Or perhaps Sandy might be able to fill in a bit of the story.

'Pity about Roger Killick,' she said suddenly.

'Not being here?'

Sandy said nothing, glanced around again and smiled mischievously. 'That as well.' Scott gathered there would be more later. 'There you are, dear,' said the tea lady. 'There's plenty sangwiches . . . Enjoy yourselves.'

They found a quiet corner but were joined by George Gordon,

who seemed to treat Sandy like an old family friend. She started to introduce Scott, but Gorgeous George held up a hand to stop her. 'Mr Scott and I are old friends, Sandy. One of the brighter stars in the firmament of my recent junior clinics. But how are you, my dear boy, and what are you up to now?'

Scott mentioned his surgical attachement and said that the first week had been quite interesting, and Gorgeous George confided that he had found it interesting too, as an undergraduate and for only about a week, and that all he knew about surgery these days were the names of a couple of good surgeons. Then he asked Sandy about the Southern and as she enthused he shook his head sadly. 'I cannot deny it,' he said. 'They are Rome to our Greece. They acknowledge and surpass us, while we decline in a superior culture.' Scott thought about that and decided it was nicely put, even if the old rogue had said it a hundred times before. 'And these plans with which they mock us . . .' His eyes rolled dismissively. 'Our dignity dictates simply that we decline, like the Greeks themselves, amid the ruins that we love.' Scott found himself liking the man, for his lucid contrariness, and for sentences that could have been translated into Latin and back again with some enjoyment.

Sandy seemed to be enjoying him too. Gorgeous George blossomed and began to gossip about Institute matters, and at one point seemed to be on the verge of saying something quite illuminating about Roger Killick's departure, at the last minute appearing to decide that there were matters of which even socially acceptable undergraduates should not hear. When he left Sandy suddenly became her efficient secretarial self. 'We probably need about twenty minutes, Andrew . . . There are a couple more things since the weekend but it's only six o'clock, so we could . . .'

'Gosh.'

'What?'

'Six o'clock. A meeting. Sorry. A six o'clock meeting I'd forgotten about.'

'What, Andrew?'

'SRC Executive. Big stuff.'

'You better go. What about later?'

'This evening?'

'Just come round to the flat.'

'Oh. OK.'

'You know where it is?'

'No.'

'Sixteen Forrest Road. Top flat. Above Sandy Bell's. See you later.'

'See you later.'

Sandy turned in the direction of Dr Ratho, Gus's father, and Scott slipped out, the first to leave and well aware that in these circles it would be seen as presumption in one so young, but the SRC Executive was serious. He had a place on it as chairman of the Medical Students' Council and, although he wasn't particularly interested in most of the things that came up for discussion, a precarious majority of moderates sometimes needed his vote. The chairman, a third year history student, was the sort of chap who, if Scott missed a meeting, would ring up to ask how he was in order to make it clear that it would have been all right if he'd actually been ill. When he got down to the SRC rooms in the Old Quad the meeting had been going for quarter of an hour and they were still arguing about the minutes of the last meeting, which, because of the long vacation, had taken place months previously. At twenty to seven they were half way through matters arising and Scott realised he could have sorted out all the MSC things with Sandy and still not missed anything of importance. The big stuff, about South Africa, student representation on the University Court and what the Trots called warmongering NATO research, would come later, perhaps a lot later.

The council room was dim and smokestained and lined with dispiriting bookshelves of maroon-bound volumes of SRC minutes going back well into the nineteenth century. Whatever tedium or passions the issues of the day may occasion, Scott mused, quite consciously in the manner of Gorgeous George, they too will pass into the silent, dusty annals of business once transacted. For the moment about fifteen people sat round a table with spaces for twenty, with Walker, in a high-backed ceremonial chair at one end, still trying patiently to get on to the agenda proper. Most of the niggling that was holding up progress came from the Trots, as usual, and most of that effort came, as usual, from their principal ideologist, a thin, pale German youth, a third year student in political science who seemed to regard the obstruction of SRC business as simply the practical side of his mainly theoretical course of studies, rather as keen medical students went to Casualty in their spare time to stitch up drunks. The rest of them sat back and smoked a lot while Dieter, in his precise, nasal English, continued to press the chair for a full account of the proposed implementation of the anti-discrimination strategy for the Council's four cleaning ladies, as agreed at the meeting of twentyseven May, as he called it. The smoke, not a prominent feature of medical student life or politics, was for Scott a nuisance that made the boredom all the harder to bear.

By eight they were moving again, into an area where most people agreed but where the intransigence of the man Walker referred to in private as the token Tory might still waste a great deal of time. The University had got rid of its South African shares some time before, but the continuing self-respect of the far left seemed to depend on finding around the place an endless series of increasingly trivial instances of what they called economic support for apartheid. Offending oranges had been swept from the shelves of the snackbars quite early on. Now they were trying to free the university from less obvious infringements, like grapes and certain hardwoods, and there was talk of a campaign to end subscriptions to learned journals with South African editors or contributors. That might give the moderates some problems, as the left was well aware, but for the moment it was still mainly fruit stall politics, about which almost everyone agreed. The problem this evening was that the exception, the token Tory, the chairman of the Law Students' Council, had turned up with a sheaf of notes and an impressive stack of books, rather as if he were about to address the central criminal court in defence of an international fraudster down on his luck.

It was another of those spare-time practicals, Scott concluded after twenty minutes or so of libertarian theory and a lot of rousing rhetoric to the effect that none would suffer more than the hapless wives and children of thousands of honest black toilers if South African tinned grapefruit segments were to be wantonly and arbitrarily excluded from the Edinburgh student market, and it still looked as though he had used only one page of his notes. Walker sat forward in his chair, leaning on one elbow and listening patiently. The outcome of the vote was not in doubt. Ranald Crumlin would attain his customary martyrdom at the hands of democracy. The only question was when. Meanwhile the left smoked steadily, lighting one cigarette from another, and variously doodling, chatting, snoozing or trying to stare down the personification of apartheid and racism so conveniently available for them in central Edinburgh tonight. Scott's attention wandered and he began to think about Sandy, not simply in terms of her contribution to the smooth and blessedly simple workings of the Medical Students' Council.

Crumlin, who wore a waistcoat and a watch chain and affected a kind of Edwardian guardee drawl, had not always thought and dressed and talked like that. According to Robbie, who had been in the year ahead of him at Heriot's, he had stood once as a communist in the school debating society mock election, perhaps because his father, a history teacher at one of the corporation schools, had for years stood in local elections for the same party. Somehow he had since become chairman of the Tory Club, the sole declared conservative on the SRC executive and had been talked of as a possible candidate for a shot at a seat in the East End of Glasgow. His manner tonight hinted at grouse moors and clubland and a lot of port after a heavy dinner. Perhaps one day his life would catch up, although the chances were it wouldn't, which would be a sad waste of performing talent. As he talked it occurred to Scott, who had watched the kind of people who seemed to want to become politicians quite closely for some time, that if they didn't get on in their chosen calling they could do worse than apply for drama school places instead. Dieter would probably make quite a decent Hamlet, in his leaden Germanic way, and Crumlin, on tonight's form, could go straight in as the chap in the *Importance of Being Ernest* who wasn't called Ernest.

When the evening's South Africa motion eventually went to the vote Crumlin got up, gathered his notes and books and swept out to genial jeering from Dieter's lot. Walker caught a mood for progress with the agenda and a sudden rush of business took them most of the way through it. By quarter past nine they were breathing fresh air again and Walker was making signals that seemed to mean the moderates were going for a pint. In the event only three of them – Walker, Scott and the girl with the funny name who was from the arts faculty – made it across to the little pub in College Street which was their usual refuge after executive meetings. The girl, Engadine somebody, was pretty and bright and sensible, and was in student politics because her father was a Labour MP. Walker, like Scott a son of the manse, seemed to be in it because he wanted to help people. After the first pint it occurred to Scott that another of Engadine's reasons for being in student politics might be the prospect of a continuing association with Walker, who was dourly handsome and very clever and might, in his quiet way, go far. After the second Scott realised that he had been summoned for a drink only so that Walker would not be left alone with Engadine who, she might have been disappointed to learn, was important to Walker, but only for her vote. When someone else joined them Scott mentioned something about still having some Medical Students' Council business to sort out, excused himself and made his way the few hundred yards across to Sandy's flat.

She came to the door in faded jeans and an old shirt. To Scott's surprise she was wearing glasses, and his surprise must have shown because she laughed and took them off, putting them into the top pocket of her shirt. 'They're just for swotting,' she said as he followed her through a shabby entrance hall with dark, varnished doors. 'Print seems to have got smaller since first year. Want a coffee, Andrew?'

'Yes, please. And a loo.'

'That door. Milk and sugar?'

'Milk, no sugar, thanks.'

The loo was old-fashioned and there was the usual girls-together clutter of shampoos and cosmetics and things dripping over the bath. When Scott eventually wandered into the kitchen Sandy was standing waiting for a whistling kettle to boil on a gas stove. 'How was the executive?' she asked, as though it might be some time.

'Odd. As if no one had been away, or maybe as if they'd all spent the long vac practising being themselves. Walker being sensible and patient, the mad Tory doing his thing and the Trots frothing away at all the usual stuff. Sorry I'm a bit late.'

'It's all right. It's neurology night. I've been looking forward to a break. All those sad things that are interesting but hopeless. There's been a sort of run of them at the Southern so I'm being good and reading them up. Did you know. . . ?' Sandy hesitated.

'Go on,' said Scott. The kettle was nowhere near boiling.

'. . . that Huntington's chorea usually starts with the person just dropping things. And because it's in the family they sort of know about it, so if they drop something they think they're going to go mad and die like their uncle or whatever. And of course a lot of them do, but then again they might just have dropped something.'

'It's pretty rare, isn't it?'

'Not if it's in the family . . . Half, but you don't know if it's your half. We've got a chap in under Dr Lauder who's been dropping a lot of things lately, an architect, about thirty, and he's got it, poor chap. Funny movements now, and his wife says he's changed, and he knows himself his work's no good.'

There was a long silence. The cooker hissed and eventually the kettle whistled. 'No sugar?'

'Right.'

Sandy made coffee in two smart new mugs. 'Let's go through, Andrew. All the stuff's in my room.'

Sandy's room was different from the rest of the flat: bright and modern, or as bright and modern as you could make it if you were stuck with dark varnished woodwork and funny old beige flowery wallpaper. She had a matching chair, desk and bookcase in light pine, a jazzy print bedspread, lots of posters that more or less swamped the wallpaper and some clever lighting that meant you could hardly see the ceiling. 'You can have the seat.'

Scott sat at the desk and admired a huge neurology book. 'It's from MacKay's library,' said Sandy. 'Cheap subscription courtesy of the Society. Quite useful.'

'The only useful thing about it.'

'Almost. They've written back about the Ball . . .' Sandy reached across Scott and pulled a file from her desk. 'They agree with me, which is quite clever of them, so that's all sorted out. And you know you've more or less got to go, Mr Chairman, and even stand at the door with Max and welcome people.' Scott nodded. 'But you can worry about that nearer the time. And there's a committee, but don't worry about that either. Catriona Heptonstall's mum does hunt balls so she thinks she knows all about it and she's actually not bad at getting people to do things. I just go.'

Sandy was sitting cross-legged on her bed with her file open in front of her. 'What about the faculty liaison stuff?' said Scott, to show a little chairmanly initiative.

'Straightforward. Nothing from the preclinicals, which means the anatomists have stopped misbehaving. No . . .' She fished out a letter. 'Sorry. Something about bacteriology practicals going on longer at the end of third term than anyone else's, and it interferes with swotting and could we please stop them. Yours indignantly, etc.'

'Might be worth a try. Does anyone go?'

'Shouldn't have thought so. We could . . .'

'. . . ask the year rep to find out and tell us.'

'I thought you were going to say do a survey.'

'And get a survey done next year if they don't drop them.'

'OK.'

'And clinical things?'

'Compulsory gynaecology residence.'

'Yes . . . D'you have the letter?'

Sandy passed it across. It was addressed to the clinical dean with a copy to secretary of the Medical Students' Council. The previous professor's name had been obliterated from the notepaper with a blizzard of x's, and 'Acting Head of Department: Dr Alan Thorburn' typed above it. The letter began with a testy acknowledgement that the results of the survey had been received, went off at a couple of tangents about medicine being a round-the-clock commitment and emergencies being by their very nature unpredictable, however inconvenient that might be for practitioners and students alike etc, and ended with a flat statement that there were no plans to review arrangements for gynaecology teaching in the foreseeable future. Scott passed it back. It was all very silly. Only the Institute still insisted that students live in, and most students now did their gynaecology attachements elsewhere.

'Where did you go for gynaecology, Sandy?'

Sandy thought briefly of the motherly, grey-haired lady in Glasgow a long time ago then said 'The Southern. I seem to have spent half my life there. All very advanced and liberal, and so organised we started at eight and got away at about three most days. Nice people, too.'

'I was here, and bored stiff for the whole four weeks. They made half of us stay in at a time . . . Two weeks in a ghastly hostel in Soutar Street, with poltergeists in the water-pipes and a strange warden who was only there because his wife had left him.'

'Blair somebody. A sort of surgeon. We knew his wife.'

'Creepy chap . . . Prowled around at night to see there was no naughtiness, but probably hoping there was and he could join in.'

'Was there?' Sandy was smiling.

Scott's compulsory gynaecology residence in the Soutar Street hostel had been made a little less boring by the presence in the residency of a friendly Dutch girl doing an elective attachement in ophthalmology who had visited him quite often, perhaps partly to avoid being visited by the warden. 'The worst thing about it was the phone. If they were serious about getting us across for emergencies they would have given us a phone in each room. There was one, out at the end of the corridor, and if it ever rang everybody used to pretend not to hear it and wait for it to stop and go back to sleep, and then they'd send a porter across. I think I just caught the end of a lady whose fibroids went critical . . . It's got to stop.'

'Futile, according to the fourth year reps.'

'But Dr Thorburn won't like it.'

'What's he like, Andrew?'

'Tense and horrible. Got right up my nose, and cornered me with a long tirade about everything, really everything, because I'd missed most of his all-star midnight fibroid suspense drama.'

'So there actually was an emergency?'

'Yes, but because he's a consultant and he'd been called out in the middle of the night he's trying to say it happens all the time. It doesn't. At least I'm pretty sure it doesn't.'

'Another survey?'

'Probably. If the fourth years don't mind.' Scott wondered whether to tell Sandy what her father had said about the acting head of department's horoscope, decided against it because she probably knew already and drank some coffee instead. She leafed through her file a bit more and when she looked up their eyes met. She put down the file and reached for her coffee. 'When I was at the Southern people seemed to think that the nice chap who does most of the teaching there might actually get the chair at the Institute. Dr Morris. Everyone's decided they're going to have him for all their babies. And he'd sort out all the nonsense about having to stay in horrible hostels.'

'But meantime?'

'A survey. I'll talk to the fourth year reps before the liaison meeting.'

'Thanks, Sandy.'

Scott sipped his coffee and wondered if Sandy was quoting Lennie rather than gossip from the Southern. Whatever the source it was an agreeable prospect, because defeat at the hands of an outside candidate from a hospital only four miles away was the kind of thing Thorburn probably deserved. Perhaps he could then start applying for chairs in places like Penang. There was a companionable silence.

'Sandy . . .'

'What?'

'What happened to Roger Killick?'

Sandy smiled. 'Well, you know he always wanted to be a professor . . .'

'Yes . . . But according to Max there was some sort of enquiry . . . that might have stopped him becoming one in Edinburgh.'

Sandy shifted on her bed so that she was lying, like the patient in a psychotherapy cartoon, with her head near where Scott sat at her desk. 'Yes,' she said, 'not an Edinburgh problem, at least not any more.'

'Oh well. That's all right then.'

Sandy laughed. 'And there's a nice wee building to remember him by. Gosh, Andrew, did you know that poor old Webster's so gaga he can hardly talk? But Roger had him chatted up with a load of nonsense about the cure being just another couple of experiments away, and another hundred thousand should do it, just sign here and all that. He'd owned a whisky bond and had pots of money but his lawyers were a bit slow off the mark, so in the end they decided just to put a good face on things and let him out of his nursing home for the opening and put it all down to experience.'

'Hmm. And Roger?'

'I think you could say he saw the writing on the wall . . . Before he pushed off he went round for a few months talking about time for a change, new challenges and all that, but I think more or less everyone knows, well, the general picture . . . Certainly in this department. But the awful thing is that his wife has gone too.'

'Really?' said Scott, remembering the night Killick's secretary had come in with an overdose but preferring to let Sandy go into all that herself if she knew about it and wanted to.

'He wasn't very nice to her.' Sandy put her hands behind her head and yawned. 'Sorry, Andrew. It's not you, it's the neurology. No, from what everyone says Roger Killick was a horrible man and good riddance to him. And everyone thinks that, except for his wife, poor her, so she's gone to Penang with three children. Four, if you include him. And she's a good doctor with a proper job, a consultant in anaesthetics.'

'Poor her. And the enquiry?'

Sandy pursed her lips and looked round and up at Scott. 'Hm. No one's supposed to know, because it was *very* discreet, very high level too. A sort of tribunal with . . . some very senior people on it. But he'd done nothing quite criminal, apart from to poor Mr Webster, so there wasn't actually a lot anyone could do. And according to . . . to people in his department . . . he was actually quite a good basic immunologist before he decided immunology would cure everything and got overstretched. So he might even do some good in Penang.'

Scott found all that quite interesting. Either Lennie or Gus, most probably the latter, had spilled the beans. Sandy, in her nice veiled Edinburgh way, was telling him things she probably shouldn't have, and though Max would be fascinated by it all he wasn't going to hear anything about it, at least not from Scott. Sandy reached round for her coffee, which she had put next to Scott's on the desk beside her bed which seemed to serve as a bedside table too. In trying to pick it up she knocked it over and about a quarter-mugful of lukewarm coffee went to the floor, a little of it splashing Scott's left knee on the way. She swung round and sat up.

'Gosh, I'm sorry, Andrew.' She reached down to a drawer in the desk and fished out a box of paper hankies and began to dab at the warm wet bit on his knee. 'I don't usually drop things,' she said, laughing again. 'And there's no Huntington's in the family.'

'That's nice.'

'One or two ghastly things, but not that.'

Scott thought about Lennie and about Sandy and wondered what they might be and if she was going to tell him any more. She didn't, so he said 'What about the carpet?' It was of an age, shade and state of neglect that rendered the question no more than a courtesy.

'Doesn't matter . . . I'm awfully sorry, Andrew.' She giggled, then said 'I suppose secretaries really shouldn't throw coffee over their chairmen.'

'It's all right.'

Sandy sat on the edge of the bed with a now damp and brownish paper hankie in her hand. 'Sorry,' she said again. Scott, who had never seen her do anything clumsily or badly before but didn't think any the worse of her for the kind of minor mishap that could have happened to anyone, thought she was taking it all a bit seriously. He finished his coffee. 'No problem. Tomorrow night's laundrette night . . . Removes coffee stains. Rests the brain . . .'

'. . . and lets you meet interesting people?'

Scott found that a little puzzling. Sandy was half-smiling. She had been quite a close friend of Theresa's since they had started medical school together. Did girls chat about things like that, and if so in what sort of detail? Scott and Theresa, still friends, sometimes went to things together that it was convenient to go to with someone from your year, but he didn't think of himself as having the kind of relationship with her that people reminded you about when they thought you were going to make a pass at them. On the latter issue he had at that point not quite decided: his indecision might have been obvious and her remark intended to help him make up his mind. All coffee nonsense apart, and even without a consideration of the implications of a final year medical student going into overt competition with a fairly rich houseman on the same unit who also owned an MGB, Scott decided to take the hint. As she saw him to the door she took her spectacles from her shirt pocket. As he left she popped them on her nose again and they both laughed.

March 1969

Robbie walked along the corridor and the patient, instead of following him as he had expected, walked alongside as though they were friends. When they reached the interview room he opened the door, stood back to let the man go in first and indicated which of the two chairs he should sit in. That was a bit silly. He could have told him instead of showing him. There was nothing wrong with the man's hearing. 'Please make yourself comfortable, Mr Govan . . . We'll only be an hour or so . . . And thanks very much for agreeing to talk to me.' Robbie was now conscious that he was overdoing it. Psychiatry was like that. It made you think about things you hadn't previously thought of as difficult or significant and then you messed them up. 'Sorry. You know what I mean.'

The man smiled his sad smile and Robbie felt even more foolish. Mr Govan hadn't talked to anyone, not even his wife, for about three months, and that was why he was here. Robbie sat down in the other armchair. There was a coffee table with a half-full ashtray and the room smelt of stale smoke. That was something else about psychiatry that Robbie found irritating. People in group therapy smoked all the time, using cigarettes as props in the awful endless play they made up as they went along, the girls punctuating their revelations with long, smoky sighs, the men plucking up courage with a few desperate drags before breaking in. Every room and hallway in the unit stank of it, but the small and badly ventilated interview rooms were the worst. Robbie thought for a moment about putting the ashtray out in the corridor, then decided against it when he had worked out how that might be discussed and interpreted if it were noticed. The man opposite was waiting for him to begin.

Robbie had been allocated his patient by Dr Bennett, the head of the unit, probably as some kind of punishment. He now had to interview the man and get the story all over again, going through the full ritual of a psychiatric interview, writing the case up and presenting it to the great man's teaching group, and he had been given a man who couldn't speak. The patient, Mr Govan, had been admitted first to one of the medical units in the Institute for investigations because he had lost his voice. No cause had been found and he had been referred to Dr Bennett for a psychiatric opinion. There was something odd going on between the patient and various members of his family, and the more that had been found out the odder it had all become. Dr Bennett's letter to the physician in the Institute, old Glaister, had dwelt on the problems the family had had concerning the pregnancy of a teenage daughter, a series of rows between Mr Govan and his wife and the general difficulties middle aged men experienced coming to terms with the sexuality of their female offspring. The last paragraph had begun 'The rest is silence . . .' and went on to assure Dr Glaister that group therapy in a predominantly younger mixed group had much to offer in cases of hysterical aphonia such as these.

So far it hadn't achieved much. Mr Govan, a moderately successful chartered surveyor, had sat amid the swirling currents of anecdote and recrimination like a man who had turned up at the wrong party by mistake but was still doing his best to enjoy himself. His clothes – collar, tie and a worn grey suit that would have passed for one of the dapper Dr Bennett's more hard-worked cast-offs – drew comment and were generally regarded as displaying inflexibility, over-identification with the medical staff and a reluctance to really participate, a view that Dr Bennett had allowed to pass without comment. He had followed the more ordinary routines about childhood experience and child-parent conflict with an air of understanding and patience and had occasionally looked uncomfortable when Alec, a depressed woodwork teacher and the only other middle aged patient in the group, came under attack. The more explicitly sexual stuff made him sweat quite visibly and Dr Bennett had commented on that, but for the most part Mr Govan's behaviour was unremarkable if highly defended. He kept his silence. His conflicts, if any, remained entirely his own. He read a lot and sometimes lay on his bed doing nothing. As the social worker had pointed out in the previous Friday's staff meeting, he was trying to pass himself off as a very quiet man by treating all the opportunities opened up by a stay in the unit as if he were stuck somewhere in a strange hotel on a wet weekend.

Now he sat opposite Robbie, nodding and grinning as though he was keen to get started. He pulled a spiral-backed pocket notebook and a ball point pen from his pocket and laid them upon the table. 'Thanks very much,' said Robbie, again without really thinking about it. Then he realised that he himself should probably have brought writing stuff for the patient. Or would that have been collusion? The man nodded again as though encouraging Robbie not to be shy. 'Do you mind writing things down?' Mr Govan shook his head. Another thought struck Robbie. Interviewing a man who couldn't speak carried with it an unexpected advantage. 'And could I have your answers, please, to keep?' He nodded and Robbie took out his notebook.

Dr Bennett, known for some reason as Wiggy, set great store by procedure and routine. To Robbie it seemed that his obsession with structure and rules, and the minute distinctions he discerned in symptoms and psychiatric disorders and personality types – things that seemed to most people all a bit blurred and scarcely worth sorting out anyway – were his way of dealing with the essential chaos of his specialty. To say so in any of his groups was unthinkable, but Robbie was sure that he wasn't the only medical student to have come to similar conclusions during his two months of compulsory psychiatry. Scott and he had discussed it once in the Union bar with one or two people from their year who were attached to other psychiatric units where different views prevailed. After a couple of pints somebody had said that they probably did what was best for the kind of patients they had, and they all had different things to deal with, like specialists in different kinds of surgery. Robbie had thought about that and decided it was plausible but nonsensical. Consultant surgeons, whose ranks he intended to join as soon as possible, were interested in different things but had a common view of diagnosis and a common approach. They tackled different parts of the body using techniques that were broadly similar; Wiggy was out on his own, it seemed, but he was a powerful and now quite senior psychiatrist with a separate unit and a strong following among the psychiatrists in training. People seemed to go along with him, joking occasionally about the more absurd distinctions he made but careful never to do so in his presence.

Robbie knew the party line on Mr Govan already, the official formulation of his personality type and disorder, and could probably have made quite a satisfactory presentation of the case to the great man simply from the notes and from what had been said in meetings, but he had been put on the spot by Wiggy himself and would be a lot safer if he had done the standard interview as well, no matter how long it took. In the chair with its back to the window, as all the best psychiatrists recommended, he cleared his throat to begin. Mr Govan sat opposite him and smiled and for a strange, suspended moment after months of silence looked as if he were about to say something ordinary in an ordinary, middle-aged Edinburgh chartered surveyor's voice.

He didn't, and Robbie thought about that, and why he had expected the ordinary, and realised it was because he had forgotten the man was a well-investigated case of hysterical aphonia. Why had he forgotten? Because Mr Govan, away from the baying pack of neurotics in the group, had reverted to social ordinariness. That in itself was odd. If he were a hysteric he would probably have become more distant and more bizarre under the threat of a one-to-one interrogation. Either he was an exceptionally well defended hysteric, a man whose pretence was so ingrained that you could have wakened him at three in the morning by pouring cold water over him and he still wouldn't have made a sound, or he was something else entirely, a man who couldn't speak and who wasn't mad either.

Mr Govan had noticed Robbie's hesitation and was waiting politely, perhaps concerned for him and his inability to get going. Robbie sat back in his chair and stopped pretending to be a psychiatrist. 'Mr Govan, how did all this begin?' The patient lifted his nicely sharpened 2B pencil and quickly wrote one word in the squarish, neat script that had been much discussed in staff meetings. He turned the notebook towards Robbie. Hoarseness, he had written.

'And how long did that last before you completely lost your voice?'

The pencil flicked neatly and the notebook was again swivelled round. Five days.

'And then you lost your voice?'

Mr Govan nodded and so did Robbie 'Anything else?'

264

Mr Govan frowned. Swallowing, came the pencilled reply.

'What about it?' Robbie asked. That was interesting: hysterics in textbooks chose a symptom and stuck to it and you often made the diagnosis on the unlikelihood of that particular symptom ever being explained in terms of conventional neurological diagnosis. The pencil filled a whole line of the notebook and then Mr Govan flipped it over to Robbie, jokily, as though they were playng the children's game of stone, paper, scissors.

Hard to describe, I had to be careful, said the neat handwriting.

'Or what? What happened if you weren't?'

Another line. Things would go down the wrong way. To Robbie that was a very important discovery, because it suddenly lifted Mr Govan out of the ranks of the monosymptomatic hysterics and into proper textbook neurology.

'When?'

About two weeks now.

Robbie felt the thrill of a diagnosis not yet made but suddenly within reach. Deep in the base of the skull lay something called the medulla oblongata and from it the twelve cranial nerves emerged. The last two between them controlled the muscles of speech and swallowing, and that was something that chartered surveyors and hysterics could not be expected to know. Robbie made a note of his own about the eleventh and twelfth crainial nerves. 'Anything else?'

The pencil wrote more quickly. My tongue.

'What about it?' Robbie asked. Mr Govan stuck out his tongue and they both laughed. It was definitely not a psychiatric interview any more, and if anyone were to come in Robbie would be in trouble. Mr Govan's quiet, happy shaking settled down and he stuck out his tongue again. Robbie got up and went across to look at it more closely, sitting on the coffee table to do so. A couple of seconds later he knew what was wrong with Mr Govan: he was not a hysteric, and he would be dead within a few months. His tongue was pink and shining, not coated or patchy or anything like that, but what made the diagnosis and sealed his fate was a strange, involuntary twitching that the books called fasciculation and described rather fancifully as a tongue that looked like a bag full of active worms. The muscles of his larynx and his throat and his tongue were twitching because their nerve supply was wasting away. He had motor neurone disease and he would die when that gradual and inexorable process prevented him from coughing and protecting his airway. Robbie went back to his seat. Mr Govan picked up his notebook again, scribbed delightedly and handed it over. So I'm not mad after all?

Robbie nodded and Mr Govan laughed a huge silent, shaking laugh that ended in a fit of hollow coughing. He took out his handkerchief and mopped his eyes then picked up his pencil and notebook and wrote something else. Robbie reached out for it. Can I go home now? Robbie thought about that and said 'I should think so . . . In a few days at least. I'm sure it can be arranged. But Mr Govan . . .' The man looked imploringly. 'I'm only a student here . . .' As they stood up Mr Govan threw his arms round Robbie and hugged him so tightly that it hurt. There was even a wet bit from his tears when he let go.

June 1969

Max led the way. Theresa, Scott and Vicky followed him from the door in the garden wall, along the green-shaded path under a series of trellises covered with climbing plants, until they reached a door in the side of the house. Pinned beneath the knocker was a little note in Sandy's writing: 'Please use front door.'

'Funny,' said Max. 'Always used this door when I've been here before.'

'It's probably the servants' entrance,' said Vicky. Max ignored her. 'It's a very interesting house, you know.' He gestured upwards. 'Especially the outside. And the front door's round this way.'

From close up the general impression given by the house was one of great size and an intricacy verging upon the eccentric: above them deep eaves were supported by elaborately carved rafters and the wall they followed was faced with a complex pattern of alternating dark and light stone in ascending zig-zags. 'Lennie picked it up for a song away back in the fifties. Twenty three rooms, apparently. Must be worth a fortune now. Probably eight or ten thousand. Yes, here we are. The carriage entrance.'

There was indeed a little gravelled drive looping through a pillared stone canopy above the front door which might just have allowed a very small carriage to deposit its occupants in shelter. Max gestured his party up the steps. 'We're not late. I mean it's *our* ball.'

'Yes, but it's *their* drinks,' said Vicky.

'Same difference.' Max fingered his medal, the presidential seal of the Ancient Society of Physic, on its ribbon around his neck. Scott and Theresa exchanged smiles. They went in. Perhaps drinks at the Society before drinks at Lennie's before the ball had been a mistake, but Max was enjoying the last duties of his presidency very much. Resplendent in his ruffed shirt and maroon velvet dinner jacket, he was met at the top of the stairs by Mrs Lennox and embraced her with an odd whoop of enthusiasm which did not seem to bother her. They went on into a big, crowded lounge. 'Everybody's here already,' said Max. 'I'd better mingle.' He grabbed Vicky's arm and made for where people were most thickly gathered. 'Poor Vicky,' said Theresa.

Vicky was a new feature in Max's life, so new as to raise the suspicion that one of his loose reserve of nurses and physiotherapists might have been ditched in her favour only a few days before the graduation ball. She was a quiet, hardworking girl who had done reasonably well throughout the course and then, to everyone's astonishment, had won the Ross Adams prize in the clinical medicine finals, an accolade that Max had spoken of quite openly as his already. Ever resilient, he had discovered in Vicky charms that had remained unnoticed until she had beaten him in his declared ambition and they had been inseparable for all of four days now. Scott watched her being introduced to the postgraduate dean's wife and decided that she could probably look after herself quite well.

A youth in shirtsleeves came round with a tray of drinks. Theresa declined. Scott took a glass of white wine. They were joined by a tall man in an ancient dinner suit with wide, angular lapels. 'Awfully nice,' he murmured. Scott nodded. Dr Fielding was a senior member of the physiology department, a pre-clinical teacher from the days of reflexes in half-dead cats all of three years ago. 'Awfully nice to see the end-product,' he murmured as though sensing Scott's reaction. 'Hello . . .' He nodded towards Theresa. 'Your face is familiar . . . I expect you sat in the front row . . .' She nodded and he smiled. Scott introduced them. Dr Fielding thought for a moment. 'I do enjoy these occasions . . . So good of Lennie to keep doing them . . . And I'll be there tomorrow too. I make a point of going to all the graduations . . . A million pounds worth of goods coming off the production line.' Theresa looked surprised. 'That's roughly what you've cost the taxpayer. As a class, I mean.' He chuckled to himself and sipped at his glass of wine. 'So I suppose I'm interested both as a taxpayer and as a teacher.'

Conversation became a little more predictable and Scott found himself explaining where he was going for his housejobs. Dr Fielding seemed to be suitably impressed then turned to Theresa, who mentioned an undemanding medical unit in one of the smaller Edinburgh hospitals and said that after that she was going to Dumfries for her six months' surgery. 'Now that's very interesting . . .' said Dr Fielding. 'They do some awfully good things down there. Best kind of job, really, especially for people who want to be surgeons . . . But of course they never go to places like that, do they? They just stick around the teaching hospitals in units that do more and more of less and less these days . . . Just as you're doing, Andrew . . . Is vascular surgery really all that important? All these poor black feet, most of which do rather badly . . . Because the surgeons are simply making local attacks on what is after all a generalised disease . . .'

'Well, it's certainly important for kidney transplants . . .' Scott was aware of the risk of sounding like a superspecialist even before he had graduated. 'If that sort of thing catches on . . .'

'As it undoubtedly will . . .' Dr Fielding, a very clinically-minded physiologist, had once astonished the class with his statement that patients with emphysema would one day be offered lung transplants. 'Are you thinking of going on in surgery?'

'Not sure, really.'

'But at least you're not thinking about psychiatry any more.' Theresa's eyes widened. Scott was being reminded of a conversation he had once had with Dr Fielding in his honours year, in the course of a long practical session on fatty acid uptake in rats. Psychiatry was now a youthful ambition almost embarrassing to recall. Then, over a pinioned and allegedly brain-dead rat, Scott had attempted to persuade his tutor that the specialty was about to achieve respectability, perhaps in only a few years, as the various neuro-chemical mechanisms of mood and perception got sorted out. Dr Fielding had shaken his head and tapped his pipe on the bench to loosen a crust of ash. 'Psychiatry,' he had pronounced, his pipe safely back in his mouth, 'is strictly for the bottom half of the class.'

'You're very lucky, you know, graduating in medicine now.' Dr Fielding had evidently decided not to go on and on about psychiatry. 'You're not going to be sidetracked for years into a war, and all sorts of interesting things are just beginning to happen . . . Of which organ transplantation is only one . . . I should make the most of it, if I were you . . . Though that's the last thing anyone thinks about when they've just got through finals. Well done, both of you.'

Scott smiled and felt that they were being ever so politely allowed to go, and that that was what should have happened anyway. The boy waiter reappeared and this time Theresa took a drink, and to keep her company Scott had another one he probably didn't need. There were minor official duties still to come. The invitation to Lennie's had said drinks at six thirty. It was already a few minutes after seven and they would need to leave in about half an hour to get down to the Assembly Rooms on George Street for eight, when Scott and Max, representing the Ancient Society of Physic and the Medical Students' Council respectively, would go through the curious charade of standing at the top of the grand stairway while a man bawled out the names of the several hundred celebrants at the Medical Graduation Ball for which they were jointly responsible.

Max, already on good form when they had arrived at Lennie's, might yet prove to be a worry or even a disgrace. Would he want to kiss all the girls, or tell everyone in the queue how he had single-handedly revived and transformed a moribund society, or even insist on suspending the proceedings of the reception line while he went off for a leak? One never knew, but it was probably worth the trouble of holding back a little. Scott decided to make his current drink his last for a while. Sandy, who had actually done most of the work for the Ball, was standing not far off with her back to the wall and smiling bravely while Mrs Wigton, her dad's secretary and for the moment clearly the worse for drink, lectured her about something in a forced whisper of nose-rubbing intimacy. Theresa had noticed too and touched Scott's arm. 'D'you think we should rescue Sandy?'

As they approached Mrs Wigton nudged Sandy with a pudgy, naked elbow and screwed up half her face in a gross theatrical wink before turning to the newcomers. 'Well, well, well. Look who's here. Mr President? Or is it Mr Chairman?' She reached out and fondled Scott's medal of office, a much more modest affair than that of the Ancient Society, as though it might reveal the answer to her question. '*Doctor* Chairman, really, though we're not supposed to call you that until the actual day you graduate, are we? Sandy and I were just having a . . . little talk . . . About something very important, eh, Sandy? But we'd actually what you might call

270

finished, hadn't we, dear? And to think I've actually known you since you were only . . . What? Ten? My oh my . . . Well, there we are. Lovely, isn't it? But you can trust your Auntie Pat . . . I mean, you know you *all* can . . .' Sandy, though a little flustered, seemed less embarassed by all this than might have been expected. Perhaps Mrs Wigton appeared regularly on such occasions, drunk and kitted out like a pantomime dame in a frothy off-the-shoulder black and white dress thick with sequins, to dispense wisdom and advice even more freely than she did at the office. And why not, Scott asked himself. Like Max with his dinner jacket run up at home from granny's curtains, as Vicky had put it, Mrs Wigton added a carnival dimension to what had threatened sometimes to become a maudlin farewell to student life. 'And are you two getting engaged?' Mrs Wigton asked suddenly. Theresa laughed and Sandy shook her head and rolled her eyes a bit. Scott could laugh too. He and Theresa were at no particular risk of getting carried away by the whole business of leaving university and starting up in real life. They were just friends who went together to things that it was convenient to go to with someone from your year.

'Mr Chairman . . .' Sandy came sufficiently close to Scott to imply that matters of grave confidence were about to be discussed. 'You look awfully smart in that rigout, Andrew. And I hope you're driving, and not Max.'

'We voted on it. It's actually Vicky.'

'Good old Vicky. I was beginning to wonder if you weren't coming.'

'Sorry . . . Got sort of held up. At the Society . . . Last night and all that. Is there a problem?'

'Don't think so. Rallied all the troops yesterday afternoon, mainly by phone. Nasty moment when the catering manager man from the people doing the supper rang up an hour ago to tell me everything was all right.'

'So everything's all right . . .'

'He was so drunk he could hardly speak. Worrying, but two minutes later I was out of the bath again . . . The head waitress lady ringing to say everything actually was all right, and not to worry.'

'Poor old you,' said Theresa. 'But you're looking super . . .'

Sandy, in an austere and expensive-looking deep green silk or silkish dress, with her hair swept back and pinned up and without

271

her glasses, actually looked quite glamorous: much more so than anyone who had seen her mainly in committees and around the medical school would have believed possible. That was something girls could do, whereas men always looked more or less the same. Scott found himself nodding in agreement and Sandy smiled again and seemed unashamedly happy to be noticed in those terms. Perhaps compliments were appreciated more by people who looked beautiful only once in while.

There was a short, happy silence then Sandy cast a professional eye round the room. 'I think little brother's slowed up a bit too early on the refills . . . Excuse me . . .' She smiled and then wove her way through the crowd, pausing here and there for polite noises but clearly still resolute in her search for the erring waiter.

'Poor little brother,' said Theresa. 'And poor Gus. Come on, let's go and talk to Prof Jameson . . . He was really nice to me over my long medical case when I was sure I was going to fail . . .'

Professor Jameson was holding court in a large bay window, perched on the back of an old leather sofa and silhouetted against sky outside. Before him on a window seat were a couple of people from the graduating class and a pushy young man from the year below who had just been elected next year's President of the Ancient Society. He was getting the full Jameson treatment. '. . . so what have you in mind for your first hundred days, which is what we're all asking of our presidents these days? What are you going to try to achieve with the Society, hm?'

The president-to-be, a tall, pale man with a ginger crew cut, paused and bit his lip. 'Well, before answering that I'd like to stress my appreciation of the, um, magnificent contribution made by my predecessor to the life of the Society.' Professor Jameson laughed delightedly. 'Of course, of course . . . But what are *you* going to do, Ewen?'

'Well, recruitment's always a problem.'

'Course it is. People just aren't as keen these days to dress up like their grandfathers in order to go and hear a lecture you could go to in jeans and a tee-shirt if it was part of the curriculum. You going to do something about that?'

The youth fingered the buttons of his dinner jacket. 'We don't actually wear this kind of stuff to ordinary meetings these days, Professor Jameson. It's been lounge suits for about five years now.'

'Gracious me, I *do* apologise. But, um, thinking of recruiting, what are you doing about overseas students, hm?'

'Well, you'll be glad to hear that our scriba secundus for next year's actually from Rhodesia. A very keen overseas member.'

'What's he called? Or is it she?'

'Morris Wasserman.'

'Hmm. You're an all-white society, aren't you? Doesn't that worry you, Ewen, particularly these days?'

'Well, professor, I'm just trying to think. We probably have one or two, um, new commonwealth members. And we've had an African president, you'll be pleased to hear.'

'Really? That's splendid.' Professor Jameson fairly bubbled with enthusiasm and the president-to-be cheered up a bit. 'And when was that, Ewen?'

'His picture's in the library . . . Chap called Kwesi something. Um, nineteen thirty something, I think . . .'

'Hmm. Could do better.' Jimmy swung round quite suddenly. 'Ah, Andrew . . . Now, you're just saying farewell to politics, aren't you. . . ? Of the student variety, at least . . . So what have you achieved over the last year that you can look back on with any satisfaction, hm?'

A minor reduction in the period of compulsory residence in the gynaecology attachment at the Institute hardly seemed worth mentioning to a man who had probably contributed more than anyone else in the world to the final battle against tuberculosis, so Scott confined himself to generalities about the importance of maintaining good communication between students and their teachers. 'Yes, yes . . . I don't think anyone would argue with that, Andrew, and we never actually came to blows, did we?'

For Scott one of the more obvious benefits of involvement in student politics was in the immediate future: he had landed a couple of much sought-after housejobs. His exam results through the course had been nothing spectacular, just a good average, enough to convince those in charge that he wouldn't be dangerous, yet he was going to spend the first six months of his pre-registration year on Sir Edgar's unit and the rest with Professor Jameson. A few ambitious people who had slogged away for years clocking up medals and certificates seemed to resent that. More in the class would probably have thought of such jobs as more trouble than they

273

were worth, worryingly high-pressured and an unnecessary burden on their early careers.

Scott did not regard himself as ambitious; it was more a question of keeping his options open. As a student he had worked efficiently but not excessively, enjoying what student life offered and making a number of friends, like Walker and Engadine and Savage, who had nothing to do with medicine. He had tackled finals by doing a safe amount of study in order to get through safely and had succeeded in doing just that. The housejobs business was more of a lottery: he had been lucky in it, with a slightly unusual ticket, but hadn't cared very much anyway.

Not everyone was as pleased with their housejobs. Robbie, sadly for him, had cared a great deal and done badly. Finals were the first set of exams in which he won no medals or prizes at all. He had even been recalled for an oral in psychiatry, not with the usual distinction crowd but with the little handful on the borderline of failure. He had passed, ingloriously, and his intended career in surgery had faltered too, at the very first obstacle. The previous year he had made a good impression on the academic surgical unit by being there practically all the time, knowing more anatomy than the registrars and going into theatre every time the professor operated. Everything had gone well, according to Robbie: a job was promised from on high, with an excellent chance of an SHO job to follow, then the professor had gone off sick having omitted to tell his colleagues any of this. When he had eventually died Robbie had gone to the next senior consultant to explain, only to be told that other arrangements now prevailed but that there were still a few vacancies out at Bavelaw and Blackridge, where there was a lot of good general experience to be had. Perhaps that and rumoured trouble on a psychiatry attachment had led to his lacklustre showing in finals. Robbie, it seemed, was no longer a golden boy.

'Now tell me, Theresa . . .' Jimmy had moved on. 'What do you think Kenneth Robinson has in mind for the Health Service now, hm? More of the milk of human kindness and lots of lovely new hospitals. . . ? Including, with any luck, our own new Institute. . . ? Or perhaps something a little less open-handed. . . ? What do *you* think?'

At about twenty to eight, when the noise in the lounge had reached an agreeable steady roar, Lennie got up on a chair and said something about not wishing to rush the meeting but there were one or two other items on the agenda, and a general move towards the stairs began. The group from the bay window formed part of a kind of rearguard, and had just reached the main first floor landing when there was a minor disturbance about halfway down the stairs. People moved round and looked down from the balcony landing to where Max was standing between Sandy and Gus, holding a hand from each above his head in a gesture that suggested to Scott something to do with boxing. On Sandy's upraised left hand was a bright, conspicuous engagement ring with a touch of green that went well with her dress. 'Three cheers,' Max yelled. 'Hip hip . . .'

The cheers were deafening, and when they died down and the party started to move again a new and happy buzz remained. Moments later there was another disturbance, this time right at the back of the crowd. Someone had fallen heavily to the floor. Scott turned round and so did Theresa and, being doctors now, both felt they ought to try to be helpful. Two men, Professor Jameson and Dr Ratho, Gus's father and now the most senior physician on the medical corridor of the Institute, were stooped over a tall, thin lady in her sixties who lay supine with a pink ballgown tastefully disposed around her. She was pale but breathing regularly. Her eyes were half closed and she was murmuring something that was not at all distinct. As Scott and Theresa knelt down Professor Jameson shook his head as though to indicate that further help was not required. 'It really was getting a bit stuffy in there,' he said. 'And poor Mopsy's never been one for the heat . . . Awfully good of you, Andrew, Theresa. But I think us older chaps will probably manage quite well. Thanks awfully. I expect we'll catch up with you in due course.'

III

THE LONG SURPRISE

December 1969

'Nothing to cry about, Lorna. Another lot of treatment this afternoon and you'll be in marvellous shape. Home for Christmas, see your baby. Wonderful, isn't it? So there's nothing to cry about, is there?' The patient continued to cry, more quietly than before, tears streaming down her face and her shoulders heaving with each sob. Dr Parkinson sat down heavily on her bed and put his arm round her. 'There there, Lorna. Think of it! Home by Christmas, see your baby. Lovely, certainly nothing to cry about ... Dr Lennox here will fix you up this afternoon and by Monday you'll be packing your bags.' Dr Parkinson, a large ungainly man who wore his underpants outside his shirt so that quite often they showed above his trousers, got up and winked at Sandy and then nodded. 'The usual,' he added quietly as the ward round left Lorna's little cubicle, 'and be very careful not to let any of it get on your hands.' At the door he turned to the patient again. 'And a very happy Christmas to you and yours, Lorna. Just in case I don't see you again before you go.'

Dr Parkinson's next patient was Mrs Jennett, an old lady halfway down the ward who had myelosclerosis and hardly any bone marrow left. She came in every couple of weeks for the top-up transfusions that kept her going. She couldn't go on for ever because, although they could keep her haemoglobin more or less steady, she wasn't making any white cells for herself and they were too expensive to give to an old lady who was going to die anyway. Dr Parkinson had vaguely decided to prop her up through Christmas and into the New Year and then let her go quietly after that. He waved at her in his odd, window-washing way. 'The top o'the morning to you, Myrtle. Now, let's see your chart.' He reached across her to the head of the bed where her chart was hanging, so that her nose was within what Sandy would have thought was probably lethal range of his armpit. 'Let's see now ... I wonder if one of you students would like to comment on this . . . Just a simple record of pulse, temperature and respiration over forty eight hours, but it speaks volumes to the educated eye, doesn't it? What do you think, young man?'

The chosen youth was about to open his mouth. 'Right,' said Dr Parkinson before he had said anything at all. 'She's got a transfusion reaction. Nothing awful, probably nothing worse than she's had a dozen other times she's been in here. Am I right, Myrtle? Indeed yes. So she's got a transfusion reaction . . . Of course at your level you're not expected to know all the ins and outs of it . . . Now if we were still in the Gambia we'd be thinking of malaria, wouldn't we? But not a great matter here in Edinburgh. No. Not malaria. Here, I suppose we'd think first of pyrogens. And of course leucocyte and platelet iso-agglutinins, wouldn't we?' The youth smiled and nodded vigorously. 'Yes,' said Dr Parkinson. 'Very good. They're the common things, aren't they? Now, young sir . . . Like to feel a spleen?'

Mrs Jennett, a well trained short case, adjusted her pillows, turned down the bed clothes, pulled up her nightie and lay flat while sister scowled and the student nurse leapt about pulling the curtains round so that the decencies were observed. Her abdomen was pale and wrinkled and there was a lump that made it look as if she had just swallowed a paving slab. The student stepped uncertainly forward, rubbing his hands together and looking at Dr Parkinson out of the corner of his eye. He laid a hand flat on Mrs Jennett's belly, across the edge of the hugest spleen Sandy had ever seen. 'No no no no no!' said Dr Parkinson. 'No no no no no no NO!' He shouldered the student aside and leant over Mrs Jennett with his arms almost encircling her and his face so close to hers that his gorilla breath must be practically choking her. 'Like *this*, see? You can't assume that every spleen you meet is going to be as easy to find as poor Myrtle's. A very difficult organ to palpate, a spleen can be . . . So we start off as if we aren't going to find it without a struggle. The left hand placed *here*, well into the left flank so as to push the organ forward and upwards so that the right hand, placed *so*, has the best possible chance of picking up the edge of the enlarged organ as the patient breathes in . . . Right, Myrtle?' Mrs Jennett took a long noisy breath in. 'What examiners are looking for is *technique*. *They* want to know that *you* will be able to find a spleen even though it might only be *slightly* diseased, don't they? Now, stand right here . . . No, right *here*, between me and Myrtle, so that *I* know that *you* have got *your* hands in the *proper* place.'

Dr Parkinson and the student stood crouched together against the bed in a way they would have been arrested for if they'd been caught doing it in Princes St Gardens at night, with the student beetroot red and holding his breath fit to burst and serve him right too. Mrs Jennett didn't seem to mind. Sandy and the ward sister exchanged a quiet smile. After a couple of minutes the pair of them got up and the student started to breathe again and Dr Parkinson muttered something to Mrs Jennett about a general improvement and how she might not have to come in so often in the New Year. She seemed pleased.

Dr Parkinson had only one other patient: a lady of ninety something who had come in to the ward when he was the consultant on for the waiting day. She'd had a stroke and there was nothing wrong with her blood but Dr Parkinson kept thinking there might be, especially on teaching rounds. He marched on past the nursing station, his white coat flapping behind him and his huge lumpy shoes crashing down so hard that the floor of the whole ward shook in time with his step. They arrived at the lady's bed and without even looking at her he pounced on the postgraduate girl from Singapore who was coming to the ward in the mornings for teaching rounds to brush up for the clinical part of the membership exam.

'Now then, Dr Wing,' He was talking a bit louder than usual and moving his lips a lot. 'As you see, this lady has had a stroke. Now I want you to think of some of the things that might have gone wrong with her blood that might have made it more likely that she should have what we call a stroke.'

Dr Wing, who was small and neat and always wore nice silk things, smiled and said 'Thrombocytosis from any cause, most commonly megakaryocytic leukaemia and haemorrhagic thrombocythaemia, and sometimes after splenectomy. And of course polycythaemia from any cause. This lady does not appear to be polycythaemic, although theoretically she might have idiopathic PRV, or one of the secondary forms, typically hypoxic or from excessive erythropoietin secretion.'

'Very good,' said Dr Parkinson, still talking slowly in short words and capital letters. 'Very good indeed, Dr Wing.' He turned to

Sandy and said 'As Dr Wing so rightly suggests, we should just check on her platelets and red cell count again, please, Dr Lennox. We might be able to nip something else in the bud.' He peered round the rest of the ward in his own bemused fashion then said 'So that's the lot then, isn't it? Thank you very much, Sandy. Thank you, sister . . .' That was the signal for the long march back to the door. Dr Parkinson smiled his idiot gargoyle smile and stamped off and made the ward floor shake all over again. Dr Wing trotted sweetly behind him like a faun following a water-buffalo and the students slouched dispiritedly after. Dr Parkinson still had about a dozen patients on the male ward downstairs.

Sandy glanced at her watch. It was only ten to eleven. Dr Marks started at eleven prompt and sometimes there were problems because he and Dr Parkinson didn't speak to each other: there was only one of her and odd things tended to happen because she couldn't be in two places at once and they couldn't discuss it, but today was all right. She jotted down the treatment for Lorna and the tests for the stroke lady and then sister made the sign for coffee. They went together to sister's room and sat down, but not before sister had closed the door.

'About Lorna,' she said firmly. 'Why do we have to go through all this again? Christmas and the baby, indeed!' She snorted and picked up the coffee pot. 'I don't think he's ever so much as glanced at her pressure areas. My girls can look after her, but her bottom's paper thin and getting redder by the minute. And her mouth's barely recovered from the last lot.'

Sandy nodded. 'Difficult,' she said, meaning impossible. Dr Parkinson had spent about twenty minutes agonising over Lorna's blood results and about one with Lorna, and he had spent it telling lies and making her cry. 'How's her husband?'

'Distraught, poor man. Absolutely distraught. Hardly surprising after nearly eight months. With Dr Parkinson keeping saying he'll see him and then forgetting all about it.'

Lorna's husband was a nice man who worked in a bank on George Street and came in a lot. There were no other children and his mother was looking after their baby. Lorna had been admitted straight from the maternity unit and had been home for just one weekend in the eight months since. Her treatment was working only in the rather limited sense that she was still alive, and officially she was unaware of her diagnosis. She cried a lot and sister now had a staff nurse organised to go in and stay with her on Tuesdays and Fridays as soon as the ward round left her room. Sandy had had a number of odd conversations with the husband, who talked about his wife's 'blood problem' as though he didn't know or, more likely, didn't want to know, and, since Dr Parkinson had never seen him and always told Lorna she just had an unusual kind of anaemia, it was all very difficult.

'So I suppose I'd better order up that ghastly stuff again, for this afternoon.'

'Daunorubicin,' said Sandy. There were two other things as well. She would check everything, including the doses, from the notes as soon as Dr Marks had finished, then give it all to sister in writing. 'Shall we aim for two o'clock?'

'Probably just as well. Get it over with, I suppose, before the admitting day cases start coming in . . . You know, she always looks so *ill* afterwards. I mean even iller.'

There was a knock on the door. It opened and Jamie Wilson's head appeared round its edge. 'Morning, sister . . . Oh, hello, Sandy. Am I . . . ?'

'Not at all,' said sister. 'Come in, Jamie, and have a quick coffee before your round . . .'

'Thanks, sister.'

'I see it's your silly tie day.'

Jamie fingered his navy and maroon striped tie and smiled. 'And why not, sister, if it keeps an old man happy?' Jamie was probably sister's favourite junior doctor. He had been a houseman on the ward two years before and had just come back as Dr Marks' registrar, and was clever and sensible and always cheerful and polite. 'Everything all right for the round?'

'From the nursing point of view, most certainly.'

'Of course, sister . . . Sandy?'

'Well, from the doctoring point of view . . .' Sister tried to frown but giggled instead. Sandy giggled too then started again. 'Mrs Hawkes is still pretty frightened and panics and thinks she's got chest pain, but it doesn't really sound like proper cardiac pain. So she's better, but doesn't believe it. And Margaret Black, the renal colic lady, wants to get home but is still having her urine strained and has only had two fasting calciums . . . You probably knew that.

Miss Clapton's just going down slowly and the ladies at the end are all very much the same.'

Jamie nodded. 'Thought so. Even the old lady who was maybe going to Sunnylea? Miss Christie? Ninety-something . . .'

'Miss Christie. She was there for a day yesterday and didn't sit down once. Kept saying it was lovely for people who needed that sort of thing but her mother was expecting her home by tea-time.'

Jamie laughed. 'Oh, all right. Good try . . . Or should we see if they'll give her a day or two to settle down?'

'I thought of that,' said Sandy. 'The social worker's not keen. Other problems.'

'What the doctor means,' said sister, 'is that Miss Christie, in the middle of a busy lounge *thronged* with Sunnylea residents, became confused and tried to use an ornamental brass plant pot for quite another purpose.'

'Gosh.' Jamie thought about that then said 'But the aspidistras get used to it, in places like Sunnylea.'

'Jamie!' said sister fondly. 'Really!' The appearance of another face and Watsonian tie round the edge of the door signified the arrival of the rest of Dr Marks' entourage. Kennie Scott, in his minor Friday walk-on role of Third Watsonian, as Sandy always thought of it, was Dr Marks' SHO. He was shepherding three other foreign postgraduates. As they went from sister's room to the door of the ward Kennie sidled up to Sandy, far closer than he had to, and whispered. 'Everything OK for the big man, Sandy?' Sandy pursed her lips like sister and nodded severely. Kennie was a heavy breather who dripped manly fragrances and had been given the brush-off by nearly every girl in Sandy's year who wasn't either evangelical or actually deformed. He didn't take hints easily, and continued to stand far too close to Sandy again as they waited at the door for Dr Marks.

Jamie glanced at his watch and did a little chin-up chest-out comic routine which meant he had seen Dr Marks on the way from his office across the courtyard. The postgraduates looked at each other in a puzzled kind of way then rallied a bit with a half-hearted Egyptian-army version of what Jamie was doing, so that both sister and Sandy had to work quite hard not to giggle. Then Kennie noticed, with a ridiculous manly ho-ho-ho that made the post-graduates realise the whole thing was obscure British humour rather than arcane British protocol. Two of them sagged a bit and looked sheepish but the little one with the moustache puffed out his chest even more and was actually putting an imaginary bugle to his lips just as Dr Marks burst through the double doors.

'Good morning, doctor.' Dr Marks boomed it straight down at the little man, who was instantly aghast. Sandy thought about it and decided that the little man probably hadn't offended Dr Marks very much at all. Of all the consultants in the Institute he was the most old-fashioned and formal, but in a tongue-in-cheek way. If he liked doing his ward rounds with full military honours, so to speak, then he could hardly object if his retinue sometimes sent him up a bit: it just meant they knew what he wanted. Dr Marks looked at his watch with affected puzzlement then turned to Jamie. 'I wondered perhaps if I had arrived a moment or two early. But no. Morning, sister. Morning, Dr Lennox. Morning, boys.' For the last bit he fingered his Watsonian tie, then he turned to the postgraduates. 'Morning, gentlemen.'

Sandy made a mental note to ask sister when and why the Friday tie nonsense had started. If Kennie or Jamie forgot to wear the old school tie on Fridays they had to pay a sixpenny fine into the coffee fund, a minor sanction which, it suddenly occurred to Sandy, might have been devised by Dr Marks to stop Kennie wearing the kind of hideous wide floral number he might ordinarily choose. Or perhaps, and on reflection it was much more likely, the Marks really was just a clannish old Edinburgh snob.

'Shall we begin,' he boomed, setting off smartly towards the doctors' room. Dr Marks did not wear a white coat, a mode of dress he considered quite improper for the consultant grade. He even referred to Dr Parkinson, whom he had once seen in a white coat with a speck of blood on one sleeve, as 'the butcher's boy'. He himself invariably wore a suit from his large and stylish wardrobe, with carefully modulated seasonal variations, lovely shirts and a floral buttonhole in summer. His juniors, however, were expected always to wear white coats of a style and freshness well above the usual standard. Sister, who was quite happy to go along with most of his nonsense, always put a fresh white coat out for Sandy on Fridays, but it was all a bit sad. Dr Marks just didn't have enough to do.

His ward round always lasted exactly one hour. It didn't matter if he had only three patients: he managed to spin it out, and even sustain an impression of haste and enthusiasm, by rushing to and fro from the doctors' room to the bedside between cases, ostensibly so that a full discussion of each individual patient, including teaching points, could take place without a muttering huddle at the foot of the bed; in fact to create a great stir with his little retinue, so as to fill the long spaces of his day.

When they were all standing in the doctors' room he boomed 'First case, please, Kennie' and they were off. Kennie ploughed his ponderous way through a perfectly straightforward forty one year old lady with renal colic who had been around for far too long already. Her pain had gone, the offending stone had passed of its own accord and been sent off to the lab to be crushed, analysed and reported on, and now they were pretending she might have hyperparathyroidism because that was a fashionable diagnosis just now, to be thought of in all cases of renal colic, peptic ulcer and confusion in the elderly. Sandy stood politely with her notebook at the ready while the smallest Arab, the bugle-boy, got a hard time from Dr Marks on the microscopic appearances of the parathyroid adenoma that Mrs Black had not got, and serve him right too.

They got through that, and the X-ray appearances of the characteristic bony changes of the thing Mrs Black had not got, and eventually they got on to the simple Reader's Digest I-am-Margaret's-kidney stuff about drinking lots and lots to avoid it all happening again and quite soon they would be saying good morning to Mrs Black and saying it all over again, because Dr Marks was a great proponent of what he called patient involvement as the essential basis of treatment, because it let him bore the pants off them and took up lots more time. And when sister reported that Mrs Black's fluid intake over the last twenty four hours had been three and a half litres there was practically a round of applause.

A couple of nice daydreams after that Dr Marks opened the door and everyone marched out in the appointed order: sister, house officer, senior house officer, registrar, post-graduates then the man himself, with the man himself holding the door open for everybody and closing it after them before resuming his place at the head of the column. Mrs Black felt well and had had no further pain, blood or gravel. Mrs Black had drunk a lot and was strongly reminded of the importance of continuing to do so. The little moustachioed postgraduate, who had got pseudo-hypoparathyroidism mixed up with pseudo-pseudo-hypoparathyroidism on top of his previous offence, was asked, to his astonishment, if he wished to ask the patient any questions. He gulped a couple of times then asked her if she had ever had peptic ulcers or what he called states confusional. She hadn't.

They retreated up the ward and went into the doctors' room again with the usual ceremony and Kennie started to present the next case. Miss Clapton, forty eight and not going to make forty nine, was a single lady who lived in a small-holding at Seafield and bred spaniels. She had come up first with a cough and weight loss, at which point Dr Marks had interrupted Kennie's droning. 'Gentlemen, one question and one question only . . . Sir?'

'Is the patient smoking, sir?'

'Good. Well, in general terms, good. Yes, Kennie? And the answer?'

'Capstan Full Strength, sir, forty a day for thirty years.'

'Poor woman. Carry on.'

Kennie droned on and eventually put up the chest X-ray from outpatients, the chest X-ray from the follow-up appointment, the admission chest X-ray and at last the one from earlier in the week. 'What can you see wrong with it, gentlemen . . . ? Sir?'

'Cancer, sir . . .'

'Wrong. You can't see cancer. Just describe the abnormalities, doctor. Cancer's a diagnosis safely made only under a microscope.'

The chosen victim laboured reasonably well through the hilar mass, the collapse, the effusion and the erosion of several ribs and was rewarded with solemn thanks from Dr Marks. 'And how is Miss Clapton today, sister?'

'Remarkably cheerful, Dr Marks. Sinking of course, but lucid and cheerful and enjoying her visits from her friend. And a lot more settled on her heroin.'

'Good. Grand. We should go and see her, shouldn't we?' Dr Marks moved smartly to his ceremonial door-opening spot and off they marched again. Miss Clapton, thin and breathless now even at rest, was sitting up in bed vaguely reading a doggy magazine but just as aware of the ritual as any member of Dr Mark's retinue. She had determinedly yellow hair and old-fashioned bright red lipstick like Gus's mum, which she put on for ward rounds and visits from her friend. 'And how are you this morning, Miss Clapton?'

The patient put her magazine down on her lap and patted it flat. 'A bit less sore, thank you, Dr Marks . . .'

'Yes,' said the consultant, still addressing her like a public meeting. 'It's good stuff and we have plenty of it. Appetite?'

'I enjoy what I can take.'

Dr Marks cast an eye over her locker. On it there were flowers, a half-full ashtray, a packet of her favourite cigarettes, a couple of bottles of Robinson's Lemon Barley Water, a couple of yellowing paperbacks and an old framed photograph of four girls in uniform. 'And you're keeping your mind active?'

Miss Clapton smiled in an odd way that involved only the bottom half of her face. Dr Marks sat down on her bed, stuck out a hand and placed it on the patient's. Looking her straight in the eye he intoned 'Is there anything you're worried about?' The postgraduates were mystified. He pronounced the question like a sentence of death, which in effect, as ward round regulars knew, it was. The patient first looked thoughtful, then laughed. 'One or two admin. things . . . KD will take care of them . . .'

Miss Clapton had a friend and business associate in her kennels venture who came in to see her every day, bringing cigarettes, flowers, books and hairdye as required. She also brought in astonishing quantities of Robinson's Lemon Barley Water, about which sister had her suspicions but which she had chosen not to investigate. The friend, whose name Sandy had at first taken to be Miss Kaye Dee or something like that, was actually called Miss Doull and the KD thing was a nickname, presumably from around the time of the butch quartet photograph. Dr Marks continued to sit on Miss Clapton's bed, in silence and without embarrassment. Eventually he said 'Anything else? Larger questions, for example?'

Miss Clapton sniffed and smiled again. 'Not really. In fact no. In the service . . . I take it you have service experience, Dr Marks?'

'Indeed yes.'

'In the service . . . We were ack-ack, actually . . .' She could talk only in short phrases now, pausing painfully for breath. 'In ack-ack we used to say . . . if your name's on it, it's for you. Bombs, you know. And we even had a silly notice – a pokerwork thing done during one of our many long spells of boredom – "If the bombs don't get you, the Woodbines will". And I was working it out the other night . . . Two o'clock this morning, actually . . . My name must have been on one . . .' She smiled. 'Perhaps the half-millionth?' She laughed and then coughed and doubled forward in spasms of painful choking. Dr Marks moved closer and held her and patted her gently on the back. When she recovered her face was reddish-purple and there was blood on her lower lip. 'I admire your spirit, ma'am,' he said, getting up to let a student nurse take his place. He shook her hand firmly and long while the student nurse attacked her tears and the blood on her lip with a paper hankie. When the nurse eventually got out of the way he nodded slowly and said 'There ought to be medals for it.' Miss Clapton smiled up at him through more tears. 'Thank you,' she whispered faintly in a chin-up, keep-smiling war-movie way, her lipstick wildly smudged.

It was corny, Sandy decided, but it was exactly what she needed. The Marks patent you-are-about-to-die routine – sit on bed, look patient straight in eye, hold hands and on a count of three say in a loud clear voice 'Is there anything you're worried about?' – was actually quite good, better than that of most other consultants she'd seen and miles ahead of the poor old butcher's boy. The putty medal for dying bravely had been a risky touch but the photograph, the army friend and the war stories justified it and it had worked. Sandy looked across at sister, who was nodding and blinking and frowning to stop herself crying too.

They marched off and then Kennie droned his way through the story of Mrs Hawkes, at least third time round. She was the lady who kept thinking she was dying and couldn't be convinced she wasn't. She had had a minor heart attack, or small subendocardial infero-lateral infarct as Kennie so boringly put it. She had done well and was far more anxious about it all than she should have been, for reasons that she had divulged in confidence to Sandy and which she, in confidence, had conveyed to Jamie, by-passing Kennie for obvious reasons. Kennie recited the details of her last couple of episodes of odd, not very cardiac symptoms and suggested that the diagnostic formulation should now include a phrase about cardiac neurosis. Dr Marks snorted. 'Really, doctor? Da Costa's syndrome? The effort syndrome? Disorderly action of the heart, as our transatlantic cousins seem to term it? I think not, doctor. Labels without meaning, substitutes for thought. The woman's worried I grant you. And on not unreasonable grounds. But as ever with clinical medicine . . . The history. . . ! What the patient tells you, doctor . . . Not what you think about what you thought she told you, but the story itself.' Dr Marks paused then glanced and nodded in Sandy's direction. Jamie must have had a quiet word with him before the round, which helped a lot. A strip of ECG tracing was produced and the postgraduate who had said least was gently exposed as knowing next to nothing about interpreting it. When the man was eventually completely tongue-tied Dr Marks stopped asking questions and brightened up. 'And in your own country, doctor, could you buy an ECG machine?'

'Certainly, sir . . .' came the proud reply. 'Many stockists of the latest machines. From Germany.'

'Alarming news, doctor. To me that is truly alarming news. I maintain a belief that these machines are like cars and aircraft. No one should be allowed near the controls until certified by public examination as safe to do so. We have no such laws here, sad to say, nor, I imagine, have you in your country, but they are long overdue. Why?' After a dramatic pause he answered his own question with pounding emphasis. 'Because incalculable harm can be done to patients by the loose or ignorant interpretation of the very precise information these machines provide.'

The postgraduates muttered briefly among themselves. It was a cruel line that Sandy had heard Dr Marks use before, in similar circumstances and to similar effect. He raised a hand. 'Quietly, thank you, gentlemen. But doctor . . . Perhaps you can redeem yourself with your stethoscope. Come this way . . .'

Mrs Hawkes was not bad-looking for somebody in her late thirties: a chubby brunette, worried with some reason and unfortunate also to be A Good Teaching Case. She had one of the odder biochemical predispositions to heart disease, with high levels of cholesterol, a family thing that gave nice clinical signs like the white margins running round the lower half of her irises and little yellowish patches under the skin on either side of the bridge of her nose: more fatty deposits of the kind also sludging up her coronary arteries.

Before letting anyone loose on her with a stethoscope Dr Marks went over all that with the lost tribe, and they all looked at the creases of her palms, where fatty lines sometimes appeared, although not in the case of Mrs Hawkes.

Mrs Hawkes was beginning to get used to all this, and also to being listened to, and as soon as the nurse had put the screens round she stripped her top half by wriggling out of her loose-necked frilly apricot nightie then sat smiling at the post-graduates in a way that they would all probably misinterpret quite seriously. 'Doctor . . .' Dr Marks ushered the quiet one forward. He pulled a stethoscope from his pocket, fumbled with it and said 'Excuse me please, madam,' lifting Mrs Hawkes' left breast as though it might have turned out to be red hot. He listened at the cardiac apex with his eyes closed, for longer than Dr Marks usually allowed, moved his stethoscope to the other standard places quite quickly then stood up and folded his stethoscope back into his pocket. He was greenish pale and there was a line of sweat on his top lip.

'Yes, doctor?'

He croaked then cleared his throat, gulped and said 'Normal'.

'Really, doctor?'

'There are two normal heart sounds and no murmurs, sir.'

'Really, doctor?'

His eyelids flickered and he gulped again. 'I think so, sir. Yes. Normal.'

Dr Marks said nothing, took out his own stethoscope and listened sternly at all four places. He stood up frowning then his face broke into a wolfish grin. 'I agree entirely, doctor. Normal. Completely normal.' He patted the patient's naked shoulder as though she were a horse that had just done something clever. 'Our patient is making an excellent recovery from her recent trouble, and can be expected to continue to do so . . . Now, if you'll excuse us, I want to have a quiet word with Mrs Hawkes . . . Jamie, if you could just take the chaps up to the end of the ward and wait a moment.'

They retreated. The ward remained hushed, as it always did for Dr Marks' round. Through the stillness Sandy could hear Mrs Hawkes' whispered confidences and Dr Marks booming and remarkably explicit reassurances that her unfortunate experience on a single occasion was a one-in-a-million mishap unlikely to recur; that it might nonetheless be prudent to avoid one or two of the more athletic and demanding practices she had mentioned, for a couple of months at least; and that – assuming her progress was maintained, as it almost certainly would be – normal intercourse could be resumed within a week or two of going home.

* * *

'Dr Roberts?' The voice drew closer as sister moved down the ward. 'Dr Roberts!'

'Excuse me a moment.' Robbie put his clipboard down on the bed and got up just as sister's face appeared at the joint of the curtains. 'Dr Roberts?' Instead of speaking more quietly as she got nearer she spoke louder than ever. 'There's a multiple on its way in from Casualty. A pelvis, both femurs and a tib and fib, if you're interested. Theatre wants to know when this one's coming and you've forgotten to cross match the two necks of femurs from the female ward. Oh, and the senior registrar wants a word with you. Right?'

Robbie looked from the ward sister to the patient and back again. The patient seemed sympathetic. The ward sister, as usual, did not. 'Right?' she said again, even more loudly.

'Thank you, sister . . .'

'I'll right you all right. Right?' She scowled and muttered 'You're in trouble, Robbie. Real trouble this time,' then smiled fiercely and said in her normal fishwife voice. 'The senior registrar would be grateful if you'd contact him at your earliest possible convenience, Dr Roberts. Right?'

'Thank you, sister . . .'

'Hmph! And theatre said this one' – she nodded in the direction of the patient Robbie was clerking in – 'this one's really urgent. Because of the multiple . . . Right?'

This time Robbie didn't say anything, but sat down again beside the patient to make it clear that she might as well go away and let him get on with it. He knew about the multiple already because Casualty had bleeped him first. The patient for theatre probably couldn't go today anyway but he needed a bit more time with him to be absolutely certain about that, and the responsibility for cross matching the two necks of femurs on the female ward lay with Peter, the houseman on that ward, but since he had gone off at lunchtime for two weeks leave Robbie was going to have to sort it out anyway, and he would have plenty of time because both of them would have to be cancelled and fasted again for theatre tomorrow because of the multiple. The man he was clerking in looked at him with genuine concern. 'Are you all right, doctor?' Robbie grinned and said 'Fine. Let's get back to you.' The man laughed and so did Robbie. If you didn't laugh sometimes you would cry.

'Sorry about all that . . . Your kidney trouble, Mr Duncan . . . How long has that been going on . . . ?'

'Well, it was the diabetic doctors that picked it up, so it must have been after I got the diabetes . . . Definitely within the last ten years.'

'We'll be able to get your notes from the diabetic clinic quite soon, Mr Duncan, and it'll all be in there. But roughly when? Just to the nearest year, and what was it you first noticed?'

'My ankles,' said the man, and Robbie had a curious, amused premonition of what he was going to say.

'I complained about my ankles, but they said it was my kidneys. Couldn't understand that at all.'

'They were swelling?'

'My kidneys?' The man looked as puzzled as he sounded and Robbie found it hard not to laugh. 'No, Mr Duncan. Your ankles.'

'Yes. Yes, that was it. The ankles started to swell, and they said it was the diabetes going for the kidneys. So they sent me to a kidney doctor . . . Nice big chap, he was, but sort of dreich. "Leaking kidneys, Mr Duncan," he says to me. "We'll do a couple of tests." So they took me into the ward and kept me for nearly three weeks. Radioactive tests, split new, he said, and I was in the forefront of medical progress.'

'Good. Now how often do you get up at night to pass water?'

'You wouldn't believe it, doc. Six, maybe eight times. And always quite a lot, and I'm nearly always thirsty, as you'd expect from that.'

'Thanks, Mr Duncan . . . We're probably going to have to do a few more tests – on your kidneys and your diabetes – before we can get on and sort your ankle out. Now I'll just have to excuse myself again and let them know in the operating theatre. Excuse me.'

'Eh, Dr Roberts . . .' Another face had appeared at the corner of the curtains, at least a foot below where sister's had been. It was the theatre orderly, Jip, a little red-faced man with staring nostrils. 'Dr Roberts . . . From the senior registrar, sir . . .' He lowered his voice slightly. 'If you dinnae get your arse along tae theatre in two minutes flat you've jist started the most miserable two weeks o' your life . . . Sir. Right?'

The face disappeared. Robbie excused himself yet again, and as he rose to answer the summons the patient reached out and grasped his hand and asked if him if he was sure he really was all right.

'I've got leukaemia, haven't I?' Lorna was lying back on her pillows looking straight ahead. Sandy, who had been just sitting beside her waiting for the three horrible drugs to come up from pharmacy, couldn't think of anything to say. Lorna turned and looked at her, her eyes filling with tears. Sandy still couldn't think of anything to say, and held her hand instead and squeezed it. Lorna looked at her intently, straight into her eyes, her tears flowing faster. Sandy nodded. Lorna let go of her hand, sat forward and reached for her big box of paper hankies. 'I've known for months,' she said, dabbing her eyes. 'And the treatment's not going to help, is it? Not much anyway.'

That was more difficult. If you were Dr Parkinson looking at a dozen different results from your haematology lab and drawing little graphs of what you called the troublesome cell mass, you might gibber and lie and do some sums that tried to balance drug dose and effect against the possibly measurable mass of malignant cells. Flattening the curve, he called it. 'Look, Sandy . . . See how we've flattened the curve,' he had grinned over his little graphs. But there was nothing on his graphs about the bleeding, the ulceration, the infection, the sickness, the pain and the misery of Lorna's last eight months. Sandy ran through the whole ghastly story in her mind, faced Lorna's gaze and nodded again.

Lorna had been in the ward when she had taken it over. Her predecessor, a calm, slightly hardened chap from Ayrshire, just finishing his pre-registration year, had explained it all to her over the case notes, before she had even set eyes on the girl still dying slowly in the same bed months later. 'Basically it's Love Story. We've had the book and the film. This is the patient . . . Lorna, or Parky's pet patient. And she's supposed to not know – All Dr Parkinson's patients are supposed to not know. Transferred straight from the matty, and the wee baby's fine. Gets the poisons about once a fortnight, after he's read the tea-leaves. And try not to get them on your hands. Apparently they can kill doctors too.' Almost unconsciously, Sandy checked that there were gloves and a mask on the procedure trolley still waiting for the drugs.

'I thought so,' said Lorna. 'Would he be terribly upset if I refused the treatment this time? Or would it help get me home? For Christmas and to die.' Sandy thought about that and nodded again, not knowing whether she was telling the truth or not. 'Good,' said Lorna. 'I'll have it. And I've really known since the start, because the way they do bloods over in maternity's different. Nearly everybody's routine, after their baby, and they leave the blood forms on your locker with the pink tubes and then the doctor comes round and picks them up when he does your bloods.' She took a deep breath. 'Mine, my form, said acute leukaemia, in big capitals I could even read upside down. I suppose the nurses do them. So I've known for months. Since the twenty second of April, in fact.'

'Gosh,' said Sandy. 'I'm sorry.'

'That was the date on the form. Then a couple of days later Dr Parkinson came over and said that I had a kind of anaemia that would need a bit of treatment. I thought that was a bit funny, so I said I've got leukaemia, haven't I? And he looked completely shocked. Oh dear me, why do you think that, he said. So I explained. There must have been a mistake, he said. There's been a terrible mix up about those forms. I'll speak to them.' Lorna smiled and even laughed. 'He got very flustered about it all. It was really quite funny, now I know him and know how upset he must have been.' She reached for another paper hankie and blew her nose. 'So I asked if I could just go home and he said No no no no *No*, we've still got this anaemia to sort out. So I knew. In fact I've always known. But I really do want to go home now . . .' Lorna paused and sniffed and blinked then put her hands up to her face and howled and howled and howled.

'Okay, okay, wonderboy, I'll give you that one. The ankle's a diabetic with wrecked kidneys so I can't have him this list. But what about the two hips? Huh? When the anaesthetist went to check them over in the ward she found you hadn't cross-matched them. Two hips and no blood, huh? How am I supposed to sort out a couple of intertrochanterics, both over eighty, with nothing to give them if they decide to bleed out, huh?'

'Well, OK. They're not cross-matched yet. But when were you planning to do them? I mean, there's the multiple.'

'Great. I see. You're not only smart, you're telepathic. There was nothing about a multiple an hour ago. Just an ankle and two hips. That's the list. That's what we planned. And now the ankle's unfit and the hips haven't been cross-matched . . . You see what I'm driving at? I have theatre set up, everybody waiting, and there's fuck all to do because a smartass house officer hasn't got his act together.'

'But the multiple . . . I mean it's just as well, really. The ankle's off anyway, and the hips are going to have to wait till tomorrow, so I can cross-match them now, and theatre's ready . . . For the multiple. So I don't think . . .'

'Nobody's asking you to think. You're a fucking house officer, Robbie, and you're no fucking good. End of story. Now fuck off.'

Jip, the theatre orderly, folded his *Daily Record* and looked up at Robbie as though he had just noticed him. The senior registrar turned to go back into the theatre and Robbie, not wishing to be left alone with Jip, rushed at the exit from the theatre changing room and found himself pushing vainly against a door marked 'Pull'. Jip smiled and opened his paper again. 'I told ye, son. I did ma best. Ye canny say I didnae warn ye.'

Out in the corridor again, Robbie tried to put the whole thing in perspective so as not to get unnecessarily worked up. The key thing seemed to be that the multiply injured patient would get dealt with quickly, going into theatre almost straight away and being operated on by Hamish Cruickshank, the consultant who was interested in major trauma. And that was probably why Goodison, the senior registrar, was getting all upset about things: he had thought he was going to be the big man doing the operations that had been planned – the ankle and the two hips – and now, through the fault of no one, least of all the houseman, he wasn't. He was going to have to go in and assist Hamish instead, and Hamish didn't like him and the feeling was mutual and that can't have helped. So bawling out the houseman, in front of the theatre orderly as a bonus, might have relieved his feelings. Meanwhile, it might be sensible to cast an eye over the multiple, after which there would be plenty of time, perhaps, to finish making sense of Mr Duncan's various medical problems, because there was no one else in the orthopaedic unit who would want to try; and he could even look in on the female ward and cross-match the two hips for tomorrow that Peter should have done for today.

'So how did all this start, Mrs Johnson?' Sandy picked up her pen.

'Hard to tell, dear. You know, hard to tell exactly.'

'Well, roughly. Or just tell me about the pain.'

'Pain?' The patient suddenly looked interested. 'Don't talk to me about pain. I know all about pain.'

'But where?'

'What?'

'Where was the pain?'

'What pain?'

'The pain you were talking about just now. The pain when all this started.'

'All what started?'

Sandy put down her pen and took a deep breath. 'Sorry, Mrs Johnson . . . You said downstairs, in Casualty, to Dr Wilson, that it had really started about three weeks ago. So I was wondering . . .'

'Oh, my pain?'

'Yes.'

'Terrible. I mean really terrible. Never had pain like it, not even with the bairns, and I've had five . . . All boys too. How many have you had, dear?'

Sandy picked up her pen again. 'Mrs Johnson, you were starting to tell me about how you first got ill. How the pain came on, and anything else that happened around that time. Were you sick? Or did you just feel sick?'

Mrs Johnson smiled and nodded. 'So you felt sick?' Sandy said.

'That's right, dear.'

'So which came first, Mrs Johnson, the pain or the sickness?'

'The sickness. Definitely the sickness.' Sandy wrote that down, with a feeling that at last she was getting somewhere. Mrs Johnson smiled and nodded. 'The sickness. Every time, dear. With all five of them . . . And how many have you had, dear?' Sandy put her pen down again. There was a GP's letter, something Sandy usually read only after she had had her own try at getting a story, examining the patient and making a diagnosis. This might be one for the short cut. The letter was quite legible and really quite helpful too. 'Dear doctor, etc . . . normally uncomplaining old lady who has been bothering my partners quite a lot with complaints of nausea, occasional sickness and intermittent upper abdominal pain. She has clearly lost weight and is somewhat tender in the epigastrium. No significant previous medical history. Five children (and proud of it!). Widowed many years, lives alone. Sons, daughters-in-law visit regularly. I think she may well have a gastric ulcer. Thank you for admitting her, etc. PS She is inclined to have become a little forgetful of late.' Thank you, doctor, thought Sandy to herself: she probably has.

'Mrs Johnson . . .'

'Yes, dear?'

'Mrs Johnson, your doctor says you've been ill for three months off and on . . . With pain and sickness . . . So how did it all start?'

'I remember now . . .' Sandy picked up her pen. The old lady's eyes misted over. 'It all started . . . It all started when they came to my door one Thursday. Two big policemen. Mrs Johnson? they said, so I said yes, I'm Mrs Johnson. And one of them said I'm sorry tae have tae tell ye, Mrs Johnson, but Mr Johnson's had a serious accident at his work. It was a Thursday. And from that day on I was left on my own with five bairns tae bring up . . .'

'How awful . . . But did anyone come into hospital with you, Mrs Johnson?'

'No, dear. I'm all on my own. For years and years now. One Thursday afternoon two big policemen came to my door. Mrs Johnson? they said . . .'

'Sandy?'

'Oh, hello, Jamie.'

'How are you getting on?'

Sandy got up and went outside the screens to talk to Jamie. 'Sorry about this,' he said. 'Just do a quick admission. You won't get much of a story, but do your best. Upper GI symptoms and weight loss is what it comes down to. So we'll just observe her over the weekend and start sorting her out on Monday. A couple of sick people on their way up, and probably two more I'll have to go back down and see. You feeling strong?'

'Fairly.'

'It's all experience . . . Invaluable experience.' It was a Dr Marks phrase, pronounced by Jamie with a hint of the authentic Marks boom.

'So what have we got, Jamie?'

'An overdose – tricyclics and quite ill – and a woman with bleeding varices who probably isn't going to do, but we'll have a go: Sengstaken tube, I'll see to that . . . And I crossmatched her from casualty so some fresh blood should be up quite soon. She's got a drip up, running saline for now, but I'd say give her three units fairly quickly when the blood appears.'

'Half-hourly readings?'

'Quarter-hourly. She really isn't very well . . . Sorry Sandy.'

'It's all right.'

'Any students about?'

'There might be one on the male ward.'

'Tut, tut,' said Jamie. 'Don't know what the younger generation's coming to. Oh, and could you ask staff to set up all the Sengstaken stuff, please, Sandy? Say seven o'clock? Thanks.'

Jamie went off and Sandy sat down again with Mrs Johnson, this time just to ask a few more questions before examining her. She was the fourth admitting day case since the ward had gone on take at three o'clock, and it sounded as if there might be another four to come in quite soon. Sandy asked Mrs Johnson a few more questions and started to examine her, asking the rest of the questions at the same time, just like the busy, rude doctors in out-patient clinics, and as she did so she realised how they got to be like that. There was really nothing much to find: flabby wrinkles that fitted the story of weight loss; a bit of tenderness when she was prodded really hard under the ribs, worst in the centre but definitely still there a bit off to the left; a puzzling collection of upper abdominal scars that probably meant someone had had a go or two at an ulcer, a gallbladder or perhaps both years and years ago, though the doctor's letter hadn't mentioned it and Mrs Johnson couldn't remember anything about it; and some fairly terrible toenails – long, yellowish and curled together in a way that seemed to indicate that she hadn't had shoes on for months and months.

When she had finished Sandy popped the covers snugly up round Mrs Johnson again, drew the screens back and went off to the doctor's room to write her up. Sandy was normally proud of her admission notes but this lot was going to look a bit apologetic, with phrases like 'Detailed history not obtainable – patient confused', which always looked as if you hadn't tried very hard. The most informative bit would be the little diagram of the abdomen, with cross-hatching for the tender area and lines for the scars, all located in proper relation to the ribs and navel, and the little summary at the end: 'An eighty-five year old lady with history of weight loss, vomiting and upper abdominal pain, all of uncertain duration. Evidence of weight loss and previous GI surgery, together with epigastric tenderness but no masses. Probable gastric ulcer, possible gastric carcinoma. For routine investigations, FOB's x 3 and barium meal.'

When Sandy had been on Sir Ronald's unit as a student the admitting day had been Thursday, and she had known when she applied for the job that if she got it she would have Friday admitting days for her whole six months. She had known in advance about some of the disadvantages of admitting on Fridays and had discovered a whole lot more in the time she had been in the job. It wasn't just the obvious things, like being up all night on Friday and working until lunchtime on Saturday even when it was your weekend off. Fridays were busy because patients and doctors tended to want to get things sorted out before the weekend proper, and there was less help around for clerking people in because students nowadays didn't seem very keen on spending Friday nights in the Institute. The saddest bit was the overdoses: weekends seemed to be when people broke up with their boyfriends, or just got drunk and decided life wasn't worth living, so even if Saturday and Sunday were worse Friday was bad enough, and they were mostly sad, unhelpable people. And last but not least, Sandy reflected as she sat waiting for her next two customers, Christmas was next Friday and it would be business as usual, or maybe just a bit quieter, but no going home to Spylaw Road for a proper family Christmas lunch, her last as Miss Lennox, spinster of this parish, but with Gus being there too, which he would have been if she weren't admitting, and which would have been quite nice. There was always next Christmas, and whatever happened she would somehow avoid being on call then too.

'Dr Lennox . . .' The second year student nurse was standing at the door of the doctors' room. 'Dr Lennox, staff says would you mind coming and taking a look at the overdose? Not at all well, she says.' They walked quickly down the ward to the sick patients' bay opposite the nursing station. In a corner bed the staff nurse was stooped over the latest admission, the one Jamie said had taken an overdose of tricyclic anti-depressants. She seemed to be having difficulty recording her blood pressure. 'Quite well when she came in, considering,' said the student nurse. 'Now she's sort of gone off . . .' The staff nurse, pink-faced and with her hair falling loose from under her cap, looked up then tried again. 'Sorry, Sandy . . . Her systolic's suddenly gone right down . . . I mean, less than sixty . . . D'you want to try?'

'What's her pulse?'

'One twenty. At least.'

'Gosh.'

'And the drip they put up in Casualty's sort of stopped.'

'Tissued?'

'We think so.'

The patient, a fairish girl in her mid twenties, was pale and inert and probably about to go unconscious. She had the grey, bedraggled look people usually had after gastric lavage, and Sandy had learned not to worry about that; but the pulse and blood pressure were more serious. 'Do we know what she took. . . ? How much. . . ? When . . .?'

'Lentizole. A lot, they think, and not a lot came up the tube. So probably a long time ago.'

'What's her name, staff?'

'Eleanor. Eleanor Goldie.'

Sandy picked up the girl's right wrist and tried to check her pulse. It was a hundred and twenty or more and irregular too. 'Eleanor? Eleanor?' The eyelids barely moved. Sandy counted the pulse carefully for ten seconds and got to twenty five. 'More like a hundred and fifty now. We'd better get an ECG and probably monitor her too.'

'Fine. But we'll have to borrow a monitor from along the corridor . . . Carol, can you go to sixteen?'

The student nurse disappeared. Sandy wrapped the blood-pressure cuff tightly round the girl's right arm and pumped it up, feeling for a pulse at the wrist as she did so. As the mercury climbed towards sixty the pulse disappeared. She pumped it up again and released it cautiously, listening at the elbow with her stethoscope. 'Nearer fifty than sixty, staff . . . I'll put up another drip just in case.' Sandy checked the pulse and the blood pressure again then opened the girl's dress and listened to her heart sounds: a frantic pattering jumble, not sinus arrhythmia, perhaps atrial fibrillation, more likely something worse. They needed the monitor quickly. Antidepressant overdoses were dangerous because they caused ghastly unpredictable cardiac arrhythmias: Sandy stood feeling a bit helpless, responsible for the life of a girl no older than herself who, for whatever reasons, had tried to kill herself; or who had made a dramatic gesture not meant to kill but which might still do so. Mousey blonde, vaguely pretty – though that was hard to tell after a washout – and still dressed in standard C&A office girl stuff, she lay limp and unconscious now, not shifting much air, her face distorted in the semi-prone position on a firm hospital bed without pillows. Sandy checked the intravenous line: it was hopelessly clogged, not even worth fiddling with.

'I'll get the drip trolley.'

'Thanks, staff.' Sandy took the girl's blood pressure again, more for something to do than because she thought it would have changed. In the event it was a little better, the systolic now around eighty, and her pulse had slowed down a bit too. Sandy picked up the chart and marked in the more recent, less alarming readings and noted the time as well: to her surprise it was ten to eight. The staff nurse came back. She had everything ready and had even run saline through the intravenous line. Sandy inflated the cuff again and worked at the girl's forearm, finding a nice vein in a good position and getting the cannula in first shot. She moved the little slide valve right back and watched saline streaming freely through and was just about to tape it all in place when the forearm moved, bending upwards as the girl's elbow flexed, at first slowly then with a series of rapid jerks. She was fitting.

The limp form on the bed was suddenly energised, twisting sideways as the girl's spine arched and her head was thrown back. Her forearms jerked fiercely and her legs straightened out, her toes pointing down like a ballerina's. The IV line was shaken free and hung streaming fluid to the floor, and the cannula from which it had detached itself threw bright arcs of blood into the air until the staff nurse seized it and pulled it out, clamping a thumb over the puncture wound on the right forearm. Gradually the movements lessened and within a minute they had ceased. The girl lay back paler even than before, her mouth slackly open and her eyes staring sightlessly ahead. Sandy grabbed her wrist again and felt for the pulse. There was none.

'Call a cardiac arrest, please, staff.' The nurse sprinted to the phone a few yards away at the nursing station. Sandy felt deep under the girl's ears with her fingertips, checking for both carotid pulses at once and finding neither, then she made a fist and hit the girl hard in the middle of her chest. Nothing happened, so she got up and knelt on the bed and leaned over and with lots of weight on the heel of her hand compressed the lifeless chest six times in as many seconds. Still nothing happened. She was just bracing herself for the sick-making business of mouth-to-mouth breathing when the staff nurse came back with the arrest tray and the short perspex airway that made it all a lot less nasty, and rather than handing it to Sandy she inserted it in the girl's mouth and blew in it herself, nodding when she had finished so that Sandy could compress the chest another six times.

Soon Jamie would come, and so would the duty anaesthetist, and all the clever things could start to happen. For now the aim was a regular, forceful repetition of the pattern of one deep breath and six firm jabs to the chest, with pauses only long enough to check whether the heart had re-started and that the pupils had not gone wide. Sandy and the staff nurse worked steadily at it, engrossed in the urgency of their effort and the precariousness of any chance of success. Jamie arrived first and got the drip going again. A couple of porters wheezed in with the resuscitation trolley: a reassuring fire engine-red assemblage of cardiac monitor, defibrillation equipment, emergency intravenous fluids and all the drugs that might ever help *in extremis*. They ran in the standard dose of bicarbonate, wired up the monitor, stripped the patient's chest and shocked her, convulsing her six times with the defibrillation paddles. Nothing happened.

By the time the duty anaesthetist arrived they had tried everything, even intra-cardiac adrenaline, and only then did they give up hope. Just after half past eight Jamie made the final checks on the girl's eyes – pupils fixed and dilated, retinal circulation stagnant – and the sad, slow business of tidying things away took over. There was no one around to report to, no relative, flatmate or neighbour who had come up with Miss Goldie on her last journey. The nurses would prepare her body for the mortuary and tell the police, and they in turn would find someone somewhere and pass on news of the death. Jamie would inform the proper legal authority, the procurator fiscal, on Saturday morning. For now, there would be other admissions to look after, and perhaps some more deaths too. Sandy stayed for a few minutes helping to tidy up. As she was removing an ECG lead from the girl's left wrist she noticed for the first time an engagement ring, a cheap solitaire, the kind of thing the nurses called a wee sparkler, and found herself feeling suddenly very sad, wondering what would happen to it.

* * *

The multiple, a motorcyclist who had been hit by a lorry, was in theatre until after seven. When he came out he went straight up to the Institute's little intensive care unit and Robbie, who had expected him to return to the ward where he would take up a lot of time when there was plenty else to do, was quietly relieved. He was sitting doing blood forms for next day when Hamish, the youngest consultant, wandered into the doctors' room and sat down for a smoke, as he often did after operating. They chatted a bit, about the motorcyclist and his injuries, then about the way things had worked out for time off over Christmas and New Year. Peter, Robbie's opposite number, had originally planned to work over the Christmas weekend and take the New Year weekend and the following week to go off to a house party somewhere in the Highlands. Robbie, who would have had Christmas off, together with a couple of days of the following week, had been quite happy with that. As it happened, Peter's step-father had died a few days before and he had claimed his right to compassionate leave over Christmas, to run on into his planned time off over New Year. Robbie would be on his own and running two wards unless some student help – unlikely over the festive season – could be obtained. Hamish was sympathetic and almost effusively grateful. 'I suppose if worst had come to worst we could have waved the big stick and got some of the registrars to sleep in and be first on call, but most of them these days have wives and families so it wouldn't have been terribly convenient . . . So essentially if it weren't for you we'd be in trouble, Robbie, and I want you to know it's been noticed and much appreciated. Were you thinking of orthopaedics in the longer term? Because if you were, going the extra mile like this is the sort of thing that we'd obviously stress in references and the like.'

Robbie thought about that and wondered if Hamish were being exceptionally devious or just very simple. As the most recently appointed consultant he tended to have most to do with the house officers, and perhaps saying things like that, when most likely he knew that Robbie had had a declared interest in the more prestigious business of general surgery all along, might be a way of anticipating Robbie's reasonable objections to fourteen days and nights as first on call for the orthopaedic unit. Or did he simply think that Robbie welcomed such an opportunity to demonstrate his devotion to the specialty? Robbie just smiled and Hamish laughed and said 'Glad you see it that way, Robbie. But you know, if you *are* thinking of making a name for yourself in orthopaedics, there are one or two things I might just mention. And don't take this amiss, please. It's very much in your interests that we sort out any . . . little problems . . . as early as possible.'

Robbie swung his chair round so as to be facing Hamish, who was puffing nervously at the last inch of his cigarette and perhaps not quite sure what to say next. 'It's about what you might call the *personal* aspect of the job. I know you're terribly bright. Seen your CV, and we're all jolly glad you applied for the job when you did. Looked as if we were going to be left with a gap, and have to fill it with some awful Iraqi, or a woman from Birmingham or something. God, it doesn't bear thinking about . . . What I'm trying to say, I suppose, is that it's great to have you, you're a bright chap. And I've noticed – indeed we all have – that the medical care of our patients has greatly improved . . . But there's still the . . . *personal* side.'

Robbie took a deep breath and was about to ask Hamish what he meant when the consultant launched off again. 'I expect it's particularly difficult for you because you're so bright. You know, people joke about us walking around on our knuckles. We don't mind. We get by. But when we get a chap like you that's won half the medals in the course, knows everything and everybody. Well, what I suppose I'm trying to say, Robbie, is . . . just try not to upset people. Please.'

'Like who?' As soon as he had said it Robbie realised that it sounded belligerent.

'Well,' said Hamish. 'I don't suppose I'm thinking about the medical staff. Most of them can stand up for themselves. But perhaps a chap like Goodison, you know. Senior registrar, been around for a bit . . . And, frankly, not having done awfully well at quite a number of consultant interviews now. Chaps like that are always a bit sensitive . . . particularly if you're right, as seems to have been the case in this instance. Peter, no doubt very upset about his poor dad, seems to have pushed off without cross-matching a couple of old ducks, and you and old Goody had a bit of an up-and-downer about it. The point is, Robbie, you have to make allowances. People get tired, and cross sometimes . . . But there's no need to keep showing you're cleverer than they are. There's a good chap.'

Robbie nodded. 'Anything else?'

'Yes,' said Hamish, bending over to stub his cigarette on the heel of his shoe. 'Actually there is. The non-medical staff. Chaps like Jip, girls like sister. I don't know if you know you're rubbing them up the wrong way, but you are. Small things, but they mount up and create a . . . certain impression. Know what I mean?' Hamish paused and groped feverishly in his pockets. 'Cigarette? Fancy a gasper? I'm having another. Sorry, Robbie. But you see what I'm getting at?'

Robbie waved off the offer of a cigarette, although later it occurred to him that it would have been a better idea to have had one. Hamish sat uncomfortably, puffing away and looking everywhere but at Robbie. Eventually he got up and took his overcoat out of the cupboard and ambled off. At the door he paused and turned, looking down at Robbie with his big, doggy grin. 'Think about it, Robbie. And have an awfully good Christmas.'

Robbie had finished his blood forms and was just setting off for the Residency dining room and a late supper when his bleep went off again. An old lady, the victim of a minor road traffic accident, had arrived in the female ward. In the normal course of events the duty orthopaedic registrar, should have rung him from Casualty to tell him she was on her way in. Not much seemed to be going right today, it occurred to Robbie as he went back along to the female ward for perhaps the twelfth or thirteenth time since Peter had left for Surrey at lunchtime. The night staff had come on, the ward lights were dimmed and the little rituals of the late evening had begun: the fluffing up of pillows, the hot drinks round, the drug trolley's last leisured tour with analgesics and sedatives.

The old lady who had just arrived sat up in bed, alert and interested, and even looked as if she were actually enjoying herself. She was called Mrs McQuillan and she had sustained her injury, a fairly complicated ankle fracture, when a van had reversed into her in the dark on her way to the bingo. She had had good previous health and was on no medications. She lived alone and her night out, alone, at the bingo was her weekly treat. She was not in much pain and though her injury was probably worth a few hundred from the driver's insurance company that aspect of her misfortune did not seem to have occurred to her. Robbie mentioned it in vague terms but the suggestion horrified her. 'No, son. Couldn't do a thing like that. An awfy nice laddie he was, with a wife and three wee girls, he was telling me. Couldn't have been nicer, really. As soon as it happened he was out of his wee van and helping me up and when I couldn't walk he said "It's the Institute for you, I'll take you up myself" and put me in the front seat beside him and brought me straight up here . . . Now I couldn't take money off a man like that, could I, son? And him with a wife and three wee girls? No, son, never mind about all that . . . Mind you, he didn't give me his name or address or anything.' Robbie clerked her in, wrote her up for something for the pain and something to help her sleep and was just about to leave the ward when the registrar bleeped him to tell him about the patient he had just seen. He reached the Residency dining room at half past ten, in good time to eat before the usual wave of battered drunks started to roll in from about eleven onwards.

Sandy, who had also asked for a late supper to be kept, was standing disconsolately in front of the warm cupboard in the dining room pantry. 'Oh no,' said Robbie. 'Not the phantom meal-snatcher again . . .'

Sandy shook her head and lifted the aluminium cover from a dinner plate on which there was a portion of steak pie, now unappetisingly dried, two scoops of mashed potato also beyond enjoyment, some processed peas and a large and not very lively cockroach. 'And the ice cream's melted,' she said quietly. Robbie took the other dinner plate from the warming cupboard. His didn't have a cockroach but was otherwise identical. He looked from one to the other then said. 'Let's not. How about chips? Hold my bleep, Sandy, and I'll nip across to Charlie's. Fish supper? Chicken supper?' Sandy thought about that and said 'Thanks, Robbie. Fish supper. Salt and no vinegar, please . . . Um. Anything happening on your wards I should know about?'

'Not really. I've just been in both of them and there's nothing more on the way in. And I'll only be five minutes.' He handed over his bleep. 'Thanks, Sandy. Coke or anything?'

'Lemonade?'

'Sure. Five minutes.'

Robbie loped off and Sandy watched him go. He would probably leave his white coat in Casualty, nip across the road in his shirtsleeves, meet someone he knew in the chip-shop queue and come bouncing back as though it had all been good fun. He was someone she hadn't known particularly well until they had both joined the house staff of the Institute. Although they had graduated together Robbie had started the course a year earlier and taken an extra year doing honours physiology, so for the first few years he had been one of the big boys: a dashing figure in the medical reading room and later at the Society, a chap with a reputation for brains and for falling in love easily but not for long; someone she had always thought of as laughing a lot. Now he was more subdued. People still asked him things and he knew the answers, and he knew more people around the Institute than anyone else she knew, but somehow, probably since finals, when he had not done as well as everyone had expected, he wasn't the same old Robbie; but he was still the kind of chap who volunteered right away to go out in the cold for chips when another Institute meal had gone wrong, and that was nice.

Sandy looked at her watch and checked her bleep. Jamie was still around, probably in Casualty, but nothing very much was happening now and the ward was quiet, mainly because the lady with bleeding varices was doing a bit better than expected. She was a hopeless drunk with cirrhosis and most of its complications, including the source of her bleeding: the congested, fragile veins around the bottom of her gullet. She had been transfused with three units of blood and Jamie had put down the Sengstaken tube, a complicated, uncomfortable-looking thing whose balloon, inflated in her gullet just above her stomach, seemed to have stopped the bleeding at least for now. It was all very sad, not least because there were things about her that reminded Sandy of her future mother-in-law: another middle-class, middle-aged Edinburgh lady drunk. Would Mopsy Ratho one day qualify for emergency admission, helplessly vomiting pints and pints of blood and pausing between retches to admit to an occasional small sherry?

Sandy thought about that, then wandered slowly round the Residency dining room looking at the group photographs from the last few years. Jamie was there with the others from his year, neat but already a little old-fashioned in white shirts and club ties. Further back there was a girl with a dreadful perm whom Sandy knew vaguely through church and who had married and had lots of children and didn't seem to have done any medicine for ages.

Before her there were hardly any girls at all, probably because there were far fewer girls in medical school and those that there were had been were too sensible to want to live in what was really just an all-male club, and an old-fashioned, ugly, smelly one at that. It was all very strange, thought Sandy for the hundred and somethingth time. In an odd kind of way, she and Dilys, the only other girl in the mess this six months, had adapted by becoming more like the men, sort of temporary acting chaps who fitted in with – or at least didn't object to – the untidy, sometimes drunken camaraderie, sat around after lunch reading the papers and pretended not to notice the way they talked about women who weren't temporary acting chaps. Perhaps, thought Sandy as she completed her round of the funny old pictures, that was one of the nice things about Robbie: he behaved more like a brother than a fellow-chap.

Tuneless whistling heralded his return. He breezed in with the fish suppers wrapped in newspaper and cradled in his arms along with the two soft drinks. 'Great to get out of the place, even just for two minutes . . . That's yours, Sandy. No vinegar. Anybody bother you from my end?'

'Nothing, and my lot are behaving too. Shall we go up to the lounge?'

'Suits me. D'you want a plate and a fork and all that?'

Sandy laughed and shook her head. The point about fish suppers, in the Lennox family at least, was that eating them with your fingers was half the fun. They went upstairs to the lounge, which smelt of whisky and cigarettes – an improvement on the dining room smell of stale cabbage, disinfectant and cockroaches – and sat in armchairs in front of the fireplace and opened their cosy, newsprint parcels and their fizzy drinks. Both ate quickly, but their bleeps remained obligingly silent. Perhaps things weren't so bad after all.

Robbie finished his meal first, screwed the wrapping paper up into a ball and threw it in the direction of the waste-paper basket, scoring with a clever bounce off the side of the piano. Sandy finished hers, tried the same trick and missed. Robbie, who was nearer, got up and fielded it. Sandy thanked him and as he sat down again she realised she didn't really know what a fish supper cost now, and wondered whether Robbie would be offended if she offered to pay her share as a proper chap probably would. In the interests of not getting women doctors a bad name she said 'Thanks very much, Robbie. Don't know how I could have coped just on steak pie and cockroach. How much was it?' Robbie shook his head and Sandy felt she ought to appeal, but he said 'Your turn next Friday,' and they both laughed.

'Are you really on at Christmas, Robbie?'

'Oh yes. New Year too. Peter's pushed off. A family death apparently. So with his leave as well he'll be away for a couple of weeks.'

'Poor you. And poor him too. Must be awful having a funeral at Christmas . . .' As she said that Sandy found herself thinking again about Eleanor Goldie, and her family if she had any, and whoever had given her the ring, and what she must have felt like to do what she had done. Perhaps Christmas was for people who were happy already. 'I had a girl today,' she said. 'Must have been depressed. She took an overdose of anti-depressants and . . . arrested just after she came up to the ward.'

'D'you get her back?'

'We tried for ages. She was twenty two, and they'd washed her out but she had a fit and then arrested.'

'Fits and arrythmias are both pretty common, but they sometimes get heart block too, so it could have been an anoxic fit. You know, rather than a straight toxic one. D'you get an ECG?'

'Not before she arrested. She went off so quickly. It was awful.'

'Probably not much you could do without a monitor.'

'We'd sent for one.'

'And it all might have been meant as just a wee gesture to bring the boy-friend to heel with the Lucozade and the bunch of flowers. What else have you got?'

'Oh, the usual,' said Sandy. 'Well, I don't mean it like that, but the usual couple of eighty year olds who are quite nice but nobody gets very excited about . . .'

'Try orthopaedics. You could get a couple of dozen quite quickly. And it's not their fault . . . You know. They've just fallen or tripped over the dog or something. The young ones . . .' Robbie paused and looked at his watch. 'The young ones work at it. Get drunk and steal a car, or get drunk and fall off the motorbike, or get drunk and get into a fight, or just get drunk . . . I mean, they ought to be starting any minute. The pubs shut half an hour ago. Where are they? And they lie there saying "I'll get him. I'll get the bastard." and end up needing twenty of valium just to get them to lie down for the operation. We've even had them from office parties this week. "Jist a wee celebration with the girls, doctor, then Ah sheemed tae trip. Hic!" '

Sandy laughed. Robbie was more like his old self. Perhaps the finals business had been some kind of temporary lapse. 'So you're quite enjoying orthopaedics.'

'God, no.'

'Oh.'

'But I had to decide . . . Stay around in the wrong job, or go away and be forgotten about within the year. I should have taken the chance and gone away. Bavelaw had two jobs going and I even thought about Blackridge. And some people come back. Sam Huntly got Sir Edgar's SHO job and he'd done both his housejobs at Blackridge. I could have done that, but I didn't and . . . Well, we'll see, but yes, Sandy, I've probably screwed it up.'

'I'm sure you're . . .'

'At least as far as surgery's concerned . . .'

'But you can still. . .'

'The only thing I've ever really been interested in. And I thought I had it all stitched up.' Robbie laughed out loud in a way that was more strange than funny and Sandy had a sudden clear new view of him: he was less normal, more fanatical than she had thought. 'Really?' she said. 'Is that why you did medicine?'

'Sort of. You haven't much clue at school, have you? You've seen your GP and *Your Life in Their Hands*. When I grew out of wanting to find cures for things I always saw myself *doing* something. Not standing around waiting for the digoxin pills to work, like a physician, or sitting for hours trying to unscrew the inscrutable, like a psychiatrist. No. Get in there and fix it. And I thought most of medicine would be like that, but it's not. Only surgery. And I've screwed it up.' He looked at his watch again. 'Six drunks by midnight, more than likely. And I'm on every night for a fortnight and I've just been told I'm awkward, bolshie and too clever by half. So I won't even get a half-decent reference out of it. You know, they actually *like* people like Peter. Big smooth thicko, goes huntin' and buggers off for a fortnight but he's *one of them*. Big, cheerful and thick. Better than them actually. I mean, he's an Etonian. Even gets pissed with the Prince of Wales.'

'Really?'

'Famous for it. You mean you've never heard this one?' Robbie leaned foward. 'A real giggle. Peter at one of those little house parties he goes to. Weekend in a haunted castle somewhere in the highlands. Gets there late and pissed as usual, sits down in some great gloomy cavern and says to the quiet young chap opposite who looks vaguely familiar "and what are you going to do when you finish?" "Oh, be king, I suppose . . ." says the quiet chap. And it was him. Not too offended, apparently.' Sandy thought it was moderately funny but Robbie gave another of his unnatural howls of laughter, squashed his Coca-Cola can and hurled it into the waste paper basket via the side of the piano. 'Good god! The navy's here!' He was staring beyond Sandy and laughing inanely again. Sandy, quite worried, quickly turned to look. 'I don't believe it,' said Robbie. 'What a hoot. Don't tell me. You've parked your admiral's barge in the bottom car park.'

'I came up by taxi,' said Scott from the lounge door. 'By taxi,' he said again, quite carefully. Robbie was writhing in his chair and rolling in wild laughter. 'What's wrong?' Scott asked.

'It's Captain Scott! He's come back,' said Robbie, still choking with amusement. 'Scott of Aunt Agatha in person.' Scott, still standing at the door, seemed a bit puzzled by all this. To Sandy he actually looked quite nice in his uniform, a dressy one with a short jacket, cummerbund, stiff shirt and bow tie. 'How was the South Pole?' said Robbie. 'What is all this? Are we at war, or is it a case of *bonjour, matelot* for a fancy dress party?'

Scott shook his head. 'Neither . . . A mess dinner. Christmas and all that.' A few years previously Scott had seen a notice somewhere offering travel and adventure to medical students who joined the Royal Naval Reserve. In return for occasional evenings at a drill hall near Leith and a few weekends spent bobbing about in a wooden minesweeper, Scott could think of himself as a seafaring man, with a vague future option of reservist service with the Royal Navy too. 'Reserve division thing down at Granton,' he explained. 'Quite good really . . . Hello, Sandy.'

'Pity', said Robbie. 'You've just missed a really good fish supper.'

Sandy got up. 'How about coffee, Robbie? Andrew? I've got some in my room.'

'Thanks,' said Scott.

'What a girl. Thought you'd never ask.' Robbie was getting up out of his chair.

'I can easily bring it down,' said Sandy firmly. 'Brown, no sugar?' Both Scott and Robbie nodded and Sandy went off to get things for coffee. Robbie sat back in his chair. 'So you all go and stuff yourselves and get pissed at the taxpayer's expense and toast the Queen sitting down.'

'It's just a mess dinner, but Christmassy, and everybody pays for themselves. But you're right about the sitting down bit.'

'No women though.'

'Well, wren officers. They're reservists too, mostly lawyers. Quite interesting to talk to . . .'

'It gets better and better,' said Robbie. 'And if things didn't pick up here I could even run away to sea. How do I join?'

Scott thought about Robbie and the medical branch of the Royal Naval Reserve and decided they would not go well together. He sat down in the third armchair by the fire. 'How's orthopaedics?'

'Much the same, alas,' said Robbie, leaning back in his armchair with his hands behind his head. 'No. The same but worse. Had a dust-up with the SR this afternoon and then he went into theatre with Hamish the human orthopod and really did me in. You know the kind of thing. Quiet word about the houseman, sir. Things you really ought to know, sir. So Hamish comes trotting out for his ciggy in the doctors' room and in his nice bumbly way tells me I'm a liability around the unit. If not a disaster.'

'But you're not.'

'I know I'm not. But if they decide you are there's not an awful lot you can do.'

'That's true,' said Scott before he had really thought about it. 'Well . . . It's difficult, but there's still a month to go. And anyway, it's not only Hamish.'

'It is, really,' said Robbie quietly. 'I doubt if any of the rest of them would know me from Adam.'

They sat in silence. Sandy came back quite soon with three mugs of coffee. Conversation remained subdued until Robbie was called away at midnight for the first of the drunks. Sandy's bleep was silent. She and Scott sat talking in the lounge until almost one, when she was called across to the ward again to clerk in another overdose.

April 1970

'Sorry about all this,' said Lennie. 'It's been bothering me for about a week. I did get hold of some ampicillin and I thought it was actually beginning to settle down by Wednesday, but it didn't.'

Max showed Lennie into the single side-room. 'Your room, sir,' he said, putting down Lennie's canvas holdall and standing solicitously by the door. 'Your personal house officer, in this instance myself, will be along shortly. So if sir would like to slip into something more comfortable and try one of our famous beds.'

Lennie laughed and sat down very cautiously on the bed. 'Hm. You're right. I'd be a lot better lying down. Thanks, Max. Tommy said about one o'clock. Said he'd rather do it sooner than later, but probably just wants to get me tidied up and then push off to Murrayfield for the match.'

'Probably,' said Max. 'But I'd like to take a quick look at you first, Professor Lennox.'

'Of course,' said the patient, still perched uncomfortably on one cheek. 'And I think for the purposes of this exercise you should call me Lennie. Then I won't feel I ought to be calling you Dr Cathcart.'

'Fine. I'll be back in five minutes.' Tommy Johnston had phoned Max an hour before and outlined the problem with his customary brevity: 'Lennie rang me this morning and he's just been round to see me. Boil on his bum. We'll do it before the match. He'll be in at twelve. Theatre at one, thanks.' Max had organised the side room and the theatre people and rung the duty anaesthetist who, when he heard the patient's name, had immediately rung the consultant on call even though Lennie would probably have preferred just a registrar and a minimum of fuss. For Max it was all fairly routine. The main attraction of a surgical job at the Guthrie Hospital was that it was a quiet number: a small surgical unit with sensible consultants and little in the way of emergency work. Another attraction, one that had dawned on Max only gradually, was that the middle classes of Edinburgh knew it was a far nicer place than the Institute just next door, and GP's played along with that, sending in only their cleaner and more presentable customers. Doctors, it hardly needed to be said, used it too when they had to be patients, because it wasn't the Institute and because its surgical and medical consultants were better than average and happy to go along with what amounted to a cosy little conspiracy against the NHS at large. Max, as house officer to the vaguely rich and slightly famous, was even quite proud of the way he handled them.

When he went back Lennie was in bed, lying on his side in nice silk pyjamas. Max sat down at the bedside with his clipboard on his knee. The VIP's got the whole routine, on Tommy's specific instructions ('Being important's bloody dangerous. So no short cuts, Max, no matter who they are.'). Lennie, one of the more sensible of such patients, was quite understanding when he explained. 'Go right ahead, Max. No problem for me . . .'

'So how did it start?'

'Pain and swelling, a week ago. Just left of centre and not getting any better when I tried a bit of do-it-yourself with ampicillin. More pain, swelling and tenderness over the past few days.'

'Fine. I'll have a look shortly. Now, how's your health generally?'

Lennie thought about that and answered seriously. 'Well, I've known better. There's a lot going on in Faculty, as you know. I take stuff home most nights but frankly I'm more tired. You know, more tired more easily.'

'How long?'

'Oh, weeks rather than months.'

'Appetite?'

'About the same. Maybe not enjoying things as much, now I think about it.'

'Your weight?'

'Down a bit. Not a bad thing in middle age, I suppose.'

'How much, and over how long?'

'You know, I don't weigh myself. Don't have to. Can still wear my first dinner jacket. But there's definitely a bit more room in the trousers . . . Say half a stone down?'

'Over what sort of time?'

'The last couple of months?'

'I'll weigh you shortly.'

'Bowels?'

'Regular.'

'Any blood? Any pain?'

'Pain. Since Wednesday. Jolly sore, actually.'

'That should get better . . .'

'. . . shortly after one o'clock.' They both smiled. It occurred to Lennie that Max was good at this: relaxed but careful; insistent, but pleasantly so. Lennie, who as professor and then Clinical Dean had been wondering for years about how you judged quality in medical education, decided a medical school was in reasonable shape if you felt safe in the hands of a chap who had graduated from it only the year before. They got through the questions and moved on to the examination. Again Max was quick but careful, prodding and listening and running his small, cool hands over Lennie in search of swollen lymph nodes or any other palpable abnormality, and ending up with the least comfortable bit, for which Lennie lay on his side, curled up but relaxed while Max examined the swelling and then popped a gloved finger in, a procedure that proved a lot more uncomfortable than Lennie had been in the habit of telling patients it was.

'That's it, Lennie . . . A urine specimen, please, and we're all set. There's a glass jar in your private bathroom.'

'They think of everything, don't they?'

Max took the resulting specimen along to his laboratory, which was just a cupboard with a bench, a light, a sink and the various bottles of reagents and test strips. He had formed a suspicion, and as he dipped the white cardboard strip, with its various patches for detecting bile, protein, ketones and sugar, into Lennie's urine he confirmed it. Middle aged man, dean or no dean, rolls up with a history of vague illness, weight loss and a decent collection of pus in a perineal abscess. What's he got? The second last patch on the stick turned slowly from beige to cobalt blue. Lennie was a diabetic. Max dropped the stick into the bin, took another from a different bottle, repeated the test and got the same result. Then he went to the doctor's room and rang Tommy at home. 'Thought he might be,' said Tommy. 'But he's not ketotic, or dried out, so the thing we can do for him is let the pus out right away. We'll just go ahead.'

Max returned to the single room and went in and sat down again. 'Well, Max?' said Lennie.

Max hesitated for a second then decided just to get on with it. 'There's sugar in your urine, Lennie. Not just a trace, quite a lot. Can we just go over one or two things again?'

Lennie sighed.

'Thirst?' said Max.

'A bit, and I ignored it. Not a lot. I took to sucking Polos. Quite good for a dry mouth.'

'Polyuria?'

'Sort of. Never used to get up at night. Always do now. And having to pop out of meetings is a nuisance.'

'You knew.'

Lennie paused. 'You know, Max, there's an amazing gap between knowing and admitting.'

'And what about family history? Anything we missed first time round?'

'Yes, actually. There is. An uncle, poor chap. Didn't live quite long enough to get insulin.'

'I see.'

'Dead at nineteen. And an aunt or two. Did a bit better, but not much. Again, one puts things to the back of one's mind.'

'People actually feel a lot better on treatment,' said Max. 'You will.'

'I'm sure I will, Max, but it's the difference between knowing and admitting. And there's so much to do. It was always something I was going to get seen to, but not quite yet. Hadn't even mentioned it to Margaret.' Lennie shook his head sadly. 'I know doctors make dreadful patients. But you'll tell Tommy . . .'

'I just have.'

'Good man. But . . .' Lennie turned and looked very seriously at Max. 'I think the reason I didn't want to know was that I didn't want anyone else to know. The sick are the people we treat, not us.'

'But you're not actually very sick,' said Max. 'and you're going to feel a lot better soon. And it's not as if it's leprosy or the clap.'

'It's a boil on my bum. As Tommy so elegantly puts it.'

'And an explanation of why it happened. You got it because . . .'

'Max, do me an enormous favour.'

'What?'

'Confidentiality.'

Max nodded but said nothing. There was something a little odd for him about the notion that confidentiality was an enormous favour; but then again the illness of Edinburgh's doctors, the more distinguished the better, was the stuff of medical gossip.

'Absolute confidentiality, Max. Not about my unfortunate bottom. That doesn't matter. But the . . . other thing.'

'All right,' said Max. He meant it.

'You can see why,' said Lennie. 'Can't you? It's political. In a way that one's bottom isn't. And I know diet isn't going to be enough. In fact in a quiet, half-conscious way I've tried it. It'll be the pills, then insulin quite quickly, if not insulin right away. And then it's needles and funny turns and gossip: how's he looking today? I wonder if he's getting it right? Is it him or the insulin talking? Does quite well, you know, *considering* . . . You know the kind of thing, Max. And I'd rather do without it.'

'I promise.'

'Thanks, Max. I appreciate it. You've told Tommy, and no one else needs to know. I'm not ill or anything, and there's really no need to bother the gasman with this. Quick whiff and he'll want to be off to Murrayfield too, I'd have thought.'

'It's OK., Lennie.'

'Good yarn though it may be . . .'

'Right. But what about follow up?'

'Oh, I'll get that right, now we've got this far. There's a physician in this town who sees an astonishing number of doctors . . . because he keeps his mouth shut, I suppose. I'll ask Tommy to give him a ring tomorrow and I'll go and see him on Monday evening. So thanks, Max. Now let's forget all about it and get the acute problem sorted out. Margaret's coming to pick me up at six.'

The anaesthetist arrived and saw Lennie and just said good afternoon. Tommy came in at ten to one and had a quiet chat with his patient in the side room with the door closed, then the three went into theatre and were there for only about ten minutes. The theatre sister wheeled Lennie's trolley back into the ward herself and Max helped her lift him, still drowsy, on to the bed in the side room then sat with him until he had come round completely. First he slept peacefully for ten minutes or so, then he flushed and stirred as though he were having an unpleasant dream. Still asleep, he shook his head and murmured odd, unconnected things: something about the roof falling in and some curious alphabetical stuff about B and A and A plus, the significance of which occurred to Max only later. Eventually his eyes opened. He yawned and stretched, smiled at Max and remarked 'Thanks a lot, Max. Gosh, that's much better.'

'Splendid . . . Just spread yourselves around. There should be enough chairs for everyone, I think . . . Good . . . Andrew?'

Scott took the first set of case notes from the heap and opened them at the little cardboard marker. He checked the name, age and address on the inside cover and launched into his spiel. 'Mrs Gorman . . . Eighty one. Widow, lives alone in, um, Thornybauk . . .'

'Good. Let's just stop there, Andrew, and see what our student colleagues think, hm? Yes? Now who's going to start? Eileen?'

The girl singled out, a lumpish redhead from Ulster, looked shiftily from Scott to Professor Jameson and back again. 'Come on now. What you've just heard about Mrs Gorman should actually tell you quite a lot. And if it doesn't it should certainly raise one or two questions . . .' Professor Jameson twinkled at his registrar, his house officer, the social worker, the physiotherapist, the ward sister and the semi-circle of students. '. . . which no doubt Andrew would be delighted to answer for you.'

The girl's brow furrowed. 'Is this woman a widow?' she asked eventually.

'Well, yes. Andrew's just told us as much.'

'Sorry. I meant does she live alone?'

'Yes indeed. Come on, Eileen. Waken up. We'll get back to you shortly. Virinder?'

'Her family. Where is her family, please?'

'Good question. Andrew?'

Scott was prepared for that. 'One son in Australia and one in Toronto . . . And a daughter in Lamancha.'

'Good gracious. The far flung Gormans, hm?' The registrar muttered something in the professorial ear and Jimmy did his short, squawking laugh. 'Oh, I see. *That* Lamancha . . . A village on the way to Peebles, I'm told . . . That simplifies matters considerably. But you're absolutely right about the family, Virinder. I take it the daughter's in touch. Andrew?'

'Sir.'

'Not terribly handy, is it? I mean, a lot better than being in Spain, but still an hour or so on the bus . . .'

'She manages in three times a week.'

'Splendid. Now, students, what else would you like to know about Mrs Gorman?'

'Is this a tenement?' The girl from Ulster had stirred to life again. 'I mean, how many flights up is she?'

'Andrew?'

'Four.'

'Well, there you are, Eileen. Anything else?'

'Does she ever get out?'

'Good. A jolly important question too. Shouldn't have thought she does, if the daughter comes up three times a week. Andrew?'

Scott nodded. 'So a much clearer picture emerges,' said Professor Jameson. They were in an attic office, scene of the ward's weekly 'social round', a duty that Jimmy took very seriously indeed. 'A widow – how long, Andrew? I see. Thank you. Widowed young, must have brought them up on her own . . . And Thornybauk's hardly the Mayfair or Belgravia of Edinburgh, hm? Know it? Rather a bleak little sidestreet off Tollcross, for those of you who don't yet know your Edinburgh. So a lady of, um, modest social background, pretty isolated now, daughter doing her best from some distance away and it's all got to be a bit of struggle. And that was even before she got ill. Just remind me, Andrew, what the problem was.'

'Bronchopneumonia, sir. Left basal.'

'Oh yes . . .' Professor Jameson put his right hand to his forehead, covering his eyes, and said 'I remember her. And an old fracture of left clavicle, bit of apical scarring on the right, and a prominent aortic knuckle.' The students were looking at each other with puzzlement: it was one of the professor's more agreeable foibles that though he sometimes forgot a name he never forgot a chest X-ray. 'And her bronchopneumonia resolved fairly quickly, as I recall. So now it's a question of getting her home again to, um, Thornybauk. Which is why we have meetings like this. Ronald . . . What do you think, hm?'

'She'll need help,' said the youth singled out.

'So how do we plan to go about getting it for her . . . Ronald again.'

'Well, it sort of depends what she needs.'

'Splendid. Mrs Irvine here will be able to help us a lot. What's she like on her feet, Helga?' The physio, veteran of hundreds of such afternoons, was a woman of few words. 'Short distances only. Won't use a stick.'

'Thank you, Helga. So is she all right for home. . . ? Eileen?'

'If it's just a wee house, probably yes.'

'I'm inclined to agree with you. And it is what you call a wee house, I imagine. But let's hope she's got a toilet actually in her flat . . . Andrew?'

Jimmy was very strong on toilets, and Scott was prepared. 'The toilet's on a half-landing on the main stair, sir.'

'Dear me. Well, there's a bit of a blow to our plans . . . Helga, have you actually tried her on our stairs? Oh. Not yet, you mean. And I expect her mobility's still improving a bit. After all, it's only two weeks since she was brought in.' The expression on the physiotherapist's face was not encouraging but Professor Jameson pressed on. 'Well, let's suppose for the purposes of this meeting that she's going to manage a half-stair up and down, or down and up as the case may be, over the next week or so. What other kinds of help might she need. . . ? Sally?'

Mrs Gorman was one of eighteen ladies aged seventy five and over in the thirty-bed female ward of Professor Jameson's unit. Anyone who couldn't go straight home when their medical problems had been sorted out was discussed in detail at the social round. It started promptly at two and on days like this there was no telling when it might finish. The students were looking jaded already. Scott chanced a surreptitious glimpse at his watch. 'Come on, Andrew, not flagging yet, are we? Sally's just about to tell us all the things we can arrange that might help Mrs Gorman get back home to Thornybauk . . .'

It was shortly after four when they descended the wooden staircase from the attic to start the ward round proper. Professor Jameson led the group from bed to bed, chatting happily with old lady after old lady, remembering all the details about their sons and daughters, stairs, toilets, district nurses and the like far more clearly than his junior staff, and still enjoying himself as relentlessly as ever. 'Ah, yes. Mrs Horne, isn't it? And how *are* you? Just been having a chat with one or two people about things generally and from the sound of it we'd hope to have you out of here and back to Craigmillar by the end of next week, hm? Now, if we can just interrupt your knitting for a moment. Sorry. Yes. That's the ticket. I wonder if we could just see how you get out of that chair, hm? Push up with your good arm, Mrs Horne . . . Splendid . . . Splendid . . .'

Scott and the registrar, like the physiotherapist and the social worker, were used to all this. The students stood wearily at the back, trying to hide behind one another to avoid Jimmy's eye and his endless, prodding questions. Only one patient seemed to interest them: a girl in her late teens who had cystic fibrosis, a fairly common congenital disease that gradually choked its victims with a gross, purulent and intractable bronchitis. She was a student – had been a student, really, since she was going to die without leaving hospital again – and her locker was piled high with philosophy textbooks. Her pale, skinny arms propped up a vast paperback in front of her. Jimmy lighted on it with interest. 'The English empiricists, hm? Rather a windy lot, I've always thought. What do you make of 'em, Yvonne?' The girl smiled wanly up at him. 'Well, I'm not really reading them for pleasure, but they're quite refreshing . . .'

'Refreshing?' The idea was clearly a puzzling one.

'Well, compared to Hegel . . .'

Professor Jameson whooped with delight. 'Isn't everyone? Gosh yes. I must admit I got dreadfully stuck with Hegel. The kind of thing that might just about hold water in the decent obscurity of the original German always struck me as either obvious or impossible once you got it into English. Simply nothing in between to get your teeth into, hm?' The girl smiled again. Jimmy sat down suddenly on her bed. 'When's the exam, Yvonne?'

'Well, if I'm all right . . .'

'Sit it in here. We'll fix something up. I'm always running into philosophers in the College Club. I'll have a word . . . Monty Smith?' The girl nodded. 'I'll have a word with him. Shouldn't be too big a problem. We used to have dozens of chaps scratching away in the sanatoriums when there was a bit more tubercle about.'

Over the last few old ladies Scott freewheeled a bit, standing behind the registrar and wondering about Jimmy and his patients: broadly speaking the young ones, like Yvonne, and the middle aged ones, like Mrs Teviot, died, of cystic fibrosis and lung cancer respectively. The old ladies like Mrs Gorman and Mrs Horne were more or less indestructible, and their indestructibility seemed to be as much of a challenge as the incurability of the young. The social round, with its heroic commitment to minutiae, sometimes got one or two of them home but most of them seemed to be around for a very long time. As Scott's predecessor had said of half dozen of them at the time of their handover: 'Don't worry about this lot, they just live here.'

The last patient, Mrs Teviot, lay quietly in the sideroom. Jimmy went in with the registrar, glanced briefly at her and came out again. 'Must have just slipped away, sister. Bit sudden, but the best thing really. Andrew? You'll do the necessary, won't you? So, um, there we are. Thank you, students. Lots there for you to think about and read up on. Thank you, sister . . . Oh, Andrew . . .'

'Sir?'

'I think we said we'd kick off at seven thirty this evening, hm?'

'Sir.'

Jimmy chuckled. 'Thought you might appreciate a couple of hours off.'

The students scattered at great speed then bumped into each other in the rush for the door. Scott went into the side room. Mrs Teviot was bluish pale and showed no signs of respiratory effort. She had no peripheral or deep pulses and her pupils were fixed and dilated. Scott gently closed her eyes then pulled out his stethoscope and listened for a full minute for heart sounds, hearing nothing. Just as he was putting his stethoscope back in the pocket of his white coat her husband walked into the sideroom, whistling and carrying a big bunch of flowers.

Scott and Irena, who was the house officer on the male ward, had been invited to supper by Professor Jameson, who lived in one of the better streets of the New Town. His instructions on how to get there had been lengthy and detailed and Scott had thought he had understood them. He had crossed the Water of Leith, turned left and then right and found himself among quite unfamiliar streets of tall, stylish Georgian houses in curving terraces. By the time he had admitted to himself he was lost, asked directions, found his way up from Danube Street to Ann Street and spotted Jimmy's car it was almost eight o'clock. He rang the doorbell and waited. Jimmy, colourful in an open-necked shirt and cravat, welcomed him in and led the way quickly upstairs, talking all the time. 'So glad you made it, Andrew. We're having a sort of young people's night. Except for ourselves, of course, and an awfully nice chap from Japan. You'll probably know most people . . . Got lost finding us?'

As he followed his host into the lounge Scott muttered vaguely about his wanderings. 'Lost in Danube Street, eh?' said Jimmy. 'I expect that's what they all say. D'you hear that, Esmee? Andrew's been casting an eye over our disreputable neighbours. I don't think you've met my wife. Esmee, Andrew's one of our house chaps. Got lost in Danube Street . . .' Scott, who had heard lurid tales of vice about the street in question and had presumed they were either entirely mythical or no longer applicable, was intrigued, but gathered from Mrs Jameson's expression that the topic was not one she encouraged. They shook hands. 'They don't actually cause any trouble, the girls,' said Jimmy. 'Discreet professionals, just like doctors, I suppose. So it's actually quite an orderly house. Even during the General Assembly of the Church of Scotland, despite a persistent Edinburgh rumour to the contrary, hm?'

Mrs Jameson now wore a pained expression. 'I'm sure Andrew would like a drink, darling,' she said. 'After all his travels.'

'Quite, quite. What'll you have? We've got most things but I'd recommend the dry sherry.' Scott was handed a very pale, very large sherry and steered by the elbow across the room towards a small oriental, middle aged and portly, in a tight dark suit with all the buttons done up. 'I expect you'd like to meet Dr Gumi . . . From Wakayama – quite near Osaka, actually – visiting us briefly en route between Stockholm and the Mayo. Dr Gumi, may I introduce Dr Scott. Andrew Scott, one of our bright young chaps. M'houseman, actually.' The handshake was warm and moist, beginning long before the man spoke and going on long afterwards. 'Good,' he said slowly. Scott smiled and expressed a hope that Dr Gumi was enjoying his visit. 'Good,' he said again without letting go. His expression became strangely mournful then brightened a little. After further thought he said 'You doctor?' Scott nodded. 'Good.' The handshake continued. It occurred to Scott that, apart from it looking a little odd, there was really nothing to prevent him having a well-earned drink from the glass in his left hand. Meanwhile, there was conversation. 'Are you particularly interested in respiratory disease, Dr Gumi?' The inquiry evoked only earnest blankness, so that Scott wondered briefly about a mime involving coughing and the use of a stethoscope, difficult with a drink in one hand and the

324

other still in the moist, persistent grip of the visitor. When it was all getting a bit silly Scott smiled and nodded vigorously, gave the man's hand a friendly squeeze, let go and had a long pull at his sherry. Dr Gumi nodded with sudden profound understanding tinged, it seemed, with professional concern.

It was not clear what, if anything, could form the basis of conversation. Dr Gumi continued his mild inspection in a way that left Scott worrying successively about his tie, his zip and his shoes, then smiled at him again and nodded. Scott smiled back. 'Good,' said Dr Gumi, now looking over Scott's shoulder. Jimmy reappeared with his sherry bottle and topped up both their glasses. 'Now, Dr Gumi,' he said, moving his lips quite a lot. 'I think you might like to meet one of our keen young immunologists. If you'll excuse us, Andrew.' Dr Gumi was led away by the elbow and Scott turned round to find himself face to face with Sandy, formerly Lennox, now Ratho.

'Well done, Andrew,' she said. 'Now Gus gets a turn. How are you?'

'All right.'

'I was coming to help. Really. And he's very important, Mrs Jimmy was saying. Something to do with the next World Congress but one . . . I suppose it's easier to look after him with lots of people around he can't talk to.'

'Except for the people, I suppose. How's surgery?'

Sandy looked around even though there were no obvious surgeons present. 'A bit sad, really. I thought my physicians were narrow-minded, but this lot . . . And they keep giving me little treats, like being allowed into theatre with the big boys and getting to hold things while they talk about their cars and dig holes that keep filling up with blood. Honestly. And they're so proud of themselves. How's Jimmy?'

'Hard to keep up with. But it's worth trying, I suppose. Enjoys everything all the time and can't understand why everyone else doesn't. The students get a bit bemused.'

'I was in his unit for junior clinics. The first time he taught us he dashed in with a dozen chest X-rays, gave us one each and said "Follow me". In no time we were out in the grounds and all standing in a circle worrying about what he was going to ask us about the X-rays, because we'd never seen any before. "Lovely day" he said. "Tutorial outside. Grass a bit wet so we'll all sit on these old chest X-rays, hm?." And we did and it was lovely.'

Scott listened to Sandy, who did Jimmy's clipped, Monty-ish tone quite well, and tried to decide what it was about her, apart from a conspicuous new wedding ring, that made her look married. She had put on a little weight, which was presumably something to do with slogging through Mrs Beeton on her nights off from the Southern, and her clothes were different too: a lot more grown up over quite a short period. Matronish would have been unkind, but there were hints of Jenners where once it would have probably been Marks and Spencers. Her hair was shorter and a bit more adventurous: wavier and possibly lighter. Scott realised that although he had known her quite well when she was a student, because of committees and politics, and when she was a resident at the Institute, where they had all been in it together, she was now a young married professional from the New Town and that was something quite different from anything she had been before.

They both started speaking together then both said something like 'You go on', then there was a funny quiet bit. 'I was going to ask if you'd got something fixed up for after house-jobs.'

'So was I.'

'You first.'

'Haematology,' said Sandy. 'Nearly sure. At least I'm going to give it a try. They've offered me an SHO job at the Southern.'

'Haematology?'

'Yes.'

'Because of Dr Parkinson?'

Sandy smiled. 'In spite of, maybe. But I actually got quite interested in it there, and it's quite good for . . . You know, looking ahead a bit. It's pretty nine-to-fiveish, and they don't mind part-timers. And we might have to move around a bit and it's easier for finding jobs in than being a brain surgeon . . . What about you?'

'Oh, not sure. Not brain surgery, anyway. Not quite a lot of things, I suppose. Remember all those funny wee subjects we got two weeks of in fifth year? And you thought no, not that either. Skins . . . Ear, nose and throat and all that . . .'

'Gosh yes. Ophthalmology . . . Public health? Venereology?'

'No thanks.'

Sandy laughed. 'I used to wonder about them. The people

teaching us, I mean. Did they sit up straight in their prams one day and say "Mummy, I want to be an ophthalmologist", or was it just something that happened to them?' Sandy paused. 'But don't just let things happen to you, Andrew.'

She had become serious. Scott was surprised. Was it just that wee girls who now had a husband and a kitchen of their own suddenly felt they could act like your big sister? Or was it a footnote to one of the occasional long chats they had had in the residency lounge at the Institute during first housejobs, most notably after the RNR Christmas dinner: one about which Scott had to admit he couldn't remember much. 'No,' he said. 'No I won't. I was thinking of running away to sea.'

'What?'

'Well, I've applied for an anatomy demonstrator's job in Glasgow. Got an interview on Monday. But somebody rang me up from the navy asking me if I wanted to go round the world.'

'You're kidding, Andrew.'

'I'm not. They're really short of doctors. The pay's not very good. Even the Irishmen have stopped joining, and quite a lot of the people who took cadetships are bailing out because they've got married or something, so they've been writing round the reserves for people.' Scott hesitated. To a well-organised young lady doctor and New Town housewife what he was contemplating might sound like social and professional suicide.

'But you wouldn't . . .'

'I just scribbled a note vaguely inquiring about it and a couple of days later somebody phoned me at work asking if I'd like to go round the world on something called a group deployment. I said I might, but I'm still going for the interview in Glasgow.'

'I'm sure they'll want you. So you'll get primary fellowship from that and then try for surgery SHO jobs here?'

'That's sort of what I thought. We'll see.'

Sandy was looking up at him as if she wanted to say something else. 'Sandy . . . Andrew . . .' Esmee Jameson had appeared with another of her young people steered firmly by the elbow. 'You probably haven't met Engadine. Engadine Morris, an old friend of the family. Sandy Ratho, Andrew Scott.'

'Hello, Andrew. Gosh, how are you? I suppose you're a doctor now?' Scott nodded. Esmee smiled contentedly and went away.

Engadine, big and pretty and smelling strongly of cigarettes, turned to Sandy. 'Are you a doctor too? Gosh. Everyone's doctors except us. And I'm gasping for a fag.' Engadine looked round the room. 'Jimmy's marvellous except for that.' Sandy looked puzzled. 'Jimmy and daddy were at Cambridge together. They're like family, really, except you can't smoke here.'

Sandy said Engadine's name was interesting. 'It's a place,' she said. 'A valley in Switzerland.' She giggled and lowered her voice. 'It's where I was conceived, actually . . . On their honeymoon. Honestly, I often wish they'd just gone somewhere ordinary like Florence instead.' Scott laughed. He had run into Engadine, usually in the company of Walker, off and on for several years and had wondered from time to time about her name. When he asked about the former student politician she said 'He's fine. He's here in fact. Over there.' Walker, who with Engadine must have arrived even later than Scott, was standing beside the grand piano that served as a bar and doing his five-minute tour of duty with Dr Gumi. 'He's just been made a junior lecturer,' said Engadine. 'In politics, of course, and he's doing a PhD all about early political influences on Chuter Ede.' She took a workmanlike sip from her gin and tonic. 'I actually wanted him to do Attlee.'

'Really?' said Sandy.

'Yes. He's boring too, but at least he got to be prime minister.'

Sandy smiled again and Scott suddenly understood what people meant by a political wife. Engadine's father's career had not prospered and he was now a life peer. Walker, still standing in silent communion with Dr Gumi, would clearly have to do better. 'And what does your husband do, Sandy?'

'Oh, he's a doctor too. In immunology.'

'Is that a research thing?'

'Yes, mainly . . .' said Sandy. 'But quite a lot of it's useful too. He's at the Southern, doing a PhD . . .'

'That's interesting.'

'Yes . . . We're actually quite keen to go on in academic medicine.' Scott listened to what might well be a ladylike piece of sparring, reflecting that there were probably medical wives as well, and then remembered that Theresa had once said something quite acid about Sandy making a good Mrs Professor. There was an awkward silence that ended only when Jimmy started hounding people downstairs to dinner.

They ate with some ceremony, twelve of them round a huge polished table loaded with crystal and silver, talking politely and generally behaving as though the whole thing were mainly a kind of deportment class, run by the Jamesons from some deep sense of public duty and aimed at young professionals of widely varying social backgrounds who were in the process of joining the Edinburgh bourgeoisie. Sandy and Mrs Jimmy flanked the distinguished Japanese visitor and plodded through basic English conversational exercises across him, maintaining all the while a courteous pretence of including him too. Scott was sufficiently near Walker to catch up with things other than the PhD on Chuter Ede. Jimmy and Engadine at the far end were almost flirtatious, and a quiet man who edited bibles for a publisher and turned out to be one of Jimmy's sons coped nobly with Irena at her most hysterical.

For coffee they adjourned upstairs again and sat in a big circle while Jimmy probed and prodded and tried to get everyone to say what they were doing or going to do that might make the world a better place. Dr Gumi beamed silently around and listened as Walker talked rather self-consciously about social justice and Gus explained yet again how immunology would transform almost every branch of medicine in the next few years and Irena agonised between her aspirations for Poland and her equally deep concern for the Polish community in Scotland. Engadine, suffering visibly from her separation from cigarettes, sketched her duties as a research assistant in a medical sociology project that might or might not lead to something called targeting of primary care. Scott got off lightly by talking vaguely about surgery, probably thoracic surgery, and the need for basic research, with Sandy looking at him as though daring him to say anything more about running away to sea. At ten thirty precisely Jimmy brought proceedings to a close by remarking that Dr Gumi had a plane to catch quite early next morning. Coats were fetched and everyone said nice things about the evening. The party broke up with Dr Gumi nodding his head off, the Jamesons smiling and waving and Engadine kissing both of them on both cheeks.

Outside it was still and mild and the whole street was fragrant from its gardens. Like students just released from an especially tough tutorial, the Jamesons' younger guests stood around on the pavement and chatted for a little while before dispersing, then Sandy and Gus set off on foot to their flat in Darnaway Street. Engadine offered Scott a lift back across town and Irena made it clear that she would like one too. They all got into the car, a not very new Mini, and even before she had started it up Engadine was scrabbling in the door-pocket for her cigarettes. 'Anyone else? God, I thought I'd never make it.' Engadine, Irena and Walker all lit up. Just as they were moving off there was a loud knocking on the roof. Engadine drew up again and slid back her window so that a rising cloud of cigarette smoke engulfed the figure standing over the car. It was Professor Jameson, coughing and choking and gesturing with his left hand at a small shoulder bag held aloft in his right. 'Someone left this,' he spluttered. 'Yours, Irena? Or Engadine?' Irena, cigarette still in hand, reached past Engadine for her bag. 'Yes. Sorry. Thanks. Thank you very much.' If there was an emotion visible on Jimmy's face it was probably disappointment. He coughed again and walked sadly back to his front door as the Mini roared off down the street with everyone inside it giggling insanely.

A few days later Scott took a train to Glasgow for an afternoon appointment with the professor of anatomy. He found the department deep in the tangle of Victorian Gothic on Gilmorehill and, on the instructions of the professor's secretary, waited for some time in an outer office. After twenty minutes she summoned a technician to show him round and he followed his taciturn guide through the museum, the library, the lecture theatre, the dissecting room and back to the outer office. Forty minutes after he should have seen the professor, the secretary invited him into her office for a cup of tea and a chat, at the end of which she confided that Professor Kerr, normally a punctilious and considerate man, had probably forgotten all about the interview and, since the weather was quite nice, had almost certainly gone off to play golf. She apologised on his behalf in a way that suggested she had done so before and told Scott she would arrange another appointment. Scott made his way back to Queen Street station.

    With almost half an hour to wait for an Edinburgh train he had a cup of coffee then, on impulse, checked through his pockets and found the RNR circular about the shortage of doctors. From a station call box he phoned the Staff Officer (Medical) to the Admiral Commanding Reserves. For reasons unspecified the staff officer was unavailable, but his chief petty officer was pleased to hear from Surgeon Lieutenant Scott, Forth Division, RNR, and on the spot offered him a job as medical officer in *HMS Panther*, a frigate bound from Pompey to Pompey via Simonstown, Singapore, Panama and Roosie Roads: a great party-going steamer, according to the chief, off on a trip he only wished he was going on himself. When Professor Kerr rang later in the week to offer a demonstrator's job on the strength of Scott's references and the impression he had made over tea with the secretary, a letter had already arrived from a civil servant instructed by the Board of Admiralty to inform the aforementioned officer that he had been appointed to Her Majesty's Ship PANTHER with effect from 15 JULY 1970 and accordingly should contact her Commanding Officer forthwith.

November 1974

'You've got to do it,' said Jimmy, 'And you'll do it well. But it won't do you any good.'

'Yes, that's what I thought you'd say.'

'On the other hand, it might be quite fun.'

'You know what it reminds me of?' said Lennie. 'A skit in a Fringe show, taking the mickey out of our lot in the Forces. "What we need now is a futile gesture that will improve the whole tone of the war . . ." '

'Oh, I don't think it's quite as bad as that.' Jimmy reached over and topped up Lennie's sherry glass. 'Might even hit the spot. A crisp, no-nonsense report that not many people will like but everyone will respect. It would rattle round a few committees for a while. Years, maybe, alas. Couple of little concessions here and there, but that wouldn't matter because you'd have pitched it fairly strong in the first place. And five or perhaps ten years from now we'd have the kind of hospitals we need, where we need 'em. But no new Institute. That's the point. You know, I think you might even have quite a lot of fun.' Jimmy sat back in his chair with his chin up as though contemplating with satisfaction the report of a committee which had not yet even found a chairman. Lennie put down his glass on the green leather of the table that occupied the centre of the Fellows' room.

'Terrible mistake if you turned it down,' said Jimmy. 'An opportunity missed, from the point of view of everyone we're trying to help. And for you.'

'Come on.'

Jimmy chuckled. 'Truly, Lennie. Professing endocrinology's not stretching you. You'll do your big Deaning sooner or later anyway, and even you have to admit it's the sort of thing you're rather good at. Ever been to Vienna?' Lennie shook his head. 'You should go. Take Margaret. Marvellous city. You'd both enjoy it enormously.'

This was cryptic even by Jimmy's standards. 'Vienna?'

'Should have thought it was obvious. You mean you've never wondered? Never asked yourself why Vienna's so big when Austria's so small, hm? Imperial decline, but done rather well. Our problems here are more or less exactly the same.'

'Up to a point. Perhaps . . .'

'One wouldn't overstretch it, but Edinburgh – meaning the Institute, mainly, of course – used to do everything that mattered medically from the Tay and the Tweed. So now that Fife and West Lothian and the Borders have all got their own set-ups we've got too much. And the Institute's the main problem, of course . . . Big, old, falling down and far too far gone to be worth spending money on. And whether we admit or not we've missed the bus for the big scheme. So no new Institute. Never. And you and your little committee – once you've been to Vienna and had a think about it – can report accordingly. Prepare people. Let them down gently. And chop things back to what we need. What we can afford, too, because we certainly can't afford to go on the way we're doing.' Jimmy sat back again. 'I'm sure you can see why your efforts would be much appreciated.'

Lennie, who had his arm twisted by Jimmy oftener than he cared to remember, sat silently and wondered about this latest and most alarming project. The proposed committee would report to the Health Board, of which Jimmy was a member, and it was probably in that capacity that he was speaking now, but – as usual with Jimmy – there was a lot more to it than that. Even the timing of this little meeting was significant, and nicely judged to add quite a bit of pressure on Lennie simply to say yes and get on with it.

'I don't want to rush you into anything,' said Jimmy, 'but the other chaps will all be along shortly and it might be helpful if I could go back to the Board next week with some kind of indication one way or the other. And of course you're perfectly free to turn me down flat, though obviously I hope you won't.'

'Quite. But wasn't reorganisation suppose to sort all that out. If not immediately . . .'

Jimmy found the idea uproariously funny. 'Come off it, Lennie. Drawing lines on the map and shuffling a few desks around was never going to do anything in the face of a hundred years of Hapsburg pretension. No. This is the real thing, and you could have great fun doing it. Right up your street. You'd have as small a committee as possible. Mainly good chaps, of course. Perhaps one dinosaur, but if you choose a dim one he more or less won't matter. And a senior nurse. I'd say Maggie Young, myself. She'd stop the doctors talking nonsense. And you'd need a chap from the minor specialities and a chap from the minor hospitals. Could even be the same chap, couldn't it?'

Lennie, who found himself agreeing about Maggie Young and thinking already of the kind of dim dinosaur who'd fit the bill, was still reluctant, but was beginning to come round to the view that taking it on might do him less harm than not taking it on.

'I can see you have reservations,' said Jimmy. 'Is there something. . . ? I mean just tell me, and I'd perfectly understand. If you've run off a quiet cardiogram on yourself and decided to take it easy for Margaret's sake – and indeed your own – you only have to tell me. We'd find somebody, I suppose.' Jimmy clutched his brow. 'There *must* be someone. No one else that springs to mind immediately. I must confess.' He sat back resignedly. 'Or perhaps *you* can come up with some ideas, Lennie. The Board's terribly keen to get on with it.'

Lennie sat at the green table in the Fellows' room of the Royal College of Physicians and looked across at the leafless trees on the other side of Queen Street. Rebuffed, Jimmy sat mournfully nursing his sherry glass, somehow a slighter figure than his great Presidential chair seemed to deserve. It was an odd occasion in a number of respects, Lennie decided. He had never encountered the Jameson mixture of soft soap and brute force served up so strong. He had never ever actually turned him down flat. Even the Fellows' room seemed quieter than ever before, but that was because he had never been in it on a Sunday morning. And he had never been in it on a Sunday morning because he had never before been a member of the committee which was about to meet: the one composed of local holders of B merit awards and chaired by the only A plus holder in town; the one which decided who got and did not get the comparatively lowly C, from which Lennie had just been promoted; and the one which in practice was the only route to the comforts of an A award, the really agreeable step up, the one that doubled one's salary.

From outside the Fellows' room came the distant murmur of

conversation on the College's main stairway. Jimmy cocked his head and looked at his watch. 'Reprobates . . . we give 'em all that money and they can't even make it to the committee on time. Lennie. . . ?'

'Yes?'

'You will do it, won't you?' Lennie took a deep breath and nodded. 'Splendid,' said Jimmy. 'We can have a little chat about it after divine service.'

May 1976

The best thing about being on call in Lavrockdale was the bath, the worst being summoned from it by the bleep. The duty doctor's quarters were a bedroom, a sitting room and an immense bathroom in the second floor of the old physician superintendent's villa: a building now occupied mainly by the social work department but still maintaining in its upper reaches an Edwardian splendour of scale and comfort. Scott lay stretched out in the biggest bath he had ever come across, moving sometimes to turn the hot tap with his foot, sometimes swirling the water with his hands to keep the temperature even throughout, and consoling himself with the thought that if he were to be summoned it would most likely be to a half-expected outside call which he would take in his bedroom, naked except for a towel, and after which he could return to the warm, pale-green expanses of the bathroom and another half hour in the bath.

The rest of Lavrockdale had little to commend it. Formerly the Haddingtonshire County Asylum, it was twelve miles east of Edinburgh and set deep in its own wooded park three miles from anything aspiring even to the status of village. A night on call there, especially a Friday night, was a curious suspension of the normal: a matter of being there rather than doing anything. The remoteness of the hospital meant the duty doctor had to live in, but the stability and experience of the nursing staff and the general robust health of the patients meant that only very rarely was there any cause to go across to the wards. A duty there was an evening devoid of all temptation except that of working for exams; for Scott, a fully fledged Member of the Royal College of Psychiatrists with all his exams behind him, it was now simply a good place to have a nice long bath.

When his bleep eventually went off he got out and took a towel through to the bedroom with no great haste. He settled comfortably on the bed and rang the exchange. For two or three minutes there was no answer: unusual but hardly surprising at Lavrockdale, where there was rarely any reason to hurry. An unfamiliar telephonist, male and gruff, eventually answered.

'Dr Scott here. You bleeped me.'

'Sorry, doc. Sorry about that.'

'What?'

'An outside call. Rung off just before you answered.'

'Oh, I see,' said Scott.

'I suppose she might ring back,' said the telephonist. 'You never know.'

Scott followed his trail of wet footprints back to the bath, wondering if whoever it was – and he had a fairly short list of possible female callers – would ring back immediately and get him out of the bath again. Rather than dry himself or wait around dripping he stepped back into the huge Edwardian trough and lay there not enjoying it very much. When his bleep went off again it was a relief. 'Death in eleven, doctor,' said the telephonist. Scott grunted non-committally. 'Oh . . . Thought you'd probably want to go over straight away . . .'

'Um, thanks,' said Scott.

'Any time . . .' said the telephonist. 'Don't mention it. I'll tell them you're on your way over now . . .'

Ward eleven was a ward Scott had had little to do with. It housed forty or so demented souls and a handful of what the specialty called 'graduates', meaning people who had come in with a touch or more of schizophrenia in the 1920's or 30's, and over the course of the next thirty or forty years grown old without ever leaving. While in the acute wards of Lavrockdale a death might be a cardiac arrest, in the back wards it was simply a death, often one which, in terms of foreseeable quality of life, was long overdue. Scott dried himself and dressed without hurrying, partly because there was no hurry and partly because the unknown lady caller might just try again while he was still near a phone.

Outside, he walked through pools of late sunshine between the trees, then diagonally across the lawn in front of the main building and round to the wing of long stay wards extending unseen behind it. The long stay corridor was empty and sunlit, its big sash windows open and its air a good deal more pleasant than usual. Ward eleven, on the right at the end, was as far from the villa as it was possible to be, and tonight something odd was going on: even from a hundred yards away it was clear that normal routine had been disturbed. At the ward entrance an old man sat on the floor, his feet sticking out across the corridor. Opposite him, also seated against the wall, was a nurse in uniform. As Scott approached he was surprised to see that each held a can of beer, the familiar red MacEwen's Export. The ward door was open and from within came the sound of a small band greatly amplified. The music, Scott decided, might have been familiar if it had been played better: only when he was quite close did he recognise it as *When The Saints Go Marching In*, played harshly on a few brass instruments. The man sitting in the corridor beamed up across the top of his beercan at Scott, and the nurse winked. It was all rather odd, but the new telephonist had definitely told Scott about a death in ward eleven.

Inside, with their backs to the door, were four middle-aged men in shirtsleeves, swaying, stamping and blazing away on trumpets, trombone and euphonium. In front of them, half the ward had been cleared of beds and there were twice as many patients as usual: rows of old men and old women sitting on benches, in wheelchairs and on the floor. Most, like the two outside in the corridor, held beer cans or, in the case of some of the ladies, glasses. And since eleven was a male ward and ward ten had been quiet, it was simply a matter of ward eleven having invited the nextdoor neighbours in for a drink and some musical entertainment. Good luck to them, thought Scott, and if someone had died they seemed to have managed to do so without spoiling the fun.

The charge nurse, standing near the back, saw Scott coming in and waved, beckoning him to the far end of the ward. He stepped carefully along the wall past the rows of patients and was led to a curtained single cubicle where a man in baggy trousers and a stained tartan shirt lay supine and inert. 'Old Bob,' said the charge nurse in a soft highland accent as Scott stooped over the bed. 'Old Bob Heading. A graduate, you know. Been here twenty years at least and a real gentleman, always talking to people. Always the same thing, mind you. But very peaceful at the last, doctor, just as the band was setting up. He mentioned chest pain, we moved him in here and he just passed away.'

Scott lowered the bed-light close to the old man's face, opened his eyelids gently and confirmed that his pupils were never going to contract again. In the circumstances, auscultation to ensure the heart had stopped was a formality, but he did it anyway. The charge nurse opened the dead man's shirt and for half a minute Scott listened with his stethoscope in his ears to *Yield not to Temptation* played as a jazz march. 'May he rest in peace,' said the charge nurse when he had finished, 'but I'd really like the remains to stay here until the entertainers leave.' Scott nodded and they switched off the light and went back on to the main ward. 'There's a drink for everybody, doctor, if you'd like one,' said the charge nurse. 'The entertainers have been most kind.'

Scott was handed a can of MacEwan's Export. He opened it and leaned on a windowsill halfway back in the crowd and listened to *Makin' Whoopee, I Dream of Jeannie with the Light Brown Hair, Loch Lomond, Rule Britannia* and *Scotland the Brave*, all arranged for two trumpets, trombone and euphonium. Then the ward piano was wheeled out and while one middle aged man in a shiny black waistcoat played, another, a tenor with a fine old-fashioned timbre, sang *Duncan Gray, O wert Thou in the Cauld Blast, Ae Fond Kiss* and *John Anderson my Jo, John.* An old man sitting in his pyjamas in a wheelchair bit his bottom lip and sniffed and was helped to a messy half-spilled gulp of Export by a nurse kneeling at his side. Quite a lot of the old ladies cried, mostly at the last two songs, and a little enrolled nurse was going busily around with a box of paper hankies.

'Marvellous,' said a deep voice close to Scott. 'Not a dry seat in the house.'

'Oh, hello, Toby.'

'Nice to see the junior staff supporting the patient entertainment programme. Sort of makes up for drinking on duty.'

'Oh. Sorry.'

Toby chuckled and shook his head. 'Had a tiny sherry myself, just to be sociable when they got here.'

Scott said something polite about the band and the singer. 'They do pretty well,' said Toby. He yawned. 'Come up here twice a year. Christmas and about now. You know, I could even get quite fond of *Yield Not to Temptation.*'

The piano was being heaved off to the side once more and the band set themselves up again around the microphone. 'I might just slide away now,' said Toby. 'Things might begin to happen t'were better for a consultant not to know about . . . See you on Monday, Andrew . . .'

Toby Russell, a tall, fit-looking man in his fifties, all the more striking for being completely bald, wove his way forward through the audience, stopping here and there for a quick word with a nurse or to pat some old lady on the shoulder. When he got to the front he spoke briefly to the euphonium player and was gone. Scott, still leaning on a window sill and wondering if another can might not be a good idea, watched as the band struck up a kind of circus march and a little conga of nurses and the fitter patients gradually took shape. Fifteen or twenty in a bobbing, heaving line eventually closed to make a ring of dancers that cavorted, in approximate time to the music, round the space at the front. Most of the nurses by now had their hats off, a lapse which, back in the Institute, would have been viewed as roughly the equivalent of streetwalking, but which seemed to matter a lot less in places like Lavrockdale. They skipped and writhed and hugged and were hugged in a stomping line that circled the band and its amplifying equipment, going faster as the music changed from the circus tune to something they could sing too, and then faster and faster still as the band drove them on in the new tune. Scott sang along, as did a few others of the audience, and lots who couldn't sing just clapped and shouted and waved.

'Haul 'em down, you Zulu warrior . . . Haul 'em down, you Zulu chief! Chief! Chief!', rang out a dozen or more times, each time quicker and louder. However, the hint of mischief implied in Toby's parting remark failed to materialise: the ward floor first shook in time with the beat then, when the dancers could no longer keep up with the band, simply shook, but nothing of note was hauled down. With a sudden shout and a mighty blaring flourish they finished, the dancers leaping into the air with their hands above their heads and the band reaching gratefully for their cans of beer. Dishevelled, pink-faced nurses helped patients back to the benches at the front. Most people clapped and one thin old lady just kept on clapping. Eventually the euphonium player put down his can and tapped the microphone and solemnly announced 'Ladies and gentlemen, the Queen.'

The four musicians, now in a straight line, stood silent and solemn as any Armistice-day buglers ever seen in Whitehall, then rolled softly and reverently into the first line of the national anthem. At first a few cracked voices sang, then more and better joined in. Scott stopped leaning on his windowsill and stood loosely to attention without actually having thought about it. Most of the audience remained seated, but someone on the far side of the front row – a solid little man with a rough hospital crew cut – was struggling to rise from his wheelchair. He wobbled and gesticulated and was eventually helped to his feet by two nurses. Held up by his armpits, with his shoulders squared and his arms stiffly by his side, he continued to sway dangerously. His face was bright with tears and for some reason he was wearing only trousers and a string vest. Scott wondered how much he had to drink and only belatedly realised that, however much the man had had to drink, the main problem was that he had lost a leg: most probably, given his determined military bearing, for king and country. Scott watched. Was it just a triumph of conditioning over dementia, or something a bit more elevating? Whatever it was, the two nurses were crying as well.

The last notes faded and the charge nurse, whose lay-preacher manner was strangely at odds with the rest of the proceedings, went down to the front and gave a little vote of thanks '. . . to our six dear friends, the Port Seton and Cockenzie Occasional Entertainers. We thank them from the bottom of our hearts for a wonderful evening and wish them a safe journey home. Good night, gentlemen, and God bless.' There was a faint cheer and the very mad lady continued to clap alone. Scott suddenly remembered the graduate he had been called over to the ward to certify dead.

He made his way to the front and stopped to talk for a moment with the band. 'It's the least we could do for the folk here,' said the euphonium player, pink from beer and effort. 'A service, a small service, to our fellow men.' The man paused as though uncertain whether to impart a confidence, perhaps about a poor mad auntie. He gripped Scott's hand firmly and muttered 'Actually, we're the Cockenzie and Port Seton masons . . . A wonderful organisation that many a young man joins to his credit and to the aid and comfort of his fellow man.' Scott smiled and nodded much as if it had been about a poor mad auntie after all, and went off into the ward's duty room, found the book of death certificates and signed Mr Heading out with the very ordinary verdict of myocardial infarction, secondary to coronary artery disease, secondary to generalised atherosclerosis. In death there is no schizophrenia.

On the way back down the corridor he dropped in on ward ten, where a solitary nurse sat at the desk opposite three old ladies already tucked up in bed, presumably too frail or ill to have gone next door. The staff nurse got up when Scott came in. Uninvited medical visits to wards like these were not always welcome, so he said quietly that he was on duty and had just been in ward eleven, then asked politely if there was anything that needed seeing to while he was across.

The staff nurse pointed in the direction of the nearest patient. 'Hetty's pretty low.' Scott raised his eyebrows. 'But I think she'll last the night.'

'Thanks, staff.' Scott went over to the lady the staff nurse had indicated. She was very old and thin and her skin under the dimmed bedlight was almost transparent. Her head moved on the pillow as he approached. In a tiny voice she said 'What was all the music for, please?'

'It was a band,' said Scott. 'Band music, songs and some dancing.'

'Dancing?' The old lady raised her head a little from the pillow then settled back smiling with her eyes closed. 'Lovely,' she said. 'How lovely . . . And tell me, were the ladies all wearing long dresses?'

'Hello? Andrew?'

'Oh. Hello.'

'I tried to ring you earlier.'

'Yes, the switchboard said . . .'

'Someone came in.'

'I see.' There was quite a long pause, then Scott said 'Has someone come in again.'

'No, silly. It's just me. How's Lavrockdale?'

'All right, really. Nothing to do, nice views and a wee band came in to play to the patients.'

'Some day I'll sneak out when you're on call.'

'That would be nice.' There was another long pause, then Sandy said 'Is it a single bed?'

'Sorry, but the bath's enormous. Easily big enough for two.'

342

'Mm,' said Sandy. 'Never tried that. Andrew . . .' She sounded suddenly businesslike. 'Where'll you be about two-ish tomorrow afternoon?'

'Oh. I could easily be at the flat.'

'And I could be visiting my poor sick father.'

'Oh. Is he. . . ?'

'He could be. Just in case someone comes in, can we fix that? I'll know by two or perhaps two thirty, and ring you. There, all fixed. Now we can just chat.'

Being told to be standing by at the flat for a phone call between two and two thirty wasn't quite the same as everything being all fixed, but it was a lot better than many of their recent arrangements. 'Fine,' said Scott.

'Golf's a marvellous game for husbands,' said Sandy. 'Takes ages, and doesn't kill them off the way squash does.'

A highly regarded local gastro-enterologist, still only in his thirties, had provoked much anxiety among Edinburgh doctors by dropping dead on a squash court a few weeks before, having complained only of a bit of heartburn. 'I'm meeting Max for lunch, but quite early . . .'

'Good. And Andrew . . .'

'What?'

'Be careful.'

'On the phone?'

'That as well, but lunch too. Please.'

'I'm terribly discreet, honestly. He's having a sort of round of farewells. I must be quite important, because I got Saturday lunch and he's off on Monday.'

'A nation mourns. Where's he off to?'

'Somewhere tremendously famous that I've never heard of. Bow something.'

'Bowman Gray?'

'That's it.'

'It's quite big in infectious diseases. A good BTA.'

'What? Oh.'

'Been to America . . . Will you have to go, Andrew?'

'Doubt it. Might. But probably won't have to.'

'I hope not . . .'

'What about you?'

343

'Couples don't usually, if they've both got careers. Might eventually, I suppose . . . It depends . . . '

She sounded sad. What she probably meant, Scott decided, was that whether she and Gus went somewhere abroad together depended mainly on if and when they had children. They loomed large in her thinking, and though they never discussed it Scott was permanently aware that she had picked him up more or less on the way home from the infertility clinic.

They had met again a few months before. She had been browsing in the section of Bauermeister's bookshop devoted to conquering nerves, curing rheumatism with squashed flowers and naming your child. He had assumed she was pregnant and had said something friendly but silly. She got upset, they went for a coffee and an hour later were comfortably together in bed in Scott's flat. Since then Sandy had been crisply efficient about her double life. Scott, having made good progress through the basics, was beginning to discover more and more about the limitations of the form. There were a great many things people like them couldn't do together in Edinburgh and for quite a lot of the time he never knew when he would see her again, sometimes even whether. At its worst, the whole business meant that he spent hours hanging around for phone calls which didn't always happen. At its best, it made him wish that there might be more to it than in the long run there probably would be. And if the faint prospect of an evening stroll through the grounds of a county asylum was one of the better items on offer, was it really worth all the trouble?

'Gosh, Andrew. I can't wait for tomorrow . . .'

'Mm.'

'D'you mean that?'

'Mm-mm.'

Sandy laughed. 'Dad actually is a bit ill. Funny. He's very good at medicine and yet he's not actually very good at being ill. D'you know what I mean?'

'Won't go to the doctor?'

'That sort of thing. And he lets it get him down. You'd never know from the way he is at work – Faculty things, and the wards. But mum says he just comes home and mopes. Has a gin, puts his feet up and isn't even much fun.'

'He works pretty hard.'

344

'He always has done. But he's always enjoyed it before.'

'I suppose things have changed a bit.'

'He's not against change. I think he's against . . . things getting worse. His lot came home from the war and everything was going to get better. And for ages it did. Now they're all older and sadder and things have stopped getting better. Gosh, Andrew, I bet you're thinking I want to see you tomorrow just so we can sort out all the problems of the poor old Health Service . . .'

'Hadn't occurred to me.'

'It's lovely just chatting to you, even rattling on about nothing. Are you in bed?'

'Yes.'

'What's it like?'

'Single.'

'You said that.'

'Narrow, and it squeaks.'

'Oh.'

'But there's never anyone else around.'

'I should jolly well hope not, Dr Scott.'

'I meant in the villa.'

'I know. I was just being silly and possessive. Oh, Andrew . . .'

'What?'

'Gosh. Sorry, Andrew. See you tomorrow.'

The phone went dead. Presumably someone had come in. Scott set his alarm clock, rang the exchange to say he was going off the bleep and settled for the night in his narrow, squeaky single bed, thinking that it would have been nice to have had another few minutes just to have told Sandy about the Port Seton and Cockenzie masons.

Max and Scott had arranged to meet in the pub opposite the Institute at half past twelve. Scott left his car outside the flat in Marchmont and walked across the Meadows with plenty of time in hand. Just as he was passing the side entrance of the Institute at the top of Middle Meadow Walk Robbie emerged, sauntering watchfully, as though looking out for someone he had arranged to meet or – and with Robbie it was more likely – simply looking out for someone to pass the time of day with. Scott had not seen Robbie for some months and was on balance quite happy to have run into him now. There was no doubt where he was heading, although he was only a moderate drinker, and if he subsequently decided to have lunch with Max and Scott then there was no particular harm in it. Max might even appreciate an unexpected doubling of his audience.

When he saw Scott he waved, for Robbie no half-hearted matter but the kind of thing people in the crowd at Murrayfield did so that their friends could see them on TV. 'Hello, Andy! How's Lavrockdale?' The question was put from some distance, as though Scott might suddenly decide to turn and go back to Marchmont because he thought he had left the gas on. 'Hello, Robbie.'

He loped up, grinning broadly. 'You heading across the road? Thought so. Great. Haven't seen you for ages. Did you pass?'

It was one of Robbie's more endearing traits that he regarded himself as being in continuous conversation with people he ran into only once or twice a year. Scott nodded. 'Pass rate's about sixty percent, isn't it? And a lot higher if you can put together a bit of English for the oral. Different in anaesthetics. Talking to people's hardly part of the job at all, is it? So how's Lavrockdale?'

They went into the pub, with Robbie buying the first round on the strength of Scott's exam pass of some months ago. Robbie had his usual lager and lime, and smacked his lips a lot. They talked about Lavrockdale. Robbie was quite interested in the Port Seton and Cockenzie masons and the euphonium player's odd hint that Scott might think about joining. 'I don't know about psychiatry – maybe, maybe not. You never know – but it's supposed to be a bloody good investment for anybody seriously interested in anaesthetics in Edinburgh,' said Robbie, looking carefully around. Most of the people in the pub seemed to be nurses and he was reassured. 'Too late for me now, though. Apparently they hold it against you if it's sort of obvious why you're joining, and then it actually marks you down . . . They've got a word for it.'

'Square-bashing?' Scott meant that as a joke but Robbie took it seriously. 'No. Not that. Something about . . . Hey! Guess who? Well, look. How about that? Over here, Max! Come and join us. I thought you were supposed to be off at Bowman Gray . . .'

If Max was displeased he had concealed it quite well. 'Monday. Hello, Scott. Everybody says the beer over there's lousy so I'll have a pint of export.' Robbie leapt to his feet. 'Let me, Max. My round.

And it's not every day we see chaps off across the pond. Another, Andy? Or a half pint?' Scott shook his head. Robbie loped off to the bar. 'He gets odder and odder,' Max muttered. 'Must be sniffing all those halogenated hydrocarbons. Have you noticed that? Or maybe it's sitting around listening to surgeon's jokes all day. How are you anyway?'

'All right. You all set?'

'It's like going off to old Plomley's desert island. "You are allowed sixty-six pounds, including the Bible, Shakespeare and one luxury . . ." Makes you think. And they don't have downies, so you have to take one. Doesn't weigh very much, but there isn't really room in your suitcase for anything else. And where I'm going goes from hot as hell about now to brass monkeys in winter. So maybe I'll go native – Bermuda shorts, parkas, all that stuff – and just buy it over there. You hear about him?' Max nodded in the direction of Robbie, who was talking animatedly to a trio of nurses while he waited at the bar for service. 'Went into an SR interview and more or less did hari-kiri. Talked the way he talks all the time, poor bugger. They actually ended up giving it to a woman. Big. You might know her. Glasgow graduate. I mean to say . . . Yvonne, that's her. Hairy. Might even have been a catholic. Anyway, I've been off work for a week and read tons about the States, so I'm all set apart from what to take and a couple more touching farewells . . .' Max lowered his voice. 'You should try it. Tell them you're off for a year – exile, darkest America and all that – and they come over all swimmy-eyed and make fantastic efforts to do something memorable. It's amazing. You should give it a try, Scott. Ah. Thanks, Robbie. Cheers . . . Which I'm told they don't say. How's anaesthetics?'

Robbie started out on a long and complex account of the interview Max had just described. He had survived his orthopaedic housejob and done quite well on one of the non-professorial medical firms in the Institute. He might even have been invited to apply for an SHO job there, but had chosen instead to go down to the Borders to do a surgical SHO job with the hope of returning to a further SHO job in surgery at the Institute. None had materialised and he had come back to the Institute with a job in anaesthetics instead, talking at the time about how all surgeons ought to know the basics of what went on at the top end of the table, but perhaps knowing even then that he would never return to the specialty of his choice. Now a registrar in anaesthetics and getting quite near the end of a year's extension on a two year contract, he was making the best of it and still not doing very well.

'. . . then Eric came out and said Dr McCafferty, please . . . You could have knocked Nigel and me down with a feather . . . Of course you never really find out, but I'm pretty sure what happened was that Jim Bowie and old Alastair were for me, with Eric Chalmers and the boss rooting for awfully smooth Nigel and they took ages to make up their minds, an hour at least. So we think they probably just agreed to differ and went for the compromise candidate – the woman, Yvonne, who's married and who'll probably push off quite soon when her husband gets an SR job in ENT somewhere else, so it kind of puts the job on hold, but not for long, so it'd be just me and Nigel again next time. You can see their point . . . I was pretty pissed off at the time, but what the hell? It's only a game . . . What about you, Andy?'

'Oh, I don't think . . .'

'They don't actually have SR's in the States,' said Max. 'Everybody who isn't a houseman or a consultant's a resident, and consultants are called attendings. Different system altogether. So somebody like me would be a resident. Oh, and there might be something called a chief resident as well, but a bigger deal than an SR is here. More like head boy at school. All the really big names in US medicine have been it at Harvard or somewhere . . . And most of the anaesthetics are done by nurses . . . Sorry, Robbie. Cheers. Great pint.'

To Scott's surprise they stayed in the pub for only one more round then walked across the road, through the medical quad because Max wanted to see it once more before he left, and over to the Men's Union for lunch. Its upstairs dining room was unusually full for a Saturday. Several tables had spaces for three but Max seemed disinclined to share, perhaps because most of those already seated were undergraduates. They stood uncertainly for a moment with an elderly waitress hovering nearby then Max said 'Come on. Down here . . . Nobody at the old buggers' table . . .' The idea appealed more to Robbie than it did to Scott. The table in question, the biggest in the dining room and the only circular one, enjoyed pride of place furthest from the door and the servery and was unofficially reserved for a loose group of life members, mainly senior medical staff at the Institute. 'Why not?' said Max. 'I'm a life member and you lot are my guests . . . And we could be practising to be old buggers ourselves one day, couldn't we?' The waitress smiled. 'Right, Millie?' Max led on. They sat down, were handed menus and proceeded, with detailed advice from Max, to order what he considered a proper British clubman's lunch. As the waitress hobbled off Scott glanced at his watch. 'Hell,' said Max. 'We should have asked her for the wine list.'

'Gentlemen . . . I wonder if you would be so good as to share a simple bottle with *me*? Dr Scott. . . ? How very pleasant to see you.' Scott got up to shake the proffered hand. 'And my much-bemedalled young colleague Dr Roberts?' Robbie was shaking with delight. 'And I am afraid I have not yet had the pleasure . . .' Max, who seemed to have assumed that Gorgeous George would know who he was too, suffered being introduced to him by Robbie. ' . . . and he's actually just about to go off for a year in the States, Dr Gordon.'

' "But westward look, the land is bright . . ." ' Max found himself transfixed by George's magician stare. 'D'you know I never cease to be amazed by the number of young men of the highest scientific and clinical promise who set off for a sojourn in Boston, Chicago, New York or even San Francisco and return to these our shores . . .' He paused and grinned. ' . . . *quite* undamaged by the experience.'

Robbie hooted and Max managed a brave grin. George sat down, a performer now fully assured of his audience. 'And may an old man risk boring you with his troubles? I too am celebrating, though in a much smaller way.' His face filled suddenly with gloom. 'I am become a grandfather.' Robbie asked him if it was for the first time. The face became even more lugubrious. George held up both hands spread wide and nodded. 'Tenth,' he mouthed. To his enormous satisfaction Robbie's reaction had heads turning many tables away. 'So bear with me, my dear young colleagues. Millie? Ah, Millie, dear . . . Champagne, m'dear. House will do perfectly well. *So* sorry to trouble you. *Again*.'

Scott was less than half way up the four flights of stone steps to his flat when he heard a phone ringing far above. He sprinted desperately and reached the top landing in time to be sure it was his own but not in time to answer it. Still fumbling for his key, he fell cursing against his door just as the ringing ceased. He looked at his watch. It was two forty three, a time by no stretch of the imagination between two and two thirty. He rushed in, dialled Sandy's number and stood breathless as it rang and rang and rang. If she had just given up trying and left her flat, she too might hear it on the stair and turn and rush up as he had done. The absurd symmetry of that, together with George's champagne and Max's claret, induced in Scott an odd certainty that it was actually happening. He stood listening, waiting for the kind of silly breathless relief that would have welcomed her if he had been home only thirty seconds or so earlier, but as the ringing went on and on and nothing happened he became more and more angry with himself. Max, Robbie and Gorgeous George did not matter; Sandy did, a great deal, and he had acted as if she didn't, in circumstances in which she was taking risks and he wasn't and which might reasonably lead her to believe he didn't want to see her ever again. He put down the phone and was half way to the loo when the doorbell rang.

Sandy stood smiling, a carrier bag in each hand. 'Aren't you going to invite me in, Dr Scott? This lot's actually quite heavy. Mm. Good lunch?'

'Yes thanks.'

'And I can see you're expecting me.'

'Hm?'

'Your zip's undone.' Sandy turned her face up to be kissed then nuzzled into his neck. 'Mm. Nice to see, you, Andrew.' They stood for quite a long time hugging and nuzzling until Sandy shook him off. 'Can I put all this stuff in the kitchen?'

'Sure.'

'Andrew. . . ?'

'What?'

'I . . . feel a bit silly. I didn't check . . . Is it all right? I just sort of presumed . . .'

'What?'

'Dinner. Us. Here. I mean, you've not got someone else lined up or anything?' Scott shook his head and Sandy laughed. 'I shouldn't presume, but I did. And I really wanted to cook for us.'

'Lovely.'

'It's a serious golf day for husbands. Luffness, drinks, dinner, speeches and all that.'

'I see.'

'Medical golf and good for the career. And home around midnight, so we've got ages.'

Sandy picked up her carrier bags and Scott followed her through to the kitchen. She looked round and smiled then started to sort things out on the kitchen table. 'We should probably put that in the fridge about four . . .' He was handed a bottle of white wine, then a bottle of red. '. . . and open that one about the same time. And is it all right if I stick these in the fridge too, Andrew? I'm really sorry, I should have phoned when I said I would but I felt so happy and silly about this evening that I just wanted to get all this stuff and come straight round and see you . . .'

Rather than explain how he hadn't actually been there Scott joined in the muddled domesticity, helping Sandy with her various bottles and packages and trying to clear up a bit at the same time. 'I know I've only made coffee here,' said Sandy, 'but I've sort of had a look round too. Women do. Is your oven OK?'

'Seems to keep Chinese carry-outs warm.'

She stooped and opened it. 'I actually like gas. I'm sure it'll be fine. And have you got a garlic crusher thing?'

'Sorry.'

'I'll just use spoons . . . Mmm. Hello, Dr Scott . . .'

They kissed again in a way that meant they would go straight to bed. 'It's been months,' said Sandy. It had been three days. For Scott one of the many surprises of the affair was how Sandy had contrived to be with him so often, if only for a half hour around breakfast time before she went to work in the Institute and he left to drive out to Lavrockdale. Sometimes she rang from her parents' house and dropped in on her way home, and on afternoons when he was up in Edinburgh for clinics or lectures they often managed lunch together, usually just a sandwich in bed. In an odd sort of way, being at five minutes notice for a series of logistic challenges often involving rapid changes of plan and a bit of subterfuge quite suited Scott: it was the kind of thing the Navy threw at you on leadership exercises and probably made you a cleverer if not a nicer person, and on the whole he had managed fairly well. If anyone suspected anything it was probably Toby, though Scott's duties to the mentally unwell of East Lothian had not suffered significantly from the demands made upon him by his private life. The greater challenge, the deception of Gus, now a dedicated and ambitious lecturer in clinical immunology at the Southern, was Sandy's responsibility, and she seemed to be more than up to it. She was a busy doctor with a lot of reasons for being in different places at odd times and she was also very organised. But was she too becoming cleverer and less nice? As she pulled his shirt loose and ran her fingertips up over his shoulder-blades Scott stopped worrying about it, at least for the time being.

'Mm . . . Come on . . .'

'Won't be a minute.' Scott got to the loo at last. By the time he went into his bedroom Sandy was sitting naked on the bed flicking through the paperback from his bedside table. 'I've heard about this, Andrew. Is it any good?'

'I suppose it's more interesting if you know the people.'

'Gosh. Imagine putting people you knew in a book? What happened to him?'

'Nothing very much.'

'Come on, Andrew . . . I'm getting cold.'

They snuggled together under the downie, which these days more or less continuously carried the smell of Sandy. As usual, there was at first a kind of silent discussion about contraception. This time Sandy shook her head, rolled Scott on to his back and applied herself with a passionate expertise that started, so to speak, from cold and went on until she was lashing about, her hair flying and her face flushed, and making the kind of noises that in a more decorous era would probably have frightened the horses. Scott lay under her, holding back until the noise really was quite alarming then letting go more or less just to avoid complaints from the neighbours. Sandy convulsed in response then collapsed moistly all over him. It took about five minutes for her pulse and respiration to return to normal. She opened her eyes and smiled. 'Coffee?'

Whoever was on top at the end always offered to go and make coffee. Scott, who because of the lunch had felt quite like one even before they had gone to bed, now needed it rather more than usual. 'Mm. Yes, thanks.'

Sandy rolled off and sat on the edge of the bed, her hair sticking damply around her forehead. 'Won't be a minute . . . Gosh, I meant to tell you . . . Something quite important. I think there's a job coming up soon that might quite suit you.'

'Hm?'

'In Edinburgh. This is the sort of thing I don't normally do, Andrew . . . Talk about things I hear at home, I mean, from dad. But there's something rather odd going to happen soon, a new joint department, and they'll be looking for a lecturer-senior registrar sort of chap. It's all a bit preliminary, but there'll probably be something advertised by autumn. I really meant to tell you before we went to bed.'

'Joint with who?'

'Oh. Yes. Psychiatry and medicine. Dad and Jimmy got fed up with nobody doing anything about old people, so they're going to set up a wee joint department. Psychiatry and medicine, probably calling it care of the elderly, but really more psychiatry. Are you interested in old people?'

Scott thought about Jimmy's valiantly interminable social rounds, and the man standing to attention while the Port Seton and Cockenzie masons had played *God save the Queen*. 'Never really thought about it. Maybe I am.'

'It would mean you could stay in Edinburgh,' said Sandy, reaching round and stroking his hair. 'That would be nice.'

'Mmm.'

'Coffee?'

'Yes please.'

They had coffee then spent the rest of the afternoon in bed making love and listening to Radio Three, which had to compete from time to time with Sandy's noises. At around four they fell asleep and were wakened by the phone ringing. When Scott answered it, whoever it was just put the phone down: a slightly odd thing to have done if it had been the person who had wanted to talk to him just before Sandy had arrived. From time to time through the rest of the evening Scott wondered who it might have been, and whether people out at Luffness ever worried about how their golf widows were managing to cope without them while they advanced their careers in medicine.

In the evening Sandy cooked, a gas oven posing no particular problems for her, and they ate an oddly formal little dinner together in the kitchen: dressed crab with salad; beef Wellington with new potatoes, green beans and rather garlicky mushrooms; profiteroles with cream; Brie and grapes and coffee. Scott had stuck candles in saucers with wax and the cutlery, glasses and wine bottles gleamed in their light. They talked about Sandy's work – she was now back at the Institute as registrar in haematology to Dr Parkinson – and Scott told her a bit more about working with Toby, and about the strange musical evening out at Lavrockdale. The phone remained quiet and at about eight o'clock they went back to bed again. Sandy got more carried away than usual and ended up breathless and sweating and flushed, heaving helplessly like one of the patients in the labour ward. As she came to, she asked Scott if he knew what it felt like to want to make a person with someone. He hugged her and kissed her and they lay without talking for a long time, until Sandy had to go at around eleven. The phone did not ring again.

'Sorry, doc, I really don't see how you can help. It's a security matter. Maybe I should just go now, and see somebody who's a bit more up on the security angle . . .'

Scott sat back in his chair and tried to look interested rather than offended. The man still had not accepted his invitation to sit down. He was thirty two and looked older, a portly, slightly harassed man with thick dark curly hair and heavy glasses. He looked out of the window then glanced round the room and smiled at Scott. 'Special Branch, I suppose . . . They could deal with it. Some of it, anyway.'

'What about the rest?'

The man laughed as though Scott had said something genuinely funny then shook his head. 'Not sure. But definitely not you.'

'Perhaps if you tell me about it. Just the rest.'

The man snorted. 'I wondered about telling the training major.'

'What sort of chap is he?'

'Oh, he's . . .' The man stopped himself suddenly. 'Why do *you* want to know, doc? Nothing to do with you, really. As I was saying, it's a security matter . . . You'd have no idea.'

'I might,' said Scott. 'Depends on the clearance . . .'

'So you know a bit about it.'

'A bit. You can talk to me if you want to. You don't have to, but if there's anything I can do . . .'

'Does Bikini Red mean anything to you, doc?' Scott nodded. The man was if anything more suspicious. 'Bikini Amber?'

'Yes.'

'So what's the other one?'

'Black.'

'OK. What are we now?'

Scott smiled. 'I know *about* them, but I don't know what we're at now.'

'Amber,' said the man. 'And it only happens when we're at Amber or Red.'

'What happens?'

'The security matter I want to report. To the proper authorities, that is.' Scott nodded. The Bikini code denoted grades of alertness in service establishments and was based on current assessments of IRA activity and assessments. The patient, described by his own general practitioner as a Post Office fitter and keen TA sergeant, had been referred because his wife had become increasingly worried about his behaviour. His GP had elicited only that the man seemed to feel he was at some risk because of his access to classified military material, and that he was doing a number of odd things, like driving for hours on end, coming home very late and sometimes not coming home at all.

'And it's never happened at Black?'

'No.'

'Every time we're at Red?'

'Sir?'

'Does it happen every time we go to Red?'

The man looked thoughtful. 'Not sure. Really not sure about that. But it only *definitely* happens when we're at Red or Amber.'

'When you say you're not sure. . . ?'

'Well, just that. Maybe yes. Maybe no.'

'And when it definitely happens?'

'A security matter.'

'Pira?'

Again the man looked a little bit surprised. Pira was forces jargon for the Provisional IRA. 'Could be. Could very well be.'

'Have you spoken to anyone about the security angle? If it really is Pira, they'd be . . .'

'On the other hand, are they trying to fit me up? Complaint without evidence. Odd chap. Get rid of him. Then I wouldn't have access . . .' The man looked round the room again. '. . . and they'd really make trouble.'

'Any trouble so far?'

'Not trouble as such. As I keep telling you, it's security.'

'Sure,' said Scott. 'But obviously it's getting you down.' The man nodded. 'Can we talk about that?'

'If you want.'

'You'd be most welcome to sit down.'

'Thanks, doc.' The man took a last quick glance out of the window, enough to suggest to Scott that he thought someone was following him, then sat down suddenly.

'It's . . . getting you down?'

'Yes.'

'Worry? Worrying about the security matter, perhaps?' The man nodded. 'Going on for . . . how long now? How long have you been worried?' The man sat silent. 'Sorry,' said Scott. 'I should have asked . . . What are we at just now? Amber?' The man nodded and slumped forward with his face in his hands. 'So obviously you're worried . . .' The head nodded. 'Just tell me how it all started, Mr Struthers.'

'Outside, in traffic, usually. One or sometimes two of them in a car. Sometimes with Ulster number plates . . . You know, one extra figure, and always an I in the letters. Sometimes just an ordinary car. And they'd be there, tailing me to or from work, never for very far in any one car, but there would always be another they'd hand me over to . . . And drill nights were the worst . . . So I started setting off early . . .'

'And?'

'Going a long way out of my way to try and shake them off . . . Just once in a while it would work . . . But as soon as I came out, there they would be. One car on another. Usually a man on his own, sometimes two men, sometimes a man and a girl . . .'

'And how about other times? When you're not travelling.'

'You can't be too careful. Tibble? That policeman. In his civvies, but they got him. That was in the street. And MacWhirter. At his house. And the Dutchman. Well, kidnapped and kept for long enough then handed back. And if they're going to the trouble of trailing me . . .'

'But you've never actually reported it to anyone . . .'

The man sat up suddenly. 'Because I never knew who I could trust.'

'I see.'

'*They* certainly don't trust me.'

'They don't trust you . . .'

'Two junior sergeants promoted over me.'

'I see. Anything else?'

'My work checked . . . My TA work. Things they never used to do, like double-checking my decryptions. Things *I* used to pick people up on . . . And now *they're* checking up on *me* . . .'

'I see. So you're worried. Just tell me about that, maybe. How it's affecting your life generally.'

'I was going for promotion. For officer, I mean, in the Royal Signals, Territorial Army. But they've blocked that too. You know I'm a Catholic? Security risk, see? Because of them.' The man lowered his voice. 'Pira.'

There was a long silence. 'How are things at work, Mr Struthers? It's the Post Office, isn't it?'

'Bloody difficult, really. Because of the threat, you know. I have to be careful all the time, and that means avoiding routine, and of course they don't like that.'

'Have you thought of taking some time off. . . ?' The man looked across at Scott for a long time, then relaxed just a little. 'We could call it sick leave, and we'd look after you.' The man nodded.

'It's like everything else.' Toby Russell lay back in his armchair, his face hidden by the huge left foot propped up on his right knee. 'Delusions aren't what they were. When I was a lad 'twere all Nazis, and I suppose the occasional Bolshevik. Then in the fifties we went through a phase of atomic radiation . . . Droves of people rolling up saying the neighbours had atomic piles and the rays coming through the walls were interfering with their thoughts. So in his funny way your chap's giving aid and comfort to the Queen's enemies. If the IRA's finally appeared in the official register of things people feel are getting at them, in an odd sort of way they've made it. Unless of course they really are after him. You had thought of that, hadn't you?'

'Well . . .'

The foot started to shake as Toby laughed. 'No, doctor, I'm sure you're right. A couple of weeks of fresh country air out at the Lavrockdale Rest Home for Troubled Folk should get them off his tail and give him a bit of a fresh start. Any family history?'

'Says he's not in touch with them any more.'

'It figures. In the trade we call that schizoid.'

'I thought of that.'

'Oh dear, not getting paranoid about our work situation, are we?' The foot wobbled cheerfully. 'There's no need. No need at all. I'm sure your patient will do very well, doctor. Nice case, Andrew. Anything else?'

'A couple of follow-ups . . . Margaret Sorlie.'

'Oh God. I'd forgotten about her. How's she doing?'

'Came in with a sheaf of letters. Brush-offs from the BBC, the General Medical Council and the Gas Board. All proving her case, so she's quite happy. And a man at work's on the point of proposing to her.'

'May every earthly blessing be showered upon them. Anyone else?'

'Routine things. An old lady feeling better on the tablets. Depressed, a bit paranoid too, but everything's settling down. Mrs Morris. Felt dirty all the time, but OK now.'

'Grand. I remember her. Cottage at the back of Musselburgh. Cats.'

'That's her. Nothing else, really.'

'Thanks, lad. That call was grand old-fashioned lunacy, the kind of thing I used to think I'd be doing all the time. Lad of twenty-five, teacher, single. Sitting in Tranent police station explaining to the sergeant how the secret of the universe had been vouchsafed to him personally in visions at midnight on Thursday and hadn't been to bed since. On cracking good form and if I'd left it another half an hour Mr Plod could well have found himself signed up. And the jargon . . . Don't know where they get it, but in this case I suspect Dylan Thomas. Came like a lamb, though. Just sat nicely in the car all the way out to the Dale, chatting happily about how everything would be better and everybody would be grateful to him even if they didn't all understand right away.'

Perhaps people came like lambs a bit more often for psychiatrists who were softly spoken, good-humoured, quite a bit over six feet in height and permanently weatherbeaten from climbing holidays in places like Spitzbergen. Toby got up. 'There must be work to do somewhere. Just a question of finding it. Anything else in?'

'I rang in at the end of the clinic. Nothing doing.'

'Grand. Acute Kardex in Ward Six at two . . . You could be slippin' off for a quiet lunch, doctor . . .'

'I was just going to eat here.' Sandy had a regular haematology meeting at the Institute on Mondays at lunchtime.

'Might even risk the paupers' dining hall myself.'

Consultant and registrar headed together for the dining room. Once a week Dr Russell did a general psychiatry clinic in the Medical Outpatients Department at the Southern ('Not a bad thing for the likes of us to try to keep in touch with the proper doctors.') where patients from southeast Edinburgh could be seen without the inconvenience or stigma of a trip out to Lavrockdale. Scott, who had taken the clinic at short notice when Toby had been called out to Tranent, was happy enough to be joined by Toby, if only because it might help ward off the slender risk of his finding himself lunching with Gus. And there was also a matter on which some advice from an experienced but disinterested party might be of special value. He got round to it over the pudding. 'Toby . . . There's word of something happening about a joint department. Medicine and psychiatry of old age . . .'

'Ah, yes. Little birds whispering here and there. You think you got a vocation, doctor?'

'Might be interesting.'

'There's certainly a lot of it about. Old age, I mean. But it's all very preliminary. How d'you hear about it?'

'A little bird told me.'

'Hm. And did this little bird give you any details? Like who, where and when?' Scott shook his head. 'Where and when aren't so important. It's the who that's a bit worrying.'

'Really?'

'Far be it from me to cast aspersions on the motivation of a fellow-psychiatrist. Heaven forfend. But there are rumours that a colleague who very much wants to be a professor might be interested. In the professorial chair at any rate. "A chair at any price," as one of the chaps remarked. "Even if it's only a wheelchair . . ." You know Wiggy Bennett?'

'Heard of him.' Gus had emerged from the serving line, lovingly in pursuit of a mixed bag of prestigious consultant physicians. 'Don't know him.'

'Not a man I'd sup with myself, even with a very long spoon.

Determined. Devious. Disingenuous. Articulate, of course. Even quite clever. A shit though. Premier cru. Mind you, probably just the kind of shit the job needs. They have to decide. To go ahead knowing it'll almost certainly be him. Or to leave things the way they are, knowing that quite probably nothing much'll happen round here for years in the care of the elderly.'

'Who'll have to decide?' Scott, who could never talk about Sandy, sometimes found himself nudging conversation in the direction of her father as a poor substitute.

'The usual crowd. Jimmy Jameson. Gavin Lennox. And of course our own dear leader, who has no views either way, in this or any other matter. So he'll do what he's told. And Wiggy's quite pathetically keen. Get himself a name at last, and see patients at the standard professorial rate of one a month . . . God, aren't psychiatrists a bitchy lot?'

'And based where?'

'The Institute, would you believe, if it's still there. And there might even be a certain perverted logic in that. For every acute medical patient in there they've got a decent old gran waiting for somewhere to spend her declining years, and some other poor wandering soul who needs locking up except we don't ever have a bed. And it's very rarely in the National Health Service you have a problem and an answer in the same hospital, now isn't it? Assuming the hospital's still there.'

'As bad as that?'

Toby ran his spoon determinedly round his plate to capture the last traces of ginger pudding and custard. 'I was on a quiet little committee once, a couple of years ago. Token shrink, I suppose, but it was a good little committee. Took a long brave look at some awful problems around here. Came up with all the right answers, the most important of which was that we haven't needed a Royal Charitable Institute of Edinburgh for at least these past forty years. We worked bloody hard, told people things they ought to have known years ago. Got no thanks for it, and good men suffered with no good coming of it. But if the bloody place is still going to be there at least it ought to be looking through the right end of the demographic telescope. And Wiggy Bennett might be just the right kind of shit to help them do it.'

Scott tidied up the last of his cheese and biscuits. Toby was sitting back looking at him as though he might be handing in his notice that afternoon. 'It all sounds quite vague,' he said, to reassure him. 'I'd never really thought about it, and I wondered what you thought.'

'If I had me time over again, lad, I'd jump at it. No. I'd take a close look at it. It might not be the answer, but at least it's a start. Recognising the problem. You know what we're up against at Lavrockdale? It was designed for the able-bodied pauper lunatics of Haddingtonshire. It had a farm of four hundred acres and they did it all themselves. Even in the twenties they regularly fielded three football teams. And look at us now. Commodes, wheelchairs and zimmer frames everywhere. We'd be hard put to it these days to get enough fit patients together to keep an eye on the window-boxes, assuming of course that the public service unions would allow it. And lads like him this morning are light relief now. The serious stuff's dementia. Little old ladies wandering through North Berwick in their nighties worried because they're going to be late for the Sunday school. Old miners from Danderhall who wake up in the morning and don't recognise their wives, even though they've changed the sheets for them three times through the night. Medicine's the same. We looked in the wards, all round the Institute, our little committee did. We had meetings with the GP's. What do you want for Christmas, lads? A decent service for the elderly, they said. The same here at the Southern. Half the beds filled by old people waiting on something else, something the Southern hasn't got. They've had their obscure diagnoses thought about, and they don't have anything that anybody's interested in. They've had their serum marmalade levels checked, not once but on several occasions. And they're sitting waiting in a bed that costs three hundred pounds a week and they're not even being properly looked after.' Toby stopped and grinned. 'I could get quite carried away about all that if I let myself go. I really could. Shall we go and have some of their filthy coffee?'

Over coffee Toby talked about Dr Bennett. 'Odd chap. It's as though he wants to be famous but hasn't quite found anything yet to be famous for. Did a line in disease classification for a while. You can always tell when a doctor's getting bored and dangerous. He starts putting diseases before patients. Then he had this thing about the mental health of the physically ill. Another boondoggle. But it took him nicely in the direction of this latest little ploy. He'd have a couple of proper doctors working for him too, of course, sorting out the constipation and the old thyroid trouble, the ills that flesh is heir to, while he worked at developing a philosophy, because if it comes down to it that's the only thing he's any good at. So if you're still thinking about it, lad, don't say you haven't been warned. Or to put it another way: it would be a challenge.'

'There's not an awful lot else coming up.'

'You mean in Edinburgh?'

'I suppose so.'

'Have you got . . . reasons for staying around?'

'Up to a point.'

'People do, even though they shouldn't.' Toby was looking quizzical again. 'Andrew, you don't mind me asking . . .' he had lowered his voice. 'You're not gay, are you, lad?'

'No.'

'Nothing personal. Just wondered . . . Single. Navy. Your funny lunches. Nothing against it meself. It just wouldn't suit Wiggy one bit. That's to say he'd feel he had to pretend it didn't matter, but it would. But then if you're not it wouldn't be an issue, would it?'

'Quite.'

'So if you're just looking for a challenge, doctor . . .'

August 1976

'Dr Ratho?' The first year nurse, the one with grubby, chewed fingernails that upset sister, looked round the edge of the door and when she saw sister was there too withdrew her hand, leaving only her head sticking out, like a puppet show on its side. 'Telephone for you, Dr Ratho. It's a man.'

Sister raised her eyebrows, but jokingly, and Sandy got up to go to the ward phone, which was in a stuffy little box near the staff loo: not one of the Institute's more pleasant phones, but conveniently private for certain sorts of conversation.

'Hello. Dr Ratho speaking.'

'Oh hello, doctor,' said a man, but not one she knew, which in its way was a relief. 'Dr Gray here. Gorgie Road practice. Got an old lady you'll probably remember. A patient of yours . . . Well, of Dr Parkinson's, but you've done all the letters. Chronic lymphatic leukaemia . . .'

Sandy was getting used to phone calls like this. They tended to go on and on until whoever it was eventually got to the difficult bit. The sooner they did the better. 'Who is it and what's wrong?' she said, sounding much snappier than she had meant to.

'Well, doctor,' said the GP, who was probably quite a nice chap when he wasn't trying to off-load some ghastly problem on to a ward that had enough of them already. 'As I was saying, you'll remember her perfectly well. Forrest, Mrs Forrest. Chronic lymphatic leukaemia.'

'Yes,' said Sandy. Mrs Forrest was an old lady whose leukaemia was among the least of her problems. 'What's wrong with her now?'

'Well, you know she has leg ulcers, and diabetes . . . Usually not too difficult to control . . . And the district nurses have really done quite well considering. But she's just . . . not right.'

Sandy bit back a few sharp sentences about had he done her

haemoglobin and a white cell count to see just exactly how her leukaemia was doing, and a blood sugar because that was often quite useful in diabetics, and did he know that just about as many people died with chronic lymphatic leukaemia as died of it.

'Her blood sugar's all right,' said the man. 'I'm waiting on other results, the haemoglobin and all that. And to be frank I don't think it's going to be any different from the last time. But her downstairs neighbour's about ready to give up . . . So maybe if you could just take her in for a wee while and try and sort things out.'

Mrs Forrest was easy to remember. As well as her not very serious leukaemia and her diabetes, she was blind and getting a bit senile too. If she was rattling around in a fourth floor flat in Gorgie, with the downstairs neighbour – a nice woman who had come in a lot the last time she was in the ward – going bonkers worrying about her then it was time she was in again. 'That's fine, Dr Gray. Just send her in.'

'Oh,' said the man as if he had been expecting to have to shout at her. 'Thank you very much. Thank you very much indeed. I'll organise the ambulance right away. Good day to you.'

'Thank you, Dr Gray.'

'Thank *you* . . .'

Sandy put the phone down. That left one haematology bed for half of Edinburgh, and she was meant to have two and at least another two just for the haemophiliacs who came to the Institute from all over Southeast Scotland. So if a haemophiliac butcher boy in Selkirk got attacked by a bacon slicer or even just fell off his bike there would be none left for the whole weekend, and once Mrs Forrest was in she might never get out again. Perhaps the really surprising thing was how long she had managed since last time, and perhaps if she died quite quickly and comfortably of whatever it was this time that might even be the best thing. Sandy went back to sister's room to finish her coffee.

'Well, Dr Ratho,' said sister. 'Was it a nice man?' It was a joke but perhaps a probing one. Sandy had been spending quite a lot of time in the stuffy phone box over the last few months, and sometimes, just sometimes, when she wasn't carrying the registrar's bleep Andrew rang her on the ward and if sister had ever happened to pick up the phone she might just possibly have recognised his voice because he had done six months there a few years ago as Dr Marks' SHO.

'Mrs Forrest's GP.'

'Oh dear,' said sister. 'That leaves us with just one bed. What's wrong with her?'

'He's not sure, and I was nearly quite firm with him. But at least she won't get here until after Dr Parkinson's been round.' Dr Parkinson had been getting very strange recently about what he called 'these wretched social admissions' and had written some distinctly odd letters about them. One old lady, a woman with a stroke who cried and giggled for hours on end, he had formally abandoned, although she remained on the ward blocking a bed just as immovably as when he had recognised her as his patient. Sister and the nurses looked after her just the same as before, and Sandy kept an eye on her, not that she needed much in the way of medical care, but the label at the top of her bed now read 'Dr Smith' because Dr Parkinson had decided that she was the responsibility of rather a silly man who sat in an office somewhere up under the Institute's clock tower rejoicing in the title of community medicine specialist, but who in practice was just the administration's tame doctor.

'You'll probably get away with it,' said sister. 'Unless he's decided to bring someone in from the clinic and forgotten to tell us. Honestly, Sandy, I'm getting more and more fed up with him. I've even tried to sow the seeds of early retirement, but you might as well be dropping hints at a brick wall for all the atttention he pays.'

'He'd be miserable,' said Sandy. 'He wouldn't know what to do with himself if he didn't have his patients. Sadly for him.'

'And for them,' said sister, sniffing. Sandy, if anyone had asked her for her views on whether Dr Parkinson ought to retire early, would have said he should definitely work until the last possible minute. He was sixty one and if he went in four years time she would probably be the right kind of senior registrar – local, competent, academically quite successful and just the right seniority – to pass muster for the resulting consultant vacancy.

Although that was not the sort of thing you would go confiding in a ward sister, Sandy and Gus had actually discussed it more or less in these terms. He would work his way up the local hierarchy by giving the Southern a far better clinical immunology service than it deserved. With luck he would get a senior lecturer job quite soon, and she would stay at the Institute and be the kind of consultant haematologist that nobody raved about but who at least knew when it wasn't worth poisoning people any more just to improve the survival figures. Then – and after that stage it all became a bit iffy – Gus might start going for chairs in other places. Edinburgh was fine, and where they both came from, but if he wanted to be a professor, which he actually did quite a lot, they might have to go to somewhere like Sheffield or Leicester and she would just fit in with that, resigning and taking a chance on something suitable coming up at the other end, or just having a few years at home with the children, if there were any. And in the long term, and that was something they had discussed too, they might eventually come back to Edinburgh, because quite a lot of the people who got chairs there had actually been professors before in what you weren't meant to think of as one of the lesser medical schools. And the children, if there ever were any, could still get a chance to do at least a bit of their growing up in Edinburgh.

With sister watching her, Sandy picked up another biscuit that she didn't really want and started to do something she had tried for years to stop herself from doing, recently with a lot less success. With a silly and unnecessary half-coated chocolate digestive in her hand she thought again about the non-person, the non-event who would have changed everything for better or for worse, the non-child now not aged eight and a bit, the chance they had been given that had not come up again. It was like one of the really cruel fairy stories, the kind that left you feeling angry and sad, where someone got what they wanted, didn't know it, spoiled it and regretted it for ever: wishes wasted, magic caverns glimpsed and then closed off for eternity, awful punishments for moments of thoughtlessness, and whoever it wasn't, non-boy or non-girl, was not now eight, not in primary school and not rushing home each afternoon to tell them things that didn't matter but mattered hugely when you were eight. Or not eight or not ever. Perhaps never ever.

'Are you all right, Sandy. . . ?'

Sandy smiled and put down the biscuit. 'I'm not hungry. Just greedy. Sorry, sister.'

'Oh there you are . . . Yes. Sandy . . . Ah . . . Sister. The top of the morning to you. Come on, Sandy. Nothing to be glum about . . . And where's Laurence? Sandy, would you mind bleeping the houseman. I don't know where he gets to on Friday mornings. Should know perfectly well by now. And aren't we supposed to have some students? Sister, you haven't seen the students this morning, have you? And how many beds do we have for the weekend?'

Sandy slipped past Dr Parkinson and made for the phone box to bleep Laurence Simpson, the houseman. With any luck he would take ages to answer, and sister could listen to the usual nonsense about how am I expected to run a regional service and what about all my leukaemia patients and what if a plane crashes at Edinburgh airport with a full load of haemophiliacs taking off for Lourdes. The exchange took ages to answer and so did the houseman when they eventually bleeped him, and Sandy stood in the stuffy telephone box waiting and thinking a number of silly things, like what they would be having for tea if they had a person aged eight to feed as well, and what to do about Andrew and what if Gus, who now seemed more interested in children than he was in sex, started messing about the way she was doing, even if it wasn't with someone as nice as Andrew, whom she was on the point of phoning when the houseman finally answered his bleep.

'Laurence? You know that Dr Parkinson's ready to go round now?'

'Oh. Sorry, Sandy. Dr Marks wanted me to come round his men with him so I knew about them for the weekend. He's just finishing. Another two minutes?'

'Hmm. Two minutes at the very outside. He's not very happy.'

'Neither is Dr Marks, but I'll come up as soon as he lets me.'

Dr Parkinson and Dr Marks were still not speaking, and still trying to inconvenience each other as much as possible without appearing overtly to be doing so. 'Do your best,' said Sandy. 'I'll try to stall my one a bit. Thanks, Laurence.'

'Thanks, Sandy.'

Instead of going back to the emergent ward round to detain Dr Parkinson with a lot of boring results he didn't really need to know about Sandy picked up the phone again. This time the exchange answered straight away. 'Oh. Hello. Could you please bleep Dr Scott, the senior registrar in the Care of the Elderly Unit, and ask him to ring this number? Thanks.' Sandy stood and waited in the airless booth, but at least Andrew always answered his bleep really quickly.

'Hello?'

'It's me.'

'Thought it might be. How are you?'

'Getting fed up with silly ward rounds. How are you?'

'Oh, all right. Wiggy and Kevin are off being famous somewhere, so I'm getting to mind the shop.'

'Busy?'

'Not really, but don't tell anyone.'

'Andrew . . .'

'Are you all right?'

'Yes. Andrew . . .'

'What?'

'If I'm a golf widow tomorrow, are you around?'

'Yes. Well, sort of. I said I'd go to something in the afternoon . . . You could come too.'

'Could I?'

'You could. Honest. Absolutely no one you'd know, I promise. And miles away. I'd love you to.'

'What is it?'

'Somebody being thirty. And nobody's a doctor.'

'I'd really like to see you.'

'It's miles out. Eddleston. And really nice people. You'd like them. And they're not remotely medical or nosey or anything.'

Sandy hesitated. It was tricky. She wanted to see Andrew, but just for a nice quiet afternoon in Marchmont and he, quite reasonably, had arranged something else because she hadn't phoned him for nearly a week. But if it was something they could go to together then she probably ought to go if he really was sure no one who knew her would be there. He had a lot of odd friends outside medicine, which was nice, and if he was inviting her to one of their things at least it more or less proved that none of them was his girlfriend as well. And he had been really patient for ages and ages about not doing anything except lunches and afternoons in Marchmont, which was sweet of him considering all the other things people normally did. And Laurence was about to appear and then Dr Parkinson would begin to think things about her for being still stuck in the phone box. It was all very tricky.

'Perhaps if we left around two-ish,' Andrew said in a very matter-of-fact, married sort of way.

'All right. But I might want to wear dark glasses and a headscarf, at least until we're a bit out of town.'

'Fine.' He was laughing in a way she could see and practically feel. 'Good idea.'

'I'll come to the flat. Two-ish. See you tomorrow, Andrew.'

'See you tomorrow.'

Sandy put the phone down and had a momentary panic about what she had just agreed to, then another, lesser one about what you were supposed to wear to the thirtieth birthday party of an unknown Bohemian out in the country in August, given also that you were attending it with someone you were committing adultery with and were actually at the same time trying quite hard to stop committing adultery with. '*Dear Marje Proops . . .*' And the answer was probably something with a bit of scarlet in it, but not too much. On her way back to the ward round Sandy admitted to herself that the problems presented by poor sincere uncouth Dr Parkinson and his unfortunate patients were actually quite simple compared to some of the other things in her life, and she even beat the houseman to it by a good half minute.

'Come on, Laurence.' Dr Parkinson shook his head menacingly, like a bull about to charge. 'We can't wait all morning. Where have you been? Surely by this time you know the routine.'

'Sorry I'm late,' said Laurence, still breathless from the stairs. It was a convention that housemen on Sir Ronald's unit, who had to work both for Dr Parkinson and Dr Marks as well, did not mention either of the latter two in the presence of the other. 'Very sorry, Dr Parkinson.'

'All right. But try to do better in future . . . And Laurence, what about the students?'

'Um, I think they might have been detained . . . on the male ward, Dr Parkinson.'

'The male ward? Oh. I see. Well, we'll just have to manage without them, won't we, Sandy? So who have we got today?'

They moved into the ward. Not having the students helped a lot, and Dr Parkinson got round in about half the time he would have taken if they'd been there. A good teaching spleen went untaught on and lot of the usual nonsensical things were left unsaid. The poor old lady now nominally under the care of Dr Smith even got a smile instead of the usual huddled tirade she was probably getting quite used to, and the matter of the precarious bed-state for the weekend was not discussed or even mentioned again. At the end, just when they were getting ready to go downstairs and do the men, Dr Parkinson suddenly stopped and put his hand on Sandy's shoulder. 'You feeling all right, Sandy?' She nodded but he looked at her even more closely and said 'You sure, Sandy? Not our usual cheerful self at all today, are we?'

Sandy smiled and sister frowned and Dr Parkinson took his hand away. 'All right? Good. Shall we pop downstairs now and see the gentlemen? But only if you're sure you're feeling all right, Sandy . . . You sure you wouldn't prefer to take it easy? Maybe just go straight down to the lab or the library . . . I could quite easily manage the rest just with the houseman.' Shrieking at him wouldn't help, either for now or for when it came to references and senior registrar interviews. Sandy smiled more determinedly than ever and decided that if that was what happened to her less than an hour after agreeing to a proper date with Andrew it really was time she gave him up, even if he was lovely in Marchmont.

About halfway through the afternoon, when she was sitting in the lab looking at reports that about four people had looked at already, initialling them because she alone among the scrutineers was the proud possessor of a medical degree, Sandy realised that she actually did feel a bit odd: not ill, and not swimmy as she had felt in the sweaty phone box in the morning, and certainly not just guilty, but odd in a faint yet quite specific way that she had felt only once in her life before. She was pregnant. She stopped with her pen in mid air and looked out of the lab window, across the car park and the Meadows, to Marchmont of all places. People sometimes said that they knew about the second time really early because it felt like the first time, which didn't really feel like anything because you didn't actually know what it was. And she was certain, and after a minute's calculation even fairly certain it was Gus, because the main reason she hadn't been seeing so much of Andrew recently was that she had been half-consciously rationing him to times when nothing much could happen. She looked at her watch and noted the time, the date and the month in her head, and even that it was nine years and five months since the last time, which had officially ended two months later in Glasgow, but really at the pirate rock on the beach at North Berwick the month before that. This time it would all be very, very different.

In the event Sandy did not wear a headscarf. She just put her hair up and wore sunglasses until they were safely through Auchendinny and out into open countryside. Then she took off her glasses and Andrew reached across from the driver's seat and held her hand for a bit, which was sweet and sad, because she knew what he was thinking about and back then it would all have been very much simpler. When he stopped holding her hand she let her hair down and shook it out and he reached across to her again, this time to ruffle her hair before she combed it. He was a loving and sincere person and in lots of ways more innocent than he knew, and it wasn't going to be easy for him, but it might be at least a little bit easier if she told him after the rural birthday party rather than before. Sandy thought about it and decided exactly when she would tell him, then sat for quite a long time before she could think of anything else to talk about.

'So what sort of people will it be?'

'No one you know. Honest.'

'I believe you. But what sort of people I don't know?'

Andrew thought about that all the way round a long corner and into an upland straight going on for miles across a sun-baked moor. 'Nineteen sixty eight people, mainly. You know, from student politics then but getting a bit serious about themselves now.'

'And who's the birthday boy?' As she said that Sandy realised she had assumed, for reasons mainly to do with possessiveness about Andrew, that it wasn't a birthday girl.

'Nice chap. Not a student politician.' Sandy laughed but Andrew went for a serious explanation. 'He appeared the year before from down South, and was a kind of administrator for bits of the SRC.'

'Making sure the sit-ins ran on time?'

'Publications mainly, and seeing to the offices. And the rest will probably be mainly retired student politicians, not famous for anything else yet but working on it. A couple of them are in TV and journalism and that kind of thing. And his girlfriend's really nice.'

'There's bound to be someone I know.'

Andrew reached out and held her hand again. 'Probably not. And I think quite a few of them got their first marriages over quickly, so nobody's going to report you to the Kirk Session.'

'Andrew . . .'

'What?'

'I've never actually done anything like this before.' He laughed and squeezed her hand. 'Am I wearing the right sort of clothes?'

'Marvellous.'

She was actually wearing very much the same as she had been wearing the night he had come round to the Forrest Hill flat and hadn't taken her clothes off, something he might or might not have noticed. 'Good. That's one less thing to worry about. And Andrew . . .'

'What?'

'My wedding ring.'

'Oh. I'd forgotten about that. Up to you. But nobody's from the Church of Scotland thought police.'

'Sorry, Andrew, I'm being silly. Put it down to inexperience. What's he called?'

'Charles.'

'What's his second name?'

'Savage. But it's honestly not going to be a second name kind of afternoon.'

'Good,' said Sandy. 'I'm glad about that,' but she had already decided to keep her wedding ring on anyway, because it really wouldn't have been fair to him to do otherwise. This time she squeezed his hand. 'Sorry for being so silly, Andrew. I'll drive us home if you like, if you want to get a bit drunk.'

'Thanks.'

They turned off the main road and up a gravel track shaded by trees and found the party, which was in a big garden outside a little stone cottage standing by itself on the edge of a wood. People were sitting around in groups on the lawn simmering in the sun and from a quick first look round there seemed to be nobody Sandy knew. The birthday boy, a large, softly spoken man with glasses, seemed quite pleased to see Andrew and said hello to her without staring at her left hand, which probably just meant that this was the sort of party where most people came with other people's wives. Then the birthday boy introduced someone called Crumlin, who had mutton chop whiskers and a suit left over from an Edwardian shooting party. He had just been adopted as the prospective Tory candidate for West Fife and was full of it, being amusing about the local Tory ladies and chatting Sandy up as if she were a very important local Tory lady too. Andrew, who didn't appear to like him very much, was at least quite amused by all that, and seemed to enjoy her being there, which was fine for this afternoon but a bit sad in the longer term.

Then Sandy spotted somebody she did vaguely know, a girl from school who had done the big sixties revolt to the extent of having joined an ashram somewhere in Stockbridge: a Jane somebody, though she had probably changed it a couple of times for reasons to do with Indian religion. While Andrew was talking to Charles she sidled up and said hello, obviously dying to know what Sandy was doing at a thing like this, so Sandy talked firmly about medicine to stop her asking about that, and the girl went off on a helpfully long tangent about a series of outrages that had happened to her in the course of what sounded like an averagely ghastly NHS confinement. The child, it turned out, had not suffered much, and was rooting around among the lettuces at the bottom of the garden. It looked blissfully happy there and they stood for quite a while just watching, then Sandy suddenly found herself having to go to unexpected lengths to avoid telling Jane that she had just found out that she was going to have a baby too.

The second person she vaguely knew was the big Roedean socialist they had met at Jimmy's, who had seemed to know the Jimmies awfully well and would almost certainly remember that she had been there with Gus. Quite quickly it became obvious that Roedean prepared you for that sort of thing a lot better than Easdaile did, and they had a civilised conversation about the delights of living in the country, which neither of them had actually tried but which passed the time quite nicely while Walker and Andrew talked about David Steel, who had been SRC senior president at Edinburgh within living memory and had just been elected leader of the Liberals: an honour which Walker was convinced would not in the long run turn out to be much of an improvement on his previous eminence.

There was lots to drink, mainly Pimm's, and dry white wine with soda water, and plenty of non-alcoholic things for drivers, and a bit after four there were things to eat, sensible for a hot day like vichyssoise, salads and cold fishy stuff and some nice summery puddings. They ate on the lawn with Walker and the Roedean girl and someone who sounded half-American who talked a lot and wanted everyone to know he was in television. Andrew, who turned

373

out to know quite a lot about lots of things that were nothing to do with medicine, coped well with the half-American, who was the only one who was anything like really drunk, as though they had known each other for a long time and had been drunk together before. Sandy sat happily in the sun with her soft drink and the summery food, listening to them talking about the politics of the university, and about NATO and about journalism, both student and grown-up, and found herself being quite proud of Andrew: he was sensible and sometimes funny too and would probably find someone else nice fairly quickly when he had to, which was sad for her and probably for him too, but in the new circumstances now absolutely inevitable.

At about six coffee came round and by half past people were beginning to make going-away noises. For a few tricky minutes Sandy wondered if Andrew was going to offer one of his drunker friends a lift home with them, which would have made the next bit a little awkward, but they reached his car by themselves and he handed over the keys without saying anything, as though they had been married for years. Adjusting the driver's seat turned out to be quite difficult, with Andrew having to heave and grunt down in front of her in a way that made Sandy want to grab him and pull him into the bushes. Instead she altered her plans for the rest of their time together just a little, mainly because of that but at least partly because Gus had said he wouldn't be home until about eight.

All the way back Andrew was quiet but not relaxed, as though he knew what was going to happen. They talked hardly at all, except for one silly conversation about seeing cars with the new registration letter, R, which once you started noticing them seemed to be everywhere. When they got to Marchmont he acted as if she wasn't going to come up and instead was just going to cross the road to her own car and drive away, so without saying anything she held his hand and looked at him earnestly until he invited her up for what they had found themselves over their few months together calling a quick coffee. Once in the flat they made straight for the bedroom, stripped off as if it were a race and hurtled naked towards each other in the middle of the bed, with neither of them thinking even for an instant about contraception. Twenty minutes later they had got to the point in Sandy's revised timetable where she was going to tell him, and instead she lay in his arms wondering for a while if she needed to now, because he had been so sad and loving and intense that she was sure he knew already. Then after that, and still in his arms, she had a long and silly silent conversation with herself wondering if she really had to at all, and whether they might not just go on for a bit longer much as they had done over the last six weeks or so, seeing each other less often but no less intensely and, if she were honest with herself, enjoyably, until it was absolutely definite, by the most rigorous laboratory standards, that she was completely and irrevocably pregnant, and therefore seriously married to Gus and no longer in a position to be any of all the nice things she had been to Andrew as well.

January 1979

'Just so long as you understand our position, doctor . . .' The man was standing far too close, so close that Gus could smell the chips and stale beer on his breath. The other two, one on each side of him and a bit ahead so that they formed a short, enfolding barrier to Gus's further progress, seemed to be quite enjoying his discomfiture.

'I don't actually work here,' Gus said, as politely as he could. 'But I do understand your position . . . It must be terribly difficult.'

'Terribly,' said the man in the middle. The man on the left, who had set the whole thing off by shouting 'Hello, doctor', started to laugh, and Gus recognised him. Menacing now, in a large and battered anorak with its hood up because of the sleet, he looked very different. He had aged quite quickly, the way working class men seemed to, and had put on a lot of weight and hadn't shaved for a day or two, but there was no doubt about it. He was called Bobby or perhaps Billy and a good number of years ago, maybe even as many as ten or twelve, he had been a junior lab boy in haematology, seconded to Roger Killick's unit to see some basic immunological techniques when Gus had been working on his honours project. Gus had always been perfectly civil to him, and had let him do simple things like nutrient dilutions and tried to explain them as well, even though he had really just been there to see how things were done and to help with the used glassware. And now, by recognising him and shouting 'Hello, doctor,' the man had triggered off a nasty little scene that was virtually preventing him from getting into the Institute.

'Maybe you'd like a pamphlet,' said the man in the middle.

'Oh, yes, please,' said Gus. Somehow that made all three of them laugh insanely.

'Jim! Hey, Jim . . . The doctor here would terribly appreciate one of our wee pamphlets.' The man in the middle shouted all that out very loud and with a silly put-on accent, and someone standing by a smoky fire in an old oil drum on the other side of the main gate came across with a whole bundle of them. 'Take three or four . . .' said the newcomer. 'You'll probably want to give them to all your friends.' Gus found himself being handed a sheaf of about a dozen. 'Thank you,' he said as coldly as possible. 'Now I really must be going.' The wall in front of him had grown to include four people and the mood was distinctly uglier than before.

'A lot of people make a wee contribution towards the printing and other strike expenses,' said the man with the pamphlets. 'It's not obligatory.'

'Quite,' said Gus. 'Now if you'll just excuse me . . .' He feinted to the right then nipped smartly to the left and past the picket line. 'Thank you.'

The four turned to jeer him as he threw the pamphlets down in a puddle and went through the gate and across the car park. The group round the brazier was shouting after him too, with one or two of them even giving him the V-sign. Gus, who had had no very strong prior views on the dispute but had been vaguely sympathetic because the lower grades of NHS worker didn't seem to be paid very much, looked back at them, once from the top of the steps and again after he had gone through the double doors of the main entrance to the hospital and into the warmth of the surgical corridor. Small and far away and standing around foolishly in the icy puddles left by the sleet, the men in the picket line receded into their proper perspective; and so far as Gus was concerned, the nastier the weather the better.

Even before all this had started Gus had come thoroughly to dislike the Institute, despite its being the hospital he had known best for the first twenty something years of his life. At the most rational level, it was as if working at the Southern for a few years now had given him an entirely different view of it. Across at the Southern there was a commitment to good investigative medicine and high-quality clinical research. Work got done and papers got published because people there were still interested in building up a reputation, while at the Institute most of them seemed to be resting on laurels earned thirty or forty years ago by surgeons like Learmonth and Dott and the physicians of his father's generation and perhaps even the one before that. That the Institute had, over the last ten years or so, outlived its usefulness was one of the few things that Lennie and Gus had seen eye to eye on towards the end.

At a more personal level, Gus had been really quite glad to leave a hospital where immunology was still regarded as rather dubious because of its association with the events leading up to Roger's departure years and years ago. But that was very much the way they thought there: in terms of personalities rather than of ideas and achievements, and on a time-scale in which events of over a decade ago were regarded as having happened only the day before yesterday. And Gus, if he were honest with himself, had not really enjoyed his pre-registration year there very much either, though most people who had done housejobs at the Institute claimed never to have worked so hard or have been so happy in all their lives. After six months of surgery, Sir Edgar had scarcely even thanked him, and on the medical side Sir Ronald had rarely spoken to him over the whole of his time there other than to pass on his regards to his father or Lennie.

Then there had been the long, miserable business of Sandy, who had been working at the Institute when it had begun to become obvious that the whole thing had been a ghastly mistake from start to finish. Now that it was all over it was as though they had agreed, tacitly rather than amicably, that the terms of their divorce left him with the Southern, which he liked, and her with the Institute, which he now disliked more than ever. But at least she wasn't working there any more, so there was no risk of running into her tripping along the surgical corridor having cheerfully and competently sorted out some haematological problem on a surgical ward, the typical haematological problem referred by the surgeons being something well within the capabilities of the average fourth year student.

Perhaps because of the strike, the surgical corridor was unusually disgusting. Years ago it had been a kind of showpiece, with maroon walls, a smart, diagonally-chequered black and white floor and an eccentric collection of paintings, plaques and statuary that made it look like a rather pretentious local museum. Now it was dull and shabby, with the paint on the walls cracked and chipped and roughly cleaned only to the level a union-protected dwarf could reach without risking life and limb by standing on tiptoe. The floor tiling was grubby and splitting and had been patched here and there with tiles that didn't quite blend in, and outside each ward, as far as the eye could see in either direction, was a drift of big plastic bags, some black, some yellow, with several days' worth of uncollected laundry and garbage, all no doubt courtesy of what were now laughingly known as the public service trade unions.

Gus turned to the left in front of the silly picture of Queen Victoria and took the stair down to the lower surgical corridor and the orthopaedic unit. It was all very inconvenient. If the orthopaedic unit at the Southern, which was perfectly all right but just didn't have very many beds, had had a place vacant when his mother had fallen at home, the whole business would have been a great deal less tiresome.

As he went into the ward the staff nurse in charge was lying in wait for him and got up from the desk at the nursing station to stop him just going straight into the side room on the right.

'Dr Ratho, can I just. . . ?'

'Yes?'

'Dr Ratho, I think the houseman would quite like to have a word with you about your mother before you go in to see her . . . The consultant, Mr Cruickshank, would have seen you himself and sends his apologies . . . But if you wouldn't mind waiting . . . Please have a seat. You could use the doctors' room.' They crossed the corridor to a large, untidy office in which every horizontal surface was covered by a hopeless jumble of case-notes and X-rays. 'Please have a seat, Dr Ratho. Doctor shouldn't be a minute. He's just seeing some relatives.'

'Thanks, staff.'

Gus sat down on the only chair in the room, which happened to be at the desk, and without particularly meaning to found himself going through the untidy heap of casenotes to see if he could find out how far they had got with the problematical case of Monica Fiona Adelaide Ratho, aged sixty two, an acute orthopaedic admission from three days before. He was still discreetly rummaging, with his back to the door of the office, when someone coughed behind him.

'Dr Ratho? So glad I could have a chance to speak to you . . .' A young Indian or Pakistani in a white coat advanced towards him with hand outstretched. Gus shook it to get it over with, and because most foreign doctors would never even begin to realise how little time the medical profession in Scotland wasted on shaking hands. 'I am Dr Gopal, the JHO. Mr Cruickshank sends his apologies, but asked me particularly to look out for you, Dr Ratho. As you know, sadly, your mother is not really at all well.'

Gus nodded. The man was standing silent and awkward as though he did not know what to say or do next. 'Mr Cruickshank is most sorry . . . He saw your father, for whom he has the highest respect, yesterday and hoped also to see you . . .' He smiled a white toothy smile. 'Would you like to go across to sister's room, where we could sit down. . . ?'

'Perhaps if you could just tell me what's happening now, Dr Gopal.'

'Yes. Yes. What is happening. As I said just now, there are some difficulties, one or two problems that have delayed the normally prompt surgery offered to a fractured hip. Your mother has had, shall we say, only indifferent previous health . . .'

Gus thought of the tantrums, collapses and hangovers, the glassy certainty of his mother when drunk, the hideous uncertainty of how each binge would end. 'Yes, really for some years now . . . But we'd been expecting her to go to theatre this morning.' What they had been expecting was that she would go to have her hip pinned or whatever the day she had been admitted, if not first thing the following morning. It had now been postponed twice, once because she had vomited some blood – which was scarcely surprising given what they knew about her liver and her oesophageal varices – and once because Hamish Cruickshank had planned to operate on her himself but had been delayed until early evening, by which time the necessary X-ray service in theatre had been discontinued because the radiographers had suddenly, in response to a call from the public service trade unions, decided not to work overtime. When Gus had phoned in that morning he had been told that his mother was once more fasting for theatre and would in all probability be taken there by mid-morning, since Mr Cruickshank liked to get his NHS operating over early. 'So has something else cropped up, Dr Gopal?'

'Yes and no, I'm afraid. There are two considerations really, Dr Ratho, one a matter of anaesthetics. Mr Cruickshank, quite correctly for a lady who is not only the wife of a retired consultant physician but also the mother of one working locally, thought it proper that the anaesthetist in such a case should also himself be a consultant.'

'I don't think we'd insist on that . . . Certainly not if it was going to hold things up.'

'A sensible view, Dr Ratho, but unfortunately it already has. Mr Cruickshank rang in to say that he would rather wait, obviously not knowing your views. And there is another matter . . . Two really.'

'Yes?'

'Unfortunately, with all this starting and delaying, your mother is not now quite herself. I thought it best to tell you that before you went in.'

Since three days was probably the longest Mopsy Ratho had gone without a drink for as many decades, that too was scarcely surprising, but there was no particular reason to discuss it all in detail with Dr Gopal. Gus nodded sympathetically. 'And the other matter?'

'I am sorry about this, Dr Ratho. We are also encountering some electrolyte problems, perhaps accounting for her acute change of mental status, perhaps arising from her poor intake because of fasting once or twice for theatre, and with her small upper GI bleed . . . But I think they will be sorted out in time for tomorrow. That is good news. So Mr Cruickshank has asked me to say that tomorrow, quite early in the morning, he will himself operate on your mother, who will find herself feeling much better very soon, I hope, and beginning to walk really quite quickly. In fact most of our patients . . .'

The man had clearly switched to automatic and was saying the kind of thing he said to more or less everyone. Gus smiled firmly again. 'Thank you so much, Dr Gopal. Is it all right if I just go in?'

'Or course, Dr Ratho.'

Gus nodded and thanked him and got away without any more handshakes. The nurse who had talked to him earlier was still standing watchfully at the nursing station. Again she approached him. 'Dr Ratho, we've had to move your mother. She's not in the single room any more. We thought it would be better to keep a closer eye on her, in the main ward . . . just meantime. She's here. Mrs Ratho? Mrs Ratho. . . ?'

Mopsy lay back with her eyes closed and her mouth open, looking awful without her teeth. 'Mrs Ratho . . .' The nurse touched her lightly on the shoulder and she woke slowly and shook her head. 'Mrs Ratho, your son's here.'

Mopsy turned towards Gus and her face assumed a dangerous liveliness. She waved her silly little quasi-royal wave then smiled and almost began to talk before remembering she didn't have her teeth in. She put her hand up over her mouth. 'Angus!' Her voice was thick and indistinct. 'How lovely! Do come in, dear . . . We're just having a drink. And where's Sandy? And how *is* your poor baby?' Gus took his mother's hand and nodded at the nurse to indicate she could push off now, then sat for a while looking sympathetic while Mopsy told him about the party, the wild animals, the squad of painters and the fire that had almost destroyed the ward the night before.

'Robbie?'

'Hello?'

'Robbie, can I just pick your brains for a minute. . . ?'

'Sure. What's the problem?'

'Not sure, and it's all getting nastier and nastier . . .'

'Tell me about it.' Caroline, the duty anaesthetic registrar on the orthopaedic rota, still in her theatre kit, came into the little departmental library and sat down. Robbie leaned back and stretched. The girl was sensible but not very experienced, very much the sort of registrar who was forever getting hold of Robbie to sort out something they didn't know about, couldn't be bothered to look up and didn't want to trouble a consultant with. Robbie, as the most junior senior registrar, fielded on average two or three such queries a day, and did so quite happily, because he knew a lot and didn't actually have very much to do. 'It's orthopaedic?'

'Yes. Hamish Cruickshank's list for tomorrow. I was just taking a look at them. Woman of sixty three. Drinks.'

'Cirrhosis?'

'Think so. And it's getting quite complicated. Came in on Sunday. Right hip, and still hasn't been done.'

'Hmm. Pass the parcel?'

'Sort of.'

'But tomorrow's the day, and you're going to have a go?' The girl nodded. Robbie approved. The worst thing that could happen to someone waiting for major orthopaedic surgery after an injury was that they could be seen by a fairly junior anaesthetist who, perhaps quite late in the day and after the patient had been fasted from ten o'clock the night before, would decide that there was some contra-indication to anaesthetising them. That anaesthetist would then cancel the procedure, knowing that by so doing they had effectively dodged the responsibility, because the following day some other junior anaesthetist would take over the duty. And there was nothing to stop the same thing happening four or five days in a row, but somehow nobody seemed to have complained about it. Robbie, in his capacity as the most experienced junior anaesthetist around, had tried to sort it out by getting people at least to put their reasons for delay in writing and then discuss them with someone more senior. It didn't seem to have made much difference. 'And the story so far?'

'They were going to do her on Monday, and she might or might not have had a small bleed, so Gerry cancelled her.'

'Clotting all right?'

'I think so. Well, she was on Monday. They screened her after Gerry cancelled her in case she might not be. She was fine.'

'Right. She in liver failure?'

'Doesn't seem to be.'

'Drunks are funny. I mean their livers are. Until they actually go over the edge it takes buckets of whatever you're using to knock them out. And then when they decompensate you can kill them with half a teaspoonful. There was an interesting review in one of the Scandinavian journals the other week. But it sounds like this lady's still the kind that's going to need a lot . . . And they get odd problems because of poor nutrition. She eating OK?'

'The odd slice of lemon with her gin and tonic, from the sound of things.'

'Oh dear.'

'And there's one other thing, Robbie.'

'What?'

'She's Mrs somebody. A medical wife.'

'Hm. Who?'

'Ratho. Monica Ratho. I've no idea who Dr Ratho is, but he seems to be quite important. And she's been cancelled again today.'

'God,' said Robbie. 'You should have said.' He got up to look at the consultant rota on the notice board. 'Don't touch her. Get your consultant. It's . . . let's see. Hm. Gilbert. Give him a ring.'

'That's the tricky thing, Robbie. I have, and he said just carry on. And yesterday they were going to do her at six, but the radiographers weren't doing overtime.'

Robbie got up. 'Let's go and have a look at her. And if you're worried I'll take you through it tomorrow.'

'Thanks, Robbie. But . . .'

'OK . . . If you're really worried I'll do her and you can just watch. Let's go and see her now and go over a few things . . .'

When they got to the doctors' room on the female orthopaedic ward the resident seemed quite pleased to see them. Robbie introduced himself and asked for the case notes. The file was thick and untidy, with letters going back to the fifties, all of which sounded much the same. Robbie flicked through them. 'Usual stuff, Caroline . . . "Charming lady, highly strung, wife of esteemed colleague etc. Probably nothing too serious going on, glad to see her again if you're worried." And either they didn't know she was on the sauce or they were too polite to put it in writing. And one son. Yes. That's the awfully nice Angus. Year above me. Bright and pushy . . . Consultant at the Southern now . . .'

'He was visiting just now,' said Dr Gopal. 'A very nice man.'

'Too smooth to be true,' said Robbie. 'And a bit of a bastard to his wife. Well, ex-wife now. Nice girl from my year. But we've still got to do the best for his poor old drunk mum. What does she admit to?'

'Occasional sherry,' said the resident. 'But perhaps more, I think.'

'I bet . . . And any signs of liver failure?'

'No.'

'And the bleed on Monday?'

'Not a very serious one.'

'Any history or investigations to suggest she's done it before?' Again Robbie riffled through the notes. 'Nothing in here going for it . . . Never had a barium meal or swallow, doesn't seem to have bled before. But we'll bear it in mind . . .' Robbie handed the notes back to the resident. 'Thanks, doc . . . Where is she?'

They went into the ward and Robbie talked briefly to Mrs Ratho, whose answers were polite but oblique when they were not frankly surreal. Once again she admitted to an occasional sherry and

Robbie did not press her very hard on the subject. He drew the screens and examined her in detail, with Caroline and the resident watching, and talked about her on the way back to the doctor's room. 'Dyed hair? Tinted glasses? Nicotine up to the elbow? Show me a wifey with all three who doesn't drink like a fish and I'll buy you a pint. Cirrhotic, but nothing going for overt liver failure. Her clotting screen was OK on Monday. I wouldn't even repeat it . . . So yes, Caroline, I'll gas her tomorrow, with you watching. Or the other way round if you want.'

'I'll watch,' said Caroline. 'I actually quite like Hamish.'

'Hmph,' said Robbie. 'Up to a point.'

'I meant seeing him operate.'

'Oh yes,' said Robbie. 'I'll give you that. As orthopods go, he's definitely one with more fingers than thumbs. But let's just check her electrolytes and liver function tests again, Dr Gopal . . . That OK?'

'Sir.'

Robbie laughed. It was perhaps only the second or third time anyone in the Institute had called him sir. 'Thanks, doc . . . Thanks, Caroline . . . So tomorrow, and she's first on the list?'

'Yessir.'

At half past eight next morning Robbie and Caroline stood beside Mrs Ratho's bed in the anaesthetic room outside the orthopaedic theatre. 'So all you'll feel is a scratch on the back of your hand, Mrs Ratho, and you'll drift off quite comfortably and by the time you wake up you'll be back in the ward with your hip fixed, and everything will have been taken care of . . .'

'Thank you, doctor. Doctor. . . ?'

'Dr Roberts.'

'Like the song?'

Robbie smiled. For a few years quite a lot of people had teased him with bits of a song, one from a Beatles LP that had come out not long before they had graduated. No one seemed to remember it now. 'That's me. Just a scratch, Mrs Ratho . . .'

Robbie emptied the first syringe of thiopentone into a good vein on the back of her right hand. Nothing happened. He raised his eyebrows and gestured to Caroline for the second syringe, then disconnected, reconnected and ran in quite a lot more. Mrs Ratho gave a contented little sigh, slid into unconsciousness and began to snore like a navvy. 'Liver still fair to middling, I'd say. Slide a tube down, Caroline, and I'll see to the rest.'

A couple of minutes later they wheeled her, comfortably gassed and with an endotracheal tube firmly in place, into theatre and transferred her to the orthopaedic horse, a complicated operating table that split, folded and tilted in every way you could think of to let them position joints however they wanted them. Mrs Ratho, almost naked and trussed, with her broken hip uppermost, lay oblivious in a pool of light. 'Robbie,' said a voice. 'How nice to see you.'

'Oh. Hello, Hamish.'

'Wasn't expecting you.' Hamish was cleansing the skin over the hip with big brown splashes of iodoform scrub. 'Have they put you back on our registrar rota?'

'Well, no. But if it's all right with you, Hamish, I'll see to this lady . . . Medical history a bit tricky, so Caroline wondered if I'd mind being around. And they've actually made me an SR now.'

'Marvellous news,' said Hamish. Green drapes flew around and were clipped into place until only a little square of skin around the hip remained. 'That's absolutely marvellous news . . . They, um, kept you waiting a bit, didn't they? But came up with the goods eventually. That's the important thing. Really marvellous, Robbie. Great news.'

'Thanks, Hamish.'

'You mentioned a medical problem? Nothing serious, I hope.'

'Bit of an alcohol history. Still well short of liver failure and electrolytes all fine now.'

'Good. Splendid. We really should have done her before now. Had a bit of bad luck with our second attempt. Rushed in the other day, got everything lined up, got her as far as the anaesthetic room then the bloody radiographers, taking their orders direct from Moscow, I suppose, like every other erk in the place these days, called everybody out . . . Not going to bleed all over my wellies, is she?'

'Clotting screen's fine.'

'Marvellous. You know your Trotskyite friends at the front gate, Robbie? The rabble that want you to stop and read their pamphlets about the imminent collapse of capitalism? Bloody man this morning actually thumped my car. Drove past him because I felt I had better things to do, heard it all yesterday, and didn't stop. Thumped my car. Um. You sure about the bleeding, Robbie? A bit soggy in here . . .'

Hamish had swept a scalpel in a firm, neat slash a foot long in the square of exposed skin. 'Hm. Probably all right . . . Thought he was going for the aerial, which would have been grounds for reversing back over his size nines. Glad not to have to do it, really, but you should tell 'em, Robbie. They won't make any friends among the consultant staff that way.'

For some reason, Hamish had decided towards the end of Robbie's unfortunate orthopaedic housejob that the problem with him, apart from his inability to get on with people, was politics. His version of Robbie, a militant class warrior who would not hesitate to nationalise farms, breweries and the whisky industry – all interests near to Hamish's heart – and abolish private medicine – another very serious matter – had no basis in fact but had sprung from a mildly political conversation they had had once over a hind-quarter amputation almost ten years before: a conversation in the course of which Robbie had taken the view that the return of a Labour government might not be an unmitigated disaster for the nation. 'And besides,' said Hamish, 'I do a lot more for the NHS than any of that lot out there warming their hands at an illegal fire in a smokeless zone.'

Caroline was smiling. Robbie shrugged and said nothing. Hamish hacked and prodded away, muttering cryptically at his assistant and mopping up blood but not in any excessive amounts. 'Did you know old Ratho, Robbie?' Robbie shook his head. 'Compared to him I'm a left-wing menace. Frightful old bugger with views on everything from hanging and flogging to the end of Empire . . . And you're sure about her clotting screen? Not that I'm one to doubt your word, but it *does* all seem a bit on the damp side. Are you working to rule too? Keeping me on my toes with a gory mess where I'm trying to get a decent run in to the neck of femur. Ah. That's a bit better . . .'

Robbie had been around long enough to accept that in some operating theatres the job of the anaesthetist was just as much to keep the surgeon amused as it was to keep the patient asleep. He and Caroline sat side by side at the top of the table while Hamish set to work with the little chain-saw thing that trimmed the bone back to accept the prosthesis that would replace the broken bone. 'Yes,' said Hamish. 'That's a whole lot better . . . So you never met old man Ratho? Creepy, humourless old bugger, lousy teacher, useless doctor . . . But everyone was always very nice to him because he used to run the wee committee that hands out the merit awards. He and another old bugger before him called Lorimer had the whole thing stitched up for about twenty years. So everywhere they went there'd be a queue of consultants, grown men with respectable jobs, waiting to open doors for them, help them on with their coats, stir their tea and for all I know wipe their bottoms . . . Robbie, you're probably overdoing it. I mean, she's hardly bleeding at all now. You sure your end's all right?'

Robbie, who knew enough about the system of merit awards to wonder how it could possibly run with anything approaching fairness, stopped thinking about that and hurriedly took Mrs Ratho's blood pressure. It was low, perhaps even dangerously so. Up on the theatre wall was an old-fashioned dial, connected to the electrocardiograph, which let everyone see the patient's pulse rate. Mrs Ratho's heart had speeded up quite a lot but no one seemed to have noticed. He checked for the pulse at the right wrist, and found it fast and rather feeble. The next place to look was the brachial artery, high in the inside of the right arm. Even there the volume of the pulse was not encouraging. Robbie slid a hand down each side of Mrs Ratho's neck, feeling for a carotid pulse. It was there and it was good enough to maintain cerebral circulation, even if it was going far too fast, but the picture generally was worrying. Mrs Ratho, for no very obvious reason, appeared to be getting into trouble. She was bleeding, perhaps even bleeding quite a lot, and there was nowhere obvious that she was bleeding from.

The proprieties of the speciality of anaesthetics were such that this was not the sort of thing an anaesthetist would trouble a surgeon with in the middle of an operation. A well-managed anaesthetic disaster, as Robbie had known since the very beginning of his training, was one the surgeon didn't know anything about until afterwards. He speeded up the saline drip running into Mrs Ratho's wrist, got up from his stool and with studied nonchalance checked to see if there was a puddle of blood gathering on the floor under the middle of the table. There wasn't, but it was still just possible that she could have quietly lost a couple of pints into the drapes around the wound. That was a more delicate matter to check up on, so Robbie strolled round the table, as anaesthetists quite often did just to stretch their legs, and over the surgeons' shoulders inspected the area around the wound. From the look of the drapes the blood loss was if anything less than average.

Back at the top of the table with Caroline, Robbie fiddled with the drip again; then, as though he were dealing with a minor problem in the clear plastic plumbing between the drip stand and the patient, deftly switched the bag of saline for one of Hartmann's and, still using the same point of access to the circulation – the green Medicut cannula at Mrs Ratho's wrist – quickly ran in half a litre. When he checked her blood pressure again it was no higher, but at least it wasn't falling any more. He pointed at the empty bag on the drip stand and nodded to Caroline. Like a well-trained anaesthetic registrar she calmly rose, put up another bag of Hartmann's and sat down again as though she too had been merely stretching her legs. Robbie winked and she winked back at him.

'What happened after the old bugger gave it up was quite interesting . . .' Robbie and Caroline exchanged smiles: Hamish was happy again. 'They decided nobody was going to be allowed to chair the wee committee for ten years and then nominate his own successor ever again. A touch of open government, really. They gave it to Jimmy Jameson, for three years only, and all sorts of extraordinary things began to happen. People got merit awards who'd never set foot in a masonic lodge in their lives. "Let's just encourage the chaps who've been trying a bit harder," he used to say, according to Bill MacMillan, who was our man with the token B award for bone-setting and rolling up his trouser-leg. Great, we all thought. And then Jimmy was all set to hand over to Lennie Lennox for a bit more of the same when everything came unstuck. Pity, really. He'd have been . . . Robbie, you sure everything's all right?'

'These cirrhotics can be a bit labile sometimes, Hamish . . She's settling down.'

'It seems Lennie had screwed it up in a big way . . . He'd once chaired a committee that had told the Board it ought to close down the Institute. No ifs and buts. Close it down lock, stock and barrel . . . So when Jimmy's three years came to an end the old buggers got their chance. They ganged up and more or less told

Lennie to push off. Pity, really. I try hard, and I'd quite like to be encouraged.' Hamish's assistant laughed, and so did both anaesthetists.

What happened next was something that Robbie remembered for the rest of his life. Mrs Ratho, still comfortably gassed and lying on her left side with her right hip opened up and ready for her Moore's prosthesis, twitched a little, like someone starting to have the hiccoughs, then stretched as though she were yawning and vomited several pints of bright red blood all over Robbie's knees and down into his boots. Caroline, without being asked, sprinted to the fridge and came back with the two units of previously cross-matched blood kept ready for every hip fracture patient who went to surgery. Just as she had connected the first and was beginning to squeeze it in, the cannula in Mrs Ratho's wrist broke free and sprayed a thin stream, first of water then of blood, across the floor of the operating theatre.

'Some problem, Robbie?' Hamish had stopped cutting and was standing with his head back, looking down over his masked nose towards the top of the table. As Robbie moved to set up another, bigger IV line Hamish saw his legs. 'Oh. I see . . . Do your best, Robbie, we're nearly there.' He stooped over the wound grumbling quietly at his assistant and heaving and tapping and grunting for perhaps a minute. 'Stitching up now, Robbie . . . All yours, really. Unless there's something I can do. Only be a couple of minutes . . .'

Getting a bigger line in wasn't easy. Mrs Ratho was in a lot more trouble than before, indeed now so near exsanguination that the veins in her neck were flat and empty. With Caroline looking on Robbie stabbed and rummaged and finally drew dark blood back into his empty syringe. 'Great. The line, please. And if someone can run down for the other two units. Oh . . . Sister? Have you rung them?'

'Rung who?'

'Sorry, sister. BTS. And if someone can run down really quickly . . .'

In addition to the two units of blood held ready in theatre, every hip patient had another two cross-matched and held in the fridge at the Blood Transfusion Service down off the medical corridor just in case of a turn of events like this. The theatre sister abandoned all asepsis and punched buttons on the intercom and shouted 'Hello?

Hello? BTS? Orthopaedic theatre here . . . The two units held for Mrs Ratho, please . . . Yes . . . Very . . . Right away . . . Yes. Very urgent . . . No . . . Well, yes. But don't you have anyone? Hell. OK. Thanks.' She turned to Robbie. 'No porters. What do you want to do?'

Robbie looked up from squeezing the second unit blood down his new central venous line. 'Could Jip go?'

Sister glared silently back at him. Jip was the duty ODA, a malignant dwarf, nominally the orthopaedic theatre assistant, in practice a bookmaker of some substance among the Institute's portering fraternity. If he was anywhere around he would be in the rest area with his feet up, reading the racing pages. Robbie and the theatre sister looked at one another without speaking. The blood was almost through. 'Perhaps if Jip could. . . ?'

Sister was still glaring mutely back at Robbie when Caroline volunteered. 'It's all right, sister. I'll go. It's no trouble.'

'Thanks, Robbie,' said Hamish. 'Thanks, everybody. I'm finished now. Thanks awfully.'

Mrs Ratho lay inert and yellowish-white, with blood still dripping slowly from her mouth and only the faintest tinge of pink over her cheeks to distinguish her from a corpse. Robbie squelched across for another bag of Hartmann's to hold things steady until Caroline came back, set it up to run fairly briskly in via the central venous line and once more tried forlornly to get a blood pressure reading.

'Milnes-Walker,' said Hamish suddenly. 'Obvious, really . . . Robbie, it's varices, isn't it?' Robbie nodded and continued to watch the Hartmann's running in. 'So we just get old Jake to pop down and do them for her here. A Milnes-Walker thingy. You crack the chest, go straight for the gullet, snip it across and sew it back together again. And look, no varices. And Jake's probably around somewhere. Sure he'd love to. I'll try and raise him. What d'you think, Robbie? Up for it? Might as well. Sheep, lamb and all that . . .' Robbie had doubts but Hamish's assistant had brightened up a lot. 'Don't wake her up or anything, Robbie,' said Hamish. 'No point. At least no point until we know whether or not old Jake's around. And we could cross-match her for a few more, I suppose . . . Say eight for starters. Yes . . . A Milnes-Walker. Her only chance, really. Might be quite fun, and after all she *is* the wife of one of our senior colleagues.'

Robbie, who had gassed once or twice for Jake, the most senior thoracic surgeon at the Institute, thought about that while he was standing at the intercom ordering the second batch of blood from BTS and decided it was quite a good idea. It was Mrs Ratho's best and perhaps only chance of survival, but there was more to it than that. If Mrs Ratho were to die straight away there would be a swift and general presumption that he, the anaesthetist in immediate charge of the case, was to blame. The more numerous and prestigious the list of doctors attending her last illness, the easier it would become for him; and Jake, a survivor from the days when anaesthetics were so dangerous that the fastest surgeons were, by definition, also the safest, might just come down from the thoracic unit, open her in a minute, slash her oesophagus and re-anastomose it in another fifteen or twenty, and thus pull off the unlikely feat of getting her out of the orthopaedic theatre alive. And if he does that, thought Robbie, whatever happens afterwards, no one will be the slightest bit interested in who precisely it was who gassed her in the first place. Hamish marched cheerfully out to find a phone.

Just as the second half-litre of Hartmann's ran through Caroline returned pink and breathless and carrying the two further units of packed cells. 'Great, Caroline. Just shove that one through and I'll set up a blood-warmer and a pump because I've just ordered eight more units and we're probably going to be at this for a while. Thanks a million. She seems to have stabilised and Hamish has just gone off to try and get a hold of Jake Leitch to do a Milnes-Walker.'

'A what?'

'Oesophageal transection. Emergency job for bleeding varices. Should have thought of it myself, but Hamish beat me to it. Might just make all the difference.'

Caroline came closer, still breathless from her run, and whispered in Robbie's ear 'Sorry about all this. Really sorry. I should just have told Gilbert I wasn't going to do it and he'd have had to come in.'

'Not sure it would have helped,' said Robbie. 'Could have happened to anybody.'

'It's the family I feel sorry for . . .' Caroline had emptied the third bag of blood and was connecting the fourth. 'Doctors, consultants even . . . And they must have trusted us – you know, the Institute – and we've sort of let them down.'

'All fixed, chaps.' Hamish came back grinning cheerfully. 'Hear that, Robbie? Great news. It's all fixed. Jake's on his way down. Five minutes. And he wants us to turn her over. Old Milnes-Walker always insisted on a left thoracotomy, it seems, so we'll turn her over. And be bloody careful not to dislocate my nice new Moore's prosthesis, if you don't mind.'

Robbie, as concerned about his central venous line as Hamish was about the hip prosthesis, steadied Mrs Ratho's head and neck and Hamish her right hip as she twisted slowly on the table in the hands of the assistant, the theatre sister, the staff nurse and Caroline, the duty anaesthetic registrar. 'Steady... Steady... Great. A touch up the table, maybe. Good. And he'll want her left arm up somewhere behind her ear, probably. D'you know about that, Robbie? Oh. I see. Thanks awfully. And you're quite sure she hasn't had any coagulation problems?'

'Hm?'

'I said you're quite sure she hasn't had any coagulation problems?'

Robbie nodded. He was quite sure. What sort of coagulation problems she might have after a thoracotomy and another half dozen units of blood was an entirely different matter, but with Mrs Ratho's blood now firmly clotted around the toes of both his feet he could be fairly certain that everything had been just fine when they had started.

'Ah, Hamish... Yes, I see.' Jake Leitch, a tall, imposing man with a mane of white hair, swept in and stood for a moment looking round. 'And it's Ranald's wife, poor thing. Yes, yes. And Dr Roberts – whom of course I know well – is anaesthetising for us...' His eye settled on Robbie and the gore that covered him from the knees down. 'Quite. Well, let us be getting on. Hamish, I'm sure you're right about the diagnosis, but before subjecting the wife of a senior colleague to a thoracotomy I'd like to see for myself what's going on. I have taken the liberty of bringing down a flexible endoscope of the kind preferred by the younger surgeons.' He tapped solemnly on the shiny black suitcase housing the instrument. 'And I have also arranged for two thoracic trays to be brought straight from the sterilising centre. They should be here in minutes... But first, the diagnosis.'

The old man opened his black case and took out the endoscope, handed Caroline the supply lead to be plugged in and knelt at the head of the table. Then he extended Mrs Ratho's neck to the usual sword-swallowing posture, lubricated the instrument, opened her mouth and slithered it smoothly down her gullet, squinting at the eyepiece all to the way. 'Yes. Yes. Some serious trouble here. And here. Yes. And here too. Thank you. We shall deal with it straight away.' He pulled the endoscope, now gorily smeared, from the patient, handed it to Caroline and stood up. 'May I scrub somewhere, Hamish? Thank you. Please just lead on.'

Jake had arrived in green theatre pyjamas already bloodstained from a previous encounter. He emerged from the scrub room masked and freshly gowned, supervised the staff nurse as she draped the patient once more then waited while sister came to grips with the unaccustomed complexity of a tray of thoracic instruments. 'Yes. Thank you, sister. A scalpel, just an ordinary scalpel, thank you.' His first cut was a huge, unerring sweep that followed a rib from spine to sternum so that suddenly the thorax yawned. Pushing the left lung forward and up he dissected down into the newly exposed depths, snipping and tying, probing behind the squirming bulk of the heart until the lower end of the oesophagus was mobilised and a couple of large ligatures snared around it. With Hamish as his first assistant and the English orthopaedic registrar as his second he worked with swift, tireless precision, first severing the oesophagus then oversewing its distended submucosal veins with firm, neat stitches that would allow no further leakage, then settling to the most demanding part of the procedure, the joining of the two severed ends of the oesophagus so that it could function as before. Hamish, the registrar and the theatre sister looked on with frank admiration as the last of the anastomosing stitches went in and the old man began to work his way back to the chest wall.

At the head of the table Robbie, watching the seventh unit of blood go in, caught the elation of the moment too, and added to it when he checked Mrs Ratho's blood pressure again and could report that it was better than it had been since she had first dropped into her slumber in the anaesthetic room. They finished shortly before one thirty, almost three hours after they had started out on a simple hip procedure that was usually over in an hour. Mrs Ratho was wheeled from the orthopaedic theatre straight to the lift which would take her up to the Intensive Care Unit on the second floor.

Robbie showered and changed and accompanied her on her way up, but not before he had overheard a brief corridor conversation between the orthopaedic surgeon and his registrar, to the effect that having half the hospital out on strike was bad enough without being compelled to work with anaesthetists who sat around talking politics while patients practically bled to death.

A little before ten the following Sunday morning Gus made his way up to the Institute again. It was his fifth visit since his mother had been transferred for intensive care after her ghastly mishap in the orthopaedic theatre, and it was quite likely also to be the last. She had been on a ventilator for almost four days now and each time they had tried to wean her off it and let her breathe for herself she had failed to do so. As each day had passed Gus knew her chances of recovery had diminished further and quite soon now they would switch off the ventilator once and for all and she would die, quickly and predictably and without regaining consciousness. His father, whose grief might well turn out to be tinged with large measures of relief, had given up already and wanted now to know only when it was all over. For Gus it was more difficult. Mopsy had been an unpredictable and unreliable mother, once glamorous, then tedious, and in the last few years so wild that her drinking had been a source not only of embarrassment but of risk: she was falling quite often now and had become increasingly dangerous with cigarettes. When she had slipped in the bathroom and broken her hip it had occurred immediately to Gus that that might be the beginning of the end. What had surprised him was how long and uncertain the whole thing had been, and how he had reacted to each turn of events.

When she had first gone in, people had been sensible and practical and had seen her drinking as just another clinical fact, as though she had been a diabetic or an epileptic, someone with a continuing medical problem that required careful handling but carried no particular stigma or blame. The little Pakistani, most probably a Moslem to whom alcoholism would be as incomprehensible as cannibalism, had been sensitive and helpful, and when Hamish Cruickshank had eventually contacted him he had been sympathetic about that and quite frank about the various problems that had delayed surgery. It can't have been easy for him trying to run an acute trauma service with only one operating theatre and no increase in staffing since the early 1960's. And the strike, to which Gus had paid a lot more attention since his stupid encounter with the men on the picket line, was not a simple matter either. Men with young families, he discovered, were being asked to live on weekly wages not unlike the kind of sums Gus regarded as pocket money.

This morning the picket line was thin and unenthusiastic, with only half a dozen of them around the makeshift oildrum fire. Once more the man who years ago had been a junior lab boy around the clinical immunology lab stood in the middle at the main gate, this time alone, which prompted Gus to wonder how they organised themselves, how they decided who had what duty in the difficult business of organising a twenty four hour picket seven days a week. Again the man recognised Gus. This time he smiled and as he smiled Gus remembered his name. 'Morning, Dr Ratho.'

'Hello, Billy.' This time, and it was another significant difference, Gus stopped of his own accord, and for a moment the two stood silent until Gus, aware of how silly it might sound, said 'How are you, Billy?'

'Och, we're doing away. It's easier now with the better weather.'

Gus nodded. 'How long have you been here this time?'

Billy shrugged. 'Six this morning. Off at noon. Are you on duty again?'

'Not really,' said Gus. I'm across at the Southern these days . . . It's . . . I'm actually going in to visit . . . my mother.'

Billy at once looked genuinely concerned. 'Sorry, doc. I mean, I hope she's going to be OK.'

Gus took a deep breath. 'I think she will, thanks, Billy. Probably fairly soon.'

'Well, give her our regards.' Billy smiled in a way that reminded Gus of the bright, slightly mischievous lab boy of long ago. 'From the boys at the front gate fighting for a better health service.'

'Thank you, Billy.'

'All the best then, doc . . . All the best.'

Again Gus went in by the Institute's main door, crossed the pretentious, shabby corridor and climbed the huge stairway, noticing for the first time a wide crack running across the wall from the corner of a window almost up to the ceiling. It was curious: once he had started seeing things like that there seemed to be no end to them. On the second flight of stairs several linoleum tiles had come loose and had been laid loosely back in place rather than fixed properly with glue. It wasn't that any single thing was particularly serious, but taken together they added up to a dispiriting impression that the Institute was now thoroughly second rate: a place that could easily get worse and could hardly, by any stretch of the imagination, be seen as ever turning itself around and making itself any good again.

The Intensive Care Unit confirmed all that in detail. It was housed in a string of cramped, old-fashioned rooms that might once, in the days of the Institute's glory, have been little offices or stores. The doctors' room, hardly more than a cupboard with a window to the outside, was tucked under the stairs and across the corridor from where the patients were. The unit was far too small, in the wrong place and had been obsolete for years. Its short-comings had been discussed often enough and long enough, as Gus knew from Sir Edgar's explosive comments whenever he had to send a patient there, but true to Institute form nothing had ever been done. People muddled on, losing all idea of how far behind they had fallen compared to almost any other teaching hospital Gus had ever visited. Lennie, he thought as he went into the shabby little unit where his mother lay unconscious and waiting to die, had basically got it right.

Two staff nurses sat by the nursing station and behind them stood the Institute's chaplain. To Gus his presence was not so much comforting as sinister, like the sombre attendance at another kind of planned death, the kind that had once taken place in prison. And besides, didn't chaplains have other things to do on Sunday mornings? The staff nurses both stood up when they saw Gus, something they hadn't ever done before. He inquired about his mother and couldn't help making it sound as casual as if she was in having a hernia taken care of. The staff nurse said simply that there had been no change, and that the consultant would be coming in at ten o'clock and would probably make a decision then. In prisons, it occurred to Gus, they were a bit quicker off the mark, and they probably avoided Sundays altogether.

'Sorry to hear about all this, Gus,' said the chaplain. Gus knew him vaguely from years ago when he had been a houseman, because hospital chaplains always vaguely knew everyone, and this one had made a habit of going round the hospital on Sunday evening making time for staff rather than patients. He was a modest and approachable man and one or two housemen and quite a lot of nurses had found his Sunday evening presence useful: a quiet time for a chat with someone who knew about the problems but was no part of the machinery of blame. But now it was Sunday morning not Sunday evening, and in local terms Gus was a relative rather than a member of staff. He nodded an acknowledgement then muttered that it had all been quite difficult.

'And your father? Is he all right? It must be very difficult for him . . .'

'I think he's expecting the worst,' said Gus. 'Probably quite soon.'

'I'm sorry, Gus. Mustn't keep you,' said the chaplain. 'Thanks, staff.' As he made to leave Gus suddenly wanted him not to. The chaplain paused. 'But I'd be happy to wait, Gus, if there's anything you want to talk about.'

'Well, perhaps I should just pop in and see her. If you're sure you don't mind waiting.'

The chaplain nodded. Gus sat for only a few minutes at his mother's bedside, listening to the steady mechanical sigh of the ventilator and wondering briefly how long it would take for everything to stop when the consultant finally switched it off. Already there was no real person left, just a lean, yellowish half-familiar figure at rest, eyes closed, tube in mouth, white gown neatly in place and hair as tidy as the nurses could make it. When Gus got up he touched his mother's hand with his fingertips, then patted it and turned to go, leaving the room without looking back.

'Dr Ratho?' Dr Ellis, the consultant in charge of the ICU, was waiting with the staff nurse and the chaplain when Gus emerged. 'I wonder if we could have a word . . . Perhaps you'd like to take a seat.' Gus sat down on a rickety wooden chair. It was obvious what Ellis was going to say and there was no need for him to look sheepish about it. 'As you know, we've tried a couple of times to see if your mother had any chance of surviving without the assistance of the ventilator . . .' Gus nodded. 'So I hope you'll understand when I tell you that there's really no point in going on. I'm sure you will.' Gus nodded again and got up without saying anything. The chaplain stood up too. 'Gus, if there's anything I can do . . . If you'd like to talk, we can sit in my office . . . If you'd like to be alone just use the chapel. You'll have it to yourself until nearly eleven.'

It seemed a good idea. 'Thank you,' said Gus. 'Perhaps the chapel, if you don't mind. Are you going down now?'

The chaplain nodded and they went downstairs together, the chaplain to his office, Gus to the little wood-panelled chapel off the corridor opposite the hospital pharmacy. It was warm and silent, and Gus sat in a pew near the back, trying not to think of what was happening up in the Intensive Care Unit, and looking round at the stained glass windows, the hymn-books, the memorial plaques and the plain oak altar table. Curiously, for someone like Gus with no particular religious views, some of the happiest times of his life had been connected with being in church, either the little Episcopalian one in the Perthshire countryside, smelling of candles and musty fabric, which he associated with the long summer evenings of holidays spent at Granny Kinnell's, or the chapel at school, where more or less compulsory attendance was actually quite enjoyable because of the music and because it gave time for private, undemanding, free-floating thought which was almost impossible anywhere else.

Being alone in church was new. Amid the oak pews and odd memorial plaques commemorating nurses who had died young, matrons who had died old and doctors killed in First World War battles whose names were all forgotten, Gus thought once more about religion and slowly began to think about it entirely differently. He had much in his life to regret already: his various pretences and dishonesties in the lab – culpable betrayals of scientific trust – and his cool exploitation of patients for research; his intolerance, his cold lack of love for the damaged child, his exasperation and eventual violence – all the icy wreckage of his marriage and the anger he still felt towards Sandy, who in leaving him had done the only safe and sensible thing for herself and for their child. He had despised his father and hated his mother. He had even hated the men at the hospital gate, who were there because they felt it was the only way left to them in their struggle for the recognition of a decent wage, and yet this morning one of them had tried to wish his mother back to health.

It seemed now to Gus that to be alone in church while his mother was dying was somehow exactly as it should be. The chaplain, by being there in the Intensive Care Unit and guiding him down here to a chapel in the heart of the hospital, had been the instrument of a higher purpose, one that became more evident with every moment Gus thought about it. He had known about belief but he had never experienced it. He had heard people talk about penitence and repentance and now he knew what they meant. He had been wrong about a great many things but he could change, and he would change. Along the pale oak of the front of the altar was carved a phrase Gus had seen often but never before understood: 'I am the resurrection and the life'. He knelt and prayed, and was still praying almost an hour later when the chaplain and a dozen worshippers came in for the morning service.

June 1979

The plane hit Scotland hard. Passengers gasped loud enough to be heard above the reverse-thrust noise from the engines, and the stewardess sitting in the little fold-down seat against the bulkhead winced and then frowned in a way she had probably been taught not to at training school. 'Welcome to Edinburgh,' said a voice so Scottish that Scott found himself laughing. For better or worse, he was home. The plane slowed then veered sedately towards the terminal, offering fine views of the Pentland Hills and the battery hen place that gave Edinburgh Airport its unique and characteristic smell, and when it stopped people got up and reached for their belongings and said very Scottish things like 'Mind your head, dear'. In general they seemed small and pale and thin.

Where he had just come from they had been large and tanned and a lot of them had been black, and Scott found himself wondering how long the foreign-ness of Edinburgh would last. At first glance the grass was a hysterical shade of green, the cars and vans dainty, and his handful of UK notes and coins, kept at the back of a drawer in his apartment for a year and retrieved only yesterday, still quite strange: the coins clumsy and the notes disreputably florid. And he had already discovered, on the way through Heathrow, that the notes and coins didn't buy as much as before. In the queue to disembark he fished the remainder from his pocket, checked it and worried about whether or not it was enough for a taxi into town.

Luggage came through only slowly, and by the time Scott got outside there were no taxis left. He waited, weary from eighteen hours travel and five hours' worth of jet lag, then after fifteen minutes gave up and hauled his bags along to the bus stop where a white double decker, for some reason entitled *Sir Compton MacKenzie*, was slowly filling with pensioners and families from package tours. On the half-hour it rumbled into life and set off for town. Gogarburn, Corstorphine and Roseburn passed dreamily as Scott dozed and woke and dozed again, Scottish voices soothingly all around.

'Right, son.' At the Waverley terminus the driver woke him. 'Your holidays is up now.'

Scott thanked him, told him to have a good day and stumbled off the bus to look once more for a taxi. When one stopped he had to load his cases in by himself, with the driver sitting silent at the wheel until they turned left on to the Mound at the Black Watch monument, when he said 'How long have you been away, pal?'

'A year.'

'You picked a good one tae miss.'

Until they were passing the Institute he said no more. Scott, who had kept in touch with events at home by reading subscription copies of the *Guardian Weekly* and *Private Eye*, was aware of some of the problems and not too sorry to have avoided them, but had had to explain sometimes to interested North Carolinians that a few strikes and a lot of headlines didn't necessarily mean the end of what they called socialised medicine. 'She'll sort the bastards out,' the driver announced without vehemence.

The fare saw off most of Scott's sterling reserves. He had just reached the top landing when he heard the phone ringing inside his flat. He dropped his cases, fumbled for his key and reached the phone in time. 'Oh, hello, Andy,' said a voice.

'Hello?'

'You took a long time to answer. Were you in the bath?'

'No. Who is it, please?'

'Oh, sorry, Andy. It's me, Robbie. How are you?'

'Fine. I've . . .'

'Listen, you've been away, haven't you? I don't know if you know, but kind of bad news . . .'

'What about?'

'Professor Lennox. I thought you'd probably want to know and didn't know if you knew already.'

'No. What?'

'I mean, really bad news. He's dead.'

'Lennie?'

'Yes. At home. Last night. Suddenly.'

'What of?'

'The funeral's this Saturday. Mortonhall at half past ten. You'll go?'

'Well, yes.'

'Good. See you there.'

'Robbie . . .'

'What?'

'What happened, Robbie? What did he die of?'

'Oddest bloody thing . . . He fell downstairs.'

IV

THE HEALTH YOU
CAN AFFORD

March 1982

'Amazing,' said Max. 'All the women who aren't going grey are growing moustaches.'

Scott looked around, checking the idea on a larger sample almost without thinking about it. They had been talking to Jennifer Norwood, now Jennifer something else, and Marion McClintock, still very much Marion McClintock. Jennifer, a tall redhead originally from Virginia Water and now a consultant paediatrician in Fife, had a few strands of greyish hair around her temples; a faint grandmotherly touch quite at odds with her former rather hysterical student persona.

'There's another,' said Max. 'I mean, really grey. God, it's Vicky! Can't they use things? They should, shouldn't they? I mean, they're in my year and they're making me feel old.'

Max, thin on top as a houseman, was now by far the baldest of his contemporaries but quite unselfconscious about it. 'I'm still going to talk to her,' he announced. 'Four kids, somebody said. You know, I thought she'd end up that way. Women just never really seem to make it in hospital medicine, but I'd better go and have a word with her. So see you later, Scott . . . Oh, what about lunch?'

Scott said something non-committal. Max marched off with his this-is-a-party-and-I'm-enjoying-myself air. Vicky seemed pleased to see him.

'Hello, Andrew.' Scott turned round. Dilys was neither greying nor moustachioed, just a little heavier and older-looking, though some of that might have been something to do with her coat, a heavy, dark blue one of the kind a well-dressed naval officer might wear to his court-martial at Rosyth in winter.

'How are you, Dilys?'

'Oh, all right. But isn't it awful? John was terribly upset. We couldn't both come, and he'd been down in Carlisle sorting

Robbie's things out, so I'm here and he's doing my morning baby clinic.'

Inasmuch as Robbie had had any close friends, Dilys' husband had been one of them. Dilys looked round. 'An odd sort of reunion, isn't it? Very sad.' People were standing in little quiet huddles. It was cold and grey, and spring was late: buds on the chestnut trees around the crematorium were still tight, but under them were a few daffodils and narcissi in bloom. 'Poor Robbie.'

'Poor Robbie.'

'Look over there,' said Dilys. Scott looked. A little knot of men in their fifties and sixties stood together, quite separate from Robbie's contemporaries. 'Nice of them to come, I suppose. But it would have been even nicer if they'd just given him a consultant job in Edinburgh.' Scott nodded. He had heard two or three of Robbie's tales of how he hadn't quite got the job this time. Dilys smiled. 'He was a very Edinburgh person.'

Dilys came from somewhere in England, but had pronounced the last bit with a strong hint of Miss Jean Brodie. Scott thought again about Robbie and the first time they had met, in his very first week in Edinburgh. After a silly walk and pub-crawl with Max they had stood on the Castle Esplanade and Robbie had pointed out Heriot's, where he had been to school, and the Medical School just next to it, where they hadn't quite started yet, and the Institute, where he was to work for most of his thirteen-year medical career. Robbie had looked across at the roofs and turrets on the horizon to the south and had said something like 'That's it, it's all there.' To Scott, who had come from Lanarkshire and had at the time thought of Edinburgh simply as a place where he would learn to be a doctor, the idea had seemed oddly parochial. Now, it didn't seem like that at all.

The older men, still standing apart, were a fair-sized senior sample of the Edinburgh consultant anaesthetists who had decided in effect that Robbie should not join their number. Scott thought about them, and about Robbie, and wondered precisely which of his classmate's oddities or misfortunes had determined his exile from the only city he knew. Robbie was – had been – gauche, but one of the men standing to the right of the steps was actually picking his nose. Robbie had sometimes drunk too much, getting cheerfully loud after three or four pints of his inevitable lager and lime, but another member of the jury which had sent him down was notoriously absent on Mondays and sometimes even for weeks at a time. Robbie hadn't published quite as much of the tail-chasing research normally expected of junior doctors in teaching hospitals, but most doctors stopped even pretending to as soon as they got their consultant jobs. Nevertheless, as Dilys had said, it was nice of them to have turned up for his funeral.

'I think there was something about Gus Ratho's mum,' said Dilys. 'John came back once after they'd been to an international together saying Robbie probably wouldn't even remember who'd won because he'd been talking the whole time about what had happened to Gus Ratho's mum, what he'd done to nearly save her and how nice Gus had been to him afterwards despite everything.'

Scott nodded. Probably everyone in the little crowd knew in greater or lesser detail about Robbie's part in the demise of a lady who was not only the wife of a consultant but the mother of one too, and perhaps the logic of Robbie's banishment was that it allowed the Edinburgh consultant establishment to dissociate itself forever from that unhappy event. And as is the custom in a well-run establishment, the whole long-drawn-out business had all been managed with scrupulous regard to form: they had interviewed Robbie five times in the space of two or three years for local consultant posts, consoling him politely on each occasion with the usual encouragements for the future, and then they had simply stopped inviting him to interviews.

'We knew he'd hate Carlisle,' said Dilys. 'And he did. He'd sometimes drive all the way up just to drag John out for a pint, and they'd have two and then he'd drive back home, except he never called it home. And then this – to feel so awful that you could just go and be very organised and considerate and efficient . . . and then do it. And there were some odd things, like giving most of his money away in one cheque to TB research even though there's really nothing left to find out about it.'

'That is odd,' said Scott, then he remembered something complicated Robbie had once tried to explain in a pub late one evening about first wanting to be a doctor so that he could find the cure for TB. They were both quite drunk and the details had remained or become obscure, but Robbie bore no grudge against the man who had beaten him to it. He was happy in his proposed career, which at that point was still in general surgery. Scott was about to tell Dilys, but she had started talking again.

'It's so sad, because it's as if he never grew up . . . The pub food diet, the string of nurses, the laundrette and all that, and then suddenly he was a consultant somewhere else and he didn't know anybody.'

Robbie had succeeded in his first consultant job application outside Edinburgh and had moved to Carlisle at the end of the previous year. He had lived in hospital accommodation, and there was talk of a friendly local nurse. Scott had last seen him just where it seemed he had always seen him, at the top of Middle Meadow Walk, one evening in February, and had forgotten that he had actually moved away from Edinburgh. They had had a short, disjointed conversation and Scott had not joined him on his way to the pub. Long afterwards, in a curious dream about being dead and in an afterlife corresponding more to the shades of classical antiquity than to Scottish Presbyterian angels or brimstone, Scott had found himself at a cold and windy street-crossing not unlike the top of Middle Meadow Walk. From the dusk a shadowy but familiar figure had emerged, and Robbie had taken Scott by the elbow and steered him towards a smoky public bar. 'Good to see you, Andy,' he had said. 'Let's just go straight in. There are lots of people we know here already.'

'And you heard. . . ?' said Dilys.

'Yes.'

In a bleak bedroom in the resident doctors' quarters of an EMS hospital a few miles outside Carlisle Robbie had set up an intravenous line on himself and run in half a litre of saline spiked with a muscle relaxant and enough potassium to stop his heart in seconds. He had been found by the cleaning lady in the morning, the empty vials laid neatly on his bedside table to help the coroner. Most people also mentioned that he had looked very peaceful, and that his clothes and books and few personal possessions had all been neatly packed as though he had been about to set out on a journey.

The last mourners from the previous funeral emerged from the chapel and Robbie's friends and senior colleagues moved quietly in to remember him. There seemed to be very little in the way of family: a couple in late middle-age, perhaps an uncle and an aunt, sat near the front looking more uneasy than grief-stricken. The clergyman was old, his voice high and ringing.

'Out of the depths have I cried unto thee, O Lord. Lord, hear my voice; let Thine ears be attentive to the voice of my supplications. If Thou, Lord, shouldest mark iniquities, O Lord, who shall stand?'

Vicky and Maggie Auld were crying and quite a few of the others were using their handkerchiefs a lot. Most people, as Dilys had said, were part of a strange, sad reunion of the class of 1969, with one or two younger girls, presumably from Robbie's complex, ultimately inconsequential past. As usual in groups like this, Scott looked round to see if Sandy was there, and as usual felt somehow relieved that she wasn't.

'Almighty God, who art ever ready to forgive, and to whom no prayer is ever offered in vain, speak to us all Thy word of consolation as we stand in the presence of death. Grant that whatever may befall us may unite us more closely to Thee, that in doing Thy will we may know . . .'

Scott sat between Dilys and one of Robbie's nurses, a plump, sensible girl who was now a ward sister in the surgical side of the Institute. Robbie, as was clear to anyone who had ever thought even briefly about such things, had killed himself because some simple calculations must, over weeks and weeks, have continued to produce the same answers: that things were bad and were more likely to get worse than better; that there were a number of people who might, if handled carefully, help a little, but no one who could be relied upon to help a lot; and that to try to go on living would in all probability prove more intolerable than an immediately available alternative. Robbie had done his sums and made his decision, and as one of the people who might have helped a little, if only by going with him in February for a couple of pints he didn't particularly want at the time, Scott felt now a kind of helpless regret that most probably at least a dozen others sitting in the chapel would share. Dilys and John, in practice together in a town a good twenty miles nearer Carlisle, had in all likelihood done more than anyone, but how many sudden visits from an eccentric, needful former classmate were enough? Had Robbie wrung them dry, or, more sadly, had he failed to go to them on a night when he might have been welcome, and instead arranged his tidy, private quietus?

'O God of infinite compassion, who art the comforter of Thy

children; look down in thy tender love and pity, we beseech thee, upon Thy stricken servants upon whom this trial has come. In the stillness of our hearts we entreat for them Thy sustaining grace . . .'

At least God, or perhaps just the author of the prayer, knew how they felt. Suicide, as all the best problem pages would put it, was a threat and a reproach to the living, even if that wasn't quite how it felt from the inside. That was much more to do with the simple arithmetic of pain and survival. Scott tried to do the sums for Robbie again, reflecting that in his own time, with similar sums to do, he had been just a little luckier.

In the awful last months of his affair with Sandy, as she had gradually withdrawn from him, retreating into her marriage and her pregnancy but still seeing him briefly and unpredictably for sad, furtive sex and long silences at Lavrockdale, at his flat in Marchmont and sometimes even at hers in the New Town, he had slid further and further into despair. Sandy, sorry for him but ever more preoccupied with Gus and the coming child, had done what she could, phoning him sometimes at work and at home, going to bed with him when she could arrange it because she thought it helped him and probably because sex, good sex, had still mattered a lot to her.

They had gone on as long as possible, far longer than Scott had expected: in the event until within a week of when she delivered. At their last meeting she had been huge and ungainly but as loving as ever, and they had improvised lingeringly around her bump, the unborn infant's slow, insistent stirrings joining them like a third participant. At the end they had lain together in their usual bed in Marchmont and held each other, Scott weeping, Sandy trying to console him, hugging him and stroking his hair for what would certainly be the last time. For the last time they had kissed, his tears salty on both their mouths, then she had held him again, and he had discovered with a kind of aching surprise how sweet the milk was that the child would drink.

Then she had gone, their relationship over, and in the months that followed Scott had learned lots of things that psychiatrists were meant to know already: about loss, guilt, anger and the various unpredictable consequences of the silent suppression of pain. Since the relationship had never officially existed, its ending had to be endured alone, with none of the usual condolences, not even the jocular sympathy of friends in a pub. Max had told him he looked as if he needed a holiday and that he knew a place that did off-season package tours to Tunisia that were just about as cheap as staying at home. Wiggy Bennett seemed to have decided that Scott's appointment to the post of lecturer and honorary senior registrar in the care of the elderly had been a mistake and had therefore treated him as if he had not existed. Toby Russell, whom he had met after a lecture by a distinguished visiting professor on recent trends in suicide, had told him he was looking hellish and ought to bugger off to the Navy for a while until he was feeling better. It seemed a good idea, and Scott had arranged to do just that, started himself on some pills that took several weeks to work, and then, like Robbie, he had packed his bags.

Even after five years, the weekend before he had gone off to the Navy still seemed to Scott the longest he had ever endured. With nothing else to do, he had his kit prepared and packed by seven o'clock on the Friday evening. For some reason everyone he knew that he could have rung up in a pathetic Robbie-ish way was out of town: Max off at an infectious diseases conference in Geneva; Walker at a Labour Party prospective parliamentary candidates' weekend; Charles Savage with his parents in Dorset; even Scott's sister, whose mildly irritating religiosity and noisy family house in Falkirk would have afforded distractions of a useful sort, was away on a cheap off-season weekend at Crieff Hydro. In an empty Marchmont flat filled with the absence of Sandy, Scott spent Friday evening drinking gin and tonic and listening to Britten's War Requiem again and again and had wakened on the Saturday morning wishing for the first time, but quite genuinely, that it was all over.

To his surprise, thinking in detail about the practicalities provided a new interest, and it occurred to Scott several times in the course of the day that it actually made him feel better. There was no particularly medical component to his range of possible plans, no inclination for the technically neat and obvious such as Robbie had later shown. In the circumstances the challenge was rather to do something that would look like sheer misfortune, with various forms of road traffic accident – epidemiologically the most likely killer of youngish men – and a number of interesting places and manoeuvres offering themselves for consideration. But halfway through the afternoon he was looking out of the window when something just as plausible, less risky to others and far more accessible sprang to mind. All the windows in his fourth floor flat were dirty, and he could clean them.

He had done nothing more than fill the plastic bucket with warm soapy water when the phone rang, and had he been more certain about his intentions he would not have answered it. In the event he did, on the faint chance that it might, just might, be Sandy just once more. 'Oh, hello Andrew,' said a male voice, familiar but not immediately identifiable. 'Jimmy Jameson here. How about popping round to see us tonight? Join us for a quiet family supper, hm?'

The quiet family supper turned out to be one for more than a dozen people: Jimmy, Mrs Jimmy, the five Jameson offspring and their various male and female companions. Scott got drunk again, and spent some time in a corner with Jimmy, who told him he'd seen him around the place and been a little bit worried about him, and also that someone had happened to mention to him that his former houseman was now nothing like his usual self. 'But the important thing with this sort of trouble is not to let it make you think you're not any good, hm? Lot of it about, lots of very good chaps indeed . . . Optimus quisque, if you see what I mean.' One of the more arcane delights of being Jimmy's houseman had been that of swapping little bits of Latin, and a response sprang to mind immediately. When Scott had muttered 'verbum sapienti satis est' Jimmy chuckled with huge delight. There was a club, and they were both in it. The rest of the quiet family evening passed in a haze of gin and a riot of holiday slides from Tabriz, Baluchistan and Sarawak.

A spell with the Navy worked much as Toby had prescribed. Scott spent three agreeable weeks on the staff of a hospital near Plymouth, leading psychotherapy groups for service alcoholics most of whom had been drinking a good deal less than he was himself. He spent his evenings drinking gin in the restful and traditional surroundings of the hospital wardroom mess, or on tour with three or four other psychiatrists, visiting cosy little country pubs where they sat till late and swapped clinical and service yarns over many pints of the strange English beer. By the time he got back to Edinburgh he was somewhat better: grateful to the service life which functioned, as Toby had once remarked, as an ideal lunatic asylum for the officers, and grateful to Jimmy too. And though the windows of his flat were even more in need of attention when he returned he cleaned them without mishap, but from that time and for a long time afterwards he was disturbed by a recurrent dream: adrift after some ill-defined but vast marine disaster and awaiting a rescue that never quite seemed to happen, he was clinging to the wreckage. Sandy came into it too. She was close by but somehow safe and dry, and she was chopping his fingers off, one by one, because she thought it was kinder that way.

'O God, who dost continue to us the solemn trust of life; forgive our past unfaithfulness, and teach us to remember Thee from whom we come and to whom we go. Help us to live in the faith of Thy Son, that when Thou shalt call us hence, we may, in fellowship with our Saviour, be prepared to meet Thee our God, and enter into Thy heavenly rest . . .'

The clergyman finished his prayer and looked out over the congregation for the words of committal. 'We therefore commit his body to be dissolved, ashes to ashes, dust to dust . . .' Robbie's coffin sank under its maroon drape and the ward sister on Scott's right sobbed and clutched his arm. ' . . . looking to the infinite mercy of God, in Jesus Christ our Lord. Amen.'

They sang 'Abide with Me' and it was all over. To anonymous, solemn music they trooped out, quite quickly because there was no one waiting at the door to shake hands and hear the kind of things people had wanted to say about Robbie. It had started raining again, in soft, fine drops scarcely heavier than mist, but beyond the hill on which the New Town lay there was bright sunshine, highlighting the Castle and its esplanade under a sky still mainly dark grey. It was a very Edinburgh picture. Robbie had been a very Edinburgh person.

The little group of older men had stayed together throughout, and now they walked briskly away to their cars as though relieved at having closed a sorry, irregular chapter in the local history of their speciality. The sad reunion continued. Scott talked to one or two other people, including Harry, the odd chap from their year who had joined the masons when Mensa had turned him down. He was in anaesthetics now, in the university department in Glasgow, and said something nice about Robbie having been the junior anaesthetist that all the other junior anaesthetists had gone to when they had got into difficulties. Had the half dozen senior consultants who mattered known that? Scott wondered when the man eventually went off. Or had Robbie just been quietly getting on with some of the trickiest bits of medical staff training on their behalf for years and years without ever getting any acknowledgement or reward?

Just as Scott was about to leave as well he noticed Theresa, whom he had seen neither at the service nor before it, standing with Maggie Auld. She was explaining something, talking animatedly and using her hands at lot, but stopped as Scott approached. The two women stood silent as though it had been something quite girlishly private and Scott had been wrong to come near them, then Theresa said 'I feel silly, Andrew. I was late.'

'I'm sure Robbie wouldn't have minded.'

Maggie laughed. 'That's what I said too. I'm really sure he wouldn't.'

'They'd decided to dismantle a bridge near Dalveen and I had to go miles round, through Wanlockhead and Leadhills, and I felt so silly because I'd only gone the Dalveen way because it's much nicer and I had plenty of time.'

'Poor old you. But it was just . . . ordinary. They didn't actually say anything about Robbie except his name. And there was only one hymn.'

'I got the end of that. Honestly, Andrew, I'm going to pray for Robbie for ages. He must have felt so awful. And I'd seen him just a couple of months ago.'

'Really?'

'He dropped in for a coffee late at night on his way back from Edinburgh. Not really on his way, but he dropped in, the way he does. Said he'd seen you. He sat and talked for ages and I really thought I was going to have to throw him out because I had an early surgery, then he suddenly got up and went and hardly even said goodbye. And he seemed very low, so I'd been meaning to ring him, but hadn't. And now I've even been late for his funeral.'

Maggie, who might well have heard most of that already, said something about having to go, and Scott and Theresa found themselves alone together, walking under the trees to stay out of the rain, more slowly than they might have done but in the general direction of the car park. To Scott it seemed that any moment now Max would thunder up and try to organise them for lunch, but he didn't, so while the rest dispersed they stood talking under a tree for quite a long time: first about Robbie, then about psychiatry in Edinburgh and about general practice in Castle Douglas, and eventually about how Scott might come down and see her some time when they both had a weekend off duty: which, as it happened, was only three days away.

'It's a bit small, isn't it?'

'No, it's not. You just think it's small.'

'I suppose so. Odd, though. Everything seems about two-thirds the size I thought it was.'

'How old were you when you moved?'

'Ten and a bit. And see that old lady standing at her door?'

Theresa tried to look without appearing to look, but the old woman noticed anyway.

'She ought to be about eleven feet tall. She was my first ever teacher in the primary school.'

Theresa laughed and the old lady stared at them. The previous evening, in the course of a long, rambling phone call, they had agreed, for a mixture of practical and silly reasons, to meet at half past ten on Saturday morning in the little cafe at the bottom of the main street in the village where Scott had once lived, about twenty miles north of the town where Theresa was now in practice. Scott had arrived first, and was relieved to discover that it was still a cafe. Theresa was about two minutes late and keen to assert that in spite of all appearances she was hardly ever late for anything. They had had coffee and were sitting in the sun on a bench outside the village hall.

'They must be awfully proud of themselves,' said Theresa. To Scott's surprise, a large notice at the roadside just outside the village and another at its centre proclaimed that it had triumphed in a contest he had never heard of, that for the European Village Heritage Best-Kept Village Award. Although he could not recall the place ever having been particularly untidy, it was now meticulously neat and bright, the front doors up and down the main street shiny with gloss primary colours, whereas before they had all been either green or grained and varnished brown. There were a few litter-bins and a lot more benches, and window-boxes and hanging baskets of geraniums were the rule rather than, as previously, a suspect exception, liable to be talked about as showing off. 'Good for them, but it leaves you wondering how they decided . . . in a competition with St Tropez and Oberammergau and all that.'

'They deserve it. It's lovely. Do you come back a lot?'

'Once, for about ten minutes, about five years ago. I just stopped off to see who had died.'

'What?'

'In the churchyard. It was even where I wanted to be buried too, when I was fifteen and heavily under the influence of Keats.'

'What was she like?' Theresa asked. The old woman had gone indoors.

'Eleven feet tall. Well, ten at least, and she dragged you along by the arms so your shoulder hurt afterwards. And there weren't enough children to have a teacher for every year, so you got three years of her. A lot of it seemed to be shouting multiplication tables, or some other lot shouting more difficult multiplication tables.'

'I had nuns. Always quiet, whether it was the rosary or multiplication. And it was nice. They didn't seem to make much of a distinction between them, so neither did we.'

A swarthy, greying man hobbled past, uncertainly wielding a pair of walking sticks. Scott tried to imagine him more than twenty years younger and came up with a rabbit-catcher: a bully and braggart who had talked a lot about Malaya and the war there, and beaten his children, sometimes even out in the street. 'Looks like multiple sclerosis, poor chap,' said Theresa. 'They seem to have quite a lot of it down here.'

Scott, who had made the same diagnosis, thought about the man, whose name might well be Taylor, and wondered vaguely which had come first: multiple sclerosis for the rabbit catcher or the myxomatosis epidemic for his prey. The sour, doss-house smell of stale urine hung in the air for a moment or two after the man had shuffled into the pub, a punctual first customer. When he had gone Scott noticed something that he had never noticed in all the time he had lived there: the village was so small that even at its centre you could hear sheep in the fields and hills that surrounded it. 'D'you want to check again who's dead?' Theresa asked.

'If you don't mind. It's a very nice churchyard. But only if you really don't mind.'

'I really don't.'

They got up and walked round to the church and climbed over a little stone stile and strolled among gravestones old and new. A few dated from the years Scott had lived there, commemorating parishioners of his father's, like an old roadmender who had died in his remote cottage of something mysterious and ineluctable called double pneumonia, and Davy, Mr Merkland's shepherd brother-in-law, never a churchgoer but as entitled as anyone else in the parish to rest by the river. A little way off, Mr Merkland was there too, his name and the name of his farm, his date of birth and his date of death a few years previously all in gold lettering at the top of a neat black gravestone: the space below indicating, Scott realised, that his wife was probably still alive. In the sound of the river and the sheep, Davy's strange, peaceful death after a day's clipping was suddenly near, with Mr Merkland, his white dome bared, leading the men in the most familiar, most fitting of psalms. Theresa drew close and Scott put his arm round her.

On the way back up the hill Scott told her about village funerals and how Roger, the milk horse, specially brushed and with his hooves gleaming black – a transformation achieved by ordinary boot-polish – and his mane plaited, pulled the hearse from the home of the deceased to the churchyard by the river, and how his career had ended when he had run amok, the full length of the main street, and had had to be destroyed just outside the cafe: an event which had occurred – fortunately, it was generally thought – during a milk run and not in the course of his other duties.

They stopped at the post office, and while Theresa bought two black and white post-cards entitled 'Dalry: the Bowling Green, from the West' Scott spotted a copy of the voters' roll pinned to a notice board and quickly flicked through it to see if Mrs Merkland still lived in the village. 'Can I help you, please?' said the woman behind the counter in a voice that caused Scott mysterious unease. 'Are you looking for anyone in particular?'

Theresa took her postcards and the lady stepped out from behind her counter to inspect Scott more closely and announced 'I'd be very glad to help you,' in a manner it would have been foolish to ignore. Scott muttered something about an old friend who might be living locally and was pressed for details. When he said Mrs Merkland's name the woman pursed her lips then said 'Thirty one Kirkland Street, but she's not there at the moment. She's actually up in Edinburgh having radiotherapy. That's just through the week. She goes down to her daughter's near Annan at the weekend.'

Theresa was open-mouthed, Scott less surprised, having long suspected that village post-mistresses steamed open all the letters. The woman continued to eye him closely, her head on one side and lips pursed once more. Scott's unease became quite specific, for reasons it might be amusing to explain to Theresa afterwards. The lips unpursed. 'You'll be young Scott.' He nodded. 'I thocht as much. I'll be back in a minute.' She disappeared behind a brown curtain into the back premises of the post office, which was really only one room of an ordinary house on the main street. Scott stood half-embarrassed, half-mystified. Theresa was giggling a lot despite trying not to.

The woman returned, accompanied by another woman of similar age and appearance. She pointed to Scott as though he were an obscure creature in a zoo and said to her companion 'Wha's that?'

'Hmph,' said the other woman, squinting at him. 'He's Scott the meenister's son.'

'There you are,' said the first, now addressing Scott. 'You're Scott the meenister's son. I kent it from the way your hair's going.' She reached out to touch Scott's left temple. 'His went jist the same way aboot your age.'

When they escaped out on to the street again Theresa held his arm and laughed and Scott shook his head in bewilderment. 'All very strange. And even telling us which breast it was.'

'Not strange,' said Theresa. 'It's because they all care about each other. And you should probably go and see her at the Southern, because she's so far from home.'

Scott nodded. 'Is Castle Douglas the same?'

Theresa thought about that. 'This is the same as Castle Douglas, but more so because it's smaller. Two hundred people?'

'Three hundred, maybe, in the village. The same again if you count all the farms and things.'

'It's so sad they don't have a doctor any more.'

'Used to have. A nice man called Girdwood. Edinburgh graduate. And I think I wanted to be a doctor too because he had a green MG.'

'Really?'

'No kidding. Well, that and deciding ministers couldn't do very much good any more. What about you?'

'A missionary nun came and told us they needed doctors in darkest Africa.'

Scott laughed. 'But Castle Douglas is all right?'

'It's lovely, thank you.'

They walked in silence, with Scott wondering what kind of social life there was for single lady doctors in a little town scarcely three times the size of Dalry, but feeling he couldn't just ask outright the way Max might have done. And had her enthusiasm for meeting him in Dalry meant that there was someone in Castle Douglas – an auctioneer? a youngish farmer? a green-wellied chap with a tweed cap and a dung-spattered Porsche? – whom she thought it better not to risk meeting in his company on an off-duty Saturday morning? It was an interesting rather than an urgent question, but it led him to speculate if she in turn was wondering why Scott, now established as a senior lecturer and honorary consultant in psychiatry, had remained single in the rather less limiting world of Edinburgh medicine? That apart, perhaps rural general practice really was a kind of mission-vocation, not darkest Africa but still worthwhile, against which marriage, children and all that assumed a lesser importance. Then another thought occurred to Scott: the speed with which Maggie Auld had disappeared when he had joined the two of them after Robbie's funeral; a curious reprise of something involving all four of them at a party in the Society's rooms a long time ago, a manoeuvre that had something to do with going for drinks and which had given Robbie perhaps the happiest few months of his life. Just opposite the green painted gates of the village school, which had shrunk by a good three feet in the last quarter of a century, he put his arm round Theresa again. She moved easily towards him as they walked, and squeezed his hand.

'She's down here, Dr Scott. Last bed on the right. And the nurses say she's just impossible.'

The house officer, an earnest girl with acne whom Scott had taught a year or two before, led the way into the ward. 'So what d'you think is wrong with her, Lorraine?'

The girl looked puzzled then said 'They just said they'd like you to come and have a look at her.'

'They?'

'Oh. The registrar and the senior registrar. She's so noisy at night and she's even hitting people. And she never walks when she's meant to, with the physiotherapists in the morning, but sometimes she gets up at night and she goes round snapping at the nurses and telling patients to go to sleep and they've even caught her fiddling with an IV infusion. So it's getting really difficult, Dr Scott.'

'What was her job?'

Again the house officer looked puzzled. 'She's eighty three, Dr Scott. I'm not sure, really, but she must have been retired for years.'

'I just wondered.'

'Here she is . . . Miss McLaughlin? Miss McLaughlin! Don't do that, please, Miss McLaughlin.'

The patient in the last bed on the left was lying on her back with the sheet drawn up over her head. The house officer snatched the sheet and folded it down over the blankets in the approved fashion. 'Miss McLaughlin, please don't do that. It means something quite special in hospitals and I know you've been asked before to please not do that . . . This is Dr Scott . . . He's . . . He's . . .'

'Hello, Miss McLaughlin. I'm Dr Scott, from the Care of the Elderly Unit. I wondered if we could talk?'

' "The curfew tolls the knell of parting day, the lowing herd winds slowly o'er the lea . . ." ' The patient recited the lines without expression and continued to lie as she had been uncovered, straight out in bed on her back, arms by her sides, eyes gazing steadfastly at the ceiling.

'Miss McLaughlin . . .'

The house officer was looking as if, for a variety of reasons, she wished she were somewhere else. Scott, who was broadly sympathetic towards housemen and their worries, still wanted her to stay for at least a few minutes more. He indicated that quite pleasantly to her and she settled down.

' "The ploughman homeward plods his weary way, and leaves the world to darkness and to me." '

That was interesting. Scott's ideas about her previous employment firmed up a little more. 'Miss McLaughlin . . .'

'Yes, young man?'

'Miss . . .'

'Yes, young man?' She had interrupted him with impressive skill and timing. 'What did you say your name was?'

'I'm Dr Scott, Miss McLaughlin. A consultant from one of the other departments . . . I'm particularly interested in the elderly patients, Miss McLaughlin. How old are you?'

The patient smiled at the ceiling far above. 'A young man like you should know better than to ask a lady her age.'

'I'm sorry, Miss McLaughlin. But I'd be most interested to know.'

' "Older than the rocks on which she sits." '

'Or, if you don't want to tell me that, perhaps we can talk about other things. Such as your work?'

'My profession, young man.'

'Your profession then.'

' "Save where the beetle wheels in droning flight . . ." '

'A very fine poem, Miss McLaughlin.' This time Scott felt he could reasonably interrupt the patient. 'But perhaps you could tell me a bit more about yourself, and your profession.'

' "A wonderful bird is the pelican . . ." '

'Let me guess,' said Scott, taking an extra turn in the interruption game. 'You were a nurse.'

'Yes.'

'And you trained here, in the Institute . . .'

'Indeed I did.'

The house officer was beginning to look interested, a useful early goal in any teaching effort. 'You must be rather proud of that . . .'

' "A wonderful bird is the pelican . . ." '

'I agree.' Nurses who had trained at the Institute and served on the staff there too were awarded a badge which featured, for reasons no one could remember, a pelican. 'And can I take it that you were in nursing for some time. . . ?'

'I was indeed, and I'm glad to say I'm still able to do the occasional duty.' Miss McLaughlin continued to avoid eye contact and was still staring at the ceiling.

'That's interesting.'

'Young man, if you knew how standards had deteriorated you would be more sympathetic. And I'm not referring simply to nursing standards . . . Are you aware this hospital is falling down?'

'Can we talk about your work a little more, Miss McLaughlin? Your last permanent job?'

'My reputation is quite sufficient to secure for me all the occasional work I need, thank you . . .'

'I'm sure it is, Miss McLaughlin, but I'd still like to know.'

'I was night superintendant at the Southern.'

'For some time?'

'Years and years, young man. And now if you'd care to make yourself scarce.' Miss McLaughlin turned suddenly and fixed Scott with a rheumy stare. 'Some of us have our work to go to tonight.'

Ten minutes later Scott and the house officer were back in the doctors' room. 'Interesting. Can I scribble something in the notes? And I'll write to Dr Wilson.'

'What they'd hoped is that you'd take her away, Dr Scott.'

That was what they usually hoped. 'I'll try . . . As soon as we've got a bed.'

'They said it was quite urgent.'

That was what they always said. 'I'll do my best. What did you think of her?'

'Well, she's not really one for an acute medical ward.'

'No. She's not. What was she sent in as?'

'Just a social admission . . . You know.'

Scott flicked through the notes in an effort to find out what that meant without making the house officer feel silly. There was a letter from a GP, beginning 'This remarkably independent former nurse . . .' and mentioning possible weight loss, poor appetite and some night-day confusion. The clerking, in the kind of careful handwriting that suggested a medical student rather than a proper doctor, started off with a plaintive 'No history obtainable because patient keeps quoting poetry.'

'D'you think she's depressed?' the house officer asked as Scott searched for the results of routine investigations.

'Quite possibly . . . What made you think of that?'

'She doesn't look at you. Well, hardly ever.'

'Anything else?'

'Playing dead with the sheet.'

'Anything else?'

'Gloomy poetry?'

' "Or that th'Almighty hadst not fixed his canon 'gainst self-slaughter"?'

'Yes . . . That kind of thing. Where does she get that from?'

'Shakespeare,' said Scott. 'Probably.'

'But it's odd she knows all that and can't tell you how old she is.'

'So what else has she got?'

'Well, her long term memory's better than her recent memory.'

'So?'

'She's a bit demented too.'

'Right.' The girl was looking quite pleased with herself. 'Very good, Lorraine.'

'So that means you'll take her, Dr Scott?'

There was nothing of significance from the routine blood tests. Scott started writing a quick opinion in the progress notes, below a scribble dated six days previously which said 'No change' and another two days later saying 'Noisy at night. Refused oral sedation. 100 mgs intramuscular chlorpromazine given. Bit nurse.'

When he had finished writing Scott got up. 'Interesting. Thanks, doctor. So we'll try her on something not too toxic for her depression, and I'll review her in a couple of weeks . . .' The house officer opened her mouth as though to object. '. . . if we haven't managed to take her over before then. The night-day stuff's interesting. Worked at night for years, but maybe a bit of it's coming from diurnal variation in her depression too . . . Not keen with the physio in the morning, feeling better really late at night. You sometimes see it, not often as marked as that . . . We'll see if it gets any better on the pills. Oh. Hello, Jamie.'

The house officer squared up a bit as Jamie Wilson, now a consultant cardiologist and technically the doctor to whom Scott was offering his own specialist advice on the management of the case, came in to the doctors room. 'Young Scott. Come to see Miss McLaughlin?'

'Yes. Interesting.'

'From a strictly cardiological point of view, not very. Can you take her?'

'I'll do my best.'

'Oh,' said Jamie. 'The usual story? Too mad for us, not quite mad enough for you. Should we try for residential care?'

'She might get better.'

'Andrew, it's not just a routine request. They really want us to cut down on the bed numbers.'

'Oh?'

'Before the floor falls in.'

'You're kidding.'

'I'm not. It's been a bit shaky for years. Everybody knew and nobody minded that very much, but yesterday they found cracks in the ceiling of the ward below and got some structural engineers in. So we're having a mild panic and they want the far end cleared. Six beds. Today if possible. We hoped you might be able to help . . . And Miss McLaughlin really is one of the ones who doesn't need to be here.'

'I'll go across to the unit and ring back in a few minutes. You know, she did mention it.'

'Lorraine did?'

'No. Miss McLaughlin.' Lorraine was nodding and laughing. 'A funny old thing. Bossy. Classic ex-nurse, trained here. And she asked me "Are you aware this hospital is falling down?" But I hadn't realised . . .'

'It's not as bad as that,' said Jamie. 'I hope.'

The Care of the Elderly Unit, which most people in the Institute referred to as the C of E, occupied a pair of wards in an outlying pavilion that had been used as a furniture store for years after the Venereology Department had ceased to need large numbers of beds for in-patients at some time in the fifties. One ward, for which Scott was in practice responsible, was predominantly psychiatric, the other, Kevin Walster's empire, seemed to be mainly concerned with bedsores and constipation. Across the corridor was a set of five former consulting rooms and a former waiting room which Wiggy Bennett referred to as the academic suite, from which he occasionally visited the wards and from which he provided what he called academic leadership.

With a psychiatrist to do half the clinical work and Kevin, a rather low-powered failed general physician, to do the other half, Wiggy's contribution was somewhat nebulous. A lot of his time was spent out of Edinburgh, either on committees in London and Geneva, or lecturing in Europe, America and the Far East about the organisation of what he called broad-spectrum integrated services for the elderly. On the few occasions on which he was seen on the wards he was usually accompanied by visitors from abroad, many of them speaking and understanding sufficiently little English for him to be able to create quite a good impression there.

Apart from travel and the pursuit of his organisational interests, Wiggy did little. He sat in his office, read a lot and was said to be in the process of writing a major work reviewing the recent history and current problems of medical education. Again, expertise was quite unsullied by practice, the bulk of the teaching falling to Kevin, who had an unrivalled collection of colour slides on constipation and bedsores, and Scott, who quite liked getting students interested in what went on in mad old lady's heads.

The unit was chronically short of resources. Essential teaching items, such as chairs and chalk, often had to be borrowed from the gastro-enterologists upstairs, and the clinical service consisted largely of juggling priorities on a potentially interminable waiting list in response to urgent, very urgent and desperate referrals from GP's and the medical wards of the hospital, few of whose patients these days were under seventy. Jamie's mad old lady was just one more, but the possibility that she might disappear through the floor in a cloud of woodworm gave her a few extra points. The waiting list was kept by a Mrs Gracie, a fat, unpleasant woman whom Wiggy introduced to his foreigners as the Clinical Services Organiser.

'Honestly, Dr Scott, I'll do my level best for you, but you know what it's like. And Kevin's just been in with five for admission from the very same ward, I don't know what's got into them up there . . . But there's that little lady of Kevin's who might be going home if her commode arrives and they can shorten the legs this week but to be honest with you, Dr Scott, I can't see it myself . . . And then there's all Kevin's patients for the High Colonic Lavage study and that's terribly important. I hate to have to put them off because research is so terribly important, isn't it? The professor's *always* telling me that.'

'There's a lady on the . . .'

'Oooh. Now I might just have the answer for you . . . There's a woman whose daughter's going to take her home for the weekend if they can get a district nurse to help with her bottom, and I'm pretty sure that before she comes back in *next* Monday there's one of Kevin's, you know the woman, Dr Scott, a Mrs Burt, a horrendous constipation . . . Well, she's planned to go home on Monday evening, her daughter's taking her home after her work, nice girl, so I can *probably* help you . . . No. Sorry, Dr Scott. I tell a lie. All that's happening on Tuesday . . .'

'There's a woman . . .'

'Hang on . . . Just hang on a minute . . . I've got it. There's one of

Kevin's who's poorly, really poorly . . . So if she were to slip away, poor thing, provided it was before next Monday, when there's a couple of lavage people coming in for you-know-what . . . No. That wouldn't work either . . .'

'Mrs Gracie, it might help a lot if I could just check the book myself.' Scott moved round so that he was standing beside her desk rather than in front of it. She reacted as though he had just made a determined effort to snatch her handbag. 'You know what the professor says, Dr Scott . . . Integrated units have to be run in an integrated way, he says, or you never know where you are with anything. So I can't have you doing my job, no more than you would want me doing yours . . . So if you'll kindly just let me explain how I'm trying to sort all this out . . . Do you know how many patients Kevin's seen this afternoon? Five, that's how many. And they're all terribly urgent because they're all either constipated or at terrible risk for a pressure sore and on top of that they're all in a ward that's going to fall down. So you see my difficulty. I've only got so many beds and everybody wants them . . . But if that lady of yours who's been held up with diarrhoea – Galloway? Garroway? – has settled herself down now I see no reason why you shouldn't bring someone across. Would this afternoon suit you?'

'Mrs Garroway went home this morning, Mrs Gracie. So a Miss McLaughlin. Ward thirty three.'

'Very well then.' Mrs Gracie opened her ledger. 'Miss Mackintosh. Ward thirty three. I'll fix that up for you straight away, Dr Scott.'

'Thank you.'

'And you did say ward thirty three?'

It occurred to Scott that if they left it much longer Miss MacLaughlin might be downstairs in ward thirty two, but ideas like that were a bit too complex for Mrs Gracie. He thanked her again and went off for coffee.

Kevin and the other secretary, whom Wiggy introduced to people as the Academic Support Manager, were sitting in companionable silence on the only two chairs in her office when Scott went in. 'Kettle's just boiled,' said Mrs Smith. That meant simply that today Scott would have to make his own coffee. The other standard signal, 'Would you like a cuppa?', indicated that she had some important information she wished to hint at but not to share, or that she was bored and lonely and would quite appreciate Scott spending anything from ten minutes to half an hour listening to the latest on her boyfriend's golf, her daughter's marital troubles or her own endless wrangles with the cowboy builders from whom she had recently had the unwisdom to purchase a small flat for her old age; the problem for Scott was that declining such an invitation invariably resulted in otherwise inexplicable delays in the typing of any dictation he might subsequently produce.

'Isn't that awful about ward thirty three?' she announced just as Scott was leaving with his coffee. Scott nodded. 'Of course Kevin knows the structural engineer, don't you, Kevin?'

'He's in . . . a club I go to. He was telling me last night the whole place is riddled. Everything's wrong with it . . . Dry rot, wet rot, dodgy wiring from the war. And there's even asbestos in there which of course makes the whole thing about three times as expensive to sort out.' Kevin shook his head like a hanging judge. 'Hard to say where it'll stop.'

'So it's not just the far end?'

Kevin snorted knowingly. 'They should be so lucky. It's all a bit hush-hush, but he's been asked to do a report on the whole of that pavilion, and according to what I hear they'll probably ask him to look at one or two other places as well.' With that last divulgence an impenetrable discretion returned. Wild horses would not drag from Kevin another syllable confided to him by a brother mason in the secrecy of the Lodge.

'That's very interesting, Kevin,' said Mrs Smith. 'Isn't it, Andrew?'

'Have we found places for all six from that ward?' Scott asked.

Kevin ignored him. 'Of course it'll be discussed tonight at the Committee of Physicians. Under any other competent business, I'm told. And from what I hear, that'll put a lot of pressure on the Board to spend a great deal of money on the Institute one way or the other. And you know what that'll mean . . .'

'Yes,' said Mrs Smith. 'The professor mentioned something about that this morning.'

Kevin had resumed his even-the-Gestapo-wouldn't-get-it-out-of-me demeanour. 'And that would certainly mean some big changes,' said Mrs Smith.

'Certainly would,' said Kevin, getting up. 'I'll be in the colonic lab, Margaret, if anything else comes up. Yes. Then the Committee of Physicians at five then straight over to the Southern for the GI Services Joint Policy Review Committee at seven if I'm lucky. Thanks for the coffee, Margaret . . . Yes, Andrew, they're going to have to spend some real money on this place at last. Cheers.'

Scott attended the Committee of Physicians assiduously, not so much in the hope that it would ever decide anything sensible, more from a well-founded fear that it might from time to time decide something very silly. It was composed of the fifty or so consultants from the Institute's non-surgical specialties and since the most recent reorganisation of health service administration it had little formal status. In theory it was part of the Board's advisory structure, contributing its deliberations to a committee that deliberated further before passing any recommendations onwards for consideration at the principal committee to which the Health Board looked for advice from its consultant medical staff. In practice, since its numbers included some fairly tough and senior medical politicians who could exert substantial influence through other channels, it could still occasionally cause trouble, if only of a minor and predominantly obstructive kind.

In the sixties, before reorganisation and with a couple of influential knighted physicians in its ranks, it had been at the height of its powers: by failing to reach any conclusive recommendations about the replacement of the Institute for a period of no less than three years and then disputing the recommendations of its surgical sister committee for a further two it had, by the kind of physicianly caution on which its members regularly congratulated themselves, delayed the decision about any radical option until an exasperated Scottish Home and Health Department had eventually reallocated the proffered funding to a less contentious teaching hospital in the West of Scotland.

Now, though its agenda was less grand, its workings were no less convoluted. It had even enjoyed a couple of small recent successes. The matter of the reallocation of registrar and consultant clinical examination rooms in the Medical Outpatient Department had grumbled on for months, but the agreed principle – that consultant duties were so onerous and unpredictable that it was never known when or indeed whether a consultant physician might drop in on the clinic for which he was responsible – was eventually upheld, the registrars continuing to double up in inferior accommodation. The dispute over clinical immunology services – simplified some years before by the departure of Roger Killick, so that there were now only two separate laboratories, both fairly reliable – had eventually also ended without undue acrimony, things being left more or less as they were.

To Scott, who had once, out of a curiosity about collective behaviour disorders, sat for an evening and read through the minutes of three years' worth of the committee's monthly meetings, it seemed that almost everything they discussed came under one of two headings: clinical freedom, which meant the inalienable right of consultants to do more or less what they wanted; and the decline of a once-great teaching hospital, the phrase itself never actually appearing on the page but reverberating in subliminal discontent beneath such trivial recurrent themes as the problem of litter in the medical corridor, delays in the linen service and the time taken to repair sixty year-old lifts that regularly went out of action; and in much more substantial concerns, such as the paucity of resuscitation equipment, inadequacy of renal dialysis facilities and the lack of an intensive care area worth the name.

A chairman of genius might have elicited and refined the main grievances of the month within half an hour or so; but since the chairmanship of the committee went automatically to the consultant physician nearest retirement the meetings usually went on a lot longer. The current incumbent, a colourless rheumatologist who seemed to Scott to be exhibiting folie de doute as an early manifestation of senile dementia, now had less than six months to serve, a fact he dwelt on frequently from the chair, usually in terms of a kind of pained relief.

'May I call the meeting to order?' Mutterings died down and people scanned the agenda and the minutes, several of them tearing open envelopes to do so. 'Since I think that by far the most important item for discussion this evening comes under any other competent business it might be best, if the meeting agrees, that we move fairly swiftly . . . Oh. Sorry, Mr Secretary . . . We no doubt have some apologies.'

The secretary intoned a list of consultants too busy or too sensible to attend and a few more names were added by colleagues present. 'And the minutes of the last meeting, Mr Secretary, can we take it that they are entirely in order?'

'Mr Chairman . . .'

'Dr Bonthron?'

'Mr Chairman, in accepting a correction – item two, para three, in the minutes of the previous meeting – referring of course to the minutes of the meeting before that . . . Mr Chairman, the list of apologies should have included both myself *and* Dr Pattullo . . .'

'Thank you, Dr Bonthron. Any other points. . . ? Dr Marks?'

'Mr Chairman, at the risk of seeming repetitious I feel I would be doing a good deal less than my duty if I failed to comment on the way the discussion of case made by our haematologist colleagues for the replacement of Dr Hewitt was summarised. "Strongly supported", if I may say so, is putting it a bit strongly, much as we value the services of a senior colleague and much as we respect the contribution made over the years by him . . . But since the case for replacing yet another cardiology consultant retiral has yet to be made in detail it would be quite wrong if the chances of that case succeeding at this and subsequent committees were to be to any extent pre-empted by an overstatement of the degree of support for . . .'

By ten to six the minute was approved and serious discussion of matters arising from it could begin. The chairman had already mentioned his own impending retirement four or five times and the vice-chairman at his side, six months his junior as a consultant at the Institute, was looking commensurately perky. To Scott, the fundamental nature of the committee had gradually become a little clearer: an image from a musical cartoon of long ago, that of a dozen or so elderly and thirsty dinosaurs plodding disconsolately round a shrinking waterhole, helped quite a lot. The world had changed and they had not, and if dinosaurs had been prone to forming committees, their deliberations would have approximated quite closely to those of the Institute's medical corridor committee: they didn't know much about change, but they were against it.

Everywhere else in Britain teaching hospitals had been rebuilt and services re-organised, yet in the Institute, a vast mid-Victorian charity hospital more than a hundred years old, hideously costly to maintain and now too expensive to replace, a group of highly qualified clinicians with no relevant skills or responsibilities had squabbled for half an hour about minuscule inter-departmental advantage in a matter over which they had no ultimate control. Scott, who at the age of about ten had developed the habit of putting numbers to things that annoyed him, looked round the room, counted heads, made a few guesses about merit awards, did some quite enjoyable mental arithmetic and put the salary cost of the meeting so far at around nine hundred pounds.

'So,' said the chairman with some satisfaction, 'we can now get started . . . And I would remind you of what I said a moment ago about the major item of business being quite far down the agenda and would again urge you to try to keep your comments brief . . . I uphold as firmly as any of you our right, indeed our duty, in the matter of full discussion of our various items of business, never more important than at times like these . . .' A further dispiriting thought occurred to Scott: in the absence of any major changes – a reasonable assumption in anything relating to the Institute and its committees – his colleague Kevin Walster would be chairman of the medical corridor committee in about 1999. It was a calculation Kevin would no doubt have made for himself already.

'All of which brings us to the major item of business for this evening . . . As many of you are already doubtless aware, yet another crisis has arisen in relation to the availability of acute medical beds . . . The underlying crisis we on this committee have followed assiduously for some time but since our advice has been consistently ignored I doubt if there is anything more we could have done to avert it . . . It arises against a background of the familiar acute bed crisis that has gone on more or less throughout the year for the last ten years at least, and if any single factor is to blame it must be the Board's failure over decades, no less, to pay any attention to our recommendations on the subject of total recon-struction of the great teaching hospital in which we work . . . Dr Wilson?'

Jamie, caught unawares by the suddenness of the chairman's summons to speak, blinked and hesitated. 'Thank you, Mr Chairman. As many of you have no doubt heard already, we've had to close down six beds at the bottom end of thirty three. Some problems with the floor, although so far we don't have many details. We've had some help placing and discharging various patients. Obviously we'll keep you posted, but it does mean we'll be able to take fewer acute admissions than usual until whatever it is gets sorted out.'

'Thank you, Dr Wilson. I'm sure we will all do what we can to maintain the level of acute services despite these additional difficulties. It won't be easy and we'll get no thanks for it, but I'm sure we'll do all we can to rise . . . to the event. Dr Walster?'

Kevin, who had arrived early in order to get a seat on the right in the front row, took off his glasses, folded them and put them in his top pocket. 'Mr Chairman, are we seriously being asked to believe that this is an isolated instance? Should we not be asking ourselves what's so special about the far end of ward thirty three and when all is said and done admitting the answer is nothing. The near end is just as old, the ward below is exactly the same age, and give or take a year or two for the building, the pavilions on either side are no different. Same contractor, same materials, same age and same use. We can't, um, pre-empt the formal report from the structural engineer, but . . . I think you'll all get precisely what I'm driving at. Um, thank you, Mr Chairman.'

'Thank you, Dr Walster. Dr Bonthron?'

'As you know, my colleague Dr Pattullo has once more had to send his apologies, but I know he shares my anxiety about the bit of ward twenty five just opposite the nursing station. It sort of wobbles, you know, with the lunch trolley, and we're always very careful on our ward rounds particularly if there are a lot of students. And of course it's two floors up.'

'Thank you, Dr Bonthron. Sir Ronald?'

'Thank you, Mr Chairman. I think it's important to keep these things in proportion . . .' There was a murmur of support which seemed to distress both the chairman and Kevin. 'In all the years I've worked here I can't remember a time when the floors were anything less than . . . shall we say well-sprung? Mind you, there was that unfortunate incident in the Indian Medical Service general hospital at Bangalore just before Independence when a whole block collapsed killing sixty three sepoys and a corporal from the Gordon Highlanders.'

Jamie looked a bit surprised and Kevin was nodding vigorously. 'Mr Chairman . . .' The chairman ignored him. 'Dr Marks.'

'Thank you. As one who, like yourself, Mr Chairman, is approaching retirement and can therefore view this problem with a little more objectivity than some of our . . . younger colleagues, may I say that for this committee simply to sit and wait while the, um, roof falls in, would be a betrayal of the trust that people put in us. Nothing less than the strongest possible representations, through the appropriate channels, I emphasise, will do.'

'Thank you, Dr Marks.'

'. . . but should these representations to the Board meet with anything less than a whole-hearted commitment to immediate action, Mr Chairman, we should not hesitate to mobilise the full power of the media.' A ripple of genteel horror spread through the meeting. 'Yes, I said the media. And since the threat to the hospital as a whole – and I very much take Dr Walster's implied point about broader structural considerations – is so grave we might also ponder, not hastily, a further option, that of contacting . . . local MP's.'

The chairman's jaw dropped. 'Thank you, Dr Matthews,' he said faintly. 'Is it your wish then, that I . . . That our . . . consternation. If you press the . . . Pavilions all and, um, planks . . .' He paused, lost for words, then his right arm slipped limply from the table. He teetered for a moment, half-focusing on the front row of consultants, whose reaction seemed mainly to be one of embarrassment, then crashed sideways to the floor. No one stirred until the Committee's secretary, a young and very highly qualified thyroid specialist, put down his pen and said 'Can someone please. . . ? Is there a doctor. . . ?' Jamie and Kevin moved at the same time, first stooping over their patient, then hauling him across to prop him up against the wall. His eyes were half-closed and his face sagged piteously to the right. Behind the table, the vice chairman of the Committee of Physicians shuffled his papers together and moved quietly across to the seat just vacated by his senior colleague.

'You want to increase your market share? You need to offer a new service . . .' Max held out his hand. 'Garlic. So we're doctors . . . Either we invent some new disease like neurasthenia or enterotoxins . . . You know all that stuff. Garlic crusher.' He held out his hand again. Rachel handed Max the instrument requested. He popped in three fat slices from an outsize clove and squeezed mightily. 'Bogus, a lot of them, but you've invented it, so you're the only guy that can handle it, and the customers just roll in. But that only works in London. Harley Strasse. You can't just invent diseases up here. Basically you're National Health Service, and private practice and fashionable self-referral is never gonna be anything more than a five percent thing down in Moray Place. But you still need a new disease. Invention's out, so you gotta discover one. Or if you don't actually discover one you gotta latch on fast when somebody else does. Oil. Olive oil.' Max took it from Rachel and used it to wash a teaspoonful or so of crushed garlic into a small crystal flask. 'That OK, Theresa? I mean Catholics can eat more or less anything on Saturdays, can't they? Like my old man with drainpipes, three quarter lengths, big shoulders, velvet lapels . . . Teddy boy gear, remember all that? He had the stuff, miles of it, serge, velvet, barathea, you name it, all black, for the orthodox market which was kinda dying out in Glasgow around that time. Vinegar. Just a few old guys so old they weren't gonna take a risk with a new suit. No. Tarragon.' Max paused to add the vinegar then shook his salad dressing vigorously. 'But he did it. He caught the wave. Hound Dog Menswear of Bridgeton Cross put me through secondary at Hutchy's, all six years with no bursaries. Gee, those old orthodox guys woulda died if they'd seen the places their stuff ended up, oy vay. But it put me through school. It even got my parents out of Auchenshuggle. Like they say, next year in Whitecraigs . . .'

'New disease, Max.'

Max looked sharply at Rachel, who smiled indulgently and continued to chop lettuce. 'And they're really happy there. And all because my dad caught the wave. It runs in the family, I guess. Catching the wave. And in San Francisco they got this great new disease . . .'

Scott and Theresa were sitting on bar stools in the Cathcarts' kitchen, a modish space lined and furnished in pale pine and spotlit from about a dozen different angles. Max, centre stage and got up in a chef's hat and a blue and white striped apron, had poured them all heroic measures of gin and tonic before setting to work on his salad dressing. Rachel, a slim Australian whom Max had met up with working somewhere in London, seemed to be in charge of everything else but making rather less fuss about it. Scott looked around again and Theresa winked at him over the top of her glass. The dining alcove was set for six and no one had as yet said anything about the third couple, but it would be entirely in keeping with Max's sense of theatre that nothing would be said about them until they arrived.

'Well,' said Max. 'Does no one want to hear about this new disease then?'

Theresa obliged. Max took off his chef's hat, tossed it in the direction of Rachel and mopped his brow. 'Maybe I'm exaggerating. It might not really be something new, maybe just a couple of things we've always had around but never seen together before. Or then again it might be so mind-blowingly new we just haven't quite realised what a big deal it is yet. But it really is the big news in the infectious diseases scene on the West Coast.'

'So what does it do?'

'Spots and a cough,' said Max, taking off his apron.

'Like measles?' said Theresa.

Max laughed. The door bell rang and he went to answer it. Theresa asked Rachel how she liked living in Edinburgh. 'No use complaining. Sure as hell beats London. In fact I love it. Oh, here they are. And I bet everybody knows everybody, because it's Edinburgh.'

Theresa and Scott knew Stuart MacGregor because, with Max, they had all qualified in the same year. Stuart, now a consultant surgeon, had been married briefly to a girl also from that year but housejobs had separated them permanently, and since then Stuart had married and divorced again. His current companion was Aileen, a pretty girl of slightly athletic appearance – in effect, a MacGregor standard – who worked as a physiotherapist but, as she put it in the private sector. Over the bouillabaisse she felt compelled to explain why: 'You can actually do more for people because there's more time, basically, and you can get to know people better. And frankly they're the sort of people it's quite nice to get to know better. And because they're paying for it they want to do their best, so it's really better for everybody.'

Scott asked her where she'd trained. She made a face and said, with a conscious effort at pronouncing it the way the grimmest of its patients did, 'The Institute, ken?' Rachel was mystified. To Scott it seemed sad. Only Stuart was amused. 'I agree with Aileen,' he said. 'I do the Inchkeith Clinic bit myself, cobbling up hernias for the upper classes, and Aileen here gets them coughing to see if she can make them pop out again.' Aileen smiled as if she'd heard that before. Max sploshed some more Sancerre around and Theresa, over a spoonful of bouillabaisse, indicated silently to Scott that private physiotherapists were not legitimate targets for canvassing on behalf of the Labour party.

'I guess when I'm filthy rich and famous *all* my masseuses will be private,' said Max. 'What do you think, Andy? Massage – public or private? One of the great issues of our times. And what about those funny little ads in the *Scotsman*? Private massage, discretion guaranteed . . . Did they all train at the Institute too?'

Aileen, unused to Max and his ways, began to look quite uncomfortable. Stuart coughed and said that the best thing about private practice was the time you could spend with the patient doing things that in the NHS were done by other people. 'I'm very happy to sit on the bed and ask about their aches and pains and what their grannies died of.'

'You could do it in the NHS too,' said Max. 'Nothing to stop you. Funny how nobody seems to. You know what I'm beginning to think? Fish or cut bait.'

Rachel got up and asked if anyone would like more bouillabaisse. 'Know what I mean?' said Max. No one seemed to. 'I'm from the East End of Glasgow. My dad was small in the garment industry. In the States I'd have graduated with a loan debt the size of my mortgage before I'd earned anything. Here it's paid for, because Attlee or somebody said this is how we're doing it. And the deal is we all go work for Mr Attlee and most of us here teach some more guys who are getting it free like we did . . . But the Inchkeith Clinic gets a free ride. On training, on what happens if anybody gets sick. I mean, would *you* want to be sick out there? On lab services. On stolen goods even. We all know stuff gets into pockets and walks out of the NHS hospitals all the way to Inchkeith . . .' Stuart was shaking his head. 'Seen it, Stuart, old Chipper at the Guthrie did it all the time. "Just a few stitches for my first aid box . . ." We should add something to NHS suture material to make it dissolve in the private sector. Imagine all the hernias you'd have popping out at Inchkeith then? That would be a start. And organise aerial photographs of hospital car parks to find out who's moonlighting all day and doing eleven private sessions in his official three. And sure, let the guys do private work, but only if their NHS waiting lists are under a week. How about that? That would sort out most of the problems. You know what? They need to get some proper doctors into administration. They should make me CAMO. Or just part-time deputy CAMO with special responsibility for sorting out the guys doing private. That would do. And Auchenshuggle would be proud of me.'

While Max went round with a second bottle of Sancerre and Rachel ladled out more bouillabaisse for Stuart and Aileen, Scott worried a little about what was happening. Like Max, he found something simple and decent about being educated to serve in a big, uncomplicated, closed system that looked after all the patients and educated all the doctors, nurses, physiotherapists and everybody else it needed as it went along. Like Max, he had seen an alternative, having worked in the USA and had found the system there kind to doctors but grotesquely greedy and unfair to patients. What was worrying now was that the people the system here had created – people like Max, himself and Stuart, who could not otherwise have become doctors – were in danger of mistaking their privilege to serve in it for a licence to trade in medicine.

Scott, born under Mr Attlee, was content, even exhilarated to be working for him still, looking after patients and teaching a bit, and if the Health Service wasn't good enough then you worked, like Jimmy's generation had, to make it better. Stuart, with a fair amount of maintenance to cope with from his second marriage, might see it differently: the worse things became in the Health Service, the longer the waiting lists for hernias, the more the incentive for patients to flash a BUPA card and be whisked off to be cared for by him in the carpeted hush of the Inchkeith Clinic, where he could spend more time with them, feel smug about it and then send them a bill afterwards. Scott, who had once sat beside Stuart for a whole term's histology practicals, tried to recall where he had come from. It was one of the bleaker pit villages in the People's Republic of West Fife: Cardenden or Lochgelly or Lochore. Scott took a large mouthful of Sancerre, glanced across at Theresa and decided it would be interesting but too unkind to ask him again about it now. With both Rachel and Max busy in the kitchen, an uneasy peace prevailed.

Max had put his chef's hat on again to deliver the roast: an elaborate circle with paper-frilled ribs sticking out of it which, he explained modestly, was called crown of lamb, and not as difficult as it looked. Along with a clever thing involving creamed potatoes and choux pastry, several different kinds of beans, a green salad and some Australian claret ('No, not a joke. Try it . . .'), it encouraged more general conversation. Max asked Scott about the curious incident at the Committee of Physicians, versions of which had been circulating for a fortnight or so. 'The way I heard it . . . OK, not exactly from reading the minutes, just from somebody at lunch at the Southern, was that somebody mentioned a secret report about closing down the Institute by nineteen ninety something and he fell off his chair and thrashed around foaming at the mouth and wetting himself . . . Is that true?'

'Not very.' There were still rivalries between the Institute and the Southern that had accounted for stories like that. 'Six beds in ward thirty three had to be cleared because somebody thought the floor was going to give way, and now they've decided it isn't. And what happened to old Weary looked like a stroke at first but he was a lot better within a week so it was probably something between a TIA and a stroke, called reversible ischaemic neurological deficit. But he's . . .'

'Oooh, clever,' said Max. 'If you can't cure the disease at least you can improve the terminology . . .'

'Max,' said Rachel.

'But he's taking early retirement anyway . . .'

'Gawd,' said Max. 'Will anyone notice? Hello, love . . .'

Amanda, the Cathcarts' four year old daughter, had appeared at the door in her nightie and stood blinking and looking round. 'Come on in, love, and meet everybody . . .' Rachel went for another chair then gave her a side plate with a bit of what everybody else was having. Amanda was introduced, sat on a big cushion on her chair and began to eat quite tidily with a little knife and fork. Stuart seemed sadder and his physiotherapist became a lot more subdued. For some time nobody said much. Amanda finished her dinner except for a few beans than asked to be excused and Rachel took her out again, returning alone only minutes later. 'Did you notice?' said Max. 'How when kids behave everybody else behaves as well?'

Theresa had been captivated. 'She's lovely, Max . . . Are you going to have lots more? You should.'

'That's what my mum says . . . "Maxie, dear, a girl is fine, of course . . . We always said that, and we meant it, but . . ." '

There was big cheerful discussion about how many brothers and sisters everybody had, and how being first or second or – like Theresa – fifth, either affected you or didn't, and about what parents could and couldn't do about power politics among siblings. Stuart talked a lot, but not about his own children. Aileen made being the only daughter of a rich farmer sound fairly tolerable. Theresa had lots of sensible things to say and Scott listened with interest, and then realised that quite unselfconsciously she was talking more as a future mother than as a family doctor or a retired wee sister; with a little more interest, he realised that he quite liked to hear her talking like that.

Over the creme brulee and some Californian sauterne, Max became suddenly nostalgic about Stanford, its lab facilities and its climate. He even seemed to be missing the challenge of his new disease, and waxed eloquent about it again: 'Yes, spots and a cough, but I mean, these are *big* spots. Reddish-purple, and they don't go away. And a cough from something that's been around for ages and nobody seemed much bothered by before.'

'Infectious?'

'Not the cough. That doesn't spread. It's just PCP . . . Pneumocystis carinae pneumonia, the kind of thing you'd have learned if you were like me and wanted the bacteriology medal. Rare, opportunistic cause of pneumonia. You see it sometimes after kidney transplants, from the immuno-suppression. But they haven't had transplants.'

'So who gets it? Kids?'

'Ah, that's the really interesting bit. It's like they immuno-suppressed themselves. And they get Kaposi's, this blotchy skin tumour the textbooks say only old Jews are supposed to get. But these guys are young, goyish and gay. And they get sick, real sick, and one or two of them die . . .'

'So where else is it happening, Max?'

'Nowhere. It's a new disease. But I know more about it than anybody else in Edinburgh . . . Or Scotland . . . Or . . . Hell, maybe the whole UK.'

'Great, Max.' Stuart was laughing. 'You're made.'

'So I caught the wave.'

'No.' said Stuart. 'You still need it to start happening here.'

June 1982

Sandy sat in the waiting room by herself and wondered again if, after nearly six years, she should have rung Andrew to tell him she might be coming back to work at the Institute; but then again she might not be, so if she'd phoned him already she might have to phone him again to say no, I'm not, but it was nice to hear your voice again after all that time and I hope you're all right and I'm glad about you and Theresa and still a bit sad about us and I know why you were so angry, and – however corny it sounds and I know it does, very – it wasn't easy for me either. So because of all that it was just as well she hadn't phoned, but if she got the job she would definitely ring him soon, most probably from work quite early tomorrow afternoon.

'Hello, doctor . . .' Sandy jumped in her seat and the man who had just come in laughed, then she laughed too.'Oh, hello . . .'

'I'm sorry . . . I did not mean to frighten you . . . But perhaps, like me, you are a little bit nervous.'

'Only a bit.'

He sat down in one of the row of chairs opposite and smiled. For some reason Sandy found herself thinking about old fashioned railway compartments and strangers on trains. 'Eight seats,' he said 'but not, I hope, eight candidates.'

'Don't think so.' No one was saying very much about it, which was a bit worrying. Normally people, meaning consultants, were very friendly and open with local candidates, most so with the one whose turn it was to get the job. It was probably all something silly and male to do with joining the gang: younger consultants were especially nice to the person they thought was going to be the next new member, so the new member would be grateful and supportive to them when they'd joined the gang. And there was also something less complicated, about being the first to pass on the good news, although at this stage if you were going to get the job people didn't actually tell you, they just behaved towards you as though they were pretty sure good news was just around the corner, which was almost as nice. No one at the Southern had done that. 'Not sure,' said Sandy. 'I think four at most.'

'Have you come a long way?'

Sandy shook her head. 'I'm sort of local. How about you?'

The man made a slightly despairing gesture, his pink palms upwards. 'I'm afraid I'm from Glasgow.'

That was odd. If he was a senior registrar over there they should have met before, probably at Scottish Haematology Society, where everybody who wasn't a consultant yet competed frantically with slides of spleens and marrows and peripheral bloods and tables of figures and as much scientific English as you could cram into a ten-minute presentation, all to show how clever you were, and get you noticed by the kind of people who subsequently turned up on appointments committees.

'I'm a locum consultant there.'

'Oh? Whose job is that . . .'

'Tom Nisbet . . . Been quite poorly for some time, I'm afraid. Not expected back now, poor chap.'

'Oh. I'm sorry . . .' Dr Nisbet was a nice man who drank. It was a possible consultant vacancy Sandy had not thought of because he was only in his fifties. And was the Indian already thinking that if neither of them got this job they would be seeing each other again in a few months in the waiting room at the headquarters of the Greater Glasgow Health Board, where he might have the advantage – because he'd done the consultant locum – and then again she might, but only because she was white? But the problem with that was that Sandy couldn't really apply for jobs in Glasgow because she had a husband whose job made him not at all portable and a child who was scarcely less so. For a moment she thought about telling the stranger in the train some possibly good news he wasn't expecting, about the competition for the permanent post in Glasgow, then decided against it.

'Is this your first consultant interview?'

'Yes.' That seemed to surprise him, and Sandy wondered if he thought she looked a bit old to still not be a consultant: which she was, a bit, for a number of complicated reasons. And if she didn't

443

get this one, on her very first application, she was in real trouble, but that wasn't the sort of thing you said to strangers in trains, even nice ones like him. Whatever it was like in Glasgow – and for practical purposes that didn't matter to Sandy at all – the problem with trying to catch up with a career in haematology in Edinburgh and for miles around was that now that Dr King had finally retired all the other consultants were really young and in the best of health. In other words, no vacancies. 'Yours?'

The Indian demonstrated a more emphatic version of his pink-palmed comic despair. 'I take the view now that it is unlucky to count.'

Sandy smiled. It was hard to tell, but he was probably a good deal older than she was, and might have run out of time as a senior registrar: after four years, if you didn't have a consultant job they said sorry, and you had to go; half-timers like Sandy got a bit longer but what use was that if everybody for miles around was still going to be young and healthy? And was this probably quite old and disappointed rival living a nomadic life doing nothing but con-sultant locums now, none of which had yet resulted in a permanent job? Was there a Mrs Indian and a tribe of little Indians, going with him from one place to another, bewildered and hopeful at the same time and always being told that some day they would stop doing that and settle down permanently? 'And how do you like Glasgow?' she asked.

The man smiled. 'Very nice. The people are so very straight-forward.' It occurred to Sandy that it was just as well he wasn't going to get a job in Edinburgh, because the people there wouldn't suit him at all. Instead she said something about how even she found it hard to understand people from Glasgow sometimes. 'The patter?' he said. 'Nae problem.' They both laughed, strangers on a train, talking happily to pass the time. 'And your husband? Is he in medicine too?'

Only my first, Sandy thought to herself, then realised that the man was just gently probing, looking for whatever other advantages she had in addition to being local and white. She shook her head. 'We are both in medicine,' he said. 'It makes careers so very difficult.'

'Oh. And what does your wife do?'

'She is a lecturer in obstetrics and gynaecology.'

'In Glasgow?'

'Sadly no. She is at the moment working in Dubai.' He watched Sandy's reaction then said 'It is not so bad. And we shall settle together some day . . . when I get a permanent job.' He said that quietly, with no real hope. 'Is no one else coming then? We are only two for this job?' Sandy said she didn't think so and for some time they sat in silence.

The next person to come in was a bit of a surprise: Laurence Simpson, a sprog senior registrar of less than a year's standing, who had been a houseman when she had been working for Dr Parkinson at the time of Andrew, and who really shouldn't have been given an interview at all unless it was just for the experience. He smiled at Sandy, ignored the nice Indian man and sat down two seats along from her, putting one foot up on the opposite knee to rub a tiny fleck of mud from the toecap of his interview shoes. Sandy had a sudden, sinking feeling that it was all going to be very difficult. 'How are you, Sandy?' he asked. 'And how's the Southern suiting you?' And he had even managed to ask that in a sorry-you're-not-getting-the-job tone of voice.

A lady in a twin set came and took away the Indian, who smiled shyly at Sandy on the way out, and almost before the door had shut the sprog turned to her and mouthed 'No chance'. He was cocky and horrible, far more so even than when he had been a houseman and Sandy had had to make excuses to the nurses about him. He might well be about to grab the last consultant haematology job in Edinburgh for about a hundred and fifty years, and now he was being nasty about a man he didn't know and that Sandy had begun to like. 'So how's the Southern,' he said again.

'All right. How's the Institute?'

'I like it a lot,' he said smugly. 'What happened to the chap from London?'

Sandy said she didn't know about the chap from London and the sprog said he would have expected to have heard if he had pulled out, but it was possible that he'd just pulled out at the last minute, because he was being interviewed for a job at the Hammersmith the previous afternoon and had been quite widely tipped to get it.

'Lucky him,' said Sandy, hoping not to sound beaten already.

'You know how it is, Sandy . . . Jobs are always coming up . . .'

He was wearing a big, slightly flashy wedding ring and Sandy sat trying to work out the rest: probably that he had been married for a couple of years or so, to a nurse or a haematology lab technician, and they had one child and a ghastly modern house in Buckstone, and if he got the job they would probably try to buy a proper house somewhere like the cheaper bits of the Grange. Her task this afternoon was to rot all that up, not because he was nasty – which he was – but because if he got the job it would be quite unfair. And if he knew as much as that about the candidates he probably knew who was on the appointment committee as well, but she still wasn't going to ask him.

When he broke his sultry masculine silence it was with something she could have done without. He coughed and glanced along at her and said 'I was very sorry to hear about your dad, Sandy.'

You horrible little man, she thought, I'm having a bad enough afternoon without that, then bits of his funeral, the worst time of her life by far, came back to her and she had to wipe them out quickly and brutally before she started to cry. 'Thank you, Laurence,' she said in a quiet, calm, Easdaile deportment-class way.

'He was a great chap . . . He spoke to our final year dinner . . . Did you know that? Really funny, lots of things we didn't know he knew about us. Teasing us, really. Lots of us. He said I had a healthy and constructive attitude to the medical establishment . . . "If you can't beat them, join them . . ." '

She was supposed to laugh, so she did. He had always said something like that about somebody when he talked at a final year dinner: at their own he had said it about Andrew, who so far at least wasn't doing all that well. And she definitely wouldn't mind him being wrong about Laurence too, at least to the extent of his not becoming a boy consultant in short trousers when it was Sandy who not only desperately needed the job but deserved it too.

'Who's on the appointment committee, Laurence?'

He was taken aback, because he had been so pleased with what her dad had said about him years ago, and because she had asked the question quite sharply, as though she were a registrar and he were still a houseman.

'Well, Nigel, of course.' He was on Sandy's list already: a bright London lab-boy who had replaced Dr Parkinson, getting the job that had come up when Sandy had still been deep in the nappy-buckets instead of being poised like an organised career person for the right job in the right place at the right time. And the committee was basically there to help Nigel to decide who he wanted to work with for the next however many years, and Laurence was his current senior registrar. So no vote. Perhaps not any votes. 'Who else?'

'The national panellist. I think it's someone from Aberdeen . . . Dykes? Dyker?'

That helped. Dr Dyker had been a senior registrar on rotation with dad at the Institute ages ago and the two had kept in touch for occasional golf and fishing through the Scottish Physicians Society. One all, maybe.

'And a couple of other people from the Institute. Dr Walster and Dr Marks.'

Dr Walster was an unknown quantity, but Dr Marks too had known her dad quite well, and appeared to have decided towards the end of Sandy's housejob on Sir Henry's unit that she was the best a woman doctor could ever be, a kind of honorary chap, and he had given her a couple of good references that had helped quite a lot earlier on. It might all turn out not too badly once the talking stopped and they started counting votes. 'And I suppose someone from the Board.'

'Yes, but not sure who,' said Laurence. Sandy found discovering a limit to his inside knowledge somehow encouraging, and if the person from the Board, as was not unlikely, turned out to be someone else who was a vague friend of the family, then perhaps it was sprog Laurence, not Sandy, who had the problem, although there was no point in thinking too cheerfully along these lines until she had been in and seen for herself and done as well as she could in the interview: which – given that she was a married part-timer with a bit of a past, an interrupted career and a husband outside medicine – might not be all that well after all. They sat in silence for quite a long time, until the twinset came back. 'Dr Lennox?'

When Sandy went in and waited politely like a wee girl until she was asked to sit down, the first thing she noticed was that the chairman was someone she had never seen before: a sharply dressed man in his early forties, fit-looking and slightly tanned as though being like that was something he did very much for his career. 'Irvine,' he said. 'Willie Irvine. Nothing to do with medicine,

except that I happen to be on the Board. Accountant, actually . . .
Now I think you'll know one or two of these chaps . . .'

Dr Marks caught Sandy's eye and winked ever so slightly, which probably just meant that he thought he'd done a fine job demolishing the Indian. Nigel, whom she should have looked at first anyway, was the first person to be introduced, then Dr Marks, then Dr Walster, with a boring Watsonian tie, then Gregor Dyker, who had once come to Sunday lunch and seemed quite pleased to see her again, then Donald, a young and healthy haematology consultant from West Lothian who had been in the year above (and whom Laurence should have told her about), then a sensible woman from community medicine called Molly Affleck, whose father had once been professor of public health and who had also been to the house in Spylaw Road about a million years ago and might be a help, not so much because of that but because she was a woman and sensible. It was still worth trying very hard.

'I think you know the form, Dr Lennox. Questions from us, going round the table, then questions from you, if any, at the end. OK?'

Sandy smiled. Any doctor chairman she'd met would have taken twice as long to get that far: whatever the outcome, it would be all be over quite quickly.

'Dr Affleck.'

'Hello, Sandy.' She was being open and friendly as usual, and that would probably go down badly with the men, who seemed to think that embarrassment, awkwardness and pain were essential ingredients of a testing interview. And she was too sensible to do the silly 'Tell me why you've applied for this job' thing. She smiled. 'We have to be very conscious these days not to be sexist at interviews, and I'm going to ask you about things that are important and relevant that might sound a bit sexist . . . coming from anyone else at this end.' The accountant had almost smiled. 'Tell me, Sandy, do you think you've found any advantages in being part time when you're doing your higher medical training?'

'I do, actually. Work's more fun if you mix it with something else, but . . .'

'I agree. But as you're aware, this post is a full time one . . . Would that be a lot less fun?'

'Circumstances have changed. And I'm actually quite lucky. I've got a self-employed husband who works from home.' The men found that surprising and Molly smiled and said 'So, if we decide to appoint you to this job, your slippers will be nicely warmed for you when you get home in the evening?' Everybody laughed. Molly had taken the difficult bit head on, made it funny and not an issue any more. Sandy could have hugged her. The rest of her questions were standard stuff, the kind of thing everyone prepared for and anyone remotely employable could handle easily: about service organisation, trends in investigation requests and how clinical haematologists related to other specialists who thought they could play around with problems like myeloma that they didn't really understand. After the last question Molly smiled and thanked her.

'Dr Dyker.'

Dr Dyker, whose wife, Sandy suddenly remembered, had been hugely pregnant at quite a worrying time, took off his gold-rimmed NHS half-moon glasses and said 'Hello again.' Out of the corner of her eye Sandy saw Dr Walster frowning. 'Dr Lennox . . .' He sounded exactly the same, as if he mucked the byre, fed the hens and checked the fat stock prices before he started out for work in the mornings. 'Of course we've known each other for some time, but rather lost touch the last wee while . . . Just tell me about what you're up to in the way of research.'

He pronounced it 'rree-search'. Sandy had quite a lot ready on that too, but went through a little charade of having to think about it, if only for a moment. 'Mainly follow-up studies, actually, because one of the advantages of a half-time job is that of course you're around for a year or two longer. I've been looking at about a hundred anaemia referrals with ESR's higher than 30.'

'Verry interresting,' said Dr Dyker. 'A good idea . . . And what have you found?'

They had a nice chat about a number of rather horrible diseases and Sandy began to feel like a proper doctor again, not just a housewife on the run from her domestic responsibilities, and Dr Marks was nodding as though all her careful research had simply confirmed what he had known for years and years from his own vast clinical experience, which at least wouldn't do her any harm.

Donald came next and was sensible and straightforward, probably because it was his first time on that side of the table, then, after him, Nigel was horrible. 'You've been away from the Institute some time now, haven't you, Dr, um, Lennox. . . ? But perhaps you'd like to speculate on the kind of developments we need there and what we might do if we had an immediate equipment budget of, say a hundred thousand for a start.' Sandy, who'd had only the briefest look round the haematology lab after an absence of more than five years and would have had to find out about current prices because she didn't keep that sort of stuff in her head, felt her mouth going dry. By strictly avoiding specifics she produced an answer that a friendly questioner might have regarded as marginal, but Nigel Worling was not a friendly questioner. Dr Walster, she could see, was looking at her as if his worst suspicions about women in medicine were all being confirmed at once. Laurence, she decided, had probably been briefed for that one and would sound ready to step in as a consultant at a moment's notice even though he was only about sixteen and nasty with it.

Dr Marks did his best, which wasn't very good, because he was so used to the sound of his own voice that his questions were almost endless and practically impossible to answer with anything other than a straight yes or no. And since he was a classic amateur haematologist of the anyone-can-have-a-go school he tried quite hard to make her say things that would have contradicted her answers to Molly on the same subject a few minutes before: answers which, she was virtually certain, he had just not been listening to. She squirmed a bit, and had the impression that the poker-faced Watsonian was actually begining to enjoy himself. When Dr Marks put her down she felt like a bone that had been licked and nuzzled by a friendly but useless old retriever. He grinned at her as though vaguely aware that he had not done a good job.

'Dr Walster.'

'Dr Ratho . . . Oh, sorry. Dr Lennox. Sorry.' Sandy flinched and so, she thought, did Molly. Her CV was lying in front of him: if he had made a mistake he was criminally stupid and if he hadn't he was criminally nasty. Sandy's decision to revert to her maiden name had been a conscious, sensible one that dumped a lot of horrible things and actually helped a bit too, because of dad, and now this idiot was making life more complicated again, upsetting her whether he meant to or not when the last thing she needed was to be reminded of that. She was aware of colouring slightly, and had to concentrate quite hard to pick up what the idiot was trying to say next. As he plodded through a long, Dr Marksish question, one about the value of routine testing that wasn't even interesting, it suddenly clicked for Sandy. He was a dim, occasional golfing chum of Gus's, who probably thought of Luffness as an exhilarating social climb, and in his dim poisonous way he was messing her up as a twisted, belated favour to his posh golfing friend. Unfortunately for Sandy, she couldn't stop herself answering his question as though it had been asked by a below average fourth year medical student. When she finished he said 'No more questions, thank you,' and even had the gall to sound quite hurt. There was no one else to ask some questions that would let Sandy show she was really a kind, sensible person like Molly. It was a bad note to end on, and she even wondered about coming up with a couple of questions herself when they asked her, just to take away the nasty taste. But only losers and the hopelessly disorganised did that at interviews, and she didn't feel at all like either of those. She smiled and shook her head.

'Thank you, Dr Lennox,' said the snappy suit, jumping to his feet. 'I'm sure you know the form. We happen to have one more candidate to see, so if you'd care to hang around in the waiting room, or perhaps take a stroll and come back in about half an hour. Thank you.'

The twin set appeared again from somewhere behind and showed Sandy the door and the five yards along the corridor to the waiting room. With Sandy standing behind her she popped her head in and said 'Dr Simpson? Dr Simpson, please.' Laurence came swaggering out, straightening his tie even though it was perfectly straight already, and walked past Sandy without even noticing her. Maybe Molly would sort him out, but the more she thought about it the more Sandy realised that she was no longer an obvious, non-controversial candidate for anything. For the first six years of her medical career she had had good fun and done well, because she was cheerful and straightforward and hard-working, clever enough to cope without conspicuous effort and good at organising people and things. Now she was what her dad in his ex-naval way would have called a welfare case: a lame duck that nice people like Molly would try to help; but sufficiently old, as these things go, and unusual, in terms of career continuity and the name changes that the nasty Watsonian had so clumsily or adroitly emphasised, for people who wanted safe, ordinary decisions to begin to feel uneasy about her. And sadly, when it came down to it, committees appointing consultants to work till they were sixty five just didn't take risks.

If there was still any doubt about it, and strictly speaking there was, Sandy had to decide now what to do with the half hour of her life after which she would know whether or not she had got the last consultant post that could conceivably be of any use to her. She looked into the waiting room. It was quiet and empty, now more of a prison cell than a train compartment going somewhere, so she went downstairs, through the foyer of the Board's offices and out on to its rather pompous stone steps. She checked her watch. By three thirty five they would have finished with Laurence and the accountant-chairman would have done his celebrated impression of a business-man of few words and great force of character harrying a lot of woolly-minded doctors to a quick decision, and it seemed obvious to Sandy that only a very long discussion indeed, with marginal figures like Molly and Gregor Dyker being allowed to talk a lot and being listened to, would give her even an outside chance. More likely, alas, was something along the lines of 'Come on, chaps, who do you want? The black, the woman or the crisp, confident young man we've just seen? Good, we'll send for him.' There didn't even seem to be much point in counting the possible votes.

Sandy walked west, to stay well clear of the otherwise quite nice part of the New Town where she and Gus had lived, then turned north along the front of the Episcopalian cathedral. A little door in the big main door was open and inside they were practising something with a choir and organ, stopping unpredictably and often and never really letting the music get going at all, the way they had done with the choir at school until everybody got so frustrated that when they were allowed to sing on they did it really well. She stood and listened, hoping whoever was in charge would just let them get on with it, but it never happened. The music in the cool space inside stopped again and again, with a man's voice shouting bossily every time it did, and Sandy found herself checking her watch absurdly often, so just gave up and walked the rest of the block before turning east again.

On the way back she looked around for the Indian doctor from Glasgow, because it would have been nice to talk to him again while they could both still pretend that either might still get the job, but there was no sign of him. With a good ten minutes in hand she went back up the stone steps, through the foyer and upstairs to the waiting room. He was not there either, and she sat down, alone again on the same chair as before, looking round with a kind of distracted concentration and finding all sorts of things she hadn't noticed previously, like cobwebs thick on the cornice and slight differences between chairs that had at first looked like a set. The sooner it was all over, and the less time she had to sit with Laurence Simpson awaiting the final verdict, the better.

When he came back, she was calm and he was clearly not. He sat down opposite, head in hands, looking like a tired little houseboy after a hard admitting night and in dire need of a word of encouragement from a nice, sympathetic registrar. Sandy let him sit for about five minutes then asked how it had gone. 'Rough,' he said. 'The worst interview of my life. That woman from community medicine?'

'Dr Affleck.'

'Practically laughed at me. And Dr Marks as good as told me I should come back when I was a bit older.' He sniffed and giggled. 'I'm sure I'll have to anyway. Somewhere. I mean, not here. And we really like Edinburgh . . .'

Sandy was just starting to tell him that he'd probably done a bit better than he thought he had when the snappy suit came bouncing in, looked straight past her and said 'Dr Simpson? Could you come this way?'

As soon as they had gone she got up and walked calmly downstairs trying to convince herself it was neither a surprise nor an injustice. Her mum would sympathise, her daughter would never understand anyway and her husband would continue to believe that medicine was a disordered profession. And she wouldn't have to phone Andrew tomorrow afternoon, or ever, which was a pity, because she'd been quite looking forward to it.

October 1984

'It's awfully good of you to come away out here, Dr Ratho . . . I really do appreciate it.'

'It's no trouble really. And they're looking after you?'

Miss Finnie closed her eyes and frowned in thought. 'I'm sure there was something I was going to mention to you. It'll come back in a minute.'

'But the most important thing, Miss Finnie . . . How are you?'

'I hardly have to tell you, Dr Ratho. You know how I suffer.'

She sank back in her chair and sighed. Gus, leaning forward in his, waited for the next bit of her litany. After a longer pause than usual she said 'And I know there's really nothing anyone can do for me.'

Normally at this point Gus agreed with her and told her how splendidly she was coping in the face of a very difficult illness. That was all very well for a consultation in Moray Place, but now that she was an in-patient he might have to be a bit more positive. He leaned further forward, with his hands in the classic fingertips-together how-are-we-today position. 'I certainly wouldn't want to raise your hopes too far, Miss Finnie, but I think that quite soon we'll be able to report some quite useful progress. You remember all the blood tests we sent off when you came in?' She nodded. 'Although there's really no doubt about the diagnosis, there are one or two things we look at – trace elements, immunoglobulins, things like that, that you and I have discussed before – that vary quite a lot between one case and another . . .' Her attention was wandering. She did not wish to hear about other people. '. . . and indeed over the course of the illness in individual patients, particularly so in difficult cases such as your own. And what we've found is that when certain things begin to pick up in the blood we can be fairly confident the patient will feel quite significantly better over the following weeks, indeed sometimes days.'

Miss Finnie smiled bravely. Gus nodded encouragement. He had once read something rather cynical to the effect that people spend hundreds of guineas in Harley Street in order to buy permission to get better. Since Miss Finnie was unlikely to get out of the Inchkeith Clinic with a bill for less than several thousand pounds, the least he could do was to offer her a little of that.

'I've just had a very close look at your results,' he said, leaning back again and talking a bit more cheerfully. 'Not just the recent ones, but going right back to the beginning of your illness. And may I say now that looking back at them it seems almost a miracle to me that you didn't feel a very great deal worse when all this started. But the key to the whole thing in your case seems to be something we call albumen-bound zinc . . .'

Myalgic encephalomyelitis had come along at a good time for Gus. Lab work bored him and the NHS in-patient workload had come more and more to resemble the leftovers from an OAP's outing. Registrars, even SHO's could do as much for them as he could medically, and since half of them got stuck in the ward for months because their families wouldn't look after them the turnover, and hence the real medical interest, had dwindled to virtually nothing. But just when NHS medicine had become almost impossible, the government, which was by no means as bad for medicine as some of the comrade consultants on the Left made out, had changed the rules a bit, so that more or less anyone could do private practice.

As a clinical immunologist Gus had at first wondered what sort of patient he might get turning up in Moray Place, and then someone from his year, in general practice in Morningside, had sent him an old duck who thought she might have myalgic encephalomyelitis. To this day Gus was uncertain whether she had or hadn't, but the old duck, who seemed to take all the Sunday papers and read them from end to end, had sat happily chatting for the full half-hour about the various symptoms she had that might well fit the diagnosis. Scientifically speaking, the disease remained a puzzle; in strictly commercial terms it had turned out to be a dazzling success.

Old ladies seemed to tell other old ladies about it, and GP's in the nicer areas began to hear quite a lot about it too. That, and a few hints dropped to GP's on golf outings and at dinners sponsored by drug firms, had been the beginning of what had turned out these days to be almost a full-time job. And somehow the fact that most of his patients were aged seventy five and upwards didn't seem so much of a problem in the private sector: Miss Finnie, now eighty three and the sole heiress of a family business that made sticky liqueurs, was really quite bearable for up to half an hour at a time.

They had given her a room on the second floor, looking out over Cramond Island and across to West Fife. As well as the bed there was a drinks cabinet, a decent sized television, a bookshelf of Nigel Tranters and Dorothy Dunnetts, some bland pictures, a coffee table and the pair of armchairs in which they were sitting. The carpet was deep, the lighting good and the view really quite pleasant. Although her own house in Heriot Row, which he had visited on a private domiciliary consultation with the GP several hundred pounds ago in the case, was more comfortable and a great deal more affluent, she wasn't doing too badly considering she was in hospital. Looking round, Gus remembered she had a complaint, probably the kind of thing he had to listen to rather than do anything about, and he would ask her about that when they had nearly finished. Meanwhile, she was getting more for her money than just permission to recover.

'. . . was a martyr to her bowels too, Dr Ratho. I'm sure these things run in families, aren't you?'

'I think one could say so . . . Up to a point.'

'And of course a lot of people say that with myalgic encephalomyelitis the whole thing becomes a lot more difficult. I could spend half the morning in the toilet and have hardly a thing to show for it . . . Could that actually be making things worse?'

'There's a fair amount of evidence these days . . . that it almost certainly won't be helping. And in some cases, of course . . .'

'You know, I thought so. It seems awfully old-fashioned to be worrying about my bowels, but if there *is* anything you could do, Dr Ratho . . .'

'I'm sure we can arrange something, Miss Finnie.'

'Remembering of course that nothing seems to work for me . . .'

Gus braced himself, and they talked about a high-fibre diet, which she had tried and hated and which hadn't worked anyway. Then they discussed drinking lots of fluid with and between meals, but that just made her run back and forward to the toilet but never for what she really wanted; and all the laxatives she'd tried, she assured him, had availed her not at all. Time was passing and Gus wondered about writing her up for one dose of the sort of thing used to clear people out before bowel X-rays, stuff that came in a bottle virtually labelled 'Light blue touch-paper and retire', but decided that making her explosively incontinent of faeces might mean the end of a long and mutually beneficial relationship. He looked puzzled, thoughtful and wise in succession then said 'We may be able to help quite a bit with that, Miss Finnie. A colleague of mine, an outstanding specialist in the field that, um, concerns us, might be able to pop out here and assess things for you with a fresh and expert eye. We can't bank on it, because I know he's an extremely busy man, but I think if I stress to him the seriousness of the problem he'll certainly do his best.'

Miss Finnie lay back in her chair again. 'I'd be most grateful, Dr Ratho.'

It seemed as good a time as any to get away. Gus rose to his feet. 'And you mentioned some other small problem, Miss Finnie . . . To do with the Clinic?'

She shook her head. 'Just get my bowels sorted out, Dr Ratho, once and for all. I've been clutching at straws for them for years.'

Gus saw the rest of his Inchkeith in-patients and looked in at the Southern on the way to Moray Place, trying off and on to remember the name of the chap at the Institute who worked with Professor Bennett and sometimes turned up for golf and was supposed to be interested in constipation. Webster was near it, Wallace a bit further away. Walster. Kevin Walster. As soon as he got back to his rooms he asked the secretary to ring around and get hold of him. She found him in about two minutes, which meant he couldn't really be all that busy. Unfortunately Walster's secretary was playing the telephone game too, and Gus had to listen while she did her 'I'm just putting you through to Dr Walster now, Dr Ratho. Just putting you through.'

'Hello? Gus?'

'Oh, Kevin, awfully sorry to have to bother you. I'm in a little bit of trouble with a lovely old duck out at Inchkeith. A Miss Finnie. Does remarkably well with quite severe ME, but the problem now is that she's become terribly constipated. We've tried most things, and it really is probably the most treatable thing about her. As you know, there's not an awful lot one can do about ME itself.' Gus could hear

Walster almost panting with excitement, as though he had to try hard to stop himself interrupting. 'But I wondered if you might be able to help a bit.'

'I'd be . . .'

'She's not exactly in her salad days. Eighty three, in fact. But I don't suppose you'd mind that.'

'No, I'd . . .'

'Good. Terribly sweet old thing. Eighty three and sharp as a tack. One of my favourite patients, really, so if there's anything you can do.'

'I could get over there this evening, Gus. This afternoon if it's urgent.'

It occurred to Gus that Walster might not have done much private work before and might not be quite up to the form. Being busy was as much part of it as agreeing with almost everything the patients said. 'Unfortunately I've got a few things lined up for her this afternoon. Tomorrow as well, actually. If you could perhaps pop out on Thursday . . .'

'Okey dokey.'

That made Gus wonder again if he might be making a mistake, but since not many people wanted to come to grips with this type of problem it was a question of needs must, and with any luck he wouldn't say things like okey-dokey in front of Miss Finnie. 'I'll just give you the details, Kevin. It's a Miss Letitia Finnie. She's eighty three and her GP's Donald Cameron . . . Yes, old-fashioned, I agree, but he's found quite a lot of ME for me in Morningside . . . She'll be out at Inchkeith until the end of next week, I'd have thought . . . So there's no desperate rush . . .'

'Okey-dokey, Gus . . .'

'Thanks awfully, Kevin.'

'Grand . . . Maybe see you out at Luffness for a game some day.'

'Most certainly,' said Gus, putting the phone down. When he had done so a possible slight snag occurred to him. Since most people did a little bit of private work now, Kevin's name was almost certainly on the list of consultants with official access to the facilities of the Inchkeith Clinic. But if he wasn't, it still might not be too much of a problem, since the nurses were very thinly spread and dozens of doctors, lawyers and assorted visitors streamed in and out of the place every day of the week. And of course if, as a result of a misunderstanding, it were all to slip through unofficially Kevin might be happy to take cash, which would probably suit both of them quite well. Gus settled in and checked the bookings for his afternoon clinic. There were two new ME's and three follow-ups, which was just about right if everyone wanted to come away from Moray Place feeling relaxed, cared for and satisfied.

'So what happens now, Dr Cathcart?'

'It's a notifiable disease . . . We've notified somebody. On a form. Every ward should have some. Officially you tell the CAMO, who isn't very interested. But in practice he tells somebody who tells somebody else who tells somebody else who comes and talks to the patients. Usually works quite well.'

'So what's gone wrong this time?'

'Dunno. Forms lying on a desk somewhere at the Board. Long weekends can damage everybody's health.'

'So what happens now?'

'Good question.' Max looked again at the girl and decided she was probably the adventurous type. 'Let's go and take a look.'

'At the Board?'

'No. At Allanshaw. Where they came in from.' The girl was intrigued but still a bit hesitant. Max grabbed patient identification labels from four sets of casenotes, stuck them on an X-ray request card, then took off his white coat and put on his jacket. 'Come on. It's so horrible it's quite interesting.' She hung her white coat beside his and they walked out to the car park. When she saw his car she looked distinctly more keen.

'Eight miles away . . . Say ten minutes. And it's the kind of place a film outfit would hire if they were making The Boyhood of Kinnock.' She was laughing as she got in. 'You know what I mean? Half a dozen brick terraces round a slagheap.' He handed her the card with the labels stuck on. 'Look. Third Street. Fifth Street. Either they thought it was going to get like New York, or they couldn't even be bothered to think of names. And everybody's poor. And that's before the strike started. God knows what it's like now.'

If he were being entirely honest, Max would have had to admit that he probably wouldn't have gone out to have a look for himself if it hadn't been for the miners' strike. He would have made one of his fairly famous phone calls to the infectious diseases section at the

Health Board and someone would have been up in the ward talking to the patients about where they'd been and what they'd eaten, usually within the hour. But whoever had come up would most likely have had to go out to Allanshaw as well, because the patients were children, and the parents, who would perhaps have been more helpful about specifics, couldn't afford to come in very often. To pass the time on the way out he quizzed the girl about the piece of practical epidemiology that every medical student was supposed to know, the tale of the Dr Snow and the pump in Soho. She was quite good, and even knew that the epidemic had begun to go away by the time he took the handle off the pump, which was more than most of them did.

'So we're doing a Dr Snow. Go take a look. Talk to people. See how they live. You don't get too much of that, do you? And these kids are poor. I mean really poor.'

Six of them had come in over four days, all with good-going salmonella, which was odd, and probably meant there were a lot more cases out there that hadn't been admitted. The patients in the ward were aged between two and seven, most of them small for their age, thin and dirty, bewildered and frightened. On the ward round they had just finished Max, with the houseman and the student beside him, had sat on their beds, trying to talk to them. The little ones had cried a lot. The bigger ones were mutely suspicious, ill at ease in the quiet single rooms, uncomfortable and ashamed at having diarrhoea, wary even of the nurses. Thinking about it, and about the parents who couldn't afford to visit them, Max began to get angry again. The girl was a well-brought-up young lady from a good Edinburgh school, exactly the kind of person who should be coming with him to find out what went on beyond the genteel southern horizon of the Braid Hills. Perhaps quite soon she would be angry too.

They left the main road for a side road that started badly, under a disused railway viaduct, and soon got worse. The village itself appeared quite suddenly as they crested a hill. 'There you are,' said Max. 'Kinnock country. In only nine minutes. Give me an address.'

Third Street was a rutted, pot-holed lane with single-storey red brick terraces on either side. A few battered cars were parked as though they would never move under their own power again. 'There we are. Fifteen. Macrae. And it's wee Norman . . . We'll take it slowly. What's your name, sunshine. . . ? So I can introduce you.'

'Heather.'

'Good. Come on, Heather.'

They got out and Max knocked on the door. A dog barked and there were scuffling noises and a woman's voice shouted 'A'right, I'm comin' . . . I'm comin'.' Max stood back from the door as it opened.

'Mrs Macrae?'

She was probably not much older than the medical student, but could have passed for forty: a thin, bedraggled woman clearly astonished to have two middle-class aliens on her doorstep.

'Mrs Macrae? Hello. Sorry to disturb you. We're from the Southern General Hospital. And I should tell you straight away that Norman's doing fine.'

The woman started to cry, and Max put his hand on her shoulder. 'He's fine, Mrs Macrae . . . I'm looking after him and I was with him half an hour ago. He's coming on nicely. Hope to get him home to you soon. But for now I just wanted to have a quick chat about his illness . . . Maybe you know, there have been one or two others from the village.'

'Come on in . . .' They followed her along a dark passageway into a bleak little room with a sofa, two chairs and a noisy television set. A toddler, thin and red-haired like its older brother, was sitting in front of an empty grate. 'Sorry aboot the state o' the place. It's no' been easy, ken? Would you like tae sit doon?'

She turned the television sound down and Max quizzed her gently about matters relating to possible salmonella sources. Her answers were oblique, not because she was trying to hide anything but because she was distressed. 'There's nae money in Allanshaw noo, ken? For naebody. It's been months and months, an' the strike pay's nothin'. Folk are daein' their best but whit can ye dae?' She sniffed deeply. 'Even the men dinnae eat right. And a few o' them tried tae feed the kids . . . Jist soup an' a puddin', ken? But the cooncil's closed them doon.'

Perhaps Max had underestimated the efficiency of the CAMO and his small army of Environmental Health Inspectors. 'Tell me about that, Mrs Macrae. The soup place.'

'Jist some women . . . In the Miners' Welfare hall . . . For the wee bairns.'

461

'So what were they getting?'

'Soup and puddin'.'

'Anything else, Mrs Macrae?'

'No' much. Some wee sangwidges.'

'Tell me about them.'

'Jist wee sangwidges. Biled ham, chicken, that kind o' thing . . . For the wee yins.'

Max nodded. 'I see. And tell me about . . .'

'But they stopped them. Jist the ither day there. The cooncil stopped them.'

'Because?'

'Dinnae ask me.' she said. 'Imagine stoppin' us feedin wir ain bairns.'

'So how are you managing now?'

'Daein' ma best.' The woman put her hands up to her face and sobbed. 'Sorry,' she said through her tears, reaching for the toddler on the floor. 'But dinnae take *him* away, will ye? There's nothin' wrong wi' him.'

Max put a hand on her shoulder again. 'No, Mrs Macrae, we won't. Of course we won't. We've just come to tell you Norman's going to be all right.'

'I'm daein' ma best,' she sobbed. The child on her knee put his arms round her neck. 'I even got him Coco-Pops.'

Max got up and the girl got up too. He ushered her on ahead and in the passageway quickly took out his wallet. He had thirty five pounds in tens and fives, and three more houses to visit. Someone was going to have to go short.

Gus had always been grateful to the Institute's chaplain for putting him in touch with St Andrew's, because the congregation there combined a vigorous spiritual life with a few traditional touches that really appealed to him, like formal communion services with the duty elders wearing morning dress. He was standing at the foot of the aisle beside the other duty elder, a down-at-heel lawyer called Aithie, waiting to take the offering up to the table to be formally dedicated. When the organist started to play, Aithie, as senior elder, muttered 'By the right' and they were off, Aithie's salver wobbling from his obvious hangover.

The tune was one Gus had known from his earliest time at

school, a vigorous march by Handel or somebody, with words that began 'See, the conquering hero comes . . .' although that did not seem quite right for a couple of elders marching the morning's collection up the aisle like a badly matched pair of butlers. He was smiling to himself about that when he became aware of another sound, a short but steady high-pitched tone, repeated once. For a moment he wondered if it might be something to do with Aithie, then felt rather foolish when he realised that it was his own Air-Call pager, in the inside pocket of his morning suit, and that he would have to slip away as soon as his duties permitted.

They arrived, quite smartly together at the steps where Gavin, the minister was waiting, and the music stopped. With both hands still holding a silver salver at least thirty inches across, there was little that Gus could do immediately to silence his bleep, but with any luck they would be well into the final hymn before it went off again. Gavin lifted his arms and said 'O Lord our God, who givest liberally and upbraidest not; teach us to give cheerfully of our substance for Thy cause and Thy kingdom . . .' then just as Gavin was drawing breath for the rest of the dedication the Air-call sounded again: a delicate problem, but one that could be solved as soon as Gavin took the salvers and Gus could get at his inside pocket. '. . . a living sacrifice, holy and acceptable to Thee; through Jesus Christ our Lord. Amen.'

Gavin took the salvers, Aithie's first, Gus's second, and Gus retrieved his pager and silenced it, but not before about four hundred morning worshippers had been made aware that Dr Angus Ratho, one of their duty elders, had temporal responsibilities as well as spiritual ones. And since it would have looked rather foolish not to, Gus moved quickly and quietly away to make use of the phone in the vestry corridor.

The Air-Call operator asked him to ring the Inchkeith Clinic, a number he knew well, and the sister on duty there asked him to come in straight away because one of his patients, a Miss Letitia Finnie, had taken a turn for the worse. Gus left St Andrew's by the back door and drove straight out to the Clinic, partly to save time and partly because Miss Finnie, to say nothing of the staff, might rather enjoy his coming straight from church in morning dress. Traffic was light and he got out to the Clinic in record time and bounced up the steps, reflecting happily that the private sector not only offered full-time consultant cover but could deliver it pretty quickly too.

The sister on duty seemed pleased he'd come in straight away, and explained the problem on the way upstairs. 'I'm quite worried about her, Dr Ratho. She was fine on Friday and I was off yesterday but nobody seems to have noticed anything amiss, and this morning when I was walking round I noticed she looked quite grey.'

'I see. And nothing to account for it? You've got readings, pulse, temp and all that?'

'From this morning, Dr Ratho. I checked her as soon as I saw her . . . Apyrexial, pulse a hundred and twenty and blood pressure a good deal lower than it was when she came in.'

'What is it now?'

'A hundred over sixty.'

Miss Finnie was ill, perhaps very ill. She lay in her bed, eyes closed and mouth half-open, breathing only irregularly, switching from swift, shallow gasps to periods of virtual apnoea. Gus glanced at her chart, which was empty of readings apart from on the day of admission and this morning. 'And nobody's noticed anything else, I take it? I think it was Wednesday I last saw her. Not expecting trouble at all, just a fairly routine ME in an otherwise quite fit old thing. This is all very strange . . . Miss Finnie? Miss Finnie?'

Her eyes half-opened but did not focus. Gus felt her pulse, which was tiny in volume and very fast. 'I'm sorry sister . . . I came straight in from church. Could you possibly find me a stethoscope? Put out your tongue, please, Miss Finnie.'

Her mouth opened only a little. Her lips were foul and cracking and her tongue was a greyish-white mess. Gus turned the bedclothes back and through her nightie gently palpated her abdomen, which was quite soft. He lifted her arms one by one and let them fall. There was no difference in muscle tone between the two sides. He flicked the ends of her middle fingers, watching to see if her thumb moved too, then lifted the bedclothes from her feet and carefully scratched each sole, looking for the abnormal upward movement of the big toe that might denote a stroke. Sister returned.

'Just been over her quickly. Wondered about a stroke . . . The likeliest thing, really, but there's not actually much going for it. Thank you, sister.' Gus took the stethoscope and listened on the left chest: that told him only what he knew already, that her heart-beat was fast but regular. Then he pulled Miss Finnie's nightie up around her chest and listened to her belly. It was silent. He stood up and handed the stethoscope to the sister. 'All very unexpected. I'd be grateful if you'd let her relatives know she's really quite ill.'

'I have,' she said. 'They're coming in.'

That was worrying. Gus said 'Good, thanks awfully, sister . . . And you're sure there's nothing untoward documented in your nursing notes since Wednesday? Not that I'm suggesting you've missed anything, of course. I just know how terribly hard pressed you all are.'

'See for yourself, Dr Ratho . . .'

That was reassuring. Gus took the folder and saw that after 'Seen by Dr Ratho' on Wednesday there was nothing but the usual banal alternation of Good day, Good night, Good day, which indicated either that nothing was going on or – and in this case it might be an important distinction – that the nurse thought there was nothing going on. 'A pretty uneventful week.' He handed the folder back to the sister. 'I'd be grateful if you'd repeat her readings half-hourly for the time being. To be frank it's not awfully clear yet what's going on . . .'

'The relatives said they would like to see you, Dr Ratho. They're on their way in.'

'Thanks awfully, sister. I'll just pop along to the medical office and scribble something in the notes. Please tell me as soon as they arrive.'

The medical office, a modern, well-equipped room twice the size of anything in the Institute or for that matter the Southern, was quiet. Gus found Miss Finnie's notes in their proper place and opened them with some trepidation. After his scribble from Wednesday there was a side and a half of neatly written notes beginning 'Thank you for asking me to see this charming old lady . . .' and ending 'K V Walster, Consultant Physician.' The bit in between described the symptoms and signs of Miss Finnie's constipation, went on to give an almost coprophiliac account of something called a high colonic lavage procedure, and included a grim little sentence about 'the small but definite risk of diverticular perforation following this procedure in the frail elderly.' According to the note Kevin had asked, in view of this risk, for hourly readings for twenty four hours, but he had clearly not talked to anyone who had paid any attention.

465

There was something else Gus needed to know and needed to know quite quickly. On the main desk was an A-4 sized loose-leaf binder titled 'The Inchkeith Clinic: Directory of Physicians and Surgeons with Consulting Privileges'. Sections were alphabetically indexed and the only entry in the 'W' section was that of Johnny Woods, a nasty little surgeon who did varicose veins. Gus returned to Miss Finnie's notes, removed the page with his own brief note from Wednesday and Kevin's longer one from Friday and rewrote his Wednesday note on the following blank page. He had just slipped the little ball of screwed up paper into the pocket of his morning suit when sister knocked at the door. 'Miss Finnie's relatives, Dr Ratho. Shall I show them to the visitors' room?'

'Thank you, sister. I'll be along right away.'

When Gus went in they both got up and practically stood to attention because, he realised almost as soon as they'd done it, of his morning suit. 'Please, please sit down . . .'

The man was in his thirties, unshaven and wearing a Heriot's RFC jersey. The woman, of similar age, wore a track suit in an unfortunate shade of pink. Both looked as if they had come straight from bed and neither looked in the least distressed. 'You must be terribly upset,' said Gus. 'This is all so sudden. And I'm afraid we don't seem to have met. I'm Dr Ratho, and I've been seeing your. . . ?' He paused, as he had intended, to let them explain the relationship. The man spoke up. 'Letty was my granny's cousin . . . We're really the only people she's got now. But she's always been awful good to us. I'm Jim Finnie. And this is Shona, my wife.'

Gus had once worked for a rather roguish old physician called George Gordon, one of whose many aphorisms was 'Where there's a will, there's a relative.' It seemed to Gus that any grief Jim and Shona might experience was unlikely to be more than they could bear. 'I've known your, um, kinswoman for quite a long time now. She kept her spirits up quite remarkably, and I had hoped that she would get over this unfortunate exacerbation of her . . . condition.'

'I didn't even know she was ill,' the man said.

'She was very brave about the whole thing,' said Gus. 'Not one to complain at all, even to me.'

'Was it something serious, doctor?'

Gus swallowed heavily. 'I'm afraid so.'

'What kind o' thing, doctor?'

'She suffered from quite serious heart disease,' said Gus, 'and I'm afraid she's had rather a massive heart attack this morning. I came as quickly as I could – ten minutes, actually – but sadly, there is so little one can do . . . So far as we know, she's not in any pain, but I'm afraid . . .'

'Letty wouldn't have wanted to be an invalid,' said the woman 'Would she, Jim?'

Gus got up. 'Shall we go in and see her now? She's really very peaceful.'

Later that afternoon Gus was called back to the Inchkeith Clinic to certify the death of Miss Letitia Broome Finnie. In the very elderly patient exact diagnosis is sometimes difficult, so rather than trouble people by mentioning peritonitis secondary to bowel perforation after colonic lavage he wrote a certificate citing something which, on clinical grounds, was almost as likely: massive myocardial infarction. It could be thought of as quite a peaceful release for a frail old lady who had suffered so much in her latter years from a remarkably troublesome form of myalgic encephalomyelitis. In the evening he rang Kevin Walster at home, gave him a brief account of events, and of how misunderstandings had been prevented, and arranged a game of golf with him at Luffness the following Saturday.

July 1986

'Not really working out, is it?'

'No.'

'Seemed a jolly good idea at the time . . . Everyone said so. But what do *you* think. . . ?' Scott hesitated. 'Come on, Andrew . . .' Jimmy Jameson reached across and topped up an already large Tio Pepe. 'Say what you think. We still might get it right.'

'I suppose the main thing, objectively . . . The main thing is that hardly anybody else is doing it that way.'

'Hasn't caught on, hm?'

'Not really. One place in England, maybe.'

'Pity. We got in early, and got it wrong. But you should have heard the chaps at the time. All terribly keen. Breaking down barriers, holistic approach. Integrated, but somebody's got to be in charge. Marvellous, we all said. Let's get on with it. Then we appointed Wiggy.' They were sitting in the sun on a terrace overlooking Jimmy's vast and orderly garden. Scott had been summoned at short notice for 'a quiet chat about something quite important.' Jimmy rolled his glass in one hand and frowned at the wooded slope opposite 'At the time I saw it as being rather like rooting out tubercle. You know the sort of thing. Team game, everyone in it together, good morale essential in what had been a pretty gloomy corner of the trade.' He emptied his glass. 'Pity.'

Mrs Jimmy came out with a tray and deposited on the table between them a small dish of peanuts and another containing what she described as some quite tasty things from the market in Kathmandu. 'Thanks awfully, Esmee . . . Andrew's kindly sharing some thoughts about what to do after poor Wiggy.'

Following a minor but widely publicised incident on the steps of a Soho club, Professor Bennett had recently gone off to Wales on a sabbatical of indefinite duration. The future of the Care of the

468

Elderly Unit was uncertain but Jimmy, who in retirement had retained an undiminished zest for medical politics, seemed to have views. 'So this time we've really got to get it right . . .' Scott might have looked puzzled at that, because Jimmy turned to him and said 'You do know I'm a curator?' Scott shook his head. 'See, Esmee? He thinks I'm just a meddlesome old buffer, poking around in things that don't concern me. No Andrew, for some reason not obvious to me the University's kindly made me a Curator of Patronage . . . Marvellous title, isn't it? Makes you sound like a chap in Pepys' diary, going round fixing appointments and pulling in sovereigns by the sackful, hm?' Esmee was frowning. Jimmy became serious again. 'In fact we're there to worry about things . . . What professorial chairs are for, and who gets them. And as one of the chaps who thought the idea up in the first place, I'm jolly glad to get a chance to sort it out. And what everybody's saying now is that what's needed is a lot more hands-on medicine. Not particularly good news for a psychiatrist like you, Andrew, but I do want to know what you think.'

Scott said what he thought, with Jimmy frowning in deep concentration until he felt he had heard enough, when he confided to his former houseman that exactly the right sort of chap who was needed to revitalise Care of the Elderly in Edinburgh had once worked locally, and might now, under changed circumstances, be persuaded to come back. Scott's glass was topped up yet again and Jimmy sat back contentedly in the sun. 'Ever been to Kathmandu, Andrew?'

Max rang the doorbell on the wall next to the odd little Alice-in-Wonderland door and waited. Nothing happened so he rang it again. He was about to ring it for a third time when a man in his twenties, casually dressed in jeans and loose white sweater, opened it and said 'Dr Cathcart?' Max nodded. 'Come on in. David's expecting you.'
'Thanks . . .'
'I'm Robin,' said the man.
Max just stopped himself saying 'And I'm Batman', because most people didn't like jokes about their names and, perhaps more importantly, there was no certainty where Robin fitted into the Pitsligo scheme of things. He followed him across a lawn, through a

conservatory full of the kind of plants that Max had seen previously only in the Botanic Gardens, and into the house. David Pitsligo was sitting in the corner of a billowing antique sofa in a sunny lounge.

'Max! Lovely to see you. Thanks for coming over. Please sit down. Drink?'

'Yes, thanks . . .'

'What would you like? We've got most things . . .'

'Beer?'

'Export or lager?'

'Oh . . . Lager, thanks . . .' Robin, who had been standing attentively through all this, slipped out of the room. David smiled across at Max. 'Marvellous weather, isn't it? But of course you'll have been slaving over all those hot patients since daybreak?'

'More or less.'

'I was out for a bit, just after lunch. You know, so much goes on in a garden that you never think about until you've got time just to sit and look. I've stopped worrying about butterflies . . . All the people who still do should come round and just sit for an hour out there. Dozens of them, and half a dozen different kinds. And did you know that when a bee goes into a snapdragon, the snapdragon goes . . .' He mimed a curious gulping gesture that ended in a smile. 'Marvellous.' He was chuckling but there were tears in his eyes.

Robin came back with a glass of lager for Max, who realised somewhat ruefully that he'd been expecting the can as well. 'Thanks, Robin.'

The companion-manservant or whatever smiled and went away. David sighed. 'I keep lists in my head of all the things I'm going to miss. Today it's butterflies and snapdragons. Summer things. The things that are around all the time aren't so bad, but passing things . . . That's a lot tougher.' He paused. 'D'you mind all this, Max?' Max shook his head. 'If I go on a bit?'

'Not at all.'

'I'm practically the only person I know who loved school. Every minute of it. And we had morning assemblies. Hymn, prayer, bit of the Bible, read by some demigod. Pep talk, announcements then carry on to your classes. And for about three days twice a year the sun would shine straight through a stained glass window above us and on to a marvellous war memorial – the kind of thing Rupert Brooke would have died for, blissfully. And as I went up the school I used to count off the number of times I still had left to see it. Coloured morning sunlight on those long, long columns of names, really only twice a year, and even then it might be cloudy . . .' He paused. 'You know what I mean, Max?' Max nodded. 'But today it's snapdragons and butterflies . . .'

David Pitsligo had lost weight since Max had last seen him. He sat now with an arm along the back of the sofa, looking for all the world like one of the photo-features at the back of a Sunday colour supplement: a room of his own, the room being a cool, mainly white one with lots of impressive modern pictures, a pale pink and grey carpet and the kind of furniture that looked to Max as though it might have escaped from a stately home.

'But one has time to think as well as to . . . repine.' Max nodded again, though less than certain about the nature of repining. 'So I rang you last night . . . Oh. The young lady? I mean the very young lady.'

'Amanda . . . Eight now.'

' "My daddy's at the hospital saving people right now but he usually rings people back . . ." '

'That's the one.'

'I'm glad I'm one of the people, Max. The second lot, I mean. And glad you could come over. There are all sorts of things I'd like to know about what it's going to be like later.'

'Later?'

'No, not for me, Max. I mean when I'm not around. I'm a . . . I'm blazing a trail, I suppose. But we don't really know yet what it's going to be like later. When there are more of us.'

'Sorry, David . . .'

'I mean is there anything one could do? You know, if the things I've read had been a bit clearer I'd be telling you. But nobody seems to know, so I wondered if you had some idea, Max, how you'll cope. Locally. Assuming no cure.' Max put down his glass. 'And assuming a hundred percent progression. From positive to, um, negative. Like not being around. Fair assumptions?'

Max was being asked questions like that quite often now. 'From what we know, David, yes, 'fraid so.'

'Not that one holds out the faintest hope . . . for oneself. But I'd like to put up a little to help you. Money, I mean, because from the sound of things you're struggling.'

'We are a bit. But later on, it's gonna be a real problem. For now we've got more experts than patients, curiously enough. We can look after people right now, because there really aren't an awful lot of them. But . . . Two assumptions, OK? Yes, we'll be in trouble quite soon. Not next year or the year after that. Say five years, six years from now. Let's talk about the people we know about. People testing positive. A handful of chaps like you and a handful of haemophiliacs. And several hundred, maybe a thousand who got it from dirty needles. They're the real worry.'

'That's what I thought, Max. So what do we do? And I don't just mean for the chaps like me. Most of us, lucky old us, are doing quite nicely thank you. We've got friends, and if we were rich enough to hit San Francisco in 1979 we're not poor. No, Max, I was sitting in my garden this afternoon worrying about people who've got what I've got and don't have gardens. Who's going to look after them?'

'Well, I am. My lot are. It's our job.'

'Good, Max. And if you'll let me, I'm going to help you.'

They sat for an hour and by the end of it had agreed the outline and remit of a trust to be set up by David Pitsligo and some of his fellow-advocates, to be funded entirely by him and administered after his death in accordance with his wishes: which were mainly that the unit headed by Max should, having been relieved of the uncertainties of reliance upon official funding, continue to investigate the possibility of effective treatment; that it should work at the same time on the control of infection; and – in the likely event of neither of these admirable initiatives succeeding – still be prepared for the worst.

Pitsligo reached for a little silver bell and rang it twice. Robin appeared and Max got up. 'I'll see you to the door,' said the advocate. 'Robin, would you mind?'

On his companion's arm he came as far as the conservatory. 'Thanks for coming over, Max. God bless.'

'Thank you, David.' Max looked back at the dying man and his friend, now framed by an arch of mossy boughs thick with orchids. 'Please let us call it the Pitsligo Trust.'

'No, Max. Partly because I think you'll probably find there's one already. Something to do with decayed gentlewomen . . .' Robin laughed. Pitsligo smiled a ghostly smile. 'But Max . . . I still want to be your fairy godmother.'

December 1988

'Hello, sister. I'm Dr Russell, the director, and this is Dr Scott. He's a clever doctor. You know, from the University Department for the Care of the Elderly, and we've borrowed him to give us a hand for a week.' They sat down. 'Thanks, sister. And you know what all this is about?'

'Not really, doctor. I've just come back from days off.'

'Well, we're just visiting, and we're here to help. That's the most important thing. Basically they like us to get round all the hospitals like this every five years or so. Friendly . . . All very friendly. And I think our predecessors were round in . . . Yes, 1982. But that would have been before your time, wouldn't it?' The ward sister nodded. Toby smiled. 'Either that or you're wearing remarkably well.' The ward sister smiled too.

The duty room was a tiny cubicle with a desk and just enough space for three chairs, and if the door opened someone would have to move. 'I think you'll find that we're interested in the kinds of things that you're interested in, and worried about the kind of things that you're worried about, so we should all get on like a house on fire. But since we've got these forms to fill in, devised by civil servants, we tend to plod through things in a civil service kind of way. That all right, sister?' She smiled and nodded.

'Let's start with the easy stuff. Accommodation . . . One of those things where you've got to make do with what you've got, isn't it? But let's just chat about it anyway. And I know it isn't exactly what you'd ask Santa for at Christmas, to go with your little nurse's uniform, is it?'

'I think you could say it's adequate.'

'But no more than that? A good building of its type, maybe, but things have moved on a bit since 1941, haven't they, and we're not as keen on temporary buildings as we were. But from the nursing point of view, sister . . . Tell us about the problems, the accommodation problems . . . First thing, are you wind and watertight?'

'Usually. The day room's a bit draughty sometimes . . . But only when the wind's coming from certain directions . . .'

'But all right on days like today? Good. And the roof doesn't leak.'

'Oh, no. Well . . .' The sister hesitated. Toby sat in contented silence, smiling at her as though he was wondering what she might look like with her hair down. When the silence became oppressive she bit her lip then said 'We did have a wee problem once . . .'

'Tell me about it.'

'We've had to have a couple of windows boarded up.'

'I see . . . And why was that?'

'They used to leak, a lot. Not just like the day room windows, but all the time when it rained.'

'And they boarded them up.'

'Yes.'

'When would that have been, sister? D'you happen to remember?'

'Just after I came here. Two years ago?'

'I see. And are they windows you miss, sister? I mean, did they think of replacing them?'

'Oh, yes.' There was another of Toby's persuasive silences. 'But because we're scheduled for demolition, Dr Russell. You know . . .'

'Yes. I see. And it's been two years now, so you just have to make do.' The ward sister nodded and smiled again.

'Toilets, sister . . .'

'Yes. That *is* a problem. We really should have at least another two.'

'That's what our colleagues thought a while back . . . But nothing's changed?'

'No.'

'And the same number of patients?'

'Yes.'

'I see.'

'But because we're scheduled for demolition . . .'

'Quite. Well, we'll certainly take a look at them, sister . . . Day room all right? With the wind behind you?' The ward sister had begun to look happier. 'So you use it a lot?' said Toby. 'Church services, keep fit classes, bit of bingo, basketwork with the

474

occupational therapist? Indeed every form of vice and recreation an old lady could reasonably wish for?'

'I just wish we could, doctor . . .'

'But you can't.'

'Well, it's really cold. Except for a couple of months in the summer. If it's nice, you know.'

'I see.'

'We're here to help, sister. Andrew? Any other questions about accommodation before we move on to something cheerier, like the food?'

'Sister, has anything else been put off because of the plans to demolish this block?'

'We'd hoped for a wee lick of paint.'

'Anything else?'

'The call bells. We have to pick and choose a bit where we put people, so that people who can shout aren't taking up an electric call bell somebody else might need more than they do.'

'How many of them don't work, sister?'

'Well . . . Quite a lot of them do. Eight? Nine? We manage.'

'I see. Thanks, sister.'

'Now, sister, the food . . . One of the things that really impressed my colleagues last time round at Cuddiewood was the way that, despite everything . . .'

Scott and Toby were in the third ward of the morning and with luck they would break soon for coffee and get another three wards done before lunch. The report of the 1982 visit had not been enthusiastic: 'The only possible justification for the continuing use of the former Polish Army General Hospital hutted accommodation at Cuddiewood Hospital would be as a very temporary expedient pending the urgent upgrading of the more substantial EMS blocks at Ladymuir.' Curiously, the ward sister did not appear to be dispirited. Perhaps it would have been better if Toby had not suggested to her that looking after patients in a temporary building put up in 1941 with an expected life of only five years was in any way extraordinary. With a paint job, two new windows, a few extra toilets and a handful more electric call bells that worked she would be happy to keep the place going for another five years on top of the forty two by which the building had exceeded its design life.

'. . . so that concludes the formal business of the meeting, sister.

But we always like to have a stroll round and perhaps a chat with one or two patients as well, and then if we can have a look at the medical case notes and maybe take a few minutes to discuss the arrangements for medical cover . . . Which I gather from one or two sources sometimes don't run as smoothly here as they might in one of our great metropolitan teaching hospitals.' Sister opened her mouth and then closed it again. 'Let's just take a stroll round, shall we? You know, you're right, you could do with a lick of paint here and there. And of course in this type of building you don't have single rooms, do you? So what happens if someone's making a bit of a hubbub in the night. . . ? Or wants a moment's peace and quiet with their loved ones before they slip away, sister? How do you manage that?'

'They were going to cubicalise the first bed on each side, doctor, but . . .'

'They decided it wasn't worth doing because the whole place was coming down shortly. Is that it?' Sister nodded. 'So you do your best with curtains, screens and all that . . .' She nodded again. 'Not the way I'd want to go meself, but there we are . . . Now, let's see . . .' Toby glanced at the name at the head of a bed. 'Hello, Mrs Lowther.'

The patient, a beefy, red-faced lady with thinning hair and a vaguely disgruntled air, said 'Yes, son? Whit is it?'

One of the minor pleasures of dealing mainly with older patients was that they called you 'son' even if, like Toby, you were well into your fifties and completely bald. 'Dr Russell. Just visiting the hospital, Mrs Lowther. How are you?'

'Not so well, doctor, not so well.'

'I'm sorry to hear that. But they're looking after you?'

She craned round in the direction of the ward sister as though to reassure her that however serious the shortcomings of the ward no advantage would be taken of the presence of an inquiring stranger. 'They dae their best, son.'

'I'm sure they do, Mrs Lowther. And from what I see they're doing a remarkably good job. D'you like Cuddiewood?'

'It's no' like yer ain hoose, is it, son?'

'Probably not, Mrs Lowther. I'd have to agree with you there, but lovely to have talked to you. Good morning.'

Scott took off on his own to look at the toilets, the duty of whoever wasn't going round chatting up the patients. The first he found was a dank, windowless space whose door had been removed, presumably to facilitate access for wheelchair patients. Under loose, shabby linoleum the floorboards were sodden and rotting, soft to the toe of his shoe. The handrails on either side of the WC pedestal were insecure and, given the layout of the building and the absence of the door, any patient using the toilet could do so only in full view of the main body of the ward. The second toilet, at the far end, was the same in all essentials. Scott did not write detailed notes. There was no need to: ward ten of Cuddiewood Hospital was very much like wards eight and nine.

'So there we are, sister . . . Not easy, I imagine, to do things the way you'd like to, but if I may say so, you're making the best of it. We don't like paper sheets, but then neither do you. The day room would be a lot more use to you if you could use it. And what you really need is a nice new hospital. And you're going to get that. Some day. Oh. One other thing. Staff meals at night. Any problems there?'

'Well, yes. It's not what you'd call very safe walking around a place like this at night.'

'So the folks bring in a bit of something and eat it on the ward? I see. Again not ideal, is it? We don't ask the day staff to eat on the wards, do we? We'll try and get back here on our night visit, even though it's officially just Ladymuir. Be nice to talk to your people here too. So that's probably it, thank you, sister. Unless Dr Scott's got something he'd like to bother you with.'

'Medical cover, sister. What happens if one of your ladies here needs to be seen by a doctor? Any special difficulties with that?'

Sister paused and frowned. Toby excused himself. 'I think I might just test the system and see. All right to use your phone, sister? In a good cause. Thanks.'

'So what would happen?'

'Well, maybe nothing. And you can never really be sure. He might be here in two minutes or two hours, and never think to tell you which.'

'Who, sister?'

'The duty doctor, but because we're a bit out of the centre of things we get left till last, or just forgotten about.'

'Do you get to know them?'

'Not really. It's kind of emergencies only.'

'I see. And consultant cover? How does that fit in.'

'You might well ask, Dr Scott . . .'

'So you don't get the house officer and consultant going round together?'

'Well . . . Not very often.'

'So consultant rounds are what? Once a week?'

'In theory once a month.'

'And in practice?'

'Once in a blue moon. No, I shouldn't say that, doctor. I mean, he's nice enough when he comes. On a Friday afternoon, usually. Or sometimes on a Sunday morning. But always very nice when he comes.'

'I'd like to see some medical notes, please, sister.'

'This way, Dr Scott.'

Again there were no surprises. Scott picked half a dozen at random and found that in only two were there progress notes dated within the previous six months. Clerkings were barely adequate, there were no problem lists and one lady had had nothing at all written about her for two and a half years.

'Hello? Is somebody looking for me?' Scott turned round. A girl in a white coat was standing in the doorway. 'I was bleeped for ward ten.'

'Oh. Yes. I don't think it's an emergency or anything. You're on call for here?'

The girl smiled ruefully. 'Here as well.'

'I'm Dr Scott. With Dr Russell, we're having a sort of look round.'

'Good. There's a lady here I wanted to talk to somebody about. She was just a bit off and I did some bloods the other day and got a sodium back at one sixty. Odd. She doesn't look too bad on it, but I wanted some help, so thanks for coming.' The girl paused and was looking at him quite closely. 'You *are* the consultant for this ward, aren't you, Dr Scott?'

On the way to coffee Toby was sombre. 'Not exactly the kind of place you'd want for your own dear old gran, Andrew, is it? How were the bogs?'

'Same as the others.'

'That's worrying.'

Eric, the nursing adviser, and Doris, the social worker attached to the team, were already installed in the smoking section of the dining room. 'Nice bunch of girls, but the wards are bloody terrible,' said Toby. 'How were your bits, Eric?'

'If the lassies in the wards are daein' fine it's no' because they're working for the greatest nursing officer I've ever met. No' a bad wee mortuary, though. Surprisingly.'

'Thank you, Dr Scroggie, I look forward to reading your final report.'

Eric had started out as a deckhand on trawlers, become a nursing auxiliary in a psychiatric hospital in the far North East ('They were aye lookin' for strong lads tae haud folk doon for various things.'), switched to general nursing training, acquired a degree followed by a doctorate in nursing and then joined Toby's team because he cared fiercely and persistently about nursing standards in the National Health Service. 'And the personal laundry's still a shambles. Tell him, Doris.'

'Oh, dear,' said Toby. 'We're still in communal knickers, are we? Three heaps in the cupboard – large, a bit larger and bloody enormous?'

'Exactly, Toby. Just the way it was in 1982.'

'And you were there, Doris. You were there. And it's probably . . .'

'. . . all the same knickers. Yes, Toby. But we shouldn't laugh, should we?'

'No, Doris, we shouldn't. The Secretary of State isn't going to like it one bit, is he? He's very against communal underwear, our Mr Crumlin. And the doctoring process isn't up to much either . . .'

Scott was quite enjoying his second attachment to the group which Toby led and referred to privately as the Scottish Hospitals Inspection Team, its official title being more tactfully phrased as well as offering a more neutral acronym. Toby had moved a few years before from clinical psychiatry to his new administrative role and seemed happy in it. Scott, though at first puzzled why someone so obviously skilled and effective with patients should have given up looking after them well before his retirement date, had now, after a couple of weeks with the team, realised why the new job was if anything more interesting. Like Eric, Toby had gone from looking after patients to thinking about how patients were being looked after: visiting hospitals, seeing things and talking to people, evaluating actual against possible standards of care and coming up with what was in effect an institutional diagnosis – in the case of Cuddiewood, that the hospital was very sick indeed, even if a few brave souls within it were doing their best. And if the 1988 report, which would go to the Health Board concerned and to the Secretary of State, added sufficiently to the case made for closure by its 1982 predecessor and the hospital was swiftly shut down and the patients moved to upgraded accommodation elsewhere, then the visit was not only good fun but also, in the larger sense, good medicine too.

'Come on, Eric. Stub it out before it burns your fingers. We've got serious work to do here. And it's such a lovely hospital. Beats me why the Polish Army didn't just hang on to it, but then their loss is our gain . . . And they scored quite wondrous high for lunch last time, didn't they, Doris. . . ? OK? We'll see you at about one o'clock back here . . . Come on, Andrew, better than working, isn't it?'

They walked along an icy path through neglected frozen grass towards a line of low huts on the edge of a pinewood. 'Give it a decent sized chimney with a smudge of black smoke and it could be Treblinka, couldn't it?' Scott had been thinking more or less along the same lines. 'But it's all going to change, doctor.'

'Is it?'

'Yes. Don't you keep up with the mighty flow of current events, lad? The forthcoming comprehensive and far-reaching review of the National Health Service? Been fully discussed and agreed in the highest councils of the state . . . The Grand Duchess of all the Finchleys announced it to the waiting nation last night. She seems to have thought it all up by herself, in the middle of an interview on Panorama.'

'Dr Ratho, Gus Ratho. I have an appointment with the . . . the professor.'

'Please take a seat, Dr Ratho. He's on the wards but he knows you're coming. It's just that sometimes he can be a few minutes late on Tuesday mornings.'

'Thank you.' The secretary occupied a large desk in quite a nice open space which was part of a conversion of one of the old tubercle wards. Gus had, he realised when he thought about it, been here before: as a student he had trailed round an odd little place, half hospital ward, half lodging house, where a dozen men of the kind that would now be called inner urban vagrants had been kept more or less under lock and key because their tubercle was still potentially dangerous to others. Jimmy Jameson had of course made it all sound very enlightened, and explained how they got free board and lodging, two bottles of stout a day and 'probably a bit more in the way of baths than they wanted'. Then, the ward had been bleak and malodorous, with blotchy stains on the floorboards and generous remnants of blackout paint on the windows. Now the ceiling had been lowered, with some quite nice concealed lighting, and the place where he had been invited to sit down, still smelling richly of new carpeting and furniture, would not have disgraced the Inchkeith Clinic. For about the twentieth time since a thoroughly unexpected and unpleasant phone call, Gus considered his options. None of them was easy.

'Ah, Gus, come on in.' Cathcart had crashed the swing doors and strode across the foyer towards his visitor.

'Thanks, Max. Awfully kind of you to invite me across.'

'No, Gus, you're doing us a favour. And I thought you might like to see the place. Any calls or anything, Zoe? Good. We'll be in here for . . . a while maybe. Coffee, Gus? I sure could do with one. Thanks, Zoe, two coffees, please, just put it on the tab. How d'you take it, Gus?'

'Just a little milk, thanks.'

'Come on in, Gus. Good to see you.'

The inner office was even more impressive. 'Like it, Gus?' Cathcart had taken off his white coat and lolled back behind a quite ridiculously large desk. 'Once they'd started we really couldn't stop them. I said spend it on the patients, they said don't worry, we'll do all that as well. It's gotta look nice, you're gonna have lots of visitors. You know what, Gus? It's kinda neat. You're the first. So welcome to the grand opening. Actually they want one of those as well, but that's next month.'

'I must say I was awfully pleased for you when I heard, Max. But of course you've worked so hard for it.'

'No,' said Max. 'I just drank a glass of beer. They did all the rest. A Heineken. Maybe a Budweiser. Anyway, it's all up and running. We'll go and see the wards in a minute. And I want you to do that, OK? Before you make up your mind about anything.'

481

'Thanks awfully, Max.'

'When did we last have a chat, Gus? Five, maybe six years ago? Just after I got back from Stanford, first time round. Yes. And you were starting to look at some neuro-immunological markers in motor neurone disease or something. Sounded like good stuff. What happened to it?'

Gus could not recall ever having discussed the immunology of that disease with Cathcart, far less having done any work on it, but a vague recollection of a grant application that had got no further than the drafting stage roused itself in his memory. 'Yes, we were rather unlucky with that. Quite a good piece of work, but the not uncommon story, sadly enough . . . One or two other groups were working along very much the same lines and by the time our results were coming through theirs were beginning to be published.'

'Tough. And what kind of things have you been doing more recently?'

Gus would have very much liked to have been in a position to tell Cathcart to buzz off and stop treating him like a bankrupt whose household effects were being dragged out into the street; but he recognised with some distress that Max, whose father had been a small businessman of some kind in the West, might quite deliberately be taking such a view of their meeting. The important thing was to remain civil and make the most of things. 'Oh, we've one or two good studies, mainly in neuro-immunology, that really are quite productive . . . In the sense that the data's accumulating to the extent that some definite trends are taking shape. The myelitis response to whooping-cough vaccine, for example. We're on the point of coming up with a really good animal model for that . . .'

'It's been done,' said Max. 'What else have you got? Oh, Zoe . . . You're a wonderful girl. Have one yourself. Cheers, love.' Gus made the most of the arrival of coffee to give himself time to think. 'Yes?' said Max.

'You know,' said Gus, 'the great challenges in neuro-immunology are still what they were twenty years ago. Multiple sclerosis . . .'

'Yup,' said Max. 'How are you getting on with them?'

'Well, Max, I have a most promising PhD student who's reviewing the methodology of clinical monitoring in MS . . . Trying to work up a reliable clinical method of monitoring disease progress

– the kind of basic foundation that has to be absolutely firm before we start to go in with our clever ideas about modifying the immune response. And no one seems to have looked at it very thoroughly in the last fifteen years at least.'

'Yes,' said Max. 'Library work. Zoe could do that for me. What have you got going in your labs?'

'I really should invite you across, Max. I hope we can arrange something in the not too distant future . . .'

'I was wondering about tomorrow, or maybe the day after. Come on, Gus. D'you want to tell me or show me? Either way suits me.'

'Really, Max, I wonder if spending so much time in the States has been good for you? I've no doubt the . . . brisk approach is very popular and effective over there. But here in Edinburgh? Well, you know the form . . .'

Cathcart was sitting back with his hands behind his head grinning at him. 'Yeah,' he said 'I do. And I'm gonna change it. That's my job.'

Shortly after being appointed to the David Pitsligo chair in Clinical Immunology Max had been asked by a joint committee of the Health Board and the University to implement a report prepared some years previously but neglected since. Its main recommendation – that the duplication and in some instances triplication of service and research efforts in clinical immunology should end and one large unit be set up to assume all relevant responsibilities – was now an idea whose time had come. It fitted well with the provisions of the David Pitsligo Trust and the Board had welcomed the opportunity to close down a number of small and uneconomic units of doubtful standing. Max had three more people to see after Gus, one or two of whom might conceivably be of use to him in the future. Meantime, he was simply enjoying himself. 'Gus,' he said. 'Thinking ahead a bit . . . Where do you see yourself in relation to the number one problem here?'

'You're thinking of AIDS?'

'Right.'

'Never really thought about it, Max. One has one's own field, indeed fields. But I've always been a great believer in cobblers sticking to their lasts, so to speak.'

'Don't underestimate yourself, Gus. For a start, you're not a cobbler. You're an immunologist who's into neurology, and some of the most interesting things in AIDS now are neurological . . . You'll see polyneuritis, transverse myelitis and, as you probably know, the guys in San Francisco are beginning to see something really fascinating. Dementia, would you believe? In guys aged twenty or thirty? That's gotta be the most interesting thing that's happened in neuro-immunology for years . . . I could get you tissue flown over, next week if you want. I got contacts there. You only have to say the word, Gus, if you want to get started before you move across . . .'

Gus sipped his coffee and contemplated life in a lab next to Max's. 'That's terribly kind of you, Max. But you know, I really don't know how we'd find the time to do much with it before, say – well frankly, quite some way into next year. We've really got an awful lot of things at quite a critical stage. So even to contemplate moving . . .'

'We're not contemplating it,' said Max, leaning back. 'We're doing it. By the end of next month. When I come across tomorrow we can decide what to drop and what's worth bringing across. I mean we can really discuss that, the two of us. And then I'll get the demented guys' brains fixed up for you when you get here. First week in November?'

'Aren't we just rushing things a bit, Max? I mean, one's PhD students. . . ? One's medical laboratory scientific officers. . . ? Senior laboratory staff far into important work.'

'We'll keep the important stuff,' said Max. 'But we don't have to discuss that today. What about the brains? Any ideas, Gus? Looking for the mechanisms of damage, I guess, in the first instance. Is it glial or neuronal? Cortical or basal? I guess plenty of people are working on all that already. What about why do some guys get it and some not? That's the really important question.'

'Max . . .'

'You're worried about handling the brains, Gus? Forget it. They're not really all that dangerous if you know what you're doing. Same precautions as for Jakob-Kreutzfeld . . . So it's simple. You know all that stuff. Ideal job for you. What do you think?'

'And of course one has one's other commitments. I mean other than clinical immunology. Not as portable as the straight science, Max.'

'You could still do private work, Gus, if that's the problem. We'd write it in. Say four clinics a week here, on the AIDS side, mainly, because it's all very immunological, and maybe two at Moray Place, the Inchkeith, wherever. I don't know much about it, Gus, I don't mind and I'm sure we could come to some arrangement. You might even corner the market in private AIDS. That'd be fine by me. Provided you did your sessions here.'

Gus put down his cup. It was simply impossible that Max had not heard about the termination of Gus's links with the Inchkeith Clinic, which had meant virtually the end too of his work in Moray Place. But if he was pretending he hadn't in order to extract the details from him now it wasn't going to get him anywhere. The regrettable Finnie business had surfaced, to Gus's extreme discomfiture, a week after her death, and though the certification details had not been contested and the poor old thing could not be uncremated the whole experience had been most unpleasant. The problem was that Walster had grabbed an auxiliary nurse and bullied her into helping with his filthy colonic lavage trick, and the auxiliary nurse had complained to the nurse in charge a few days later. Walster's unauthorised dip into private in-patient care had come to light and difficult questions had been asked. Though strictly speaking no laws had been broken and everyone agreed that accidents sometimes happened, the disagreement about the allegedly missing page from the notes had been tricky: Walster and Gus had suffered the gravest embarrassment and the episode had done no one any good. 'I've cut right back on my private work, Max,' said Gus. 'I feel that at times like this the National Health Service needs the whole-hearted support of each and every one of us. And I'm afraid I'll have to consider your very generous offer of lab and clinical sessions as just one of a number of similar options open to me at this moment in time . . . I don't think I'd be breaking any confidences if I told you that Professor Bennett has been pressing me quite hard to join him in what might turn out to be some very interesting work in the field of medical education.' Gus relaxed and smiled. 'So it's terribly kind of you, Max. But I think it's only fair to tell you that it's most unlikely I'll be able to accept. But thanks awfully. Really most kind of you.'

Max, who would not have made his generous offer unless he had been aware of the growing understanding between Gus and Wiggy Bennett, saw his guest to the swing doors at the far end of the administrative section of the David Pitsligo Unit and waved him a polite goodbye. 'One down and three to go,' he remarked to Zoe as he went back into his office. 'And I quite enjoyed that one.'

This time Sandy had resolved to be precisely on time for her interview and to leave immediately afterwards and wait at home until Molly rang her. This time she knew who was on the committee and this time she was also a great deal better informed about the competition. She had read everything she could about the job, talked to most of the people who mattered and gone to some trouble to think things through so that she could deal with questions not only to her own advantage but, by a kind of open, cheerful subtlety, to the detriment of the two more serious rival contenders as well.

There was a brigadier and he was not a problem. He was being interviewed, she had been told, because he might be a useful reserve option for a less important job that was coming up later, but his chances of today's job were nil, having been effectively destroyed by the official whose premature retirement had created the vacancy. Not that Sandy had anything against soldiers and the like, but the Health Board's first appointment to the post of general manager of acute services had been widely criticised. To begin with people had quite liked the Air Vice Marshal, as he had been generally known, because he was a charming and sociable man obviously keen to learn how the Health Service worked. But after only a few months most people had agreed that, however well equipped he had been to penetrate the air defences of Moscow, he just wasn't up to the rather more demanding task of day-to-day dealings with Edinburgh doctors. In his wake, the brigadier was not a worry.

The person from nursing was a little bit more of a threat, but not much. Sandy had known her from a couple of committees, where she tended to speak from detailed notes and more or less without regard to the general flow of discussion. She was running the Southern as its first general manager and could therefore expect to be interviewed for this job, but was discussed over coffee at Board HQ more or less as a matron without a frilly hat, a person from nursing who even after two years in general management was still sometimes heard to begin sentences with 'from a nursing point of view'. She had a big dog, a lot of female friends who also wore tweeds practically all the time, and was said to go on holidays quite

486

regularly with a night sister. Nothing against it and all very well in its place, thought Sandy, but again, not a worry.

If there was a worry it was management man, a chap who would have described himself, without realising how much it annoyed people, as one of the new breed. He was younger than Sandy, and handsome and quite bright, an economics graduate and one of the curious contemporary set of St Andrews University thugs, said also to be a close chum of creepy Mr Crumlin at the Home and Health Department. He too was a local candidate, at present running a big psychiatric hospital that he was fanatically keen to use as a testing-ground for some quite sinister ideas about hiving off non-clinical services, and was quoted as admitting openly to harbouring ambitions of a form of management success that included becoming as unpopular with doctors as the ghastly man in Glasgow.

According to Molly, it was between Sandy and management man, it was going to close but it was probably going to be all right, and Molly had been right about an awful lot of things since Sandy's regrettable interview for the last local consultant haematology vacancy for six centuries. She had rung Sandy that evening and told her she had been easily the best person interviewed and the important thing was that, and not the decision made by the committee. She had invited her over to the Board for coffee and a chat next day, and since then an awful lot of things had started to go right again.

Over coffee they had taken about two minutes to decide that haematology was a good thing to have done, since it involved both clinical medicine and quite a lot of management because of all the lab services, but was not a good thing to go on doing. Molly's suggestion, which was one that Sandy herself had briefly considered on her thirty-fifth birthday as a kind of token mid-life crisis, was to switch to what she called being a paperclip-doctor, as Molly herself had gone, from her previous specialty of pathology, some years before. Paperclip doctoring or – as the discipline was for the time being known – community medicine, involved doing a year at either Glasgow or Edinburgh which was like being back in medical school, but more serious, and passing an examination. Sandy, who had never failed an examination in her life, in school, at university or as a post-graduate, suddenly realised how much she was missing them. You just worked and passed them, and success in them was entirely up to you: nothing to do with whether you were male or female, married or not, with or without a child and above all nothing to do with whether or not you were part of the silly, wasteful and unfair system of male patronage that dominated hospital appointments.

Sandy had gone to Glasgow for her year back at school, because she had applied late and Edinburgh had been full up. She had commuted, working hard for forty five minutes there and back in the horrible train every day and staying up till midnight most nights to read a lot more, write essays about lots of interesting things and generally do better than the men. Because of all that they had kindly given her something called the Maxton Memorial Medal in Public Health, but even before that Molly had fixed a job for her in the Board's main offices, which had been quite easy because Molly had had the sense to become CAMO when her unfortunate predecessor, rather a dim survivor from the physician-superintendent-and-gentleman era of the specialty, had retired hurt as a result of the switch to general management, which meant basically that being a doctor was no longer enough.

But being a doctor still helped, especially if you wanted to succeed an air vice marshal who had annoyed in some way or another almost all of the five hundred or so doctors working in the Board's acute sector. The trick, as Sandy and Molly had agreed in the weeks leading up to the interview, was to sound as management-minded as management man, more so if you could, and let the fact that you had once upon a time – before your four varied and interesting years in management at the centre of things, in the Board – been a doctor come as a pleasant and helpful surprise to the members of the committee, who included, according to Molly, a fair proportion of the people who had appointed the man who should have stuck to bombing Moscow.

Sandy had arrived a couple of minutes early and on the stairs had run into the brigadier, quite a nice man she had met a few days before when he was looking round at the Board. They had a short, pleasant conversation and wished each other luck and then Sandy had been shown straight into the interview room, which was not the one she hadn't got the haematology job in, but a bigger, brighter room on the first floor. The people were exactly who Molly had said they would be, with Molly sitting on the chairman's right hand, which was probably another good sign. No one asked her why she had applied for the job, no one tried to upset her and when the chairman eventually asked her if she had any questions it was more as if they had all been having quite a sensible and agreeable chat about some real problems that Sandy happened to know quite a lot about, and some hypothetical ones that they had just enjoyed discussing, like what a radical review of the National Health Service might look like.

Alastair was out conducting a funeral and Sandy was feeding Barbara when Molly phoned. As soon as she had said hello, Sandy knew that everything had gone according to plan. 'You were terrific, Sandy. Again. Really terrific. So congratulations, but please don't tell anybody till you get your letter. And the sooner you can start the better because we've got a really interesting project for you to kick off with. So well done, Sandy, and a nice letter will be on its way soon. Bye.'

September 1989

'It was the oddest thing,' said Scott. 'We were keeping tabs on one of those Soviet trawler spy-ships, so we'd been wandering aimlessly round the Indian Ocean for weeks . . .'

'I know what you mean,' said Max. 'Frigging about in a frigate.'

'More or less. Then we suddenly got diverted to Colombo, which the first lieutenant cheerfully assured us was the arsehole of the universe, then we got told that after that we were going to somewhere called Male, quite close by. "Oh my Gawd," said number one. "Belay my last, I forgot about that bloody place. It's the *absolute* arsehole of the universe . . ." Anyway, we got there and did the usual kind of party for the locals, most of whom seemed to be called Ali. So after a couple of large ones and, you know, a bit short of conversation, I mentioned to one of them that there had been a chap called Ali in my year, from the Maldives. Remember wee Ali from Male? And he said "Very eenteresting, where eez he now?" I had no idea, and he pushed off. Then he came back with the foreign minister and the chief of police. No kidding. "My friend, we theenk you can help us." All very mysterious. So afterwards I asked His Excellency, the chap we'd been sent to Colombo to pick up. "Ah yes, he said, *'L'affaire Mehmet Ali* . . . I've told them dozens of times we can't simply knock on his door in the middle of the night and bring him back in irons just because he seems to have done a bunk on his scholarship. So if you happen to know where he is I'd much rather you didn't tell me." All very odd.'

'He's a GP in Bootle,' said Max.

'Sshhh,' said Rachel.

Theresa laughed. 'But that probably explains why he isn't here.'

People were gathering for the champagne reception that Max, as chairman of the organising committee, had insisted was the only possible way to launch the twentieth anniversary reunion of

Edinburgh's 1969 medical graduates. He glanced round. 'Lucky we made them all wear name badges. Look at whoever that is.' He was pointing to a man standing side-on about thirty feet away who looked as though he weighed around two hundred and twenty pounds. 'An extra refill for whoever twigs him first . . .'

'It's Woody,' said Theresa. 'Gosh, poor chap.' While Max laboured to joke about a thin young medical student trying to get out, Rachel pulled a sheaf of papers from his inside pocket and flipped through it until she found what she wanted. 'William P Wood? Psychiatrist in Florida. Hm. That figures.' Max tried to make a joke about that too then explained how the committee had worried a lot about name badges, and how as chairman he'd really wanted them to include the picture of you from the final year book and some colour codes round the edge to say whether you'd got to be a professor, how often you'd been divorced and how many heart attacks you'd had, so people could find out what they really wanted to know without asking a lot of embarrassing questions. 'And we even thought about having a special apologies section in the programme, for people who were in jail, or who'd been struck off. And I suppose the dead guys too.'

So far as the reunion committee knew, there had now been four deaths from a graduating class of about a hundred and twenty. One of the evangelical girls had died in a car accident in East Africa in her first week at a mission hospital there. A nice girl everyone had tried to sit near in the reading room had succumbed in her thirties to a malignant melanoma arising from a mole on her thigh that everybody had known about because of mini-skirts. The first fatal coronary had happened to a man with an appalling family history of the disease while he was still in training as a cardiac surgeon, and Robbie had been the first known suicide.

'Cheer up,' said Max. 'Think what it'll be like by the thirtieth. My God! Look at the five foot Pole. And she's seen me.'

Irena, expensively turned out and with a large man in tow, was heading straight for Max. Rachel and Theresa exchanged amused glances. 'Hello, Max.' She held her cheek out to be kissed. 'Lovely to see you, Max . . .' said Irena. She smiled with her mouth open in a way that Scott instantly remembered having found irritating about twenty five years before. 'And after all those years, Max. So? You're looking quite prosperous. And I'm told you're a professor . . . Max, this is my husband, Richard. Nothing to do with medicine, before you ask. And I'm in community medicine in West Dorset, which is actually a terrifically enlightened place ... Things are really happening, and we're tackling the issues raised by the White Paper head on. In fact a lot of things in it are the kind of thing we've been doing for years ... Did I mention I have special responsibility for audit? That's something we think they took from us ...'

Richard, with his champagne glass refilled, turned out under interrogation by Theresa to be a farmer with hundreds of cows and a marvellous accent, at first glance an unlikely partner for Irena, but very much at ease with himself and even, it seemed, with her. Rachel watched calmly while Irena, who appeared to have not only come a long way but also to have spent a great deal of time and money on her appearance for the purpose, continued in her efforts to convince Max of the kind of blissful lifetime partnership he had foregone forever by not asking her out even once. '... so we're just going right ahead with back-up systems for hospital opt-out and GP budgeting, because if authorities like ours can't come up with the goods no one can, and I know that a lot of you up here think if you ignore it it's all going to go away, but our view is that if it's happening – and it is – we're leading, not following ... We say you couldn't argue with her majority even if you wanted to, so you should see it as an opportunity because, as I try to tell everybody I talk to, staying the same is not an option ... We've got to change so we're going to be ahead and people trust my judgement on that. So that gives me lots of clout with both the clinicians and the managers, because if community medicine is about anything these days, it's about providing a dynamic interface for people to access to, facilitating change. That's the way I see it, Max ... And do you have children?'

Max glanced across as though referring a strictly departmental question to Rachel, who said 'Yes, darling ... Two. A girl and a boy ...' Everybody laughed then Irena turned on Rachel. 'And are you a doctor too?'

'I look after Max ... And apart from that, I guess I'm an ex-nurse ...'

'We like to think that we're carrying the nursing element along too, on a consultation basis. Because really, there's a lot in the White Paper for them as well if you think about it ...'

Scott asked Irena if she came back to Edinburgh often. She

became subdued and reached across for Richard's hand. 'Daddy died,' she said. 'Then mum. So we don't, really, except for things like this.'

The room had filled up quite a lot. Scott spotted a girl he had once worshipped from afar, actually from the opposite end of the dissecting room. Had he not seen her name on the list he would not have recognised her. In a reflective haze of champagne he worried about that, decided that time had been unkinder to her than to most and suddenly recalled something he had heard years ago in West Africa from a Canadian priest who had just been home for the first time in fifteen years. 'By far the keenest of the pleasures of celibacy,' he had announced, 'is seeing what happens to the women you aren't allowed to marry.'

Sandy's name had not been on the list. Since remarrying and changing specialities she had somehow almost disappeared. Scott had seen her perhaps three or four times and only from a distance –driving in town, once at a concert, once at a supermarket checkout grappling with a leaking bottle of squash, and recently at a meeting about the White Paper – in the ten years since her father's funeral, and for a number of years he had hoped vaguely that her husband would be called to a parish in Unst or Tiree or Geneva, because in some ways it would be easier simply never to see her again. The reunion had been a risk, with Scott half-prepared to brace himself for distant, polite noises of a few moments' duration at some point, but relieved to learn that the possibility would not after all arise. Perhaps being married to someone outside medicine made gatherings like this a bit less compelling, although that did not seem to have prevented Irena and a good number of others from turning out. Perhaps having a full time job as well as a handicapped daughter and a husband who had to work every weekend made everything a bit more serious. Whatever it was, Scott felt quite a lot more relaxed in the knowledge that Sandy was not around.

'Let's go and talk to Maggie and that chap,' said Theresa. 'Come on.' Maggie Auld, now a GP in the Borders, was the first person they had come across who looked and sounded almost exactly the same. When Scott said so she said 'Thanks, Andrew, but it's quite easy. You have your kids early, live in the country and work part-time.' Theresa laughed and squeezed Scott's hand.

'Gosh . . . So both of us must look about a hundred and fifty. What's your secret of eternal youth, Morris?'

Theresa was being nice. Morris Doig, an almost totally non-descript man whom Scott had had trouble remembering when he and Theresa had gone through the year book together in bed the night before, was now a commanding presence, tanned and well-groomed, looking perhaps a bit younger than the current class average but by no means strikingly youthful. 'Life-style, I guess,' he said without a smile, 'Money, maybe. But I guess it comes to the same thing. Like, I jog. Anybody kin jog, but I do it at a . . . real good country club?' Scott, who had spent long enough in the States to sort out some of its more obvious regional accents, thought about what Morris had said and the way he had said it, with the curious interrogative ending on a simple statement, the 'I guess,' and the 'kin': probably somewhere fairly far South. 'So where are you now, Morris?'

'Fayetteville?'

'Where's that?'

'Nawth Carolina?'

'And what do you do?'

'I'm an orthopaedist. How about you, Andrew?'

'Psychiatry.'

'Psychiatry, huh? Like, analysis?'

'There isn't very much of that here.'

'I guess not.' Scott had the feeling that he was being judged for membership of a real good country club and failing on a number of counts. 'Our guys do it a whole lot,' said Morris, 'but they still hit an earnings ceiling. Like, nobody starves, but I cain't think of one that flies a plane.'

Theresa asked him about flying and she and Scott and Maggie then listened to what Morris had clearly come all the way back to Edinburgh to tell people about. It was mostly quite interesting, and although he didn't go so far as trying to convince them you saved a lot on airline fares, he made a reasonable case in terms of times and distances between his various commitments, and the extra time that having a plane to get around in seemed to free up to allow you to do more operations and pay for your plane. Then he started to talk about the second-hand aircraft market, into which he hoped to move when his financial circumstances permitted, and became

494

frankly boring and greedy. Disappointed, Scott listened to him with one ear while Theresa and Maggie talked about children and schools. Eventually a hotel official appeared at the door and roared above the convivial hubbub 'Ladies and Gentlemen . . . Dinner is served!'

'Can't for the life of me recall where we had our twentieth. D'you remember, Esmee? Back in our salad days?'

'We missed it, dear. We were in Bechuanaland.'

'Good gracious me, I'll be forgetting my own name next. But I remember our fortieth as though it were yesterday. That's probably quite a good sign. What do you think, Andrew? Just as well to come straight out with it and ask one's personal psychogeriatrician . . .' Scott said something reassuring that probably had the additional merit of being true. 'One's wife begins to worry, but so long as one's psychogeriatrician is with one I suppose one is all right, hm?'

Jimmy and Esmee Jameson had been asked to dinner as guests of honour, and sat with the committee and their partners at a long table at the end of the dining room. Apart from chairing one or two advisory bodies, editing a journal for the Royal College of Physicians and spending three or four months a year in the third world consulting on the organisation of respiratory medicine services, Jimmy had now retired and was looking remarkably well on it; and no one who had heard him grilling Max on AIDS as a world problem would have had any anxiety about his mental capacities. His eye moved round what he probably thought of as just another agreeable little tutorial group and then settled. 'Ah, yes, Rachel. What's Australia going to do about the pressure from its neighbours for a less – shall we say restricted – immigration policy?'

Scott and Theresa exchanged glances. It was quite alarmingly like being back on the grass outside Jimmy's wards, sitting on a chest X-ray and hoping desperately that someone else would be pounced on for the next six causes of diffuse of coughing up blood. Discussion eventually moved on to the medical care of the aborigines, a matter on which Jimmy had advised in the middle seventies and on which he now wished to hear more recent information, and on that too Rachel achieved a creditable pass. Just when Scott was beginning to feel a bit uneasy again Mrs Jimmy said 'I don't know how all you people feel, but we'd almost agreed to have a night off for a change and not mention that woman and her White Paper once . . . But it's jolly difficult, isn't it, and we do want to know what younger people think.' It was Jimmy's turn to frown, so Theresa asked him how people in medicine had felt right at the beginning, when the National Health Service was just being set up.

'I was thinking about that the other day, curiously enough, when some government chap said "Well *of course* all the doctors are making a fuss, they always do when anything's changed. Look at the howls of protest in 1948, and see how happy they all are now." And certainly in 1948 the great panjandrums of Harley Street were talking about the end of civilisation as we – by which of course they meant they – knew it, and if you'd read the BMJ you'd have got much the same impression. But our lot had just been off all over the world fighting a war, or working at home in a lot of different outfits that were basically all the bits of the National Health Service just waiting to be put together and called that or something very like it. We just couldn't wait for things to be decent and fair, for everybody, that is, even though we knew they were going to be a bit shabby as well for a while . . . Everything was then, but we all mucked in. Great spirit, wasn't there, Esmee? Even the pathologists, if you can imagine such a thing as a politicised pathologist, hm?'

Perhaps Esmee had been a pathologist once, when they were making a new world. She smiled and Jimmy returned to this theme. 'But gradually the great men of the profession stopped moaning about their sacred principles and got down to talking sense about how much they were going to get paid for giving them up. Bevan didn't chase 'em quite hard enough on a couple of points, but the thing we were eventually given to run was a decent, honest shot at providing health care for everybody as a basic right . . . No more hospital flag days . . .' Four or five people in Jimmy's immediate vicinity, all toying with saddle of lamb, carrots vichy, petits pois and duchess potatoes, had paused to listen. 'And no more families missing meals to save up to pay the doctor . . .

'Bit of a queue for some things, of course, but people were used to that, sadly. But d'you know we were actually rather proud of it. For years and years . . . And it's only now – when people are beginning to forget about the ghastly problems the NHS was set up to put an end to – that you get chaps talking about the disciplines of the market and the challenge of hospital competing against hospital.'

496

Rachel said something about choice. 'Choice?' said Jimmy. 'As somebody said the other day, choice is a function of excess, which in our case we have not got. Yes, there'll be choice all right: the kind of choice the poor had all too much of in the good old days, mainly a matter of choosing what to go without . . . Choice?' Jimmy shook his head sadly. 'Doctors choosing not to take on the unfortunate, the downtrodden because the books might not balance? Hospitals choosing the patients they think they might be able to turn a profit on? And I suppose saying sorry to the rest. Oh yes . . . Lots of interesting new choices to be made. Um. Sorry, darling . . . Am I talking too much?' If Esmee thought so, no one else did. Even Max was looking thoughtful. 'Probably best to get it off me chest,' said Jimmy quietly. 'Then I won't feel obliged to say it all again as part of my after-dinner speech.'

While Mrs Jimmy, who had a remarkable facility for remembering everyone's children, quizzed Rachel about Amanda and Mike, Scott, who would have been more than happy for Jimmy to have gone on a lot longer, first listened then wondered in a vaguely opinion-pollster way what those of his contemporaries who had come to the reunion might think of the present troubles of the NHS and the solutions now proposed by a government widely believed to be responsible for them. Irena had enthused, which spoke for itself. Flying orthopods from North Carolina would no doubt prescribe lots of lovely capitalism. Country GP's like Maggie, working where sheer geography ruled out any chance of competition, would see nothing in the White Paper to do with health care in Chirnside. Everybody who was involved, as Scott himself was, with the elderly, would worry that their patients would be consigned inexorably to the lower tier of a two-tier system. And what about the terminally ill? Would they find themselves priced out of care once all attempts at cure had failed? And the handicapped, like Sandy's reputed twelve year old baby girl? Would GP's find ways of saying sorry, we just can't, or sorry, we have more than our share of those already? So who was it all for? Someone had pointed out that the ideal post-White Paper patient was a young executive driving round the M25 in his Porsche, ringing all the London teaching hospitals on his car-phone to get the best price for his hernia repair; but in twenty years of medicine, admittedly practised mainly in far-off Scotland, Scott had never met anyone like that.

Mrs Jimmy, having caught up on Amanda and Mike, turned briskly to Max. 'I think what I find so obnoxious about it is the sheer arrogance of it. D'you know what I mean, Max? We're given what's essentially a glossy brochure the content of which wouldn't get you an O-level in business studies, far less in health economics, and we're told that's it. No questions. No ifs and buts. That's it and you've all got the starting date. We've worked it all out from first principles and we know it's just what's needed. So get on with it, and we don't care what you think. Can you imagine if we tried that with patients? "We've got this marvellous new treatment, all worked out from first principles, no one's tried it but we're absolutely certain it works. You just take three big tablespoonfuls a day for ever, and you're not expected to like the taste." '

'Just swallow it down, Mr Clarke . . .'

'Exactly, Max. Think of it. No references, no evidence, no studies, no pilot projects, no data on costing, no idea even how much costing's going to cost. It's insane . . . And how are we expected to explain it to people in Kathmandu? Sensible, intelligent doctors who've been here and who know that apart from being a bit short of money the system has always worked pretty well? And all at the insistence of a prime minister with claims to have had a scientific training? *Really!* And a woman too!'

'Esmee, darling . . .'

After the pudding Max got up and said that he was conducting a study of bladder function in a cohort of ageing doctors, and that anyone who was willing to help with it should signify this by getting up and leaving the room. The large psychiatrist from Florida was first, showing a remarkable turn of speed and being rewarded with a rousing cheer; then people settled back in for coffee and a few moved around chatting at other tables until Max called them to order again, getting up to introduce Jimmy, who got a cheer too, but when he raised his hand there was immediate silence. 'Thanks, Max. And thank you all. As I recall, it wasn't half as easy as that to get you lot to stop talking and listen to me lectures . . .' That earned him another cheer, then he talked for just over fifteen minutes, telling them how he had always had a special affection for the students of the sixties; how this particular year had proved itself to be a most splendid vintage from that excellent decade; how a life spent trying to practise good medicine usually turned out to be good fun too; that there was no reason why their next twenty years shouldn't be as much fun as the last; and that there would be new changes and challenges, but every generation in medicine had had to face those. Without specifically mentioning the present troubles he dwelt a little on the importance of preserving what he called that most precious legacy of the post-war tradition, a large vision of the common good, to be pursued here on earth in minute particulars. To finish he told them that one of the greatest things of all about medicine was – just as many of them would already have discovered – that your students became your colleagues, and often your friends too, sometimes even your teachers, and if you lived long enough probably your doctors as well, and that was just as it should be, because of a tradition of comradeship, care and healing that went back to Hippocrates of Cos and stretched all around the world too, as this diverse and remarkably talented gathering had shown. When he sat down he seemed surprised by the cheers and applause, and looked suddenly small and frail.

In due course the Jamesons were escorted to their car and with the grown-ups gone the evening degenerated with agreeable speed. Someone had thought of asking people to bring along records for what was billed as a 'Late-Nite Sixties-Style Bop-Till-You-Drop Disco Event' and a number of people disappeared briefly and reappeared for it in the clothes, shoes and style of a bygone age: flares and kipper ties for men, mini-skirts and late-sixties floaty, flowery things for the women, perhaps not all fitting as comfortably as before, but soon the lights were dimmed and a couple of tracks of *Sergeant Pepper* allowed to work their magic. Shyly to start with, old yearnings across the reading room, first loves from physiology practicals and brief romances from remote fifth-year surgical attachements reasserted themselves, sweet and safe on a little dance floor reassuringly near the tables where wives and husbands sat contentedly pretending not to notice.

Irena had her way with Max, briefly, to *Strangers in the Night*. Fiona, now married to a plump engineer who had sensibly opted to go to bed early, was much in demand, with Stuart MacGregor, Morris Doig, Dilys's John and even Woody, the now vast psychiatrist, each taking his turn to gaze into her eyes or breathe into her ear to old, evocative music like *Release Me*, *Whiter Shade of Pale* and *There Goes My Everything*. Scott was content to sit drinking a few late pints, rather as he had done as a medical student, until the disc-jockey, who was a good deal younger than most of the records he was playing, came up with *Eleanor Rigby*: a song that had somehow dominated the party at the end of the Ancient Society of Physic's first mixed evening and which remained, along with the Franck violin sonata and God Save the Queen, one of Theresa's and his tunes.

When they rejoined Maggie at the table everybody needed another drink. For some reason she decided to change to lager and lime, and when the waiter came back it seemed for a few moments that a friendly, untroubled, youthful Robbie had joined them once more despite everything: something they had each thought of for themselves by the time Theresa said it for them. They talked of him and others who, for a variety of good and bad reasons, had not made it to the reunion: a Tamil girl now probably on the losing side of a civil war; a sad, solitary man who had walked away from his first house-job in Leith after three months and had never been seen again; Spike, an Orcadian whose drinking had once been a joke but who had gone on to lose his licence and then been jailed and struck off; Milly, who had had seven children and become a consultant in Accident and Emergency Medicine anyway; and Sandy, who really didn't have any excuse for not coming and who would have enjoyed herself a lot if she had, even in the company of her odd, rather dull, Church of Scotland minister husband.

For one reason and another, Sandy's really interesting project had been delayed. When she had moved into her new office and formally taken charge of the Board's acute services she had come across an awful lot of things which seemed to indicate that the citizens of Moscow had probably had a lot less to worry about than everyone had thought at the time: her first six months had mainly been spent finding out things that should have been perfectly clear on the day she started. And although the Air Vice Marshal's door had been proverbially always open, people had more or less stopped going to see him because despite his accessibility and affability he had never gained sufficient hold on how things actually worked to do much good. So there had been an awful lot of people waiting for someone else to see, and seeing them had been quite fun, even if getting them to put things in order, and in writing as well, before she saw them again had been less fun. However, after about six months she began to feel she was getting somewhere, at least with the things that should have been all right when she took over.

Another problem was how the doctors had reacted. Because for centuries they had been doing things mainly by moaning in vague committees and ringing people up on the old boy network, they had assumed that the appointment of a doctor-manager meant that that was once again the official way of doing things. Quite a few of them seemed to think that all you had to do now was shout for what you wanted, without figures or arguments, and to assume too that their traditional power of veto in the face of change had somehow been given back to them. So quite a lot of Sandy's time had been spent listening politely on the end of a phone, asking difficult questions in the nicest possible way and generally indicating that the age-old argument 'my patients will suffer' was no longer of itself an argument. So although she had tried very hard not to be nasty to doctors, they hadn't always seen it that way, and if they sometimes called her 'the manageress' when she wasn't around, as though she was running a tea-room for Crawford's, then that was all right by her provided they got their arguments together properly first and behaved reasonably on committees afterwards.

The most difficult things about the job at first had been quite unexpected, like when somebody handed you a complicated file that when you read it turned into a person in trouble: someone perhaps being paid a lot to do quite complicated things but who was being carried by other people, or was drifting into chaos or sometimes even villainy. Knowing what the lawyers thought helped, and knowing that somebody in personnel had made sure all the rules were being applied properly helped as well, but somebody still had to take final responsibility for the emerging decision, and until Sandy had learned to think of the problem people with files rather as she had thought of patients – there are patterns that become familiar, you learn the limits of intervention, you sense the longer prognosis quite early – it had not been easy. Now those files passed as quickly as all the rest, which was quite quickly, and she did not think of them again when they had gone.

To her surprise Sandy had not missed patients very much. The ones she occasionally thought about were mainly people she had looked after long ago, like Lorna, the leukaemia girl who had been so miserable in hospital for so much of the little time she had after her baby and who had died rather horribly at home, some other sad people she had got to know while they were dying slowly in hospital, and the overdose girl with the cheap engagement ring who probably shouldn't have died at all. If Sandy missed anything about proper doctoring it was probably something she had not thought about very much at the time: the fact that as a doctor looking after patients you just did your best with what you had, with a simple duty to the people you looked after and who depended on you and often said thank you, doctor, even if you weren't doing a very good job for them. That had been quite easy. Managers, and manageresses too, had to be a bit more like the grown-ups in a not very rich family with lots of unhappy adolescents, and try to help people do better rather than just try to help them or just do things for them. And at the same time you had to try to sort out the squabbles and make sure the shortages and hardships – and there were quite a lot of them now – were spread as sensibly and as fairly as possible. And still like mum and dad and the same family, you wouldn't know for quite a while whether you were really any good at it, and you would be more than a bit surprised if anybody ever said thank you.

The interesting project, when Sandy had finally been briefed by Molly and the general manager and had started on it, turned out to be quite interesting after all, and soon after she had begun to work on it people suddenly decided that it was now quite urgent too, because the Board's financial position, never good, had suddenly been declared to be really serious. Despite efficiency savings – which meant using fewer taxis and making do with a lot less different kinds of notepaper, and were barely worth the discontent they stirred up – and despite leaving vacant posts unfilled and spinning out seasonal ward closures, which helped a bit more, the Board was sliding steadily towards a seven or eight figure deficit over the course of only a year.

There were leaks to the press and angry letters, and Board meetings where people said dramatic and impractical things, and other, less open meetings where people stopped blaming one another and faced some quite unpleasant facts together. Sandy's project, now overseen by a little group of very senior people, became a top priority and she found herself working as hard as ever she had done in her year commuting to Glasgow; though she discovered also that in an unexpected way spending a given number of hours a week actually doing a job was less exhausting than the same amount of hours spent on the potentially limitless effort of preparing to do one.

It involved getting together a great many facts: from previous reports, from studies that people had done from time to time for other purposes, from in-patient statistics which would have been a lot easier to sort out if better decisions about computers and software had been taken ten years previously, and from library sorties that resulted in vast printouts from which a few useful nuggets could sometimes be gleaned. It also involved writing to people and talking to people, and Sandy had dictated dozens of letters and organised telephone mornings and visit afternoons to sound out selected sensible people who could talk from facts and think about planning problems without resorting either to greedy infantile fantasy, or to the Edinburgh disease of thinking that the way we're doing it now is not simply the only possible way of doing it, but the only desirable way as well.

The Acute Services Feasibility Study, as it was known, had made reasonable progress under difficult circumstances even before the crisis came, so putting a bit of extra effort into it for the home straight seemed quite worthwhile. Lots of headings and sub-headings on Sandy's list had been ticked off, and the list of people still to ring or see had shrunk as well. A draft outline of the report had gone round a very limited circulation for comments and the implications of implementing the main recommendations, about which there had never really been much doubt, had been discussed a couple of times with Molly and the rest of the overseeing group. In another two weeks or so the whole thing would be off Sandy's desk forever: a prospect which left her wondering a little about how she would pass the time in the office afterwards, but which would also let her get on and deal with one or two other problems, in quite separate compartments of her life, which she had chosen to defer, perhaps even irresponsibly.

Thinking about them was unpleasant, so Sandy went back to her list of people still to be phoned or seen. Some of the names were those of people she probably shouldn't have thought of in the first place: a vascular surgeon within a year of retirement who was nice and had been a friend of her dad's but probably didn't care very much about the next twenty years; a boss physiotherapist, on the list because physiotherapy was important, but whose vision of the future might not go beyond the next three hockey fixtures; and Andrew, who if life had been a bit simpler would have been nearly at the top of Sandy's list, because he would know a lot about some things that mattered a lot and needed more detail, but who had been left to the end because although she would have very much liked to have phoned him a long time ago she didn't know how he might react if she did. She thought again about the surgeon and the physiotherapist and about Andrew, whom she really wanted to talk to now for quite a lot of reasons, then rang the Institute and asked for Dr Scott's extension in the Care of the Elderly Unit.

After the reunion Scott and Theresa, with their two children and his parents, spent a week at Crieff Hydro, sploshing around a lot in a chlorinated swimming pool and going for slow, complicated walks in the autumn woods. In talking with his father on woodland paths about the parish politics of long ago, and reading endless Thomas the Tank Engine stories to his older son over a generously interpreted holiday bedtime, Scott discovered new resonances of the term middle-aged: some irksome, some frankly daunting, but amounting still to a complicated, fairly unambiguous reassurance about a lot of jumbled, miscellaneous events that at least had got them thus far along the road and might conceivably make the journey bearable for quite some time to come. And there was even a serio-comic teaching dimension – explaining to Patrick about dead birds and how much longer grandpa and the donkey might live – that in turn helped to make a bit more sense of it all. As they drove south again Theresa said that she felt as if she had been off on a kind of presbyterian family retreat.

When Scott got back to work the following Monday Kevin told him it was just as well he had, because that evening's meeting of the Committee of Physicians was probably the most important that had ever been held. According to Kevin's sources, a group of consultants, whom he would not name but who would identify themselves quite quickly at the meeting when discussion really got going, had decided that there was only one rational way to respond to the Board's policy of chronic neglect towards the Institute. They were planning to use the Committee of Physicians to float a really radical proposal that would give the Board something to think about and would probably make the vital difference between the current policy of continuing neglect and the long-deferred complete rebuilding programme for the hospital. Scott, who had heard the rumour from a more reliable source before he had gone on leave, expressed polite interest and was told that Kevin could divulge no more meantime, but it was vital for the future of the hospital that as many people turned out for the meeting as possible.

Certainly something had to be done. Coming back to the place after only ten days away from it, Scott found the Institute ever more grubby and dilapidated. The heaps of bulging polythene bags cluttering the corridors seemed bigger than before. Doors long scarred and battered by trolleys didn't fit or even swing properly. There were the usual shortages and one or two new ones, with Scott's ward sister informing him that she had run out of forks and it was just as well some of the old men preferred to use spoons. If there had been progress with anything, it had been of a fairly discouraging sort: more scaffolding had appeared around a turret that was said to be in danger of toppling into the Orthopaedic Outpatients' Department, and a bit more of the medical corridor had been fenced off for floor repairs that no one seemed to have yet got round to starting.

After lunch in the dim and grubby dining room that twenty years on still smelt of old socks and boiled cabbage, Scott was sitting in his office dictating some discharge summaries when his secretary rang through to say that while he had been at lunch a Dr Lennox had phoned again, and that she would phone back some time soon, probably quite early in the afternoon. Scott's first thought was that he ought to go and check if there were any home visits to be done, perhaps in Gilmerton or Eskbank or with luck even out at Tranent, or failing that go and spend some time in the library catching up with the journals he had missed by being on holiday. He had just finished his discharge summaries when the phone rang again. He picked it up and his secretary said 'Dr Lennox for you, Dr Scott.' He said flatly 'Hello . . . Dr Scott.'

'Hello, Andrew . . . It's me . . . Sandy.' There was a long pause then Sandy said 'It's all right me phoning you, is it?' There was another long pause. Sandy's phone voice, so familiar from hours and hours of silly, loving, inconsequential conversation, was guarded, the way it sounded when someone had come into the room, or in the kind of phone call they had had towards the end of their time together, when she didn't know if he would be pleased she'd rung him or not. 'I tried to ring you last week, but you were away.'

'Yes.'

'Anyway, you're back now.' Her voice had softened and relaxed as though she were smiling.

'Yes.'

'You're sure it's all right, Andrew. . . ?' There was another long pause. 'If it's not I'll just . . . go away.'

'Can I shut the door. . . ?'

'I'll wait.'

Scott came back to his desk and sat looking out of his window at two half-bare plane trees and the turret that still might fall down on Orthopaedic Outpatients'. 'Hello?'

'Andrew . . . It's a sort of work thing, but if it's difficult, or if this is the wrong time to phone you . . .'

'It's all right.'

'You know I'm . . . at the Board now?'

'Yes.'

'They've asked me to get some things together about acute services . . . Something called the Acute Services Feasibility Study, just going over a whole lot of things that have been gone over again and again but trying to actually do something this time.' She paused and after a silence Scott said 'Yes' again and she went on. 'So I've been talking to people and writing to people all over the place, and I suppose I should have probably written to you ages ago . . .'

Over the previous thirteen years Sandy had written and then torn up dozens of letters to Andrew, none of them about the Acute Services Feasibility Study: letters that had tried to explain; letters that had said how much she had loved him and how much she still loved him; letters that had asked for forgiveness and understanding; letters she had written in her head over days at a time and then put on paper and sometimes cried over; funny letters full of idiotic things that he was the only person in the world she would dream of telling; sad letters that would have made him cry too if she had sent them; letters from abroad full of the kind of inconsequential loving nonsense they had once phoned each other endlessly about; letters asking him to meet her again just to talk; letters wishing she could meet him again in a magical way that would allow them to go right back to the beginning and start again, so that what they had had together would not stop but just go on and on as long as they lived. But always in the end she had torn up her letters to him because even when she was on the other side of the world and loving him as much as ever, she could feel his pain and his loss and his anger. 'Yes,' she said, 'I should really have written.'

There was another long silence then Sandy said 'I still could, Andrew, if that would be easier. But can I sort of tell you what it's about first. . . ?'

'All right.'

When ten minutes later Scott's secretary brought the afternoon mail in she said 'I really should have told you, Dr Scott. That Dr Lennox has been after you for ages. And when I asked her if you knew her – you know, before I put her through just now – she laughed. I thought that was a bit odd.' Scott dug briefly in his filing system, found some of the information Sandy had requested and asked his secretary to dispatch it to her at the Board right away, with an unsigned compliments slip. Then he walked across to the clinical office and found, to his mild relief, that a couple of patients had been referred and both needed to be seen fairly quickly.

The more urgent of the two was an eighty-seven year old lady with no known previous psychiatric history who had been found when neighbours had noticed the absence of usual activity in her ground floor flat in Bruce Street, a little cul-de-sac of old and unimproved tenements beside the railway line in Morningside. The story was sad and fortunately fairly uncommon, and the general practitioner's information scanty and apologetic because he had not seen the patient for fifteen years, her difficulties having come to light only when the police had broken down the door and found her in bed beside her dead husband. His corpse had been removed earlier in the afternoon but the old lady, described as 'wasted and gibbering and stuck in bed' had adamantly refused to go anywhere and had so far also refused all offers of help, even of food and drink.

When Scott arrived a huddle of neighbours was waiting in the dank stone hallway. He explained who he was looking for and was directed towards an open doorway. 'Something'll have to be done,' said one of the women in a loud voice as he went into the house.

Scott turned and nodded. The linoleum underfoot, an indeterminate shade of brown, was sticky to his tread, the little lobby dim and its air thick with the kind of pungent stench that followed you afterwards to your car on your clothes and lingered there perhaps for hours. 'She's in here,' said a female voice. Scott followed the odour to its source, a little back bedroom where a district nurse stood, in her coat with her bag still in her hand, presumably because there was nowhere clean enough to put it down. Most of the floor space in the room was taken up by an ancient double bed and from it a skinny and wizened lady with matted, yellowish-white hair looked up at Scott as he came in. Her position in the bed was unusual, and it took him a moment to realise what had happened. Her knees were up near her chin because most of her had fallen, in a kind of forced sitting position, through a big hole in the mattress. Scott introduced himself and reached out to take her hand.

'Dinnae-dinnae-dinnae-dinnae-dinnae-dinnae!'

'She says that whatever you do,' said the district nurse. Scott, who had already resolved to have his suit dry-cleaned anyway, sat down on the bed. 'Mrs McQuaid, your doctor's asked me to come and see if there's anything I can do to help. I'm Dr Scott, from the Institute. And I'm particularly interested in older people.'

'Dinnae-dinnae-dinnae-dinnae!'

Fewer was better, a little. 'Can you hear me all right, Mrs McQuaid?'

'She's not deaf,' said the district nurse. Scott nodded. 'Mrs McQuaid, can you tell me anything about what's happened?'

'Where's-Johnny-where's-Johnny-where's-Johnny?'

'Your husband?'

'Where's-my-husband-where's-my-husband-where's-my-husband?'

'Mrs McQuaid . . . I think your husband was taken seriously ill.'

'Is-he-dead-is-he-dead-is-he-dead?'

'I'm afraid so, Mrs McQuaid.'

'Help-me-help-me-help-me.'

Scott and the nurse reached over and eased her up out of the hole and on to the better half of the bed and slowly she straightened herself out. Fragments of rotting mattress clung to her sodden, filthy petticoat. 'Should we maybe open the window a wee bit?' said the nurse. It seemed a good idea. Then they sat Mrs McQuaid on the edge of the bed. She took a deep breath and sighed and looked round. 'Would any of youse like a cup of tea?'

'That's very kind of you, Mrs McQuaid, but . . .'

'Would *you* like one, Mrs McQuaid?' said the nurse. 'Maybe I could make it for you . . .'

The nurse went off to the kitchen and Scott sat and talked to Mrs McQuaid, who thought she was about forty and said it had been nice of him to come and see her but her husband would be home soon and she really would have to think about getting out to the wee shop for something for his supper. The nurse came back with a cup of tea, and sat with Mrs McQuaid while Scott found a neighbour with a phone and arranged an ambulance to get her in to the Care of the Elderly Unit. When he went back and explained what he had done she thanked him and said she had always thought very highly of the Institute, and that a wee spell in there would probably do her a world of good and her husband would probably manage all right on his own for a wee while.

The next call took a long time. The patient lived in a farm cottage south of Penicuik and Scott got lost for twenty minutes on muddy un-signposted minor roads before he found it. The referral had mentioned confusion, blindness and possible alcohol abuse, the patient being a ninety-four-year-old retired farm labourer who lived alone and who had been managing quite well until a few weeks before. His cottage was one of a row of four, two evidently unoccupied, at the end of a farm track. As Scott's car drew up a neighbour, a young, weatherbeaten woman in an old-fashioned wrap-round pinny, was waiting. 'You're the doctor for Billy,' she said. Scott asked her if he gave a good account of himself. 'He does,' she said, 'but I'll come in with you so he knows who it is.'

The little cottage garden was tidy and well-tended and when Scott commented on that the woman said 'He does it all his self, doctor, just touching things. It was lovely in the summer there.' The door was open and they went in. 'Billy? It's me and the doctor.'

An old man sat calmly in a high-backed wooden fireside chair in a kitchen that looked as if little in it had been changed for more than thirty years. There were two coronation mugs on the mantlepiece, along with two china dogs and an eight day clock. Five cooking pots of diminishing size stood upside down above one another in a black iron potstand beside a clean and empty coal-fired cooking-range complete with pot-hook. In front of where the fire would have been was a one-bar electric heater glowing dull red. On the table, which was covered with checkered red and white oil-cloth, was a tea-caddy, together with a burnished metal sugar-tin and a place setting for one. A radio, or perhaps a wireless, with a fretted, cloth-backed speaker in the shape of a little church window, sat on a shelf at the old man's right hand and, curiously, beside it on the shelf was a large ball of grubby white string, one end of which was secured to the arm of the chair.

'It's the doctor, Billy.'

'Hello, Mr Murdoch.'

The old man reached out and shook Scott's hand firmly. 'Would you like to sit down, doctor?'

'Thank you.' The woman moved a bentwood chair from the table, turning it round so Scott could sit facing the old man.

'You'll mind and put it back, Betty . . .'

'I certainly will, Billy.'

First Scott asked him about his blindness. 'Withering o' the eyesight at the back o'the eye,' he explained without self-pity. 'A thing that comes wi' age, as you'll know yourself, doctor.' That sounded like macular degeneration, for which there was no treatment. 'And how long has that been a bother to you?'

'Twal' year, fifteen, maybe. But it came on gradual, so I'm all right.' The woman was nodding vigorously. 'Aboot the hoose, ken?' said the old man. 'But lately I've been gettin' lost . . . So . . .' He chuckled and reached out and laid his right hand on the ball of string. 'What made you think of that, Mr Murdoch?'

The old man chuckled again. 'Were ye ever a sodger, doctor?'

'No.'

'Well, I was,' he said. 'A very long time ago. And we used tae gae oot in the dark. Fighting patrols, they cried that. In Salonika. That's in Greece, aboot twa hunner mile frae Athens, on the Penicuik side . . .' He smiled and laughed. '. . . for them that doesn't know it. And if ye took yer bit string ye could aye get back tae yer ain wee trench. So I thocht, Billy, ye can dae it again. And Betty got the string.'

Sane patients took a lot longer than mad ones, but after about three quarters of an hour Scott had determined that a pleasant and sensible old man, who was blind and beginning to get forgetful too, had taken reasonable precautions and was doing as well as could be expected at home. The neighbour was happy to help. The drinking described, an occasional whisky binge ('Betty gets that too'), was within normal limits for age, sex and class. The old man could wash and dress himself, get around his house and eat food that had been prepared for him by his neighbour, who seemed to manage his pension too. He kept himself warm ('A grand thing, the electric') and could summon his neighbour in an emergency by banging on the wall.

All that was required of Scott was a detailed and tactful letter to the referring general practitioner, whose name was unfamiliar and who was therefore probably a trainee. And if things got worse over the next few weeks or months the old man could be referred again, and it would all be bit more straightforward because he had been seen once already. Finding the main road proved a lot easier than finding the cottage had been, and Scott drove back into town, against the late-afternoon commuter traffic, in moderately good time for the Committee of Physicians meeting. On the way in he thought again about Sandy and her phone call. If she had written she could have had the information she had asked for almost as quickly and an oddly disturbing phone call could have been avoided. Her voice, once she had relaxed, had been so familiar, so close, that Scott had succumbed to immediate, uncontrollable memories of the way her mouth moved when she talked, and when she had started to explain her study she sounded as she had almost always sounded: busy, happy, telling him interesting things that she knew he would be interested in, in a smiling, close, confiding way that made it almost as though they were discussing it over coffee or a gin and tonic in bed, after as well as before amazing happy sex. But what she had wanted this time was information, Scott reminded himself for the eighth or eightieth time, so he had sent it off to her.

He was still thinking about her when he reached the Institute, parked his car in the consultants' car park at the front under the clock tower and walked up the pretentious stone steps leading to the front door. As he reached the top of the steps someone – a vaguely blonde middle-aged woman in a light raincoat – hurried out and passed him. 'Can't stop, Andrew . . . Must go,' said whoever it was. The voice was familiar. Scott turned and looked as she reached the foot of the steps and hurried on to her car. It was – had been – Sandy.

'Mr Chairman . . . I think it's quite important that we're absolutely clear about this, because what we decide here this evening will have consequences long after all of us – and I don't refer here only to my senior colleagues – have retired. Every one of us, from the most recently appointed consultant upwards, will have to live with what we, as a result of our deliberations, decide here tonight. We must neither rush to judgement nor let this opportunity pass, because – however difficult it may be for us to reach a speedy consensus about what is after all a very highly complex matter – such an opportunity may never arise again . . . But we must also be absolutely crystal clear about the nature of the decision we face, because a very great deal hangs on it. A decision to express an interest in opting out is that, only that and indeed just that – a decision to express an interest. But I feel most strongly that it is my duty, as one who has thought long and hard about this, to warn you that a decision *not* to express an interest might mean the end of the Institute as we know it. And I'm not for one moment saying that I or anyone else can anticipate the outcome of the Board's so-called Acute Services Feasibility study, but there is no guarantee – no guarantee whatsoever – that it will show the regard for this hospital that we and countless others at home and abroad think is its due. And, finally and perhaps most importantly of all, Mr Chairman, it seems to me that the Board, in the way it has responded to the various serious and sometimes vitally urgent questions we have raised with it over the years with regard to the development and indeed the basic maintenance of this great teaching hospital . . . They . . . Um, the Board . . . has at best been less than generous, and while they persist in claiming that no major policy decisions have been made for the long term and indeed the medium term future, I cannot but think that what they have done – or rather, Mr Chairman, what they *have failed to do* – amounts to a policy in itself . . . I hope I have made myself clear.'

'Indeed you have, Dr Bonthron . . . Dr Smail?'

'Mr Chairman, colleagues . . . I yield to, um, no one in my admiration of the historical achievements of an integrated health service, and, indeed, in my respect for the views so cogently expressed by those of our colleagues whose support for such a concept remains unwavering . . . But may I say straight away that on this occasion it gives me considerable pleasure to find myself agreeing – for once – with a very great deal of what Dr Bonthron had just said. Because is not this matter, when we come down to it at a fundamental level, as much one of *perception* as it is of *policy*? And that is why I am so grateful to Dr Bonthron for pointing out to us so very lucidly a basic and highly relevant truth. By putting his finger so firmly on what is after all a matter of record, by emphasising what has been *done* and by contrasting it so effectively with what has been, and what doubtless will be, merely *said*, he has put the matter in the, um, proverbial nutshell. For the issue before us tonight is, I think, not so much one of how we in this hospital go on, but ultimately one of *whether or not we go on at all* . . .' There was a rustling of papers and a sharp hiss of indrawn breath. 'Yes, you may find that shocking, Mr Chairman, as indeed it is, but I would put it to you that the possibility of opting out – if I can be absolutely frank and use the phrase in common use – could not, from the point of view of this hospital, have come at a better time. And I would therefore offer you two visions of the future as I see it: the one of slow strangulation at the hands of a shortsighted and ungenerous Board; the other of growing autonomy and status, of financial and – of course more important by far – *clinical* freedom, of a chance, indeed, to determine for ourselves whatever future we as a group of responsible clinicians agree for ourselves. Mr Chairman, need I say more?'

'Thank you, Dr Smail, I think you've made yourself perfectly clear . . . Sir Henry?'

'I wouldn't for one moment wish to appear to be usurping your function as chairman, Mr Chairman, but it might be worth reminding ourselves of what we're discussing . . . A proposal, as I understand it, that we express an interest in the matter of self-governing status for this hospital. On the one hand such an expression of interest might serve to draw the attention of the Board, even belatedly, to its greatest single asset . . .' There was a murmur of appreciation and even a little stamping of feet, quickly stilled by the chairman's raised hand. '. . . and on the other . . .' Sir Henry had turned and was gazing out of the window at the clock tower. No one spoke. His attention returned after the ordinary interval to the meeting and the chair. '. . . it might just annoy them.

Then again, of course, we could just go ahead and opt out. But it seems to me that these alternatives are all a bit drastic, and we should always allow for the possibility that the Board might recognise the obvious. And it's worth reminding ourselves that at this stage there aren't any facts about the proposed review, only rumours. After all, the Board may well have decided to re-develop this hospital, taking due account, of course, of the contributions that might still be made by . . . other hospitals. So in view of all that it would be wise to choose our words very carefully. And what I was going to suggest, Mr Chairman, is that we amend the motion somewhat, maybe so it reads that we have decided *with the greatest possible reluctance* to express an interest in the possibility of opting out.' There was much nodding and murmuring and Kevin put up his hand like a schoolboy asking to leave the room in a hurry.

'Thank you, Sir Henry. Dr Walster?'

'Mr Chairman, I think that what Sir Henry has just suggested takes us a lot further forward. If there's such a thing as having the best of both worlds on a difficult issue like this, Sir Henry seems to have, um, put his finger on it. So I for one would be more than happy to second his suggested amendment.'

Since Sir Henry had taken over the chairmanship of the merit awards committee an awful lot of people on the Committee of Physicians, Kevin perhaps most enthusiastically of all, had taken to supporting his suggestions. At quarter to eight it seemed that the longest Committee of Physicians meeting Scott had ever endured might have begun to draw peacefully towards its close.

'We thought they might,' said Sandy. 'But it isn't going to do them any good. Everyone here's had enough of their nonsense . . .'

Somewhat against her better judgement, Sandy had phoned Scott at work again, mainly to thank him for the things that he had sent so quickly and that had been quite helpful too.

'That's interesting. Old Henry said that, more or less. Something about maybe just annoying them. So that's why it was "with the greatest possible reluctance . . ."'

'I can just imagine him saying that, sort of mournfully . . .'

'He did. Then everybody said what a wonderful idea, Sir Henry, and then we all got to go home, at about eight o'clock.'

'Poor old you.'

'It was actually quite fun . . . Well, the selected highlights would have been more fun, I suppose . . . Jamie being sensible and loyal about the poor old NHS. Bob Smail doing his courtly and statesmanlike number. Old Bonthron a bit paranoid, Kevin Walster saying wonderful, Sir Henry, and can I please have my merit award now. . . ?'

'He's horrible.'

'Kevin?'

'Really horrible. He was on the silly committee that didn't give me a haematology job, and he was dim and nasty and boring and really upset me.'

'Poor old you.'

'What's he like to work with?'

'Dim and nasty and boring but he might be going away . . .'

'Somebody said that . . .'

There was a nice friendly silence then they both started talking at once then both said 'You go on . . .'

'I was going to say that if it makes you feel any better more or less everybody on the committee was horrible to Kevin when he went for Wiggy's job.'

Sandy laughed then said 'I shouldn't laugh . . . Would you have stayed, Andrew?'

'With Kevin for king? Maybe. Oh, maybe not. He'd actually been acting king for months and was pretty obnoxious. And he thought it was all fixed because Wiggy had been doing a kind of "One day, my son, all this will be yours" thing with him for years. Then it all came terribly unstuck on the day.'

'Good.'

'And our new leader's really quite nice. So I'm staying.'

'Good.' There was another friendly pause then Sandy said 'And how are you, Andrew?'

Sandy saying that in that particular way had been one of the things that had always happened in their phone calls. It meant that whatever had had to be said or discussed had been said or discussed and the rest of the phone call – usually the greater part of it and sometimes a very long time indeed – would be about nothing in particular and everything in general: things that had happened since they had last seen each other or talked; things they had talked about before but not really got to the end of; affectionate, considerate oddities concerning either or both that got talked about at disproportionate, interesting, unembarrassed length in a way that made everything closer and more entwined.

Their endless, detailed, sometimes frankly silly telephone conversations, full of friendly pauses and funny nonsense and finishing each others' sentences, had stopped as abruptly and cruelly as everything else; and what had made it even worse for Scott was that they had become an important part of his life, not only as a magical realisation of the kind of loving conversation that most people had only in their heads if at all, but as one of the main ways he had of coping with things that were difficult or hurtful. And when the worst had happened what he had wanted most of all, apart from it unhappening, was to be able still to talk to Sandy on the phone. Since he couldn't, and couldn't see her, he had tried to school himself to think of her as little as possible; for months, even for years, it had been very difficult, especially first thing in the morning and when he woke, as he often did, through the night. On the few occasions when he had seen her, even recently at the White Paper meeting and only a few days previously on the steps of the Institute, he had been surprised by the force and complexity of his reactions. Now, in an unnecessary and unexpected phone call that seemed to be turning into the kind they had had all the time thirteen years before, there was something quite eerie about her question. 'I'm all right.'

Sandy laughed. 'It's lovely talking to you . . . Again. Were you in the middle of doing something serious?'

'Not really. Might stroll round the ward quite soon. What about you?'

'Not very. A meeting this afternoon I'm all ready for. So a nice quiet office morning. And my desk's tidy and it's too early for coffee. Sorry, Andrew, that sounds as if I just phoned you because there wasn't anything else to do. Thanks for your help. That's what I'm phoning about. It was really quick and useful. So thank you.'

'That's all right.'

'I've summarised it. You're most of appendix fifteen. And it was nice . . .'

'Glad to be of use.'

'That as well. But reading it was nice . . .' Sandy had been a bit surprised that Andrew's information, which was mainly about the older people who kept getting into the Institute and who didn't need hospitals like the Institute in a million years, had come without even a scribble on the 'With Compliments' slip. Or perhaps she hadn't been, and perhaps having a phone call like this was stupid and hurtful. And in two phone calls he hadn't even used her name once, not because he'd forgotten it – she was pretty sure about that – but because he really just didn't want anything to do with her any more.

'Mm?'

'Yes, nice. Like talking to you when you're being a serious, sensible doctor.' She could hear him smiling. 'So thanks very much, Andrew . . . It all helps.'

'Helps what?'

'Well, helps demolish the Institute, I suppose.'

Outside Scott's window the turret with scaffolding round it was still standing. A man in blue overalls was working alone on its sooty, crumbling stonework. 'When?'

'Oh, probably not until you've finished your ward round.' They both laughed then Sandy said 'Three years, they think. Maybe four. There's an awful lot to do at the Southern, but it's all definitely going ahead.'

'Gosh.'

'Sorry, Andrew.'

'No. It's fine by me. And I don't think anybody here's really going to be very surprised. There've been rumours for months.'

'Well, they're true now. Because the site's worth a lot . . .'

' . . . and the Institute isn't.'

'More or less. Oh, Andrew . . .'

'What?'

'I'm sorry I rushed past you the other day.'

'It's all right.'

'It's not all right. I really wanted to talk to you.' There was a long silence. 'But it probably wasn't the sort of conversation we could have had there on the steps and anyway you were in such a hurry.'

'Sorry. And I was only going to the Committee of Physicians.'

Sandy laughed again. 'That's much more important.'

'Than what?'

After a bit they both started talking at once and stopped, then Sandy said 'It would be nice to have lunch, Andrew. Again.'

'That's what I was going to say.'
'Good.'

They had arranged to meet for lunch not far from the Institute, in a fairly new restaurant in premises that over the previous twenty five years had served successively as an undertaker's office, a coffee bar and a health food shop. Scott got there first, was brought a beer by a cheerfully gay little waiter and sat wondering whether Sandy would by now have come to her senses, remembered she was a serious person in health service management, to say nothing of being a Morningside minister's wife, and would therefore have decided simply not to turn up. To his surprise she arrived exactly on time and sat down rather breathlessly saying how nice it was to see him. The waiter hovered, his hands clasped in front of his chest, as happy to watch as to take a further order. Sandy looked steadily at Scott, who asked her if she would like a drink.

'Yes, I really would. But I'd better not, so just an orange juice, please . . .' The waiter smiled and went off. 'Lovely to see you, Andrew . . .'

'Lovely to see you.'

'It's been ages.'

They both laughed then their eyes met again and there was a long silence. 'I'm sorry, Andrew, really sorry.'

The waiter came back with an orange juice and two menus and for a while they had a safe, easy conversation about what to eat, but without actually deciding anything, then Scott asked about the Institute, the closure of which had now been officially announced. Sandy explained that she didn't actually order the bulldozers herself, because that was someone else's job, but now that it was all official they were standing by for the inevitable protests and petitions and appeals to the Secretary of State. Then they talked about Ranald Crumlin, who had been nice to Sandy at Charles Savage's party out in the country a long time ago, but generally horrible more or less ever since; then a bit more about that day in the country, first just in a gossipy where-are-they-all-now way, then quietly and sadly, with the waiter hovering again.

To get rid of him they ordered, both having the same thing picked more or less randomly from the menu, but when he went away there was just another long silence until Sandy said sorry again, for not phoning and not writing, which had been silly because she had wanted to, a lot, and had worried about him for ages: worried that he had probably been drinking a lot, which was a waste of a good person; worried about his work, because there had been rumours; and most of all worried that he might do something final – not with pills and a heart-rending, finger-pointing note, but considerately and sort of accidentally, the way dad had done it three terrible years later. She did not tell him about that, although she would have liked to and probably still would if they stayed friends and met again. When the man came with the lunch that neither of them cared very much about it was still a bit of a relief.

The food was vaguely middle-eastern – kebabs with an odd sauce that had something to do with peanuts – and it came with rice and a side salad. Sitting close to Andrew and talking, sometimes about work and sometimes about things from long ago that felt suddenly as if they had not gone away and were never going to, Sandy ate her lunch slowly, looking across into his eyes and feeling indescribably sad. If she had not been so silly as to get pregnant again because of Gus and get it all wrong all over again; if she had had the love and courage just to turn up at Andrew's door pregnant and carrying a suitcase, as she had wanted to and probably should have done; if Andrew had not suddenly gone away without telling her and stayed away for more than a year; if Alastair had not been so kind and sensible and insistent about getting married despite everything; if – and the more Sandy thought about them the more important the little ifs became – if she had just kept Andrew all night in the Forrest Hill flat when he had come up cuddly and a bit drunk after his SRC meeting; if, on that silly long ago evening, she even just hadn't spilled some coffee over him; if any or all of the above, as they put it in exams, then they would have had years of calmly and happily loving each other, at least until about now and maybe even for a bit afterwards, but they would have loved each other so much they would have been able to deal even with that. And having not been very sure at first whether she was going to or not, Sandy decided over the last of her salad that she would tell him about that too, but not quite yet.

They had coffee without spilling any of it and then walked back together to the Institute, because Sandy now had a little office there where she worked most afternoons on her interesting project. They went up the steps together, slowly, and went in and then stood for quite a long time in front of the picture of Queen Victoria, all in a way that reminded Sandy of being escorted home from school by her very first proper boyfriend: you went as slowly as you could and kept finding silly excuses to keep talking so as not to have to go inside and end the magic. Andrew was close again and not angry: sad, perhaps, perhaps even as sad about everything as she was, but close and kind and amusing. In the end the time came to tell him, so she started by telling him that she had put off the bulldozers for a couple of weeks because she was going to need the Institute for herself next week. There was a long silence and she didn't have to explain. He looked at her and said 'A lump?' as she had half expected him to say because they were so close again. She nodded and he looked even sadder. 'A difficult one?'

'Maybe. Probably. I've been a bit silly.'

'Oh, Sandy.'

'I should have gone earlier. But doctors always . . .'

'. . . make such awful patients.'

'Yes.'

'Firm?'

'Yes.'

'Fixed?'

'Fraid so.'

'How long?'

'Two months. Nearly three.'

'Where?' She put her hand up to just below the middle of her left breast. 'Oh, Sandy . . .'

They looked at each other for quite a long time then he became a sensible doctor and they talked about cure rates and survival rates and how treatment was much better now, even though they both knew, from being so close again and so sad, that it really wasn't going to be like that at all. When it had got to be ridiculously late to be coming back from lunch Andrew asked her which ward she was going into. She told him. 'I'll definitely come and see you. I could be looking for a mad old lady.'

'Me,' said Sandy. 'I've been really silly about this.' They laughed, with both of them practically crying. She really wanted him to come and see her but she said she didn't. He said he would come anyway, which was what she expected. 'I'd love to, and I'm coming,' he said, 'but mainly just because I've never seen you in a nightie.'

When Scott got back to the clinical office there was only one referral waiting for him. Someone with dementia who had been in a private nursing home for several years was no longer welcome there because his behaviour problems were increasing and his money was beginning to run out. The GP had requested admission if at all possible. Scott checked that there was a bed, a matter that had become much simpler since Mrs Gracie had been replaced, and went off to retrieve his car from the muddy, lumpy car park created by the demolition of the Institute's old bacteriology department. With the car lurching and splashing towards the exit, he turned on his car radio and thought of Sandy and of the Institute, and how, if she were lucky, she might live to see it off. To great crashing chords of something that was probably Elgar's second symphony, he drove out on to Lauriston Place biting his lip to stop himself sobbing for her.

The nursing home, an unfamiliar one with an address in south Edinburgh somewhere between Bruntsfield and Myreside, turned out to be one of a row of rambling villas most of which had seen better days: many had been subdivided and some had sprouted ugly wings of small modern flats. Dalnottar, standing on its own in a rutted gravel waste, was bleakly eccentric, with spreading eaves, odd stone chimney pots and walls scarred and blotchy where vast tracts of ivy had been ripped away. Scott tried the door, found it locked and rang the bell. After many minutes a tired-looking girl in a grubby pink overall let him in. When he asked for the nurse in charge she looked a bit shifty then said that she was actually covering for the nurse in charge because the nurse in charge had been called away to an emergency elsewhere. Nursing auxiliaries, such as the girl presumably was, were officially not permitted to cover for qualified nursing staff, even briefly. It was a bad start.

Scott explained who he was and asked if he could see Mr Gordon, the patient who had been referred for transfer to the unit. 'He's right at the top, and he's actually a doctor, doctor . . .'

'A medical doctor?'

'I'm surprised the doctor didn't mention that, doctor,' said the girl, as though a minor lapse on someone else's part might distract

Scott's attention from the illegality of Dalnottar's nursing cover arrangements. 'I suppose you might know him.' They ascended two flights of stairs and the girl showed him along to the end of a narrow, malodorous corridor. 'Dr Gordon!' the girl shouted as she opened a bedroom door. 'A doctor to see you. Shall I just leave you with him, doctor?'

It would have been useful to have heard some details about the behaviour problems, but the girl was sketchily qualified, perhaps too busy to have done much in the way of observation and in any case was half way down the stairs already. Scott went alone into a little bedroom with a sloping ceiling and a small dormer window. In a bed against the wall there sat an old man in a loose white shroud-like garment that made him look like one of the less well-fed of the later Roman emperors. 'Come in, dear boy,' said the unmistakable voice of Gorgeous George. 'Come in and sit ye down.'

'Dr Gordon?'

'My dear boy . . .' The proffered hand was smeared with faeces. Scott nodded politely.

'Dr Gordon, I'm Dr Scott, and your own doctor . . .' Scott checked the name at the head of the note. 'Dr Steedman, has asked me . . .'

'Dirty little bitch.'

'Your own doctor asked me to come along and see if I could help in any way . . .'

'Dear boy, whoever you are you're a great improvement on that unfortunate creature. You know about town dogs and women doctors, of course? And what did you say your name was?'

'Scott, Dr Gordon.'

'Edinburgh chap?'

'I trained here.'

'Ah yes, but what *school* did you go to?'

'Dr Gordon . . .'

'Just tell me your name again, dear boy, and what school you went to. You know, this is all vaguely familiar. Did I ever teach you?'

'Scott, Dr Gordon. And you . . .'

'Dreadfully common name, dear boy, but I expect you have no trouble remembering it. And tell me, did I ever teach you?'

'You did, Dr Gordon. Thank you very much.'

The old man chuckled. 'Not much good to you today, I'm afraid.

Much as I'd like to.' He lowered his voice and beckoned Scott closer. 'We just don't have the patients now. Terribly sad, but there it is. Haven't seen a case worth teaching on in . . . weeks? Months, really. We had one chap a little while back, nice case really. Puffing his last, *navy blue* with his congestive failure. Exactly the kind of thing you young men need to know . . . Died, poor chap. Of course.'

'Dr Gordon?'

'Yes, dear boy.'

'I'm actually here to help if I can. And I wondered . . .'

'Yes, dear boy?'

'How would you feel about coming in to the Institute?'

Gorgeous George frowned and then grinned. 'You know, I'd love to. D'you think we'll make it in time for lunch?'

'Dr Gordon, I meant . . .'

'Marvellous. We'll go to the consultants' dining room, of course. You *are* a consultant, I hope, dear boy . . . Good, good . . . And the cellar's still all right? They used to do a remarkable claret.' He rolled his eyes. 'For only five bob. They probably still do. Yes, dear boy. That's it, we'll lunch at the Institute. And dear boy . . .' The hand came out again and Scott moved back just a little. 'Dear boy, you *must* let *me* sign for it.'

Scott eventually left the old man and made his way downstairs. On the first floor landing he paused and looked at the long stained glass window opposite. It was dull and grubby and spattered at the edges with paint, and some of its little coloured shapes had been broken and replaced by ordinary frosted glass, but he had seen it once before, a long time ago. Then, it had been radiant with summer evening sunlight; the staircase had been crowded with noisy, happy, drunk people on their way from Lennie's party to the graduation ball; Scott had been up on the landing, near the back of the crowd and waiting to go down, and from somewhere halfway down the stair below a girl in a green dress had turned and looked up at him.